Paper Girls

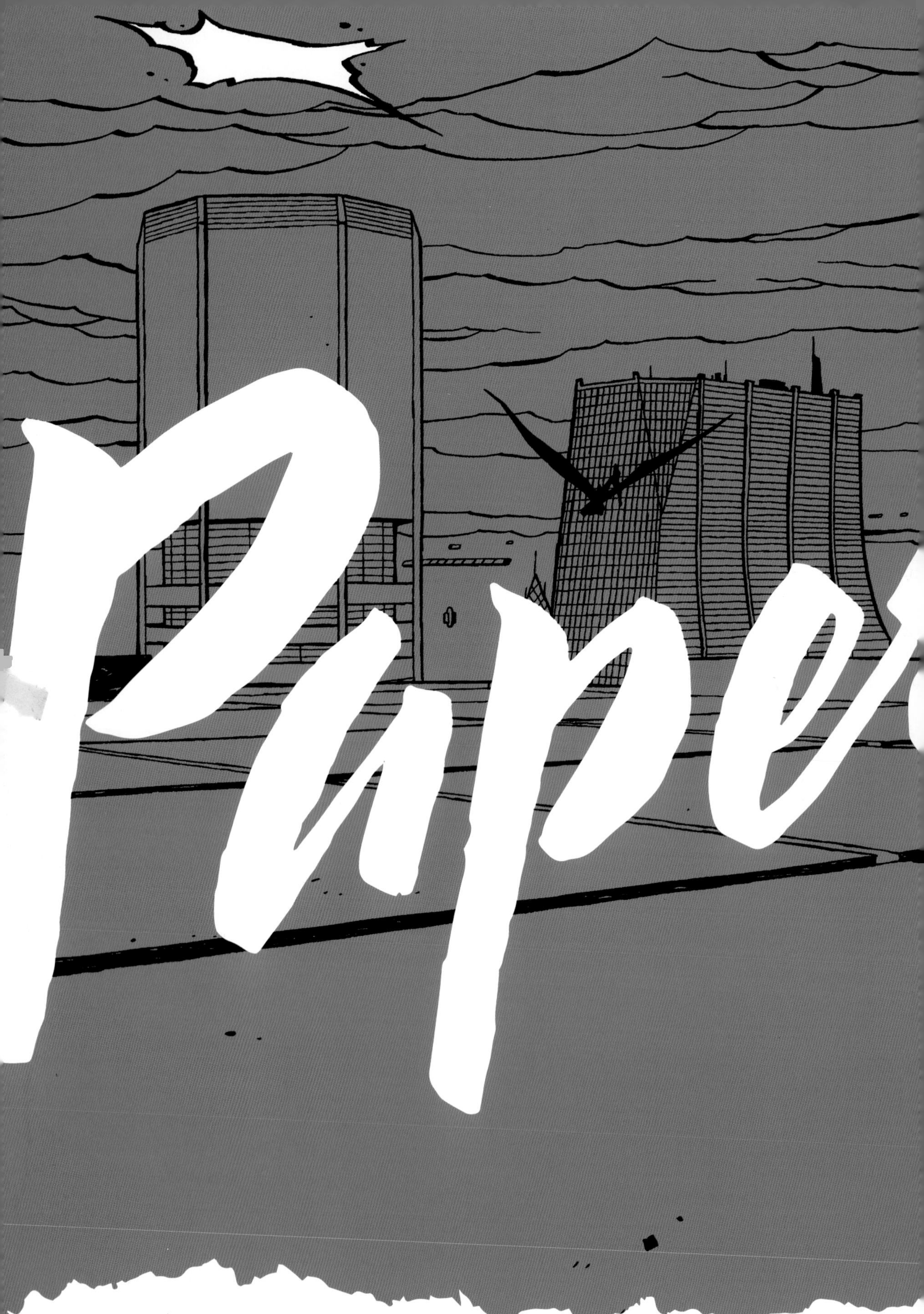
Pape

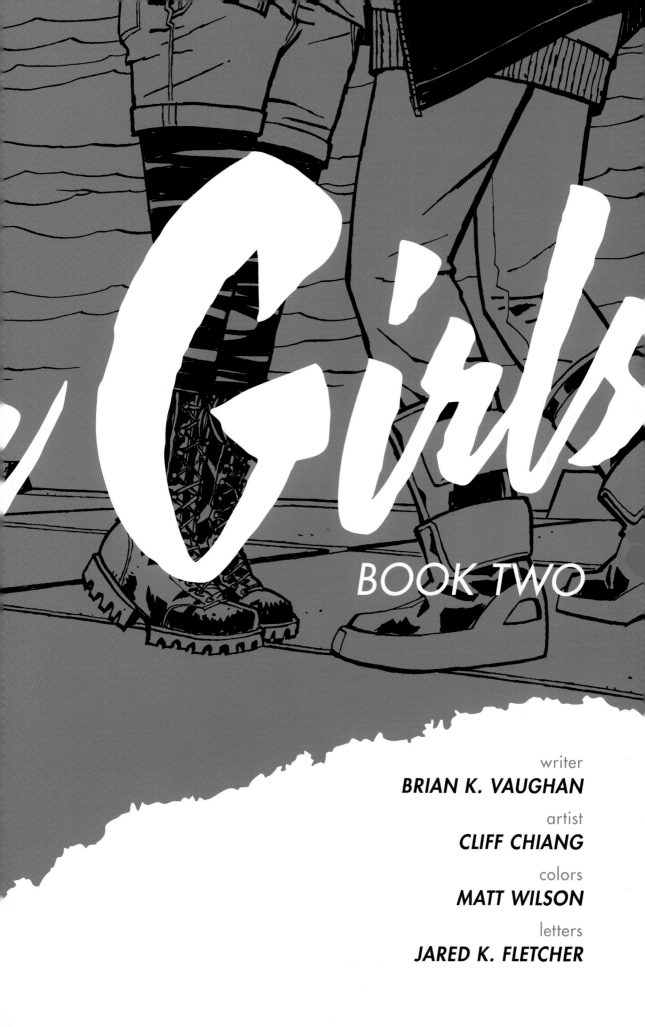

Girls
BOOK TWO

writer
BRIAN K. VAUGHAN

artist
CLIFF CHIANG

colors
MATT WILSON

letters
JARED K. FLETCHER

IMAGE COMICS, INC.

Robert Kirkman – Chief Operating Officer
Erik Larsen – Chief Financial Officer
Todd McFarlane – President
Marc Silvestri – Chief Executive Officer
Jim Valentino – Vice President
Eric Stephenson – Publisher / Chief Creative Officer
Corey Hart – Director of Sales
Jeff Boison – Director of Publishing Planning & Book Trade Sales
Chris Ross – Director of Digital Sales
Jeff Stang – Director of Specialty Sales
Kat Salazar – Director of PR & Marketing
Drew Gill – Art Director
Heather Doornink – Production Director
Nicole Lapalme – Controller

IMAGECOMICS.COM

Dee Cunniffe - Color Flats
Jared K. Fletcher - Logo + Book Design

PAPER GIRLS, BOOK 2 HC. First printing. April 2019. Published by Image Comics, Inc. Office of publication: 2701 NW Vaughn St., Suite 780, Portland, OR 97210.

ISBN: 978-1-5343-1061-2

CHAPTER 11

CAMEL

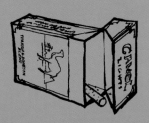

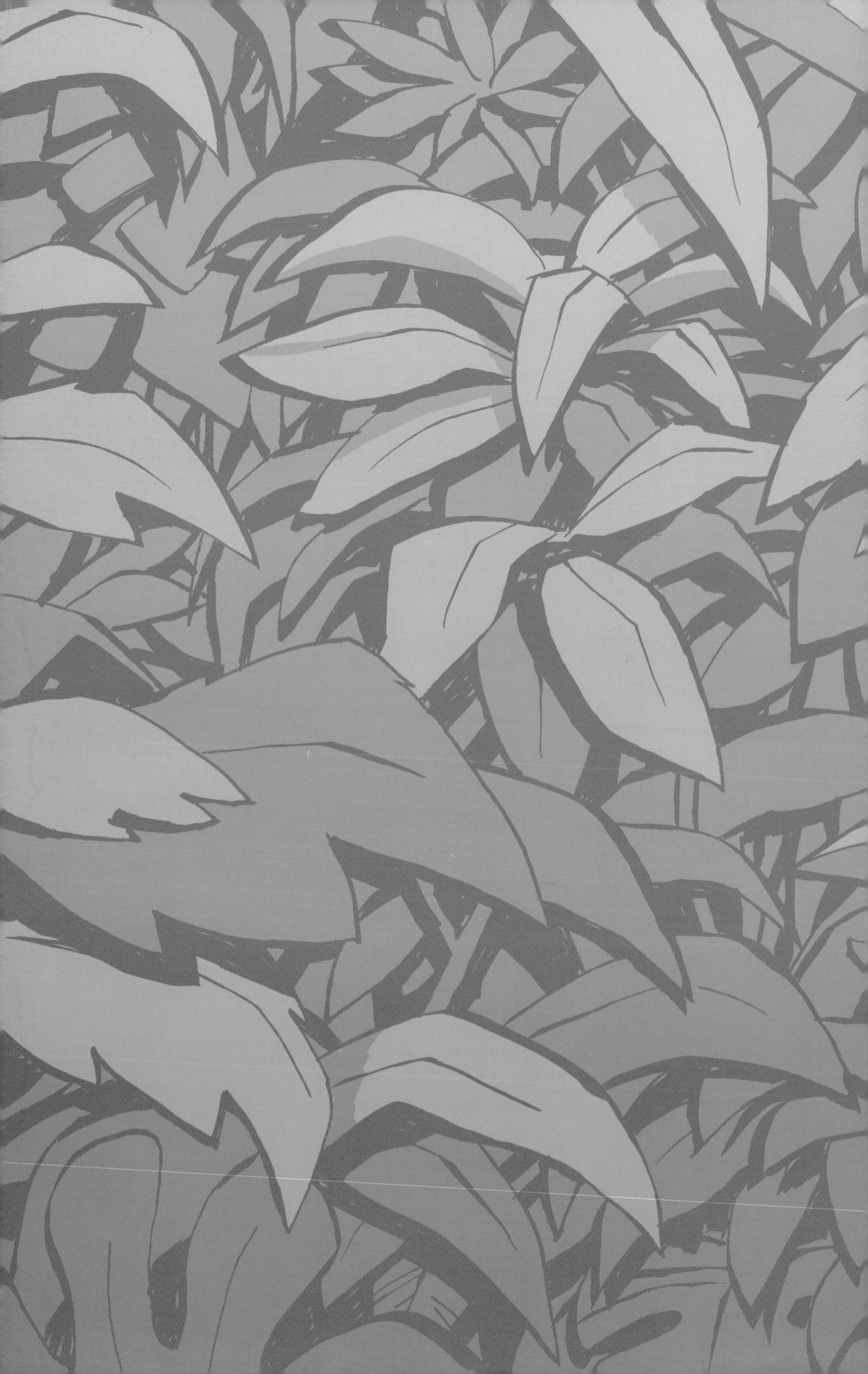

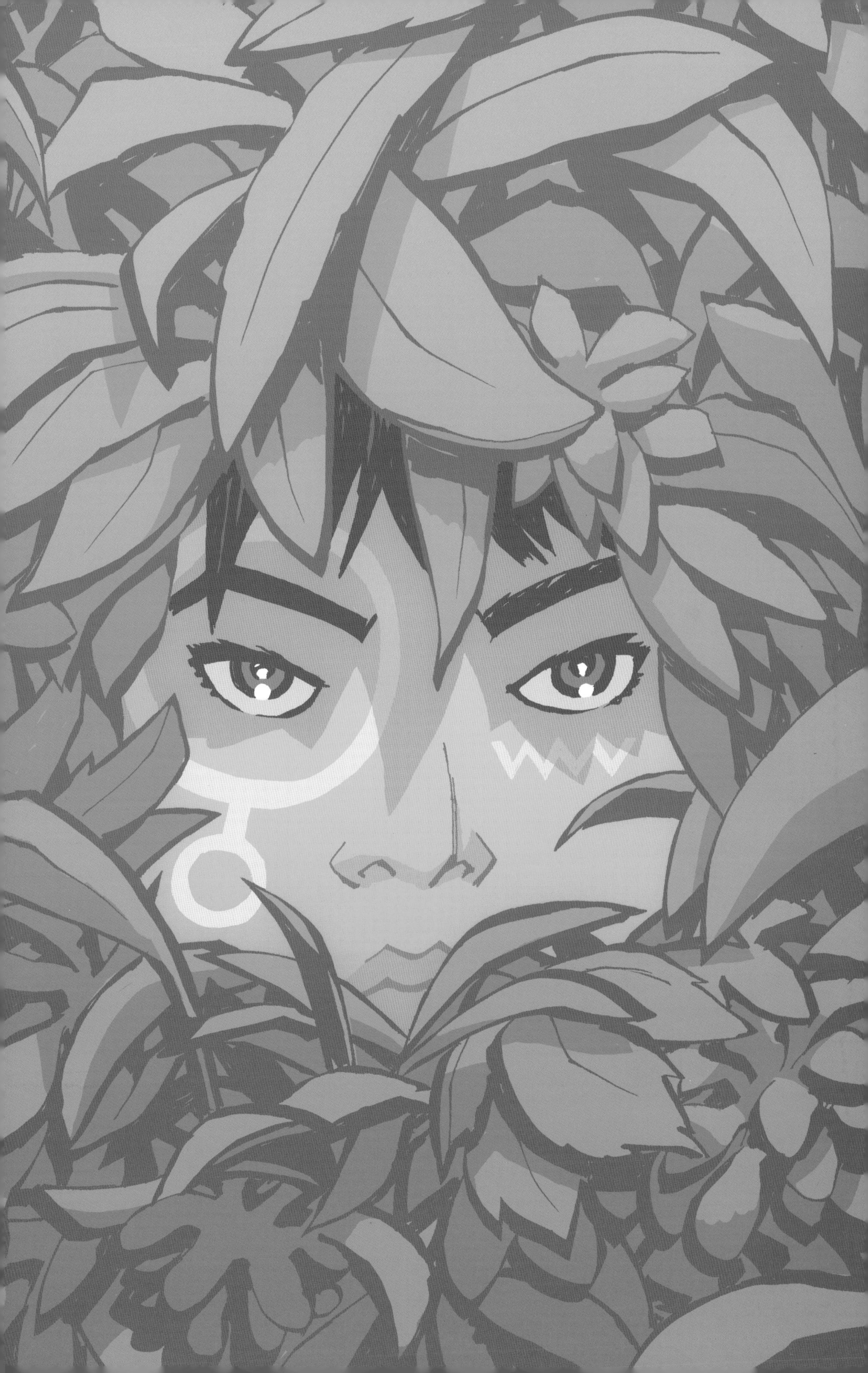

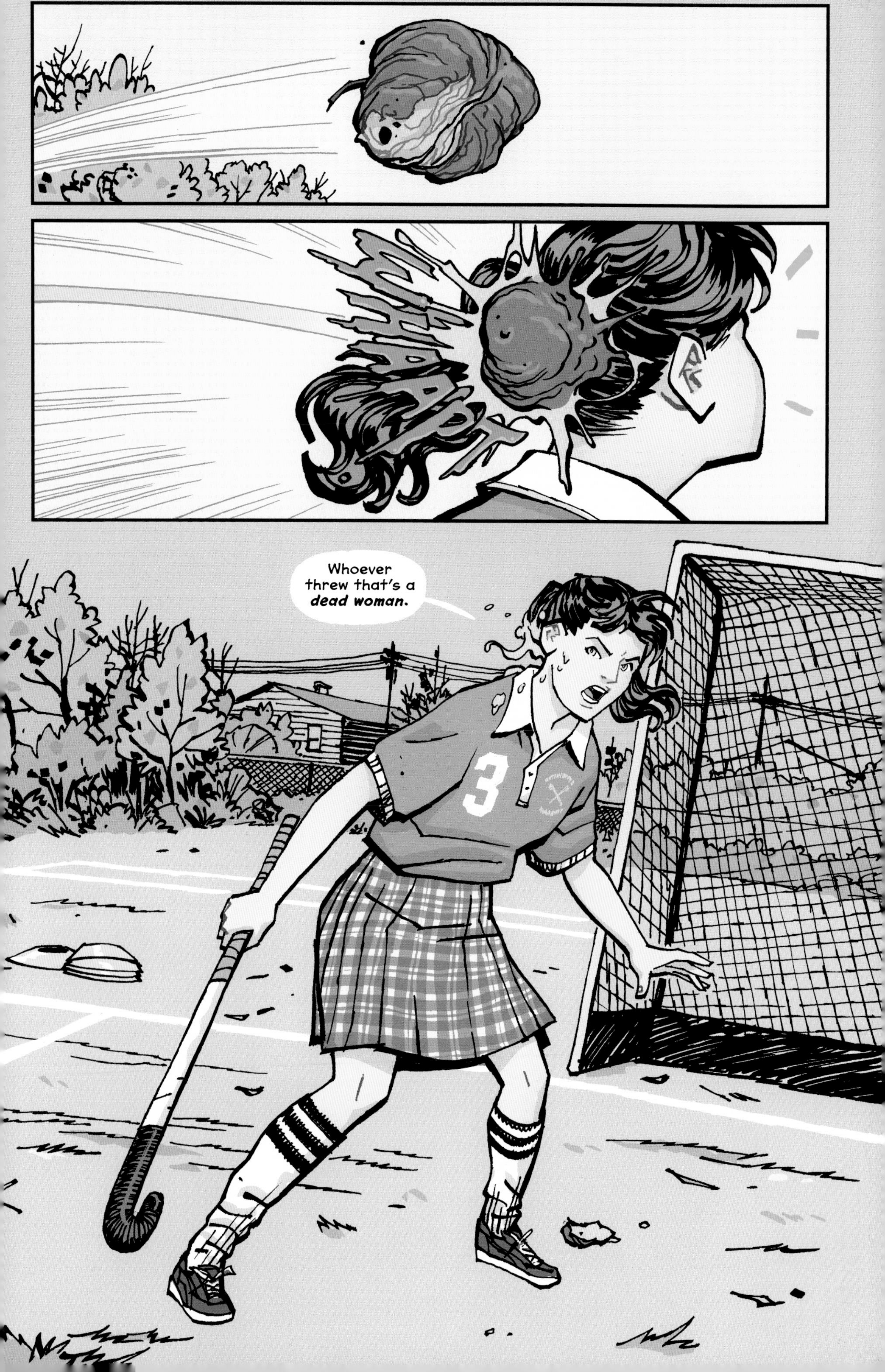
Whoever threw that's a *dead woman.*

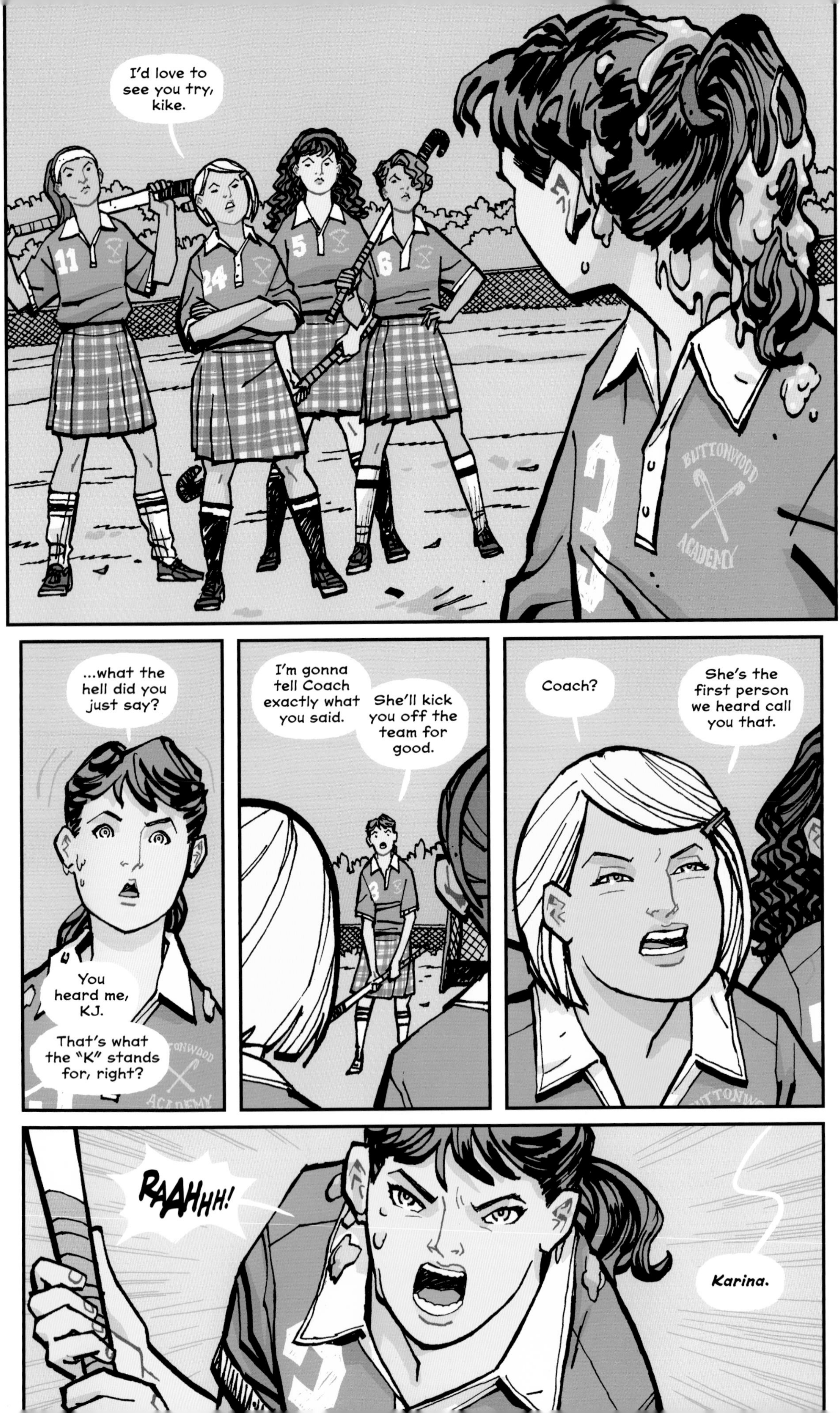
I'd love to see you try, kike.
BUTTONWOOD ACADEMY
...what the hell did you just say?
You heard me, KJ.
That's what the "K" stands for, right?
I'm gonna tell Coach exactly what you said.
She'll kick you off the team for good.
Coach?
She's the first person we heard call you that.
RAAHHH!
Karina.

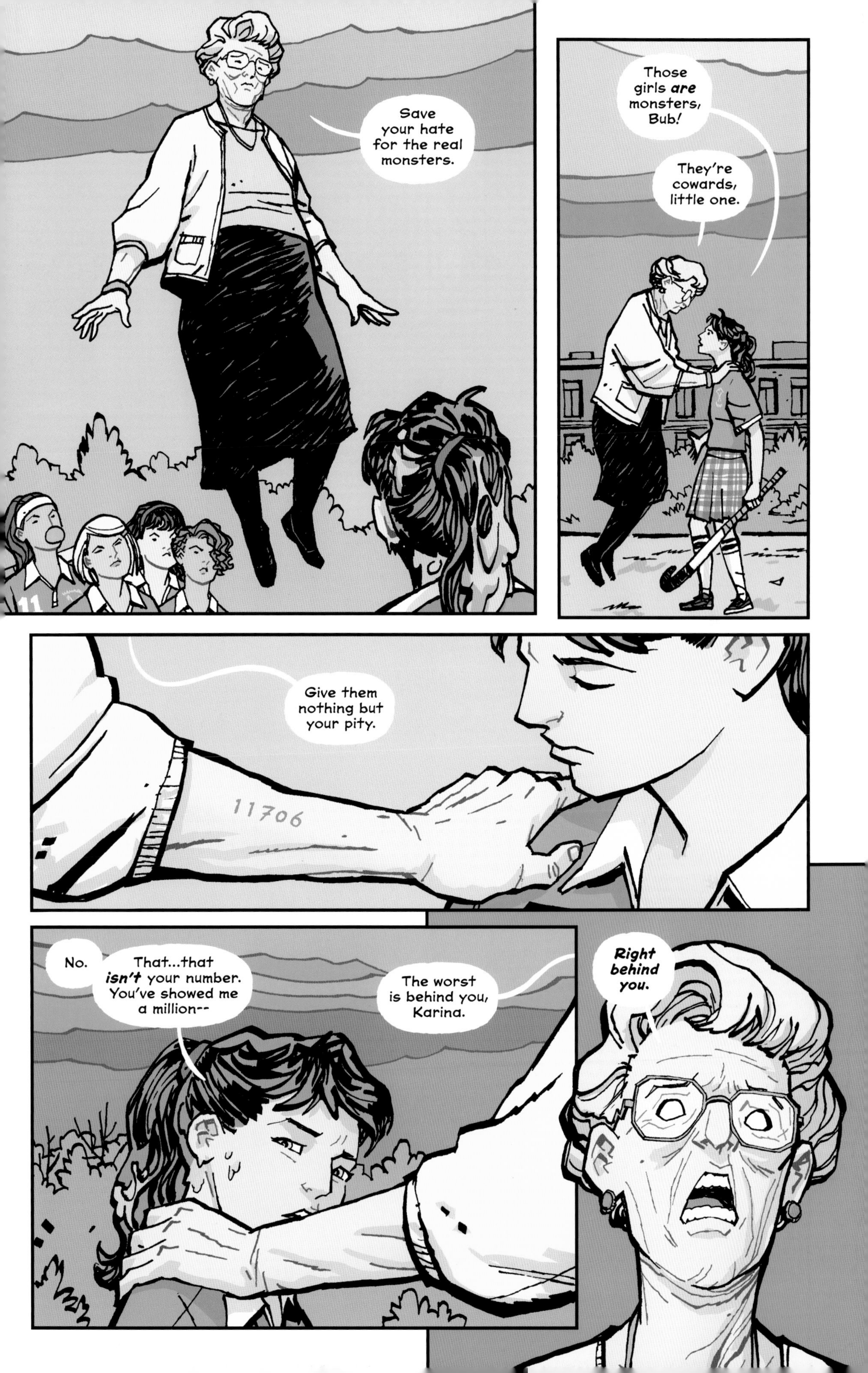
Save your hate for the real monsters.
Those girls *are* monsters, Bub!
They're cowards, little one.
Give them nothing but your pity.
11706
No.
That...that *isn't* your number. You've showed me a million--
The worst is behind you, Karina.
Right behind you.

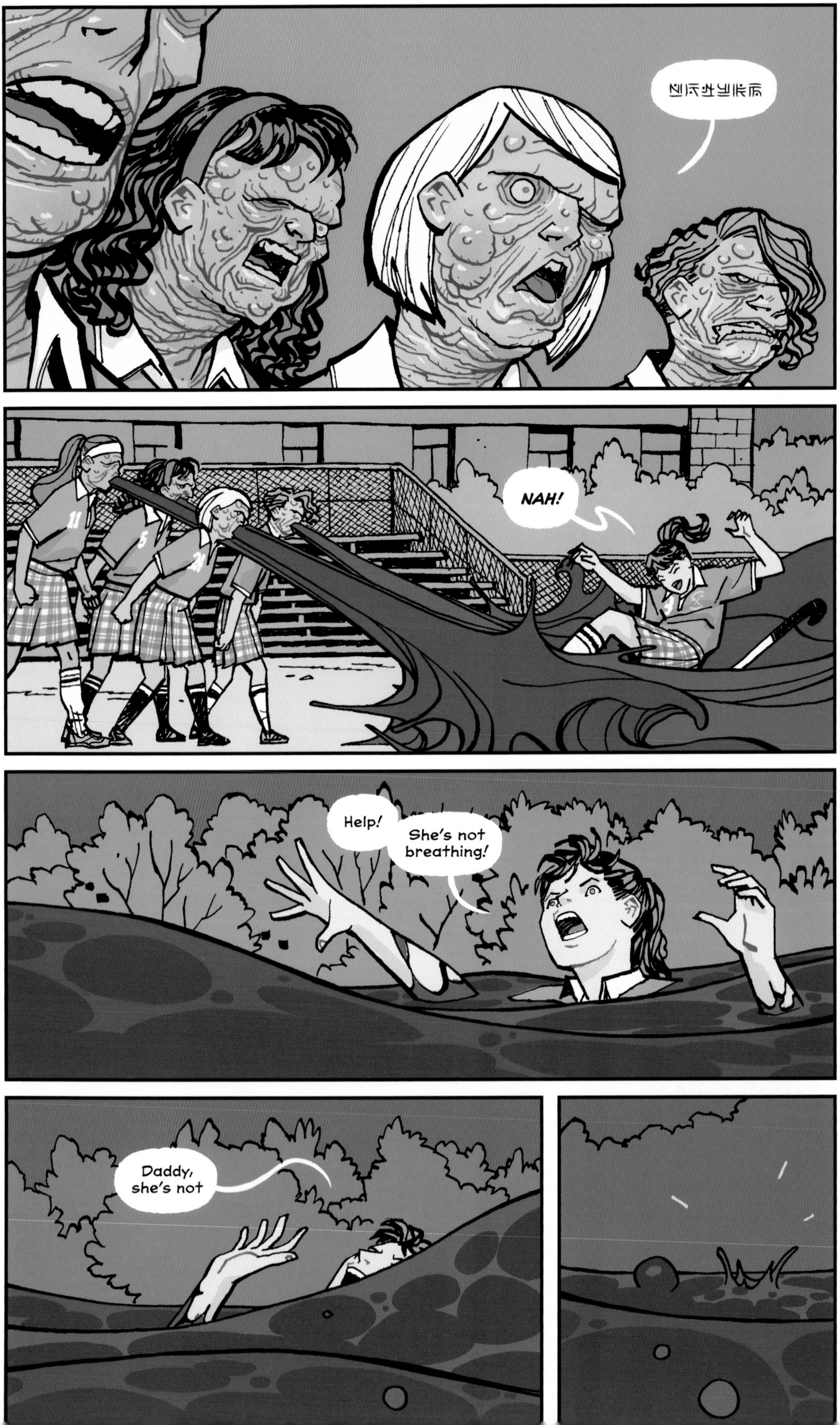
NAH!
Help!
She's not breathing!
Daddy, she's not

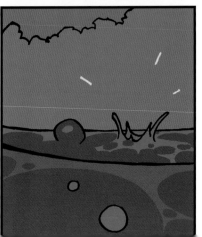

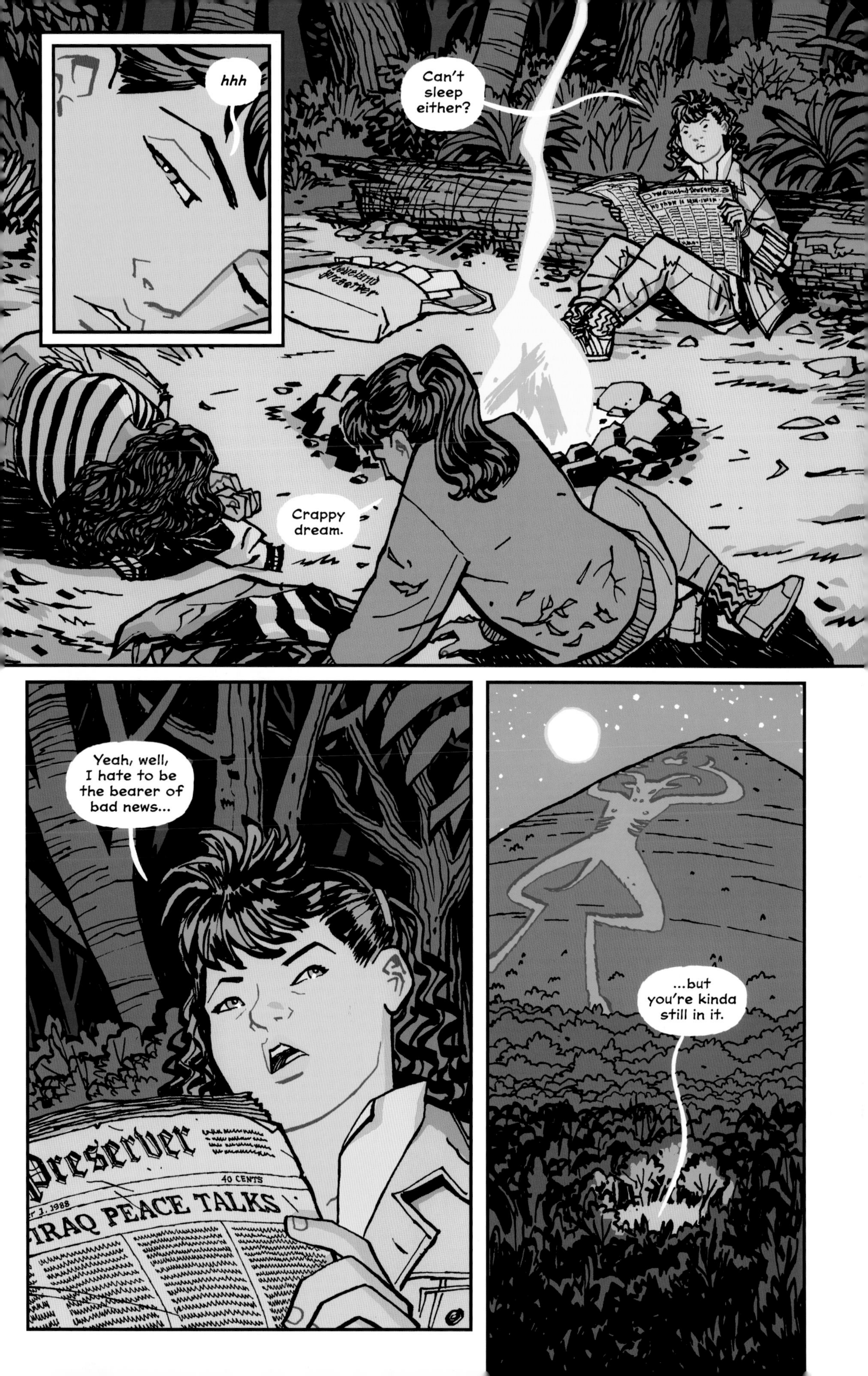
hhh
Can't sleep either?
Crappy dream.
Yeah, well, I hate to be the bearer of bad news...
Preserver
40 CENTS
IRAQ PEACE TALKS
...but you're kinda still in it.

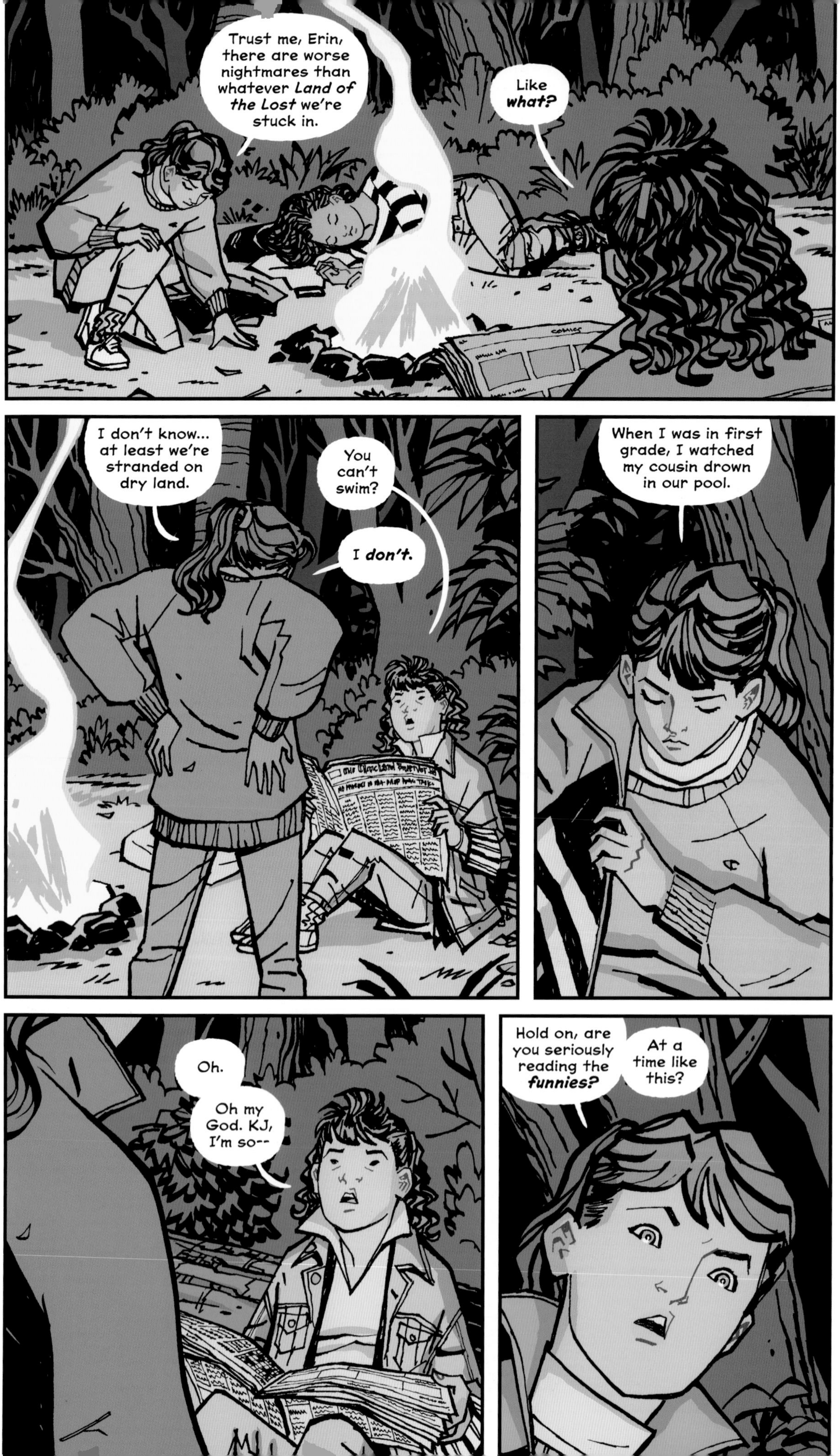
Trust me, Erin, there are worse nightmares than whatever *Land of the Lost* we're stuck in.
Like ***what?***
I don't know... at least we're stranded on dry land.
You can't swim?
I ***don't.***
When I was in first grade, I watched my cousin drown in our pool.
Oh.
Oh my God. KJ, I'm so--
Hold on, are you seriously reading the ***funnies?***
At a time like this?

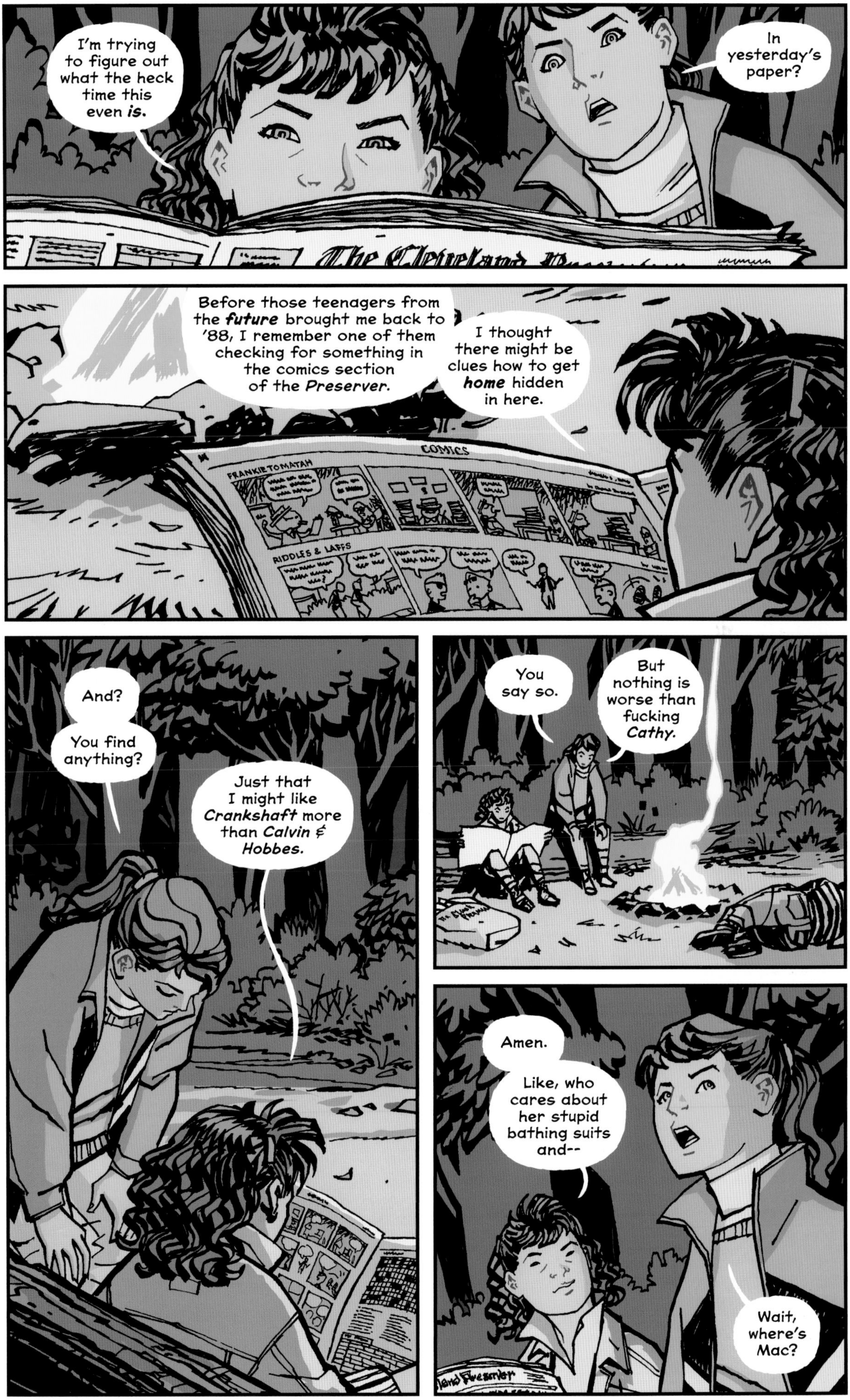
I'm trying to figure out what the heck time this even *is.*
In yesterday's paper?
Before those teenagers from the *future* brought me back to '88, I remember one of them checking for something in the comics section of the *Preserver.*
I thought there might be clues how to get *home* hidden in here.
COMICS
FRANKIE TOMATAH
RIDDLES & LAFFS
And?
You find anything?
Just that I might like *Crankshaft* more than *Calvin & Hobbes.*
You say so.
But nothing is worse than fucking *Cathy.*
Amen.
Like, who cares about her stupid bathing suits and--
Wait, where's Mac?

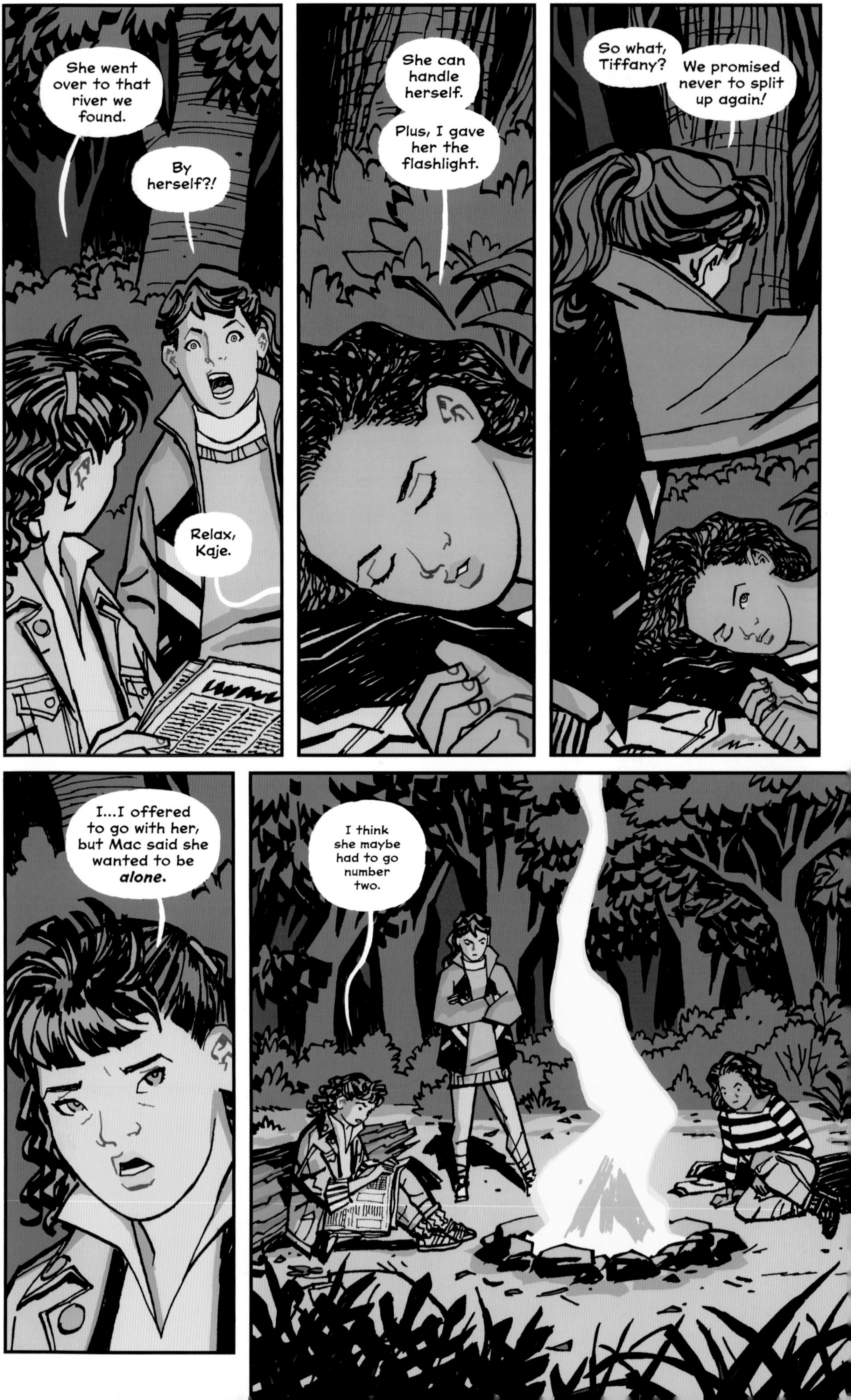
She went over to that river we found.
By herself?!
Relax, Kaje.
She can handle herself.
Plus, I gave her the flashlight.
So what, Tiffany?
We promised never to split up again!
I...I offered to go with her, but Mac said she wanted to be ***alone.***
I think she maybe had to go number two.

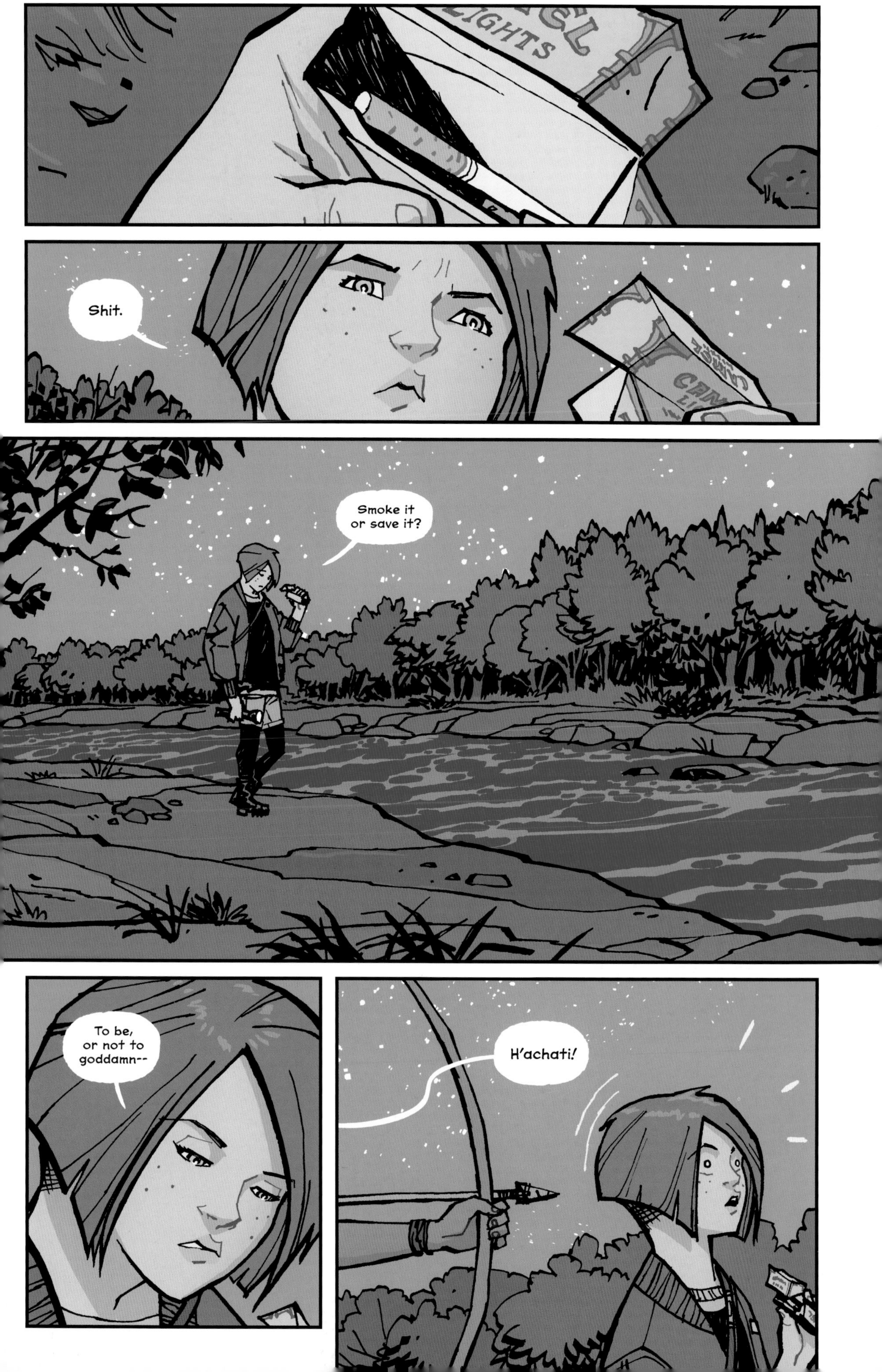
CAMEL LIGHTS
Shit.
Smoke it or save it?
To be, or not to goddamn--
H'achati!

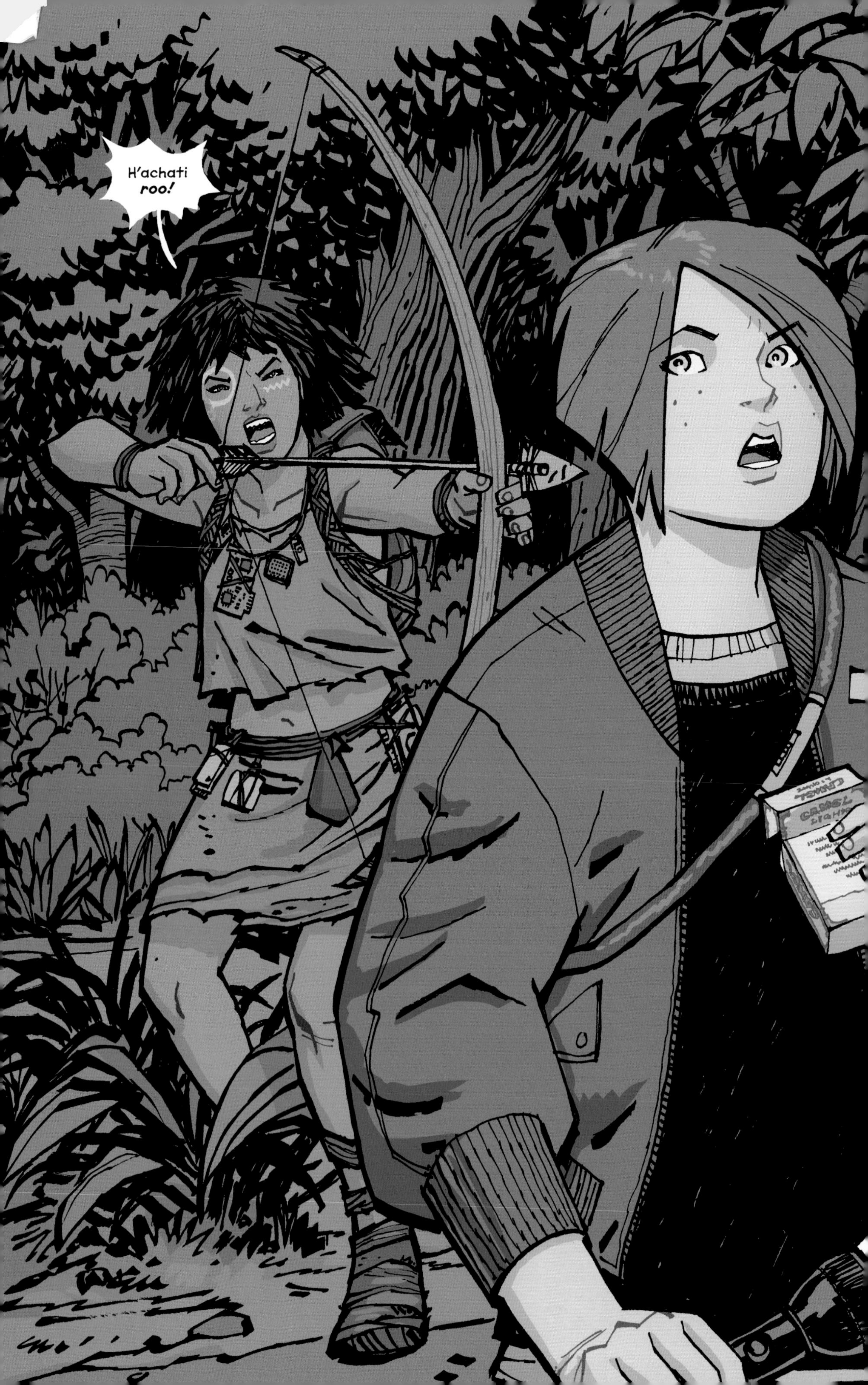
H'achati **roo!**

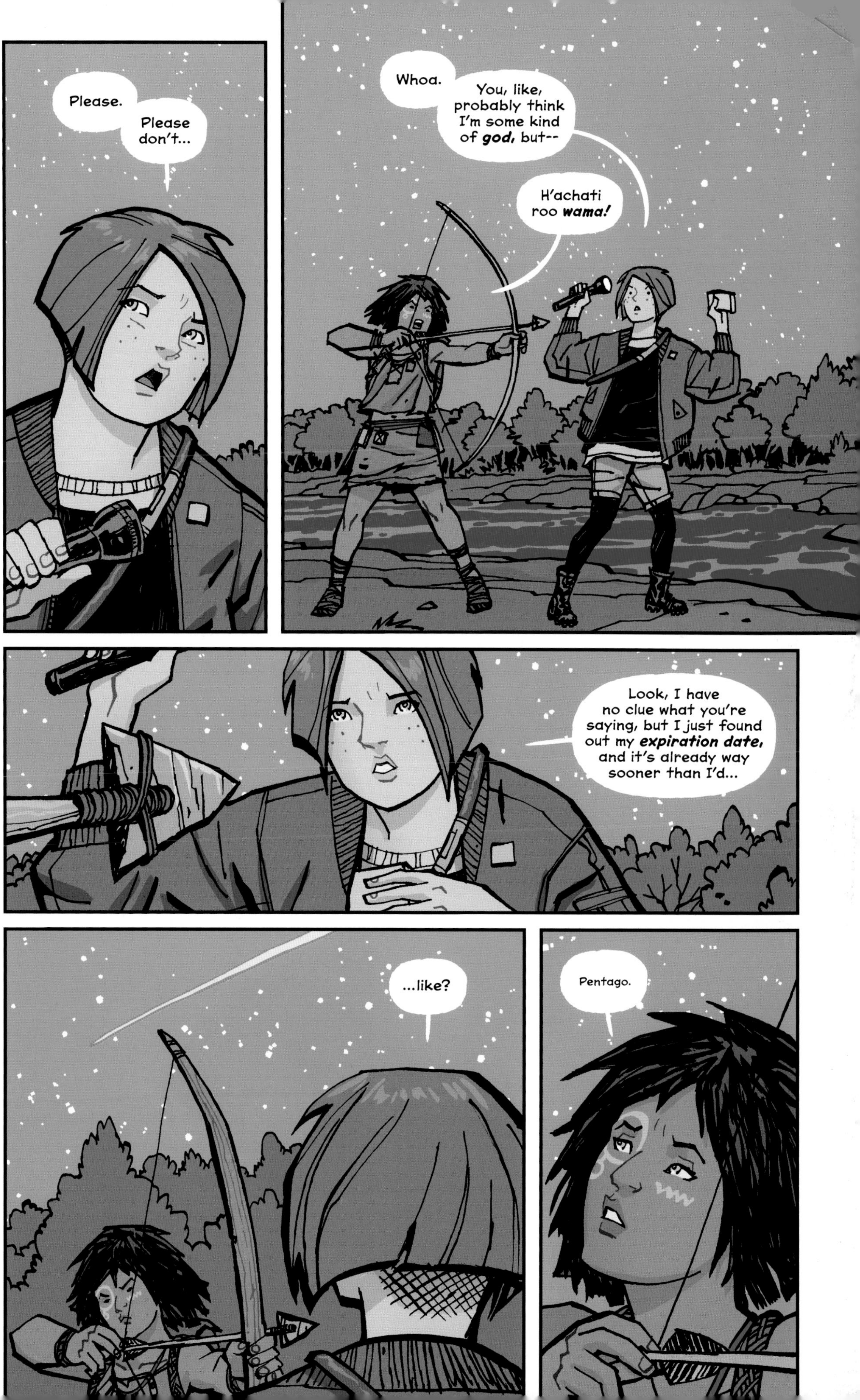
Please.
Please don't...
Whoa.
You, like, probably think I'm some kind of ***god,*** but--
H'achati roo ***wama!***
Look, I have no clue what you're saying, but I just found out my ***expiration date,*** and it's already way sooner than I'd...
...like?
Pentago.

Huhf!

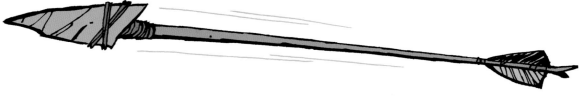

TWHOK

RRAIIIIE!

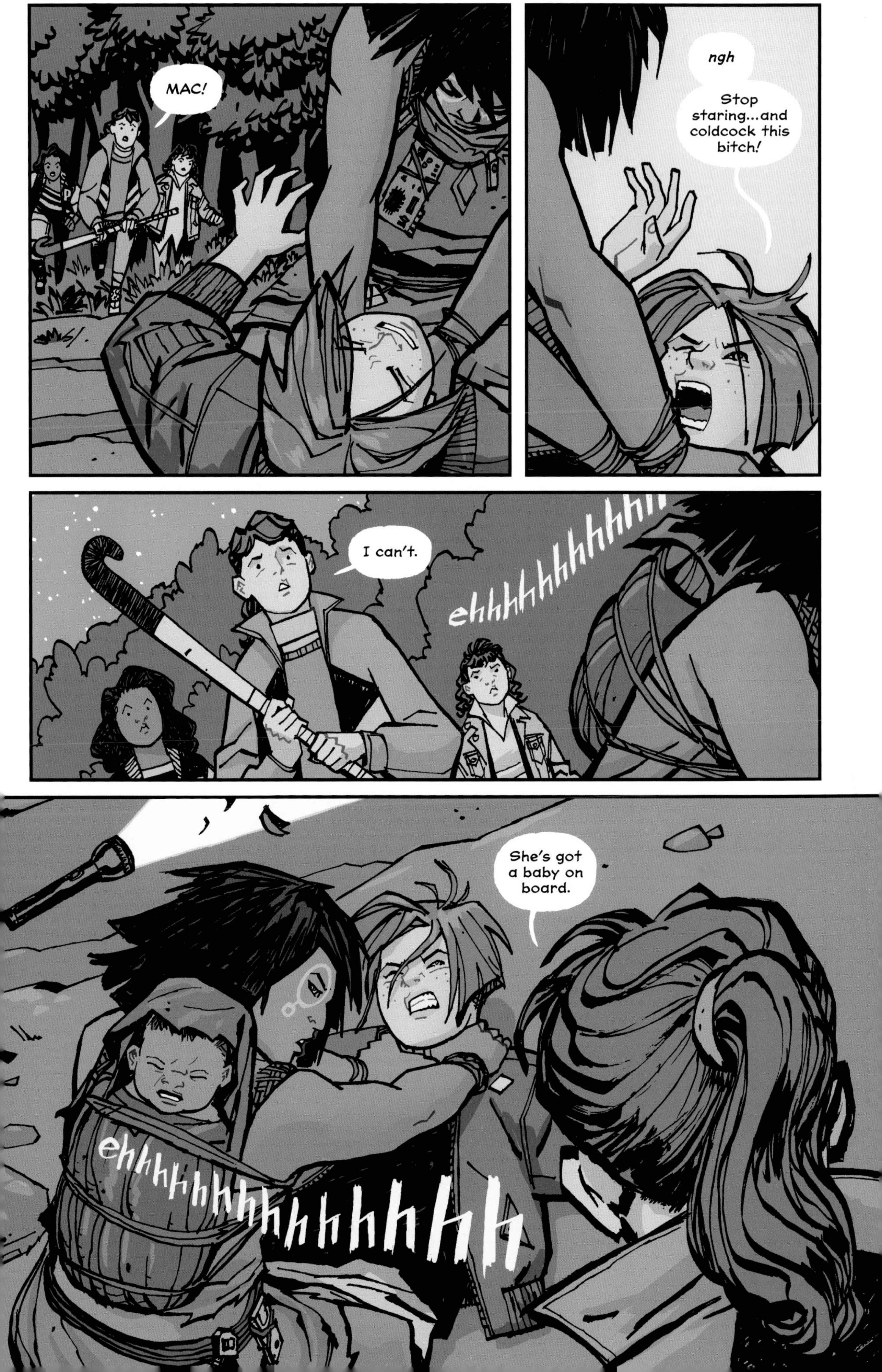
MAC!
ngh
Stop staring...and coldcock this bitch!
I can't.
ehhhhhhhhhhhhhh
She's got a baby on board.
ehhhhhhhhhhhhhhh

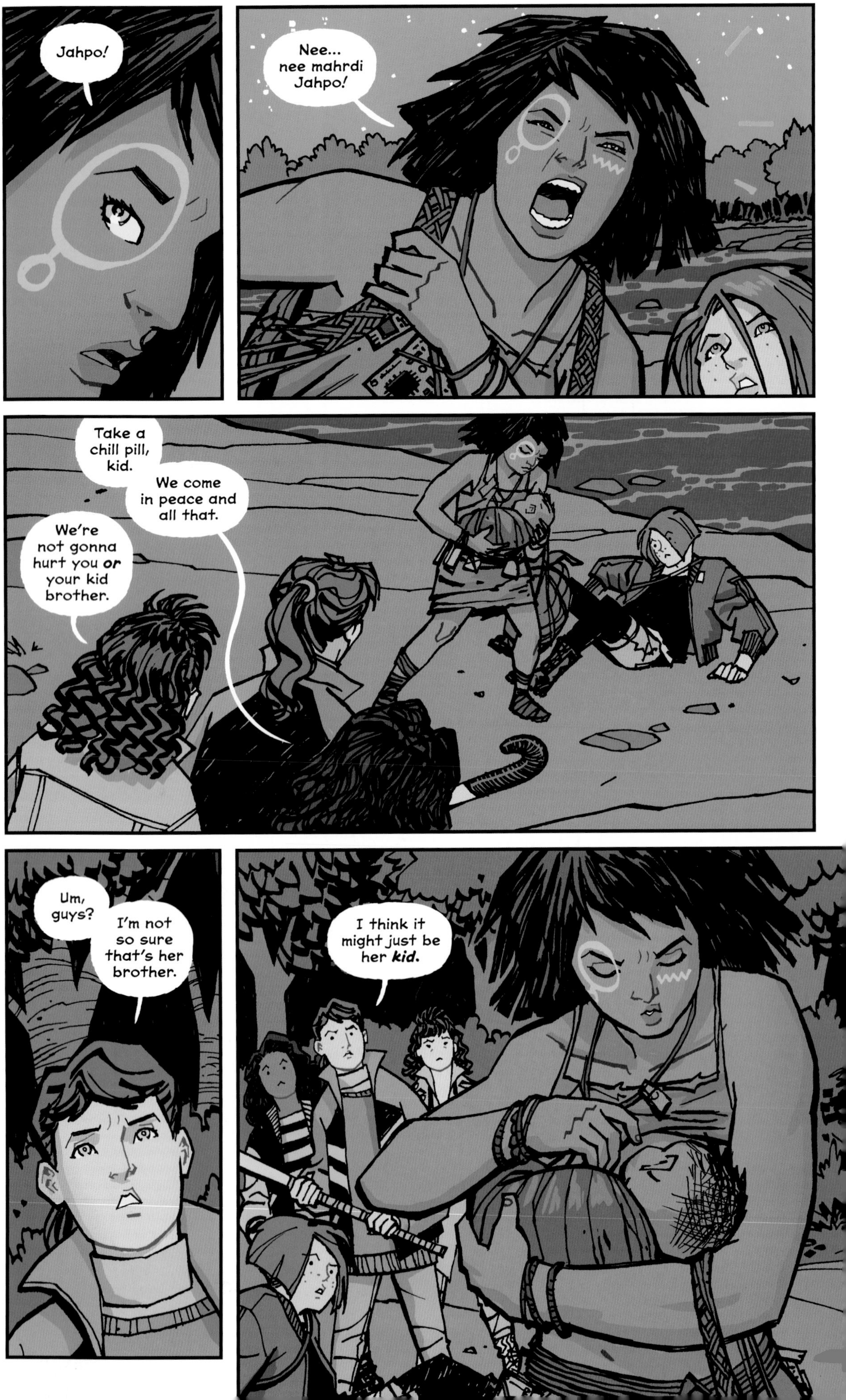
Jahpo!
Nee... nee mahrdi Jahpo!
Take a chill pill, kid.
We come in peace and all that.
We're not gonna hurt you **or** your kid brother.
Um, guys?
I'm not so sure that's her brother.
I think it might just be her **kid.**

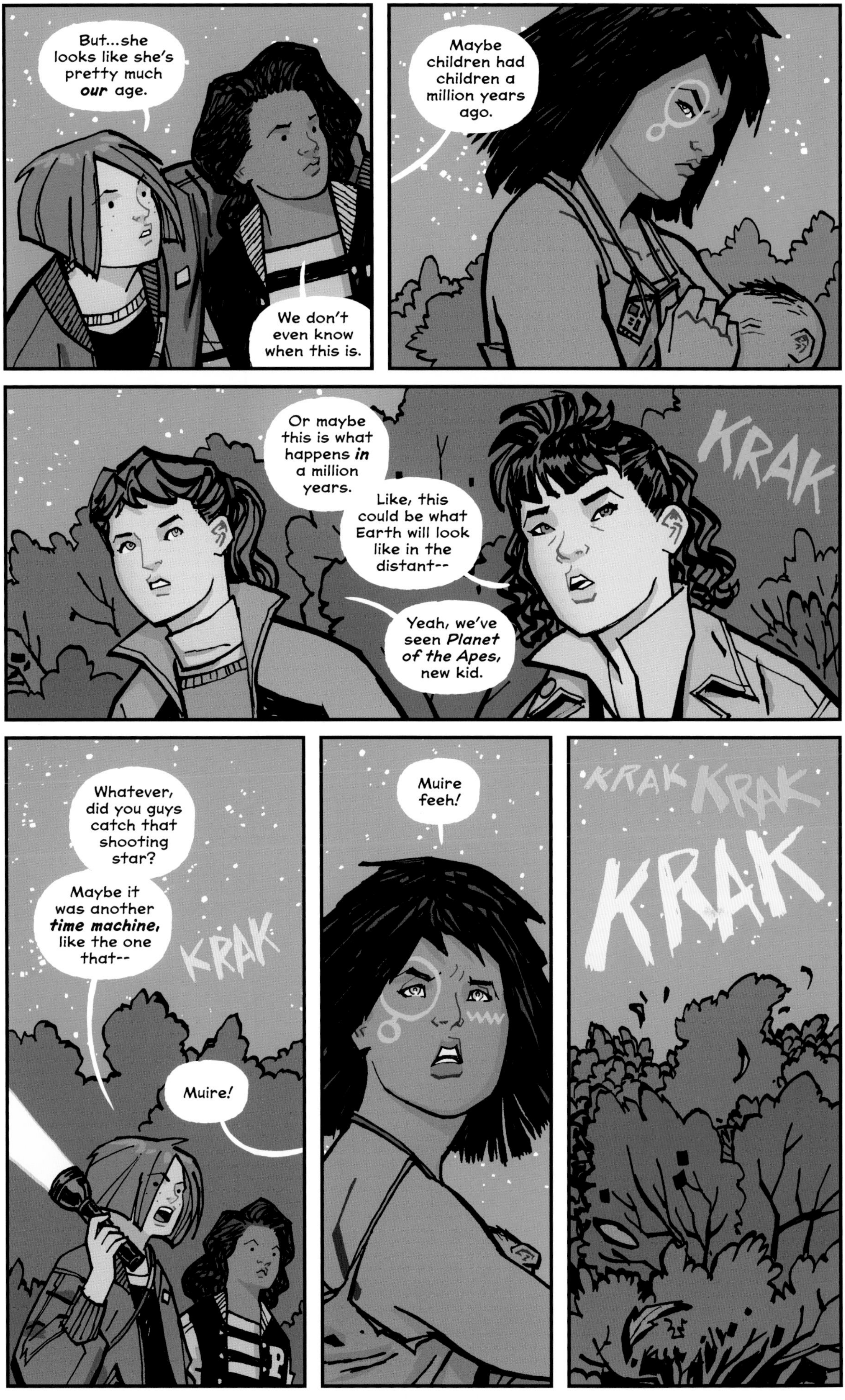
But...she looks like she's pretty much **our** age.
We don't even know when this is.
Maybe children had children a million years ago.
Or maybe this is what happens ***in*** a million years.
Like, this could be what Earth will look like in the distant--
Yeah, we've seen *Planet of the Apes*, new kid.
KRAK
Whatever, did you guys catch that shooting star?
Maybe it was another ***time machine,*** like the one that--
KRAK
Muire!
Muire feeh!
KRAK KRAK
KRAK

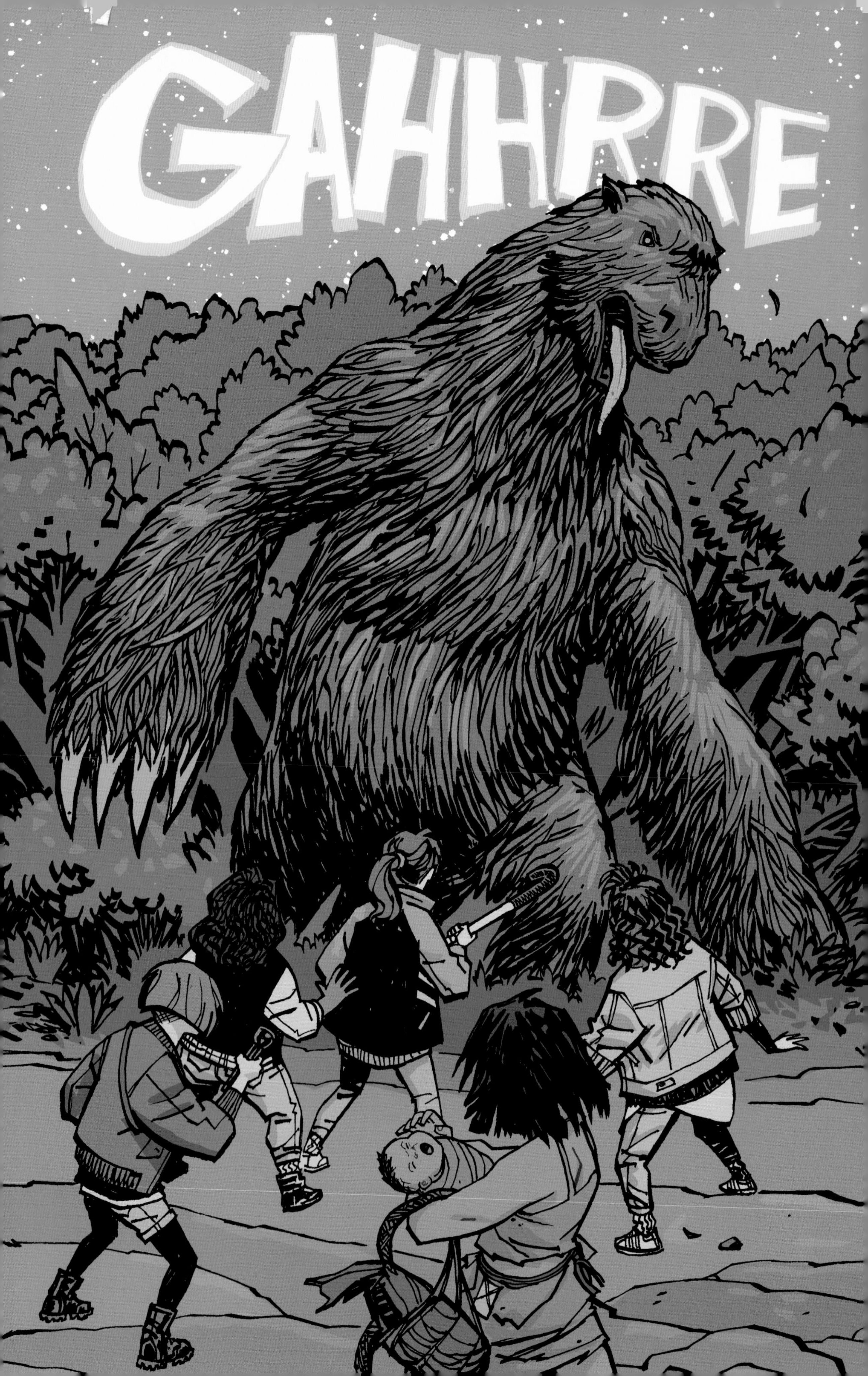
GAHHRRE

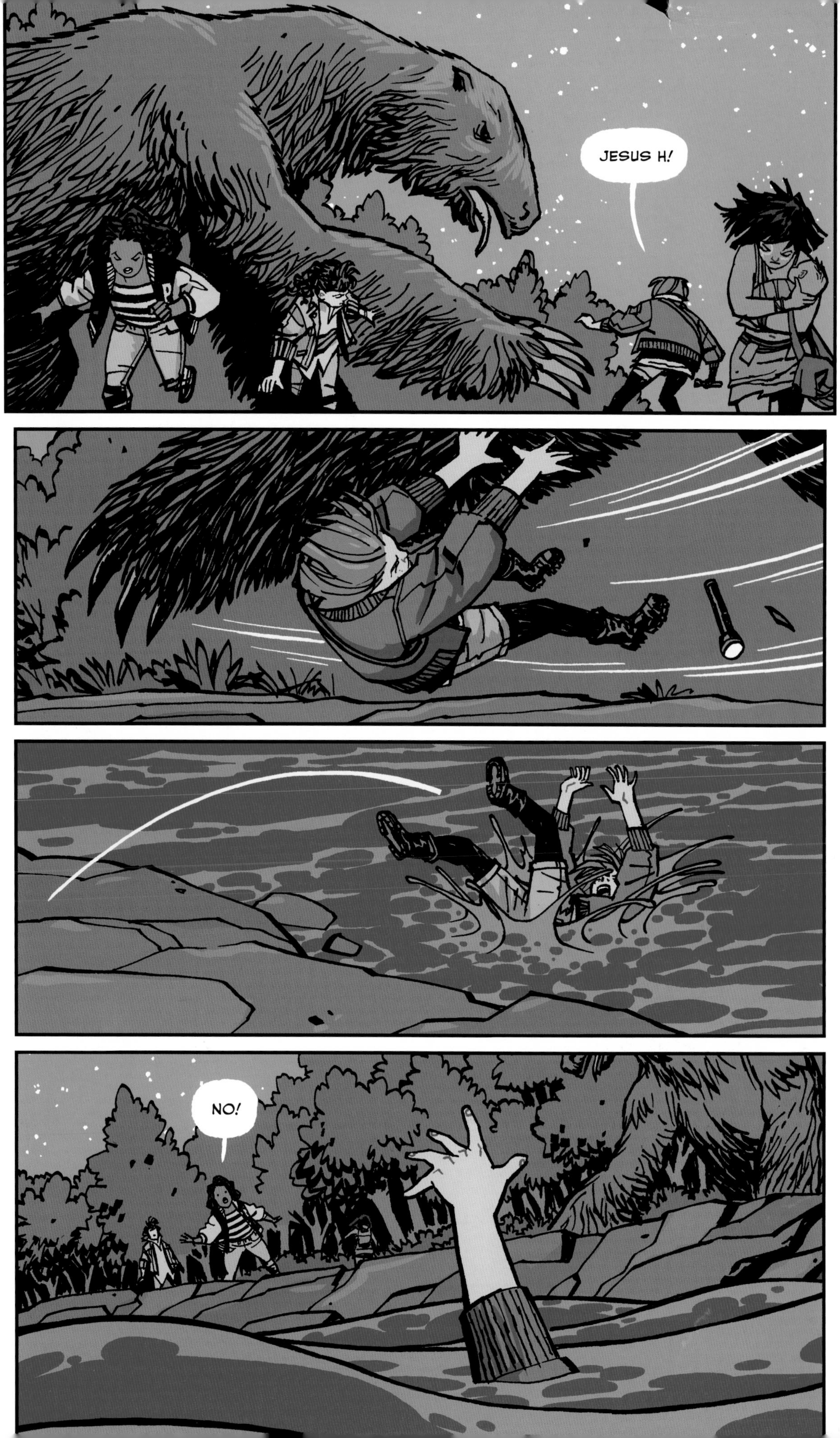
JESUS H!
NO!

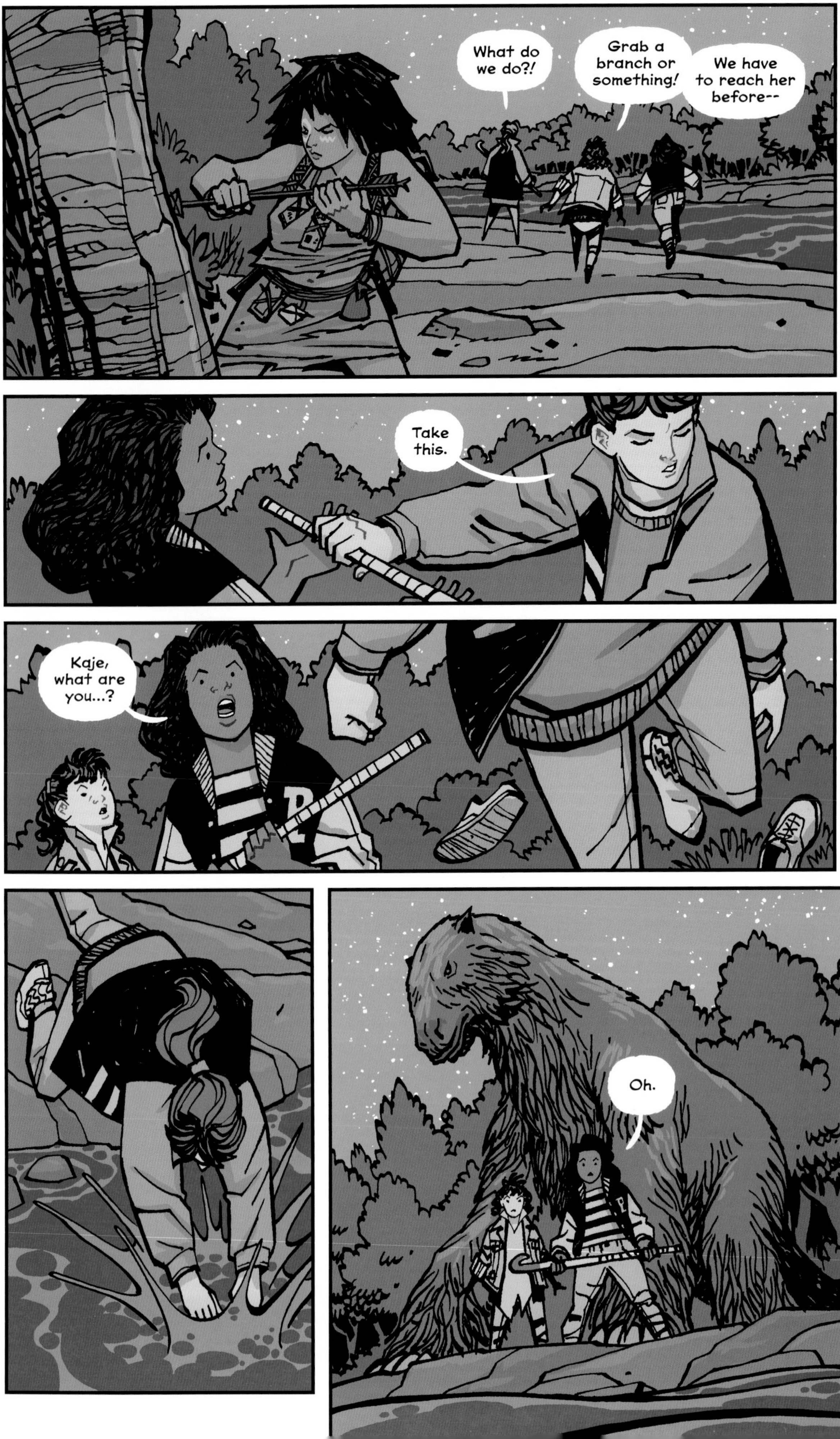
What do we do?!
Grab a branch or something!
We have to reach her before--
Take this.
Kaje, what are you...?
Oh.

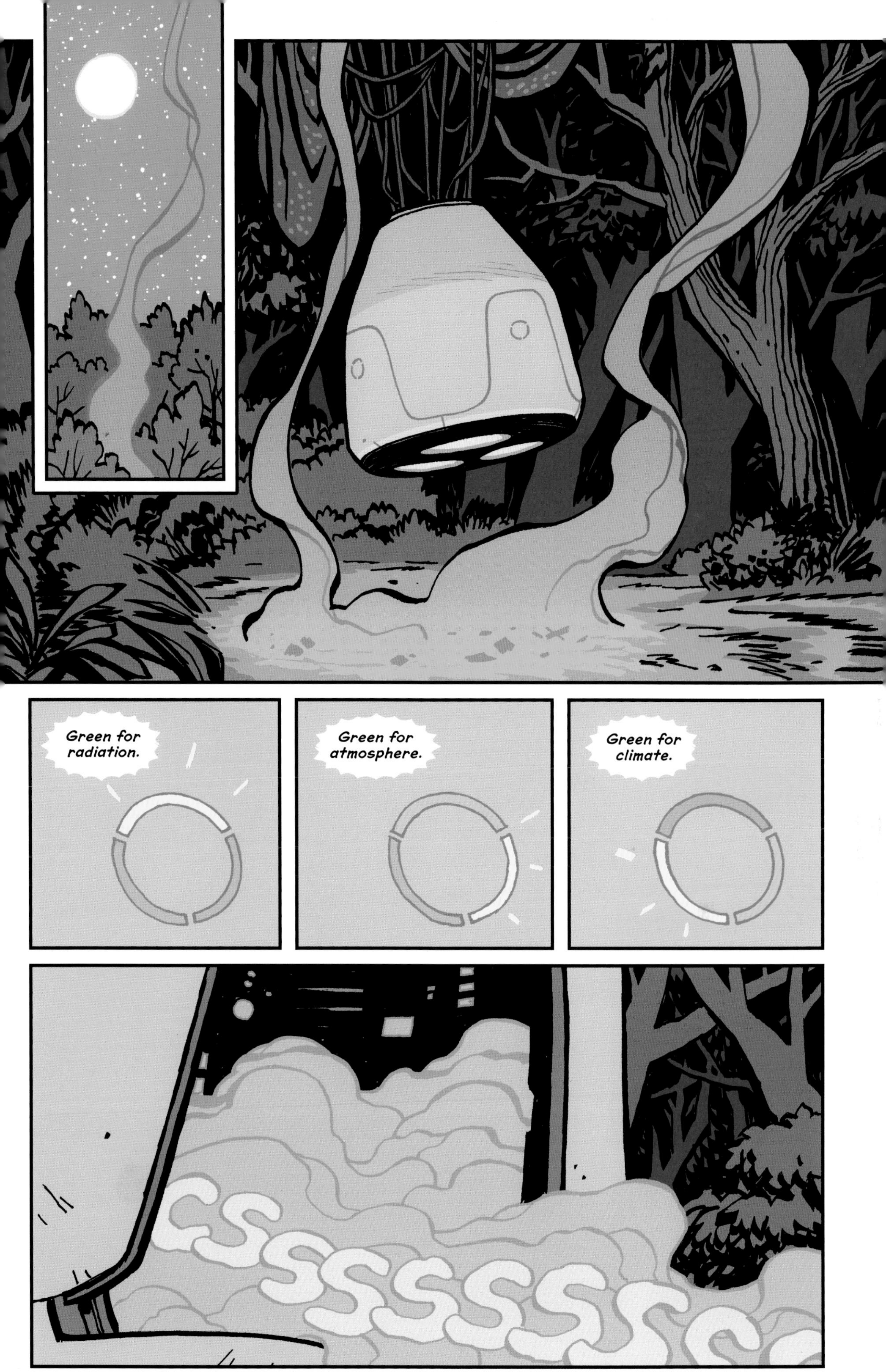
Green for radiation.
Green for atmosphere.
Green for climate.
CSSSSSSSSS

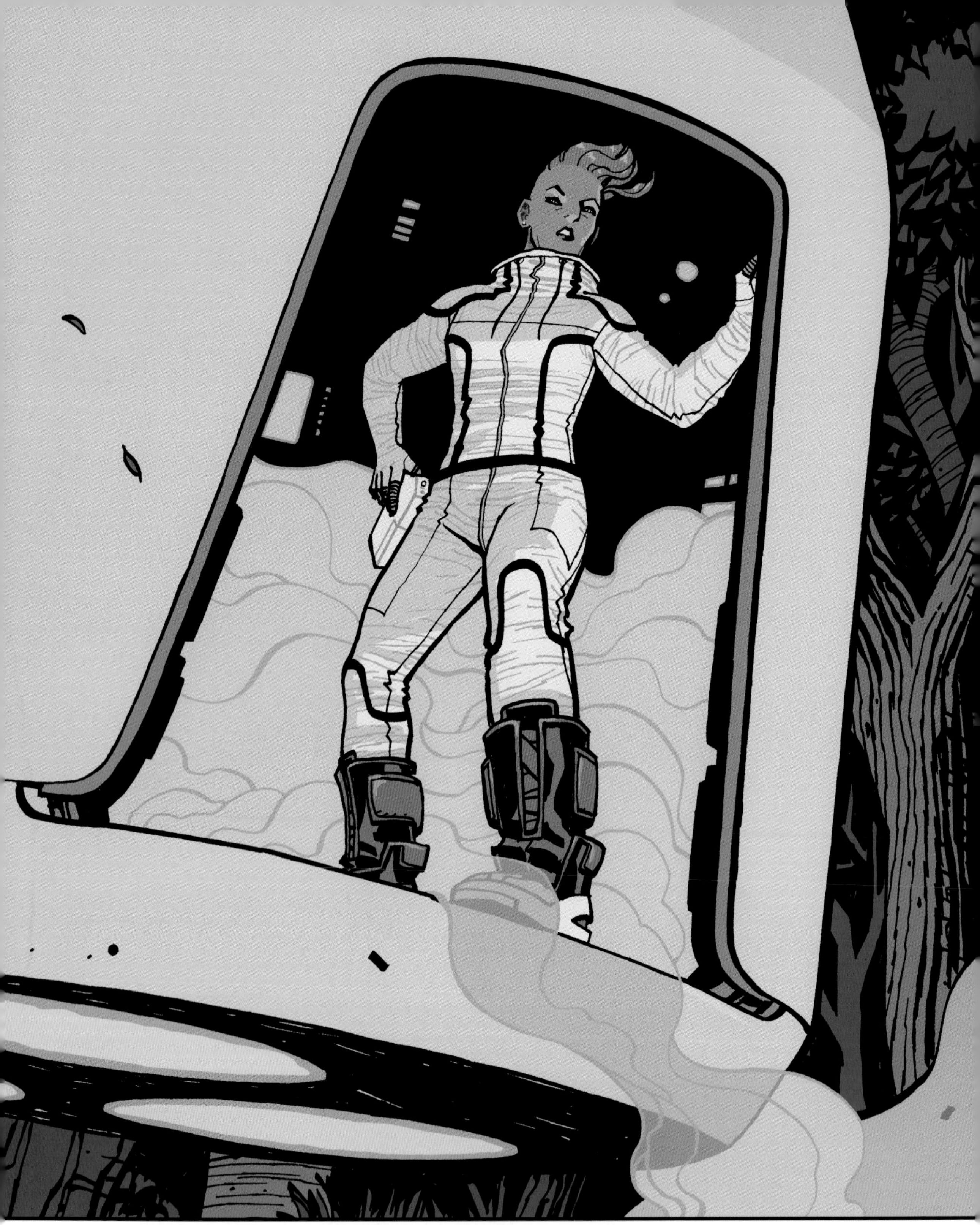

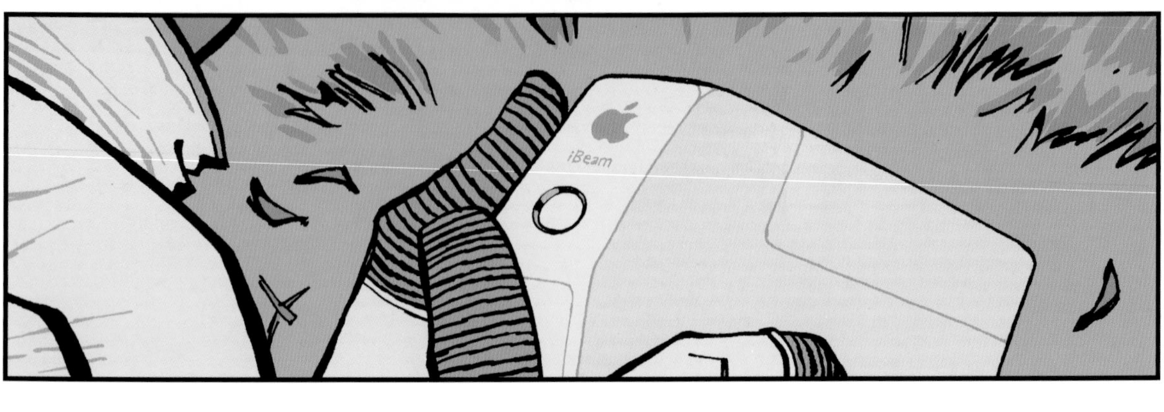
iBeam

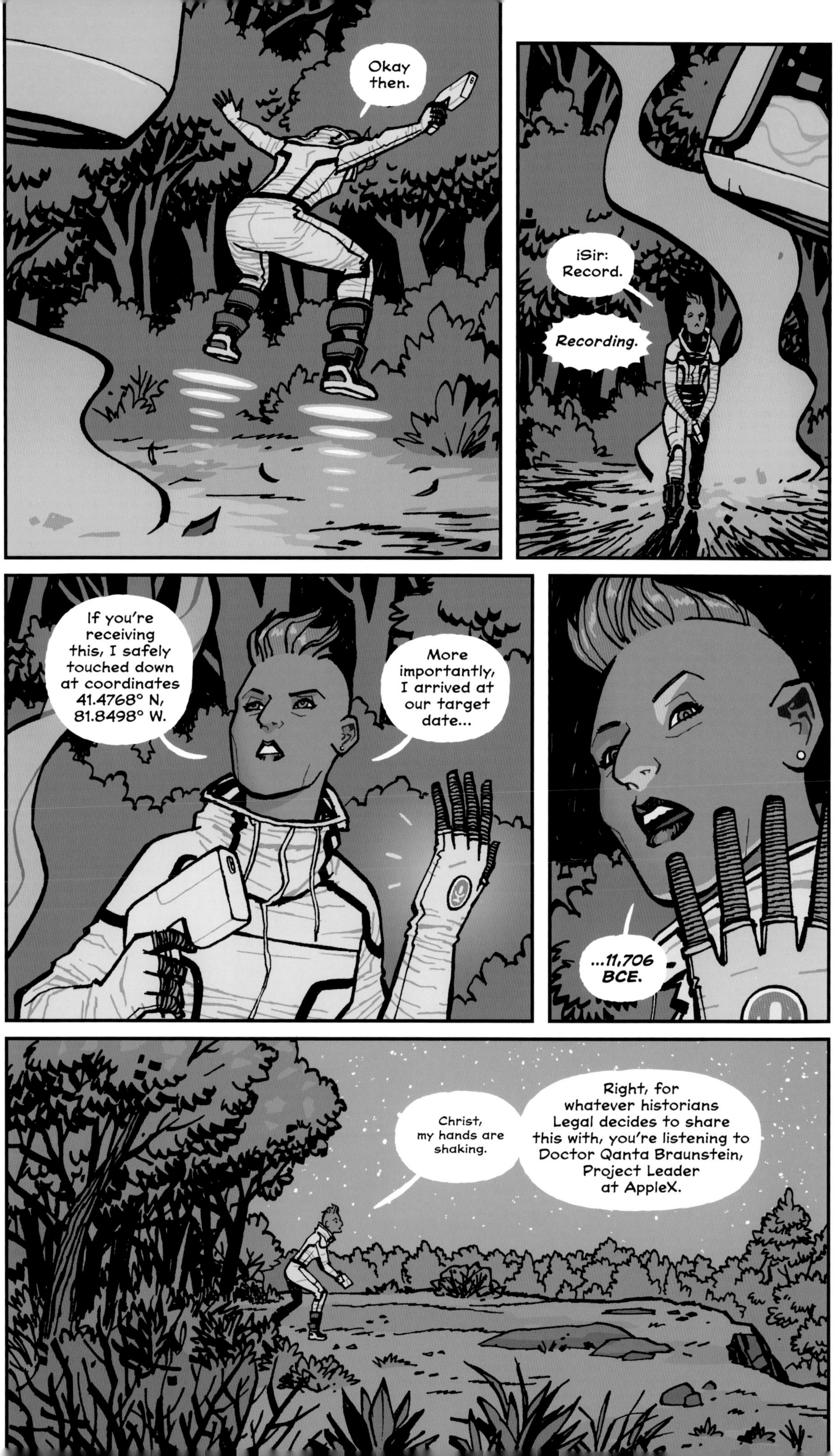
Okay then.
iSir: Record.
Recording.
If you're receiving this, I safely touched down at coordinates 41.4768° N, 81.8498° W.
More importantly, I arrived at our target date...
...11,706 BCE.
Christ, my hands are shaking.
Right, for whatever historians Legal decides to share this with, you're listening to Doctor Qanta Braunstein, Project Leader at AppleX.

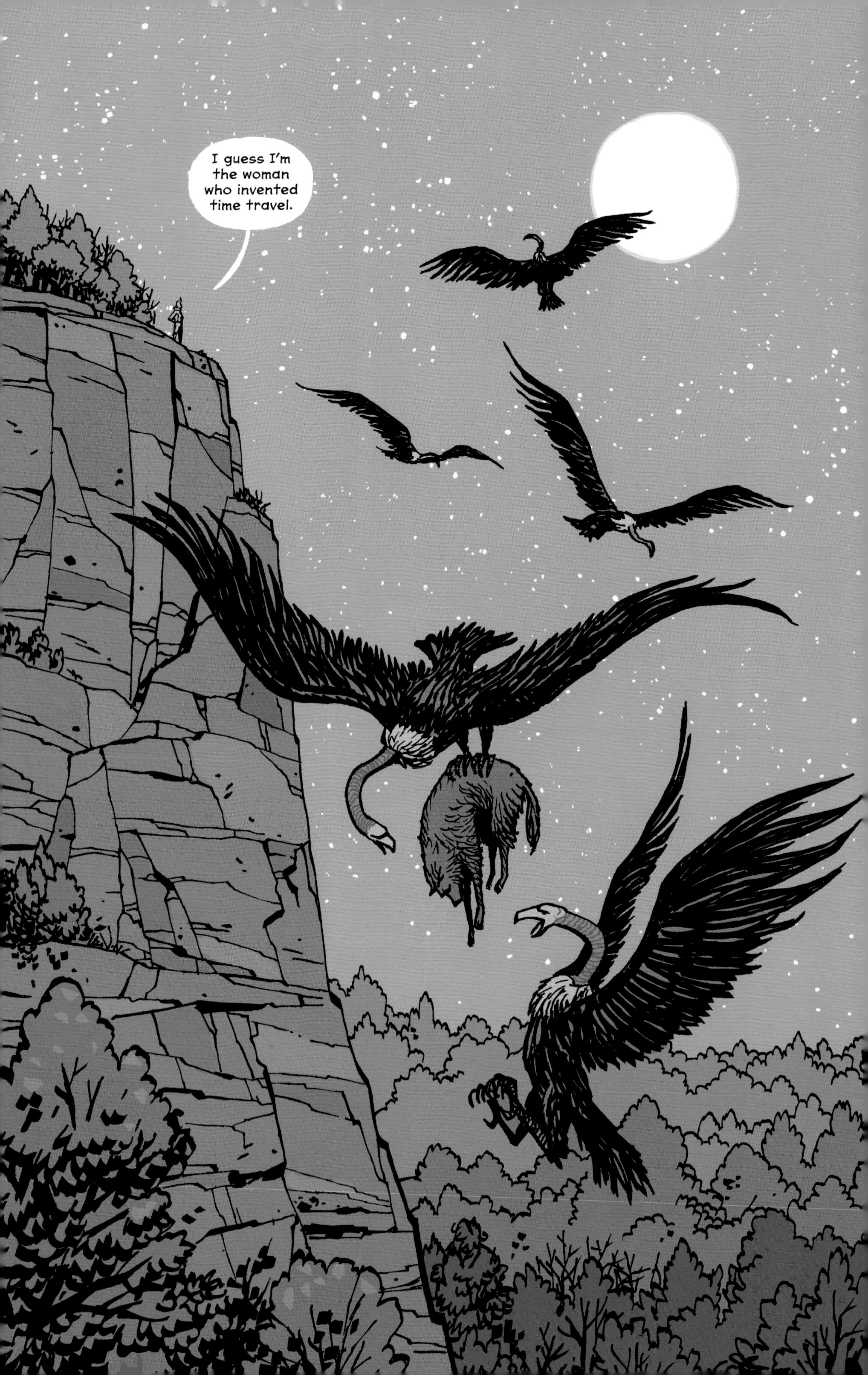
I guess I'm the woman who invented time travel.

CHAPTER
12

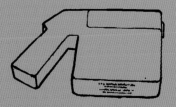

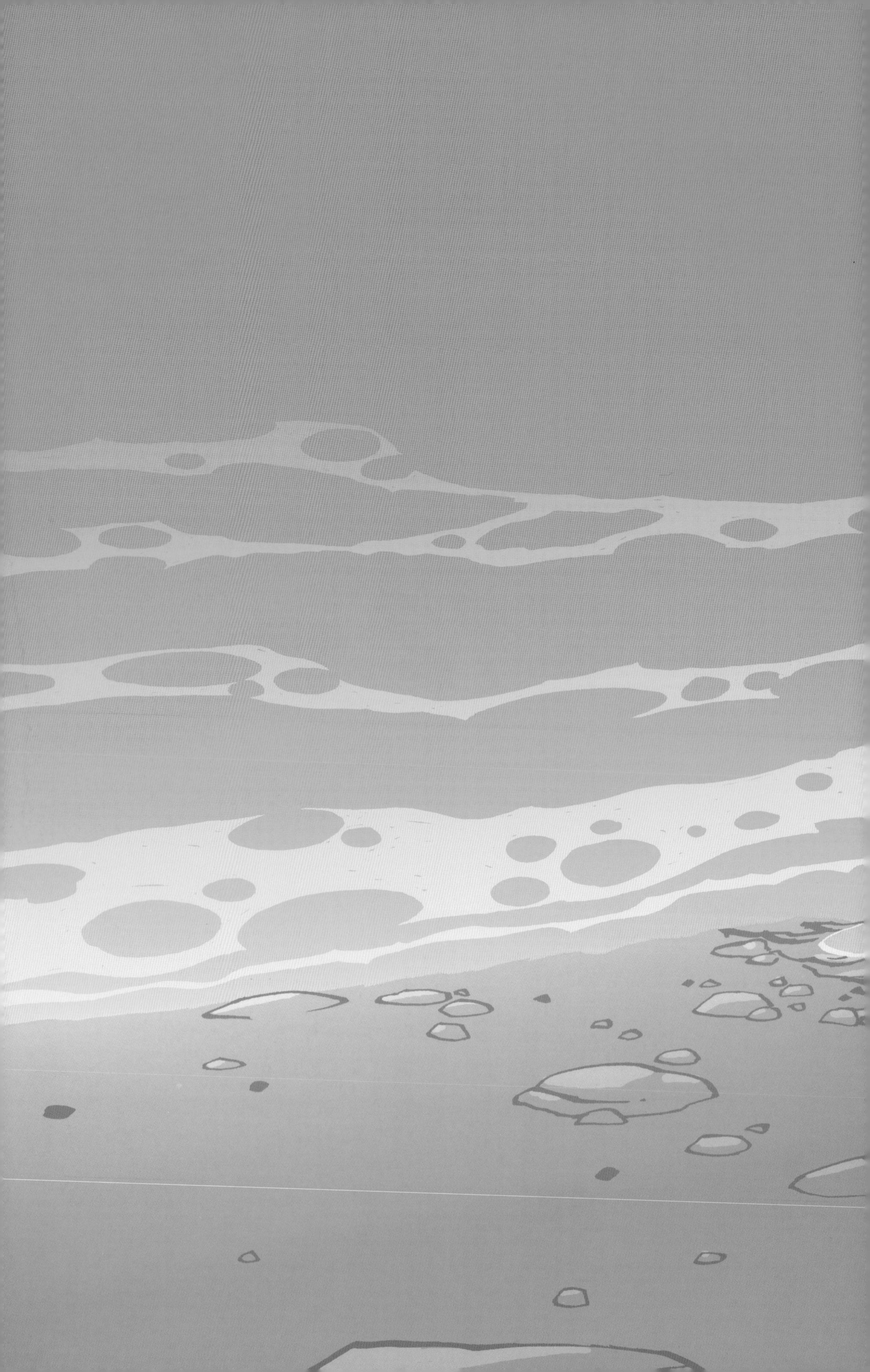

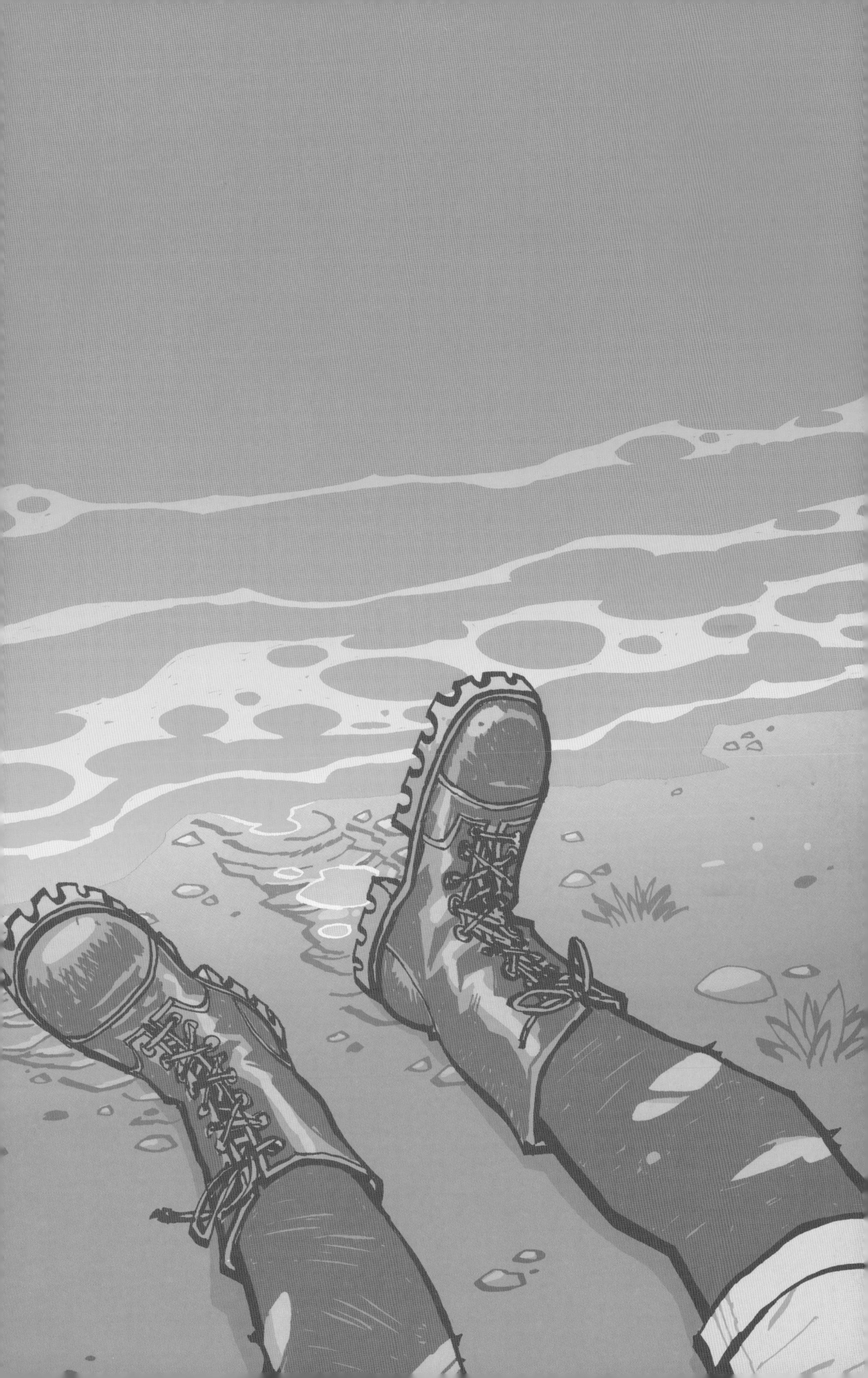

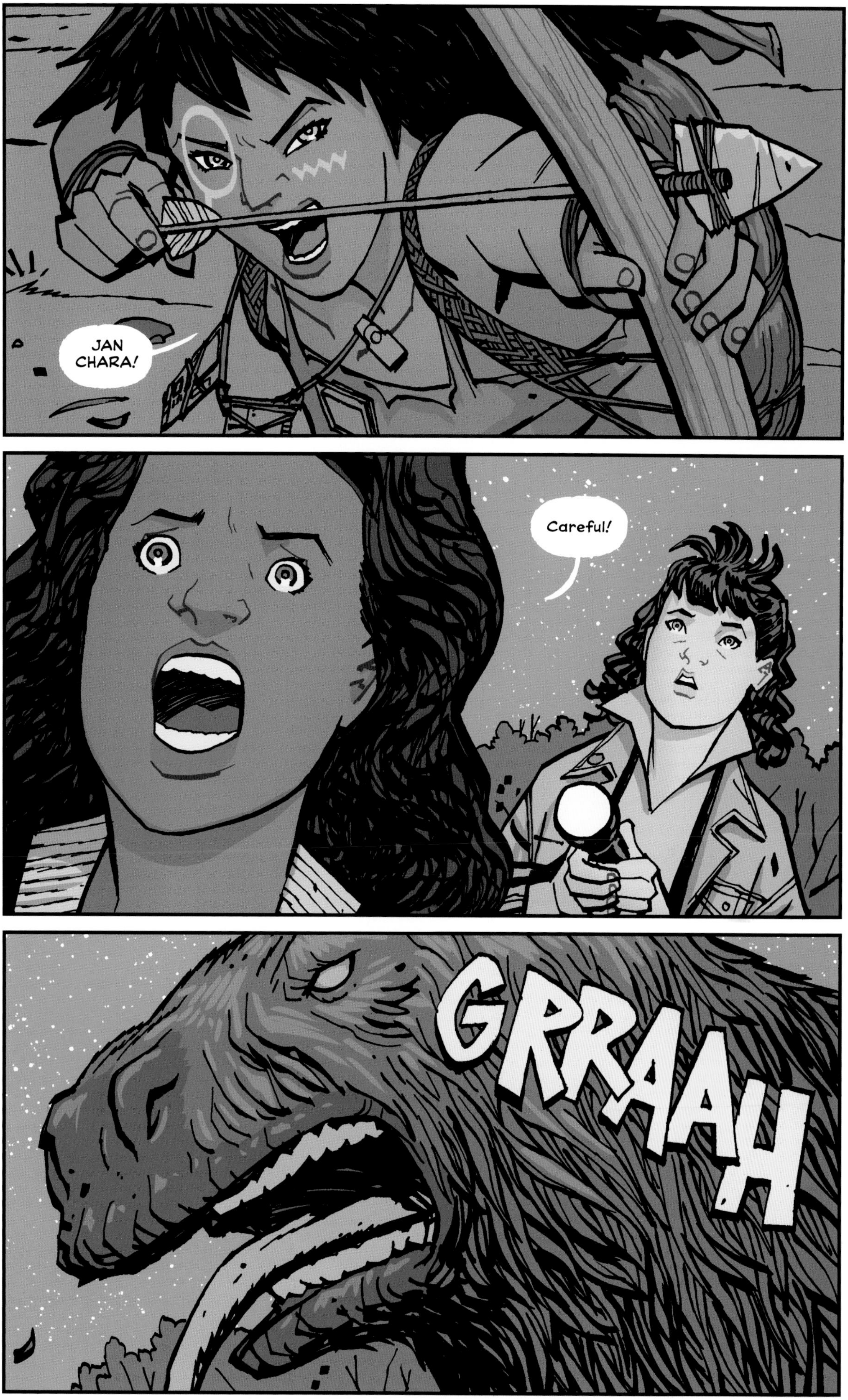
JAN CHARA!
Careful!
GRRAAH

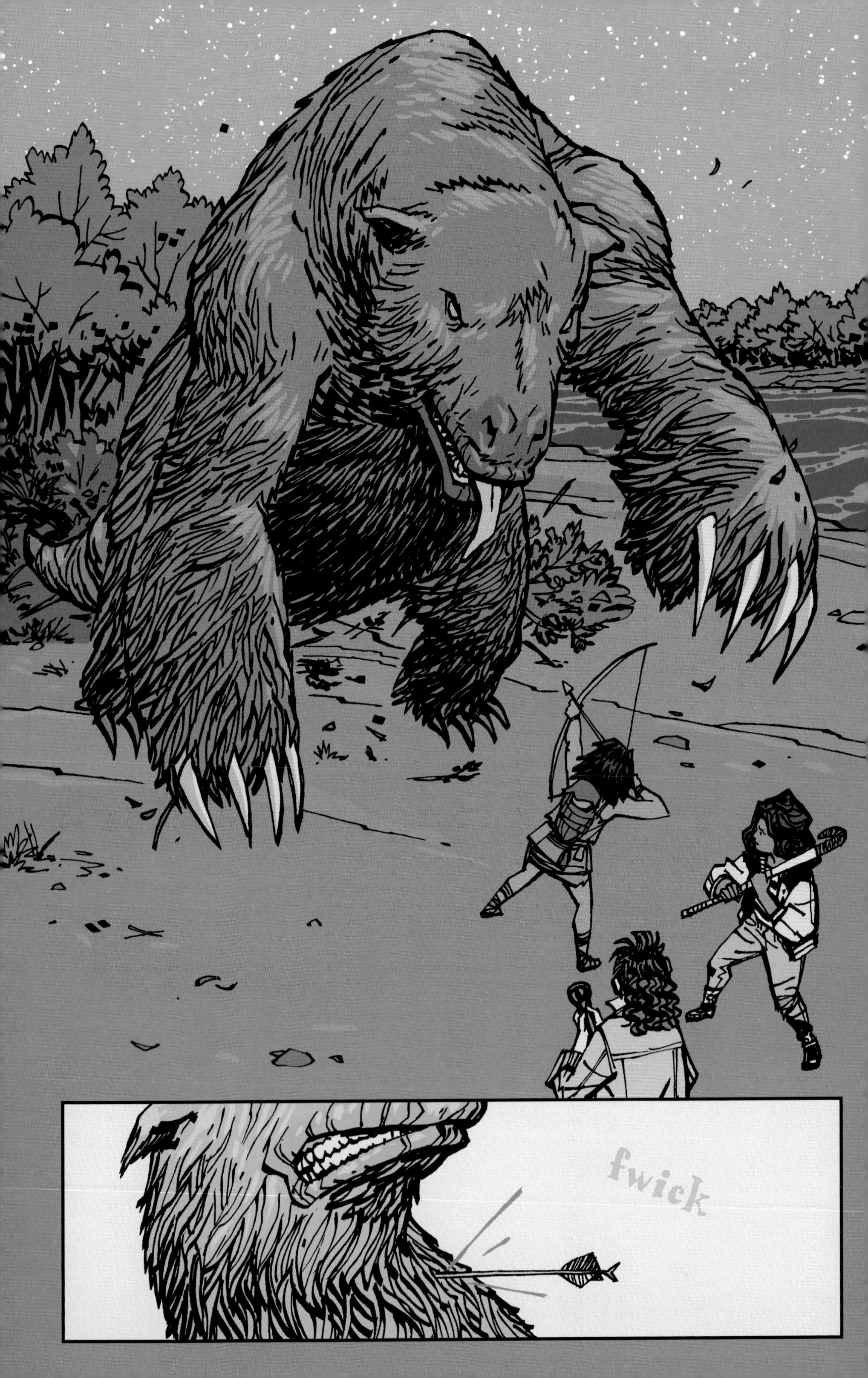
fwick

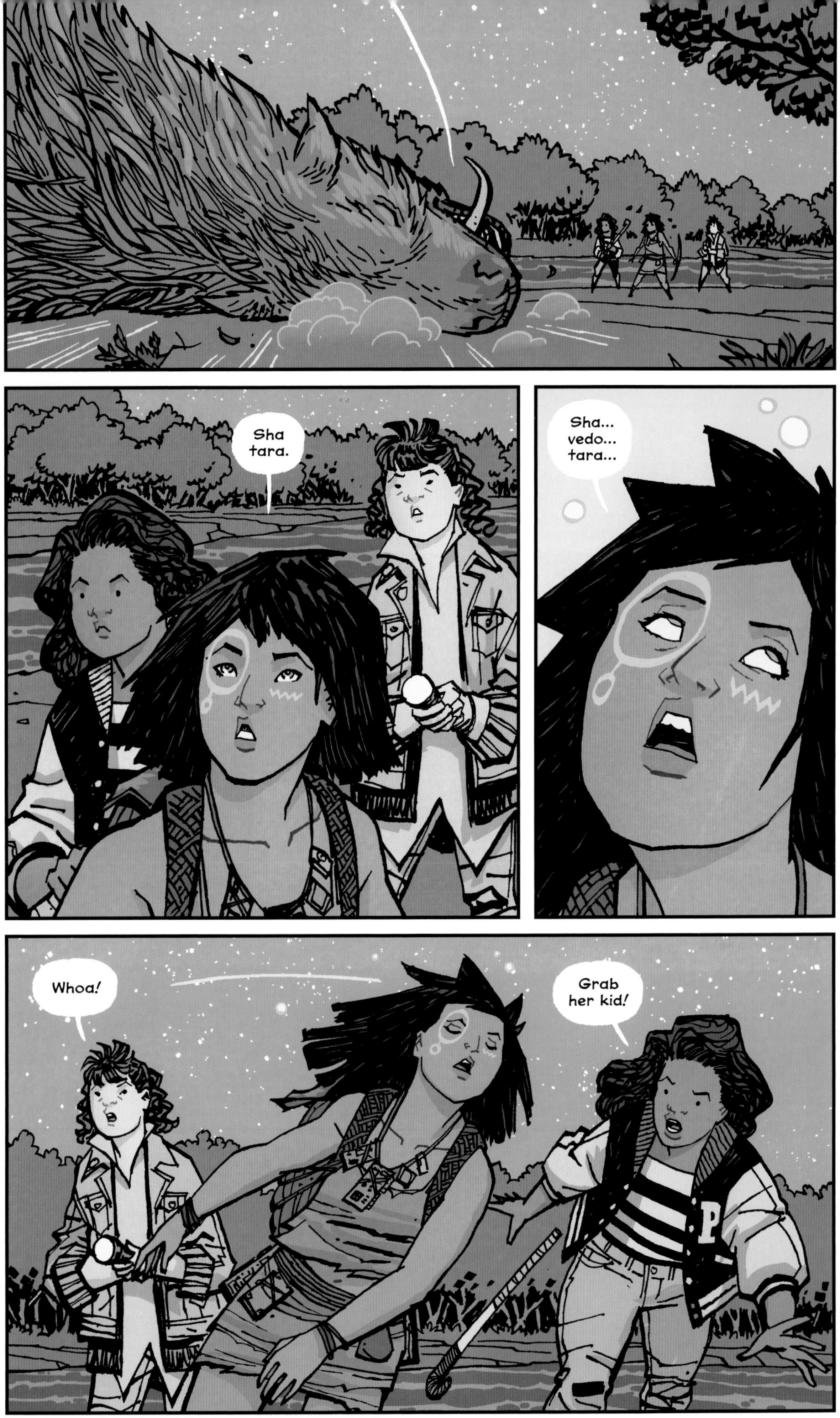
Sha
tara.
Sha...
vedo...
tara...
Whoa!
Grab
her kid!

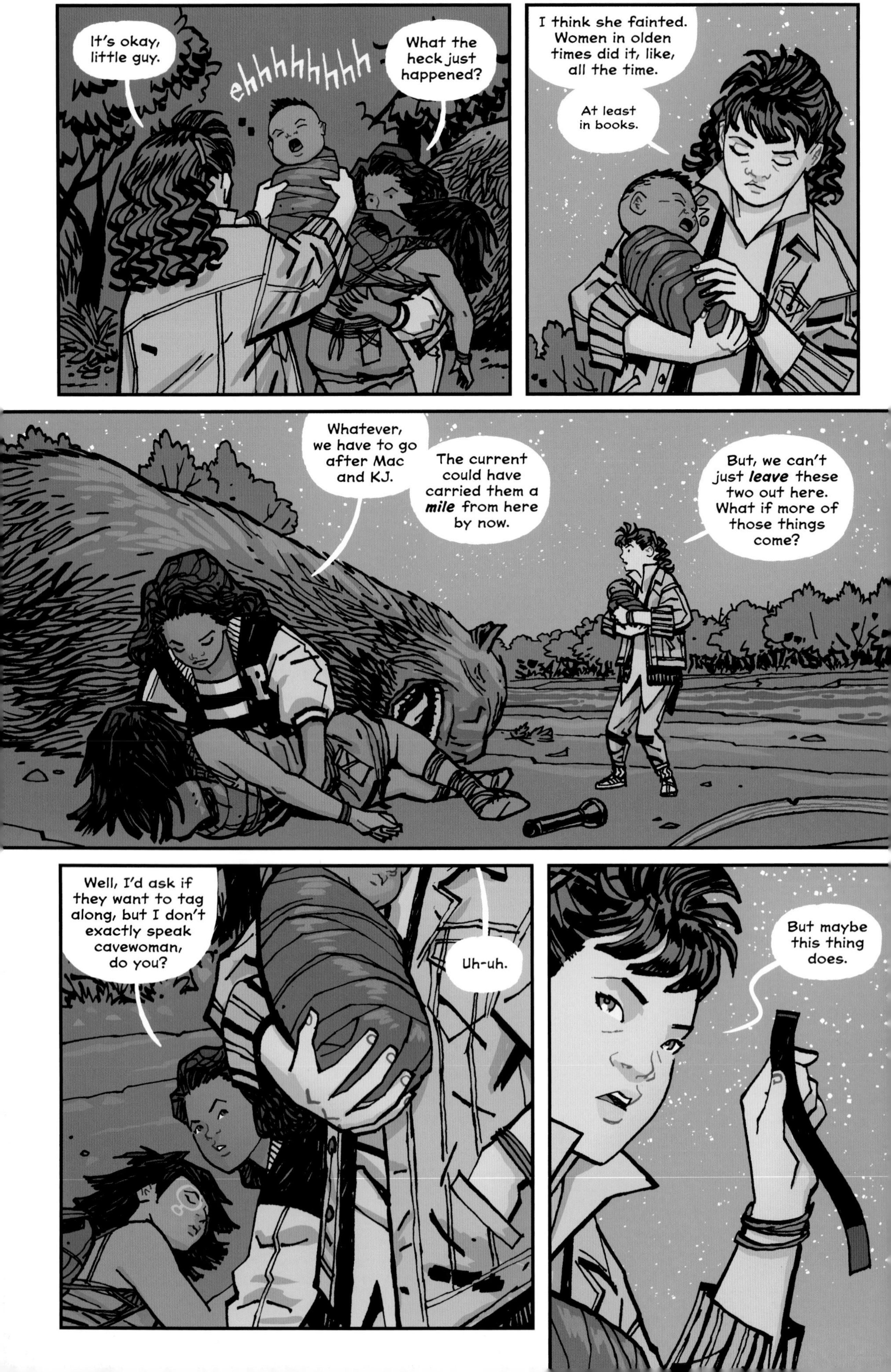

It's okay, little guy.
ehhhhhhhh
What the heck just happened?
I think she fainted. Women in olden times did it, like, all the time.
At least in books.
Whatever, we have to go after Mac and KJ.
The current could have carried them a *mile* from here by now.
But, we can't just *leave* these two out here. What if more of those things come?
Well, I'd ask if they want to tag along, but I don't exactly speak cavewoman, do you?
Uh-uh.
But maybe this thing does.

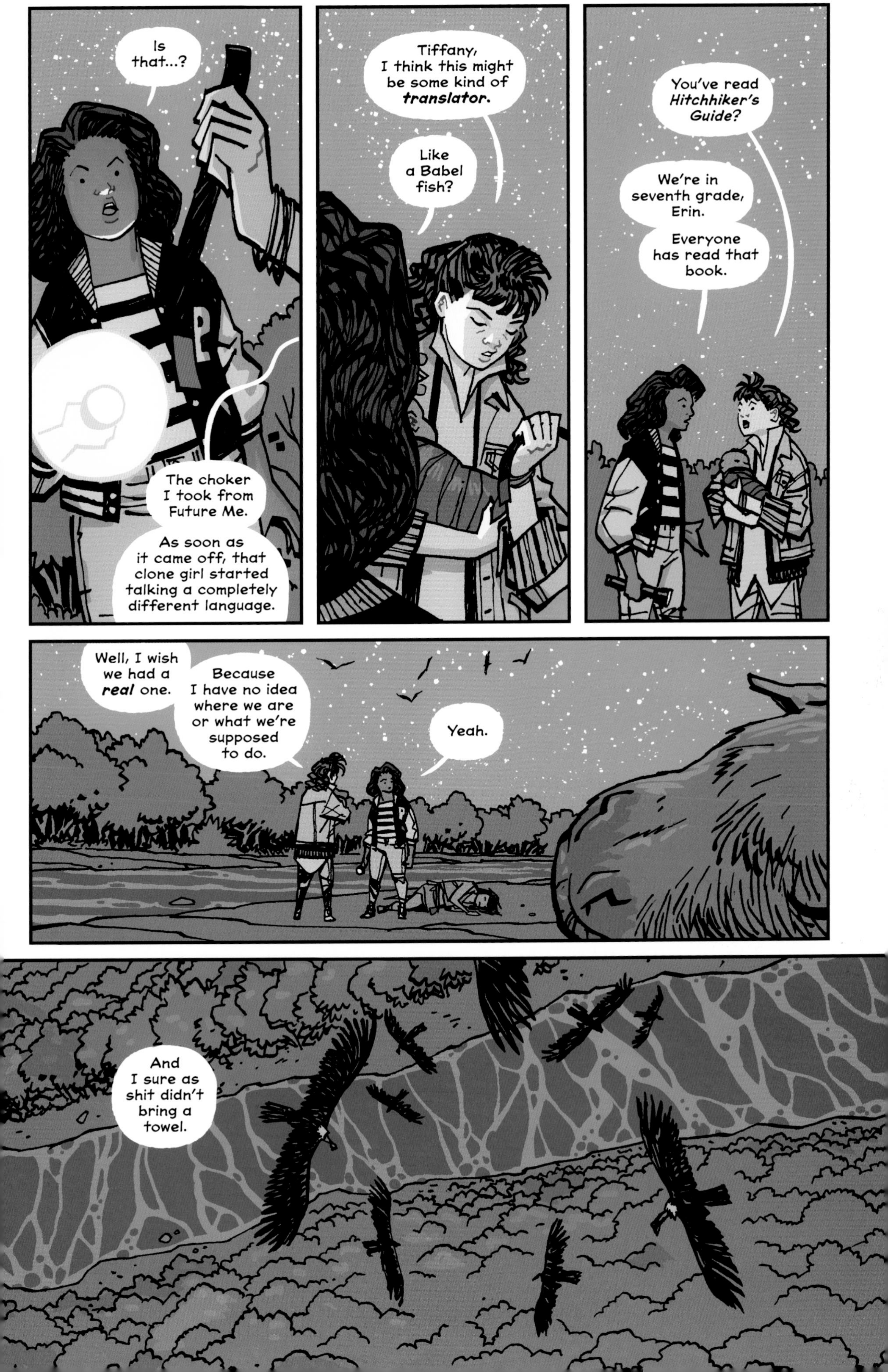

Is that...?
The choker I took from Future Me.
As soon as it came off, that clone girl started talking a completely different language.
Tiffany, I think this might be some kind of ***translator.***
Like a Babel fish?
You've read *Hitchhiker's Guide?*
We're in seventh grade, Erin.
Everyone has read that book.
Well, I wish we had a ***real*** one.
Because I have no idea where we are or what we're supposed to do.
Yeah.
And I sure as shit didn't bring a towel.

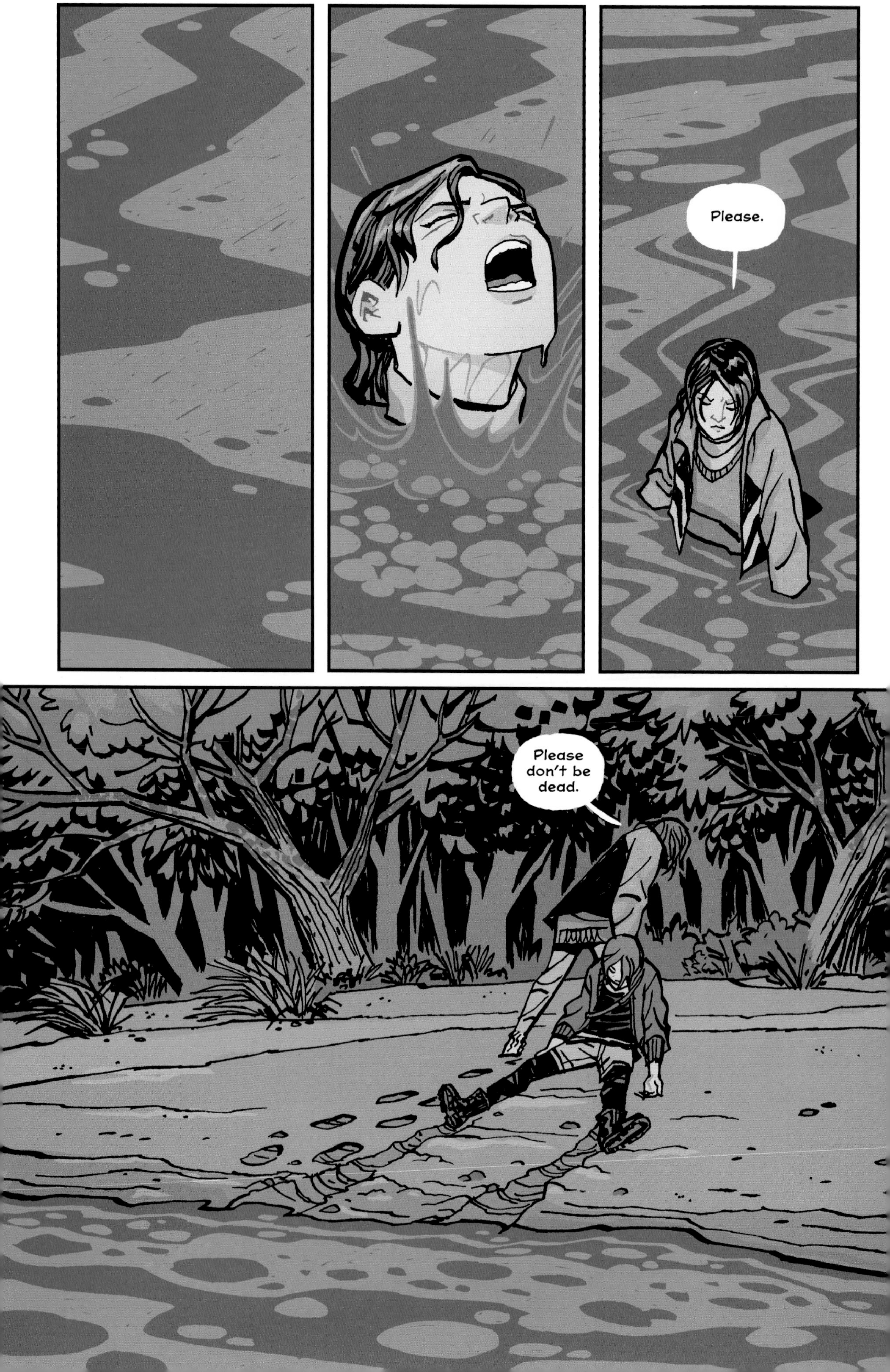
Please.
Please don't be dead.

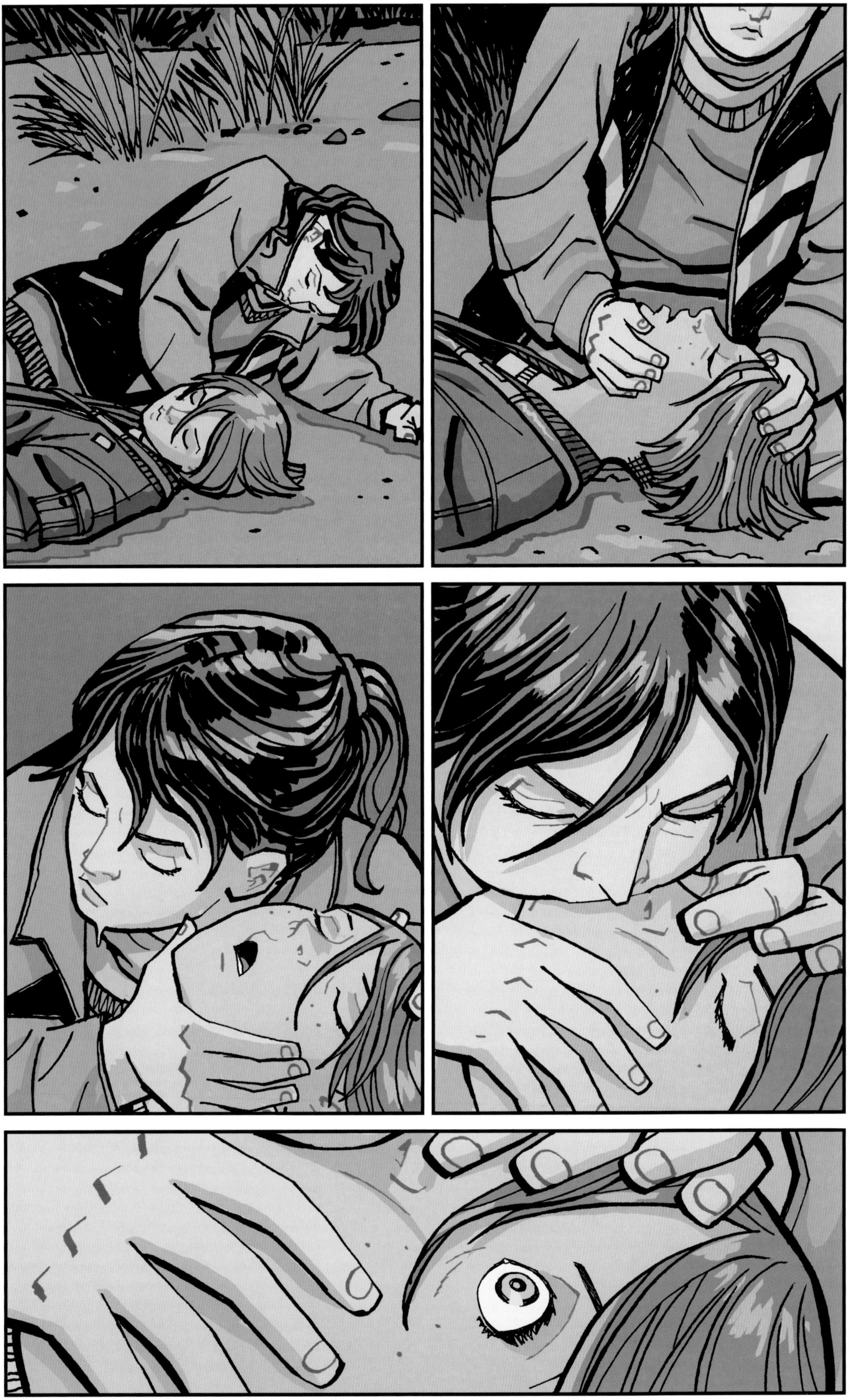

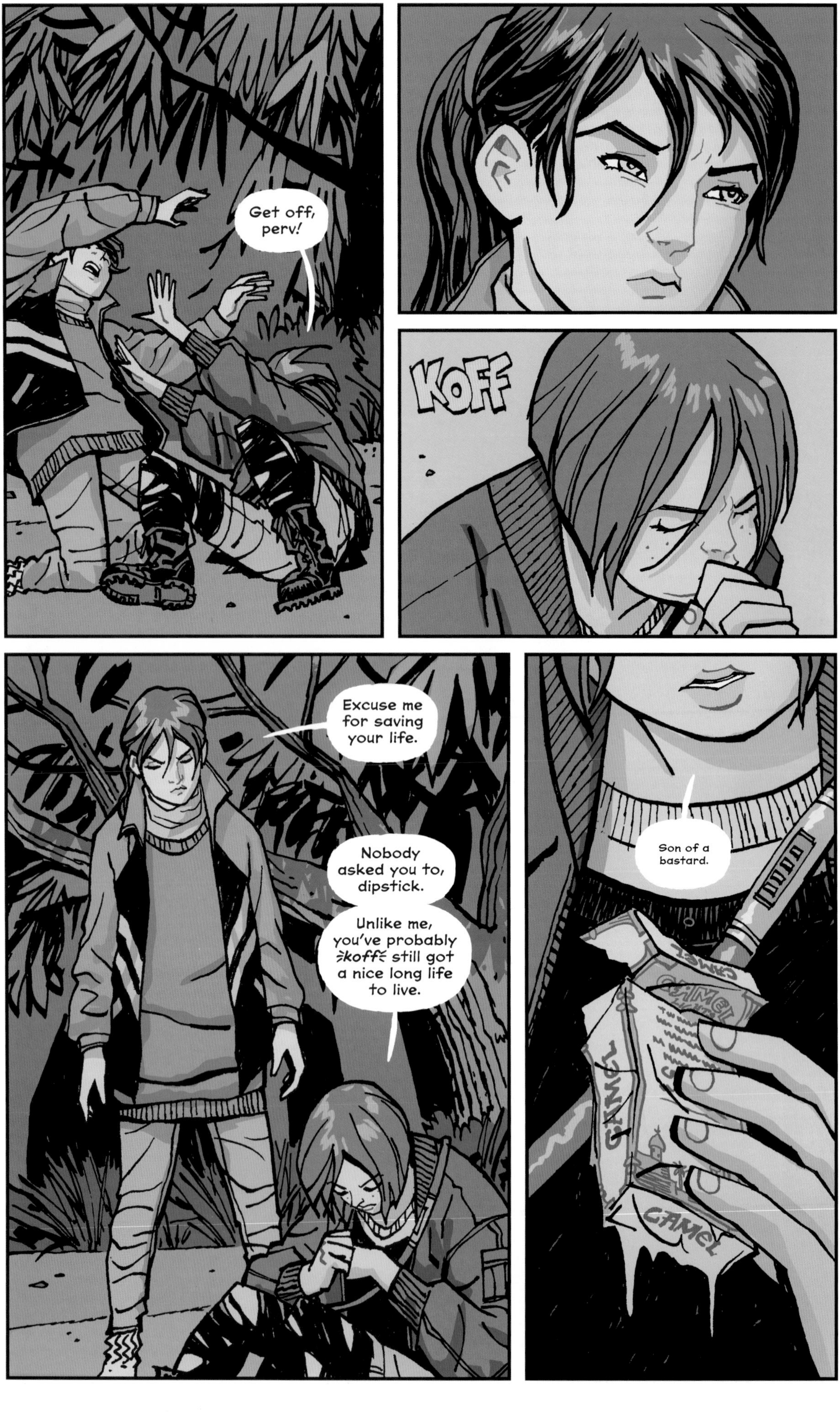
Get off, perv!
KOFF
Excuse me for saving your life.
Nobody asked you to, dipstick.
Unlike me, you've probably *koff* still got a nice long life to live.
Son of a bastard.
CAMEL
CAMEL
CAMEL

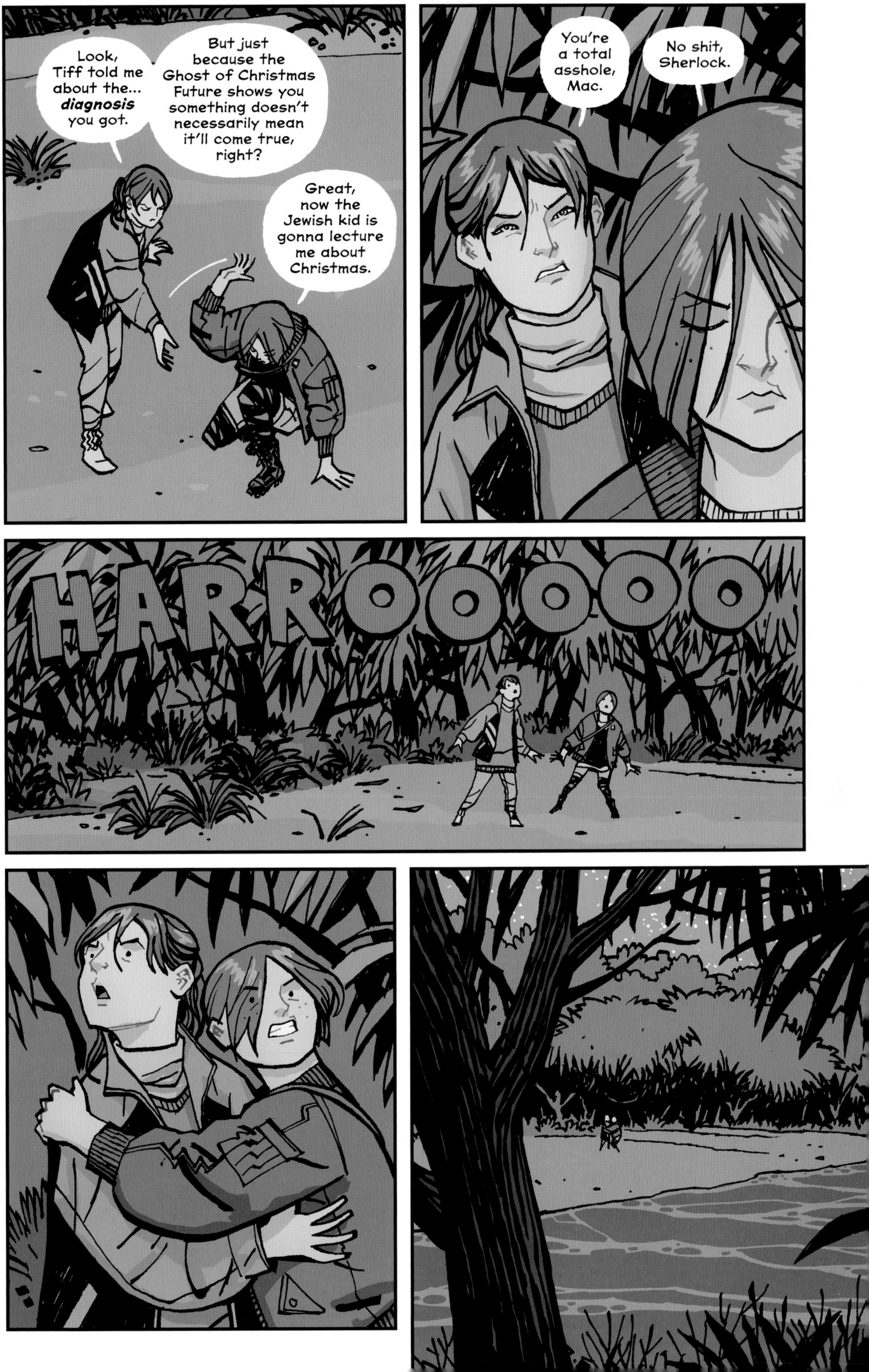
Look, Tiff told me about the... *diagnosis* you got.
But just because the Ghost of Christmas Future shows you something doesn't necessarily mean it'll come true, right?
Great, now the Jewish kid is gonna lecture me about Christmas.
You're a total asshole, Mac.
No shit, Sherlock.
HARROOOOO

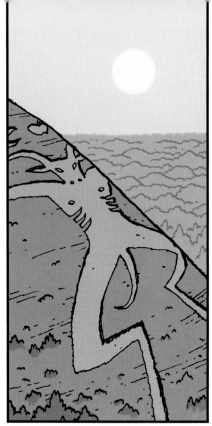

What...?

What the holy fuck?!

It works!

Little *too* well.

Don't kill my baby!

We only came to this place because I...I thought it's what you dream women wanted!

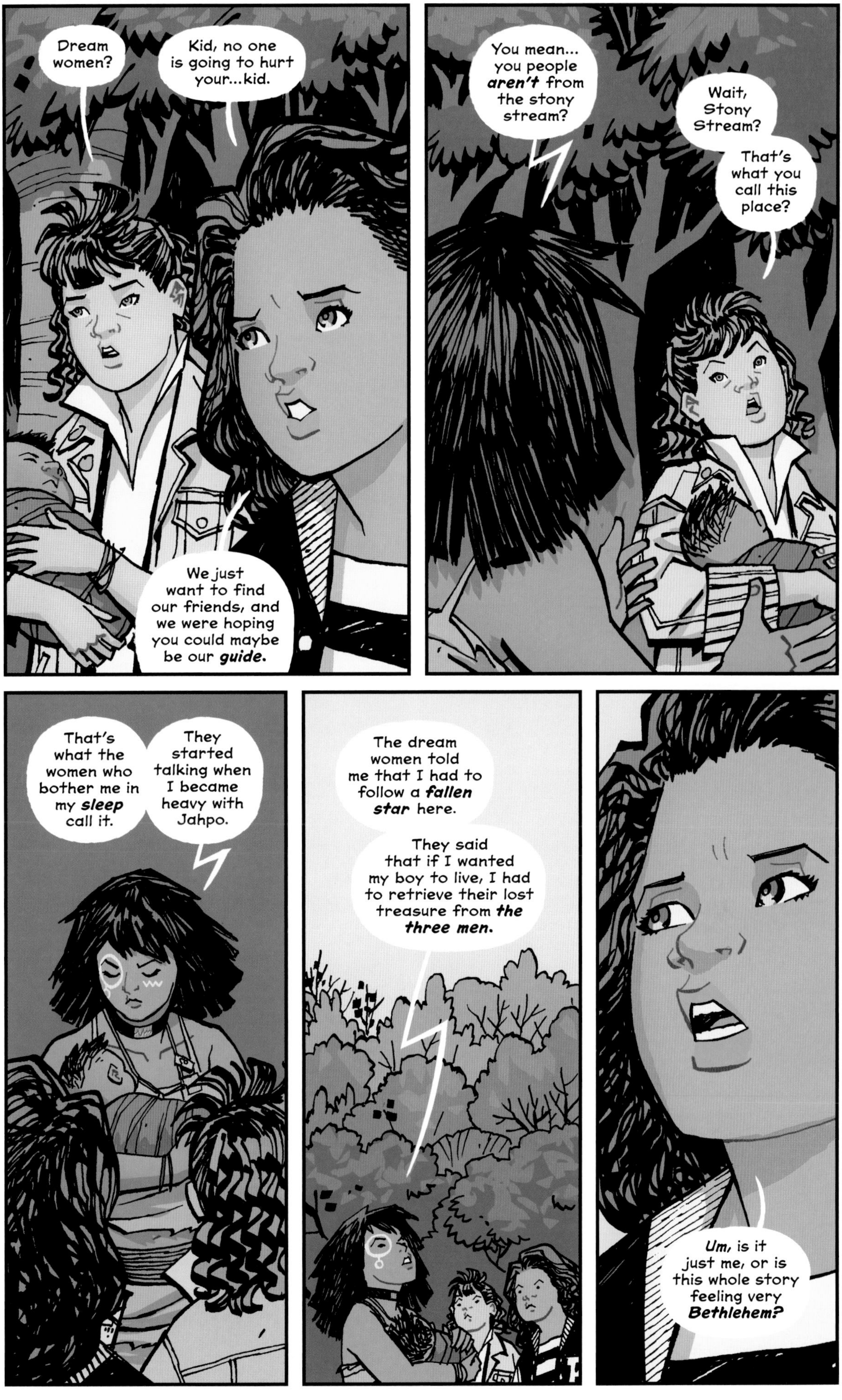
Dream women?
Kid, no one is going to hurt your...kid.
We just want to find our friends, and we were hoping you could maybe be our *guide.*
You mean... you people *aren't* from the stony stream?
Wait, Stony Stream?
That's what you call this place?
That's what the women who bother me in my *sleep* call it.
They started talking when I became heavy with Jahpo.
The dream women told me that I had to follow a *fallen star* here.
They said that if I wanted my boy to live, I had to retrieve their lost treasure from *the three men.*
Um, is it just me, or is this whole story feeling very *Bethlehem?*

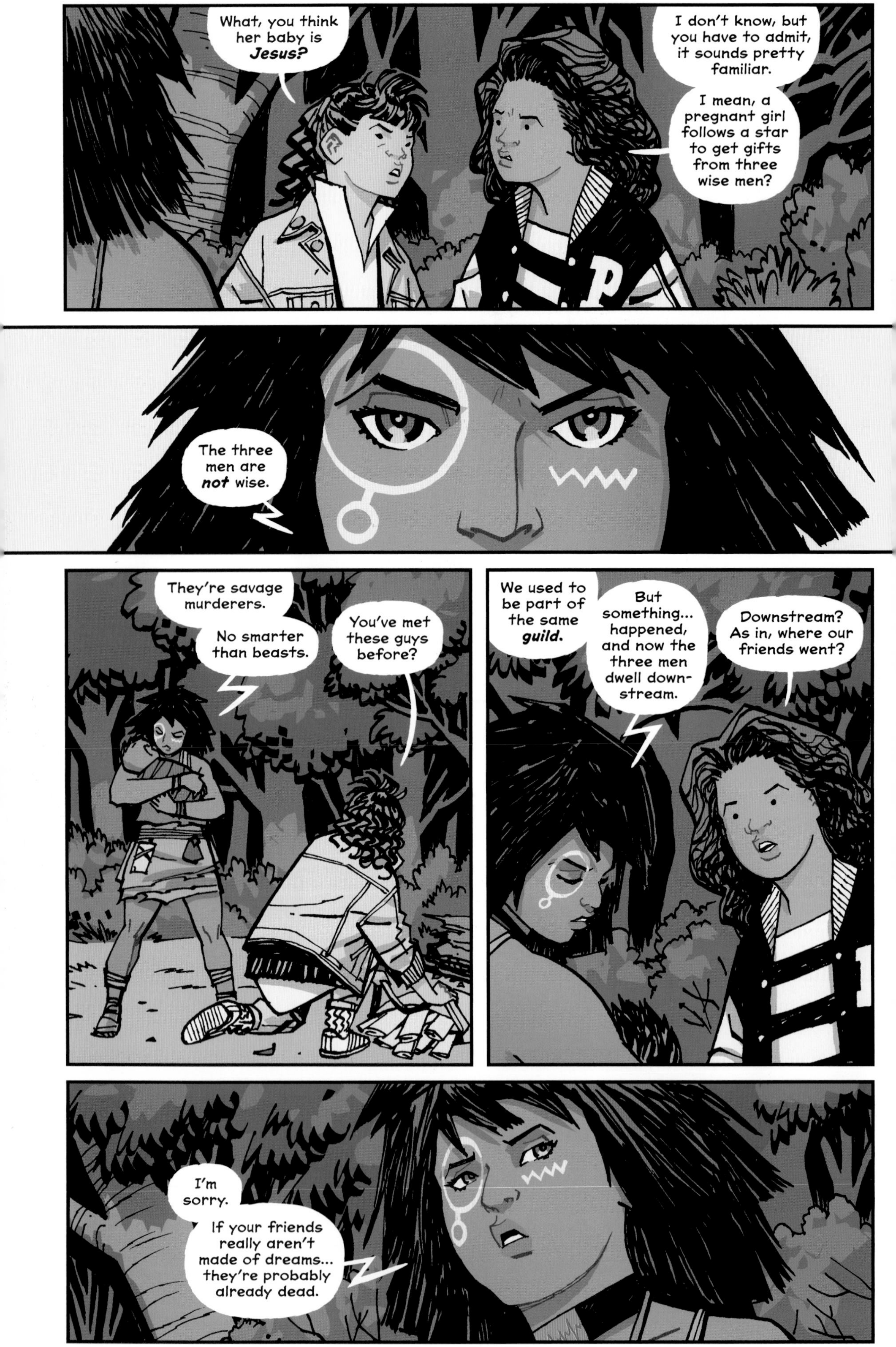

What, you think her baby is *Jesus?*
I don't know, but you have to admit, it sounds pretty familiar.
I mean, a pregnant girl follows a star to get gifts from three wise men?
The three men are *not* wise.
They're savage murderers.
No smarter than beasts.
You've met these guys before?
We used to be part of the same *guild.*
But something... happened, and now the three men dwell down-stream.
Downstream? As in, where our friends went?
I'm sorry.
If your friends really aren't made of dreams... they're probably already dead.

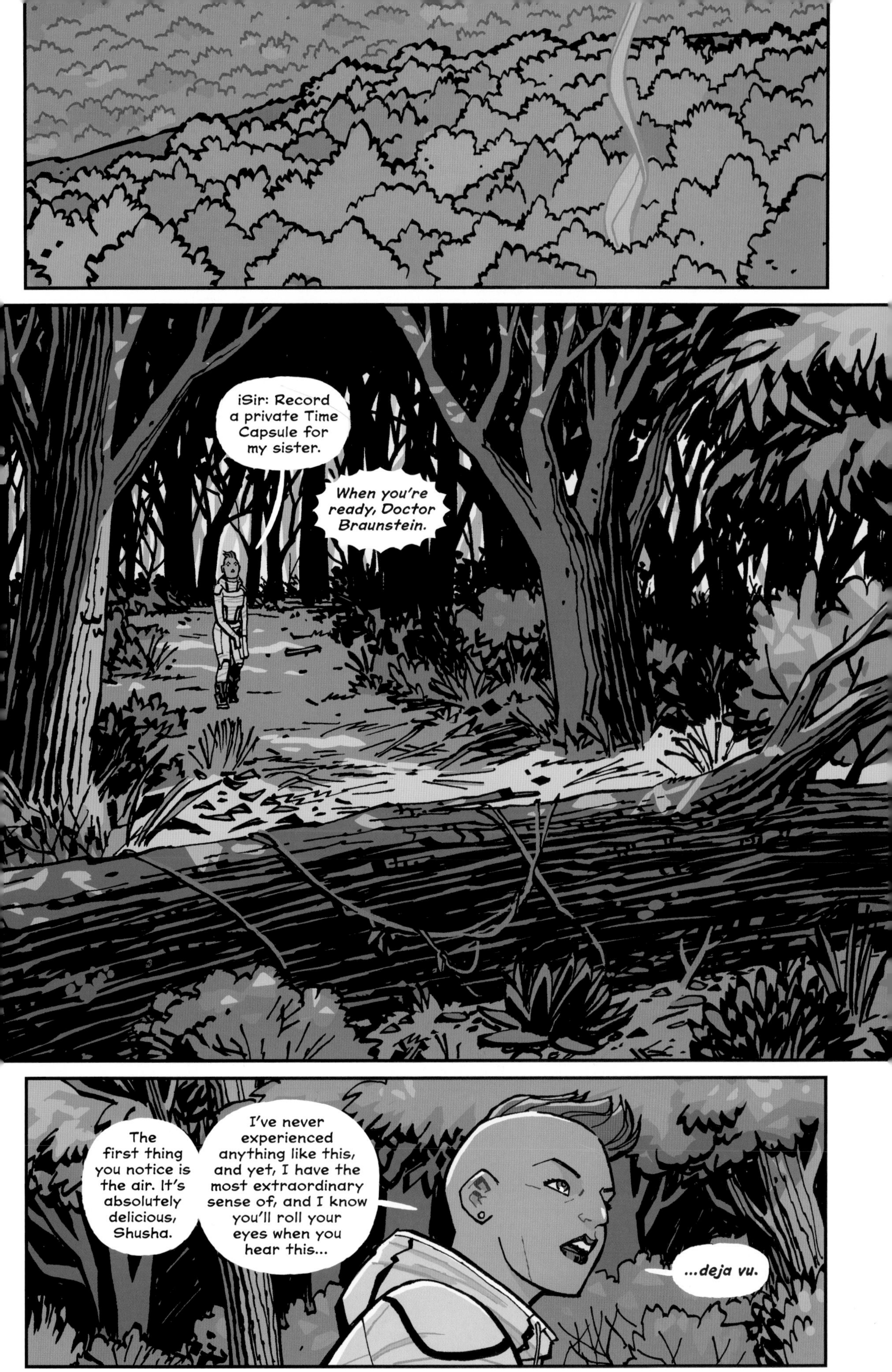
iSir: Record a private Time Capsule for my sister.
When you're ready, Doctor Braunstein.
The first thing you notice is the air. It's absolutely delicious, Shusha.
I've never experienced anything like this, and yet, I have the most extraordinary sense of, and I know you'll roll your eyes when you hear this...
...deja vu.

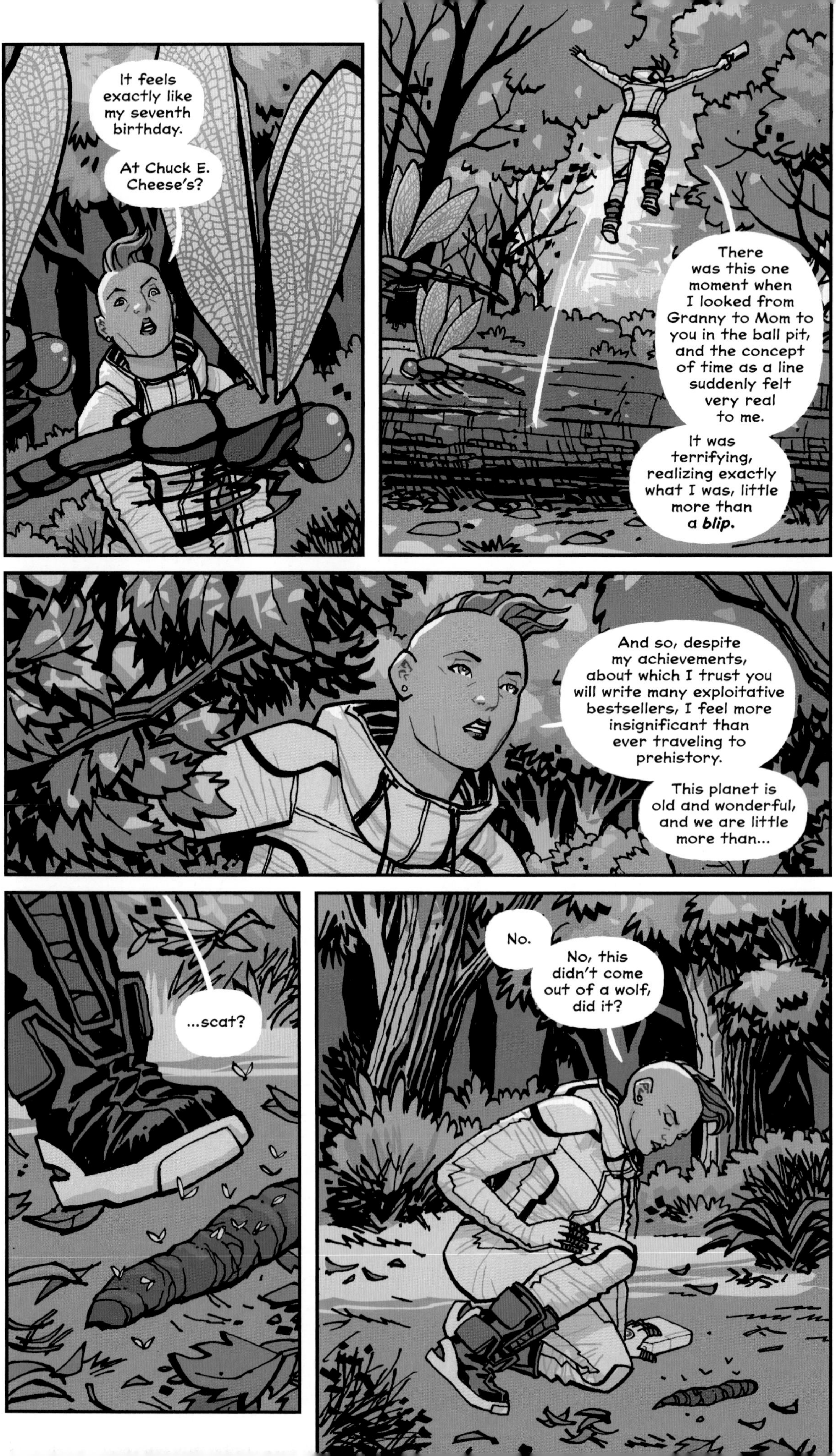
It feels exactly like my seventh birthday.
At Chuck E. Cheese's?
There was this one moment when I looked from Granny to Mom to you in the ball pit, and the concept of time as a line suddenly felt very real to me.
It was terrifying, realizing exactly what I was, little more than a *blip.*
And so, despite my achievements, about which I trust you will write many exploitative bestsellers, I feel more insignificant than ever traveling to prehistory.
This planet is old and wonderful, and we are little more than...
...scat?
No.
No, this didn't come out of a wolf, did it?

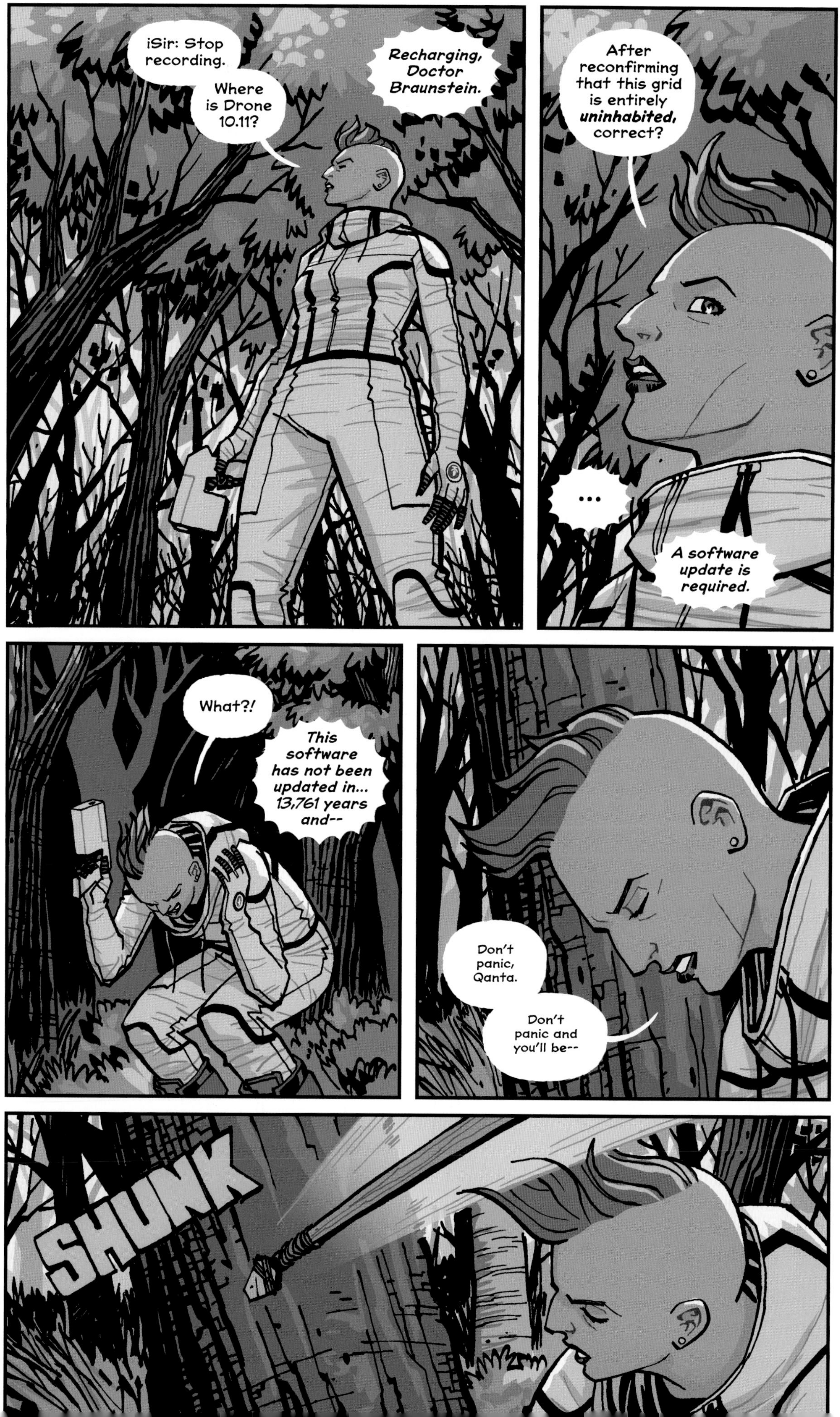
iSir: Stop recording.
Where is Drone 10.11?
Recharging, Doctor Braunstein.
After reconfirming that this grid is entirely *uninhabited,* correct?
...
A software update is required.
What?!
This software has not been updated in... 13,761 years and--
Don't panic, Qanta.
Don't panic and you'll be--
SHUNK

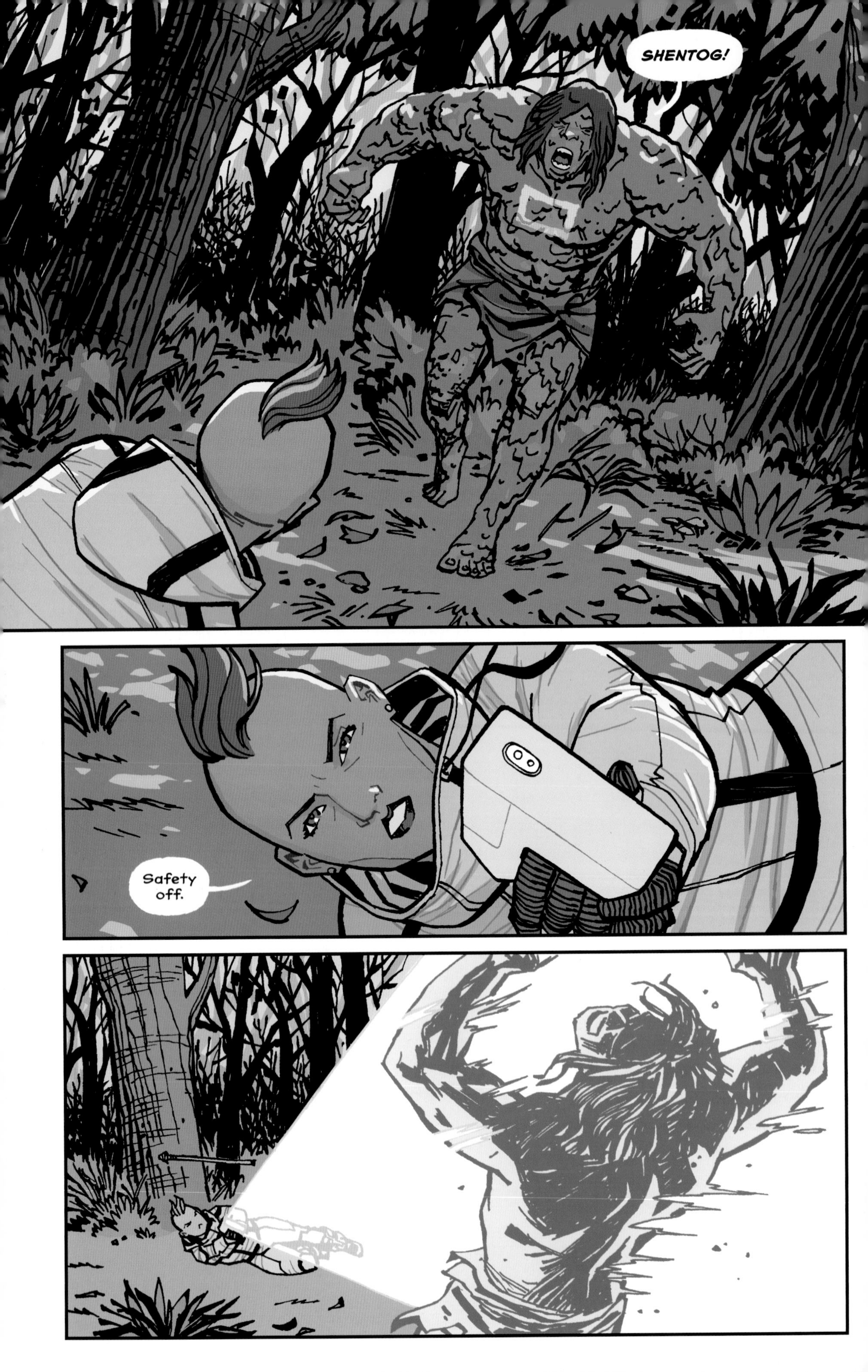
SHENTOG!
Safety off.

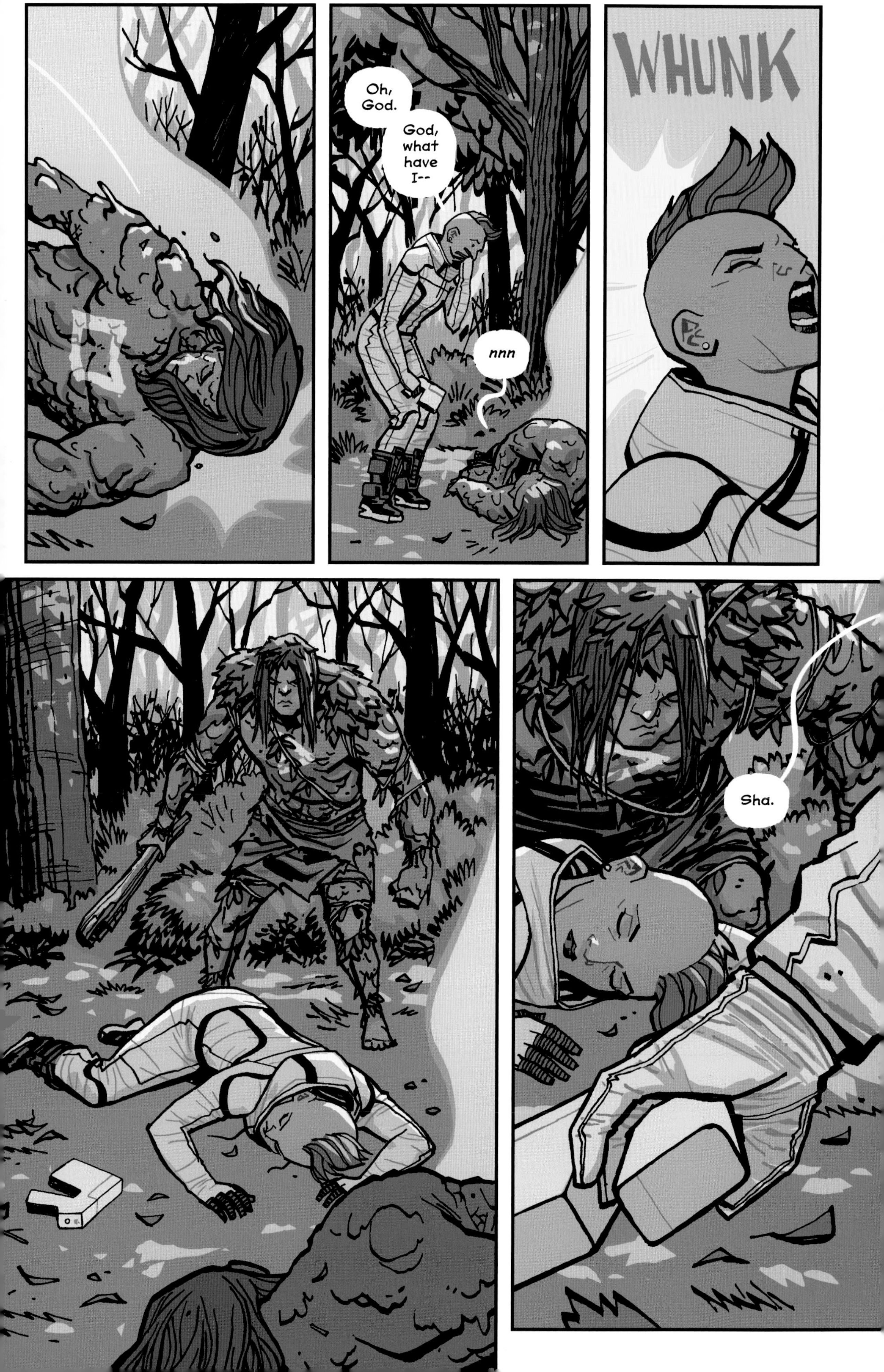
Oh, God.
God, what have I--
nnn
WHUNK
Sha.

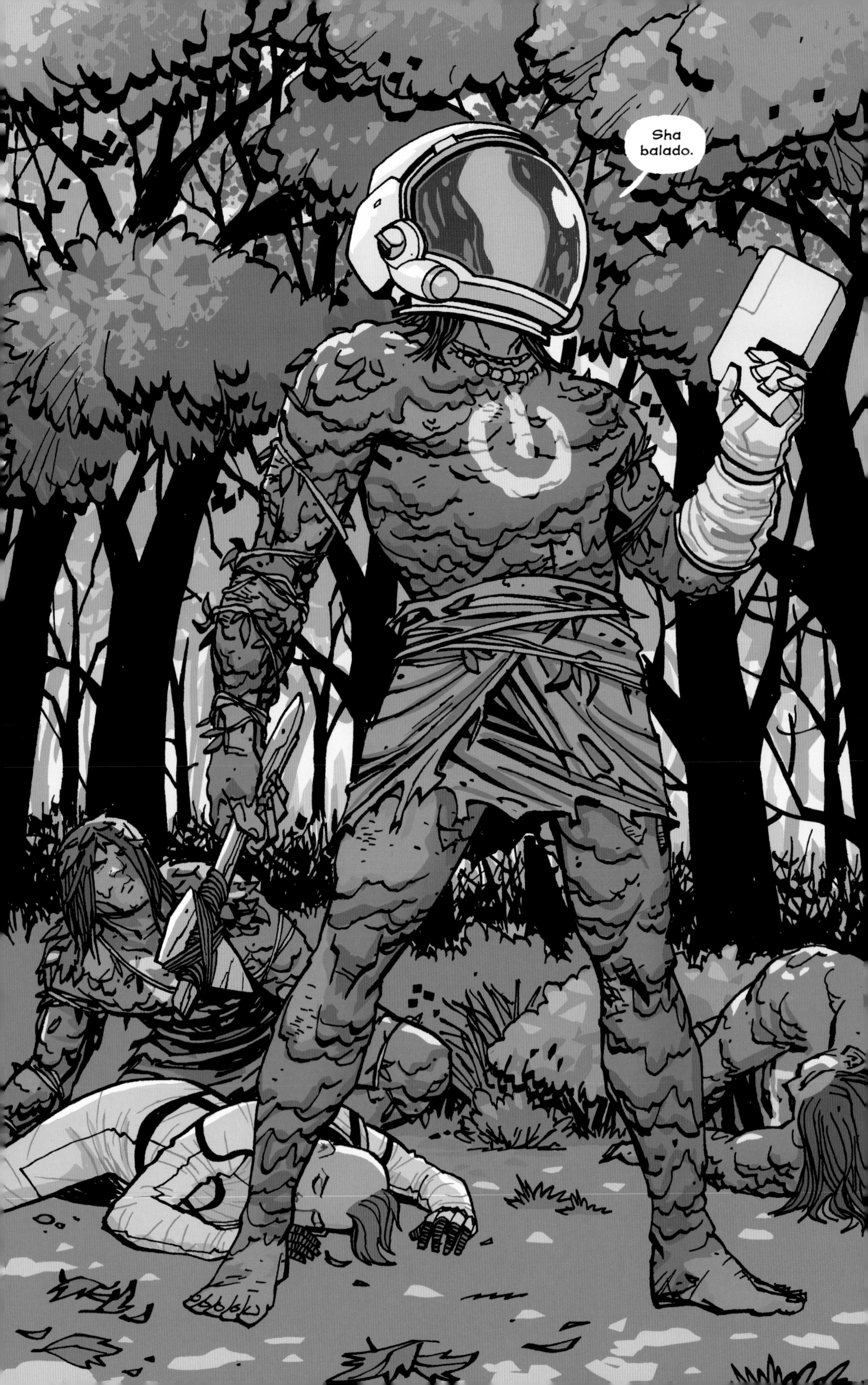
Sha balado.

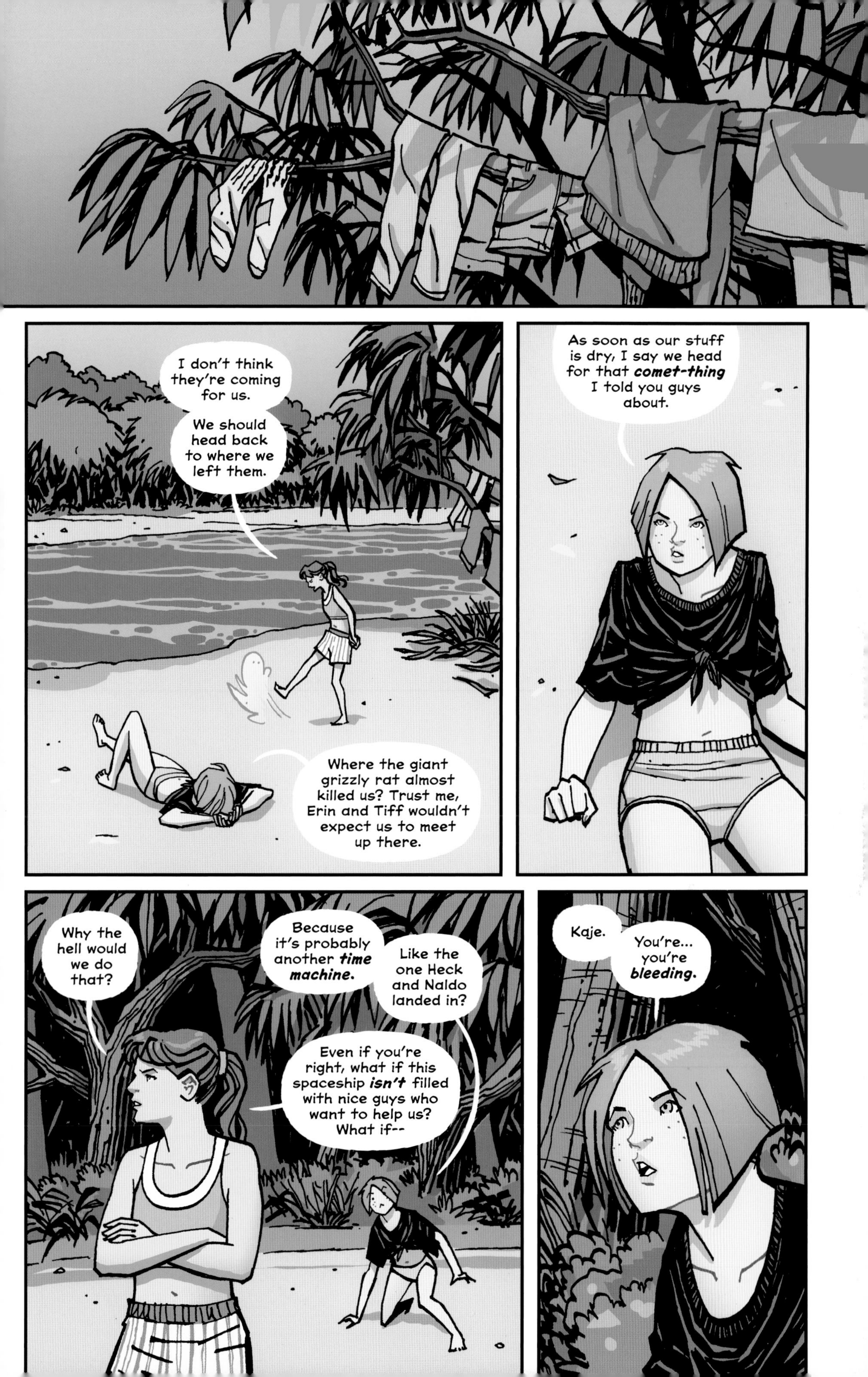
I don't think they're coming for us.
We should head back to where we left them.
Where the giant grizzly rat almost killed us? Trust me, Erin and Tiff wouldn't expect us to meet up there.
As soon as our stuff is dry, I say we head for that *comet-thing* I told you guys about.
Why the hell would we do that?
Because it's probably another *time machine.*
Like the one Heck and Naldo landed in?
Even if you're right, what if this spaceship *isn't* filled with nice guys who want to help us? What if--
Kaje.
You're... you're *bleeding.*

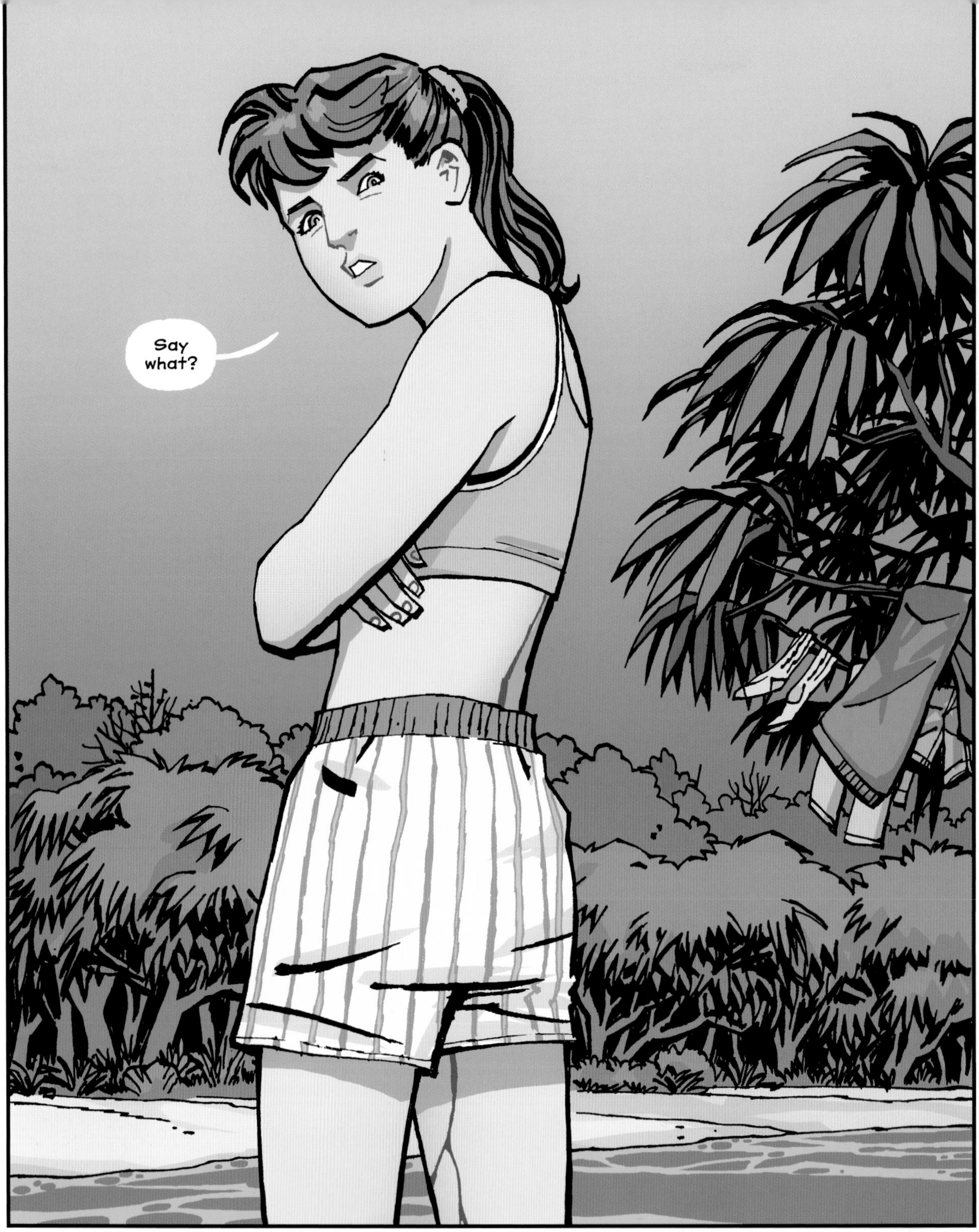
Say what?

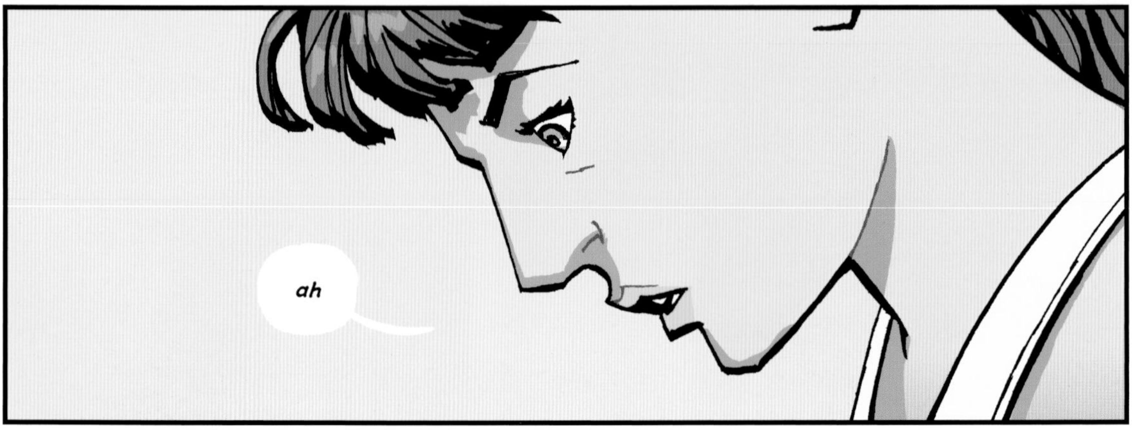
ah

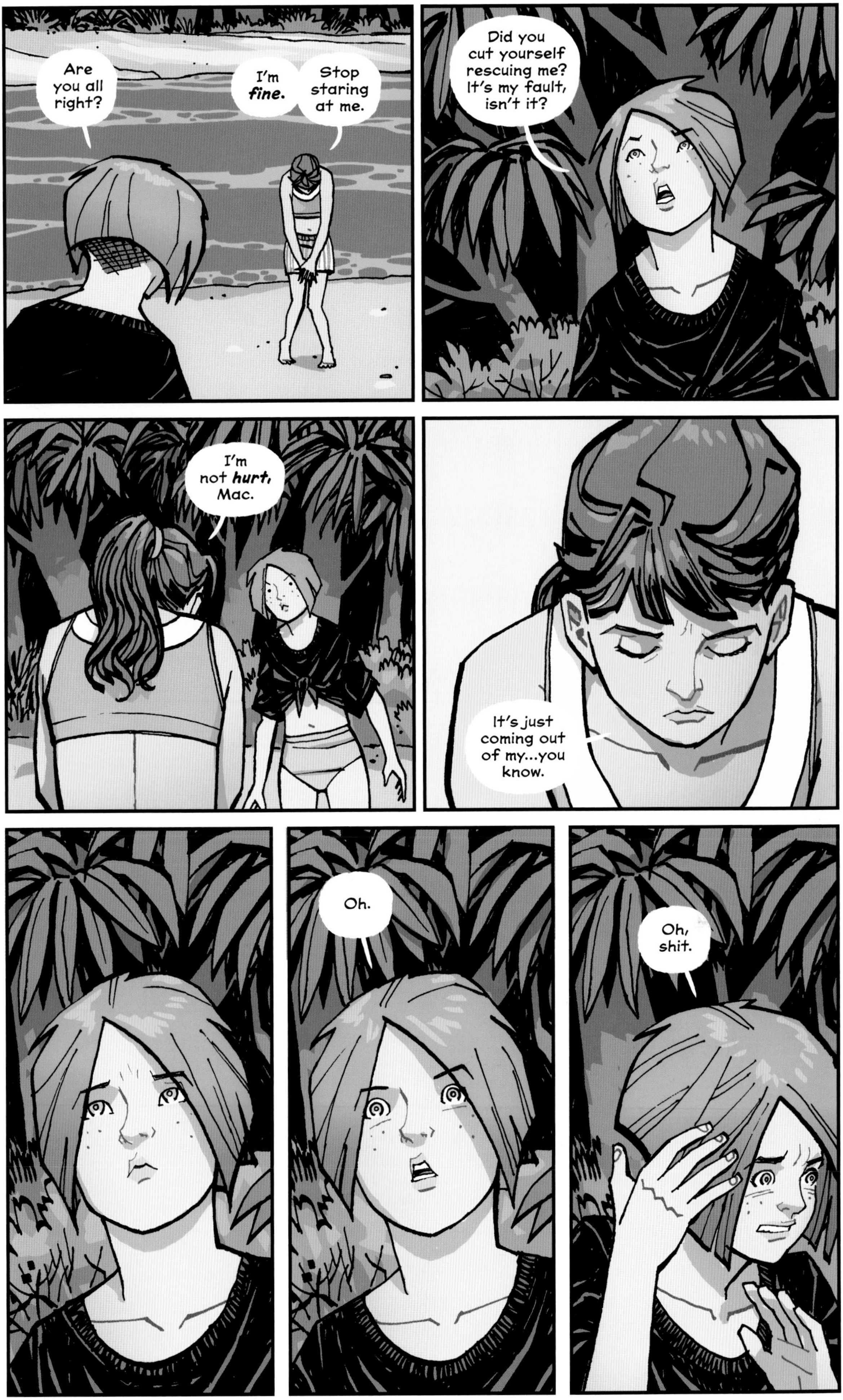
Are you all right?
I'm **fine.**
Stop staring at me.
Did you cut yourself rescuing me? It's my fault, isn't it?
I'm not **hurt,** Mac.
It's just coming out of my...you know.
Oh.
Oh, shit.

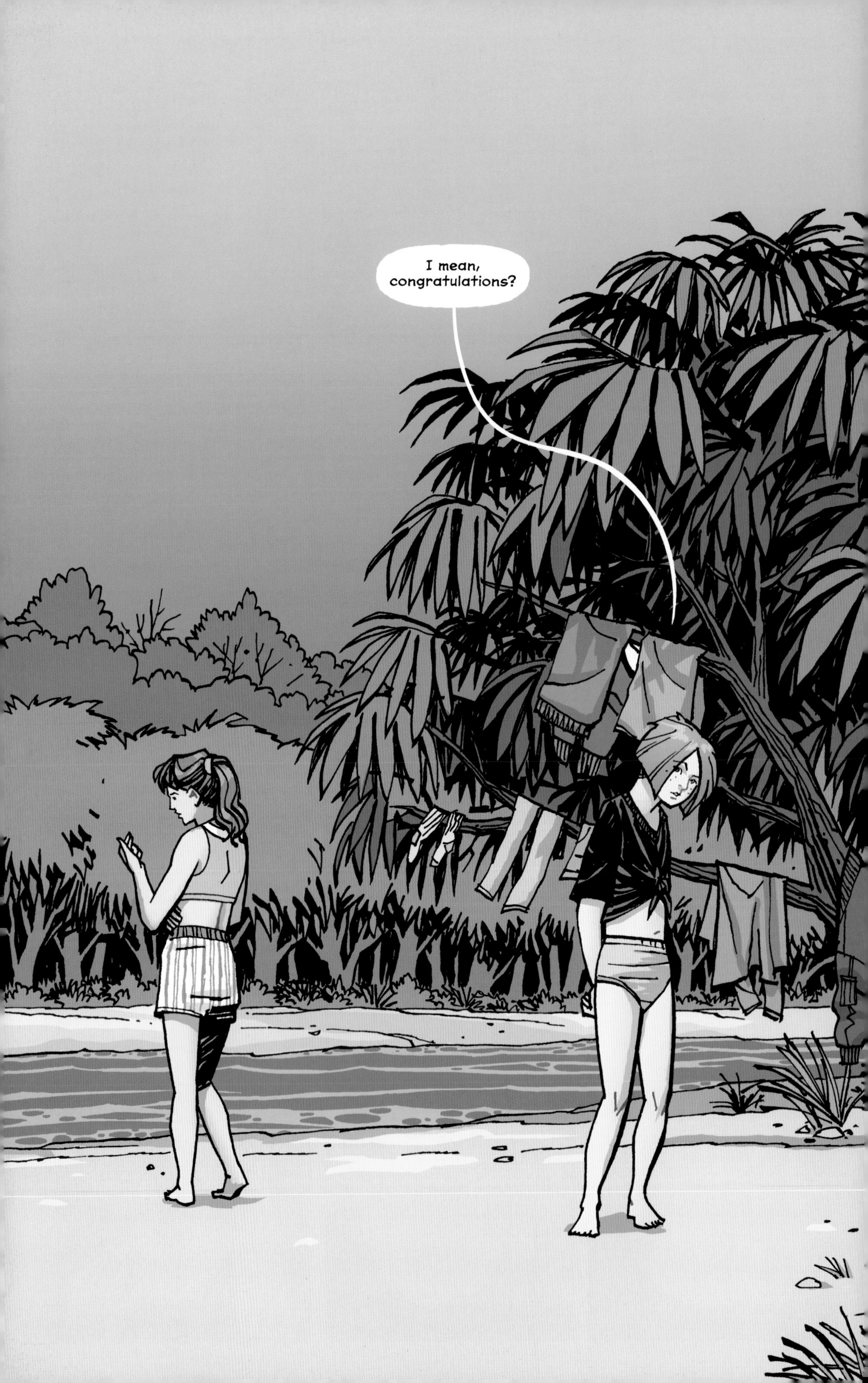
I mean, congratulations?

CHAPTER 13

DON'T TRUST OTHER ERIN!!!

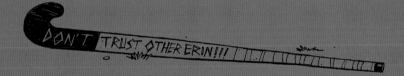

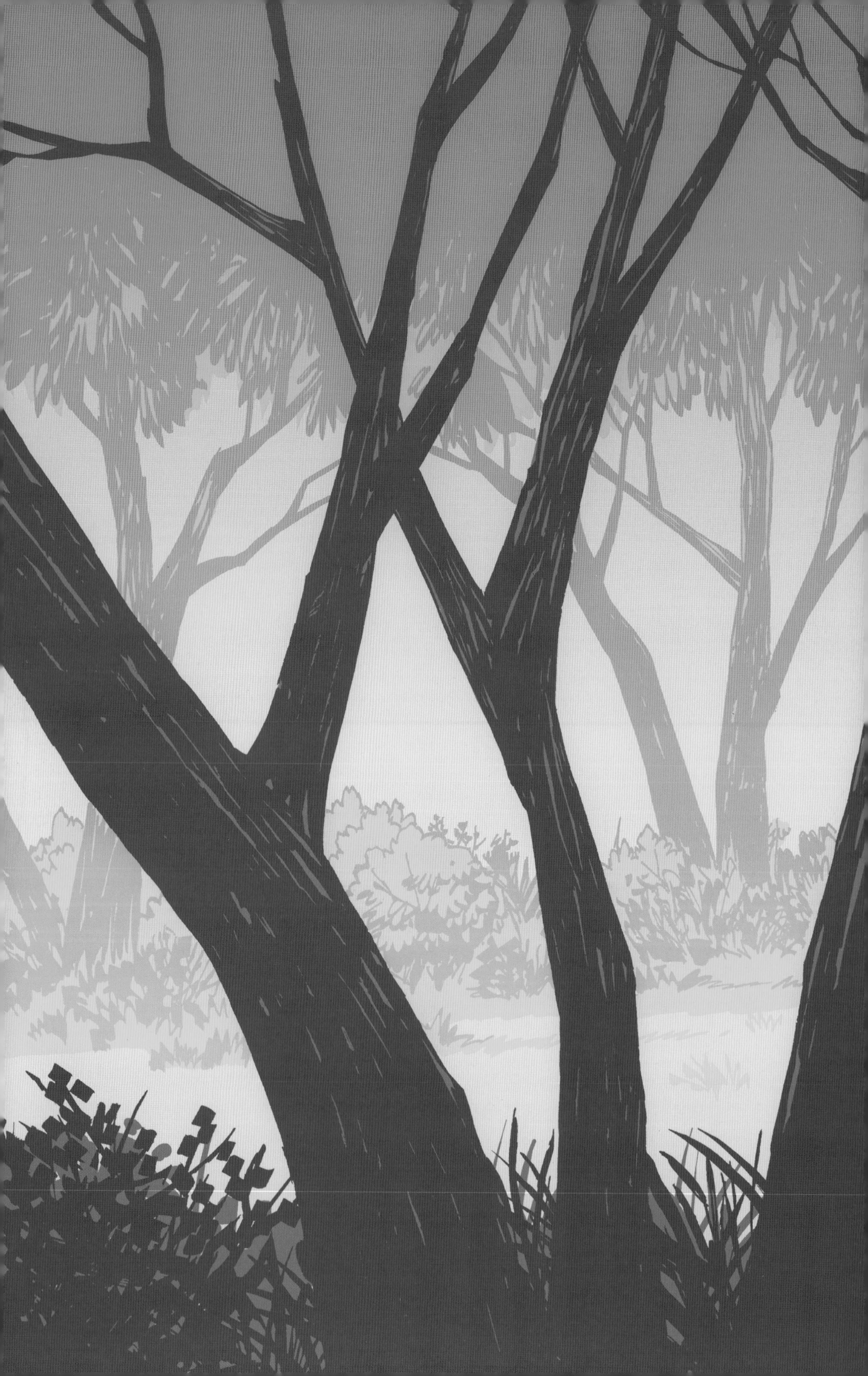

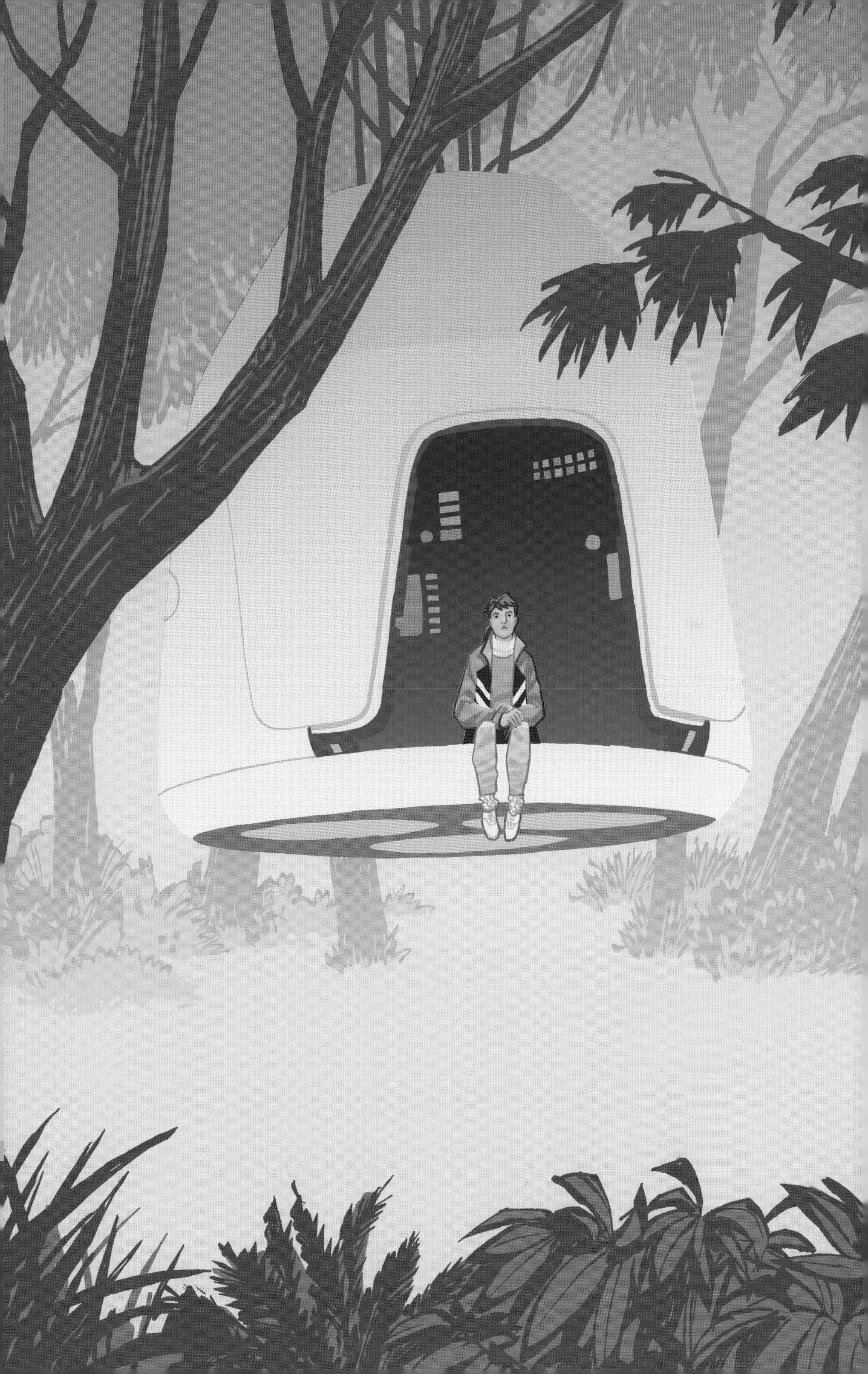

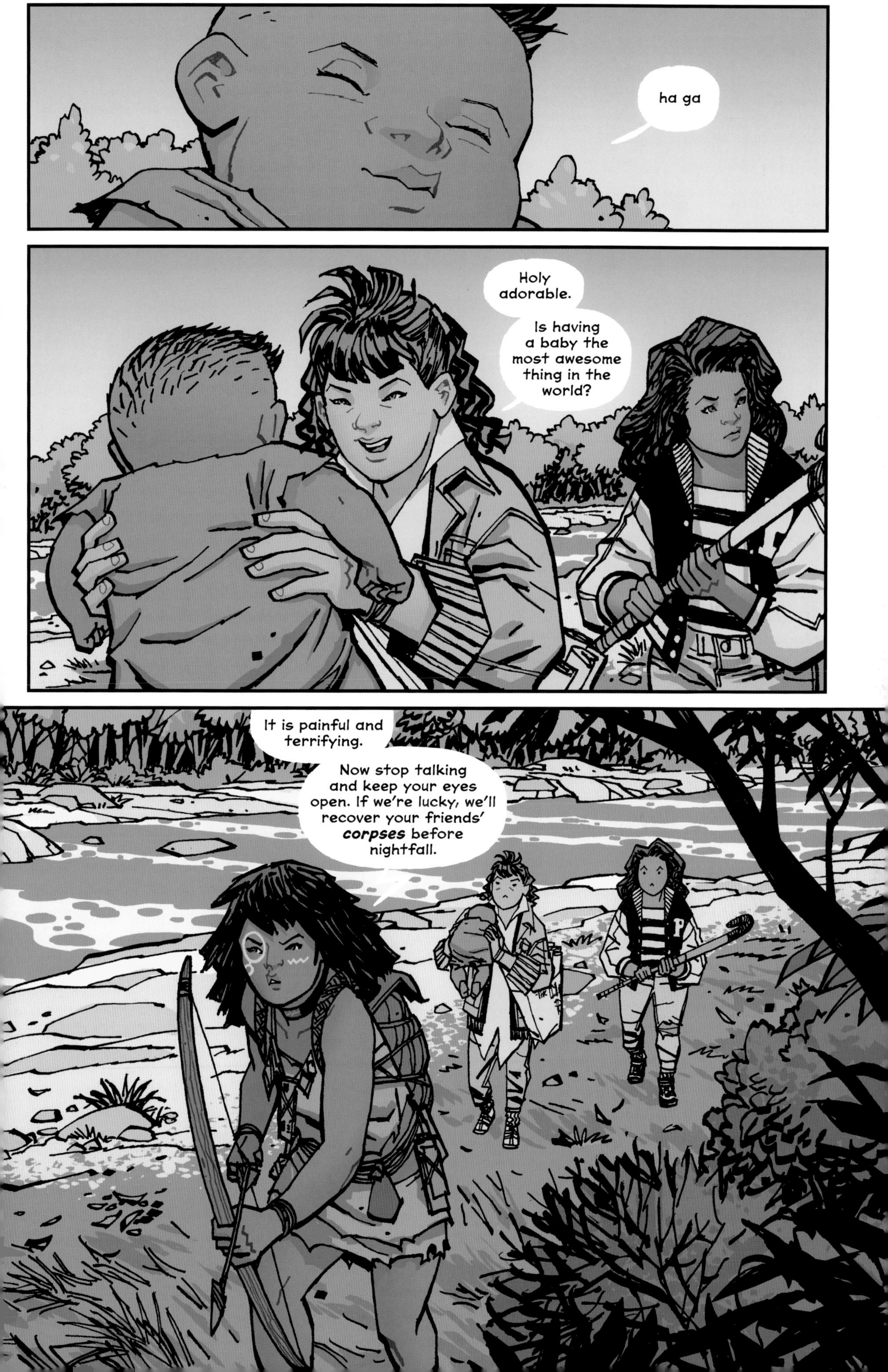
ha ga
Holy adorable.
Is having a baby the most awesome thing in the world?
It is painful and terrifying.
Now stop talking and keep your eyes open. If we're lucky, we'll recover your friends' ***corpses*** before nightfall.

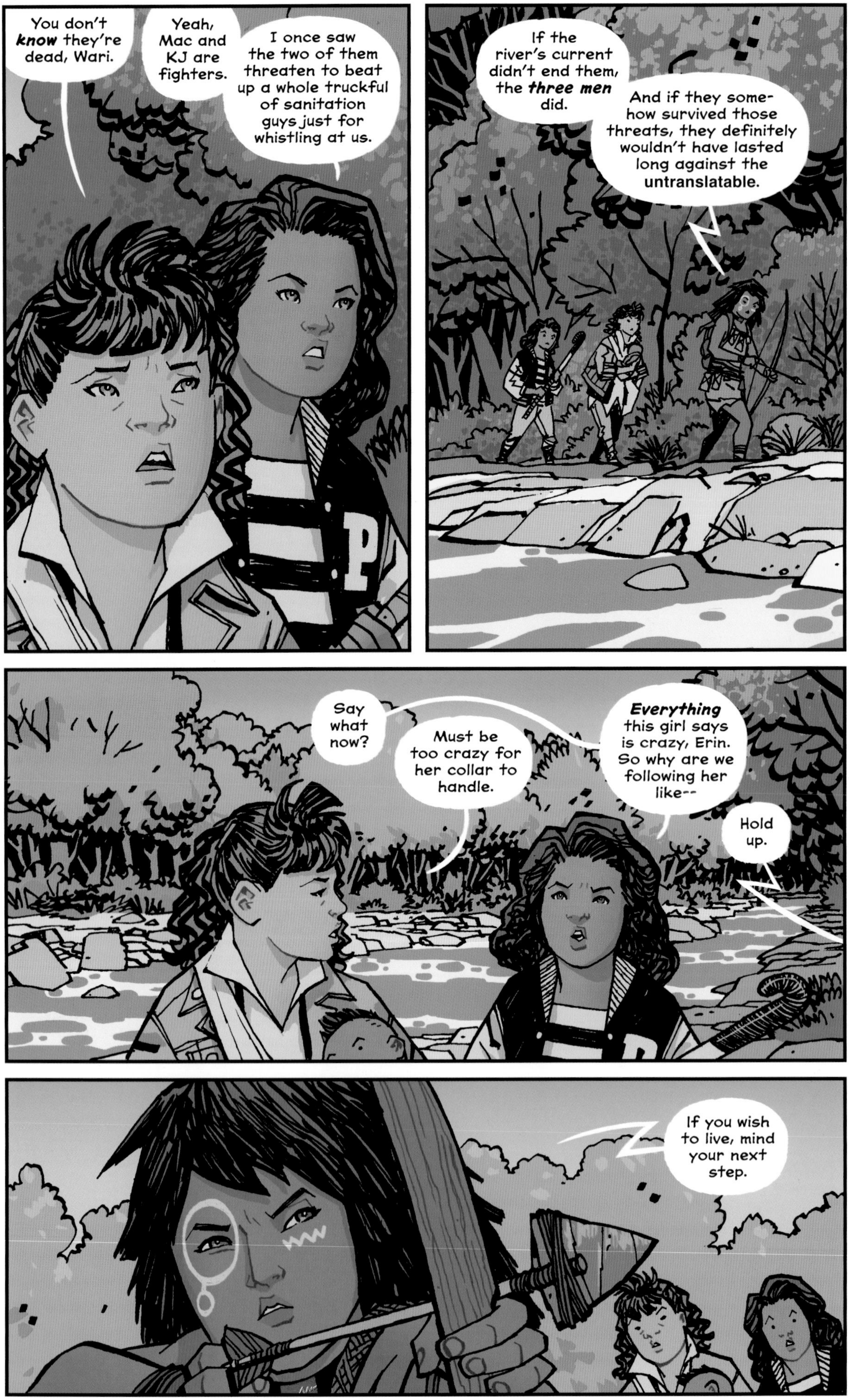
You don't *know* they're dead, Wari.
Yeah, Mac and KJ are fighters.
I once saw the two of them threaten to beat up a whole truckful of sanitation guys just for whistling at us.
If the river's current didn't end them, the *three men* did.
And if they somehow survived those threats, they definitely wouldn't have lasted long against the **untranslatable.**
Say what now?
Must be too crazy for her collar to handle.
Everything this girl says is crazy, Erin. So why are we following her like--
Hold up.
If you wish to live, mind your next step.

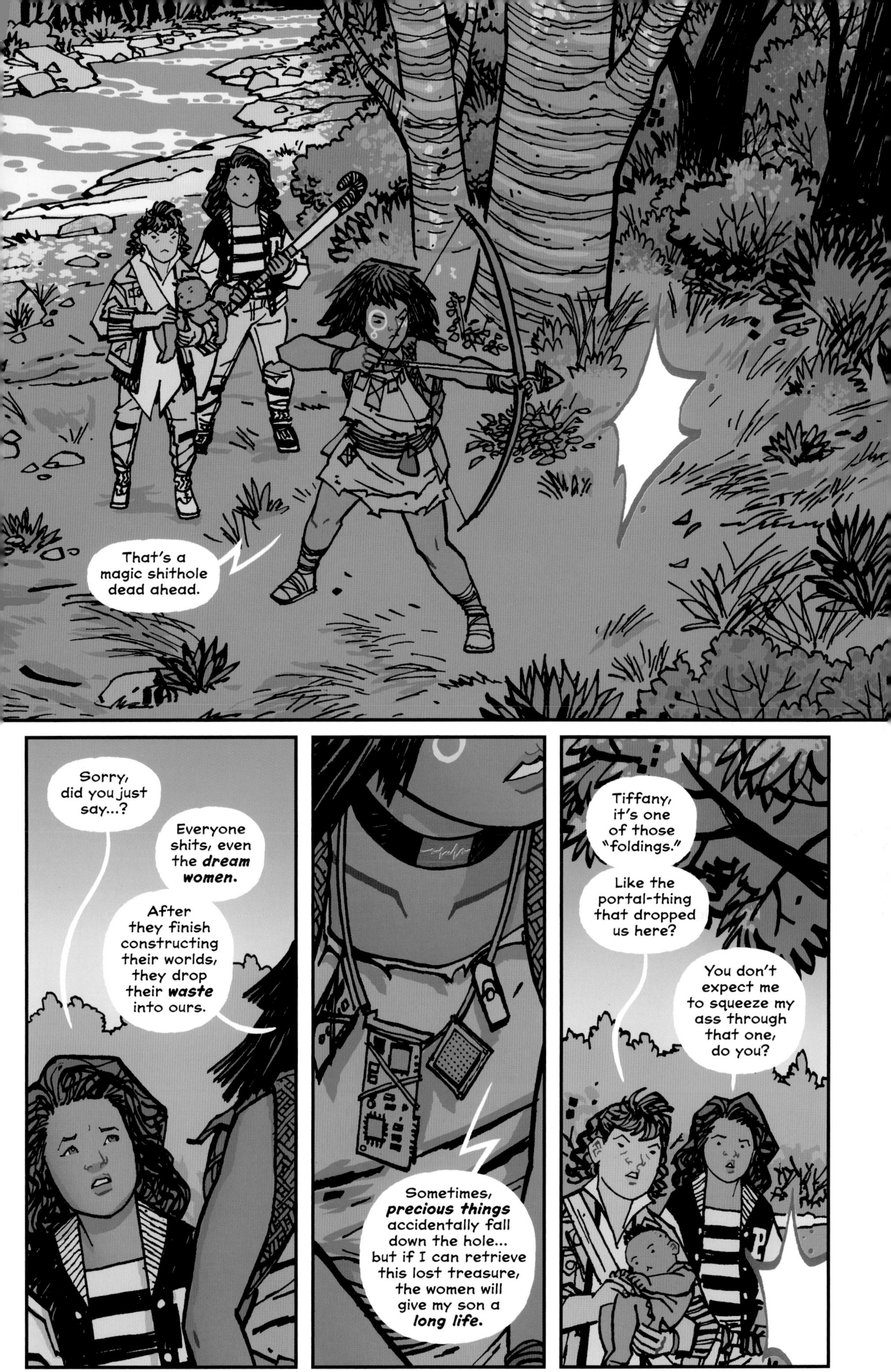
That's a magic shithole dead ahead.
Sorry, did you just say...?
Everyone shits, even the ***dream women.***
After they finish constructing their worlds, they drop their ***waste*** into ours.
Sometimes, ***precious things*** accidentally fall down the hole... but if I can retrieve this lost treasure, the women will give my son a ***long life.***
Tiffany, it's one of those "foldings."
Like the portal-thing that dropped us here?
You don't expect me to squeeze my ass through that one, do you?

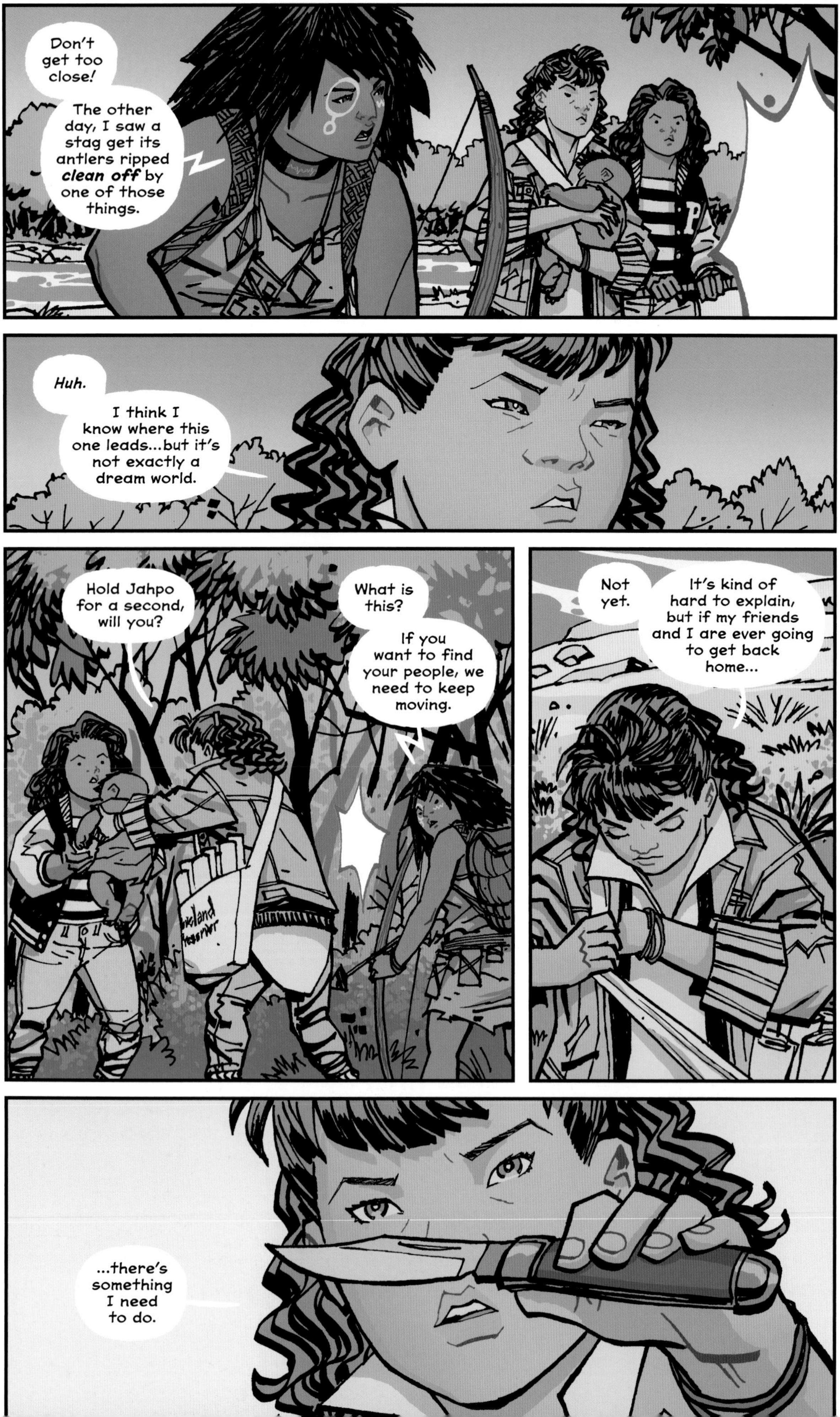
Don't get too close!
The other day, I saw a stag get its antlers ripped *clean off* by one of those things.
Huh.
I think I know where this one leads...but it's not exactly a dream world.
Hold Jahpo for a second, will you?
What is this?
If you want to find your people, we need to keep moving.
Not yet.
It's kind of hard to explain, but if my friends and I are ever going to get back home...
...there's something I need to do.

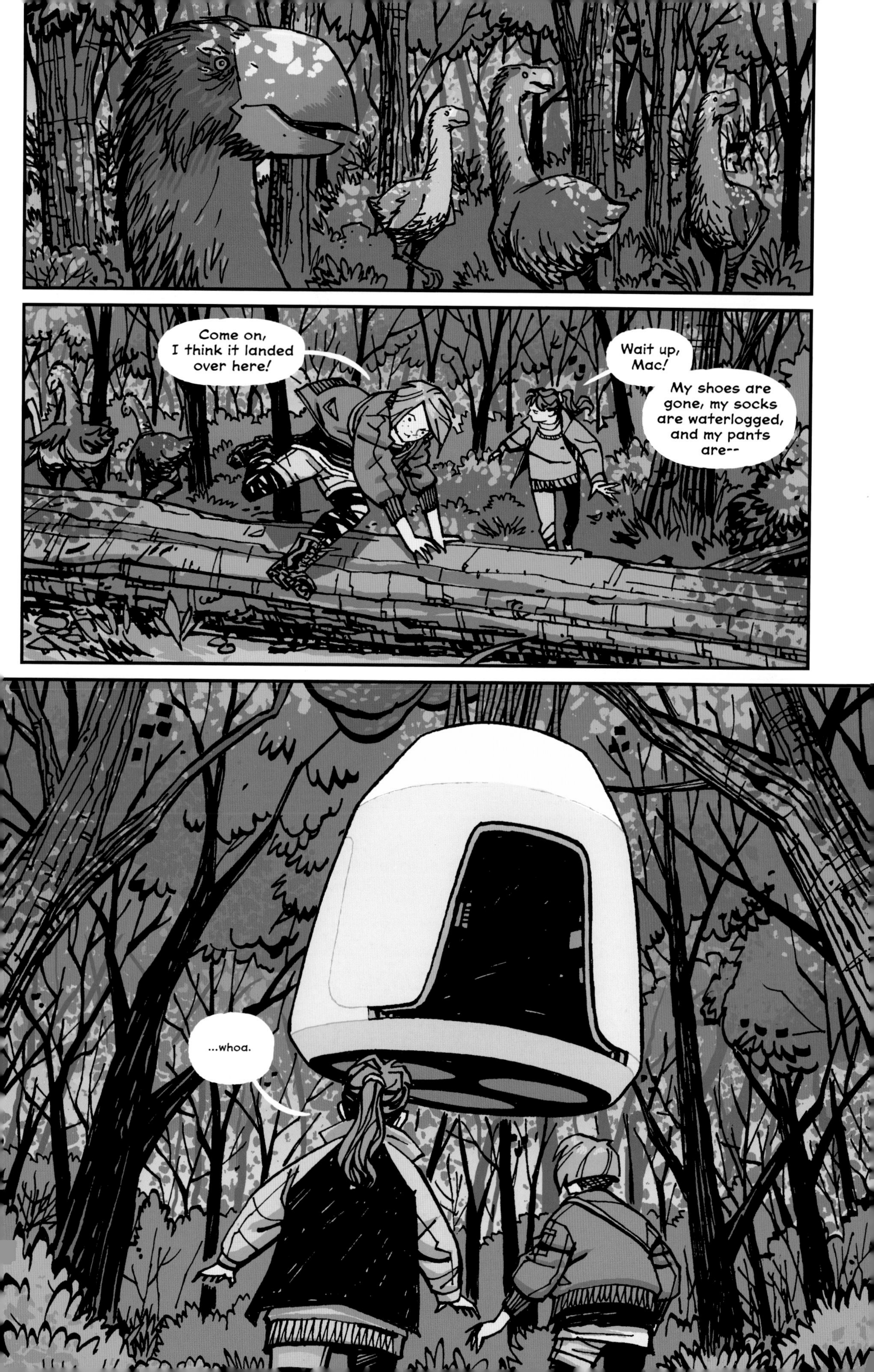
Come on,
I think it landed
over here!
Wait up,
Mac!
My shoes are
gone, my socks
are waterlogged,
and my pants
are--
...whoa.

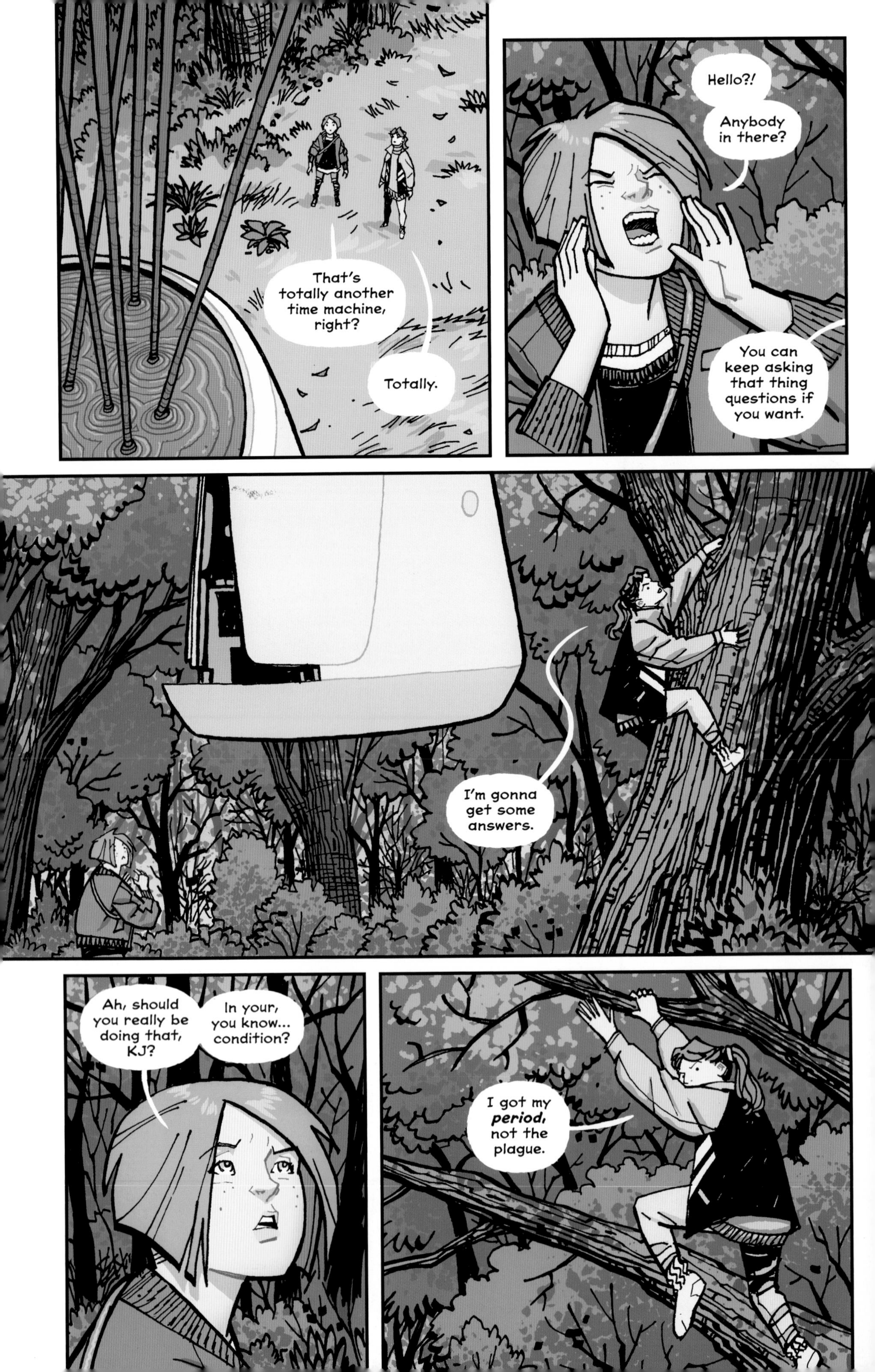

That's totally another time machine, right?
Totally.
Hello?!
Anybody in there?
You can keep asking that thing questions if you want.
I'm gonna get some answers.
Ah, should you really be doing that, KJ?
In your, you know... condition?
I got my *period,* not the plague.

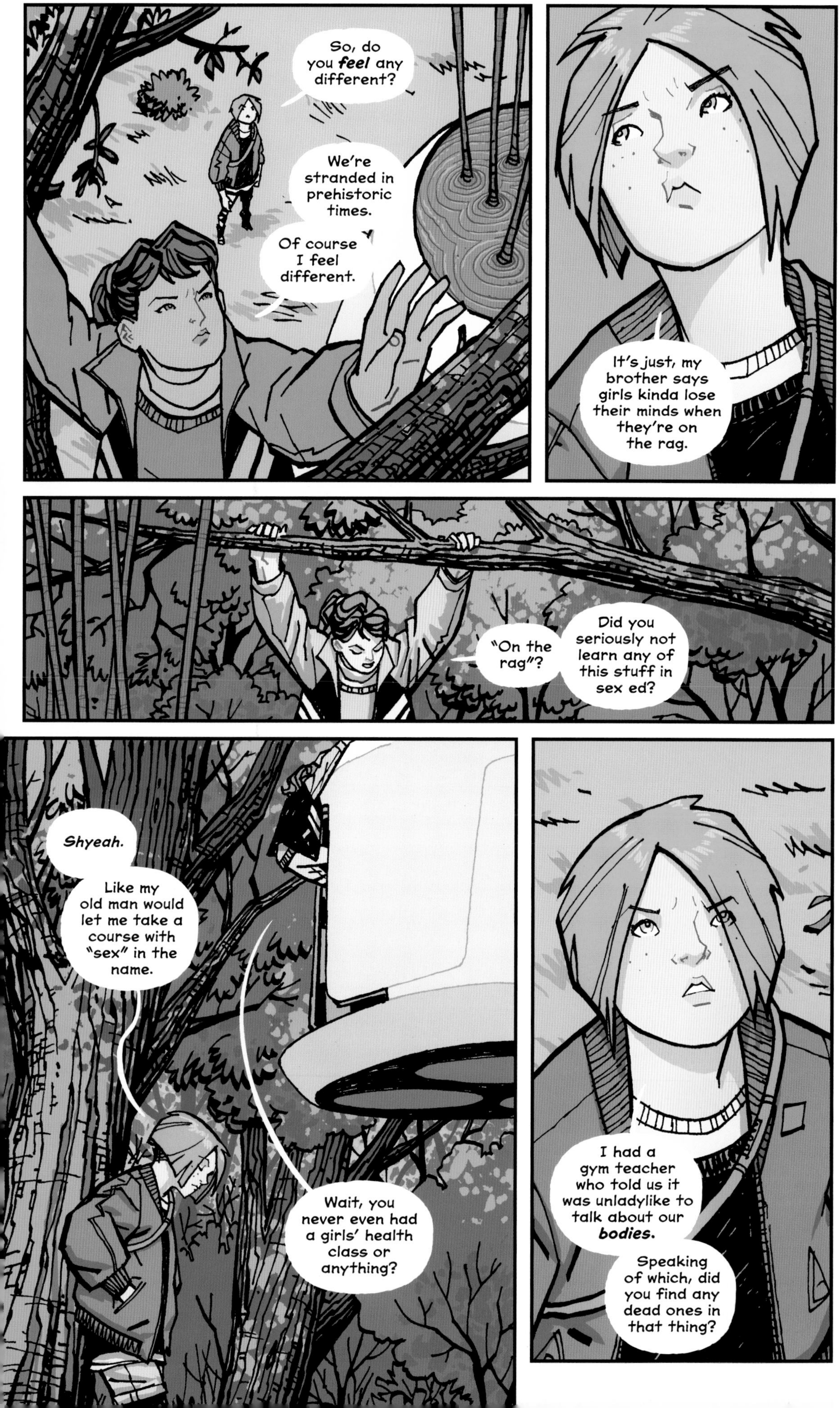
So, do you *feel* any different?
We're stranded in prehistoric times.
Of course I feel different.
It's just, my brother says girls kinda lose their minds when they're on the rag.
"On the rag"?
Did you seriously not learn any of this stuff in sex ed?
Shyeah.
Like my old man would let me take a course with "sex" in the name.
Wait, you never even had a girls' health class or anything?
I had a gym teacher who told us it was unladylike to talk about our ***bodies.***
Speaking of which, did you find any dead ones in that thing?

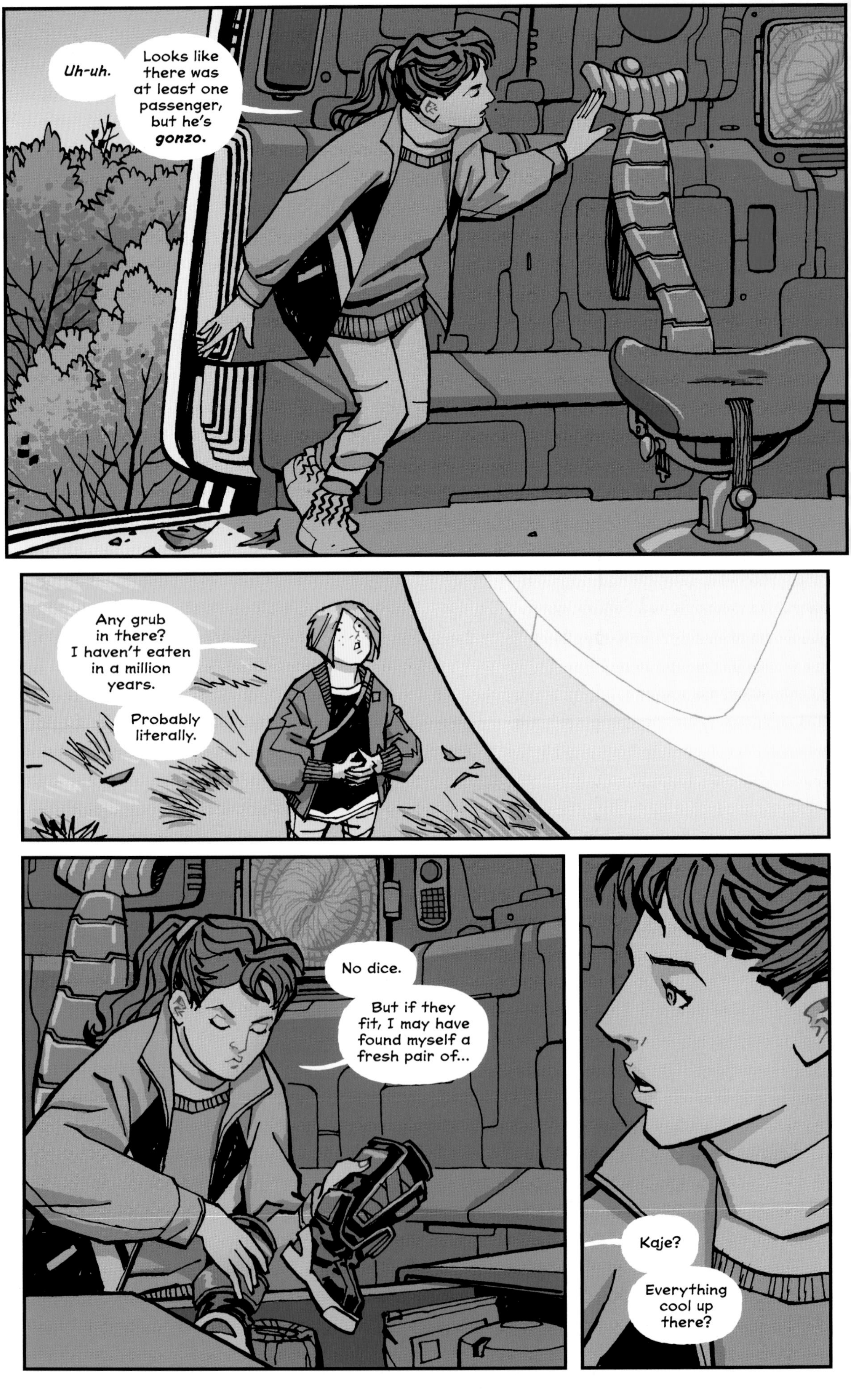
Uh-uh.
Looks like there was at least one passenger, but he's **gonzo.**
Any grub in there? I haven't eaten in a million years.
Probably literally.
No dice.
But if they fit, I may have found myself a fresh pair of...
Kaje?
Everything cool up there?

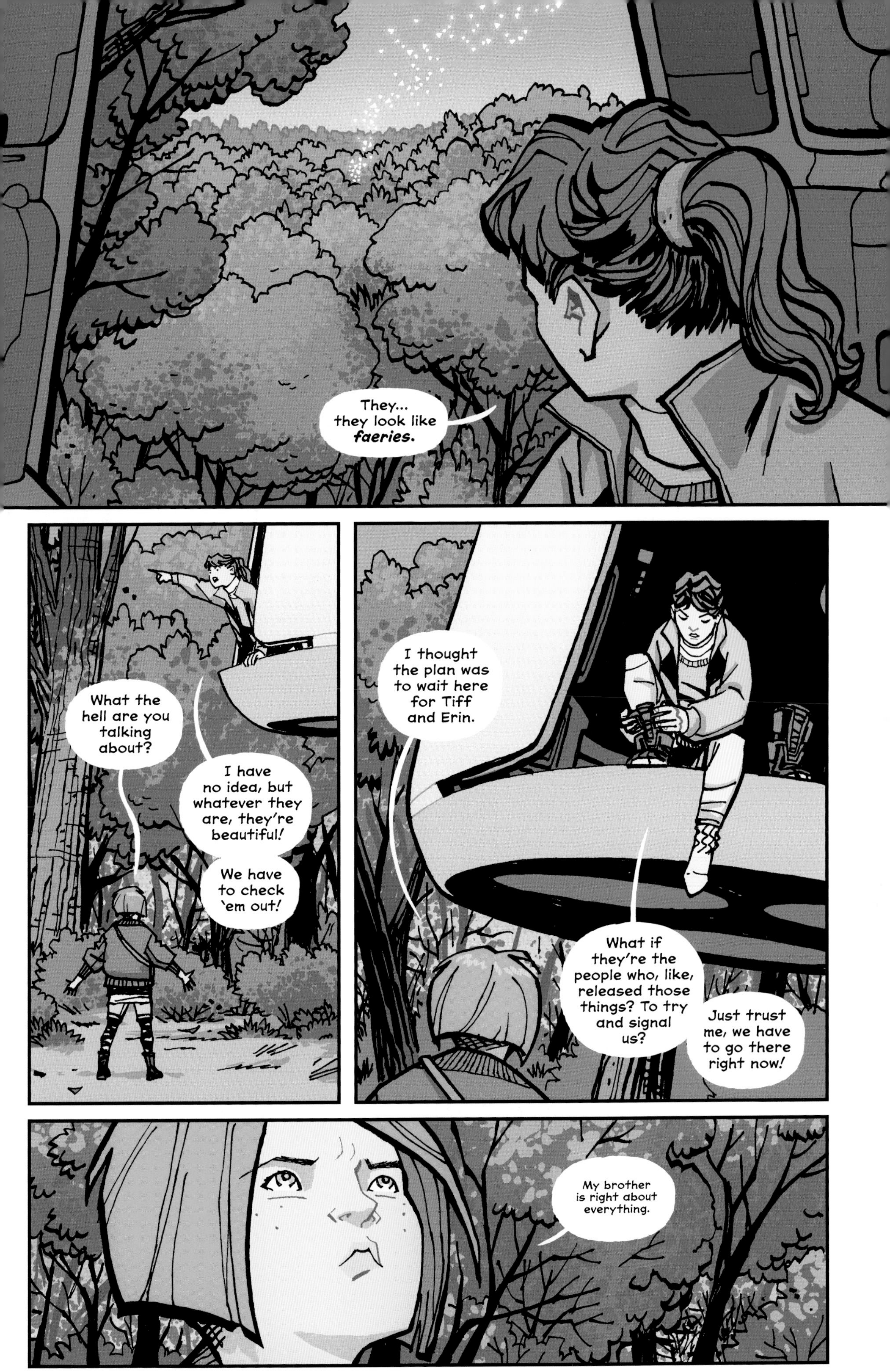
They... they look like faeries.
What the hell are you talking about?
I have no idea, but whatever they are, they're beautiful!
We have to check 'em out!
I thought the plan was to wait here for Tiff and Erin.
What if they're the people who, like, released those things? To try and signal us?
Just trust me, we have to go there right now!
My brother is right about everything.

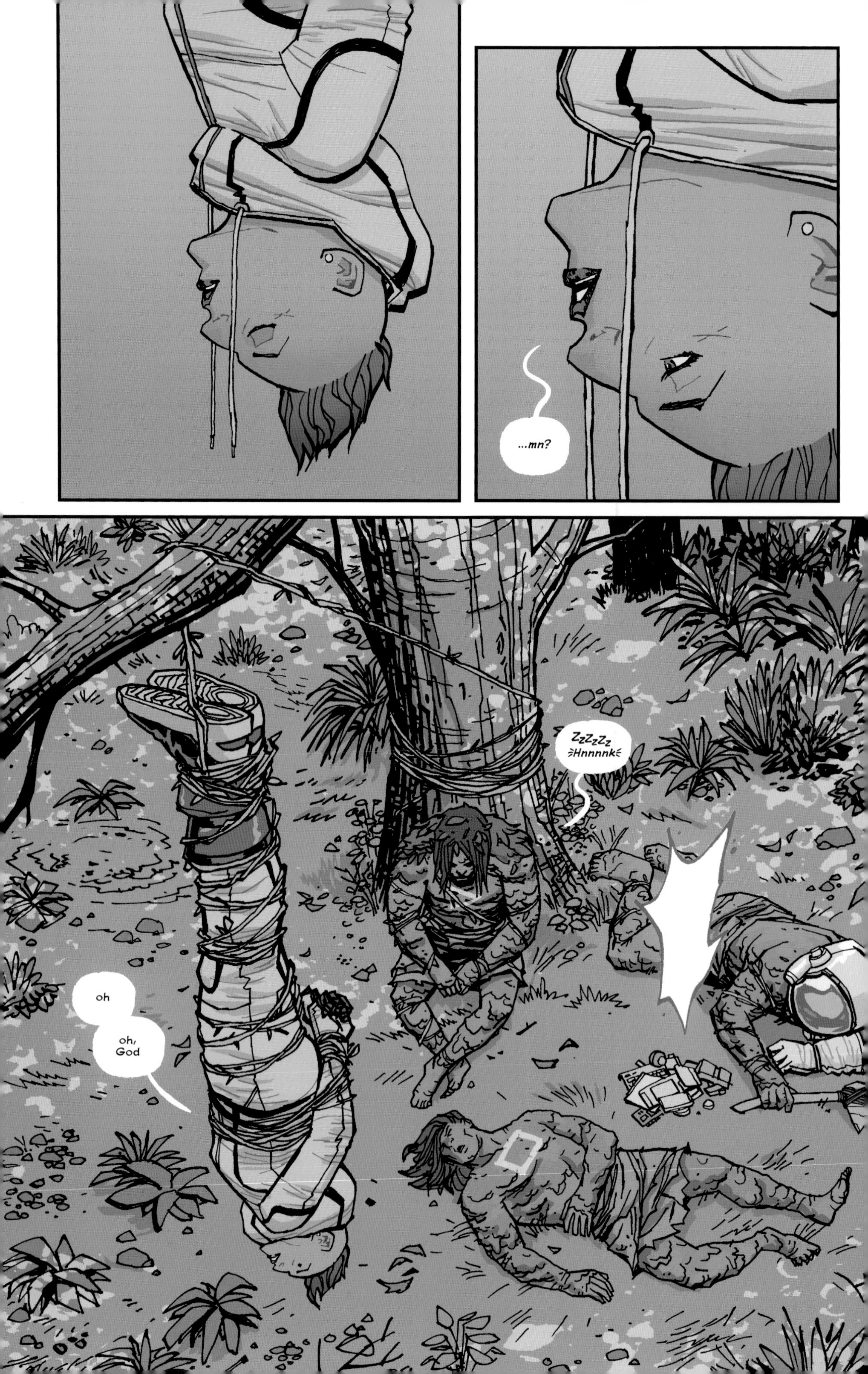
...mn?
ZzZzZz Hnnnnk
oh
oh, God

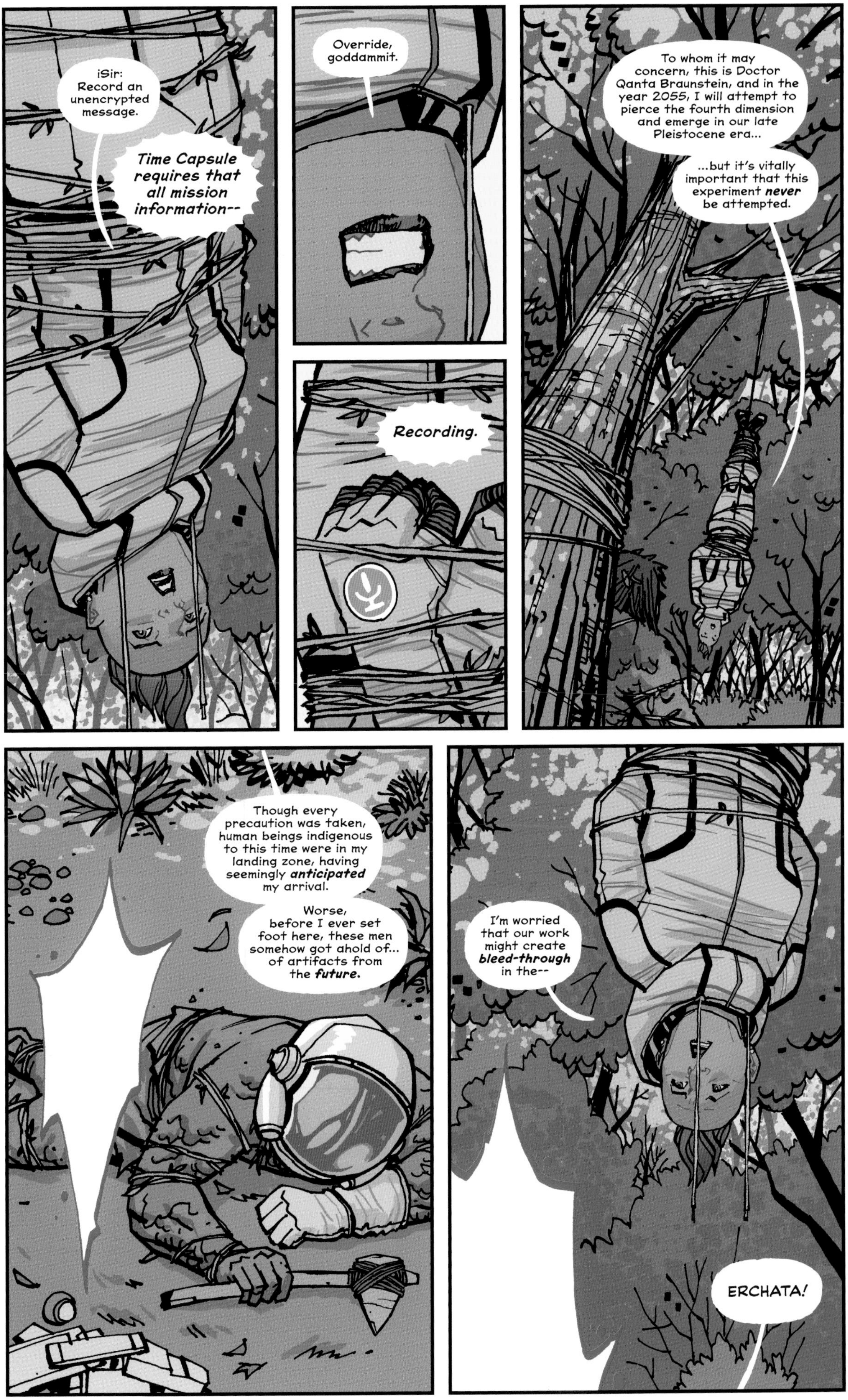
iSir: Record an unencrypted message.
Time Capsule requires that all mission information--
Override, goddammit.
Recording.
To whom it may concern, this is Doctor Qanta Braunstein, and in the year 2055, I will attempt to pierce the fourth dimension and emerge in our late Pleistocene era...
...but it's vitally important that this experiment never be attempted.
Though every precaution was taken, human beings indigenous to this time were in my landing zone, having seemingly anticipated my arrival.
Worse, before I ever set foot here, these men somehow got ahold of... of artifacts from the future.
I'm worried that our work might create bleed-through in the--
ERCHATA!

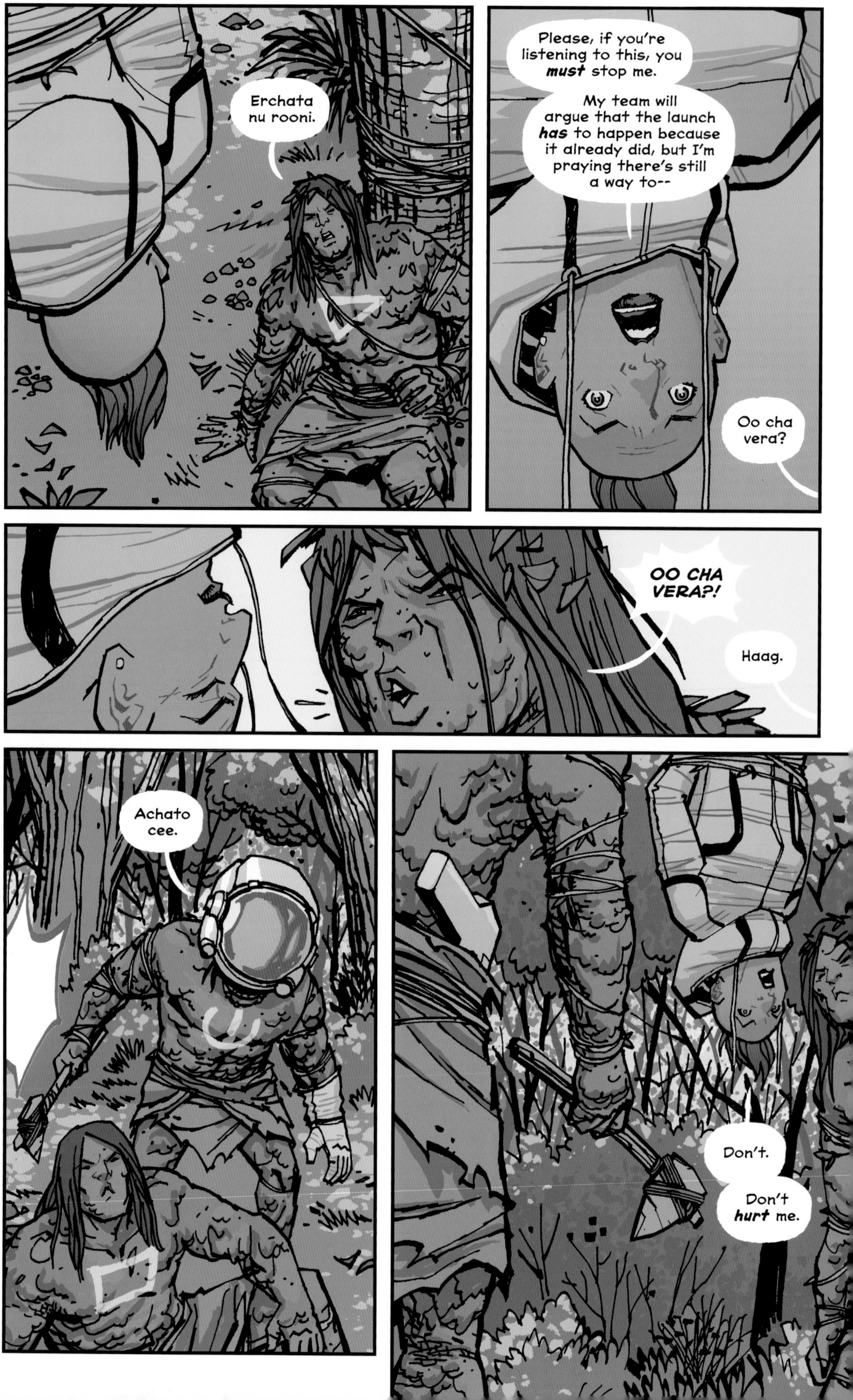
Erchata nu rooni.
Please, if you're listening to this, you *must* stop me.
My team will argue that the launch *has* to happen because it already did, but I'm praying there's still a way to--
Oo cha vera?
OO CHA VERA?!
Haag.
Achato cee.
Don't.
Don't *hurt* me.

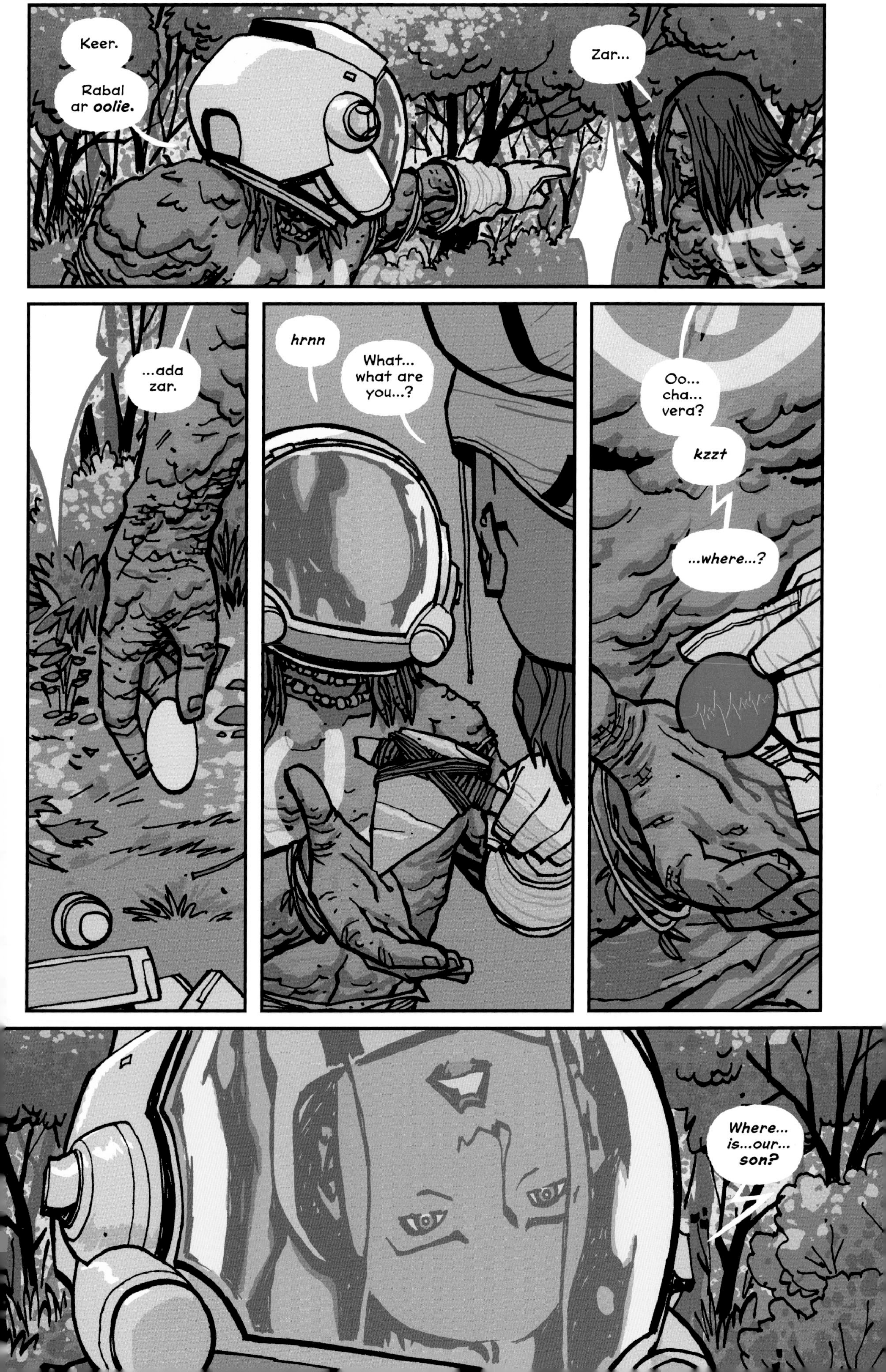
Keer.
Rabal ar *oolie*.
Zar...
...ada zar.
hrnn
What... what are you...?
Oo... cha... vera?
kzzt
...where...?
Where... is...our... son?

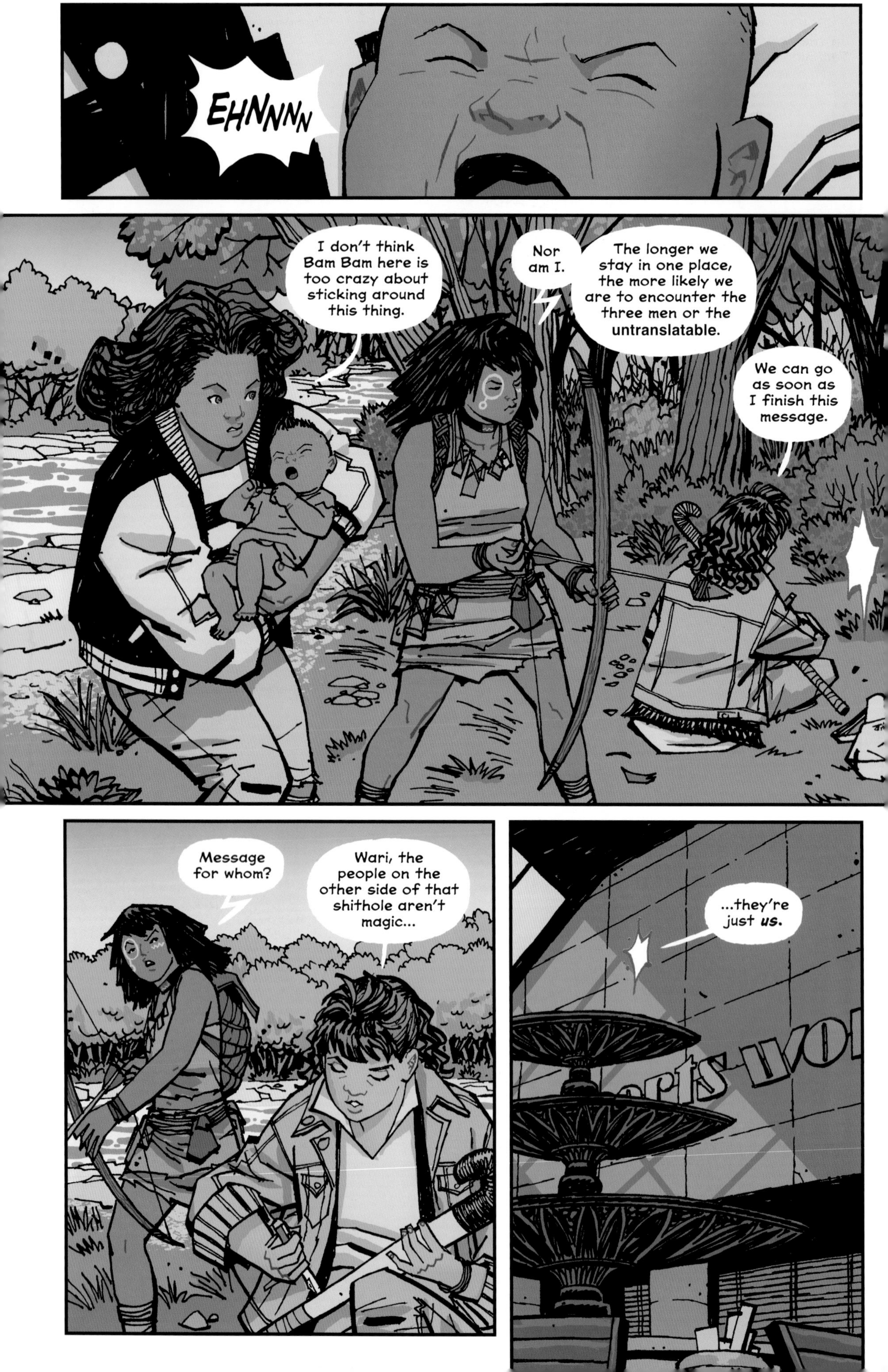
EHNNNN
I don't think Bam Bam here is too crazy about sticking around this thing.
Nor am I.
The longer we stay in one place, the more likely we are to encounter the three men or the **untranslatable.**
We can go as soon as I finish this message.
Message for whom?
Wari, the people on the other side of that shithole aren't magic...
...they're just ***us.***

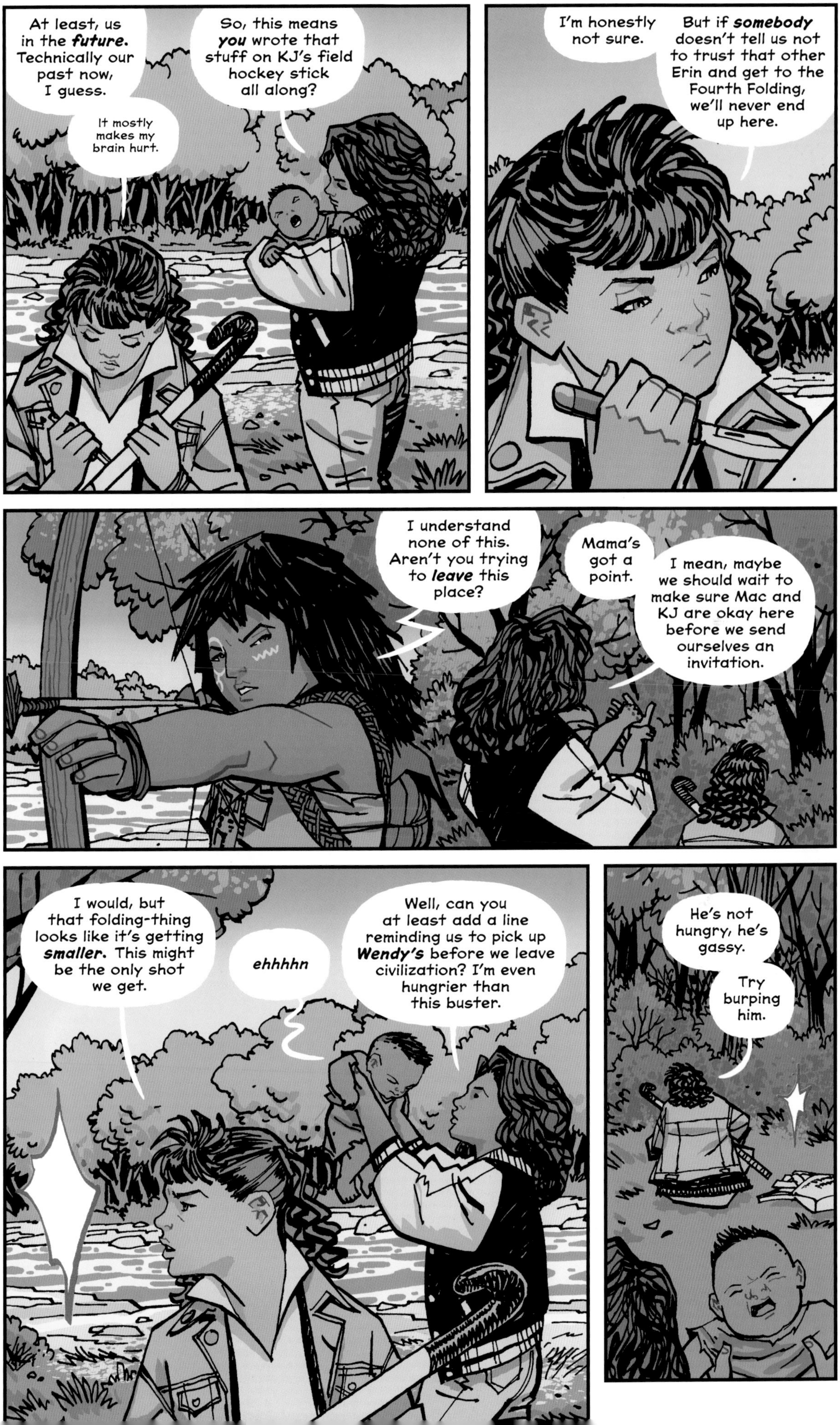
At least, us in the ***future.*** Technically our past now, I guess.
It mostly makes my brain hurt.
So, this means ***you*** wrote that stuff on KJ's field hockey stick all along?
I'm honestly not sure.
But if ***somebody*** doesn't tell us not to trust that other Erin and get to the Fourth Folding, we'll never end up here.
I understand none of this. Aren't you trying to ***leave*** this place?
Mama's got a point.
I mean, maybe we should wait to make sure Mac and KJ are okay here before we send ourselves an invitation.
I would, but that folding-thing looks like it's getting ***smaller.*** This might be the only shot we get.
ehhhhn
Well, can you at least add a line reminding us to pick up ***Wendy's*** before we leave civilization? I'm even hungrier than this buster.
He's not hungry, he's gassy.
Try burping him.

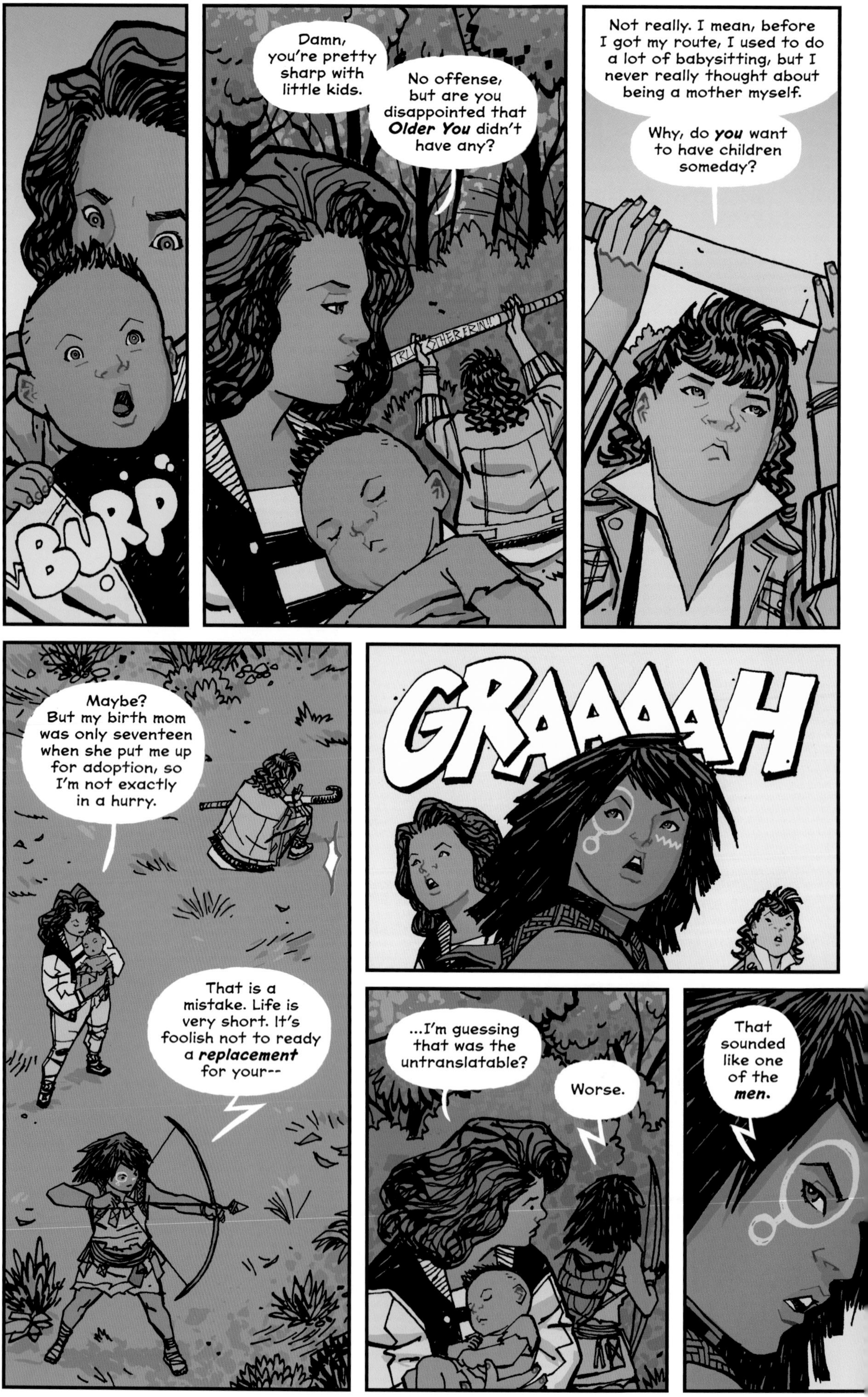
BURP
Damn, you're pretty sharp with little kids.
No offense, but are you disappointed that Older You didn't have any?
TRU OTHER ERIN!!
Not really. I mean, before I got my route, I used to do a lot of babysitting, but I never really thought about being a mother myself.
Why, do you want to have children someday?
Maybe? But my birth mom was only seventeen when she put me up for adoption, so I'm not exactly in a hurry.
That is a mistake. Life is very short. It's foolish not to ready a replacement for your--
GRAAAAH
...I'm guessing that was the untranslatable?
Worse.
That sounded like one of the men.

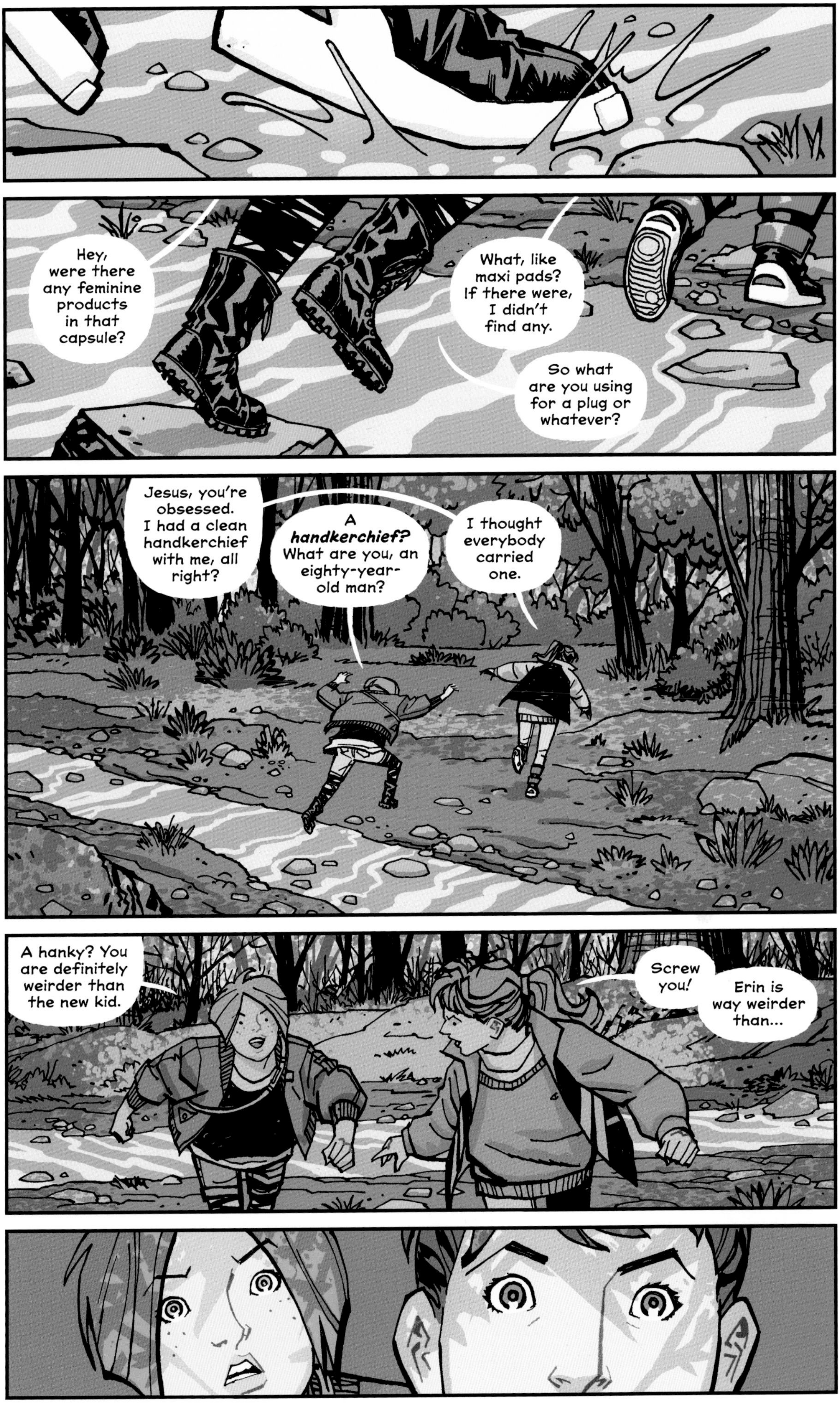
Hey, were there any feminine products in that capsule?
What, like maxi pads? If there were, I didn't find any.
So what are you using for a plug or whatever?
Jesus, you're obsessed. I had a clean handkerchief with me, all right?
A *handkerchief?* What are you, an eighty-year-old man?
I thought everybody carried one.
A hanky? You are definitely weirder than the new kid.
Screw you!
Erin is way weirder than...

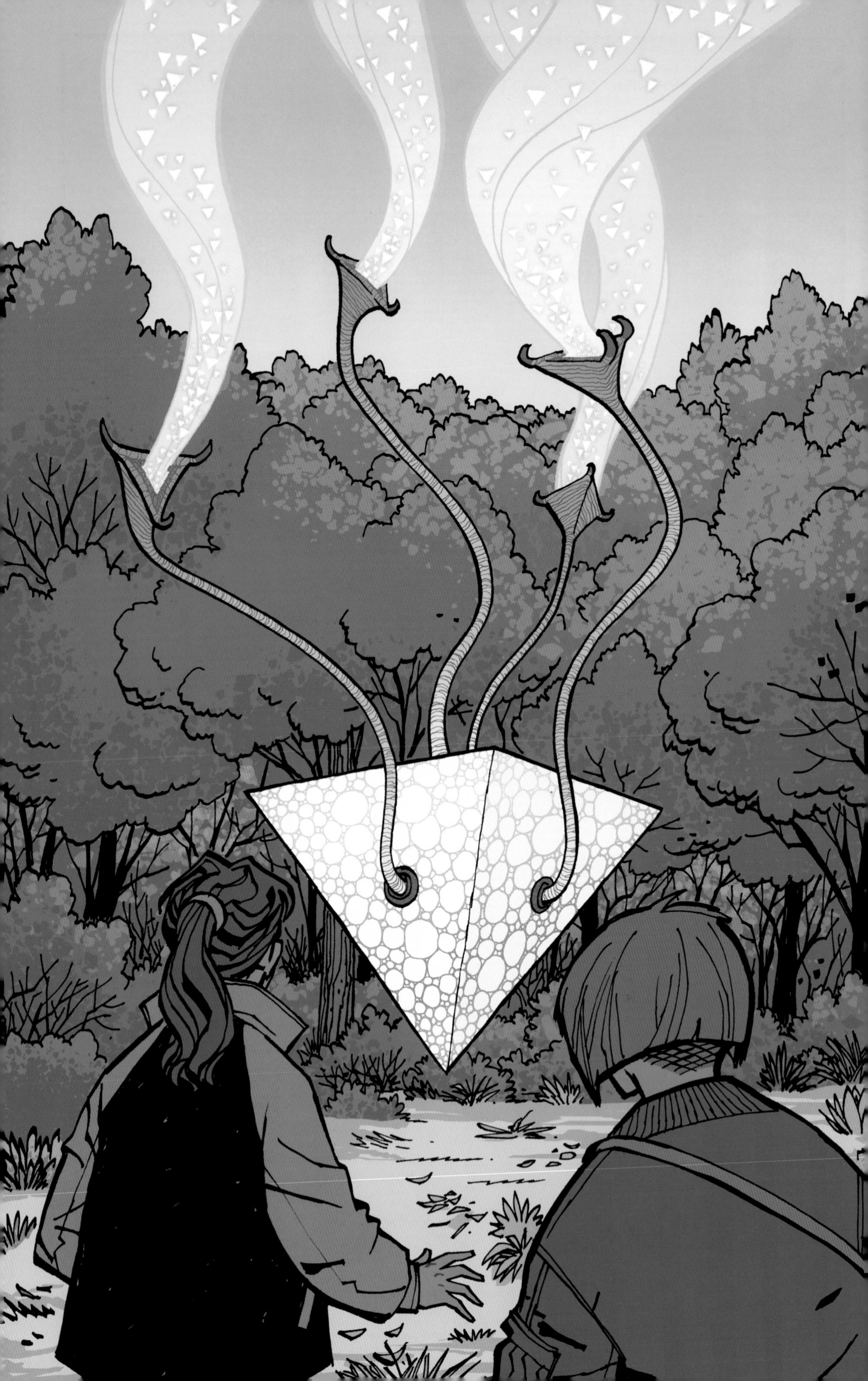

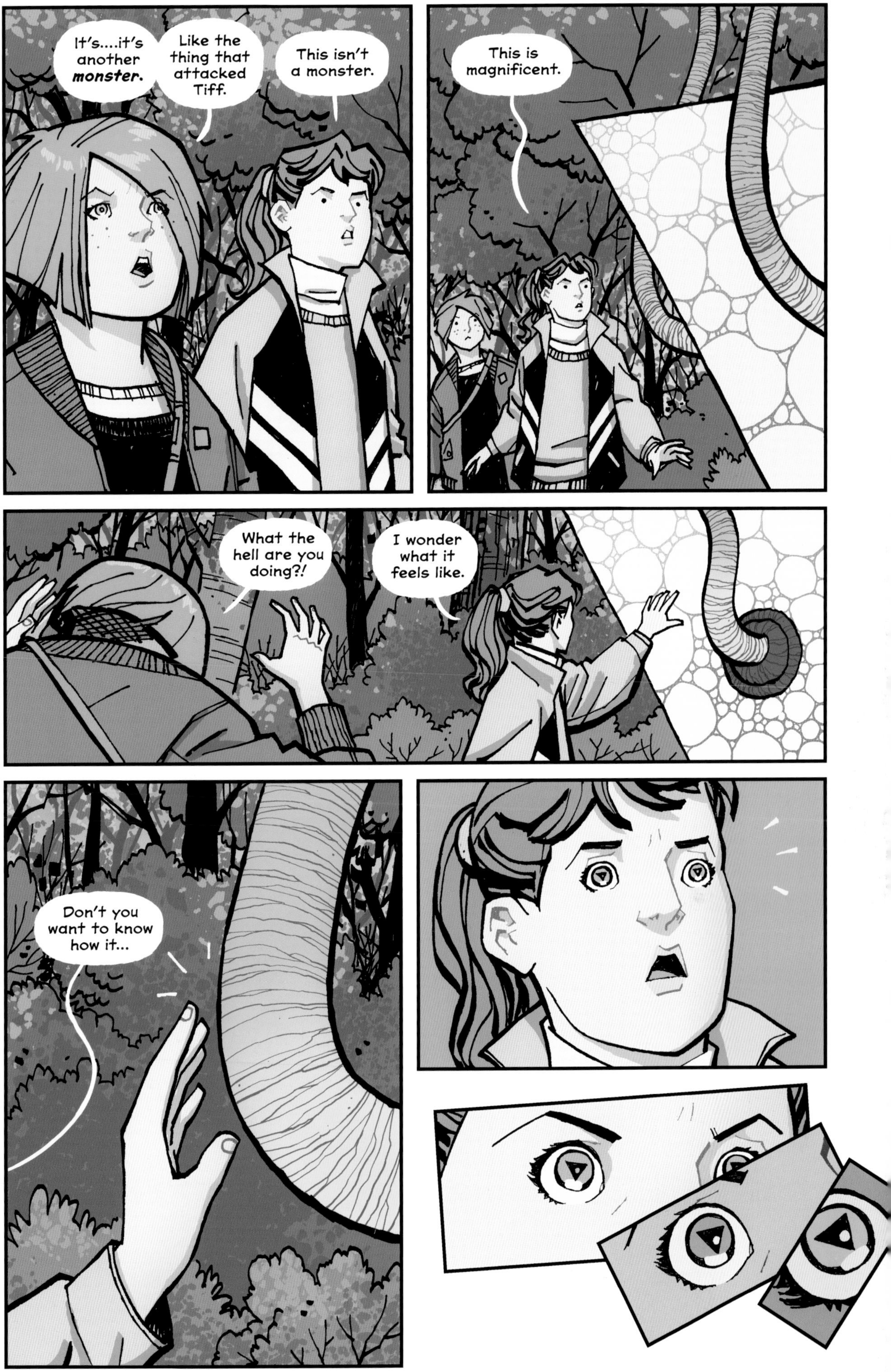
It's....it's another **monster.**
Like the thing that attacked Tiff.
This isn't a monster.
This is magnificent.
What the hell are you doing?!
I wonder what it feels like.
Don't you want to know how it...

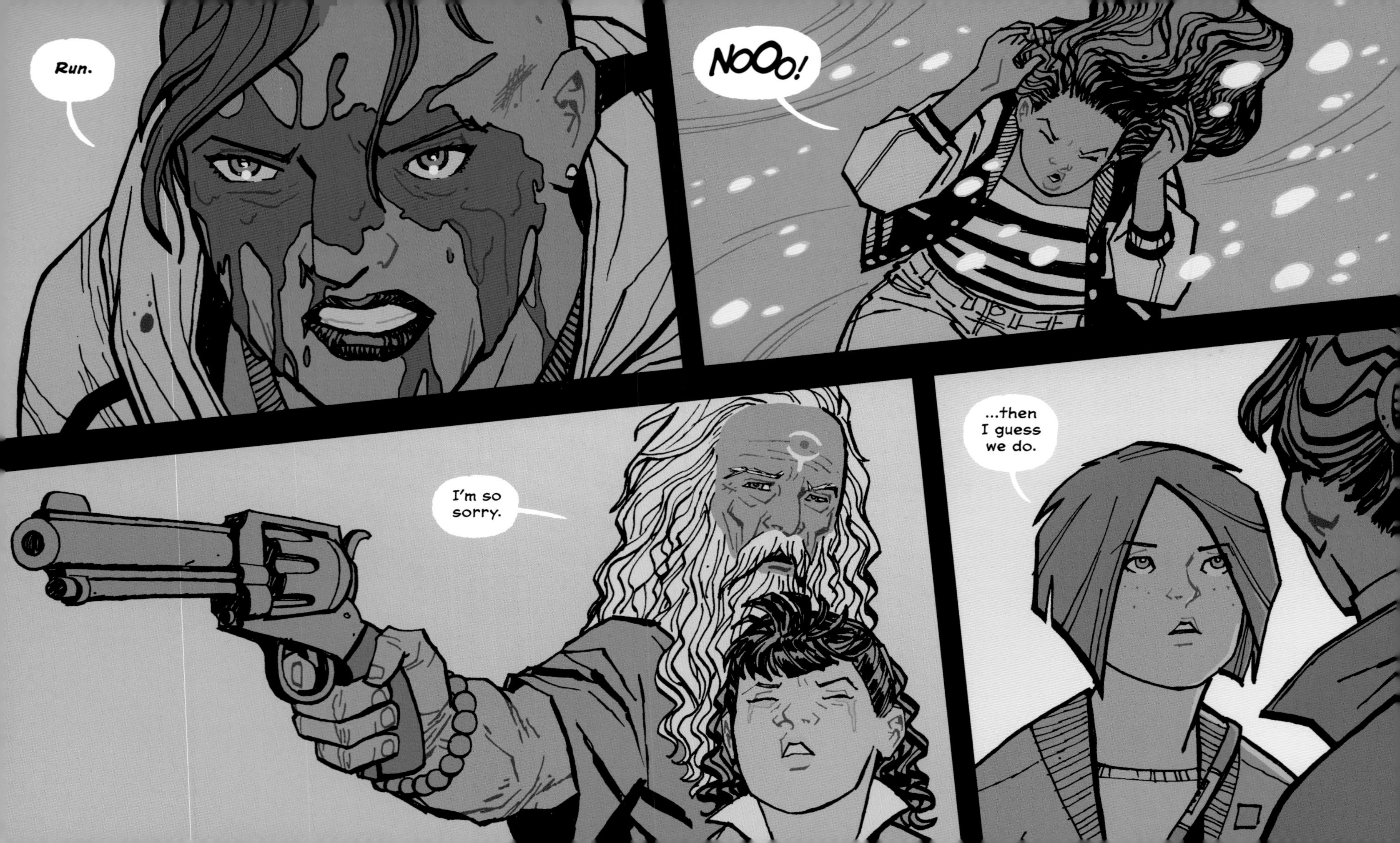
Run.
NOOo!
I'm so sorry.
...then I guess we do.

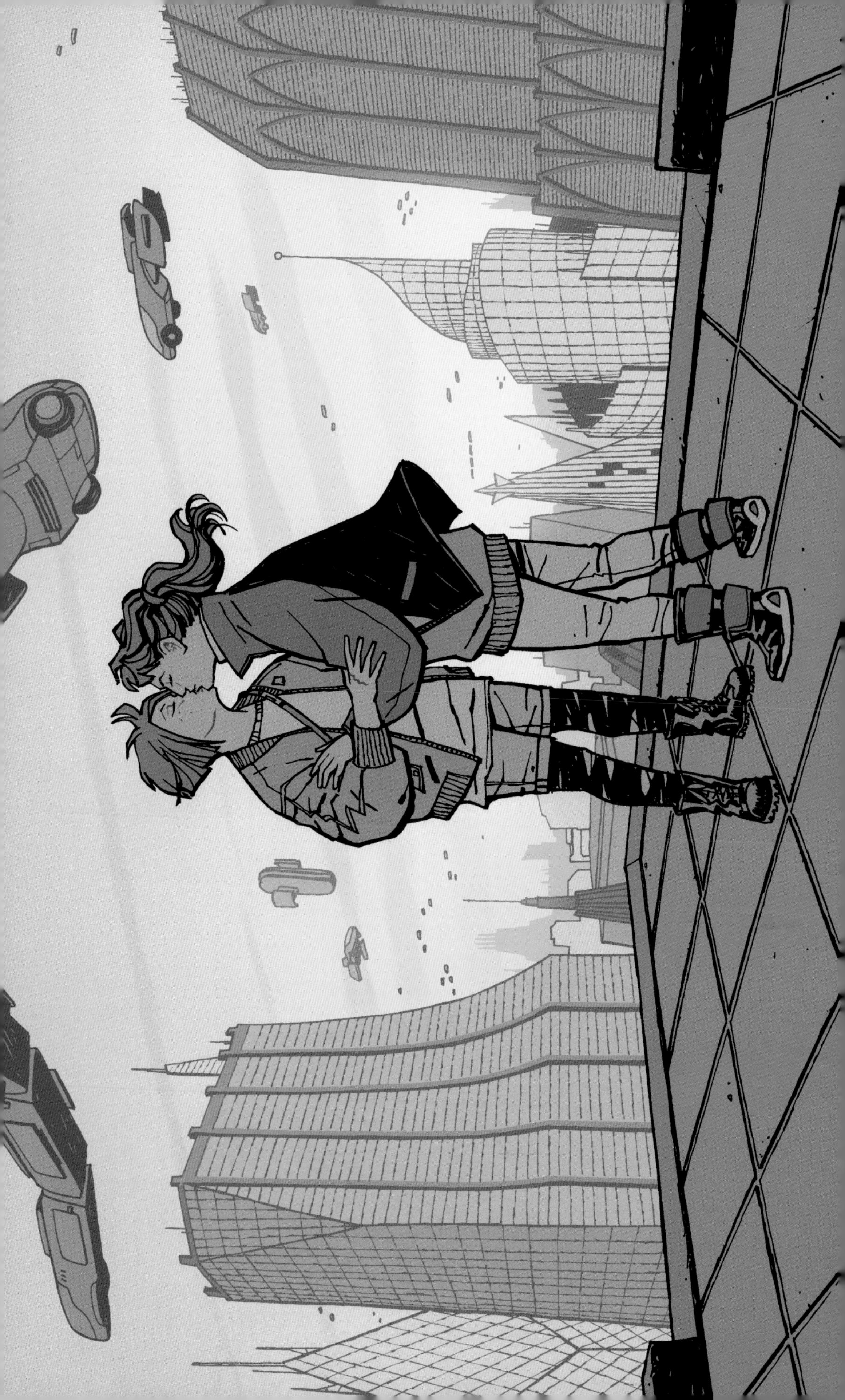

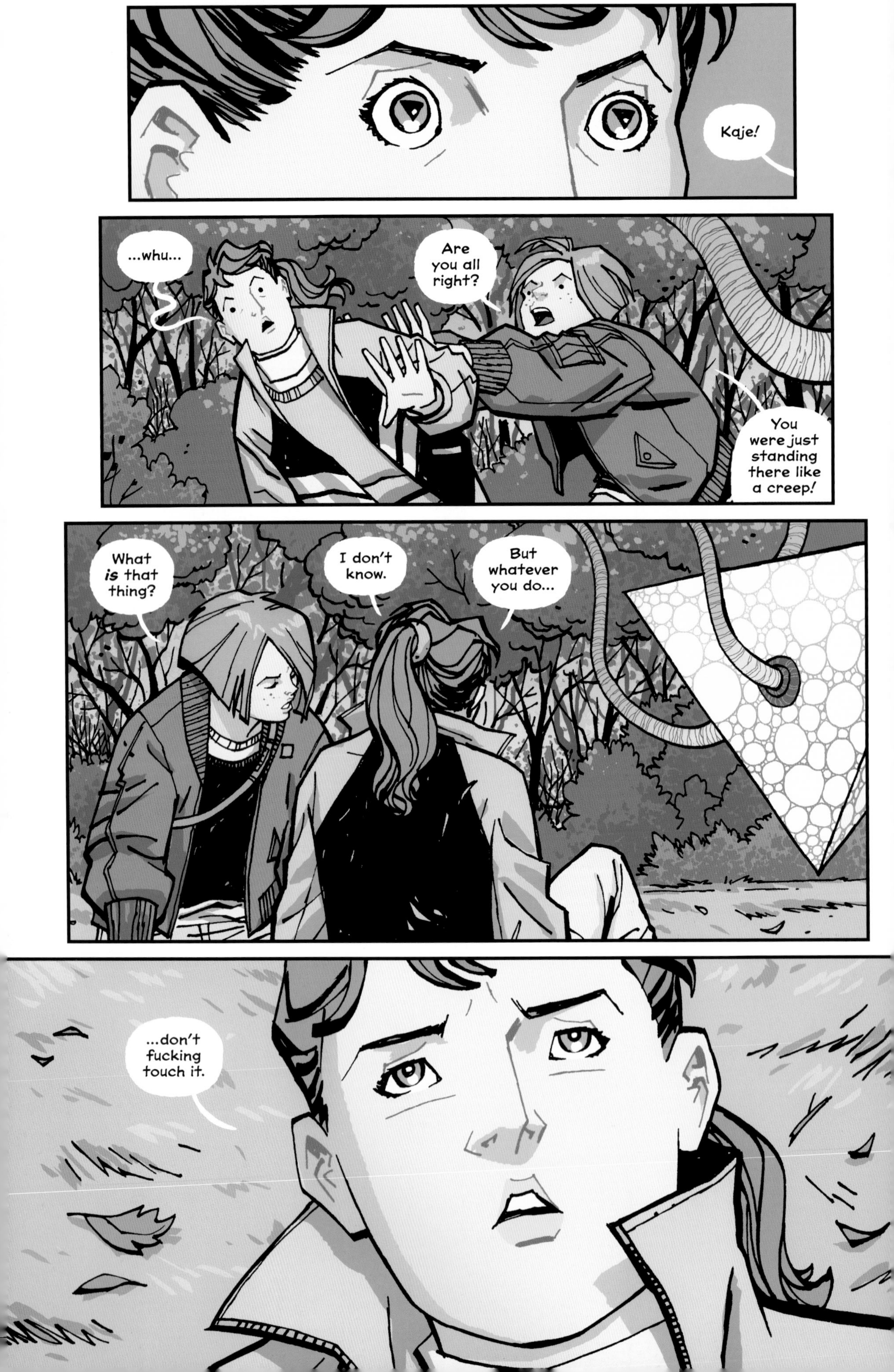
Kaje!
...whu...
Are you all right?
You were just standing there like a creep!
What *is* that thing?
I don't know.
But whatever you do...
...don't fucking touch it.

CHAPTER
14

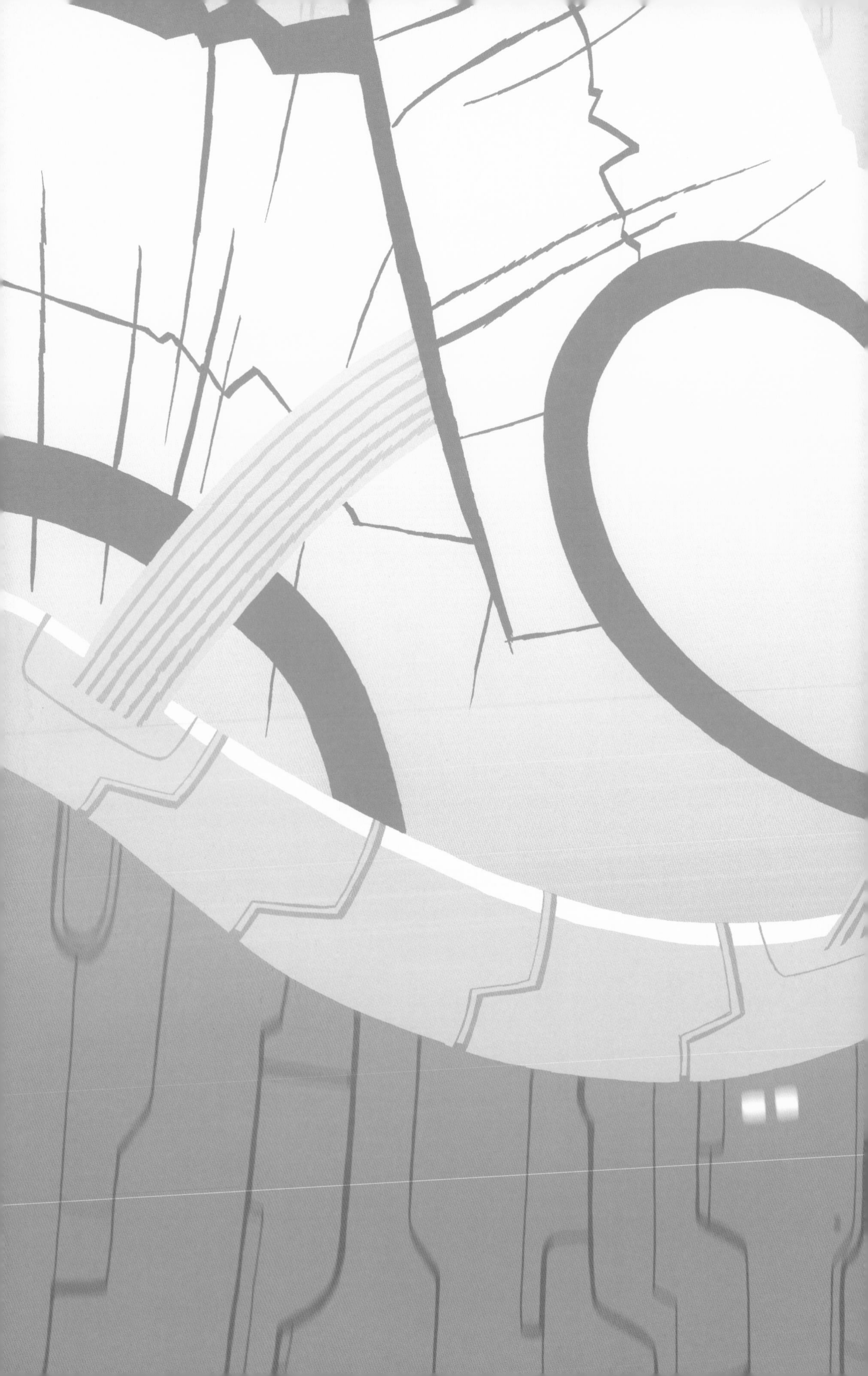

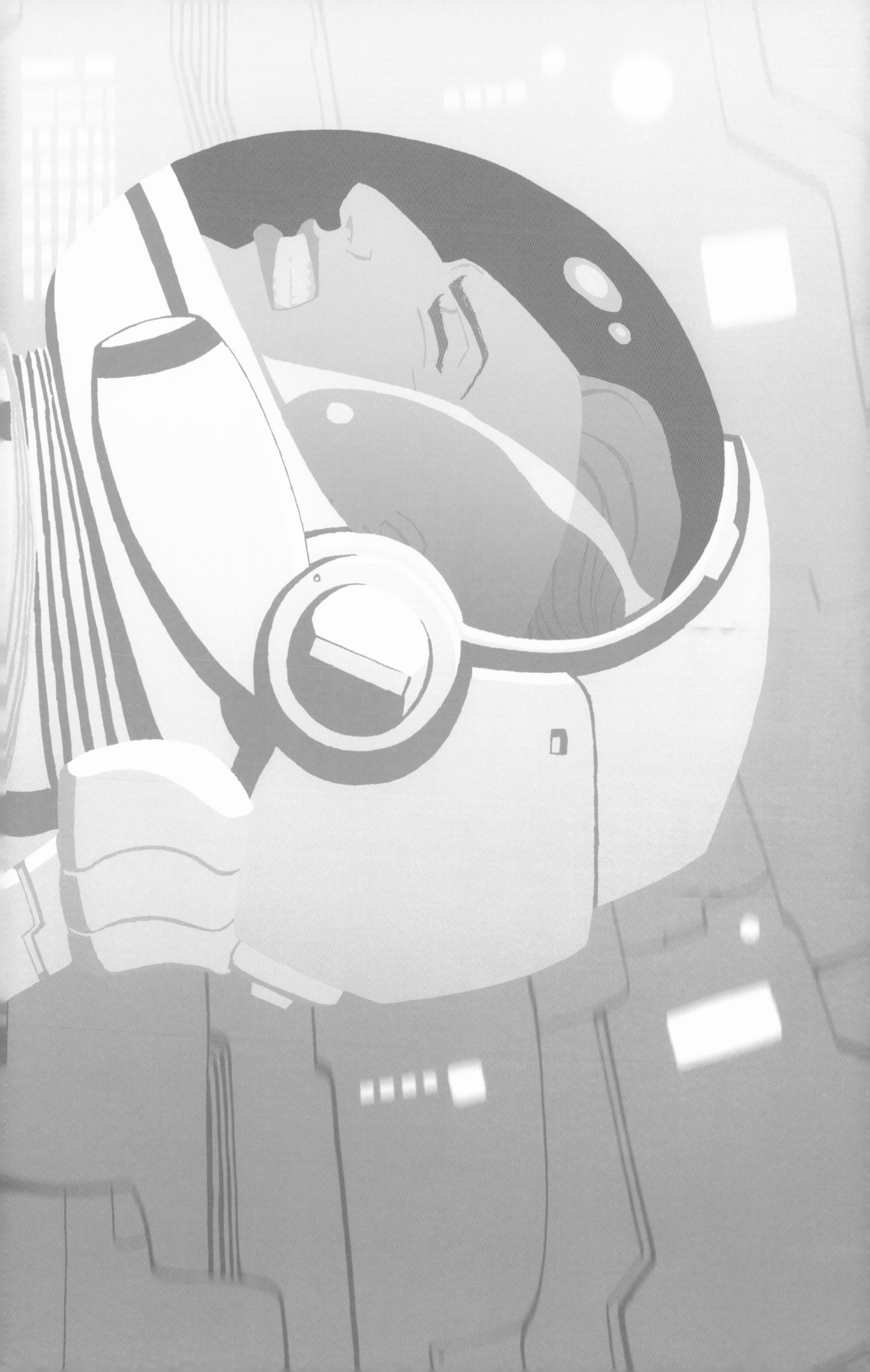

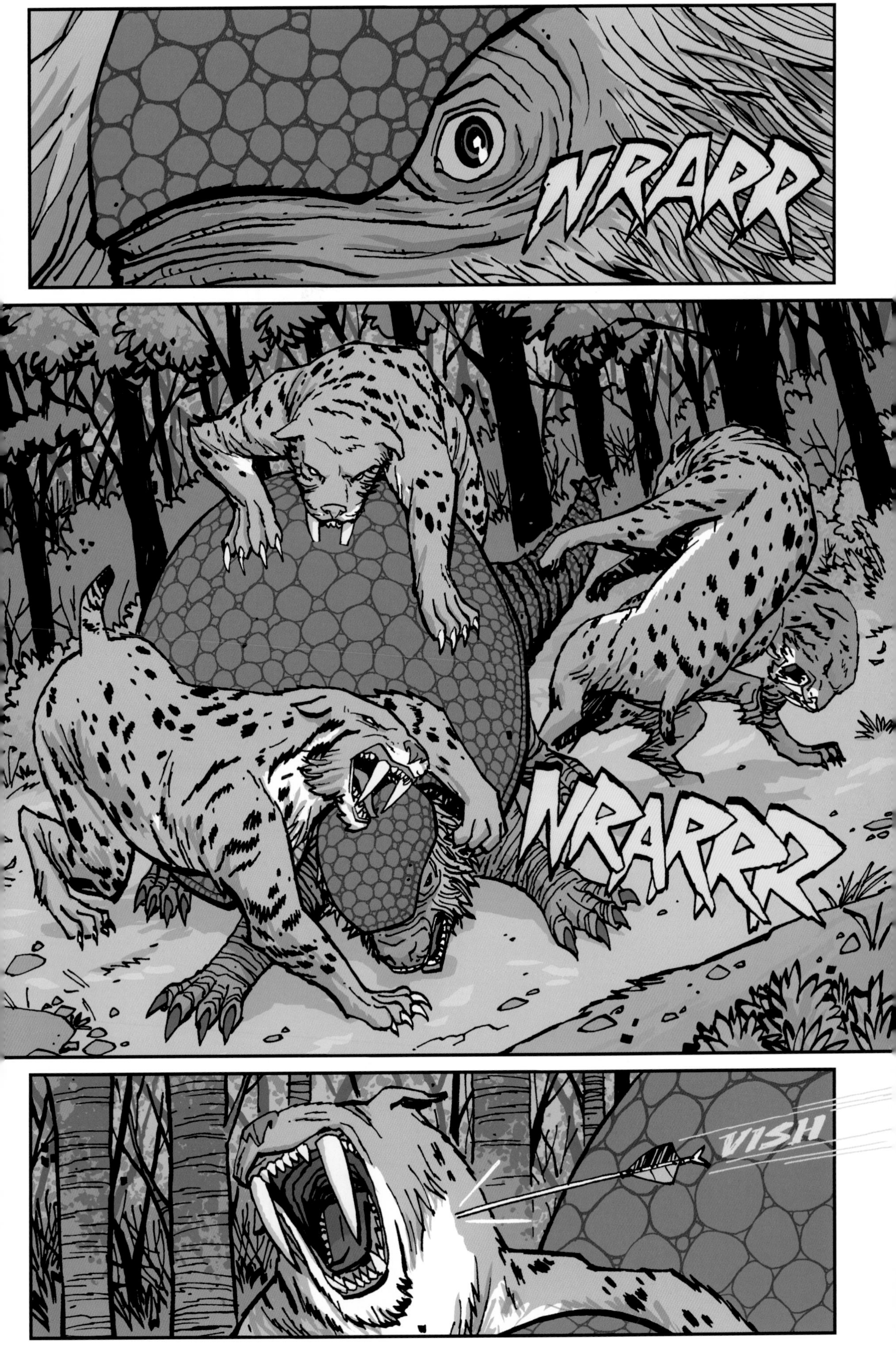
NRARR
NRARRR
VISH

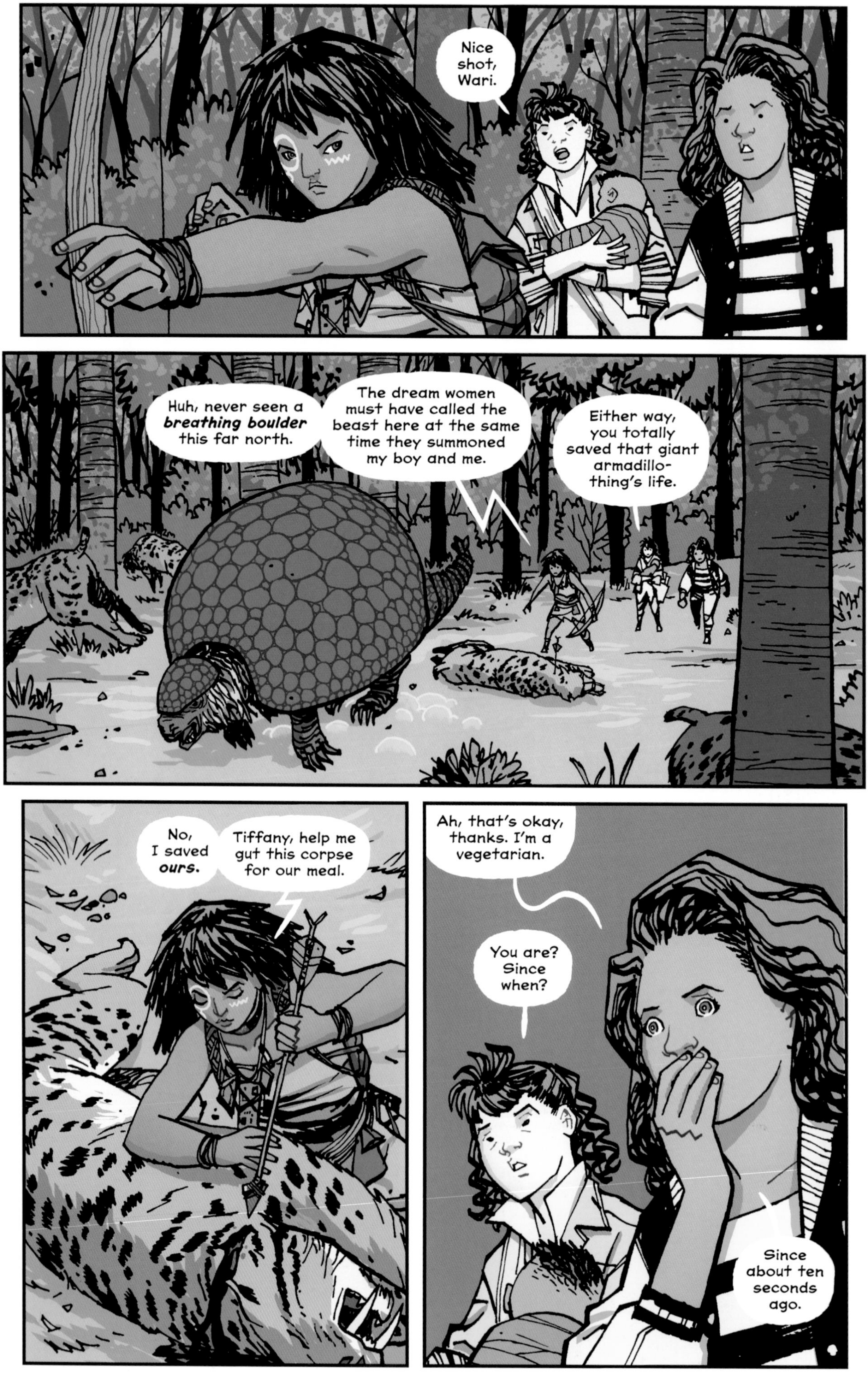
Nice shot, Wari.
Huh, never seen a *breathing boulder* this far north.
The dream women must have called the beast here at the same time they summoned my boy and me.
Either way, you totally saved that giant armadillo-thing's life.
No, I saved *ours.*
Tiffany, help me gut this corpse for our meal.
Ah, that's okay, thanks. I'm a vegetarian.
You are? Since when?
Since about ten seconds ago.

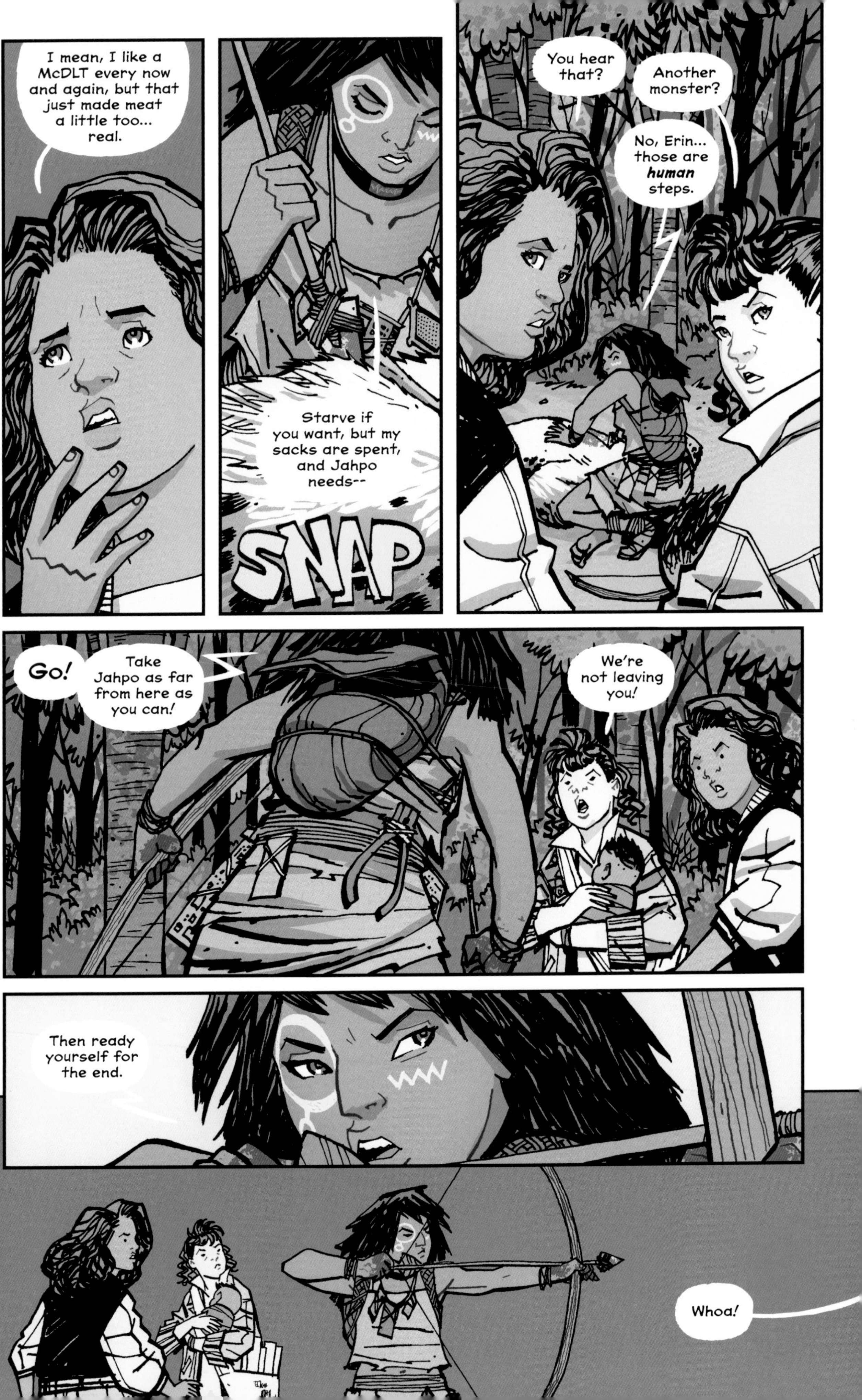
I mean, I like a McDLT every now and again, but that just made meat a little too... real.
Starve if you want, but my sacks are spent, and Jahpo needs--
SNAP
You hear that?
Another monster?
No, Erin... those are *human* steps.
Go!
Take Jahpo as far from here as you can!
We're not leaving you!
Then ready yourself for the end.
Whoa!

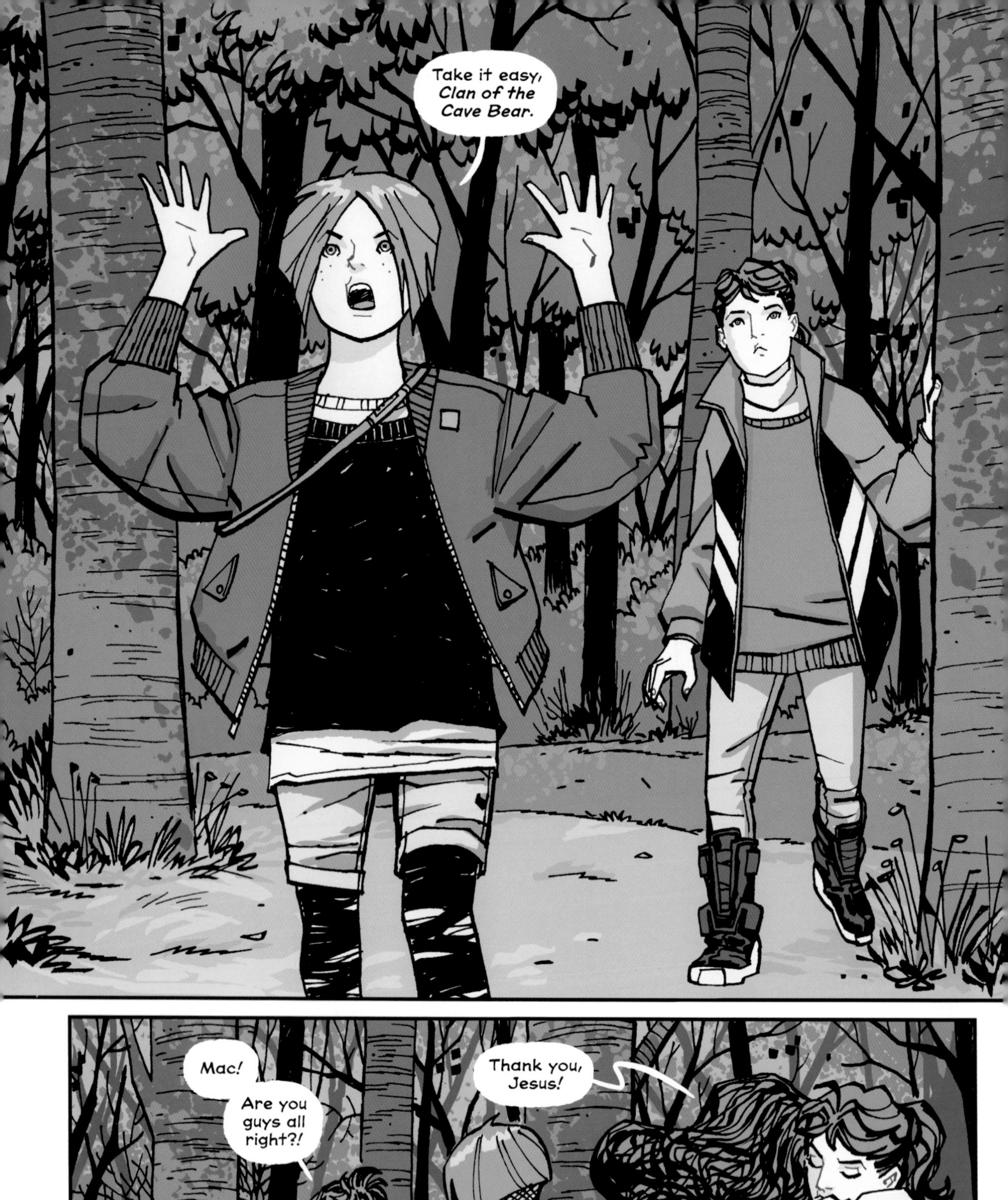
Take it easy, *Clan of the Cave Bear.*

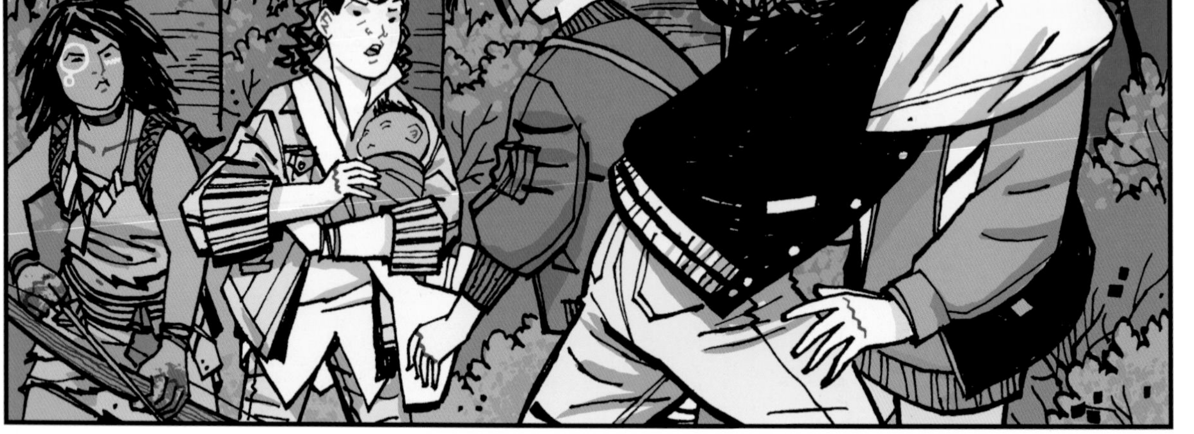
Mac!
Are you guys all right?!
Thank you, Jesus!

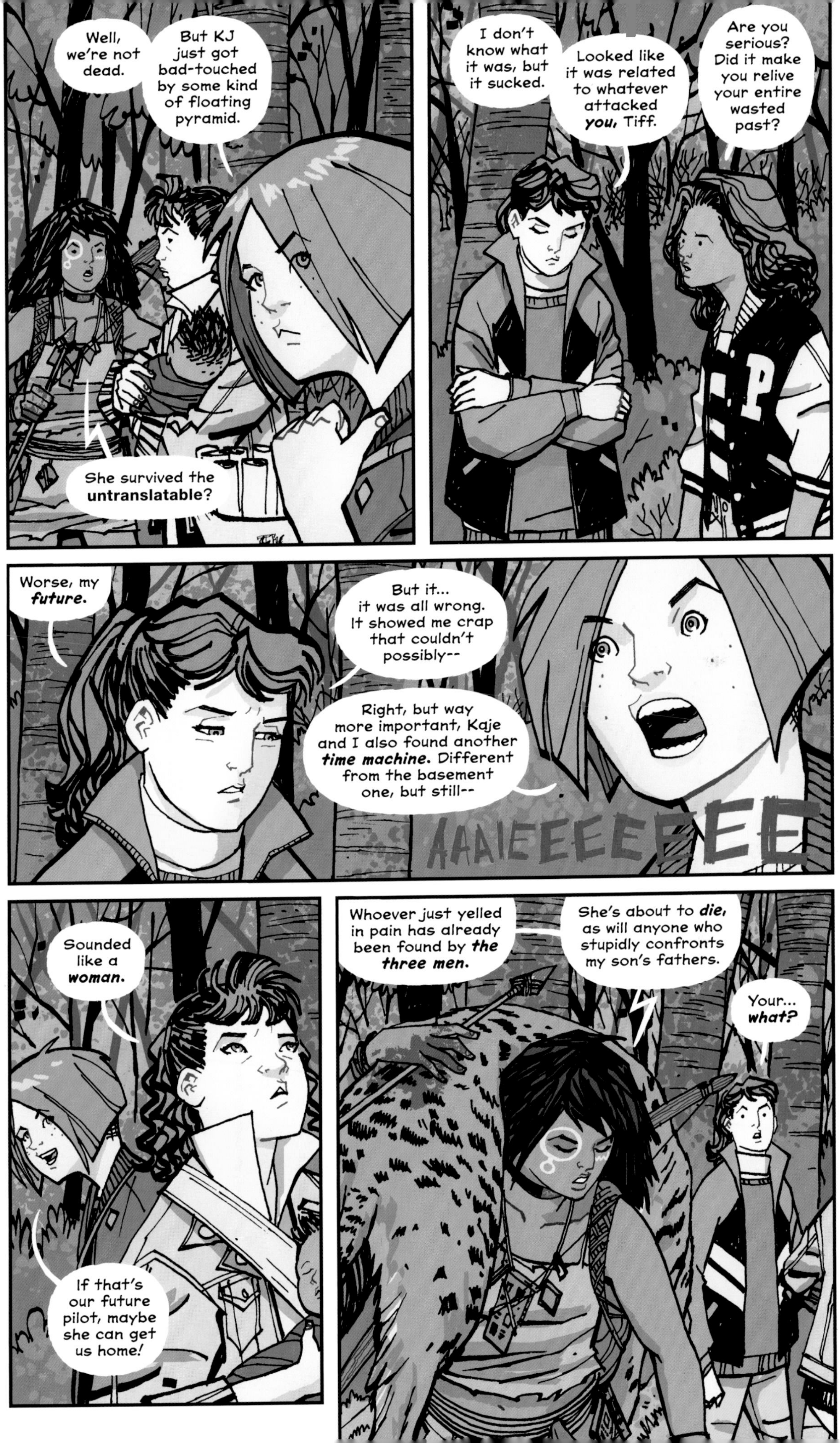
Well, we're not dead.
But KJ just got bad-touched by some kind of floating pyramid.
She survived the untranslatable?
I don't know what it was, but it sucked.
Looked like it was related to whatever attacked you, Tiff.
Are you serious? Did it make you relive your entire wasted past?
Worse, my future.
But it... it was all wrong. It showed me crap that couldn't possibly--
Right, but way more important, Kaje and I also found another time machine. Different from the basement one, but still--
AAAIEEEEEEE
Sounded like a woman.
If that's our future pilot, maybe she can get us home!
Whoever just yelled in pain has already been found by the three men.
She's about to die, as will anyone who stupidly confronts my son's fathers.
Your... what?

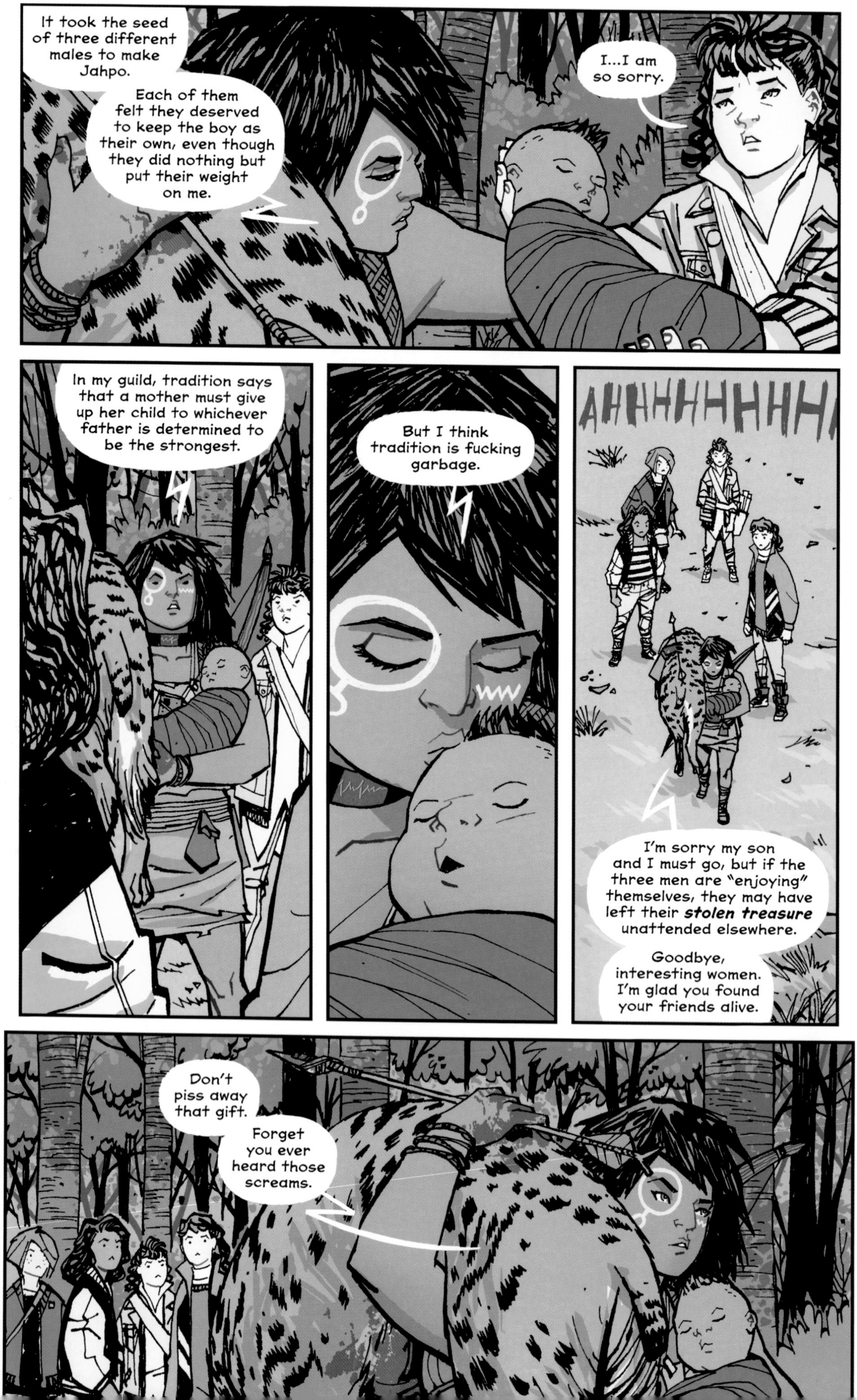

It took the seed of three different males to make Jahpo.
Each of them felt they deserved to keep the boy as their own, even though they did nothing but put their weight on me.
I...I am so sorry.
In my guild, tradition says that a mother must give up her child to whichever father is determined to be the strongest.
But I think tradition is fucking garbage.
AHHHHHHHHH
I'm sorry my son and I must go, but if the three men are "enjoying" themselves, they may have left their ***stolen treasure*** unattended elsewhere.
Goodbye, interesting women. I'm glad you found your friends alive.
Don't piss away that gift.
Forget you ever heard those screams.

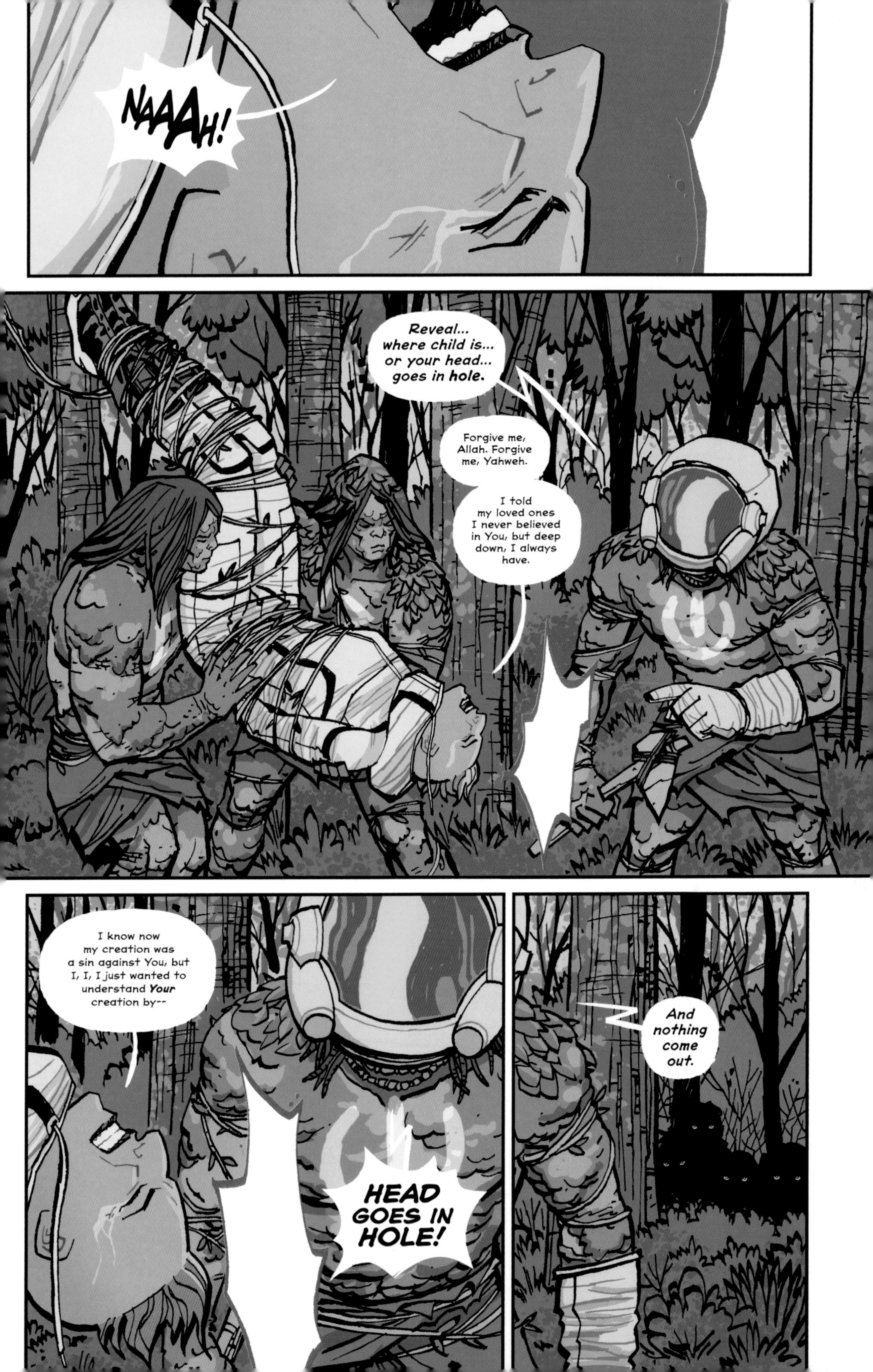
NAAAH!
Reveal... where child is... or your head... goes in hole.
Forgive me, Allah. Forgive me, Yahweh.
I told my loved ones I never believed in You, but deep down, I always have.
I know now my creation was a sin against You, but I, I, I just wanted to understand Your creation by--
HEAD GOES IN HOLE!
And nothing come out.

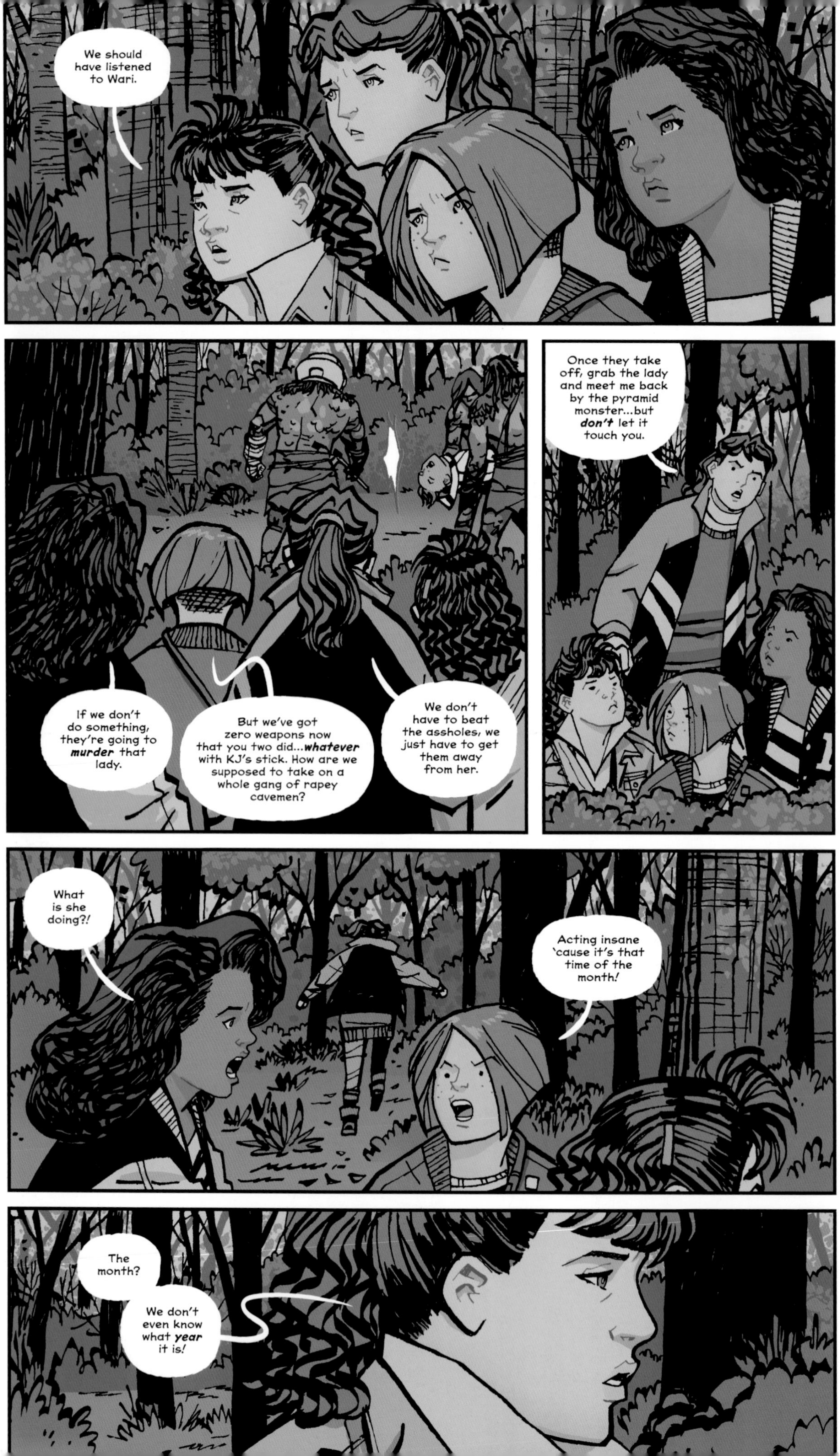
We should have listened to Wari.
If we don't do something, they're going to *murder* that lady.
But we've got zero weapons now that you two did...*whatever* with KJ's stick. How are we supposed to take on a whole gang of rapey cavemen?
We don't have to beat the assholes, we just have to get them away from her.
Once they take off, grab the lady and meet me back by the pyramid monster...but *don't* let it touch you.
What is she doing?!
Acting insane 'cause it's that time of the month!
The month?
We don't even know what *year* it is!

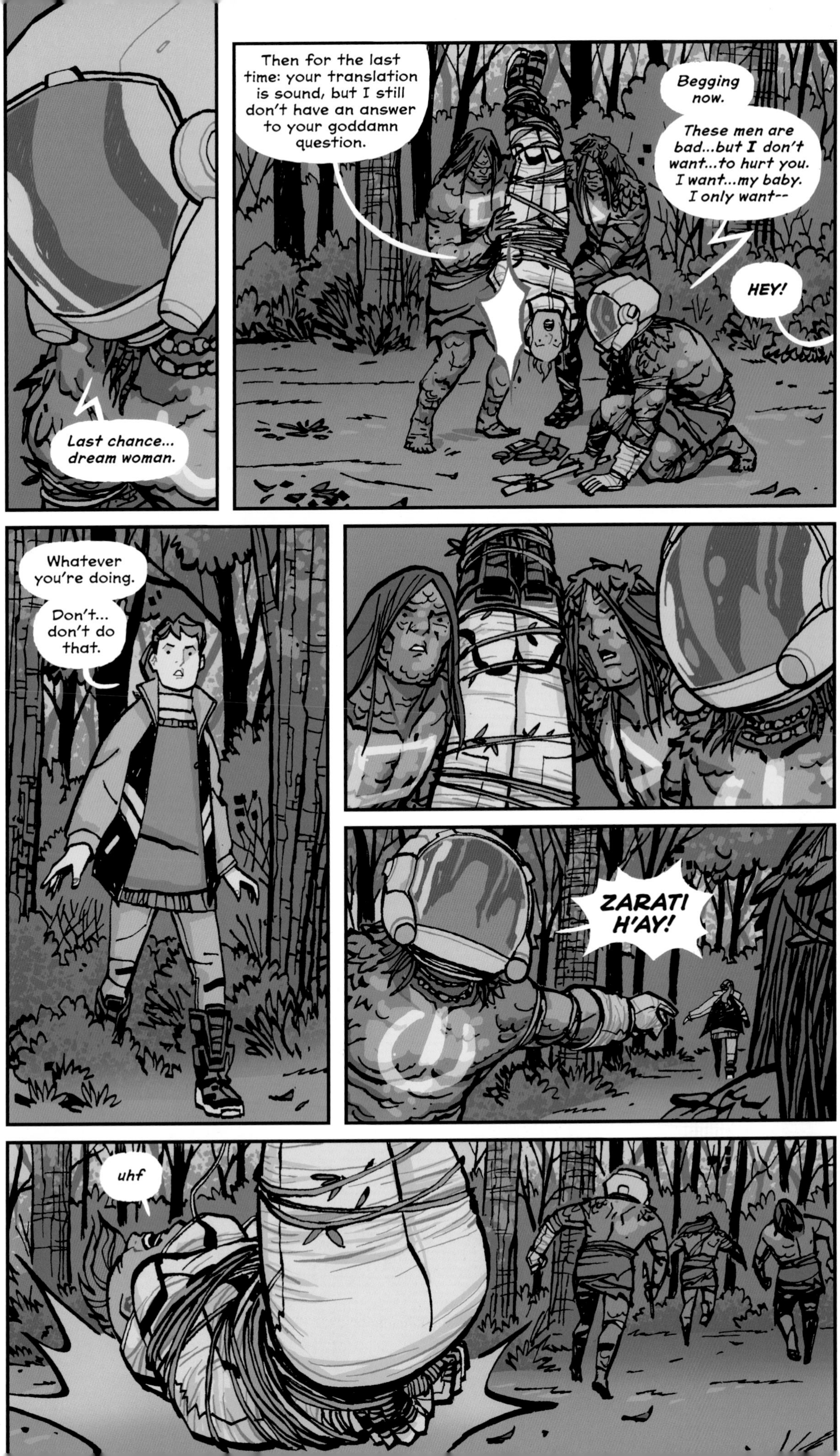
Last chance... dream woman.
Then for the last time: your translation is sound, but I still don't have an answer to your goddamn question.
Begging now.
These men are bad...but I don't want...to hurt you. I want...my baby. I only want--
HEY!
Whatever you're doing.
Don't... don't do that.
ZARATI H'AY!
uhf

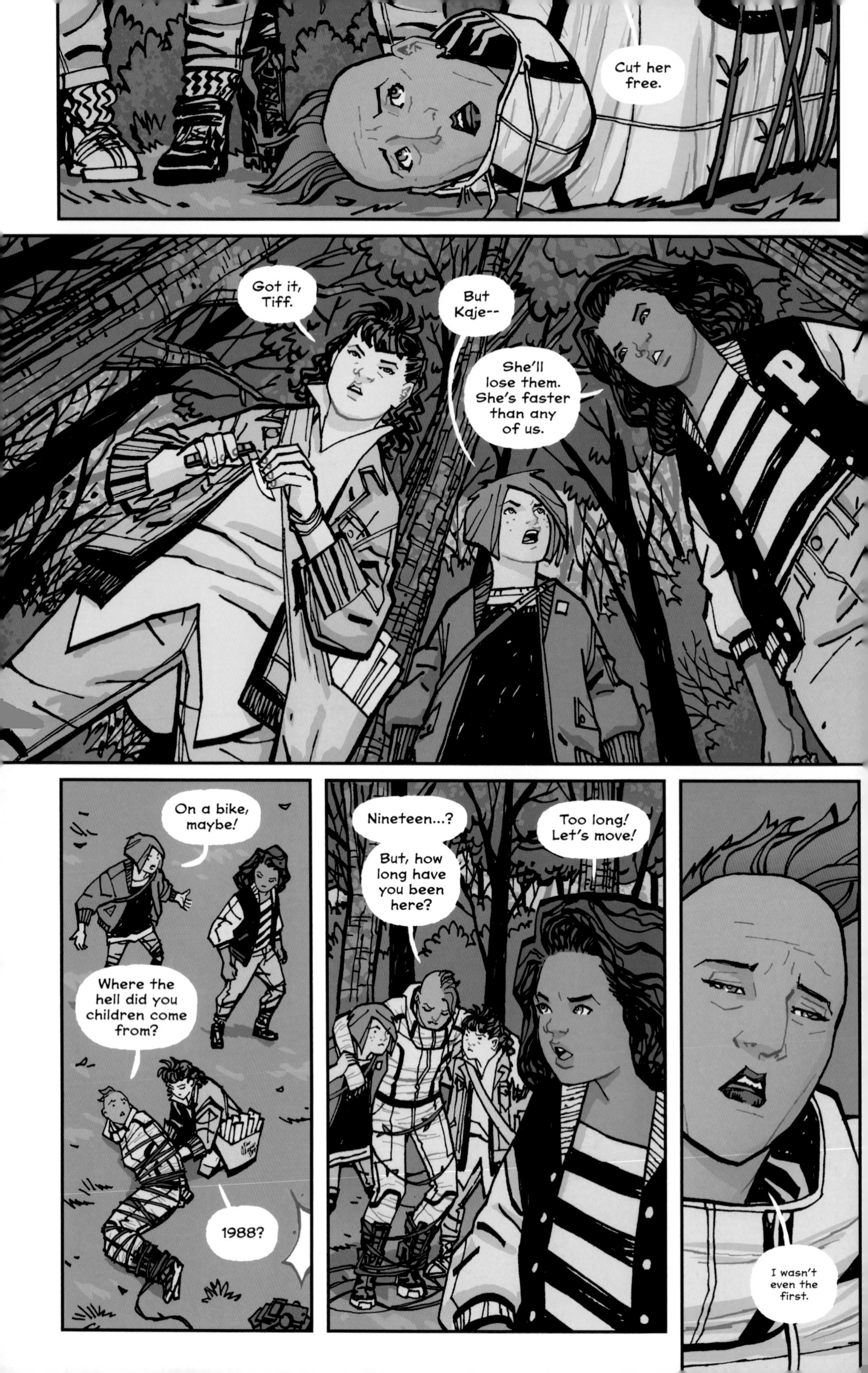

Cut her free.
Got it, Tiff.
But Kaje--
She'll lose them. She's faster than any of us.
On a bike, maybe!
Where the hell did you children come from?
1988?
Nineteen...?
But, how long have you been here?
Too long! Let's move!
I wasn't even the first.

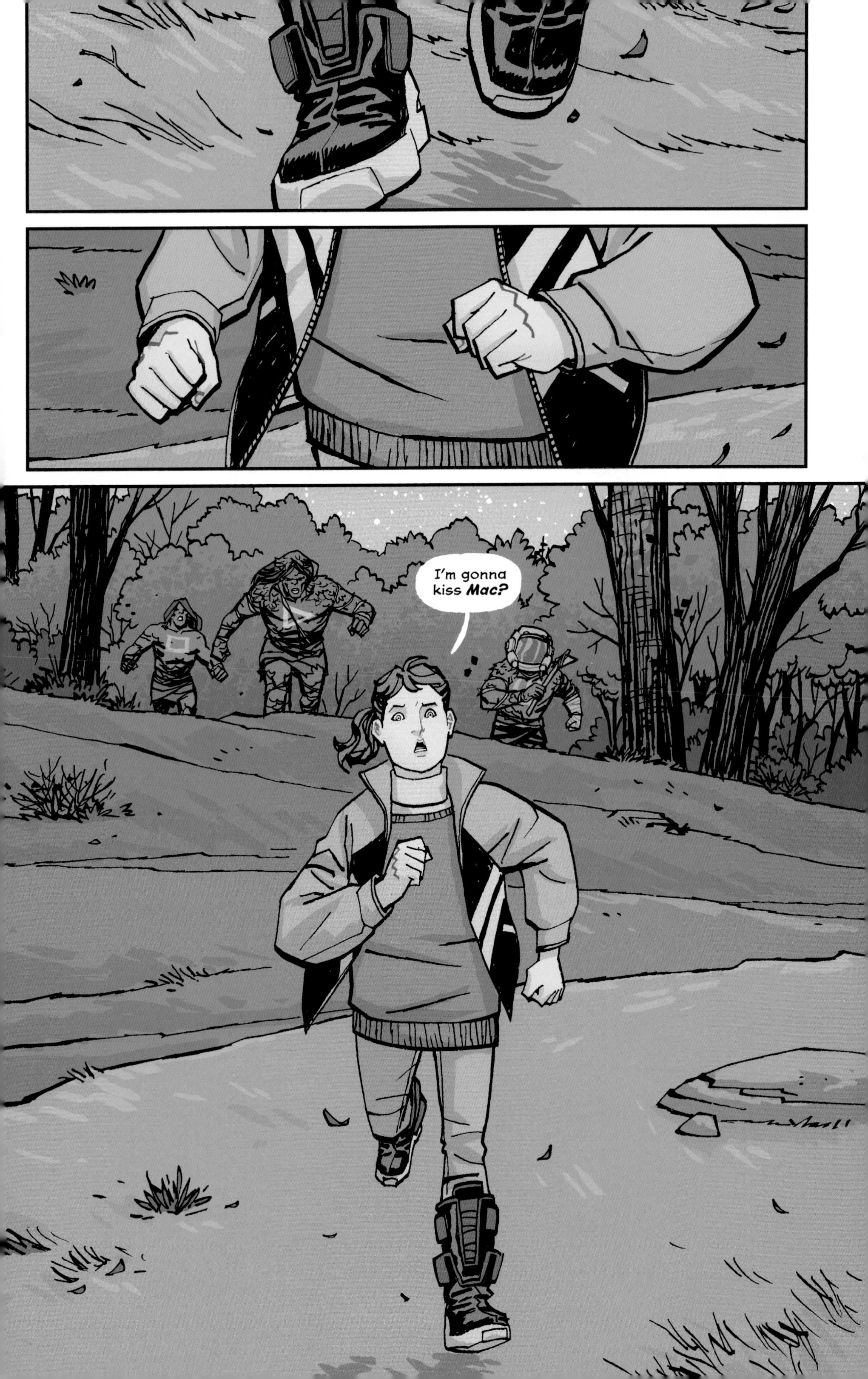
I'm gonna kiss Mac?

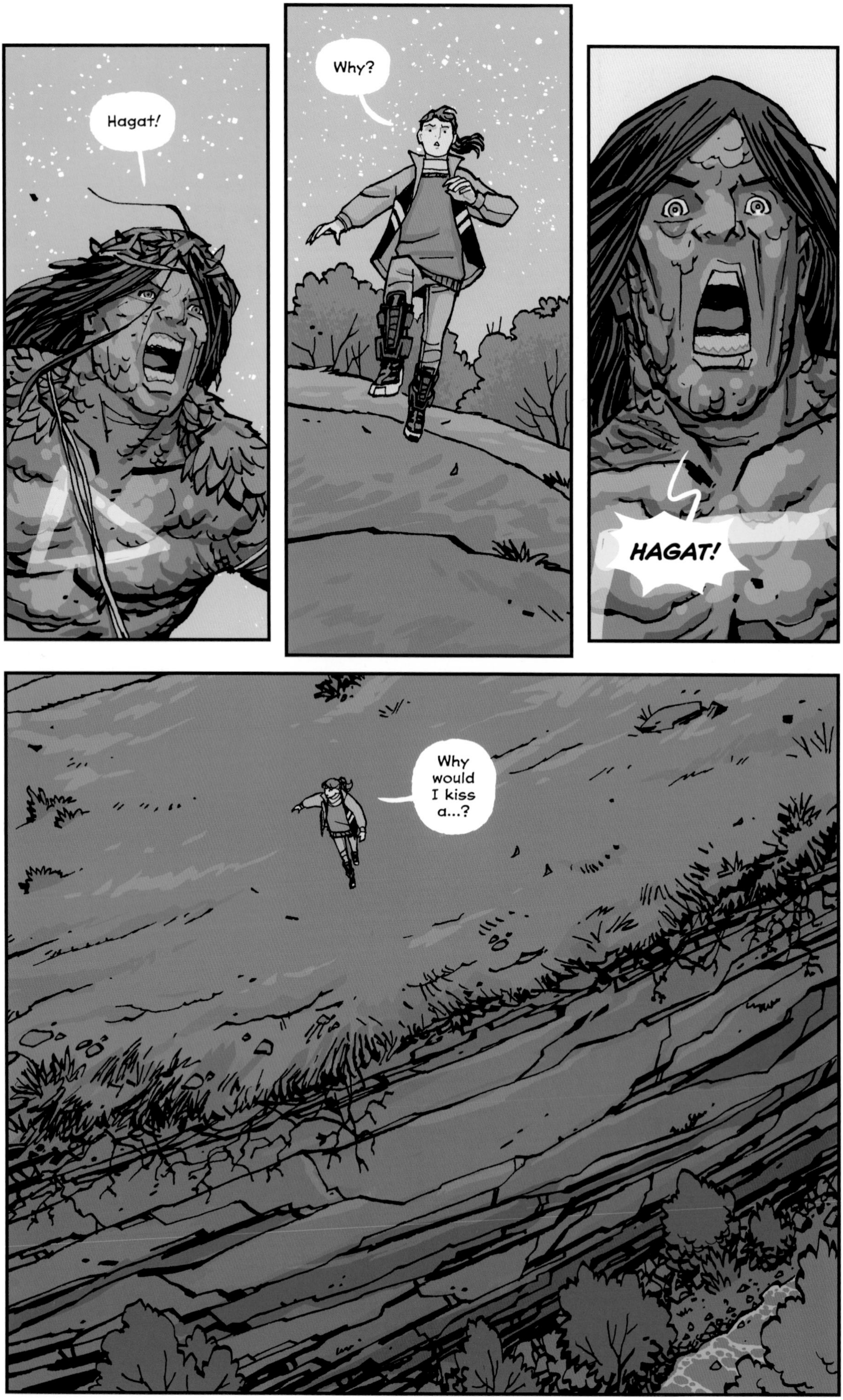
Hagat!
Why?
HAGAT!
Why would I kiss a...?

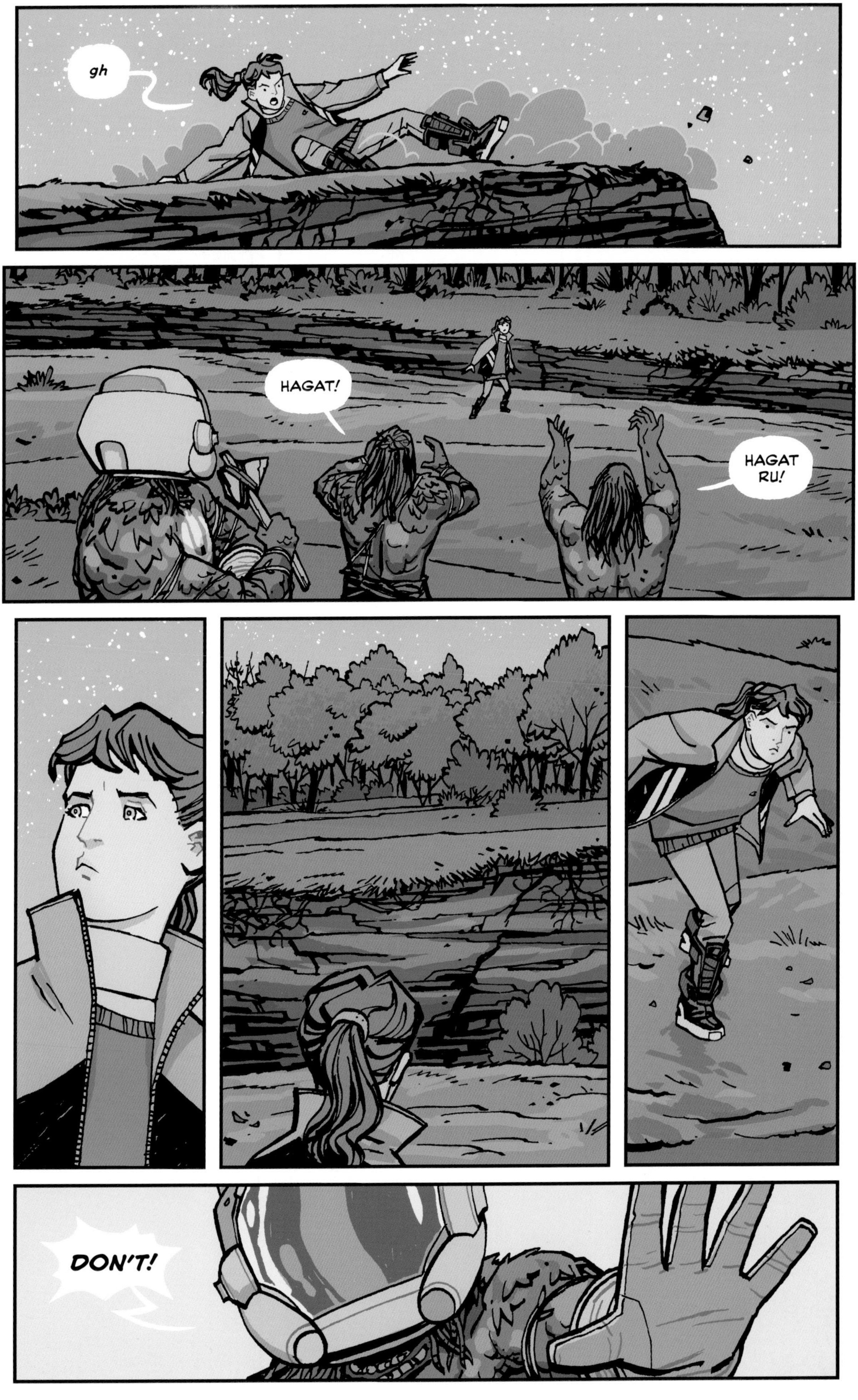
gh
HAGAT!
HAGAT RU!
DON'T!

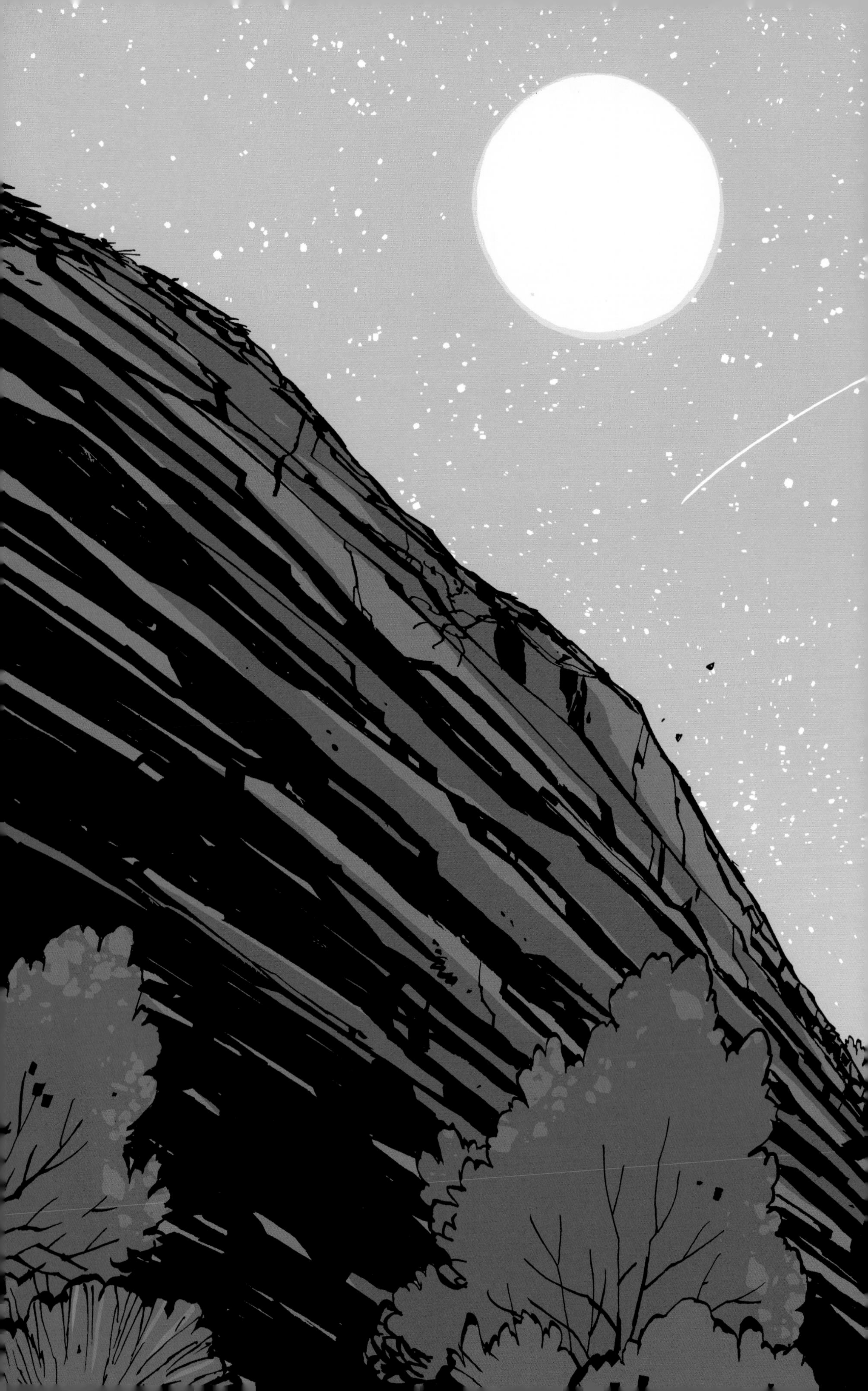

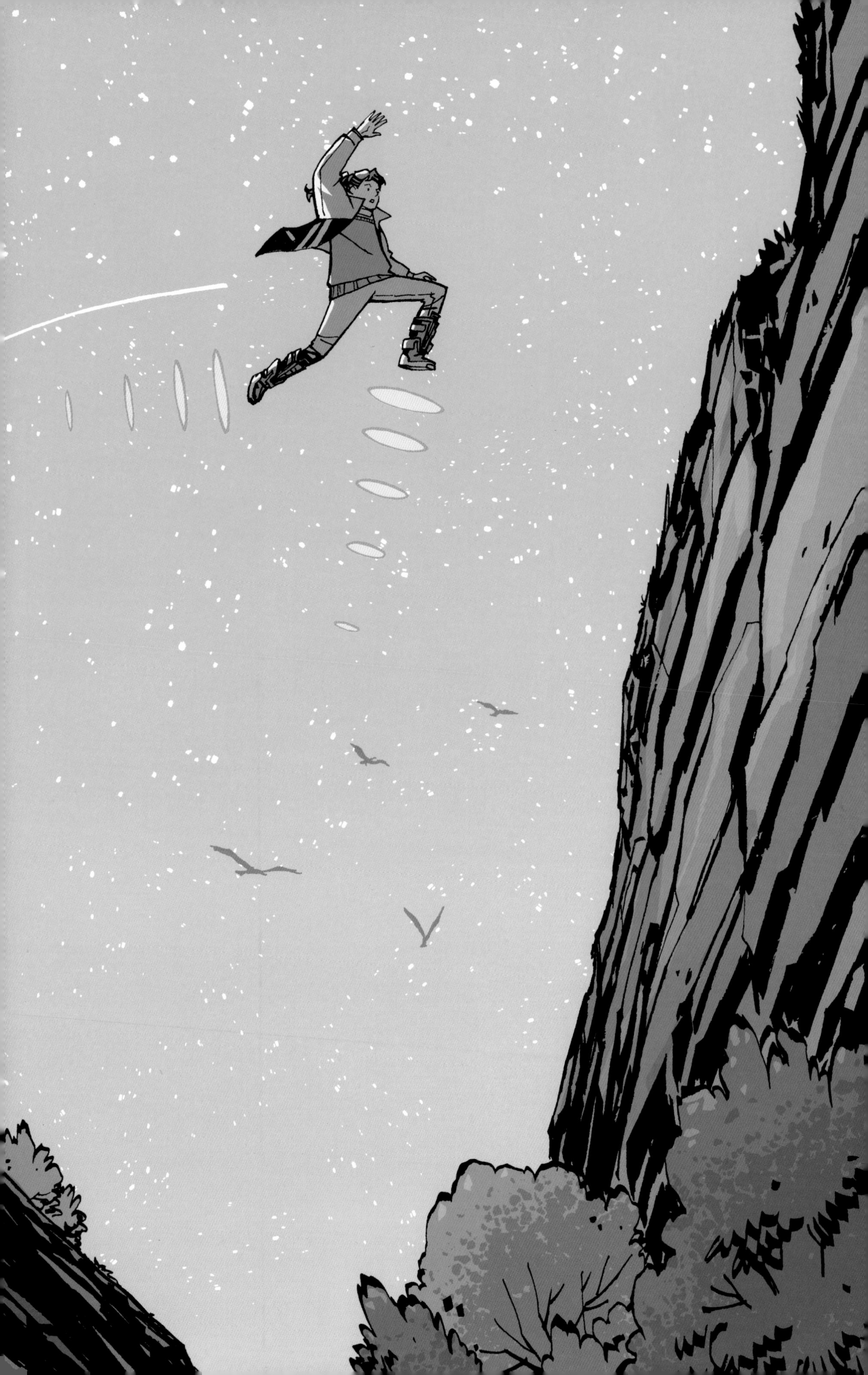

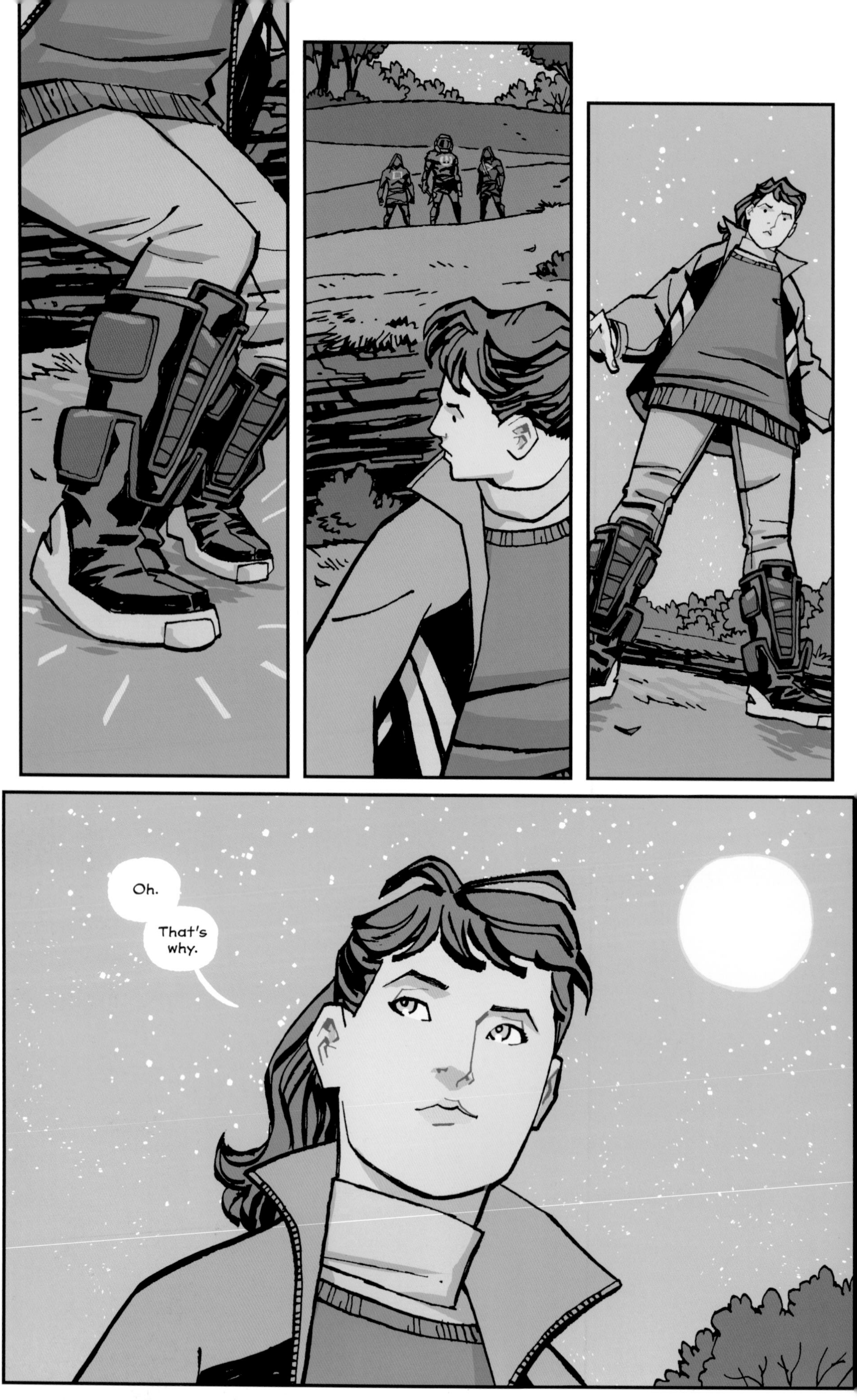
Oh.
That's why.

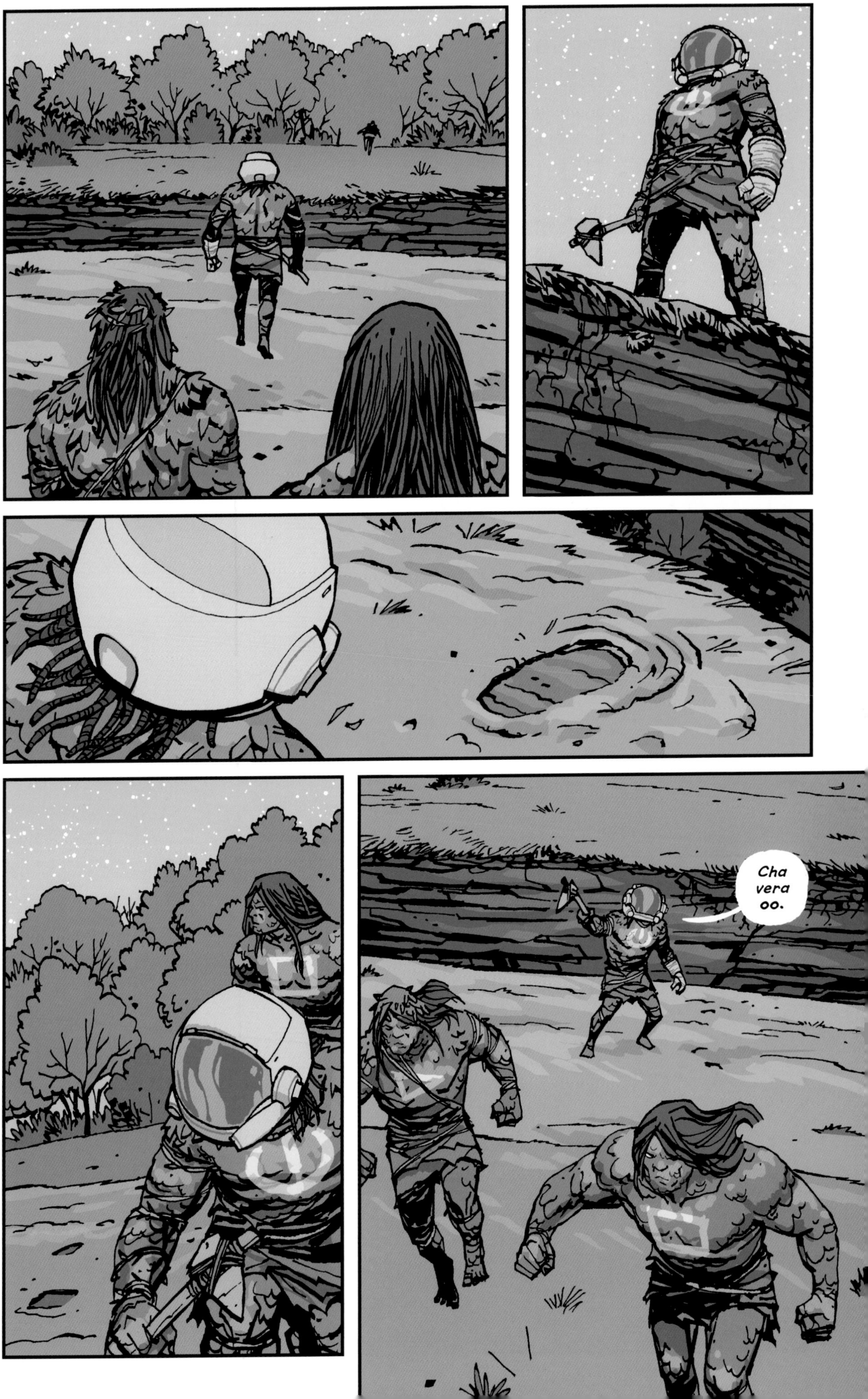
Cha vera oo.

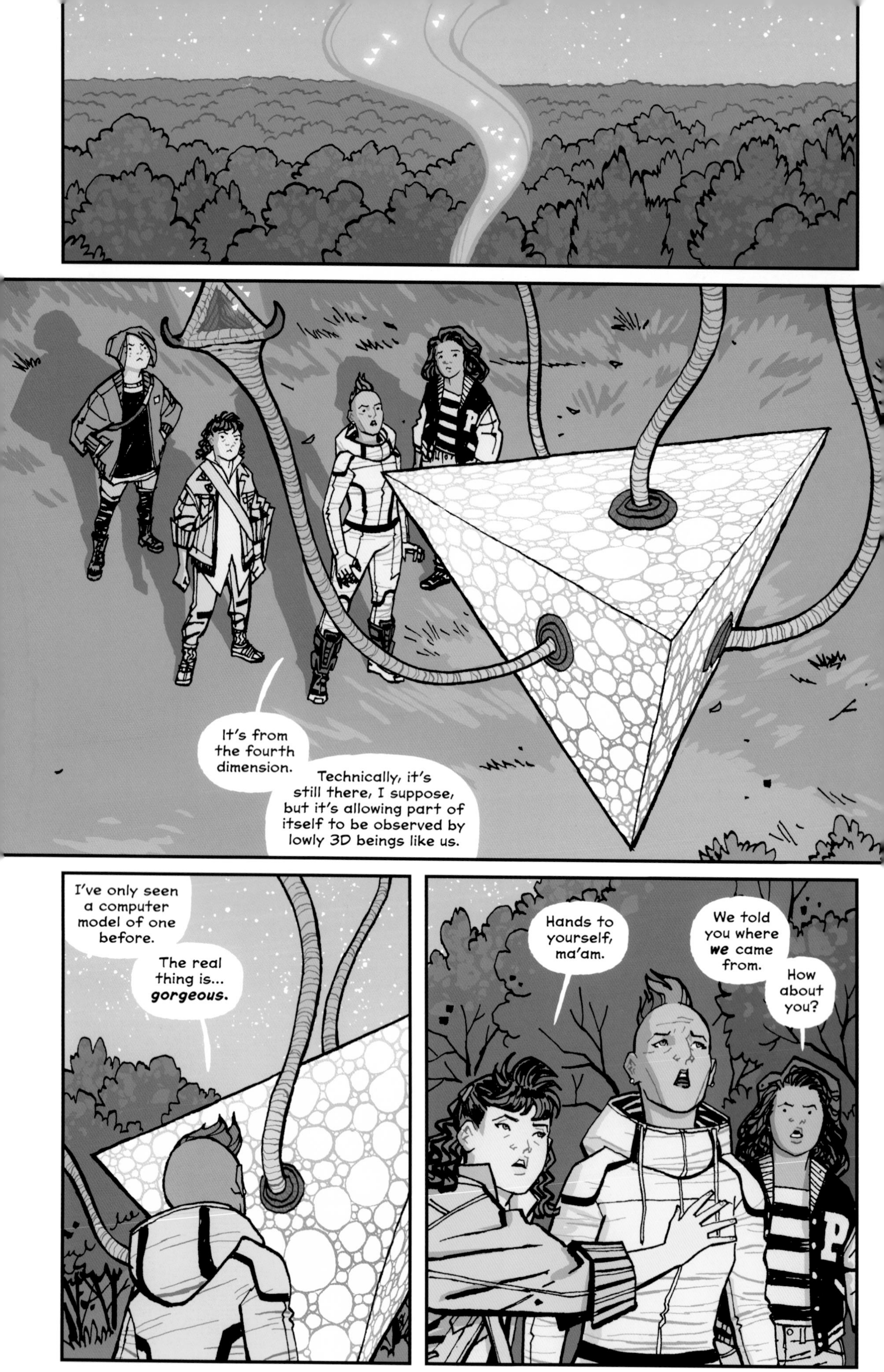
It's from the fourth dimension.
Technically, it's still there, I suppose, but it's allowing part of itself to be observed by lowly 3D beings like us.
I've only seen a computer model of one before.
The real thing is... **gorgeous.**
Hands to yourself, ma'am.
We told you where **we** came from.
How about you?

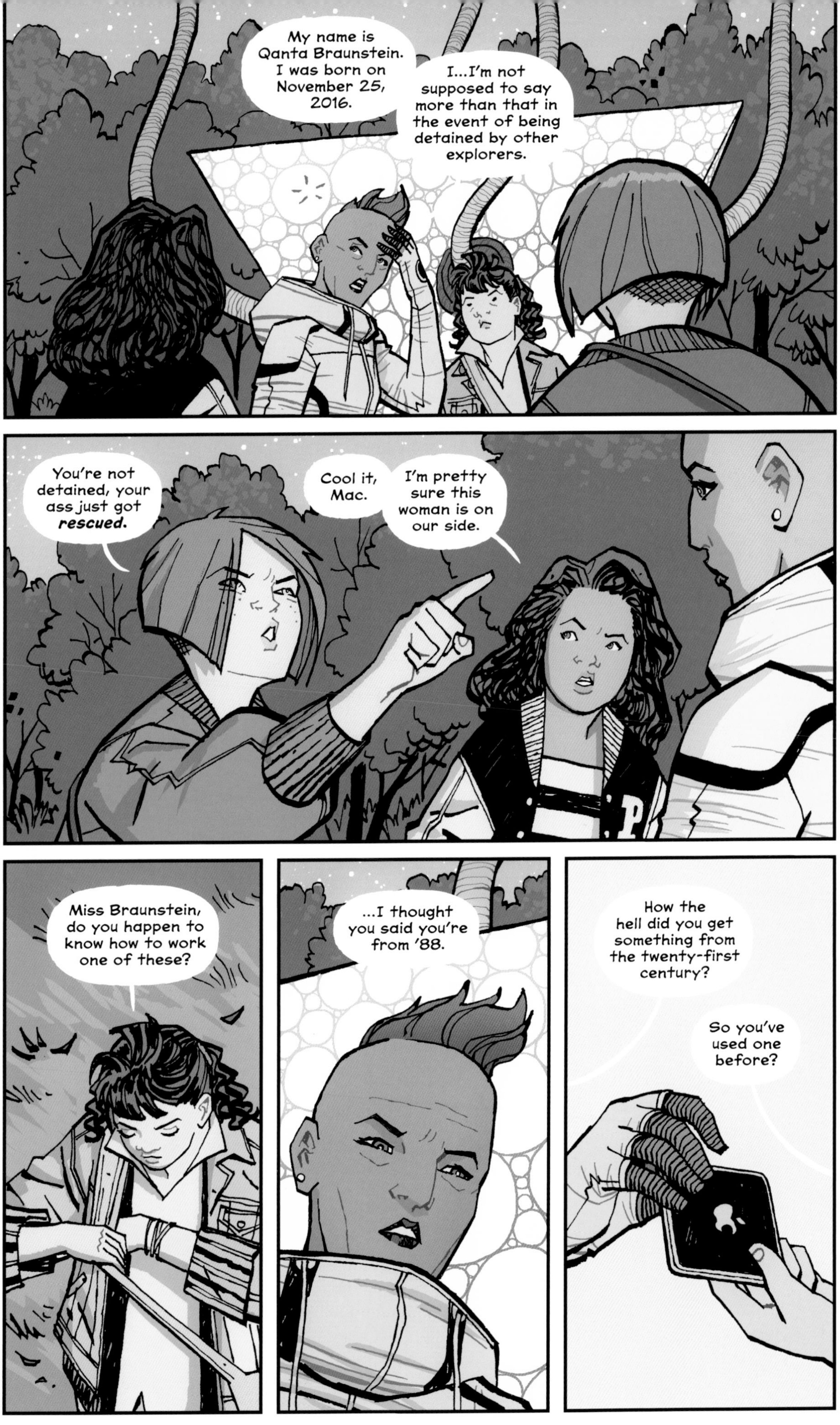

My name is Qanta Braunstein. I was born on November 25, 2016.
I...I'm not supposed to say more than that in the event of being detained by other explorers.
You're not detained, your ass just got *rescued.*
Cool it, Mac.
I'm pretty sure this woman is on our side.
Miss Braunstein, do you happen to know how to work one of these?
...I thought you said you're from '88.
How the hell did you get something from the twenty-first century?
So you've used one before?

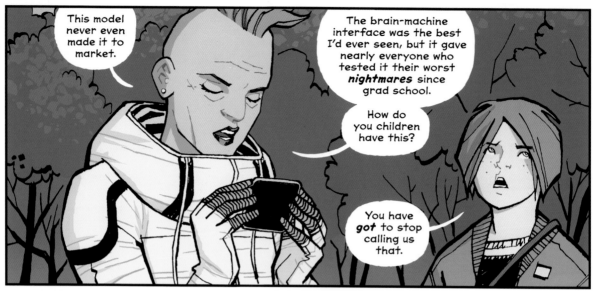

This model never even made it to market.

The brain-machine interface was the best I'd ever seen, but it gave nearly everyone who tested it their worst *nightmares* since grad school.

How do you children have this?

You have **got** to stop calling us that.

We'll tell you as much as we understand...**if** you promise to get us out of here.

I give you my word that I'll do what I can.

But the capsule is programmed to return to **my** time, nearly seventy years past your target.

Does your time at least have working toilets?

Waterless ones.

Regardless, we can't linger here. I have to get to my capsule before it automatically--

SNAP

KJ...?

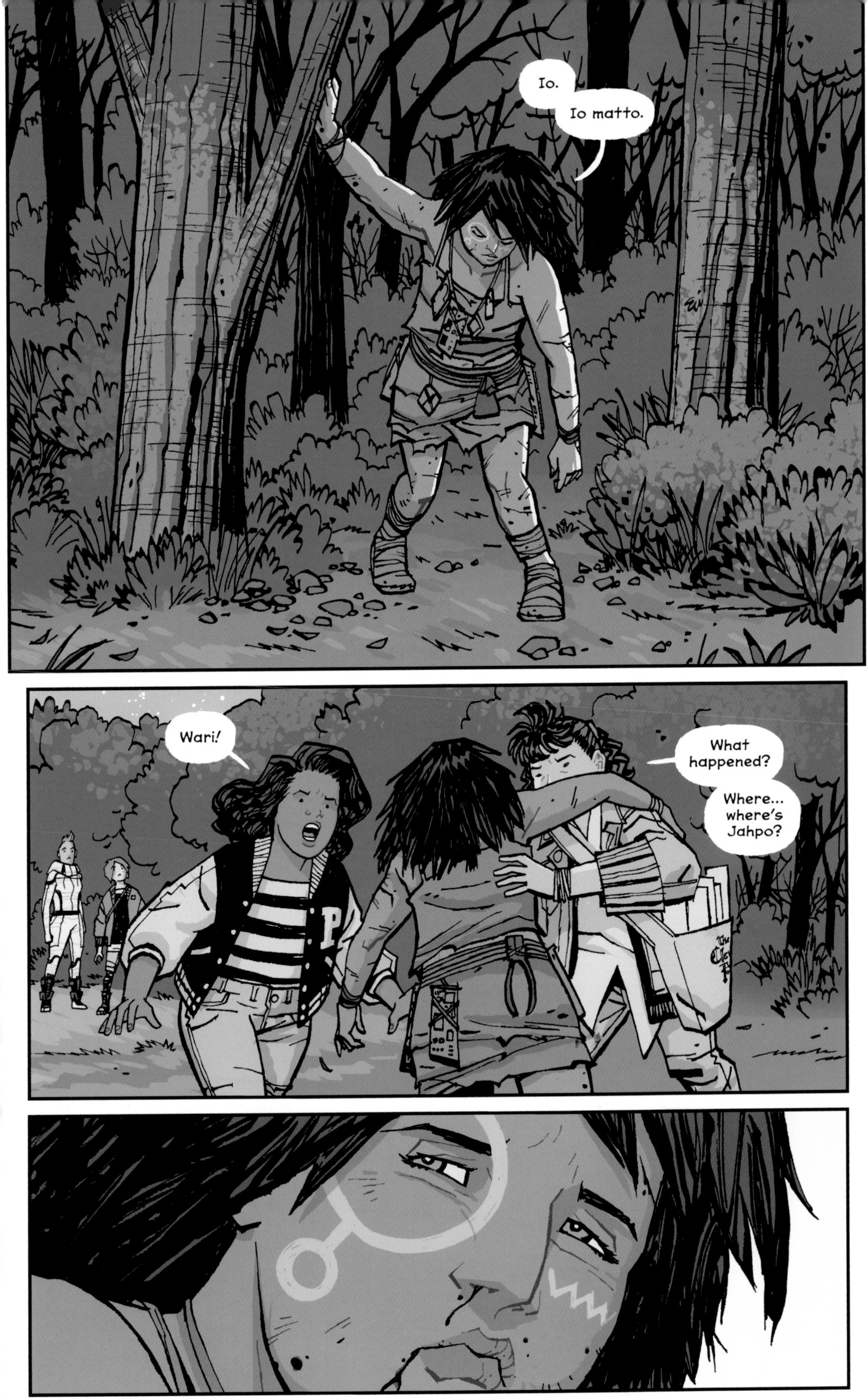
Io.
Io matto.
Wari!
What happened?
Where... where's Jahpo?

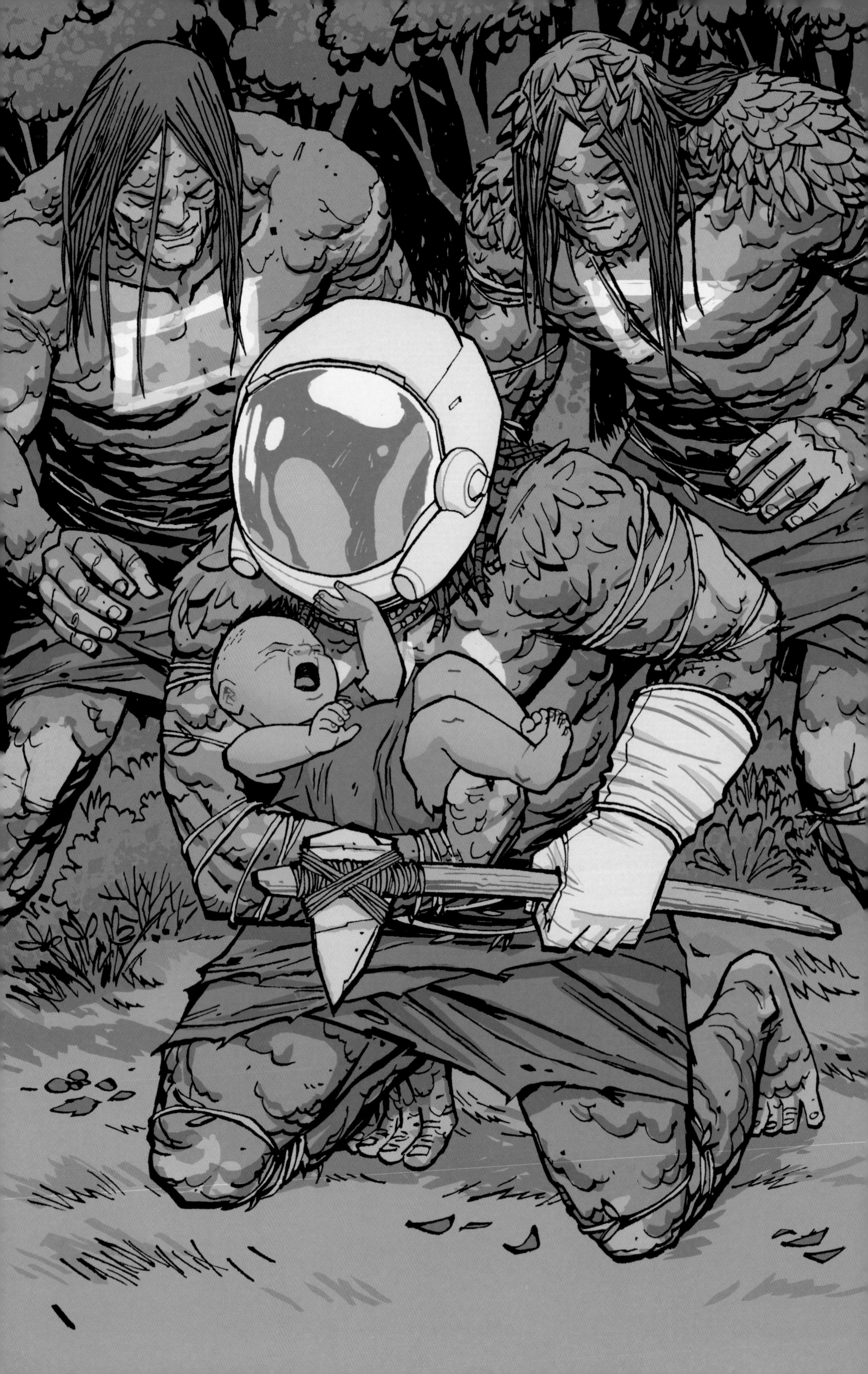

CHAPTER
15

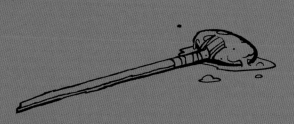

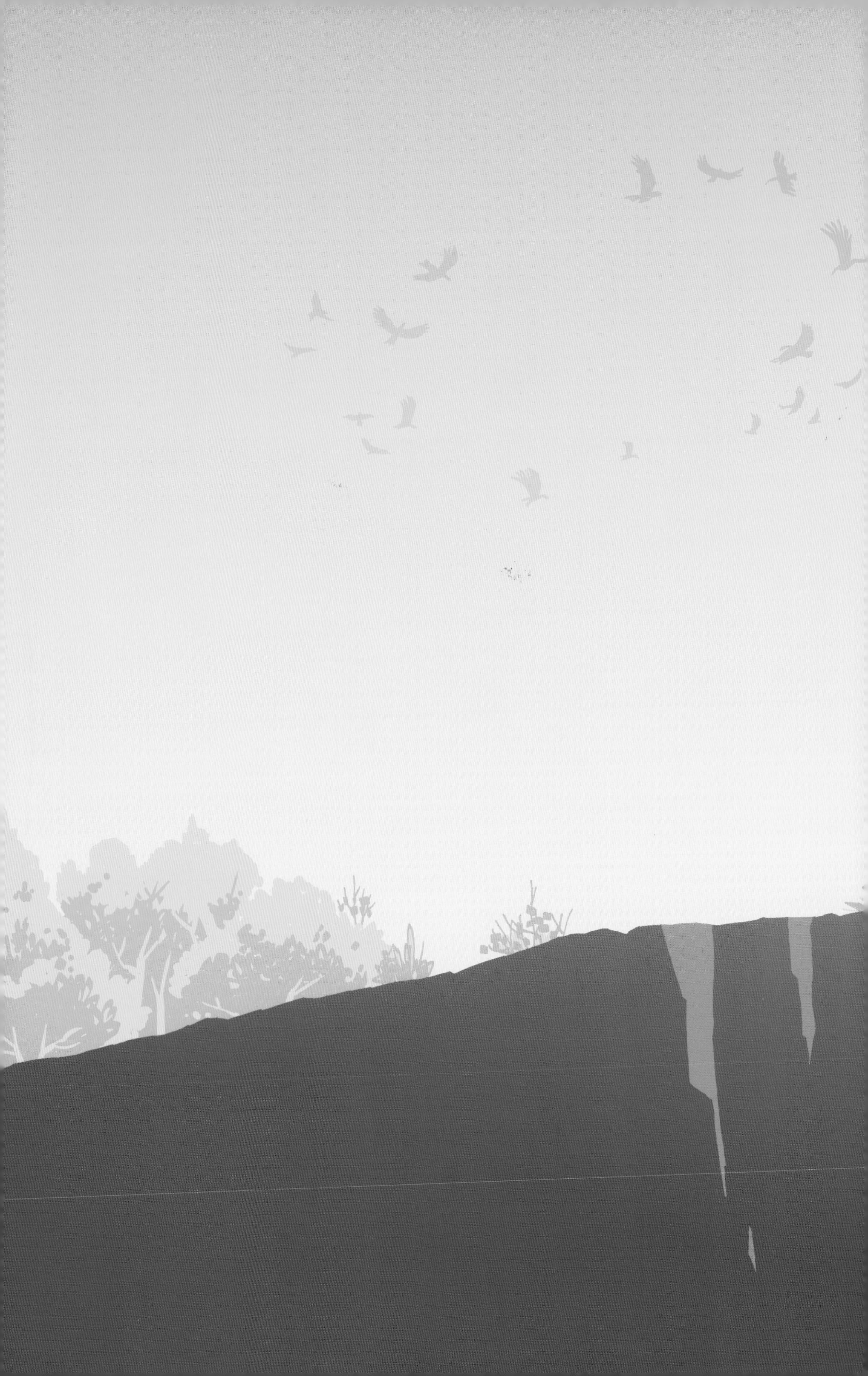

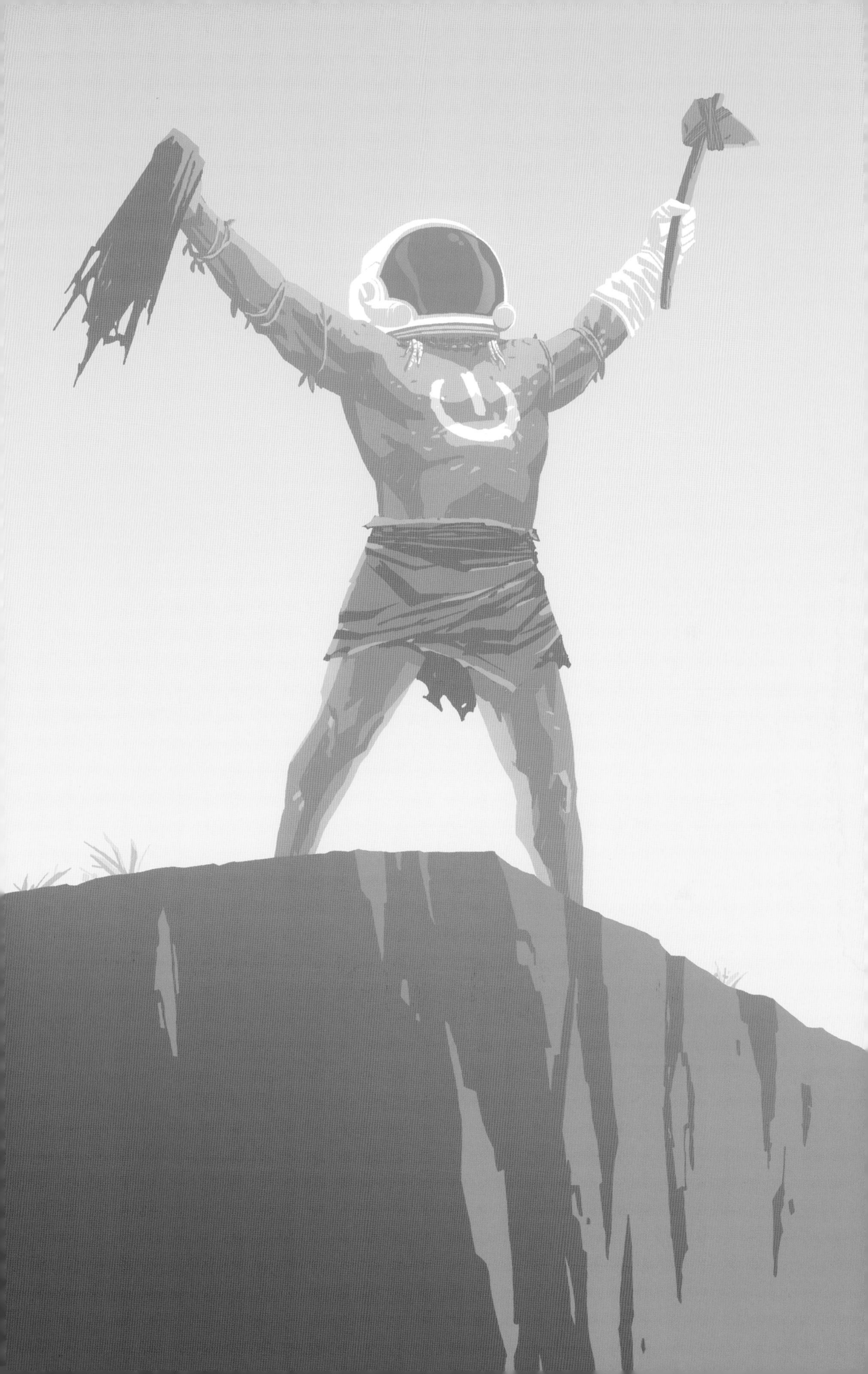

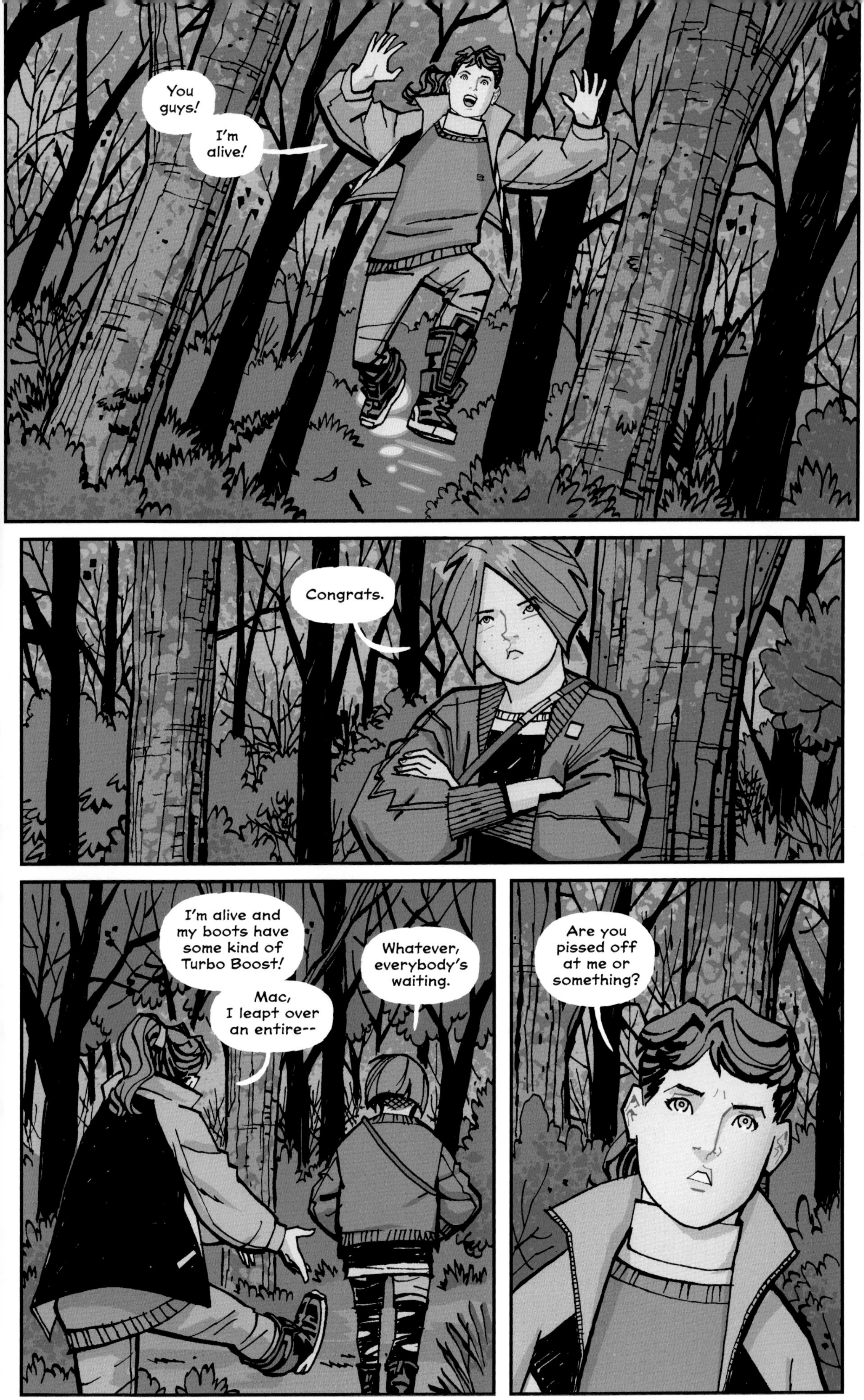
You guys!
I'm alive!
Congrats.
I'm alive and my boots have some kind of Turbo Boost!
Mac, I leapt over an entire--
Whatever, everybody's waiting.
Are you pissed off at me or something?

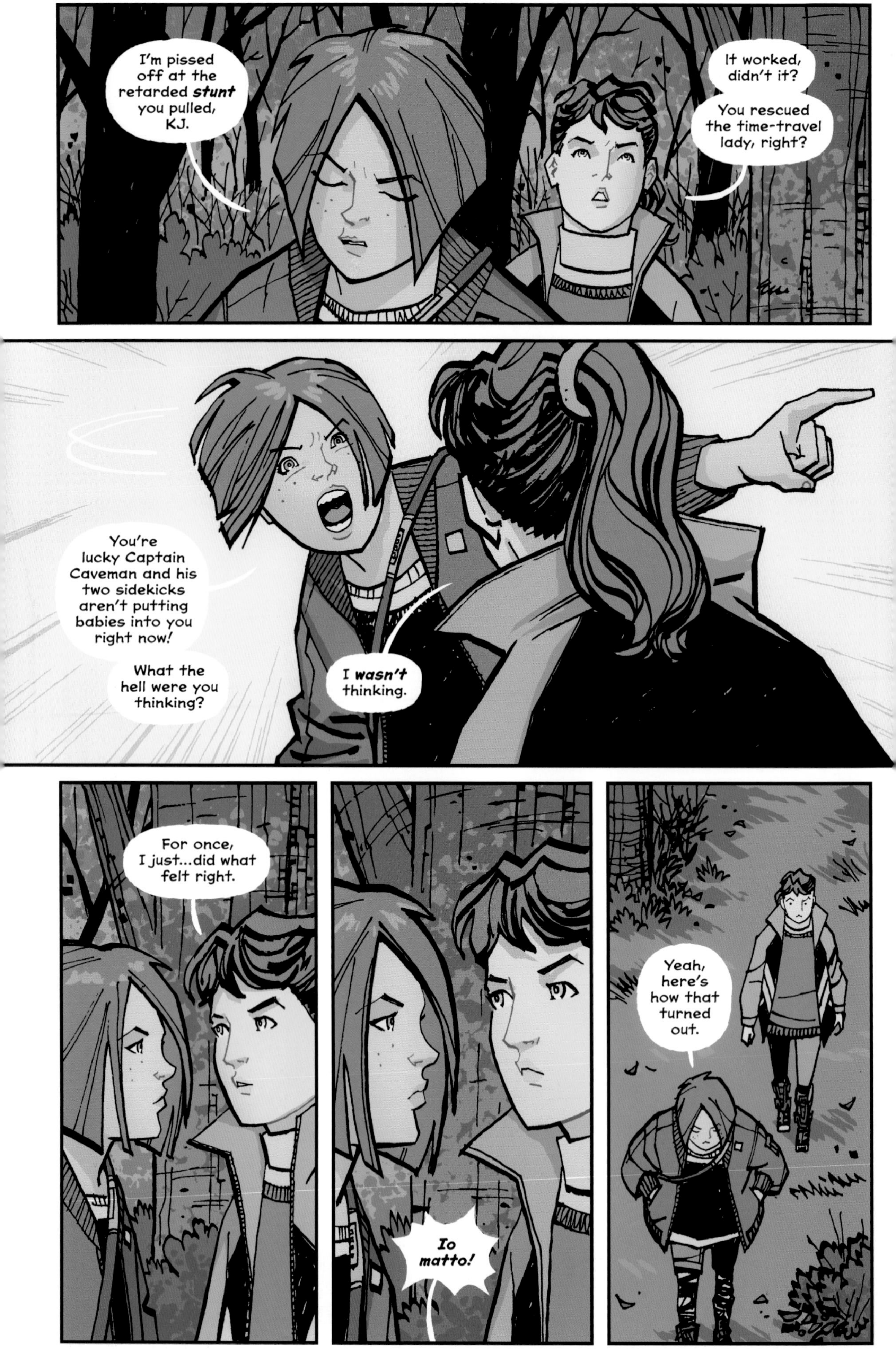
I'm pissed off at the retarded *stunt* you pulled, KJ.
It worked, didn't it?
You rescued the time-travel lady, right?
You're lucky Captain Caveman and his two sidekicks aren't putting babies into you right now!
What the hell were you thinking?
I *wasn't* thinking.
For once, I just...did what felt right.
Io matto!
Yeah, here's how that turned out.

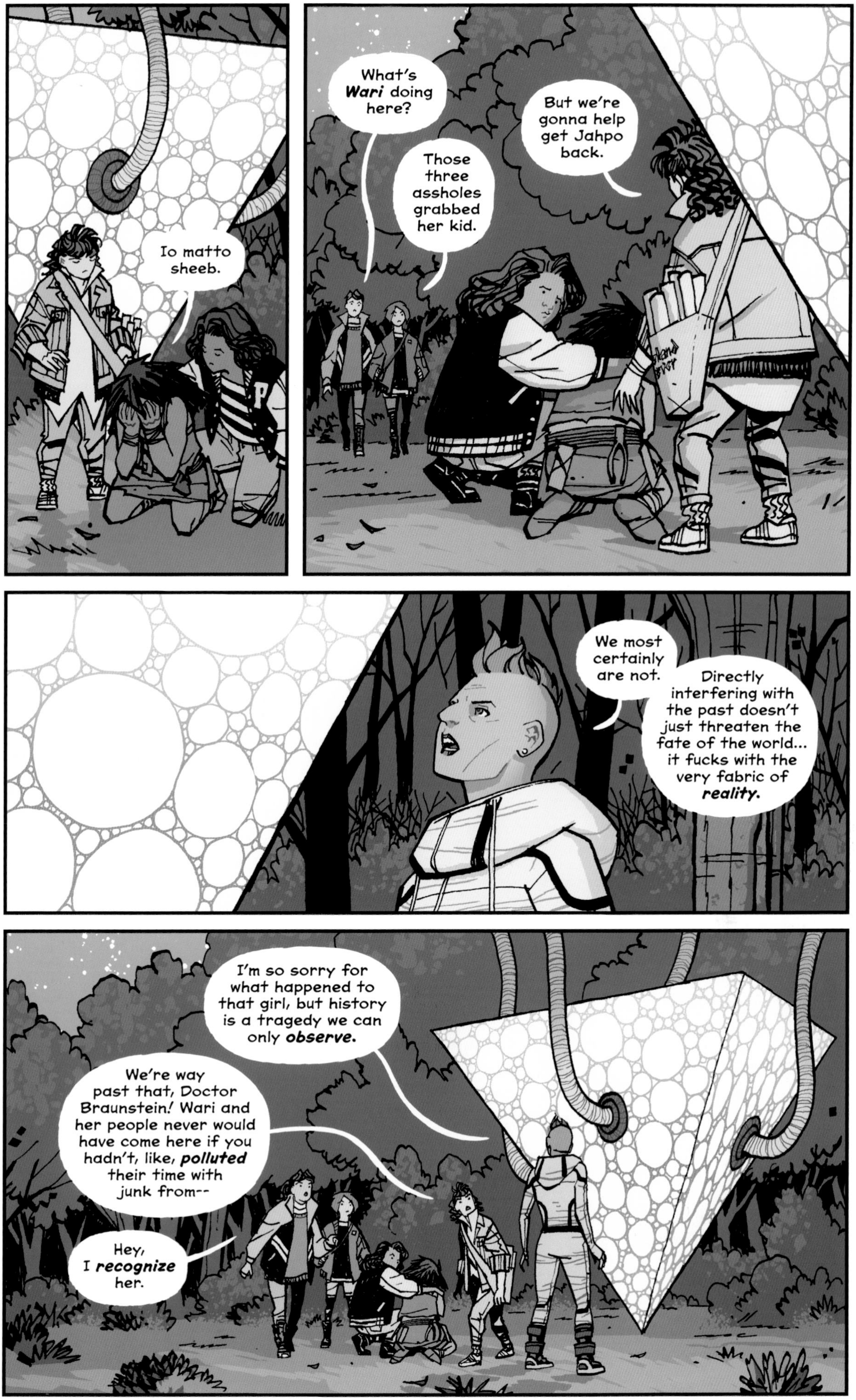
Io matto sheeb.
What's *Wari* doing here?
Those three assholes grabbed her kid.
But we're gonna help get Jahpo back.
We most certainly are not.
Directly interfering with the past doesn't just threaten the fate of the world... it fucks with the very fabric of *reality.*
I'm so sorry for what happened to that girl, but history is a tragedy we can only *observe.*
We're way past that, Doctor Braunstein! Wari and her people never would have come here if you hadn't, like, *polluted* their time with junk from--
Hey, I *recognize* her.

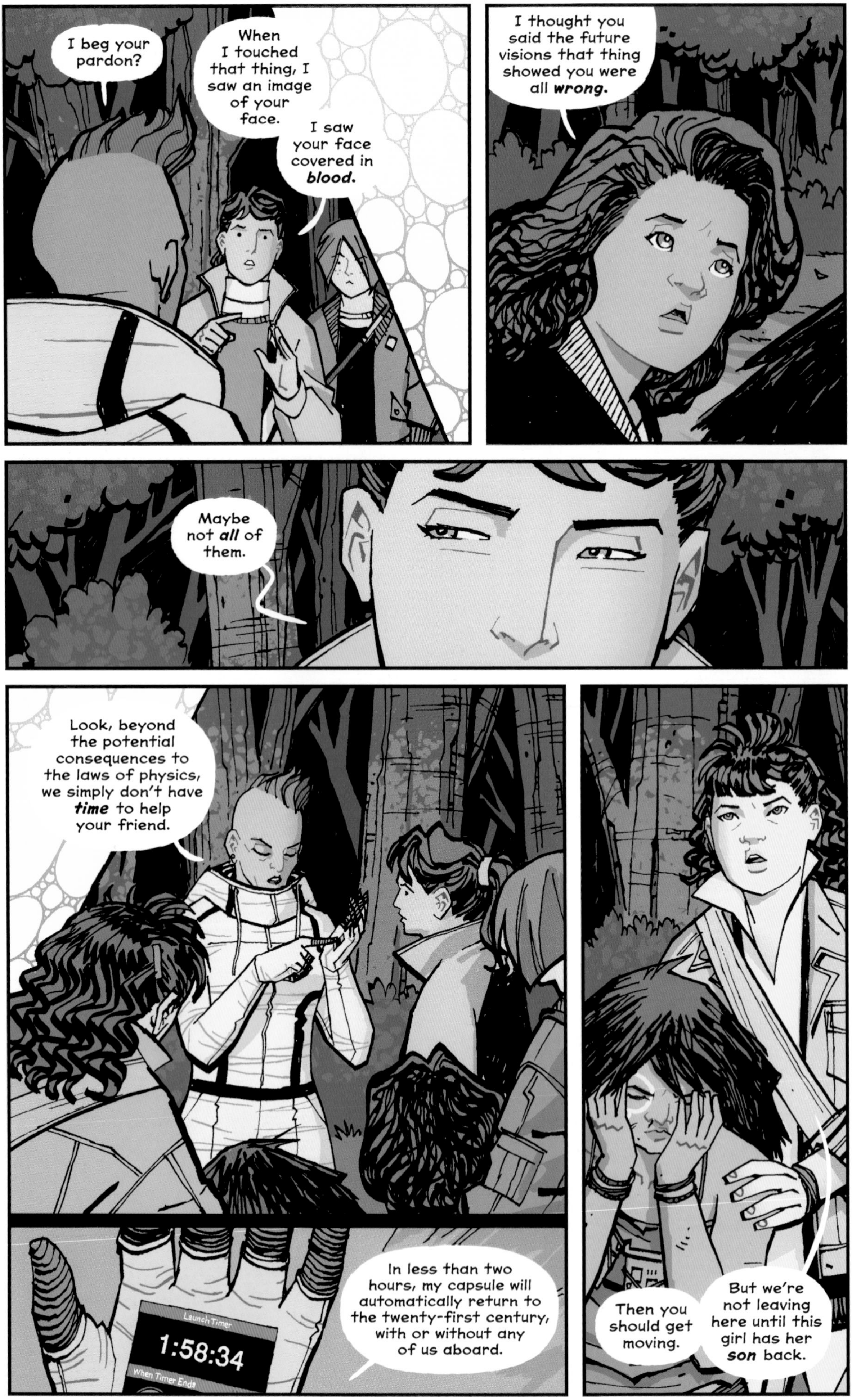
I beg your pardon?
When I touched that thing, I saw an image of your face.
I saw your face covered in *blood.*
I thought you said the future visions that thing showed you were all *wrong.*
Maybe not *all* of them.
Look, beyond the potential consequences to the laws of physics, we simply don't have *time* to help your friend.
Launch Timer
1:58:34
When Timer Ends
In less than two hours, my capsule will automatically return to the twenty-first century, with or without any of us aboard.
Then you should get moving.
But we're not leaving here until this girl has her *son* back.

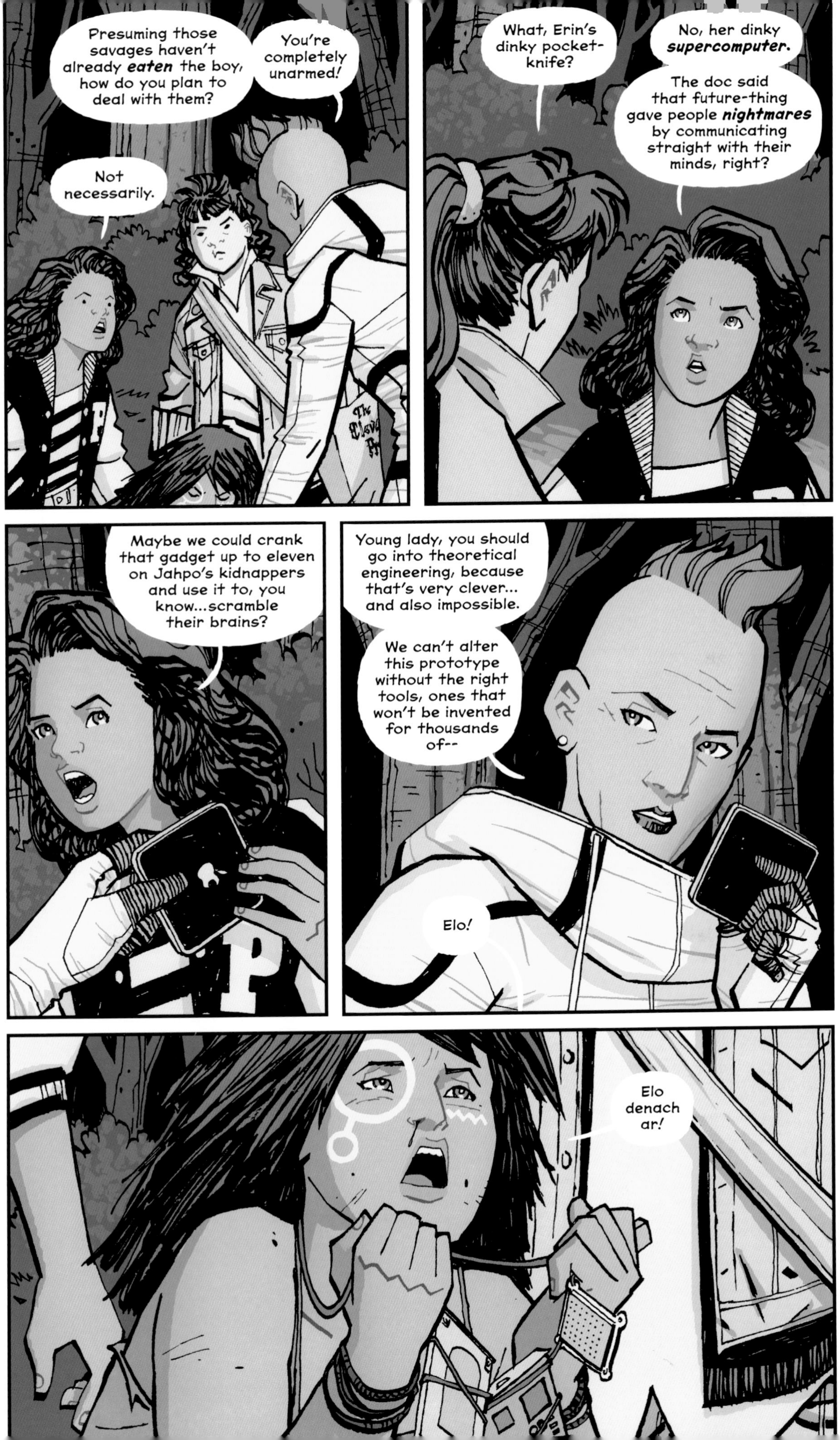
Presuming those savages haven't already **eaten** the boy, how do you plan to deal with them?
You're completely unarmed!
Not necessarily.
What, Erin's dinky pocket-knife?
No, her dinky **supercomputer.**
The doc said that future-thing gave people **nightmares** by communicating straight with their minds, right?
Maybe we could crank that gadget up to eleven on Jahpo's kidnappers and use it to, you know...scramble their brains?
Young lady, you should go into theoretical engineering, because that's very clever... and also impossible.
We can't alter this prototype without the right tools, ones that won't be invented for thousands of--
Elo!
Elo denach ar!

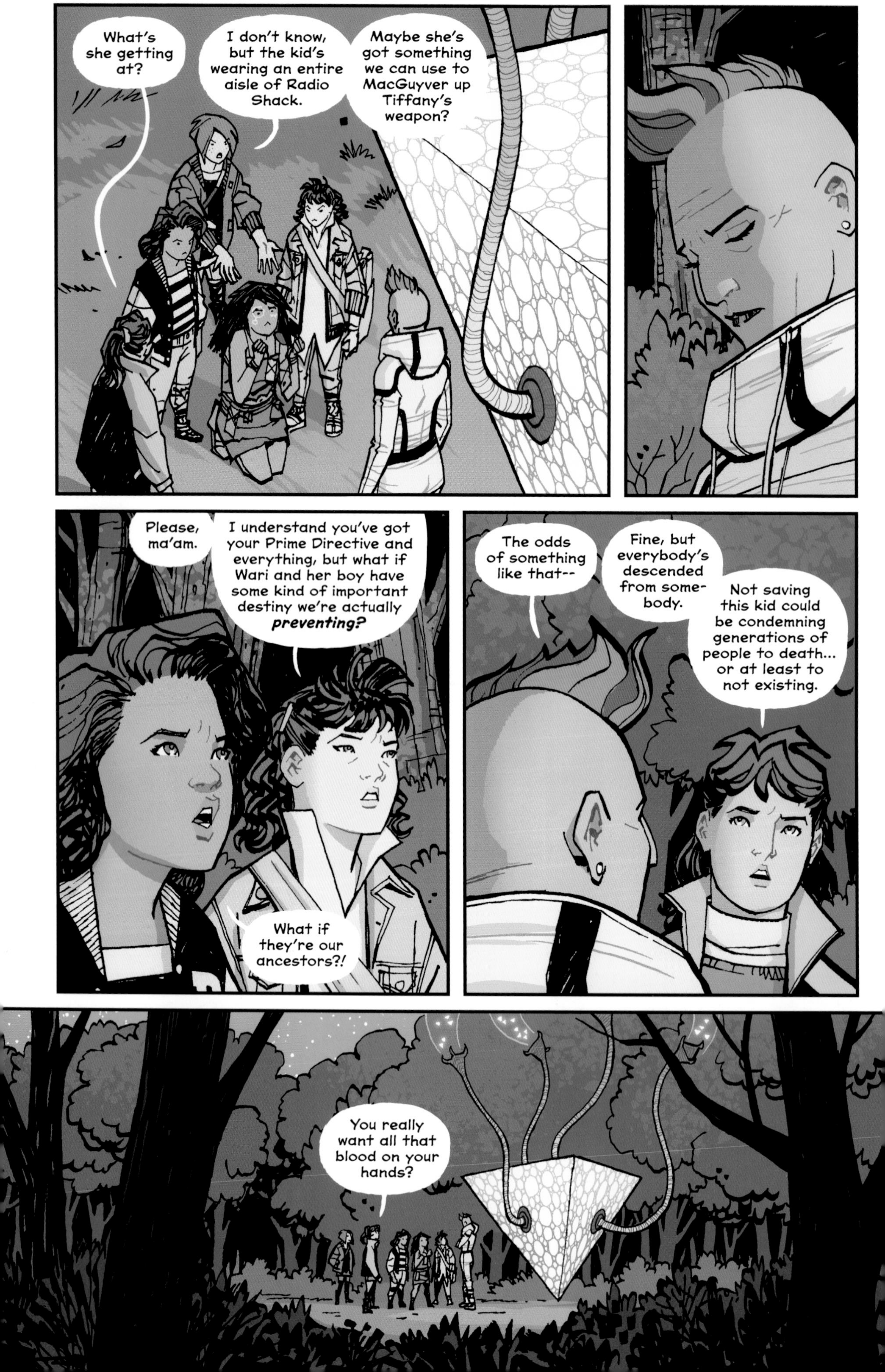
What's she getting at?
I don't know, but the kid's wearing an entire aisle of Radio Shack.
Maybe she's got something we can use to MacGuyver up Tiffany's weapon?
Please, ma'am.
I understand you've got your Prime Directive and everything, but what if Wari and her boy have some kind of important destiny we're actually *preventing?*
What if they're our ancestors?!
The odds of something like that--
Fine, but everybody's descended from some-body.
Not saving this kid could be condemning generations of people to death... or at least to not existing.
You really want all that blood on your hands?

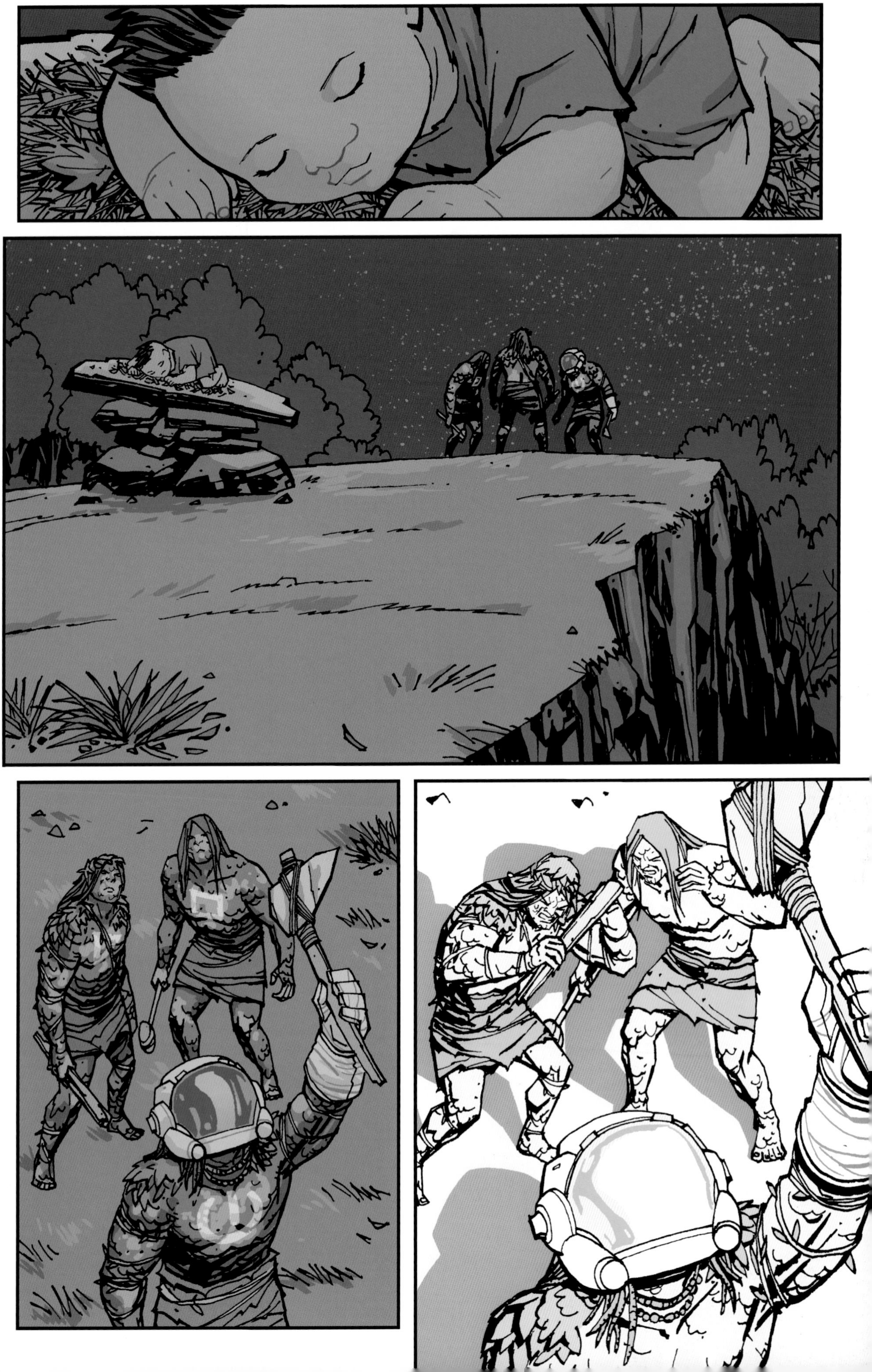

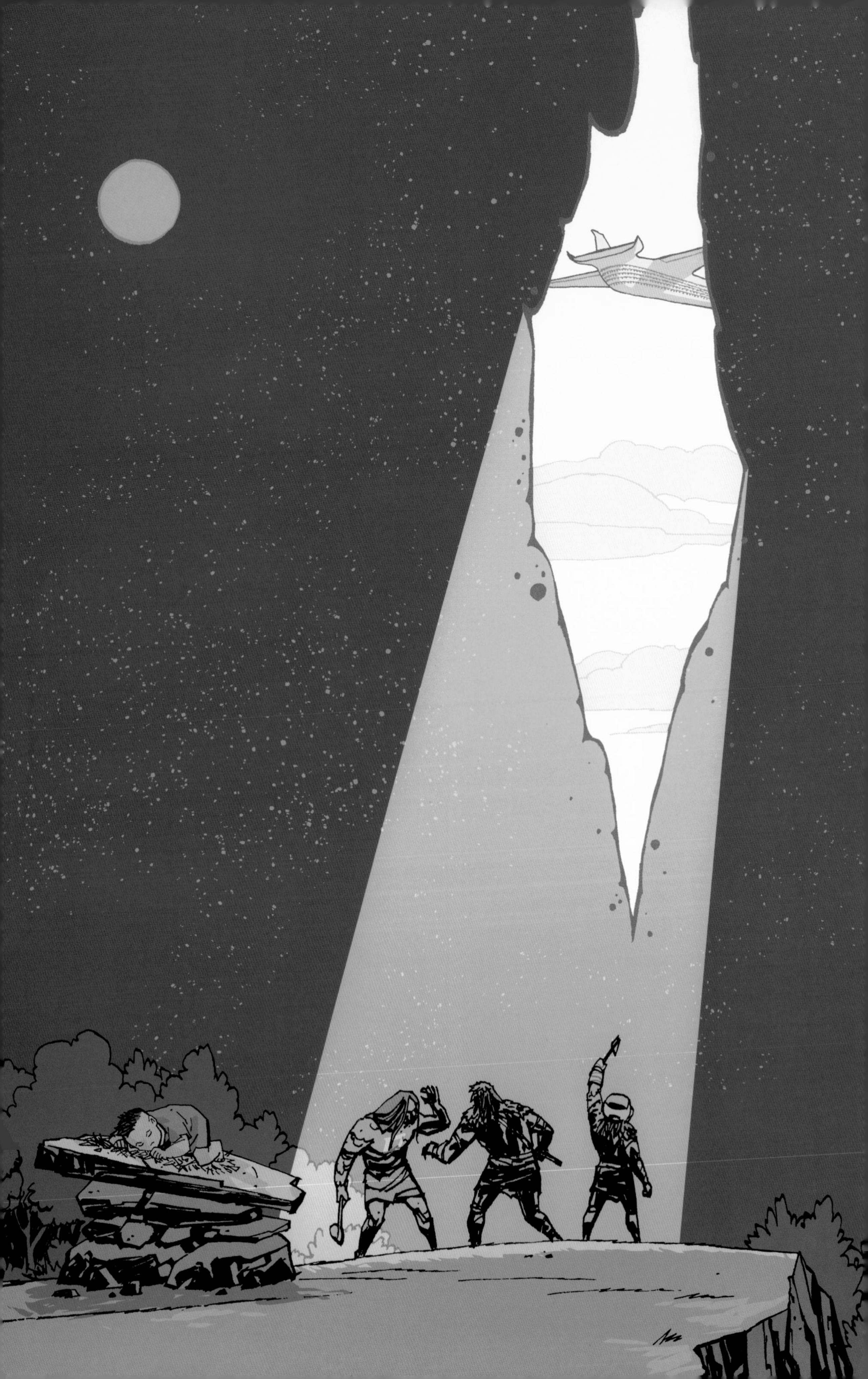

Ba.
Eldago.
Eldago sha.
Eldago sha **zaku.**

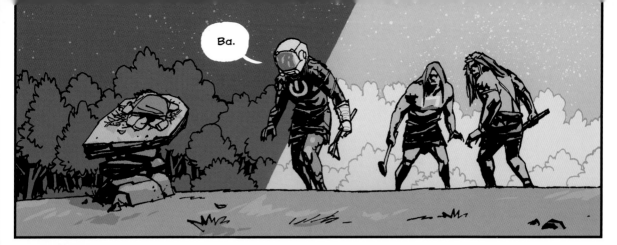

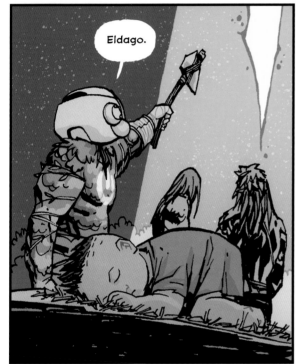

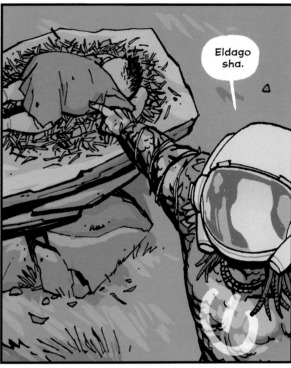

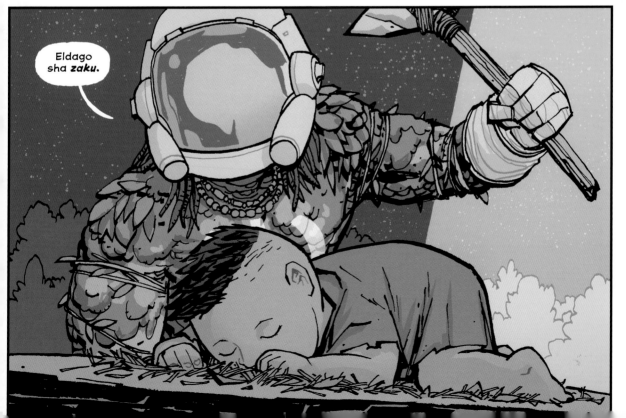

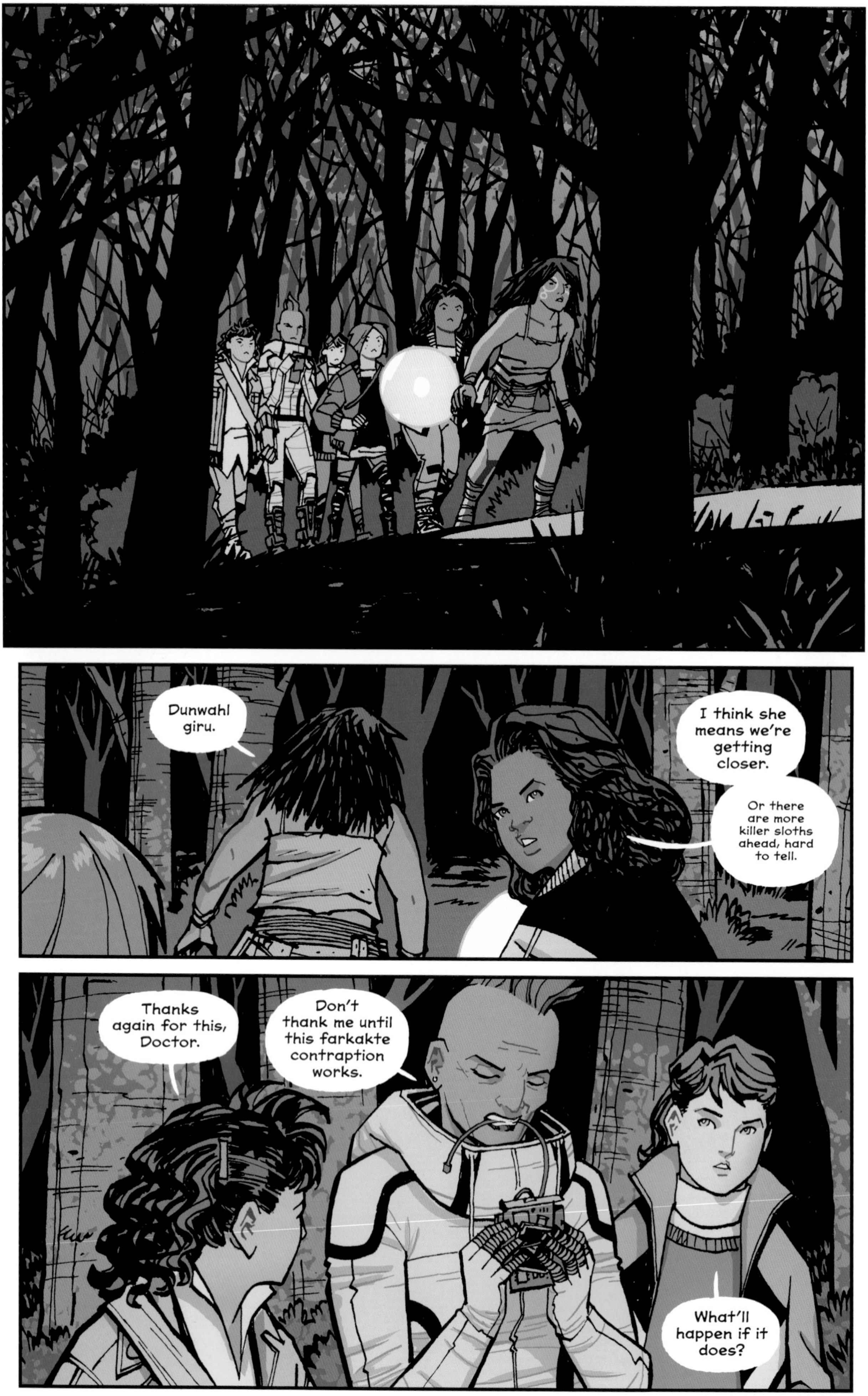
Dunwahl giru.
I think she means we're getting closer.
Or there are more killer sloths ahead, hard to tell.
Thanks again for this, Doctor.
Don't thank me until this farkakte contraption works.
What'll happen if it does?

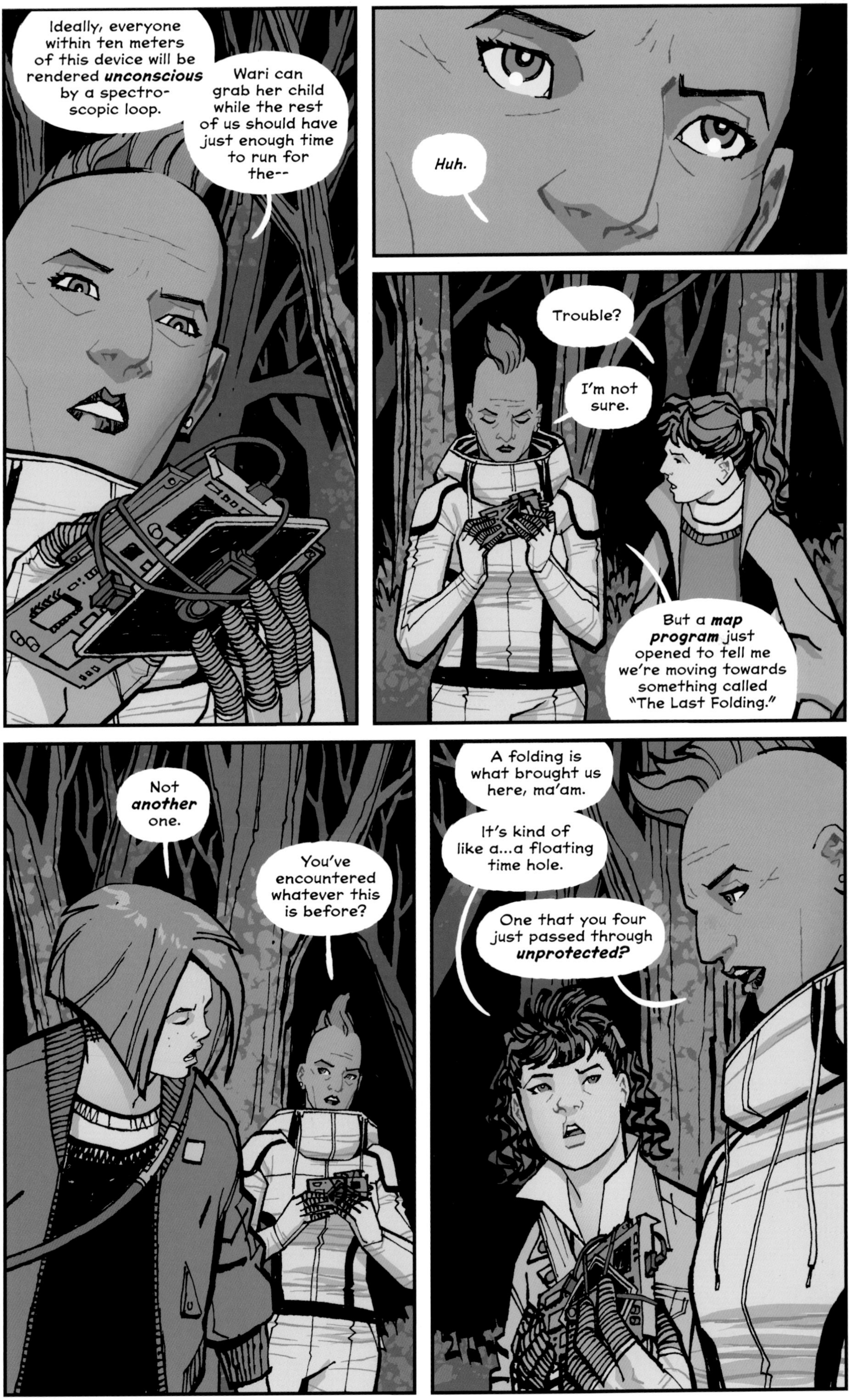
Ideally, everyone within ten meters of this device will be rendered *unconscious* by a spectro-scopic loop.
Wari can grab her child while the rest of us should have just enough time to run for the--
Huh.
Trouble?
I'm not sure.
But a *map program* just opened to tell me we're moving towards something called "The Last Folding."
Not *another* one.
You've encountered whatever this is before?
A folding is what brought us here, ma'am.
It's kind of like a...a floating time hole.
One that you four just passed through *unprotected?*

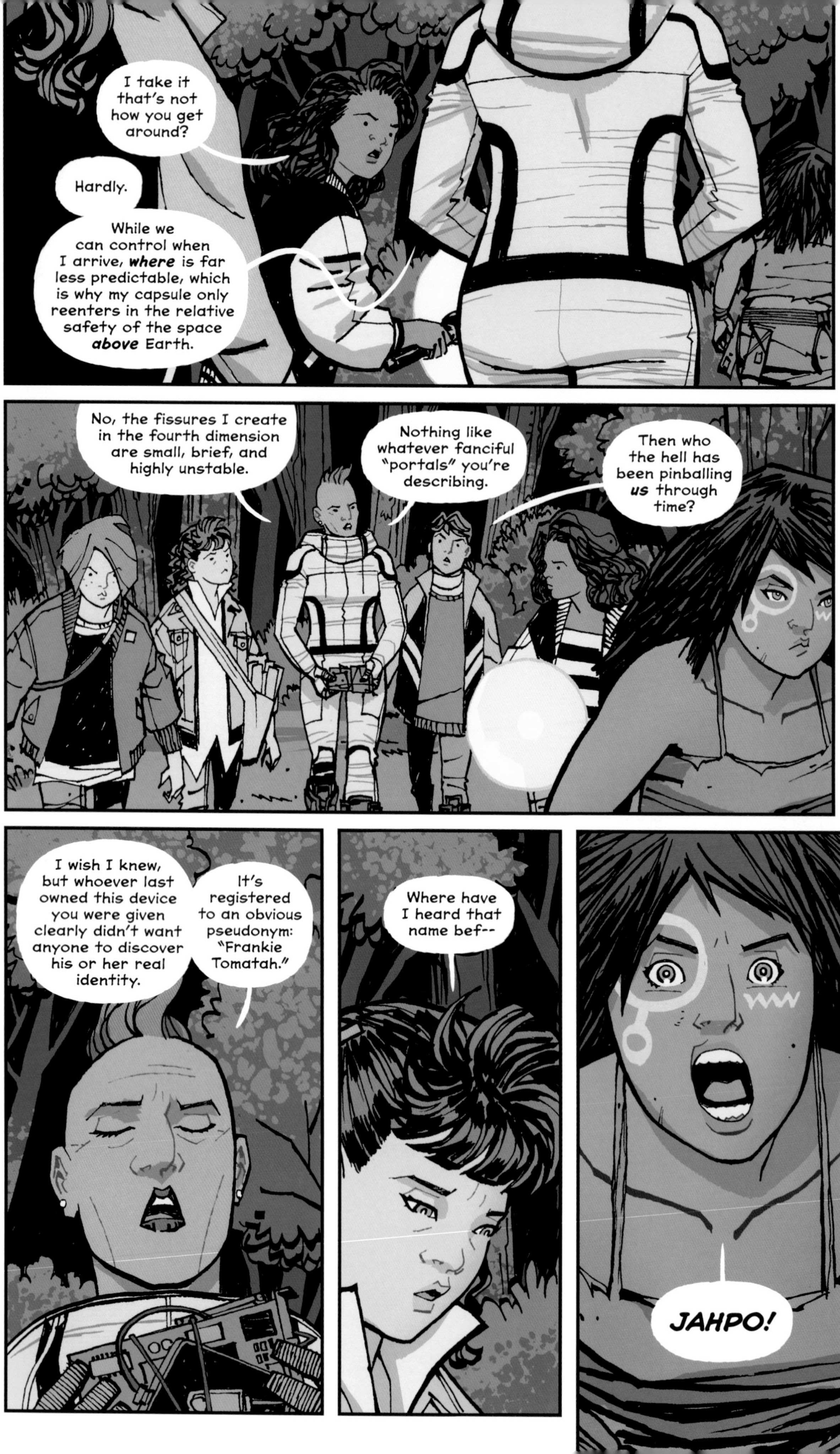
I take it that's not how you get around?
Hardly.
While we can control when I arrive, *where* is far less predictable, which is why my capsule only reenters in the relative safety of the space *above* Earth.
No, the fissures I create in the fourth dimension are small, brief, and highly unstable.
Nothing like whatever fanciful "portals" you're describing.
Then who the hell has been pinballing *us* through time?
I wish I knew, but whoever last owned this device you were given clearly didn't want anyone to discover his or her real identity.
It's registered to an obvious pseudonym: "Frankie Tomatah."
Where have I heard that name bef--
JAHPO!

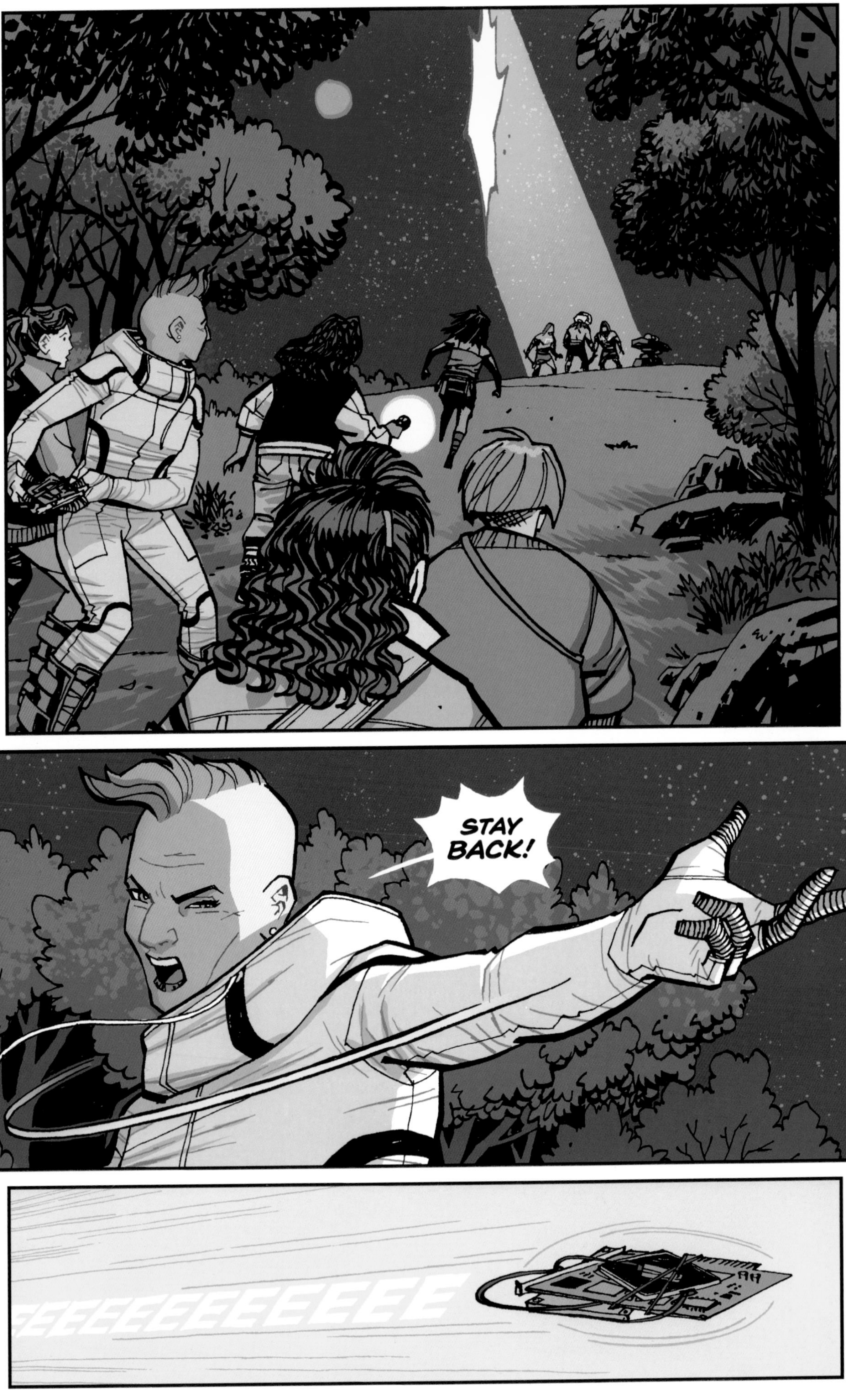
STAY BACK!
EEEEEEEEEEEE

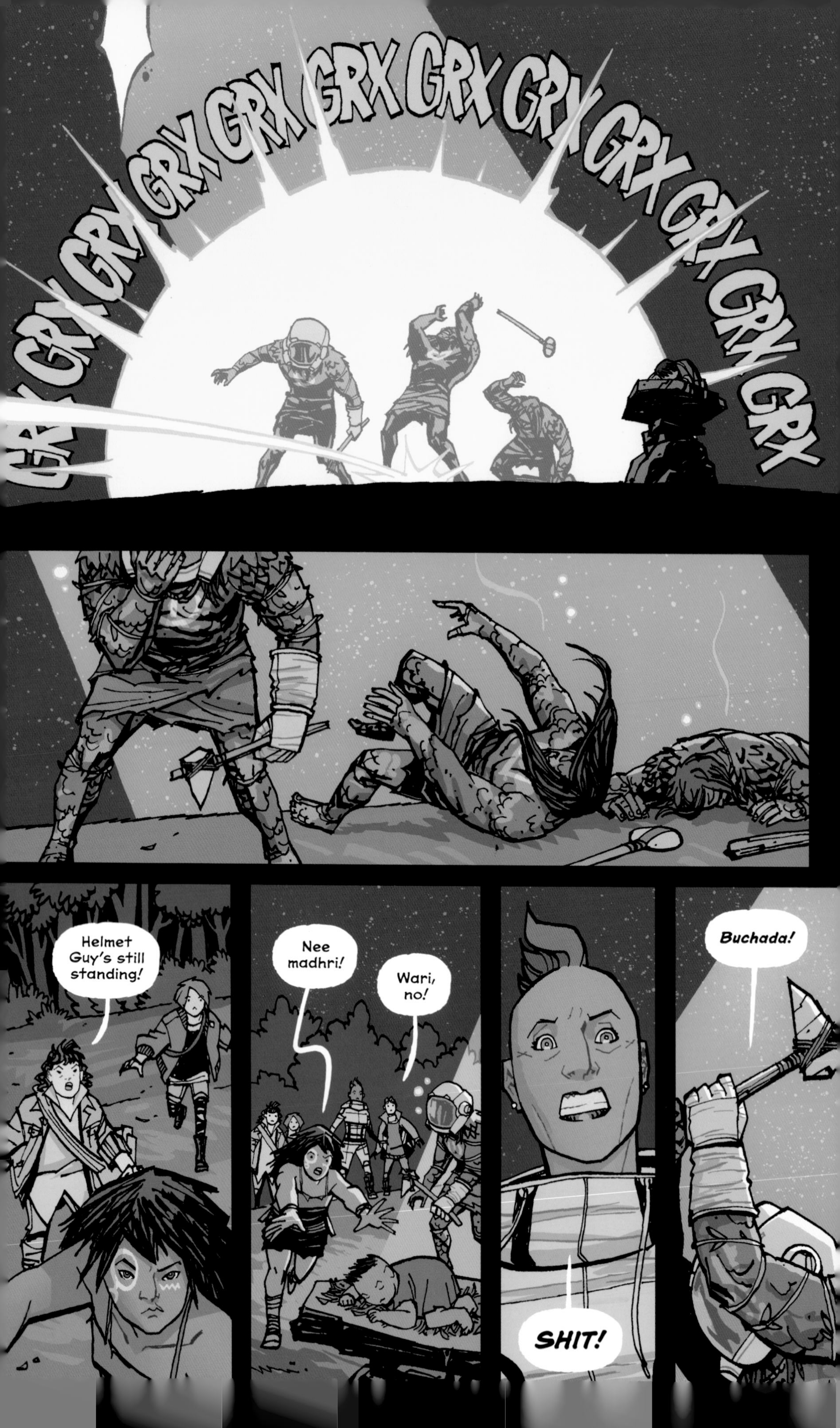
GRX GRX GRX GRX GRX GRX GRX GRX GRX GRX GRX GRX GRX GRX
Helmet Guy's still standing!
Nee madhri!
Wari, no!
SHIT!
Buchada!

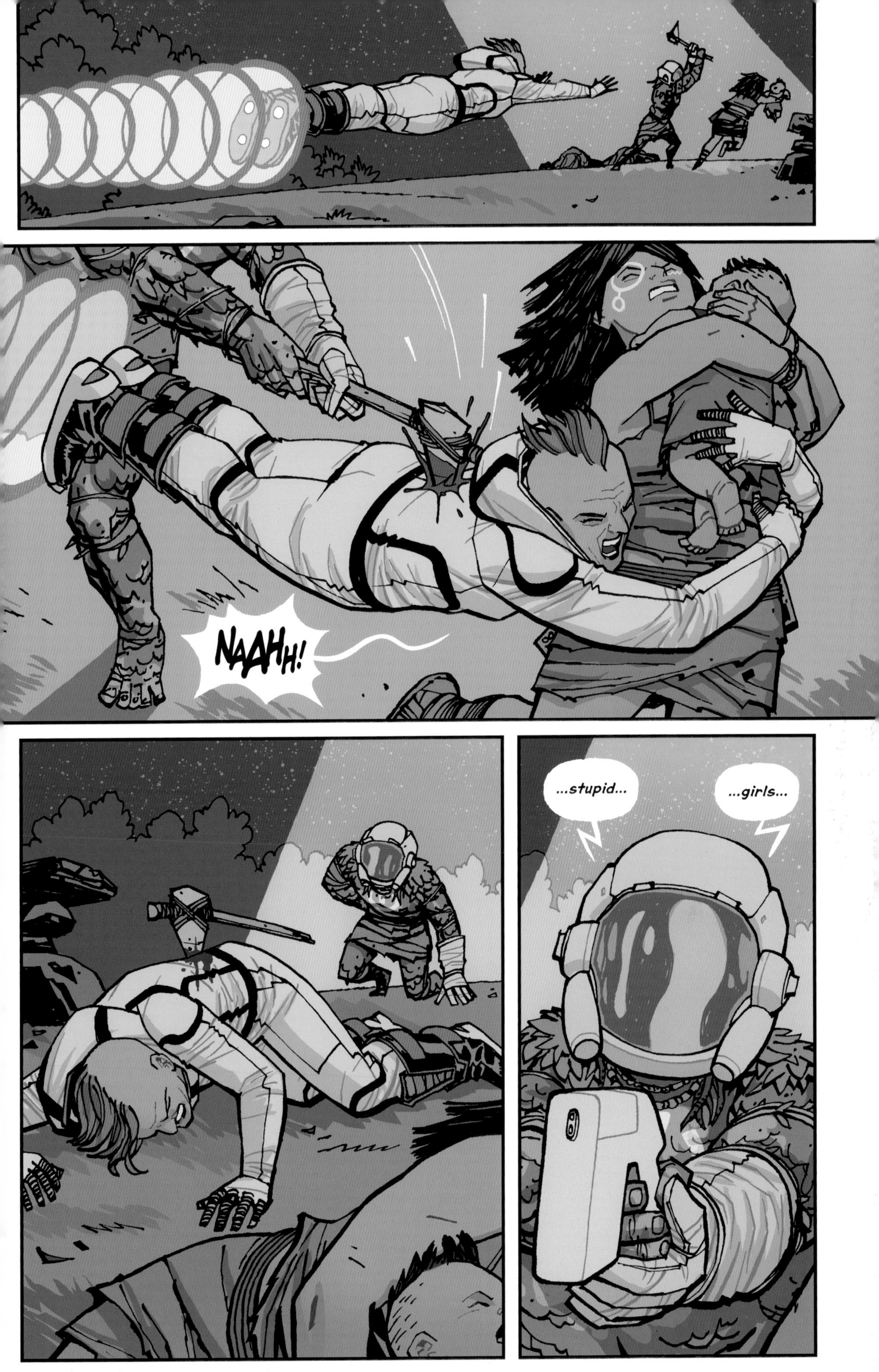
NAAHH!
...stupid...
...girls...

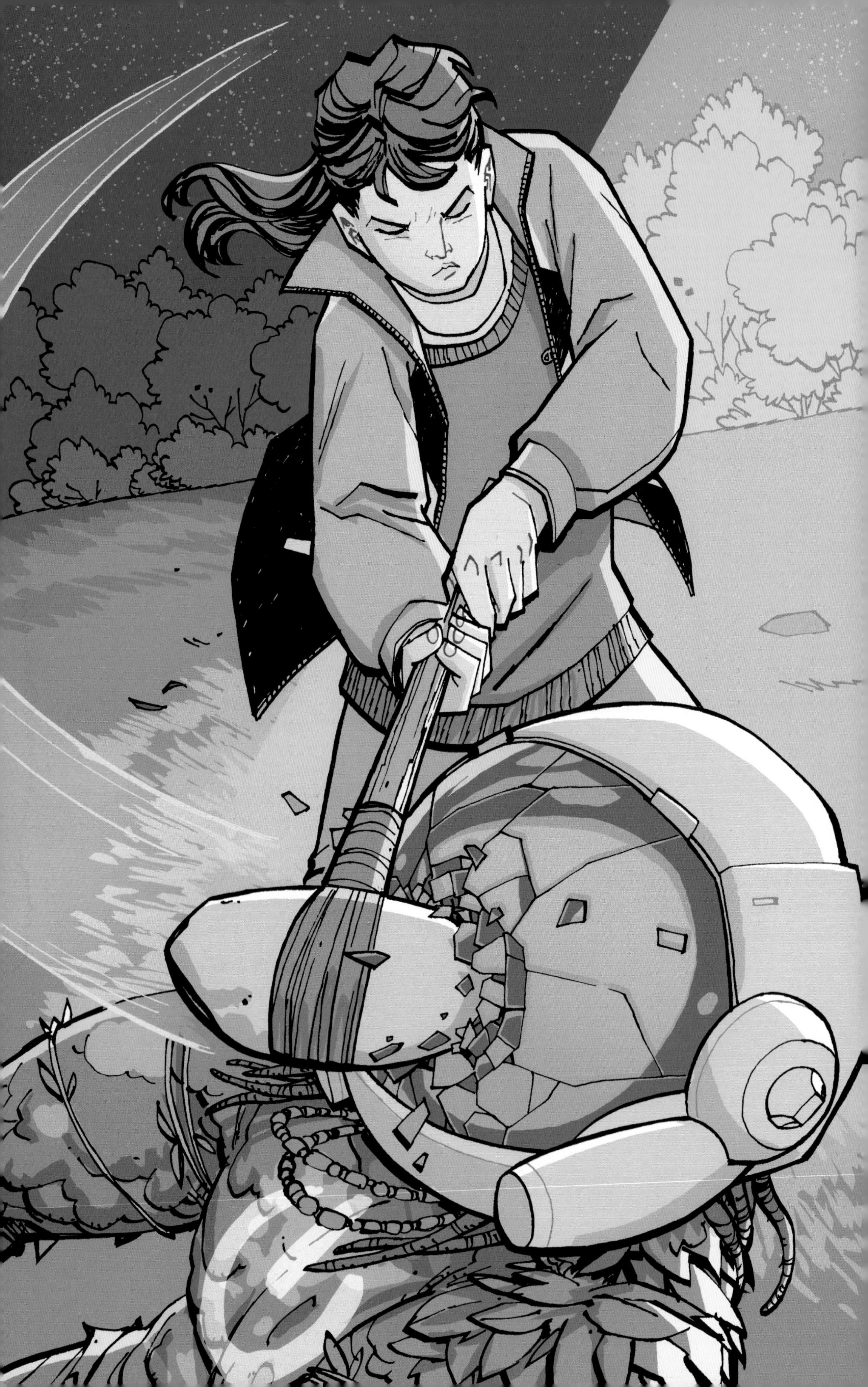

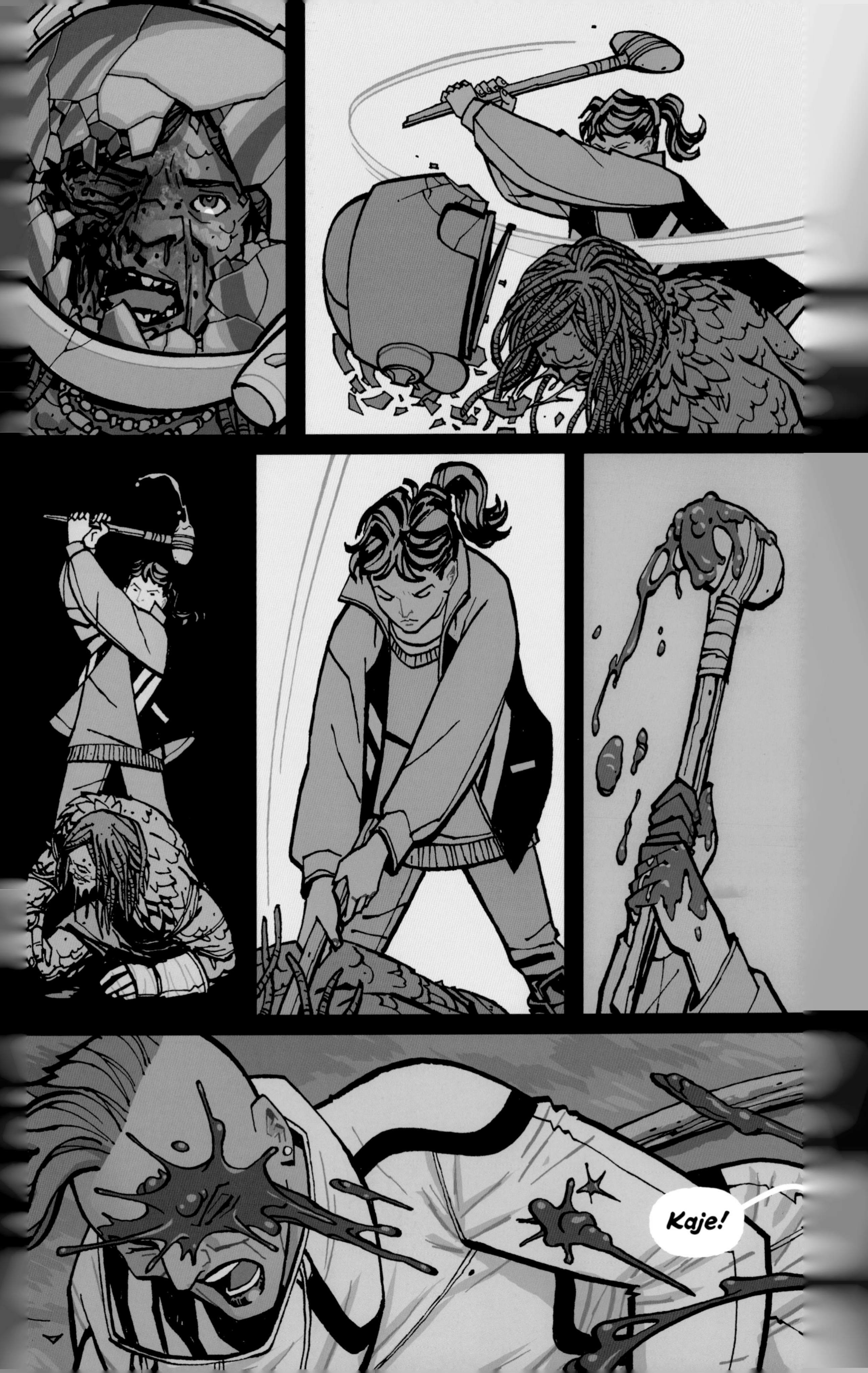
Kaje!

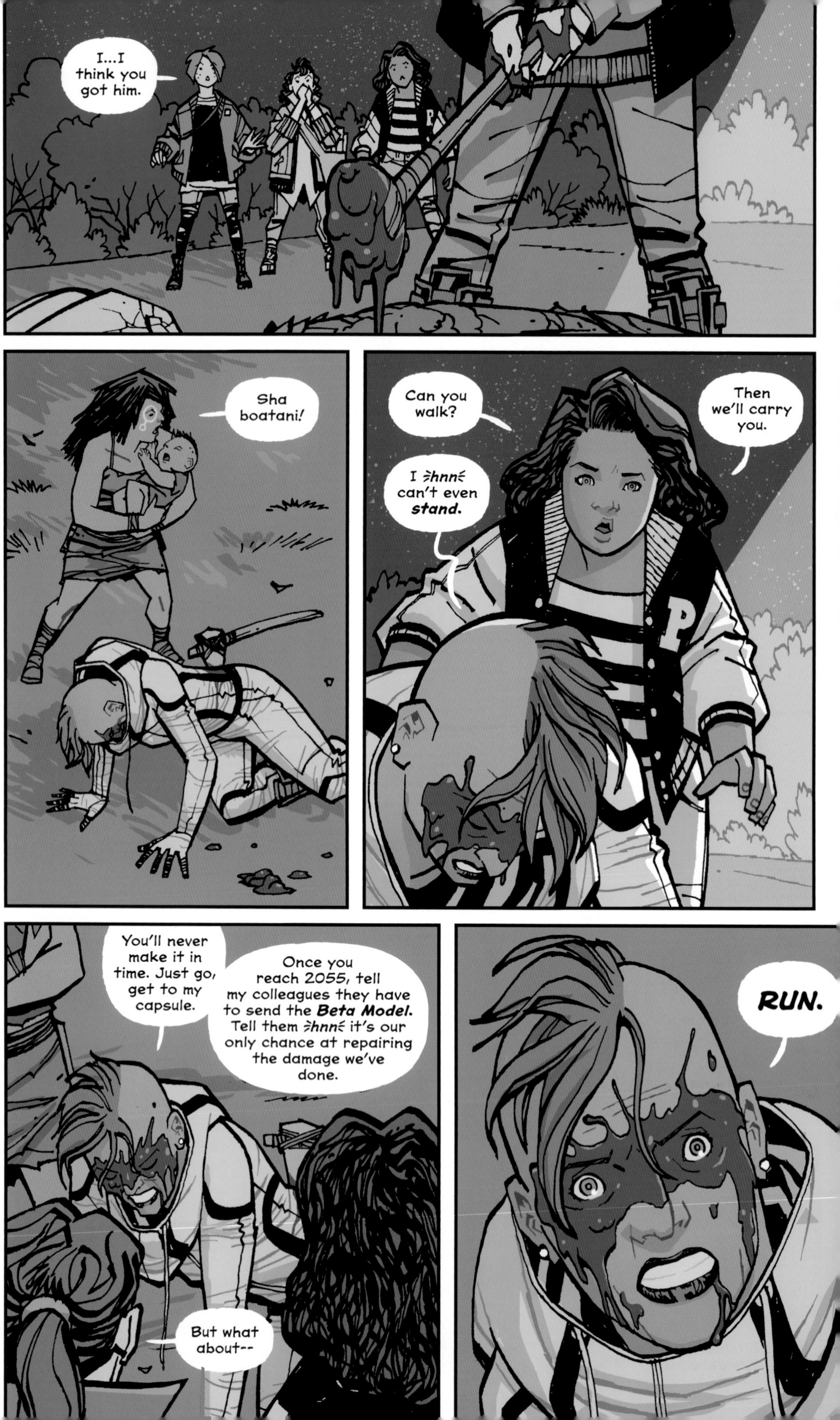
I...I think you got him.
Sha boatani!
Can you walk?
I ≷hnn≶ can't even **stand.**
Then we'll carry you.
You'll never make it in time. Just go, get to my capsule.
Once you reach 2055, tell my colleagues they have to send the **Beta Model.** Tell them ≷hnn≶ it's our only chance at repairing the damage we've done.
But what about--
RUN.

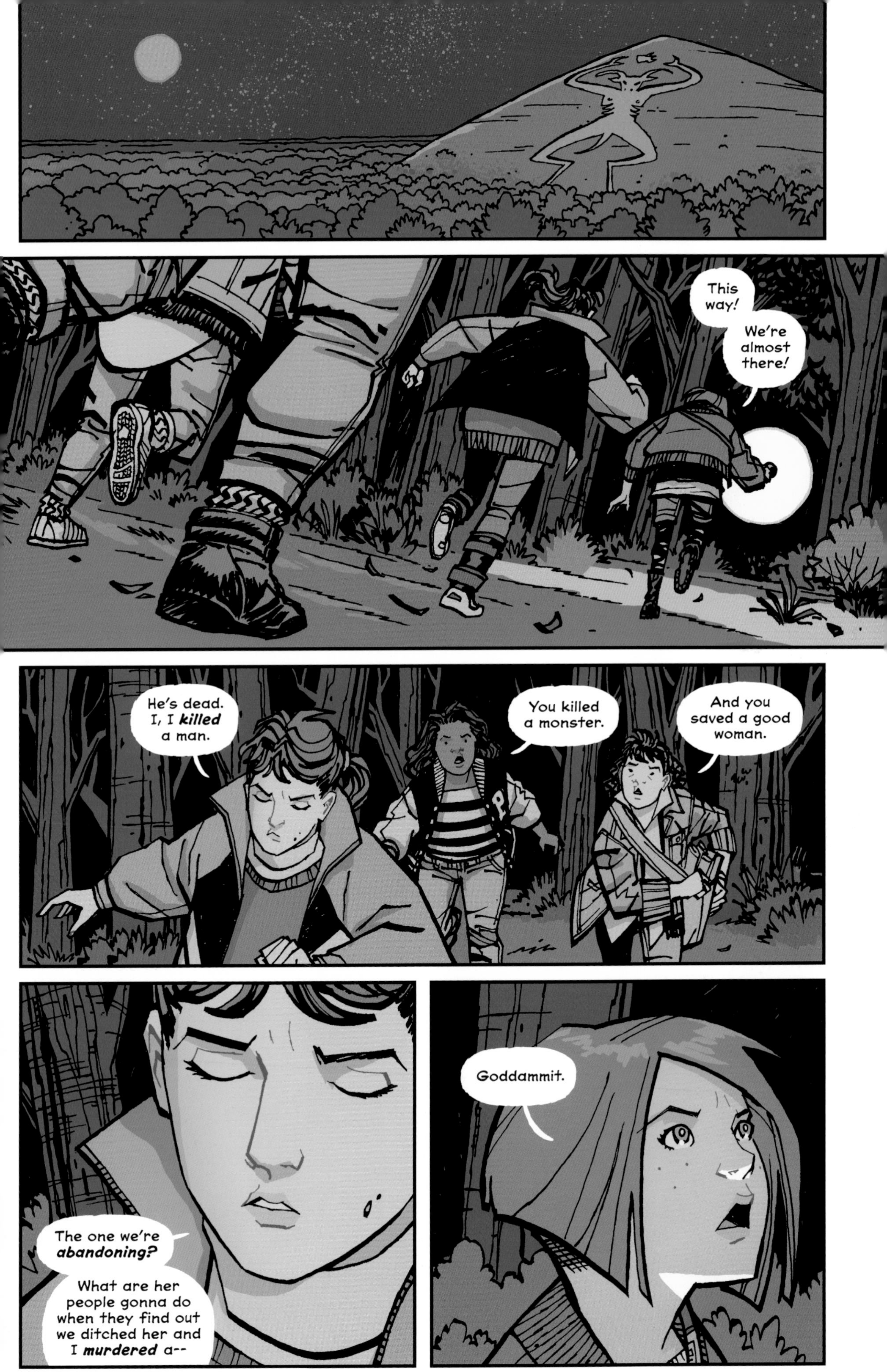
This way!
We're almost there!
He's dead. I, I *killed* a man.
You killed a monster.
And you saved a good woman.
The one we're *abandoning?*
What are her people gonna do when they find out we ditched her and I *murdered* a--
Goddammit.

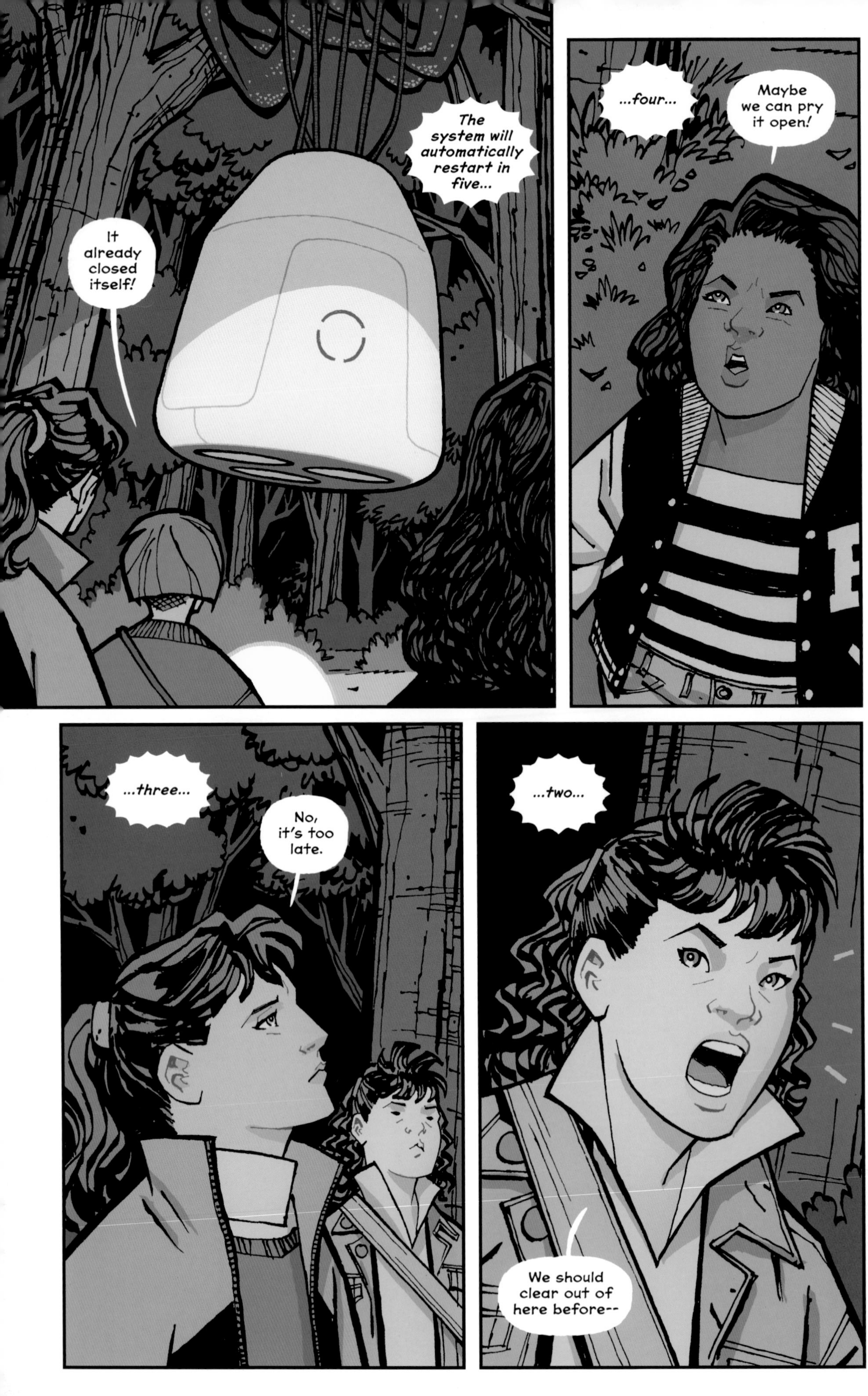
The system will automatically restart in five...
It already closed itself!
...four...
Maybe we can pry it open!
...three...
No, it's too late.
...two...
We should clear out of here before--

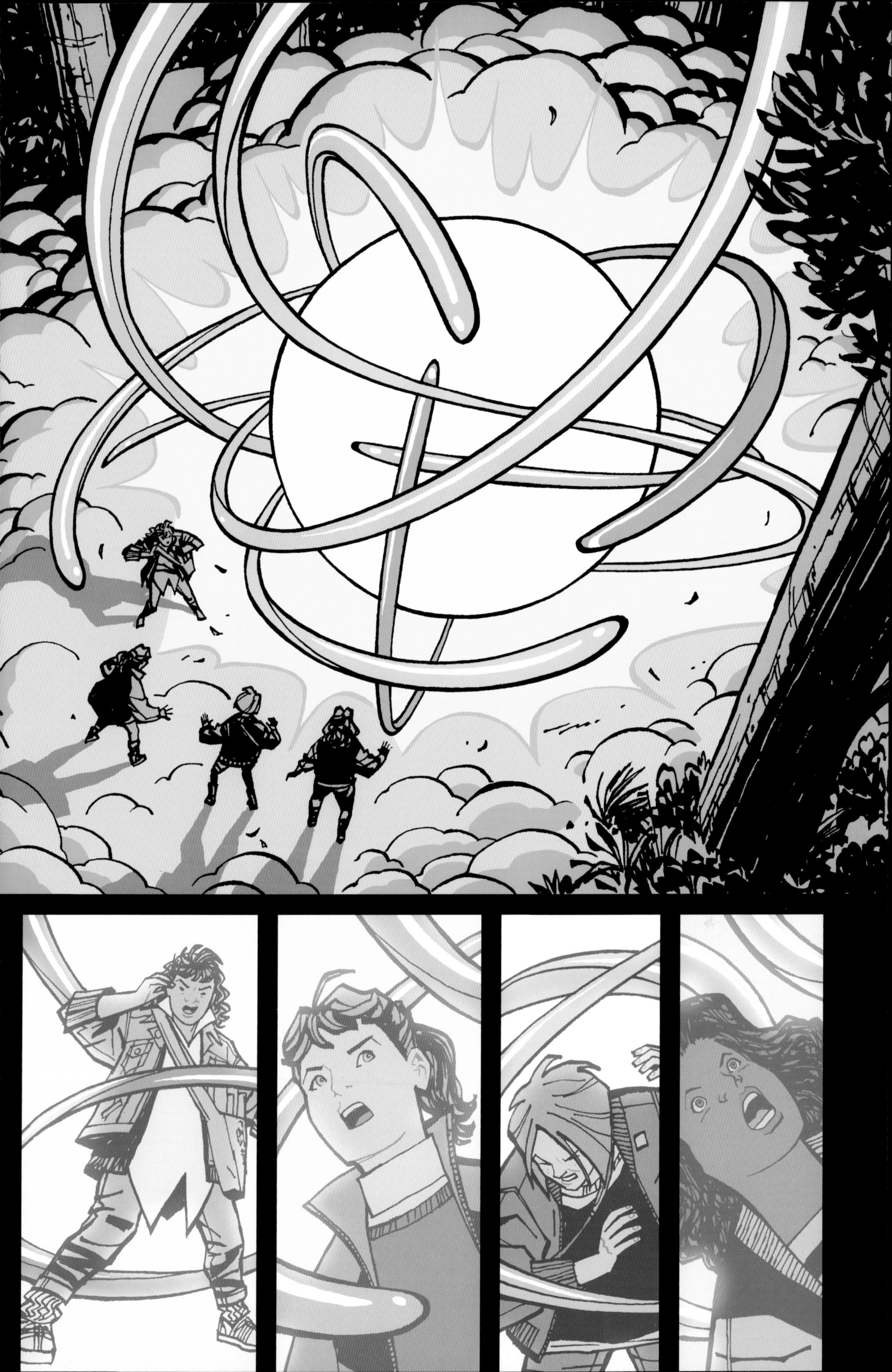

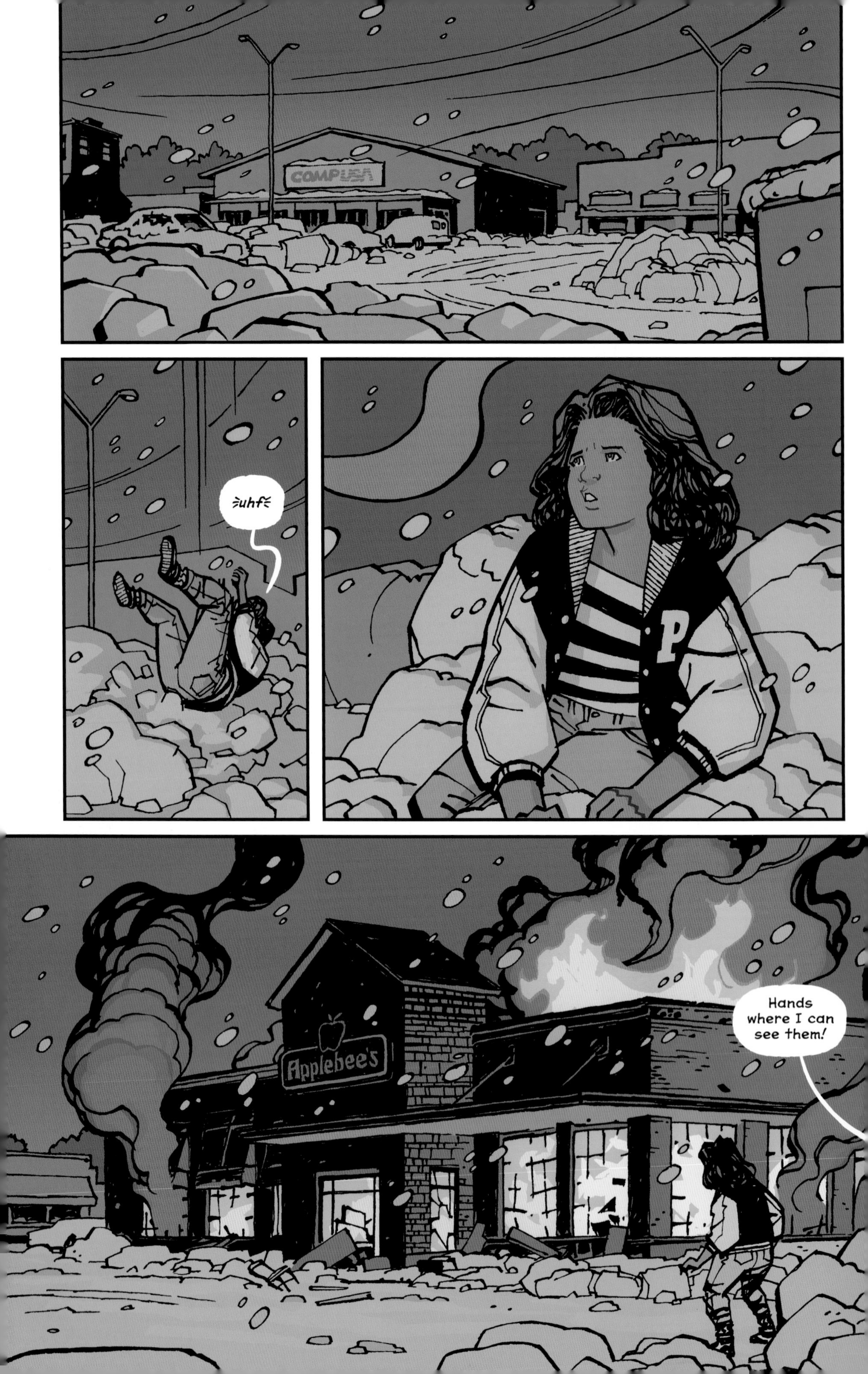
COMPUSA
uhf
Applebee's
Hands where I can see them!

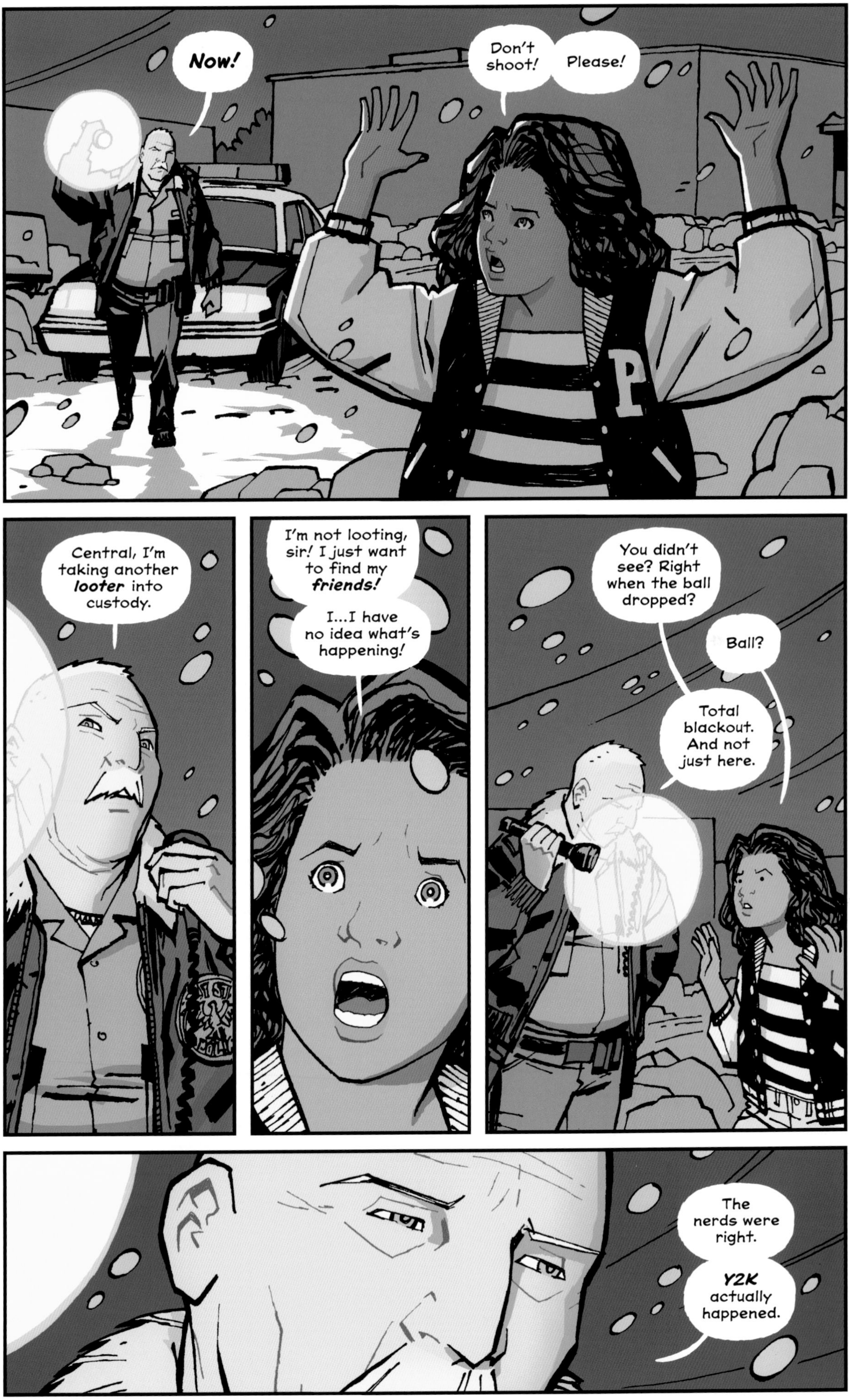

Now!
Don't shoot!
Please!
Central, I'm taking another *looter* into custody.
I'm not looting, sir! I just want to find my *friends!*
I...I have no idea what's happening!
You didn't see? Right when the ball dropped?
Ball?
Total blackout. And not just here.
The nerds were right.
Y2K actually happened.

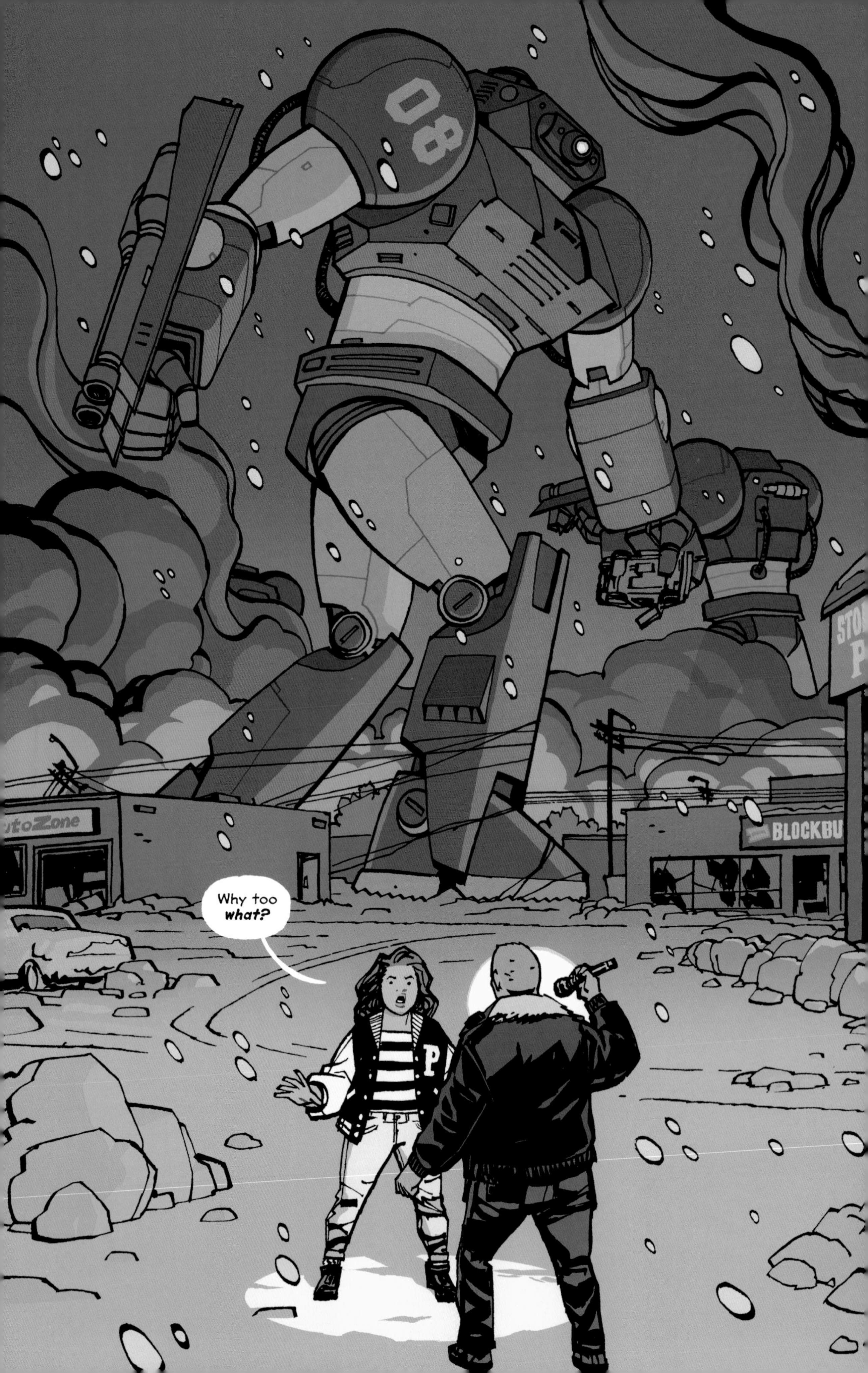
Why too *what?*

CHAPTER
16

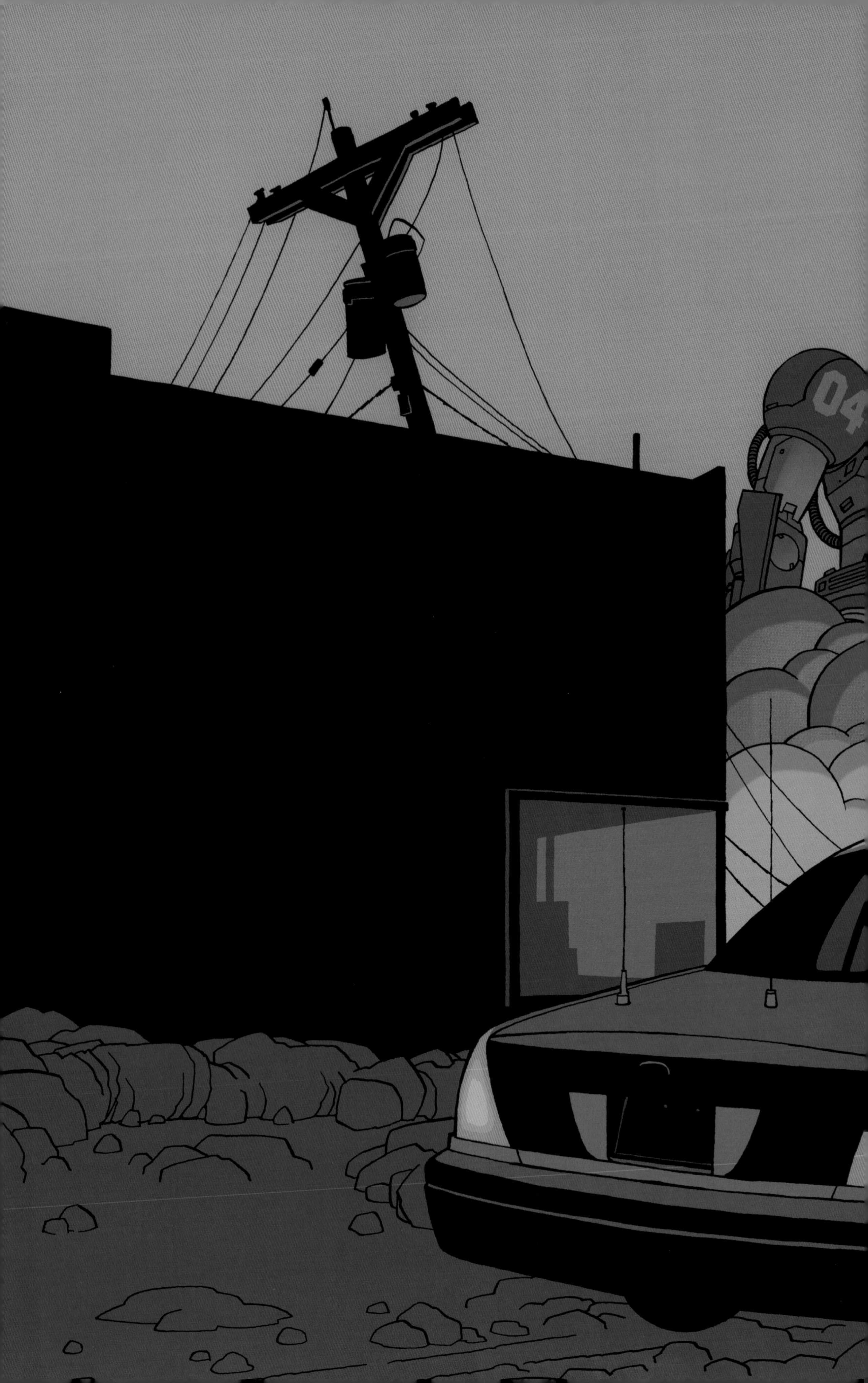
04

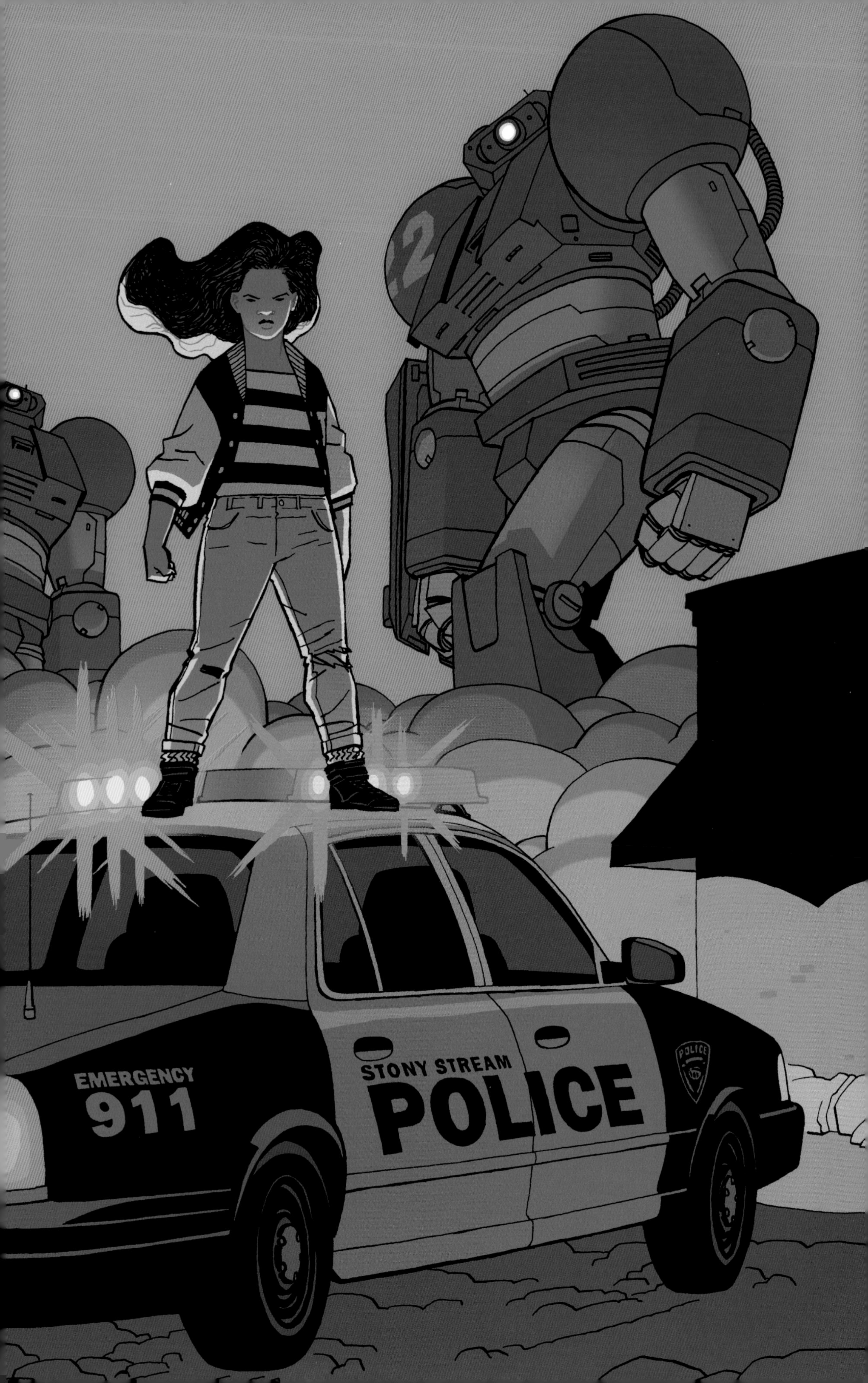
EMERGENCY
911
STONY STREAM
POLICE

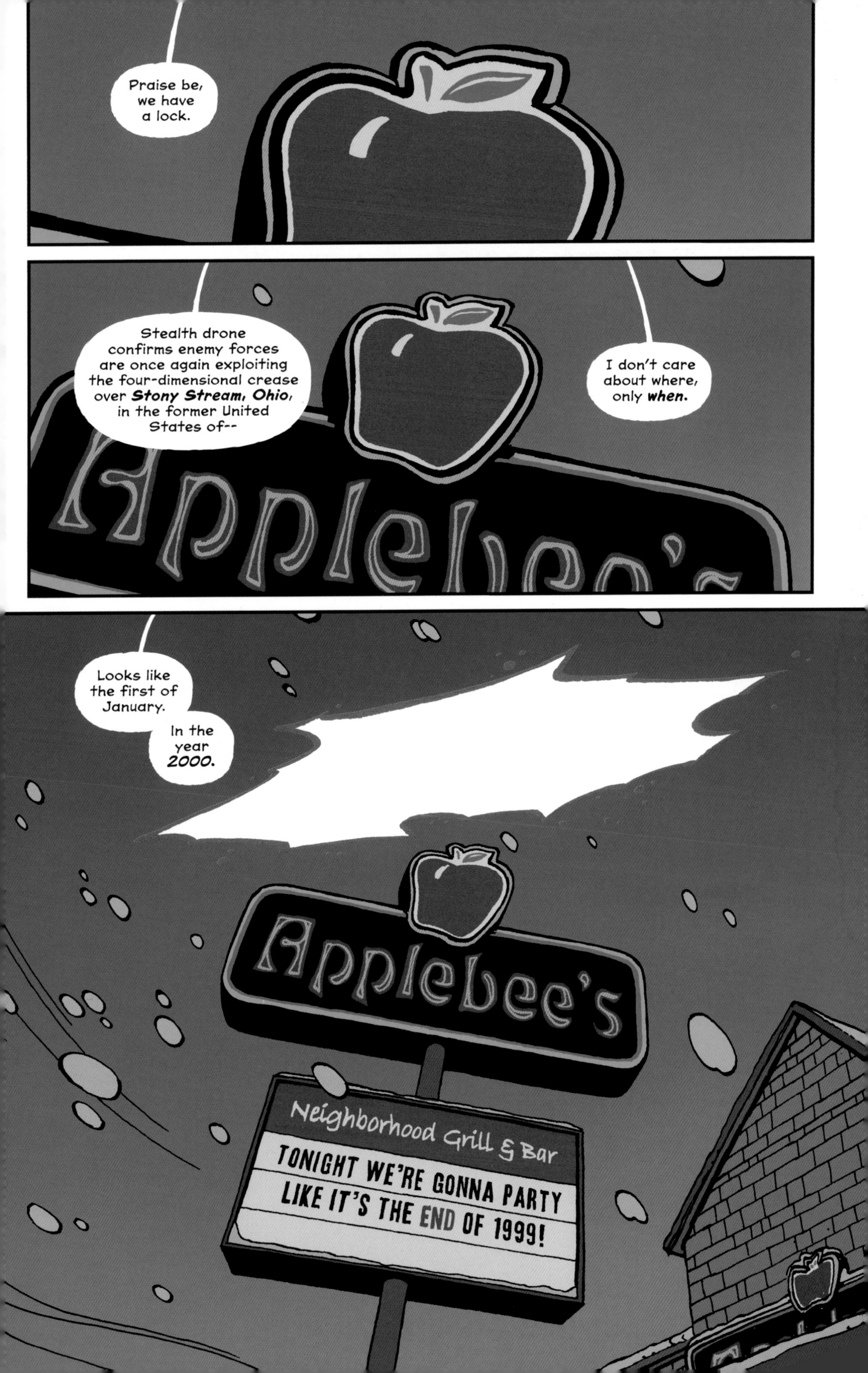
Praise be, we have a lock.
Stealth drone confirms enemy forces are once again exploiting the four-dimensional crease over Stony Stream, Ohio, in the former United States of--
I don't care about where, only when.
Applebee's
Looks like the first of January.
In the year 2000.
Applebee's
Neighborhood Grill & Bar
TONIGHT WE'RE GONNA PARTY LIKE IT'S THE END OF 1999!

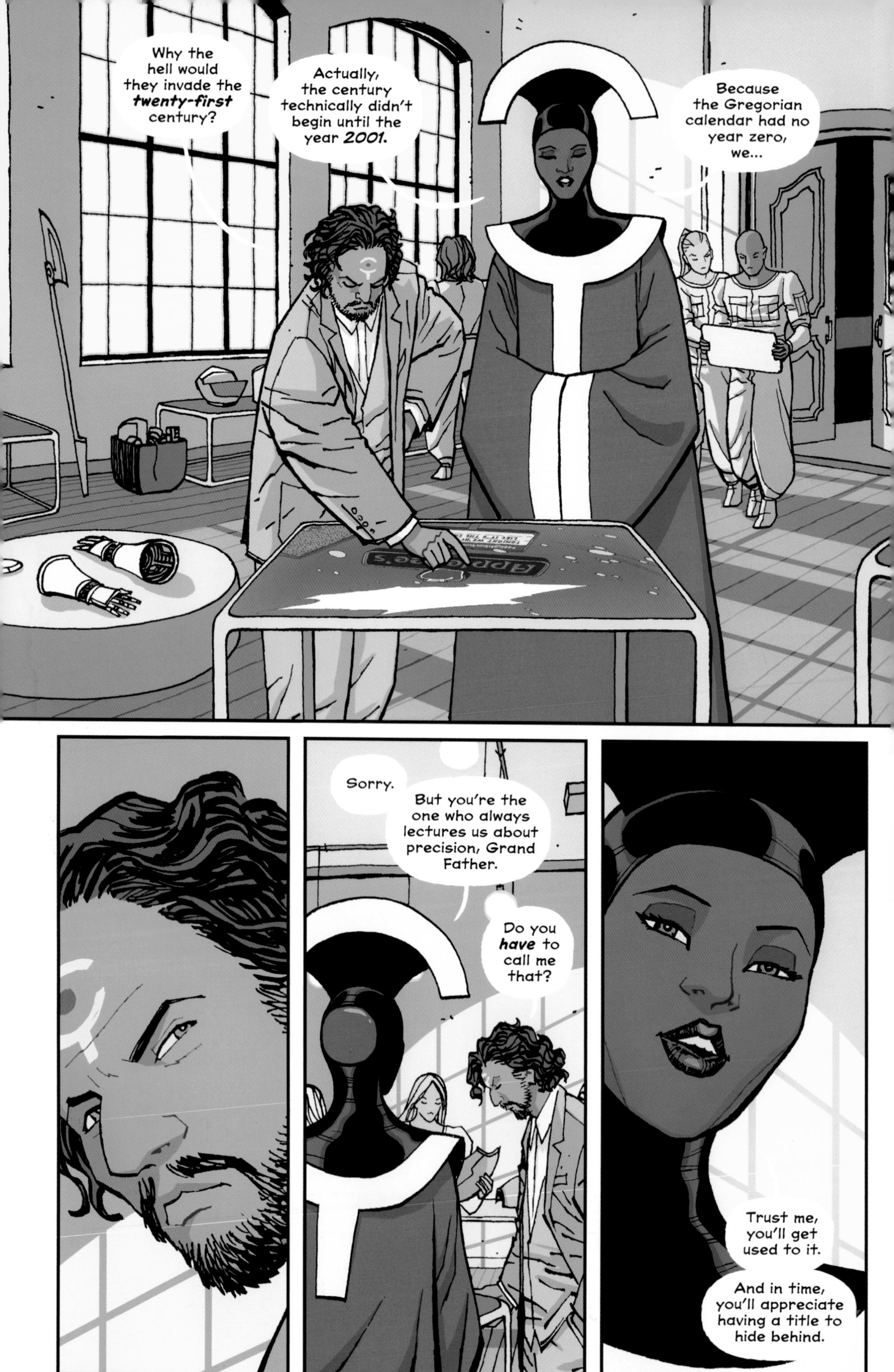
Why the hell would they invade the *twenty-first* century?
Actually, the century technically didn't begin until the year ***2001.***
Because the Gregorian calendar had no year zero, we...
Sorry.
But you're the one who always lectures us about precision, Grand Father.
Do you ***have*** to call me that?
Trust me, you'll get used to it.
And in time, you'll appreciate having a title to hide behind.

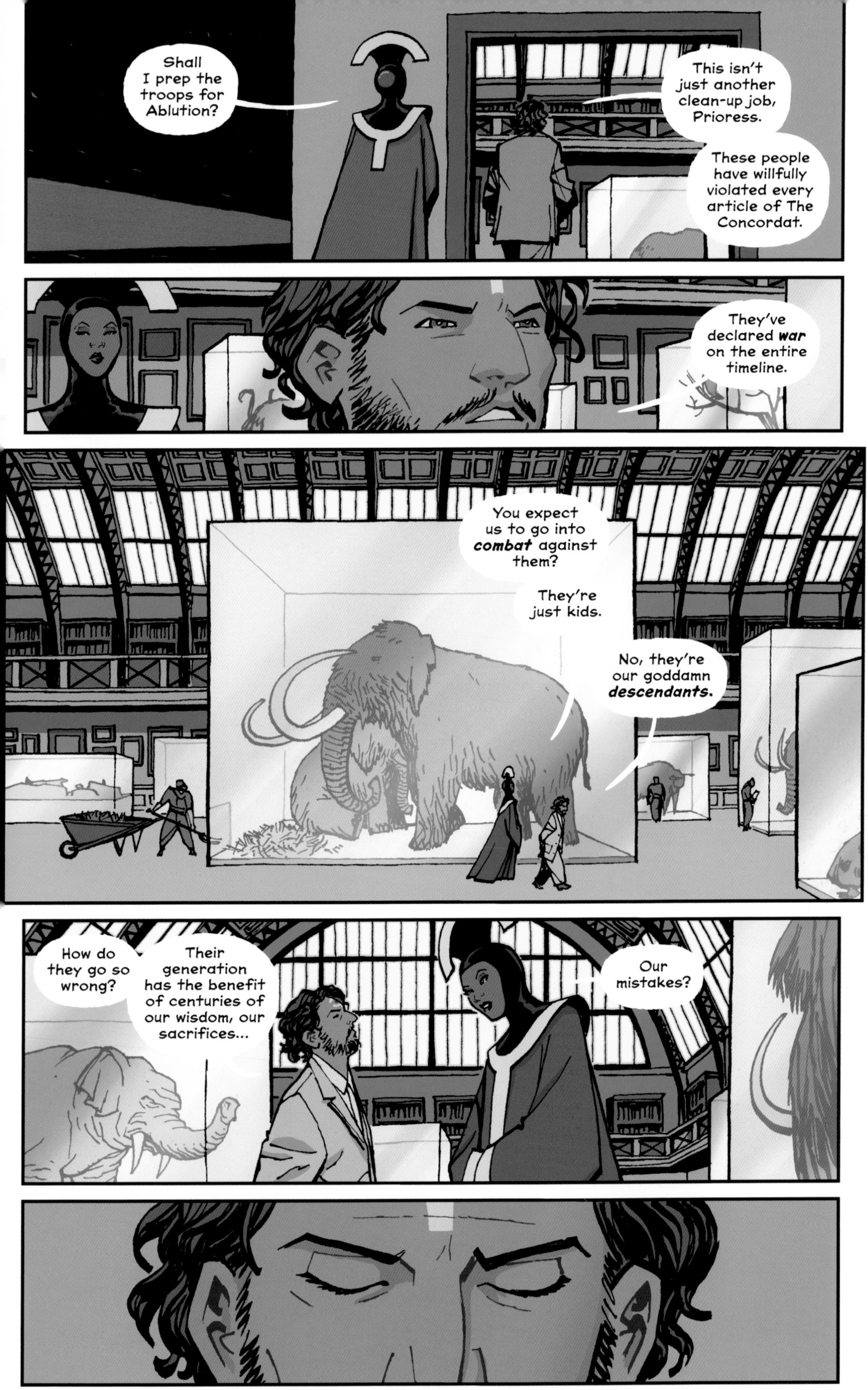
Shall I prep the troops for Ablution?
This isn't just another clean-up job, Prioress.
These people have willfully violated every article of The Concordat.
They've declared **war** on the entire timeline.
You expect us to go into **combat** against them?
They're just kids.
No, they're our goddamn **descendants.**
How do they go so wrong?
Their generation has the benefit of centuries of our wisdom, our sacrifices...
Our mistakes?

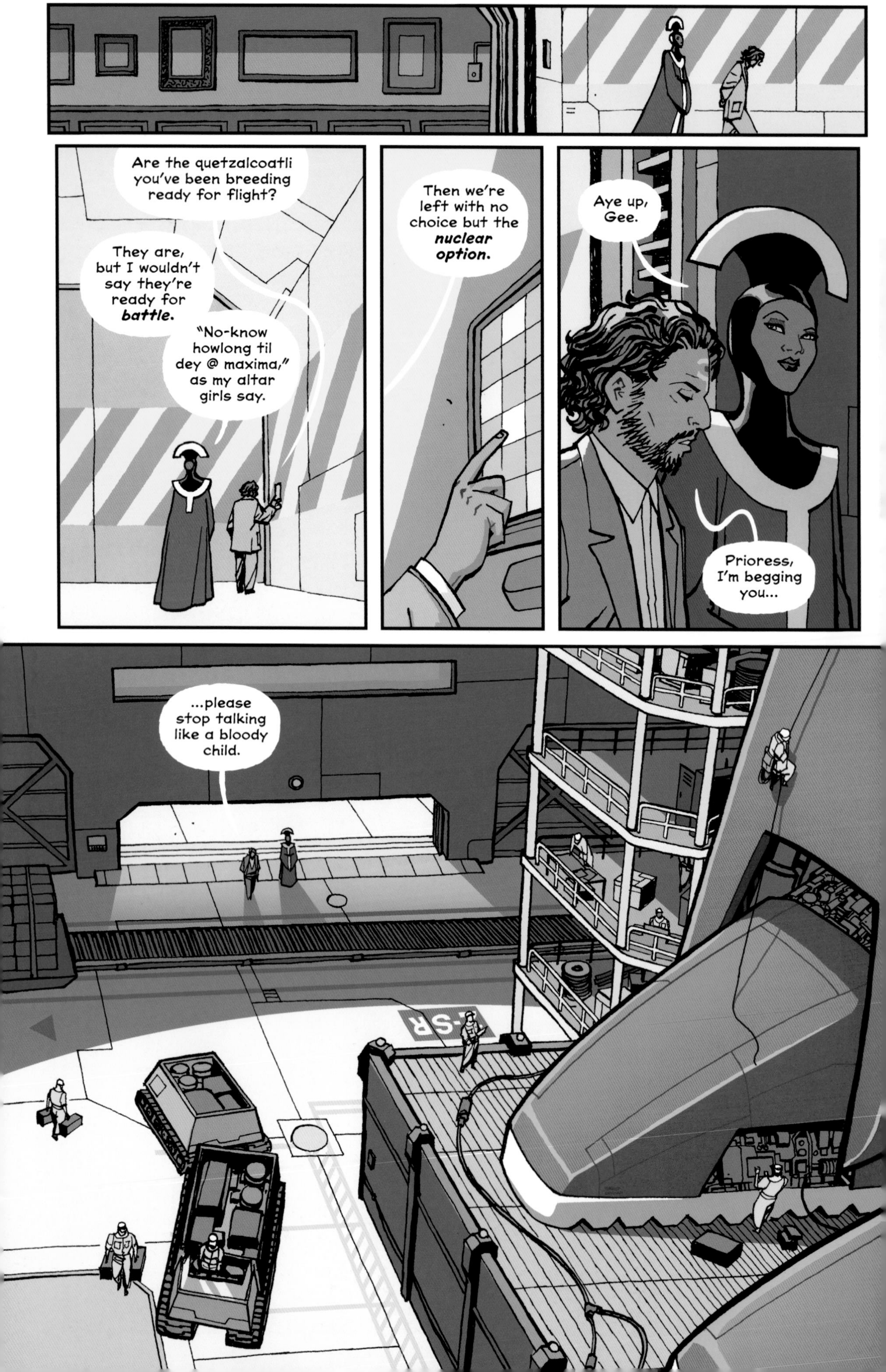
Are the quetzalcoatli you've been breeding ready for flight?
They are, but I wouldn't say they're ready for **battle.**
"No-know howlong til dey @ maxima," as my altar girls say.
Then we're left with no choice but the ***nuclear option.***
Aye up, Gee.
Prioress, I'm begging you...
...please stop talking like a bloody child.

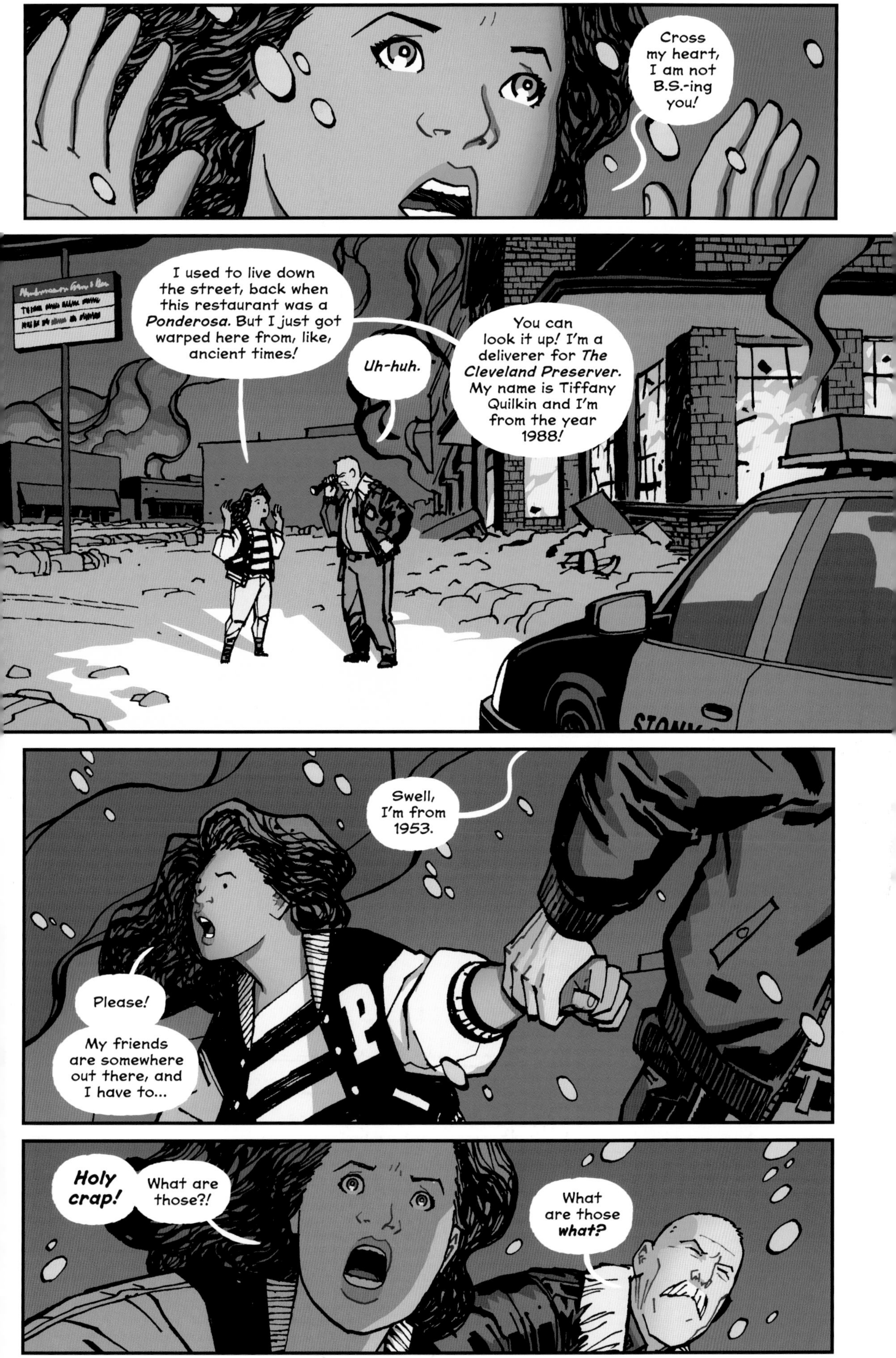

Cross my heart, I am not B.S.-ing you!
I used to live down the street, back when this restaurant was a *Ponderosa*. But I just got warped here from, like, ancient times!
Uh-huh.
You can look it up! I'm a deliverer for *The Cleveland Preserver*. My name is Tiffany Quilkin and I'm from the year 1988!
Swell, I'm from 1953.
Please!
My friends are somewhere out there, and I have to...
Holy crap!
What are those?!
What are those ***what?***

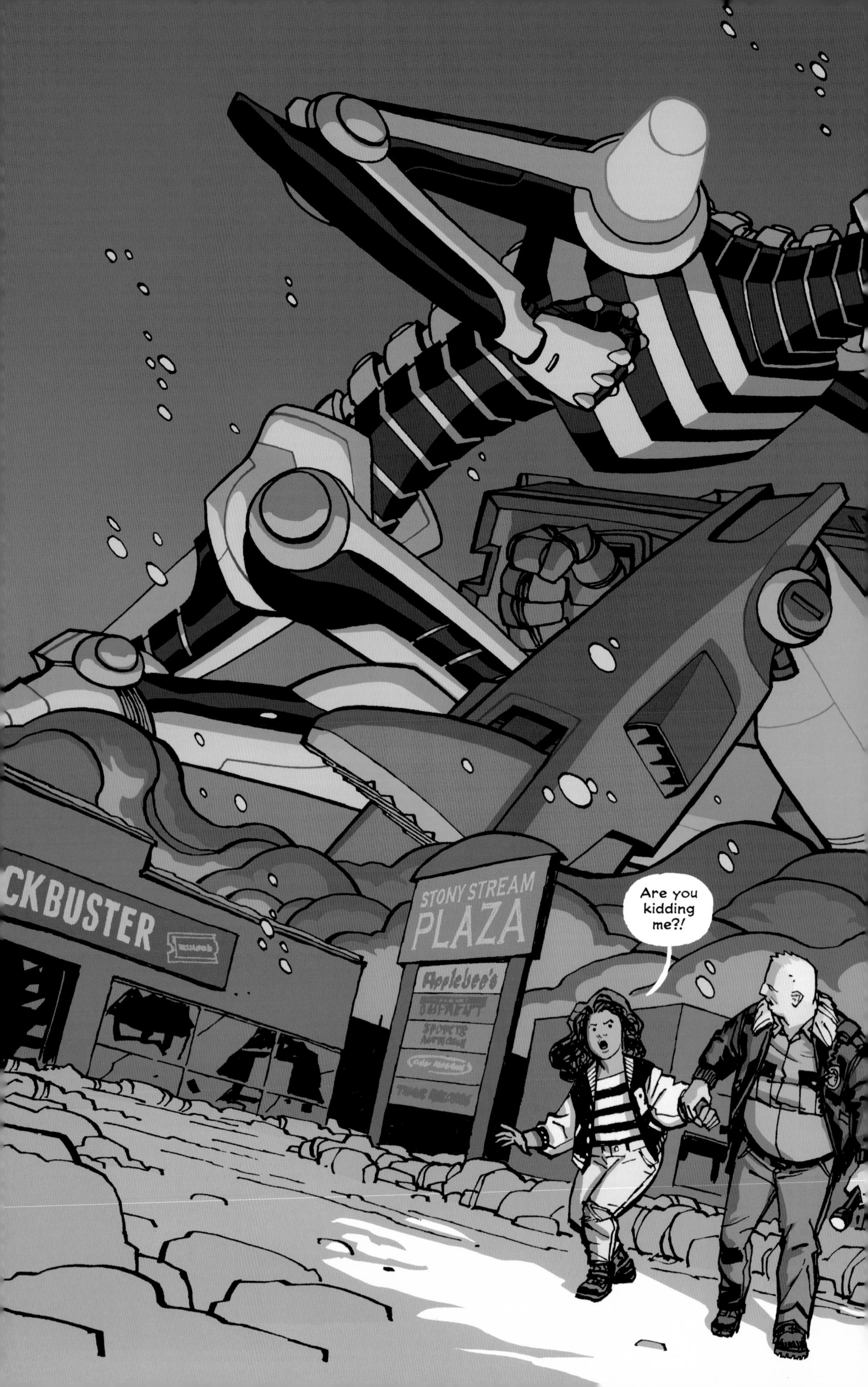
CKBUSTER
STONY STREAM
PLAZA
Applebee's
Are you kidding me?!

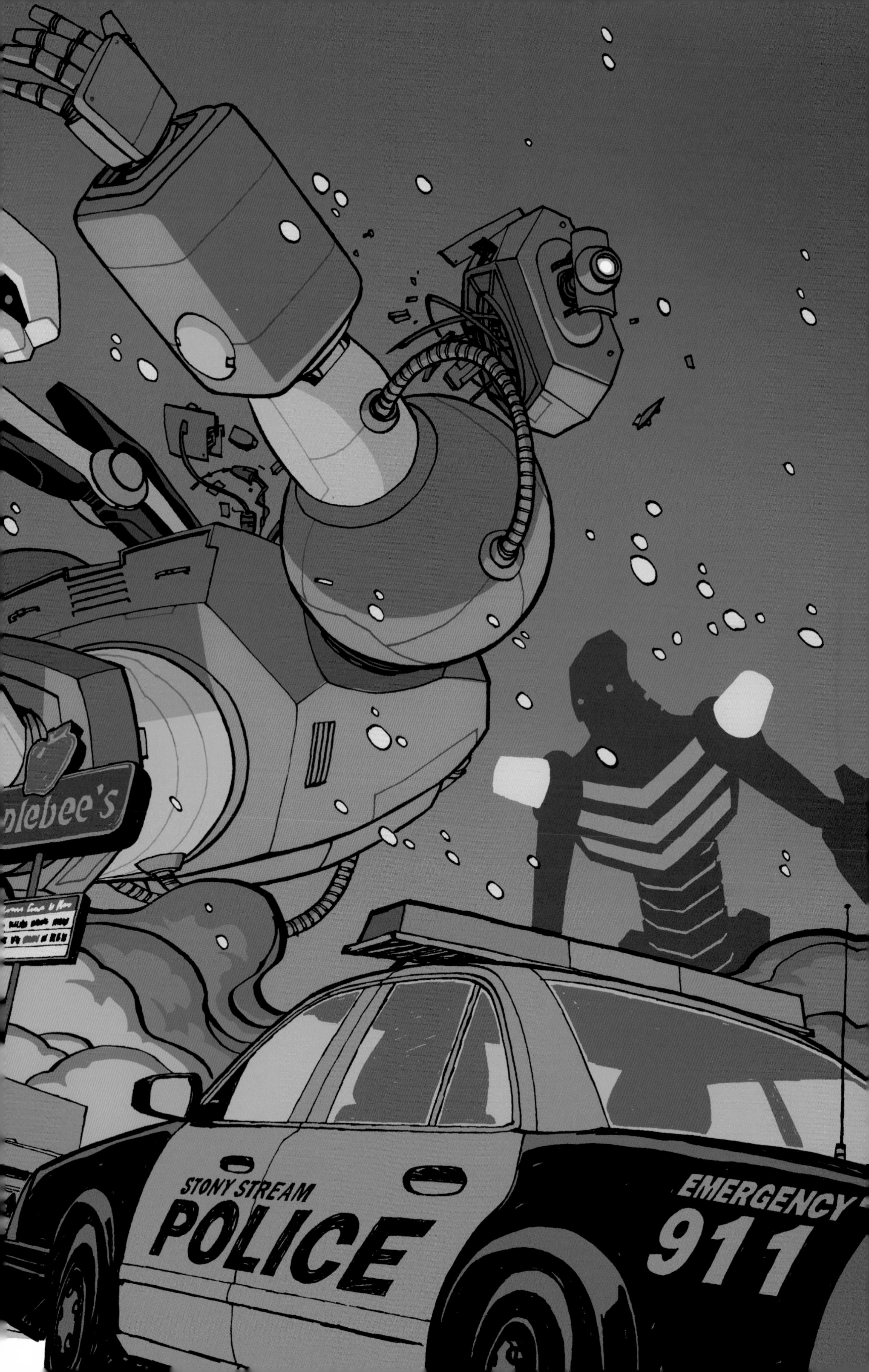

plebee's
STONY STREAM
POLICE
EMERGENCY
911

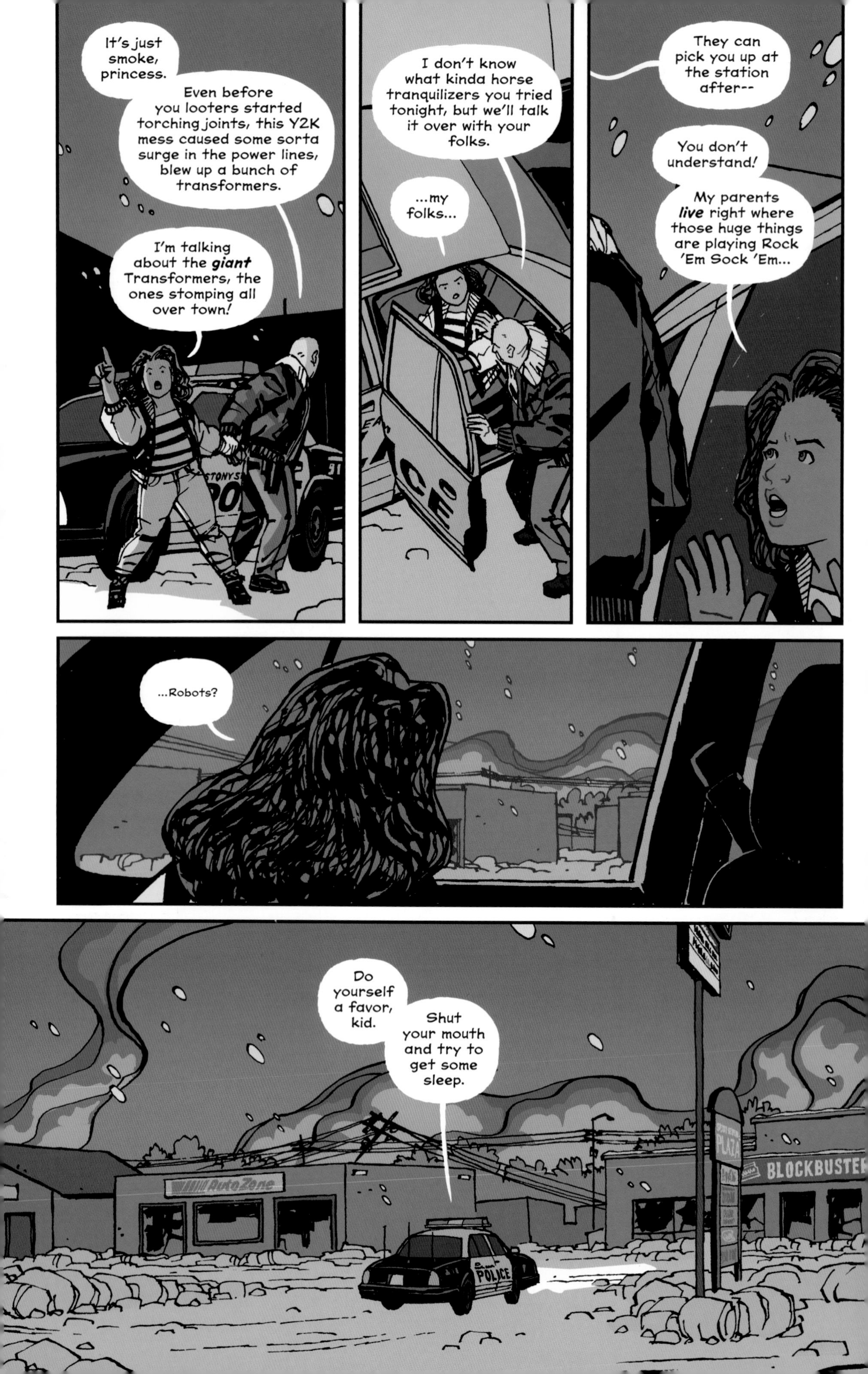
It's just smoke, princess.
Even before you looters started torching joints, this Y2K mess caused some sorta surge in the power lines, blew up a bunch of transformers.
I'm talking about the ***giant*** Transformers, the ones stomping all over town!
I don't know what kinda horse tranquilizers you tried tonight, but we'll talk it over with your folks.
...my folks...
They can pick you up at the station after--
You don't understand!
My parents ***live*** right where those huge things are playing Rock 'Em Sock 'Em...
...Robots?
Do yourself a favor, kid.
Shut your mouth and try to get some sleep.
AutoZone
PLAZA
BLOCKBUSTER
POLICE

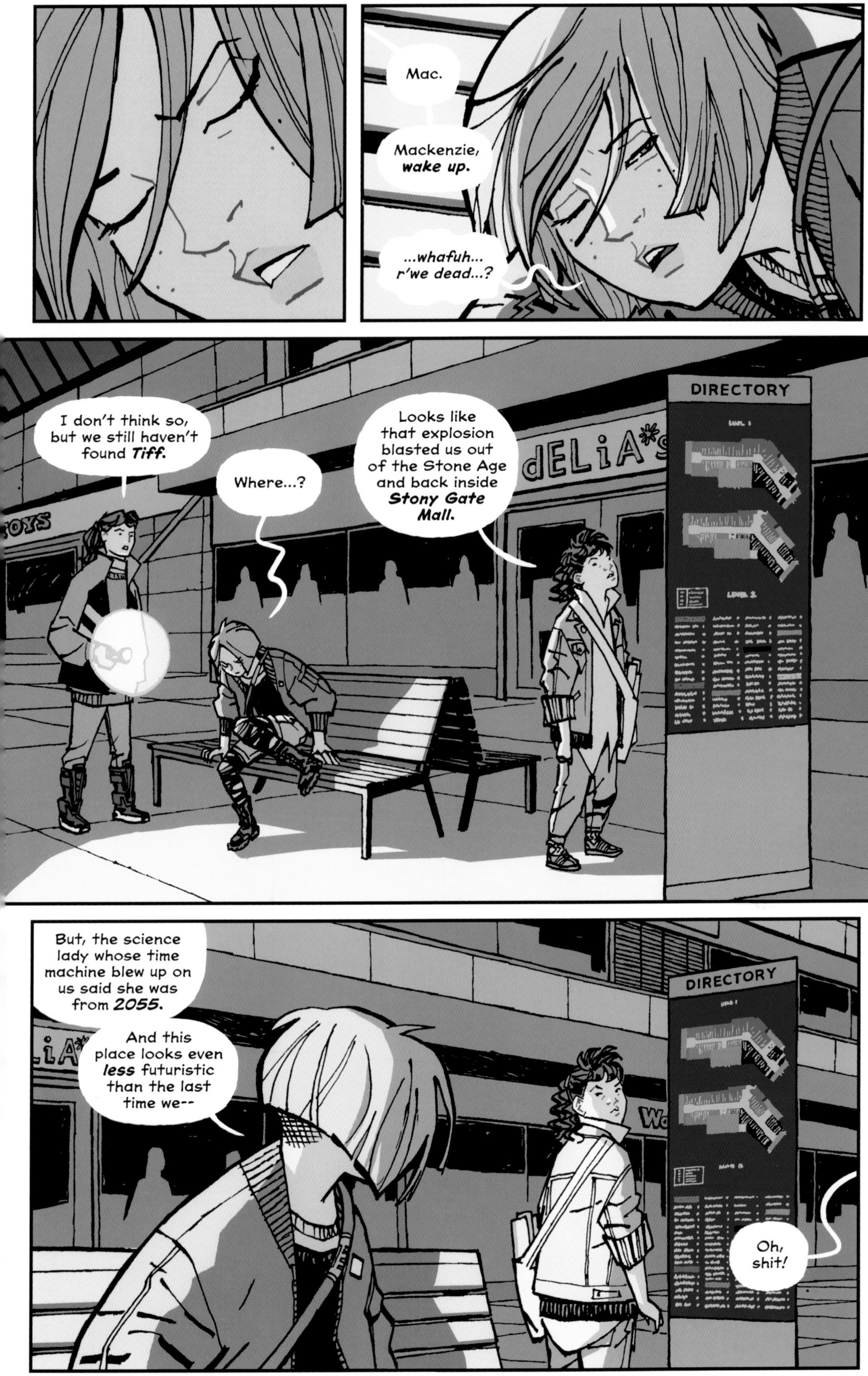

Mac.
Mackenzie, wake up.
...whafuh... r'we dead...?
I don't think so, but we still haven't found Tiff.
Where...?
Looks like that explosion blasted us out of the Stone Age and back inside Stony Gate Mall.
dELiA*s
DIRECTORY
But, the science lady whose time machine blew up on us said she was from 2055.
And this place looks even less futuristic than the last time we--
DIRECTORY
Oh, shit!

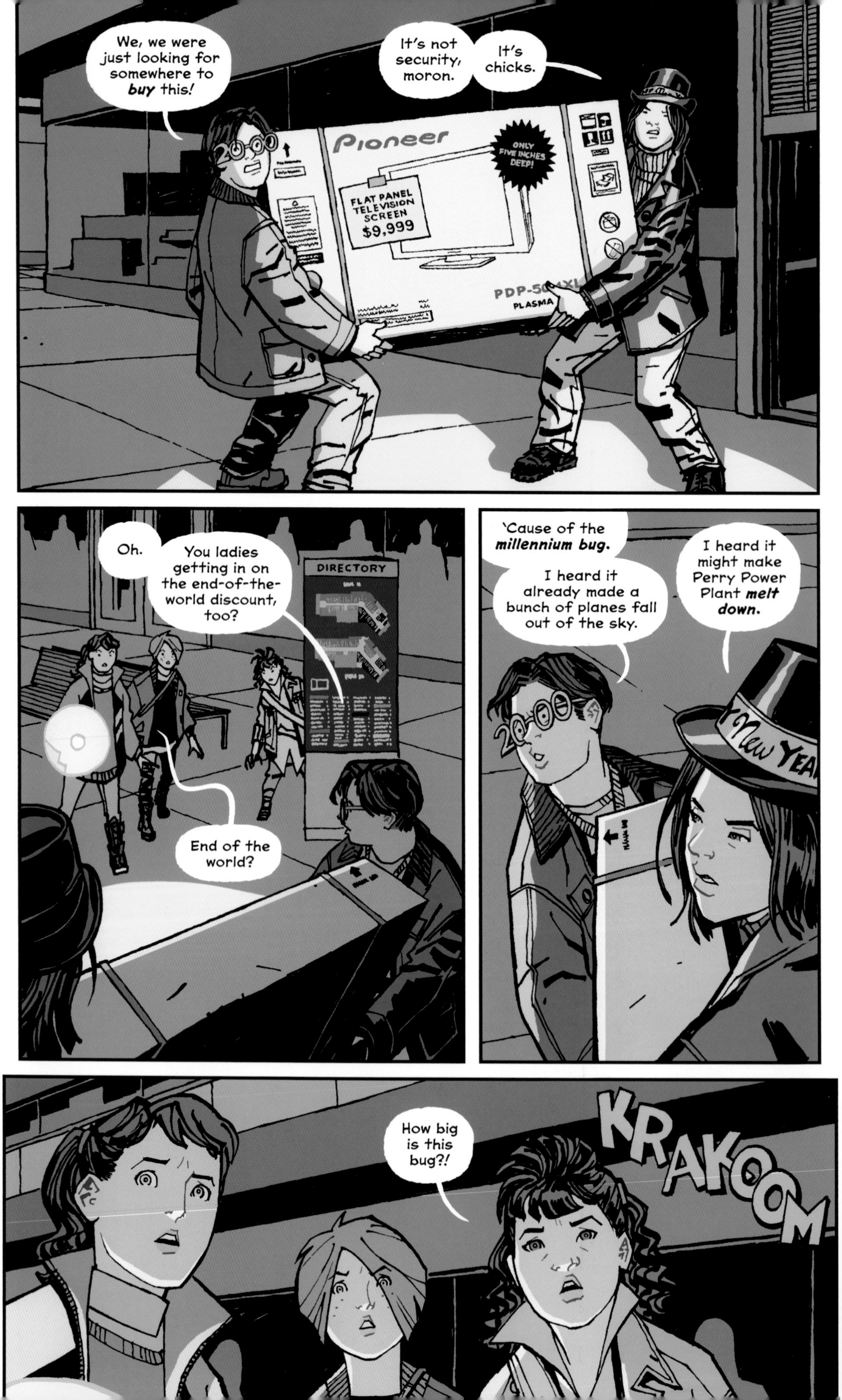

We, we were just looking for somewhere to **buy** this!
It's not security, moron.
It's chicks.
Pioneer
ONLY FIVE INCHES DEEP!
FLAT PANEL TELEVISION SCREEN $9,999
PLASMA
Oh.
You ladies getting in on the end-of-the-world discount, too?
DIRECTORY
End of the world?
'Cause of the **millennium bug.**
I heard it already made a bunch of planes fall out of the sky.
I heard it might make Perry Power Plant **melt down.**
How big is this bug?!
KRAKOOM

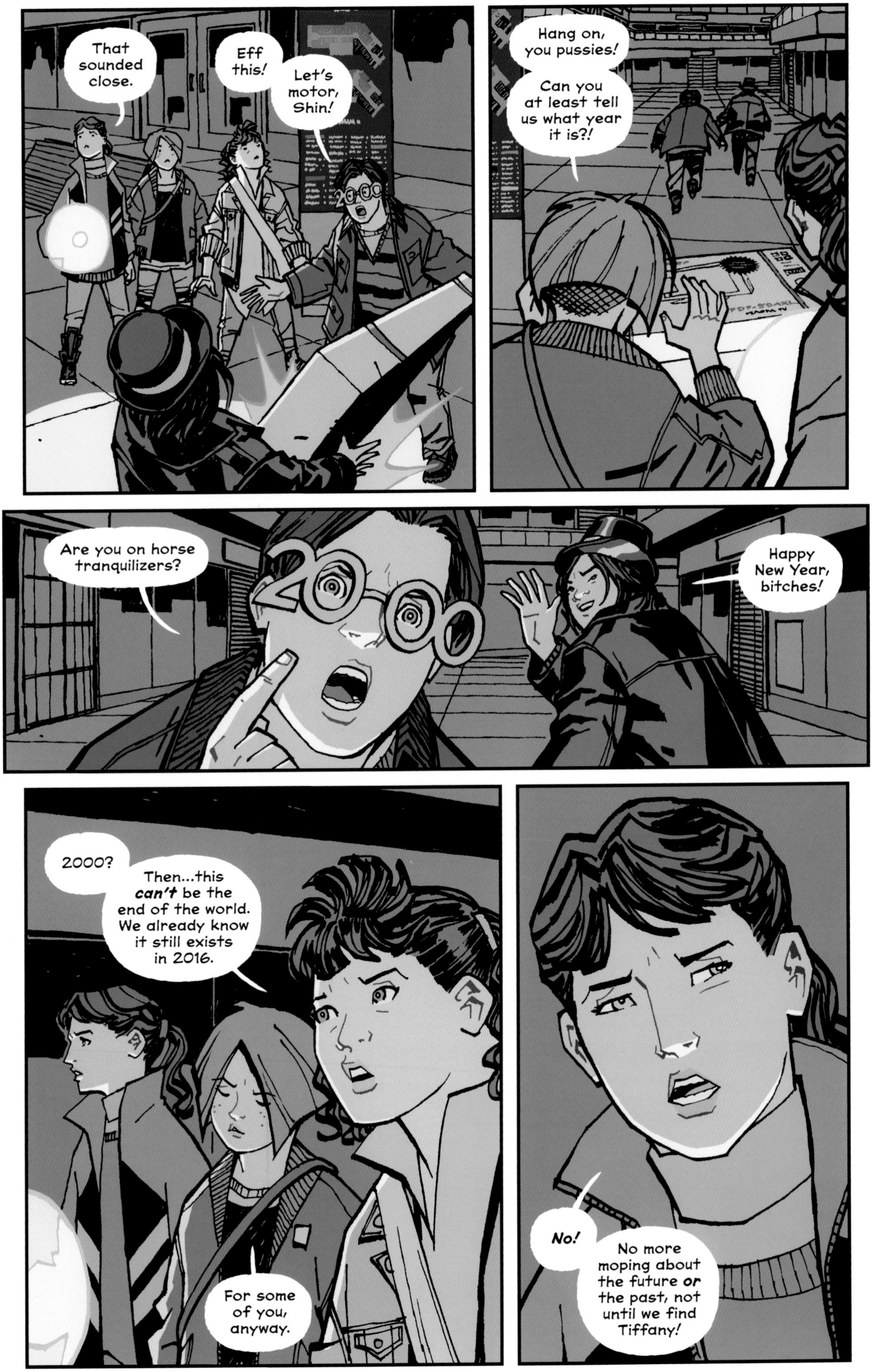
That sounded close.
Eff this!
Let's motor, Shin!
Hang on, you pussies!
Can you at least tell us what year it is?!
Are you on horse tranquilizers?
Happy New Year, bitches!
2000?
Then...this *can't* be the end of the world. We already know it still exists in 2016.
For some of you, anyway.
No!
No more moping about the future *or* the past, not until we find Tiffany!

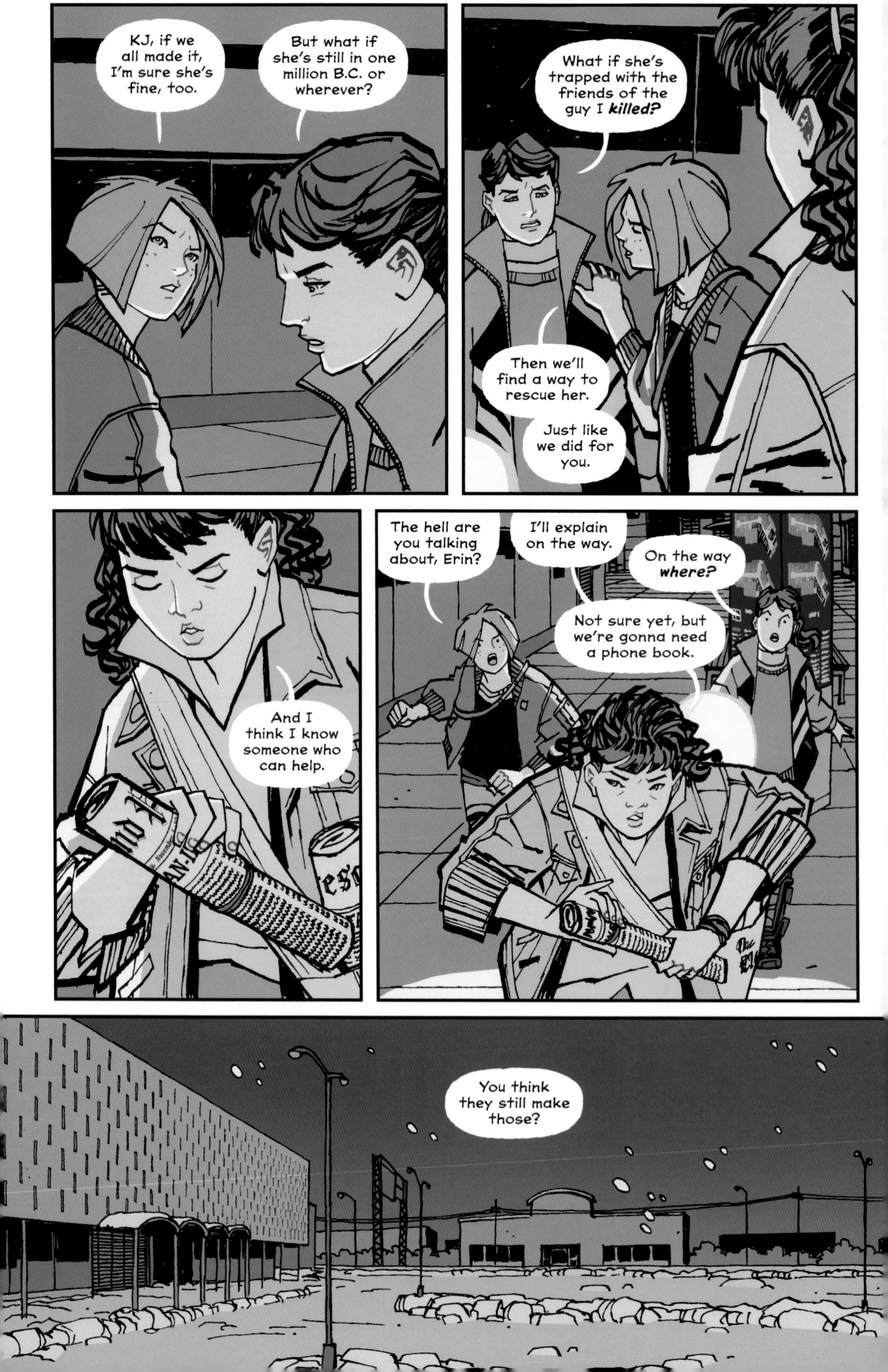
KJ, if we all made it, I'm sure she's fine, too.
But what if she's still in one million B.C. or wherever?
What if she's trapped with the friends of the guy I *killed?*
Then we'll find a way to rescue her.
Just like we did for you.
And I think I know someone who can help.
The hell are you talking about, Erin?
I'll explain on the way.
On the way *where?*
Not sure yet, but we're gonna need a phone book.
You think they still make those?

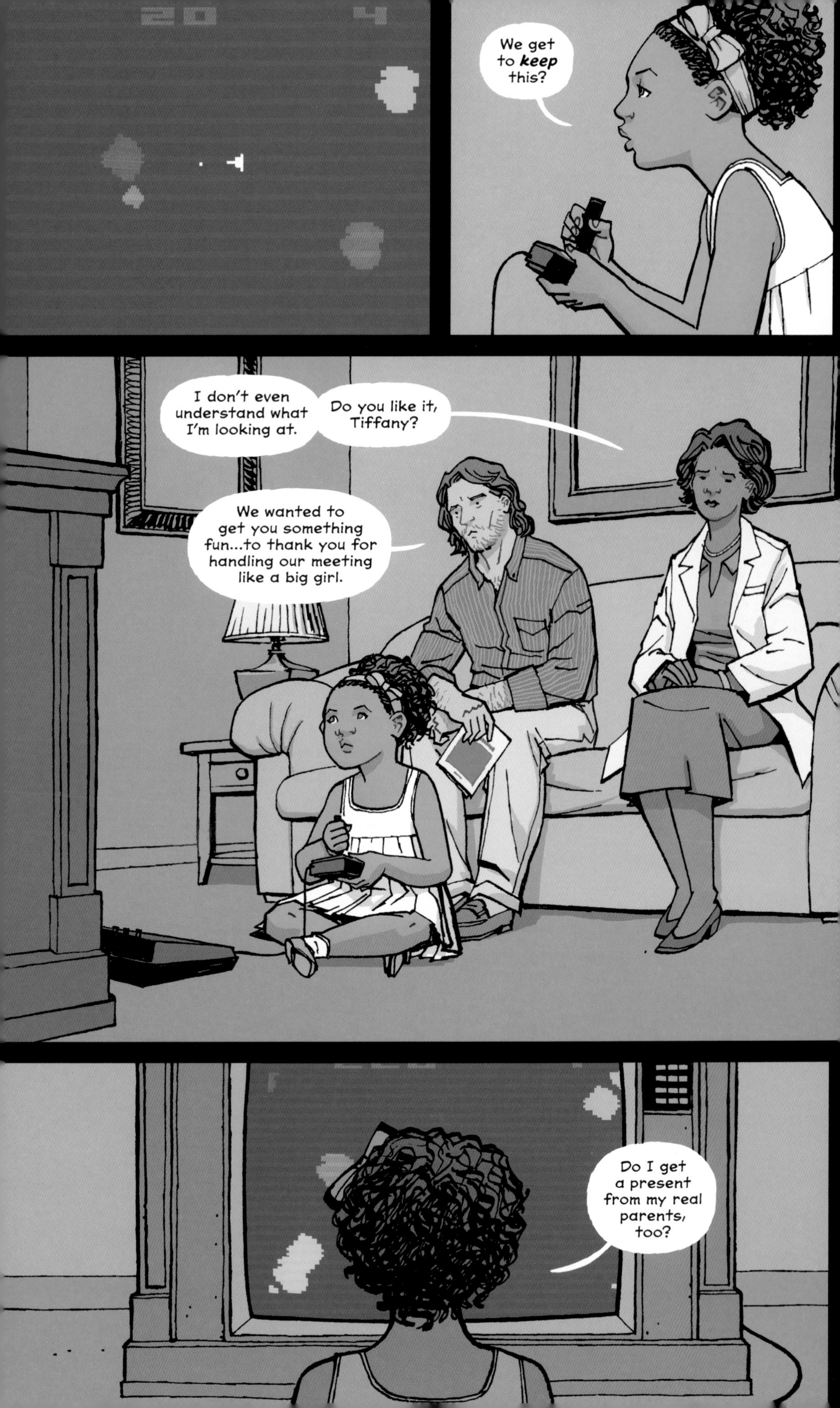

20
4
We get to *keep* this?
I don't even understand what I'm looking at.
Do you like it, Tiffany?
We wanted to get you something fun...to thank you for handling our meeting like a big girl.
Do I get a present from my real parents, too?

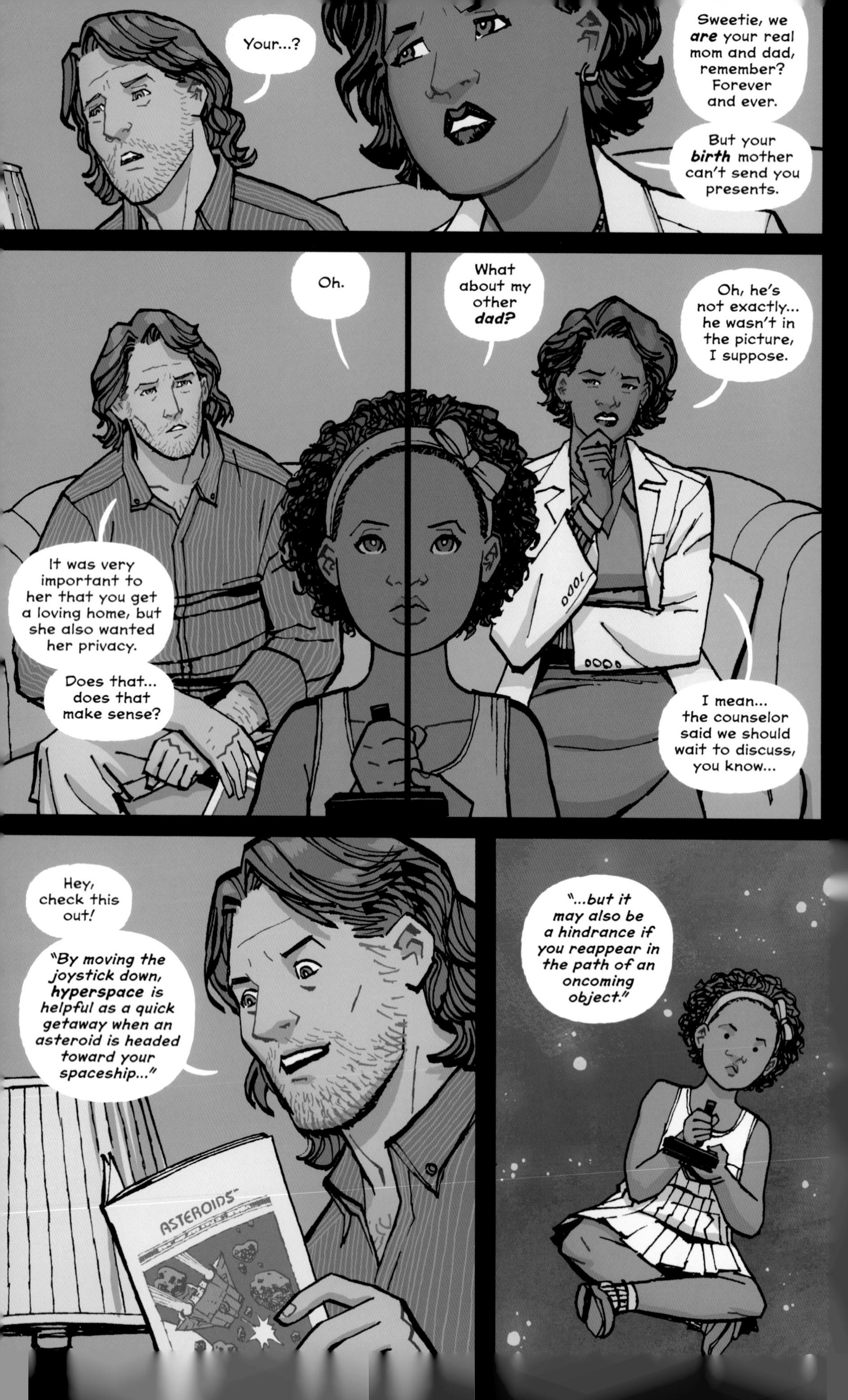
Your...?
Sweetie, we are your real mom and dad, remember? Forever and ever.
But your birth mother can't send you presents.
Oh.
What about my other dad?
Oh, he's not exactly... he wasn't in the picture, I suppose.
It was very important to her that you get a loving home, but she also wanted her privacy.
Does that... does that make sense?
I mean... the counselor said we should wait to discuss, you know...
Hey, check this out!
"By moving the joystick down, hyperspace is helpful as a quick getaway when an asteroid is headed toward your spaceship..."
ASTEROIDS
"...but it may also be a hindrance if you reappear in the path of an oncoming object."

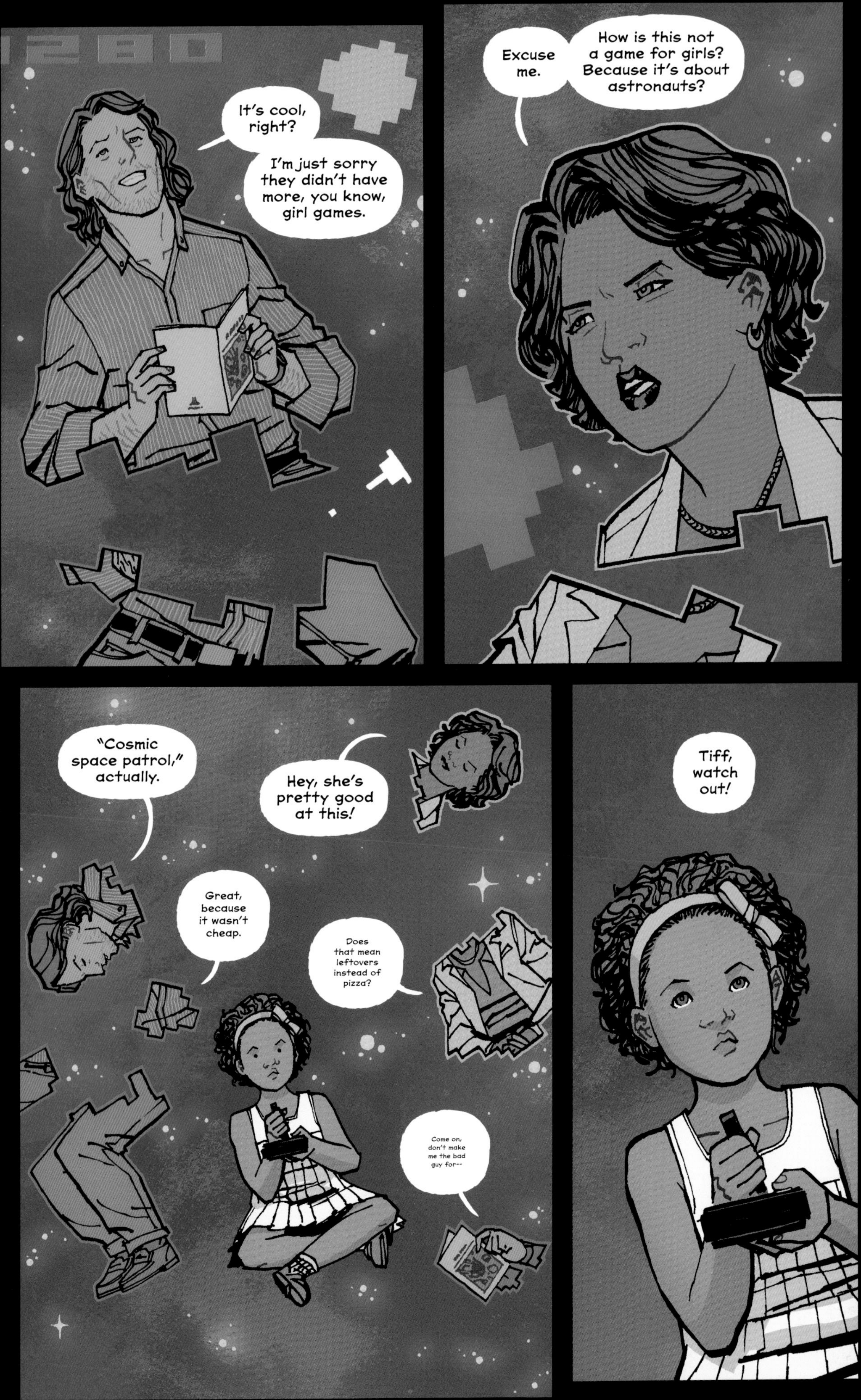
It's cool, right?
I'm just sorry they didn't have more, you know, girl games.
Excuse me.
How is this not a game for girls? Because it's about astronauts?
"Cosmic space patrol," actually.
Hey, she's pretty good at this!
Great, because it wasn't cheap.
Does that mean leftovers instead of pizza?
Come on, don't make me the bad guy for--
Tiff, watch out!

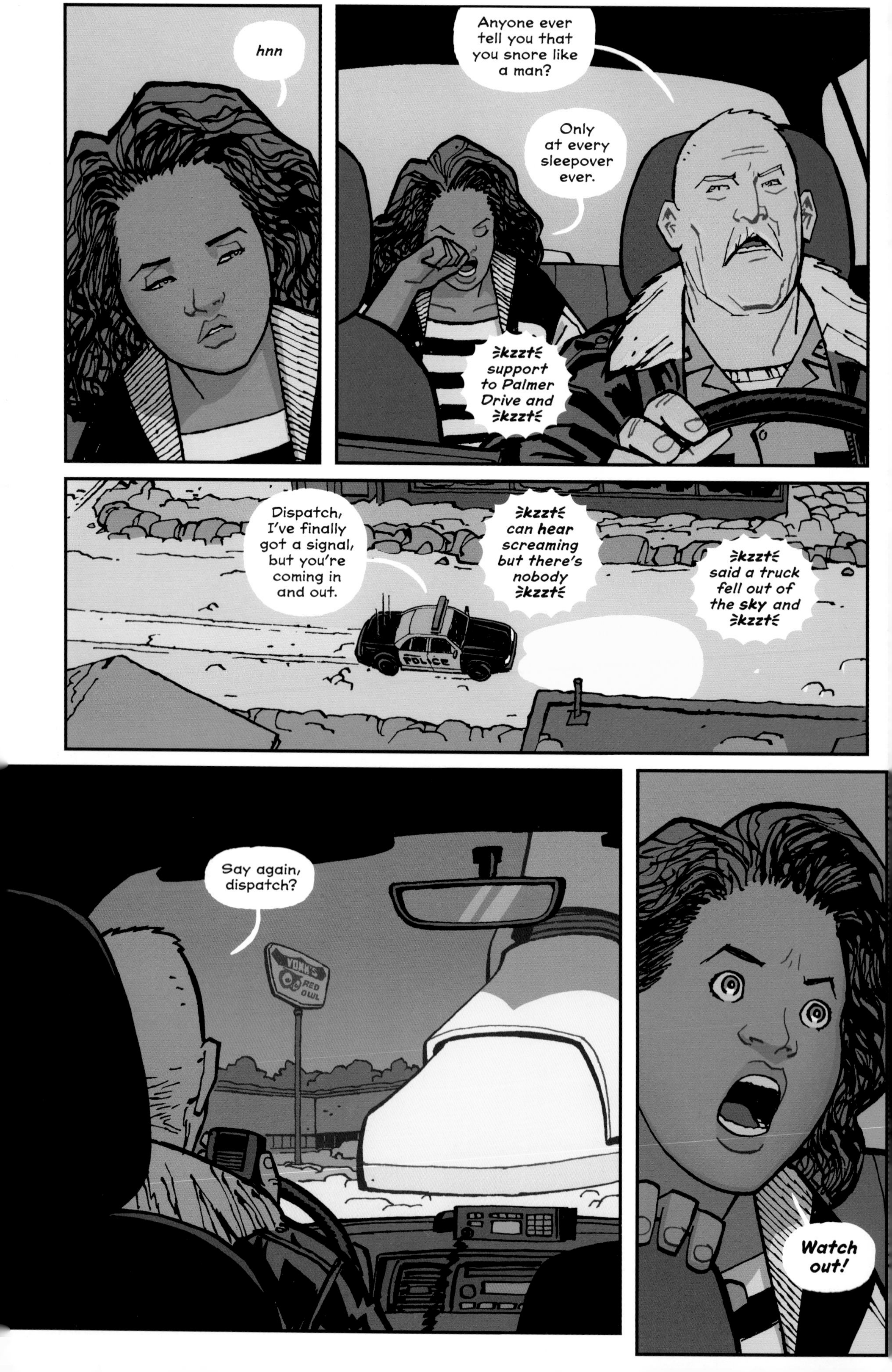

hnn
Anyone ever tell you that you snore like a man?
Only at every sleepover ever.
kzzt support to Palmer Drive and kzzt
Dispatch, I've finally got a signal, but you're coming in and out.
kzzt can hear screaming but there's nobody kzzt
kzzt said a truck fell out of the sky and kzzt
POLICE
Say again, dispatch?
YONK'S RED OWL
Watch out!

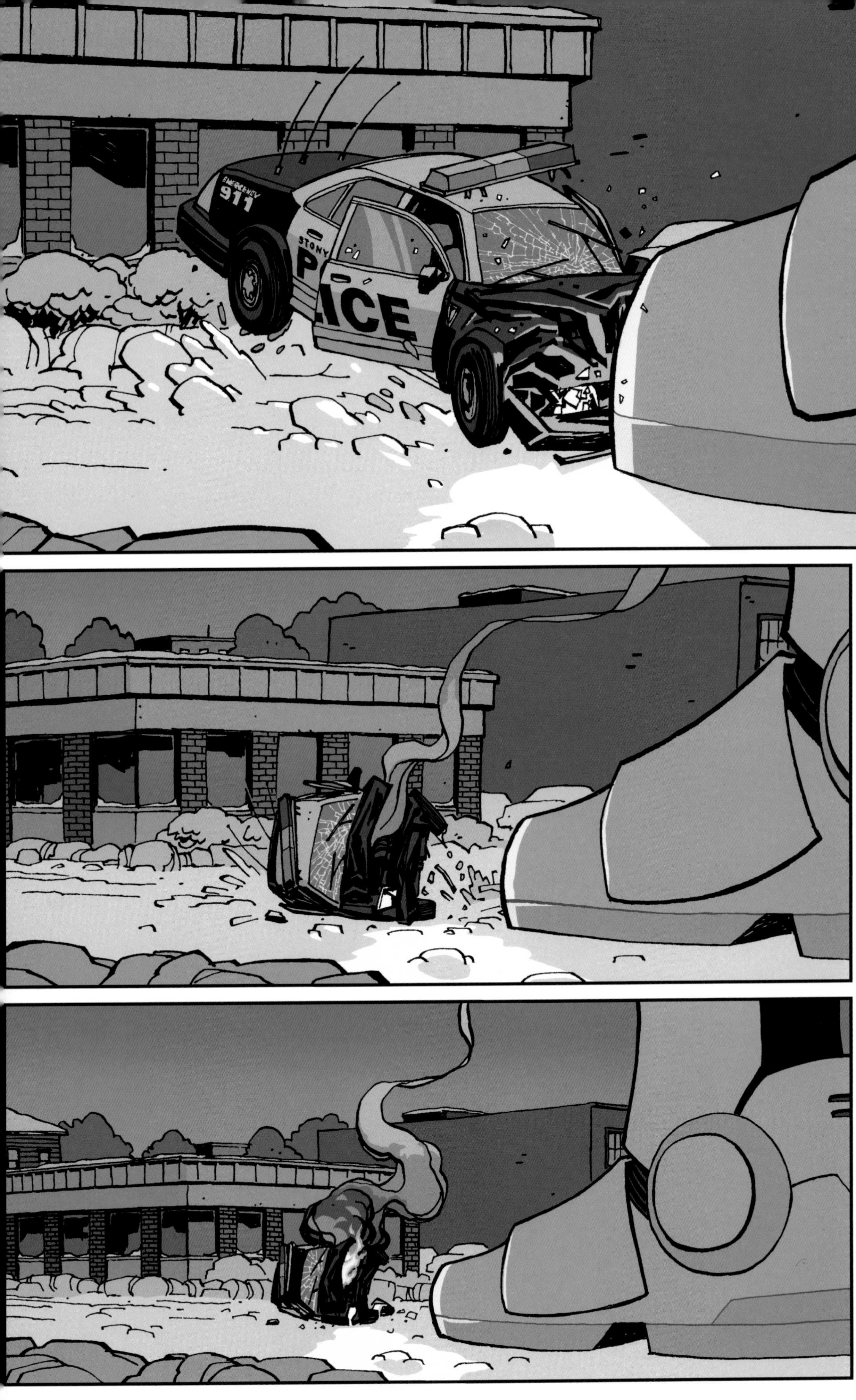
911
STONY

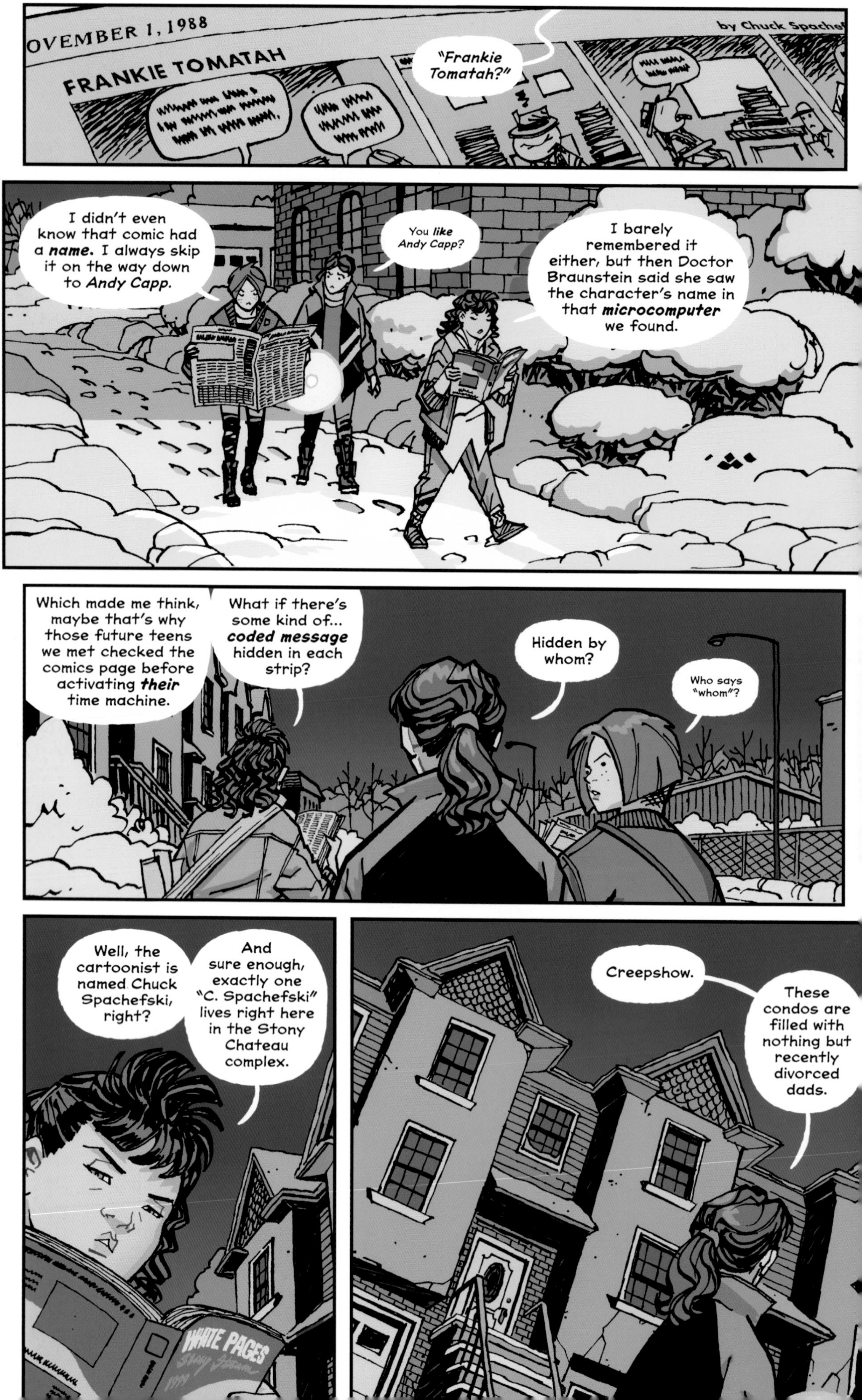
OVEMBER 1, 1988
FRANKIE TOMATAH
by Chuck Spachef
"Frankie Tomatah?"
I didn't even know that comic had a *name.* I always skip it on the way down to *Andy Capp.*
You *like* Andy Capp?
I barely remembered it either, but then Doctor Braunstein said she saw the character's name in that *microcomputer* we found.
Which made me think, maybe that's why those future teens we met checked the comics page before activating *their* time machine.
What if there's some kind of... *coded message* hidden in each strip?
Hidden by whom?
Who says "whom"?
Well, the cartoonist is named Chuck Spachefski, right?
And sure enough, exactly one "C. Spachefski" lives right here in the Stony Chateau complex.
WHITE PAGES
Creepshow.
These condos are filled with nothing but recently divorced dads.

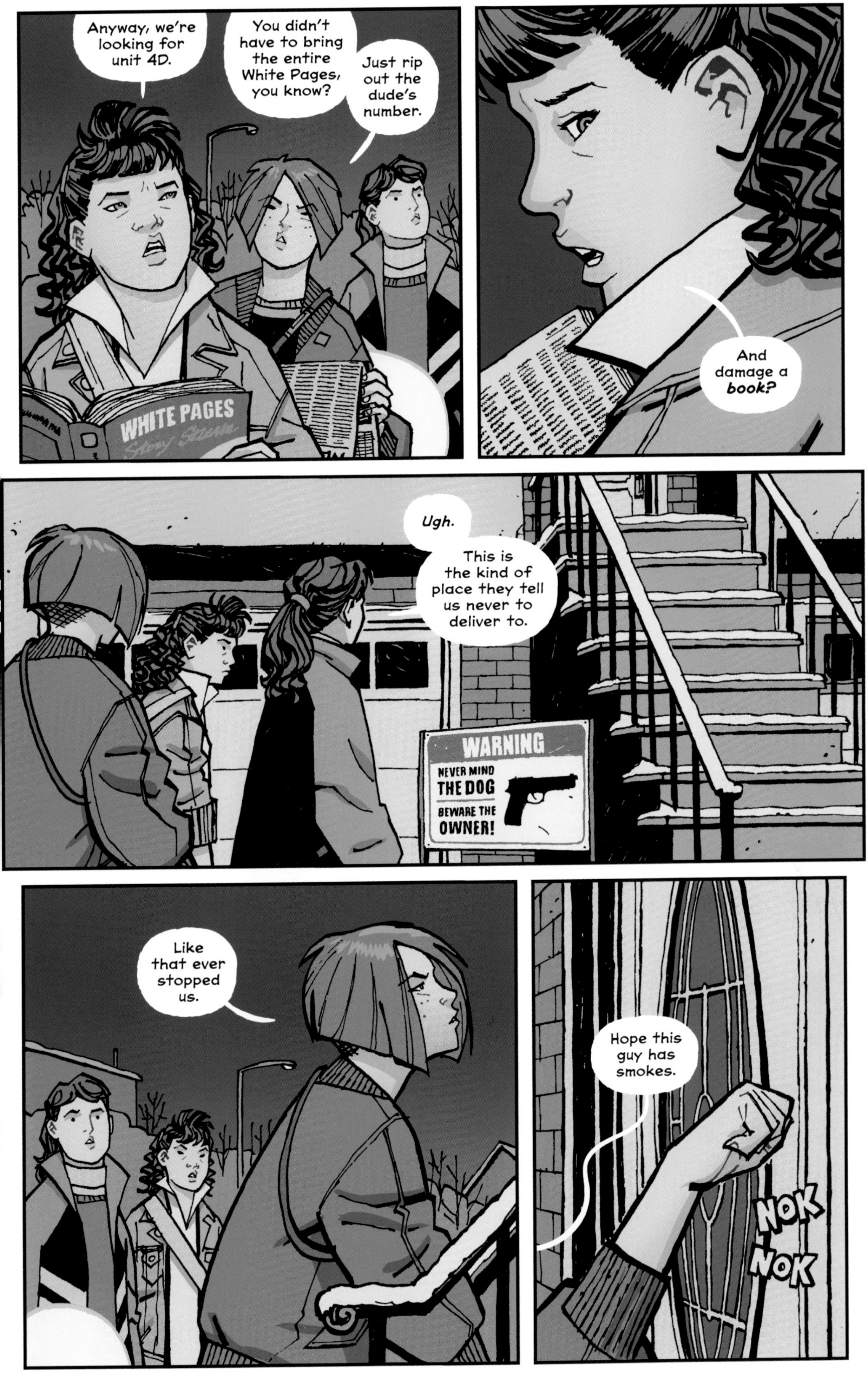
Anyway, we're looking for unit 4D.
You didn't have to bring the entire White Pages, you know?
Just rip out the dude's number.
WHITE PAGES
And damage a *book?*
Ugh.
This is the kind of place they tell us never to deliver to.
WARNING
NEVER MIND THE DOG
BEWARE THE OWNER!
Like that ever stopped us.
Hope this guy has smokes.
NOK
NOK

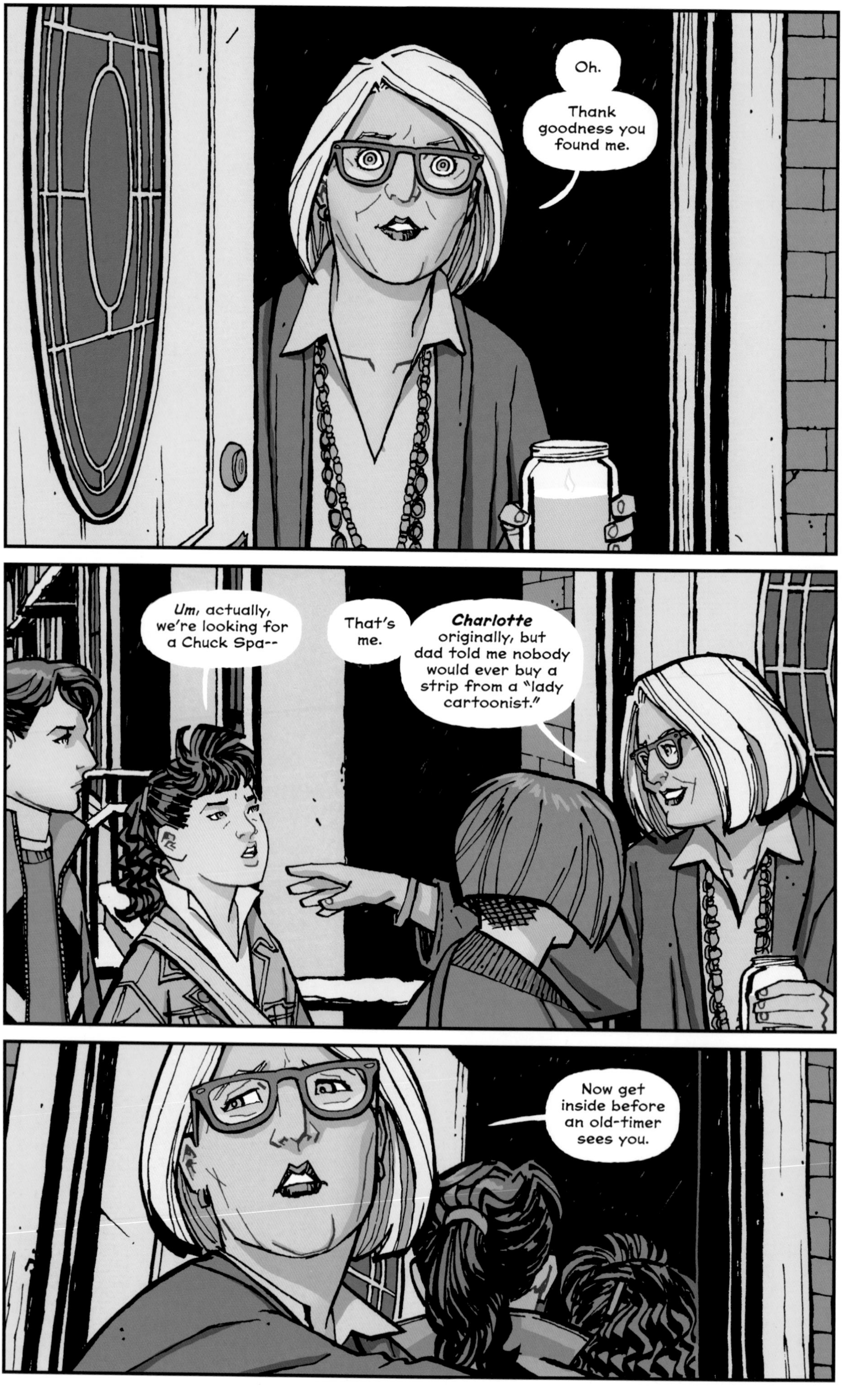
Oh.
Thank goodness you found me.
Um, actually, we're looking for a Chuck Spa--
That's me.
Charlotte originally, but dad told me nobody would ever buy a strip from a "lady cartoonist."
Now get inside before an old-timer sees you.

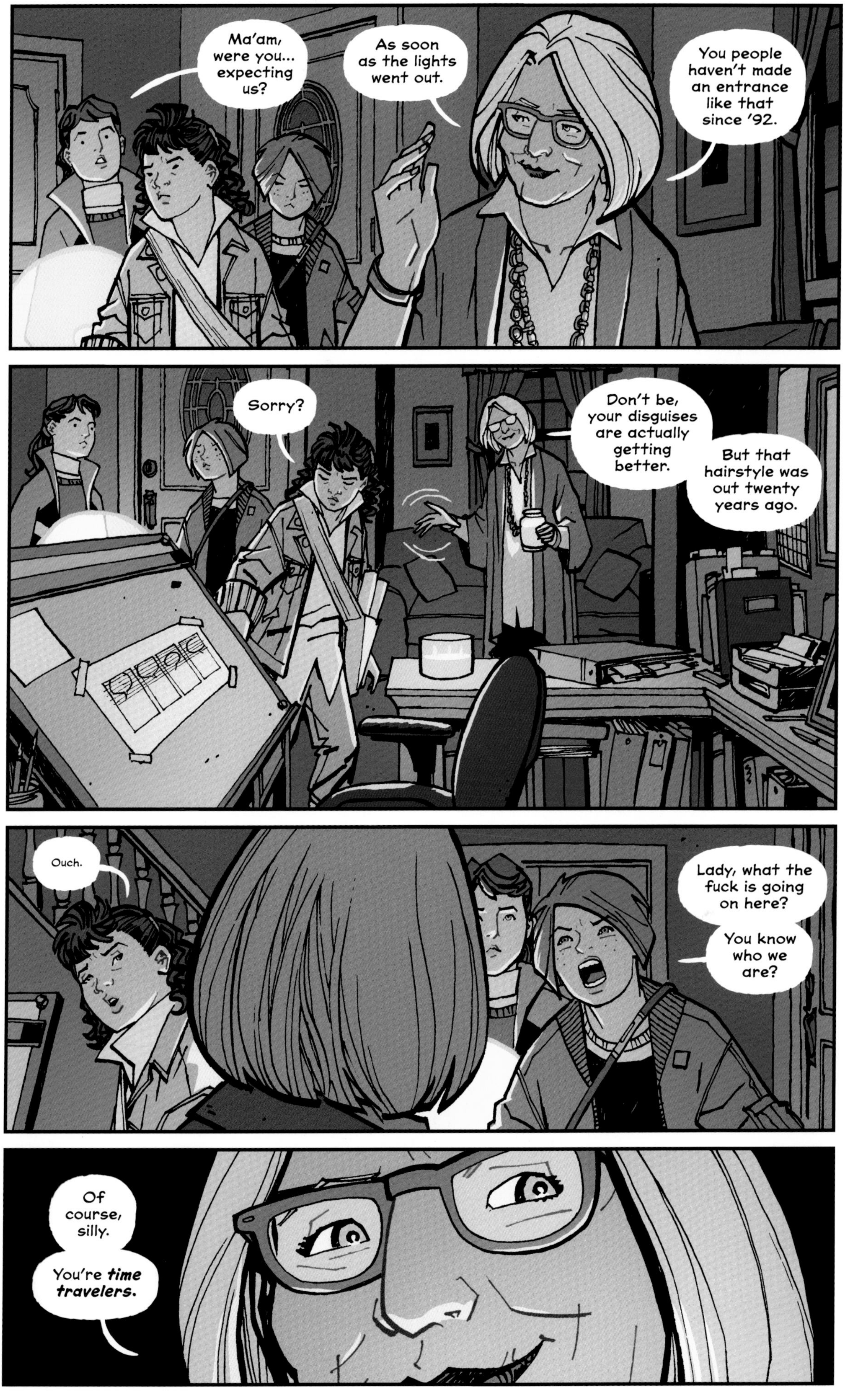
Ma'am, were you... expecting us?
As soon as the lights went out.
You people haven't made an entrance like that since '92.
Sorry?
Don't be, your disguises are actually getting better.
But that hairstyle was out twenty years ago.
Ouch.
Lady, what the fuck is going on here?
You know who we are?
Of course, silly.
You're ***time travelers.***

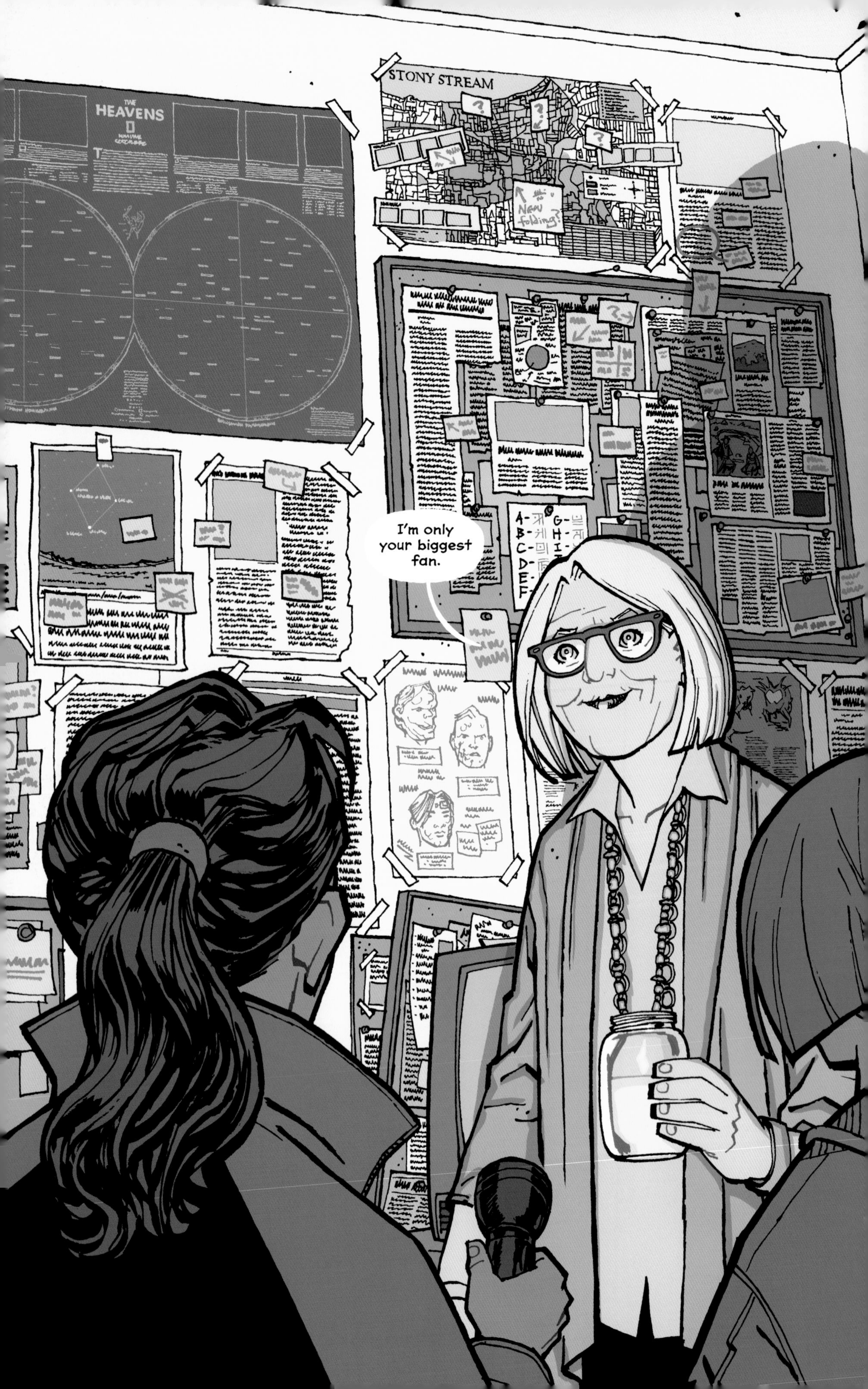

THE HEAVENS
STONY STREAM
New folding?
I'm only your biggest fan.

CHAPTER

17

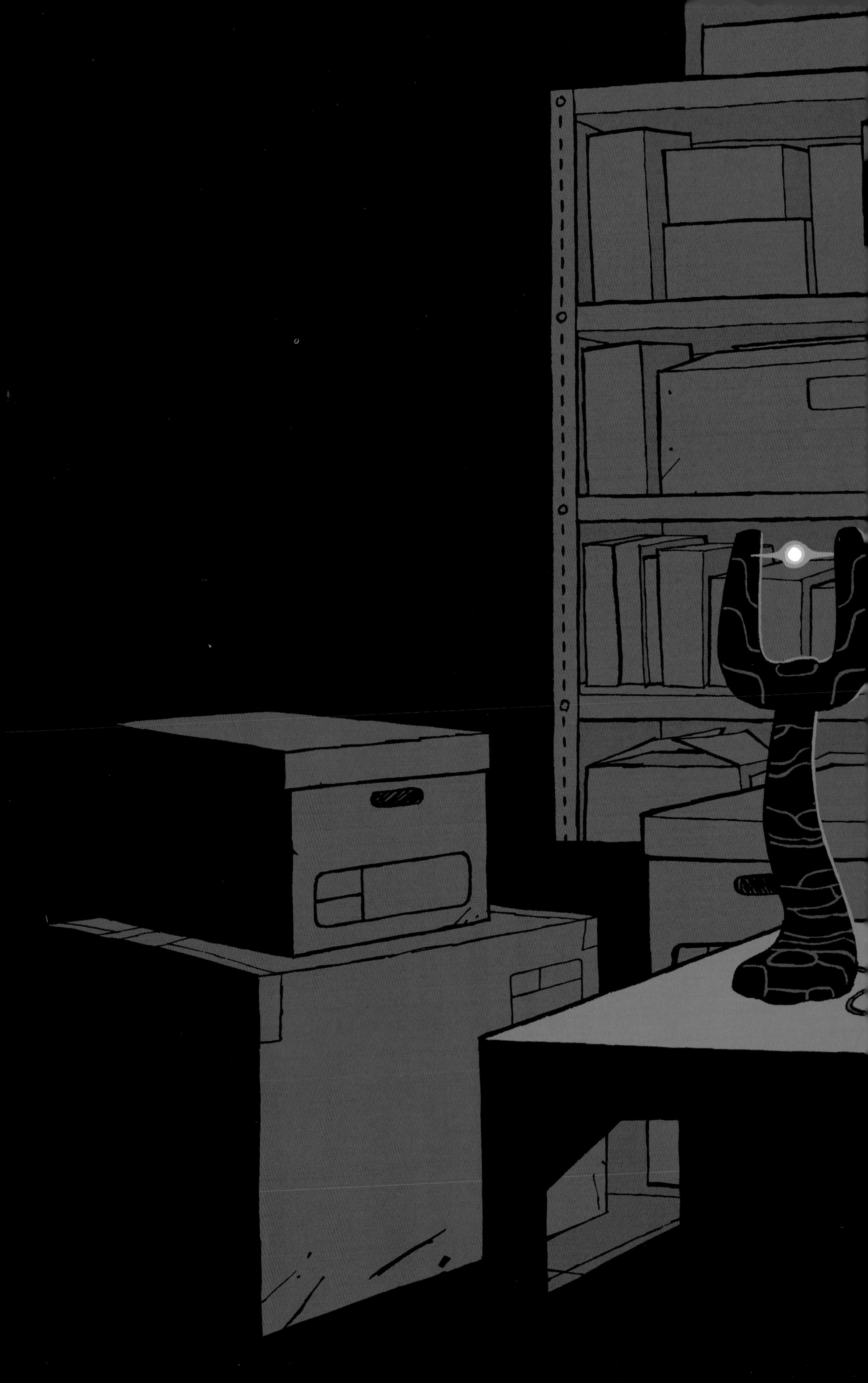

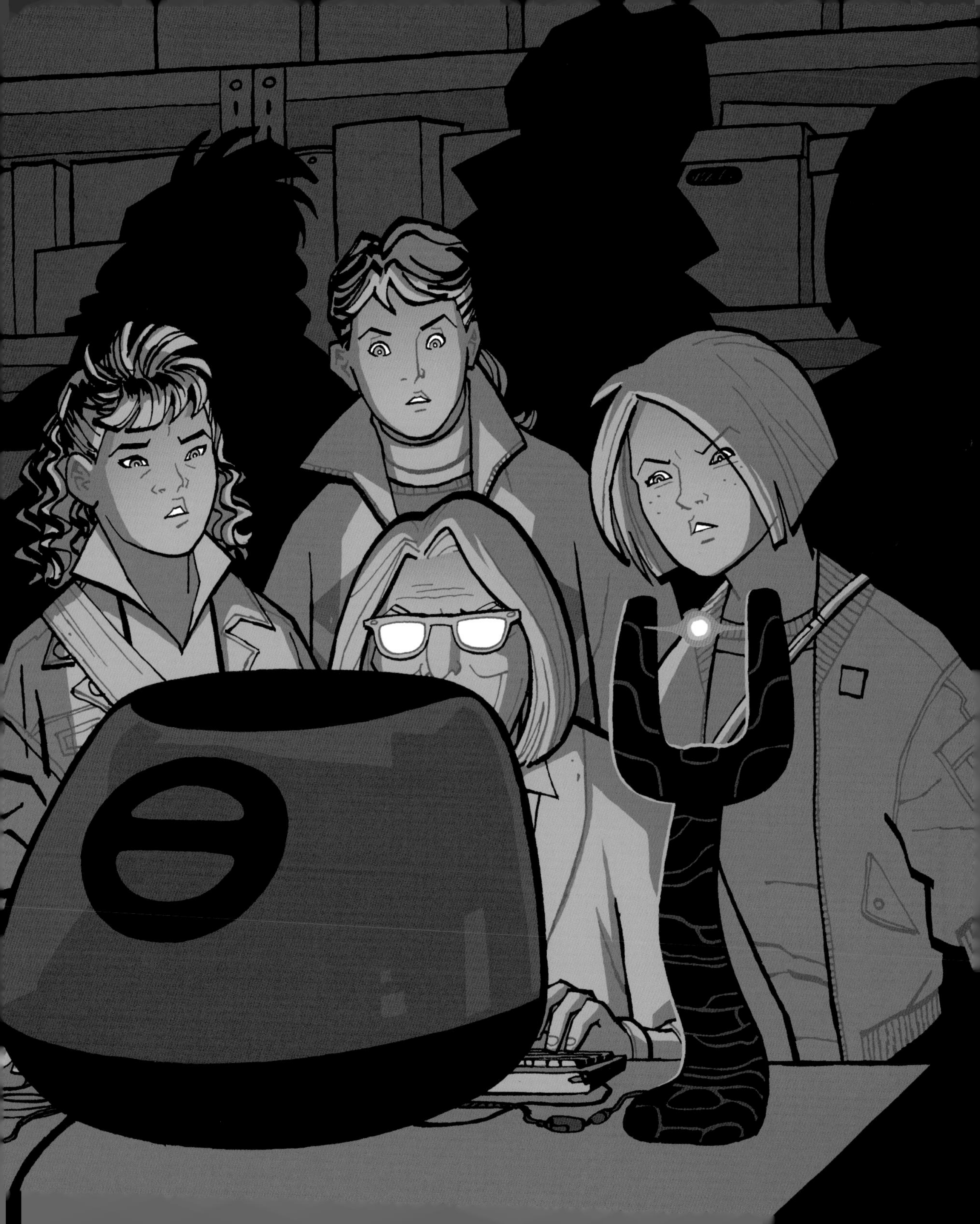

"THE END OF THE WORLD?!?
Y2K Insanity!
Will computers melt down?
Will society?"

-**Time Magazine** cover,
January 18, 1999

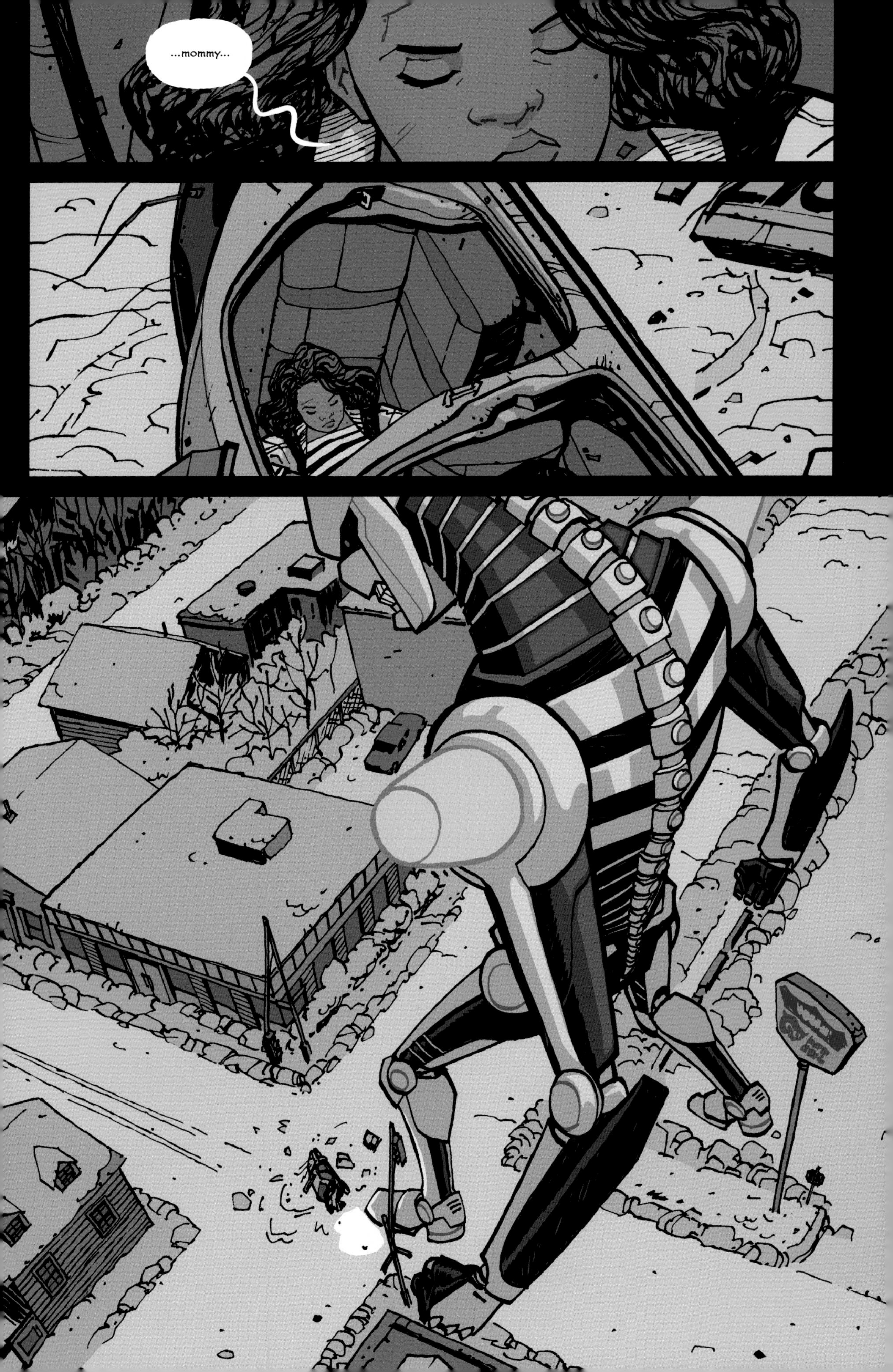
...mommy...

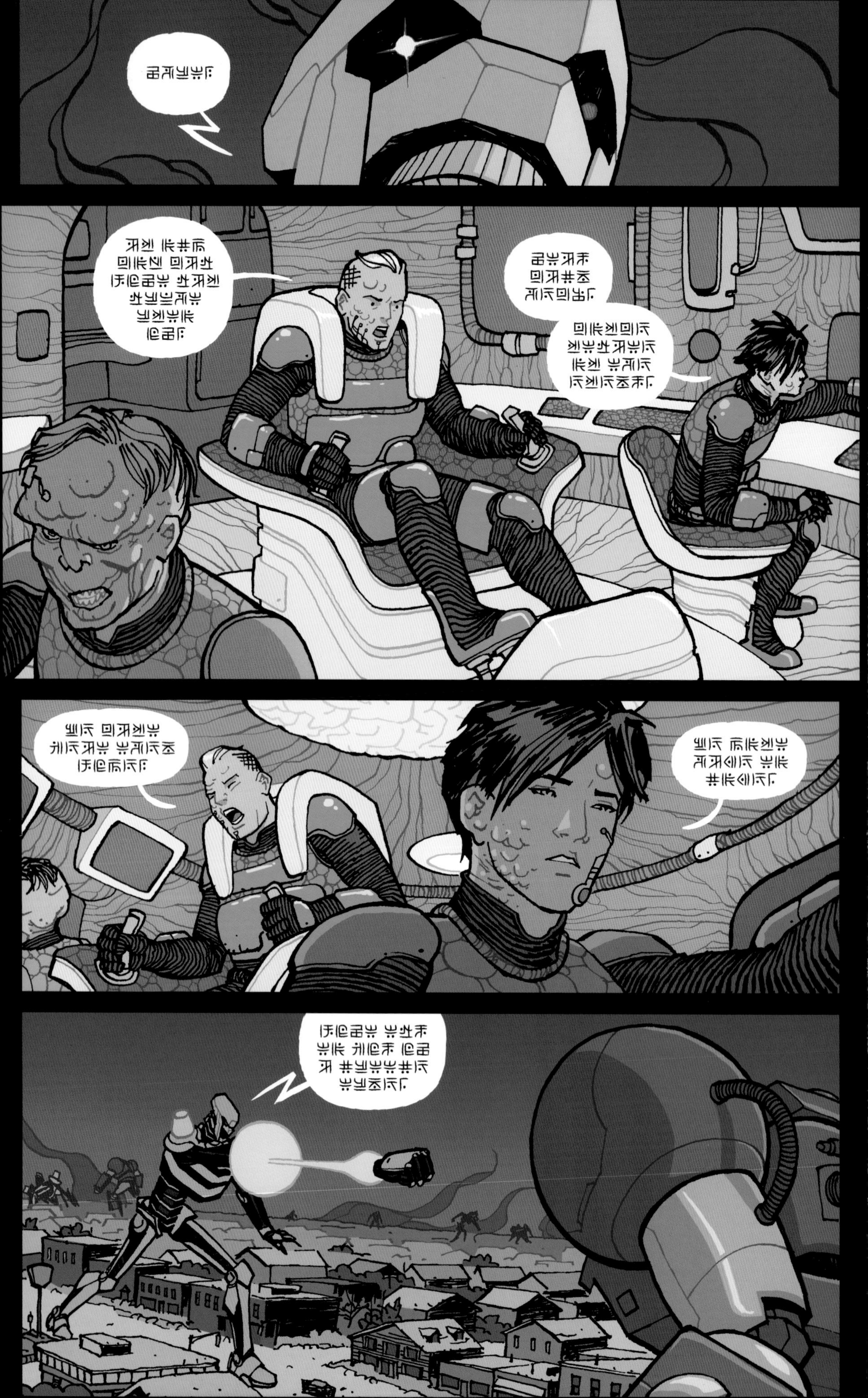

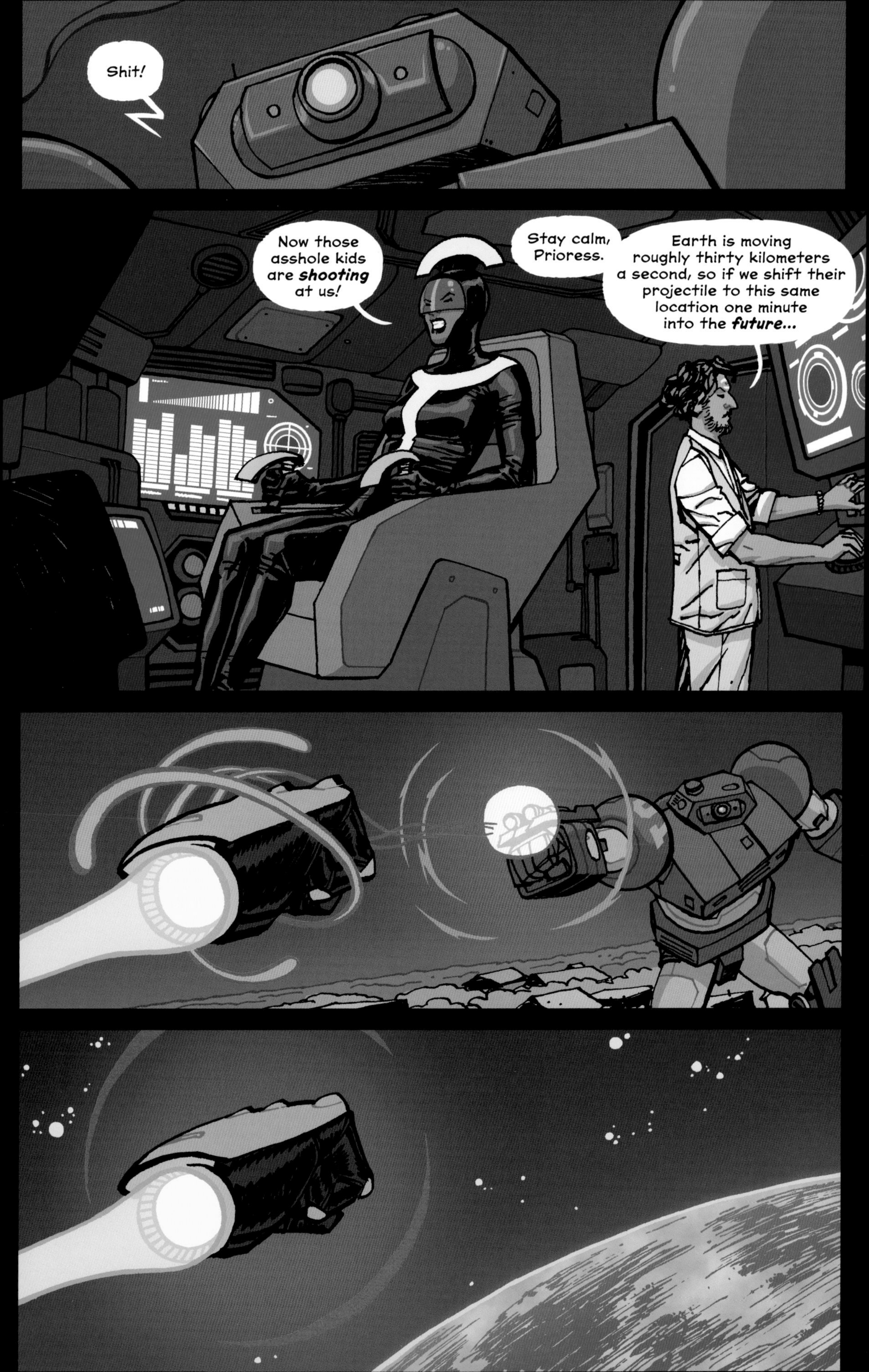
Shit!
Now those asshole kids are ***shooting*** at us!
Stay calm, Prioress.
Earth is moving roughly thirty kilometers a second, so if we shift their projectile to this same location one minute into the ***future...***

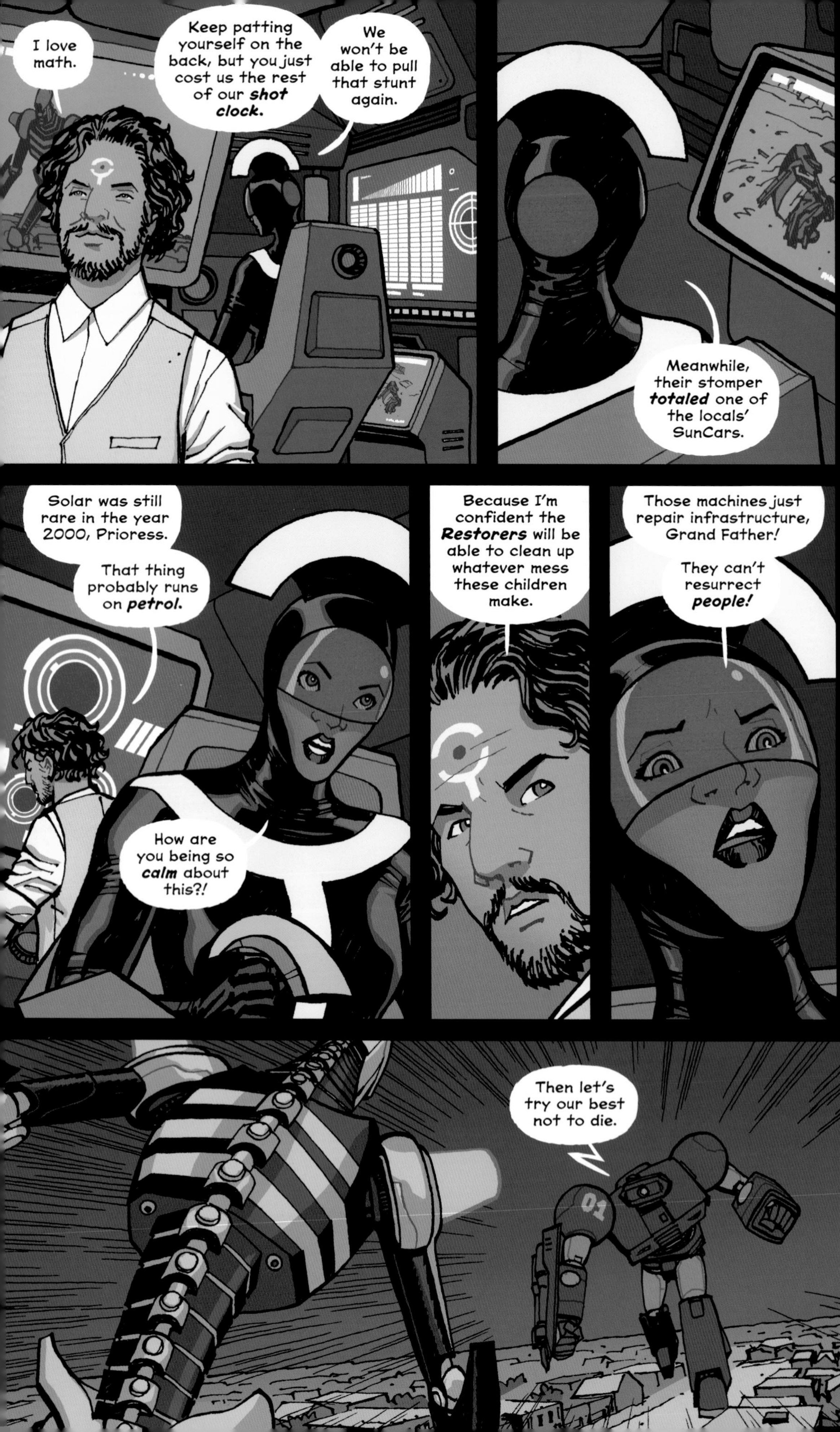
I love math.
Keep patting yourself on the back, but you just cost us the rest of our **shot clock.**
We won't be able to pull that stunt again.
Meanwhile, their stomper **totaled** one of the locals' SunCars.
Solar was still rare in the year 2000, Prioress.
That thing probably runs on **petrol.**
How are you being so **calm** about this?!
Because I'm confident the **Restorers** will be able to clean up whatever mess these children make.
Those machines just repair infrastructure, Grand Father!
They can't resurrect **people!**
Then let's try our best not to die.
01

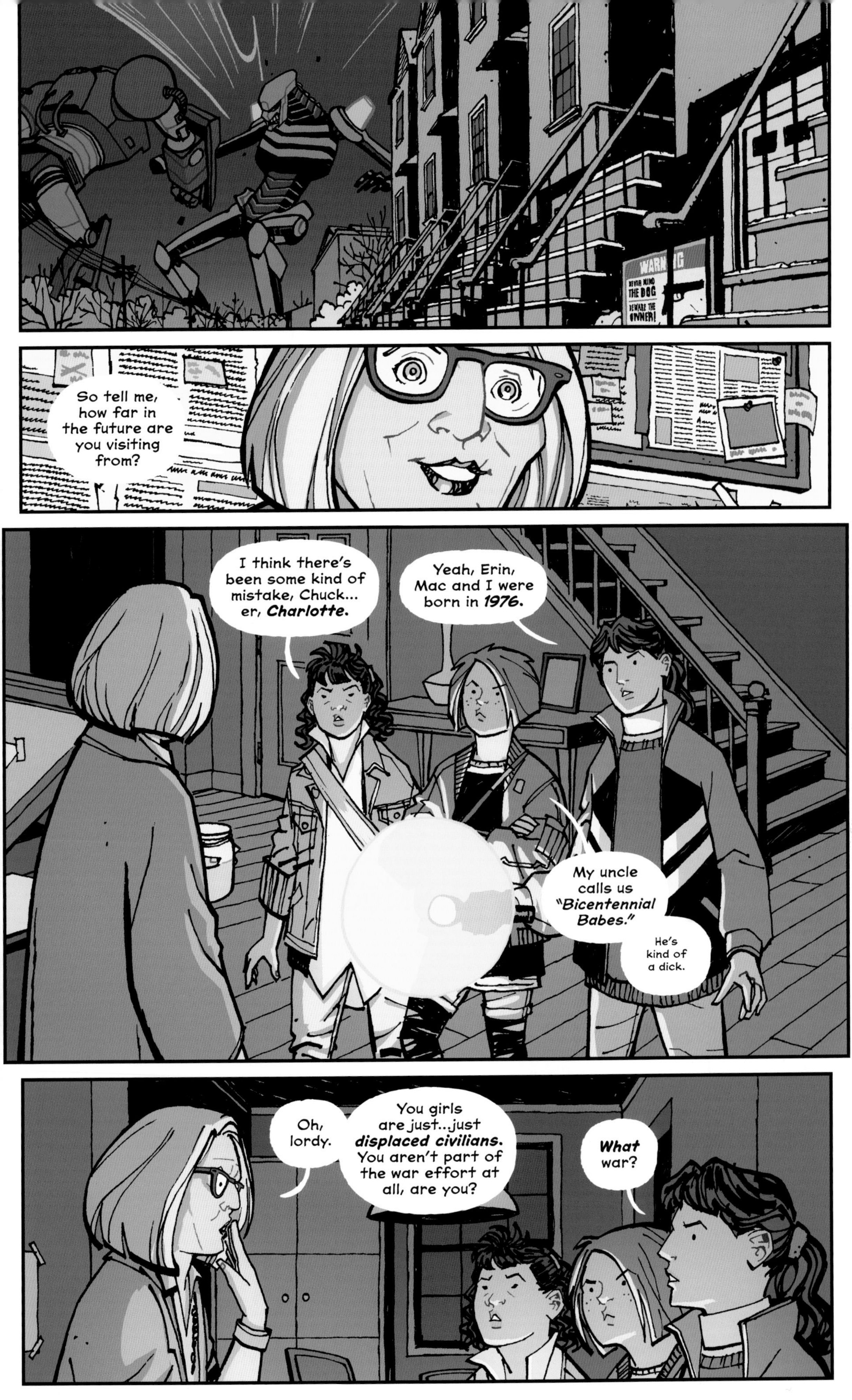
NEVER MIND THE DOG
BEWARE THE OWNER!
So tell me, how far in the future are you visiting from?
I think there's been some kind of mistake, Chuck... er, *Charlotte.*
Yeah, Erin, Mac and I were born in *1976.*
My uncle calls us *"Bicentennial Babes."*
He's kind of a dick.
Oh, lordy.
You girls are just...just *displaced civilians.* You aren't part of the war effort at all, are you?
What war?

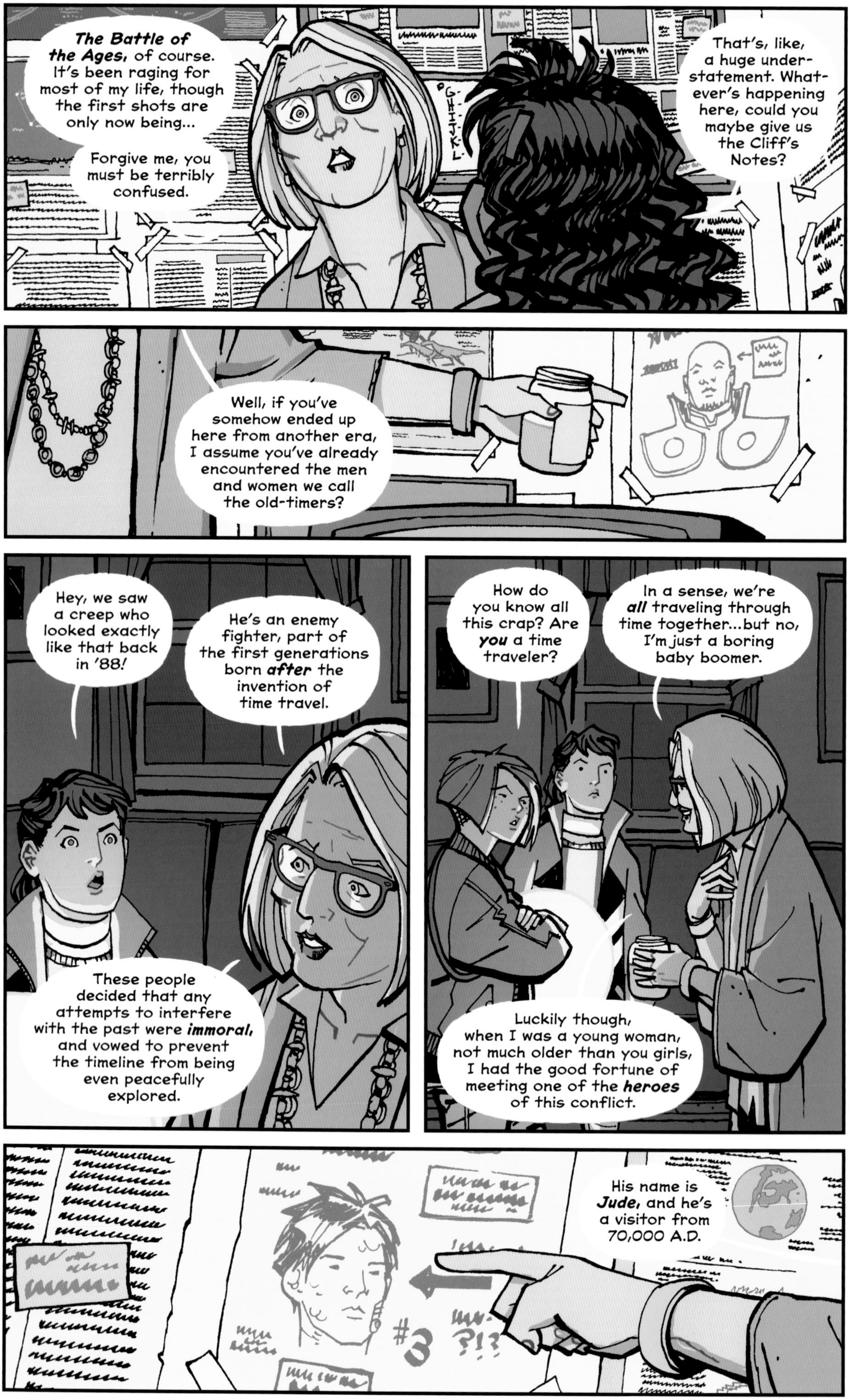

The Battle of the Ages, of course. It's been raging for most of my life, though the first shots are only now being...
Forgive me, you must be terribly confused.
That's, like, a huge understatement. Whatever's happening here, could you maybe give us the Cliff's Notes?
Well, if you've somehow ended up here from another era, I assume you've already encountered the men and women we call the old-timers?
Hey, we saw a creep who looked exactly like that back in '88!
He's an enemy fighter, part of the first generations born ***after*** the invention of time travel.
These people decided that any attempts to interfere with the past were ***immoral,*** and vowed to prevent the timeline from being even peacefully explored.
How do you know all this crap? Are ***you*** a time traveler?
In a sense, we're ***all*** traveling through time together...but no, I'm just a boring baby boomer.
Luckily though, when I was a young woman, not much older than you girls, I had the good fortune of meeting one of the ***heroes*** of this conflict.
His name is ***Jude,*** and he's a visitor from 70,000 A.D.
#3
?!?

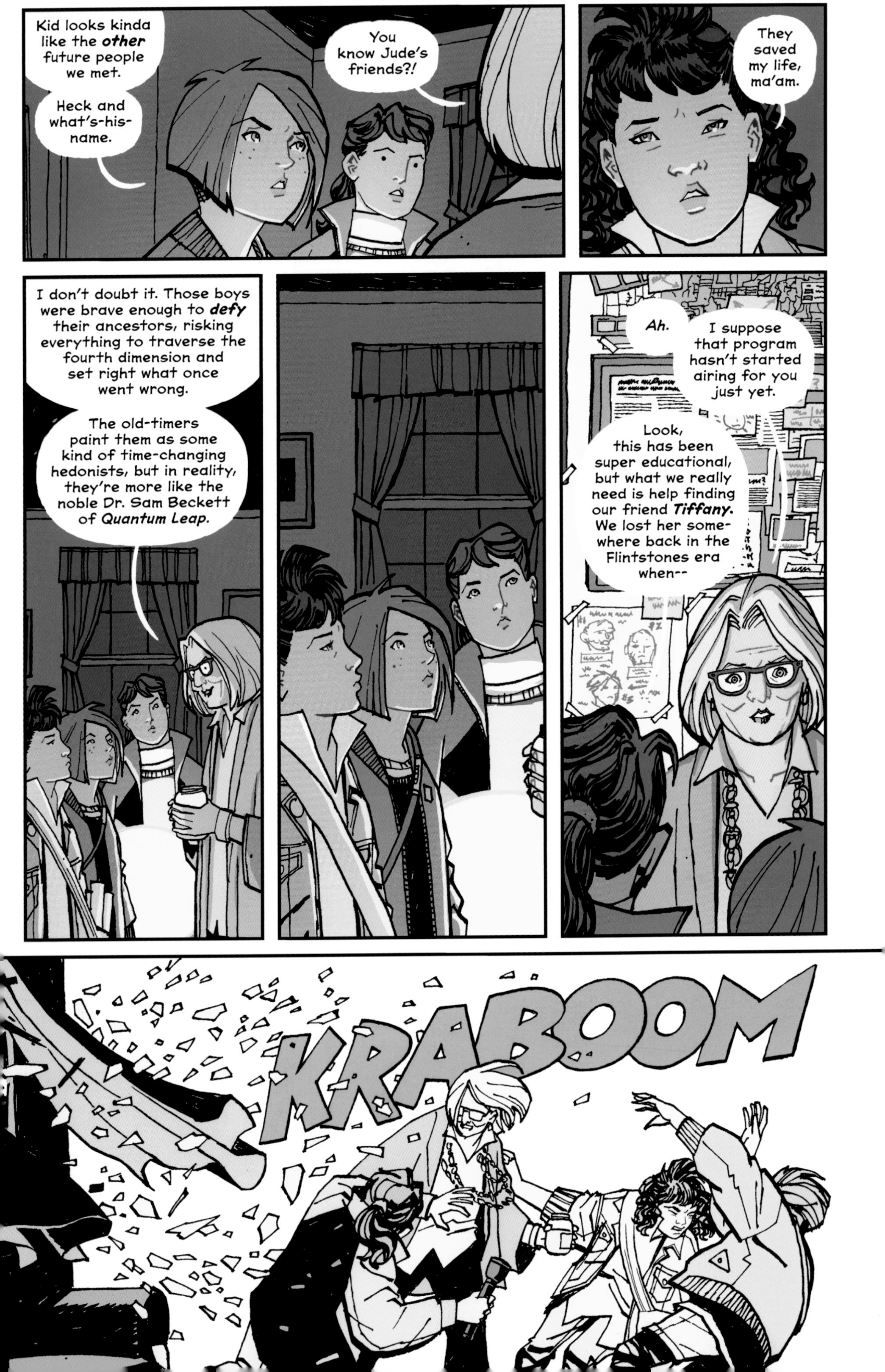

Kid looks kinda like the *other* future people we met.
Heck and what's-his-name.
You know Jude's friends?!
They saved my life, ma'am.
I don't doubt it. Those boys were brave enough to *defy* their ancestors, risking everything to traverse the fourth dimension and set right what once went wrong.
The old-timers paint them as some kind of time-changing hedonists, but in reality, they're more like the noble Dr. Sam Beckett of *Quantum Leap.*
Ah.
I suppose that program hasn't started airing for you just yet.
Look, this has been super educational, but what we really need is help finding our friend *Tiffany.* We lost her somewhere back in the Flintstones era when--
KRABOOM

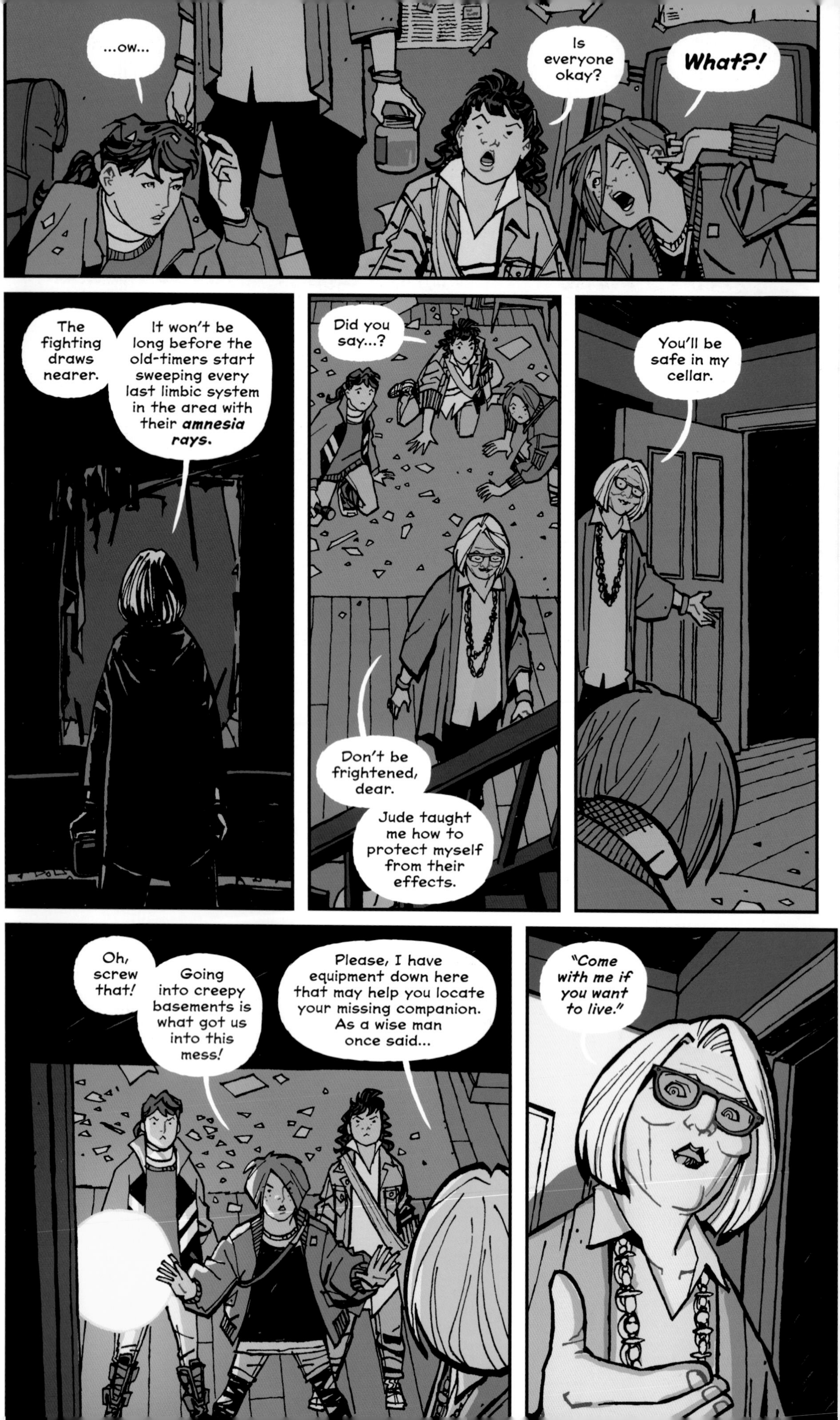
...ow...
Is everyone okay?
What?!
The fighting draws nearer.
It won't be long before the old-timers start sweeping every last limbic system in the area with their *amnesia rays.*
Did you say...?
Don't be frightened, dear.
Jude taught me how to protect myself from their effects.
You'll be safe in my cellar.
Oh, screw that!
Going into creepy basements is what got us into this mess!
Please, I have equipment down here that may help you locate your missing companion. As a wise man once said...
"Come with me if you want to live."

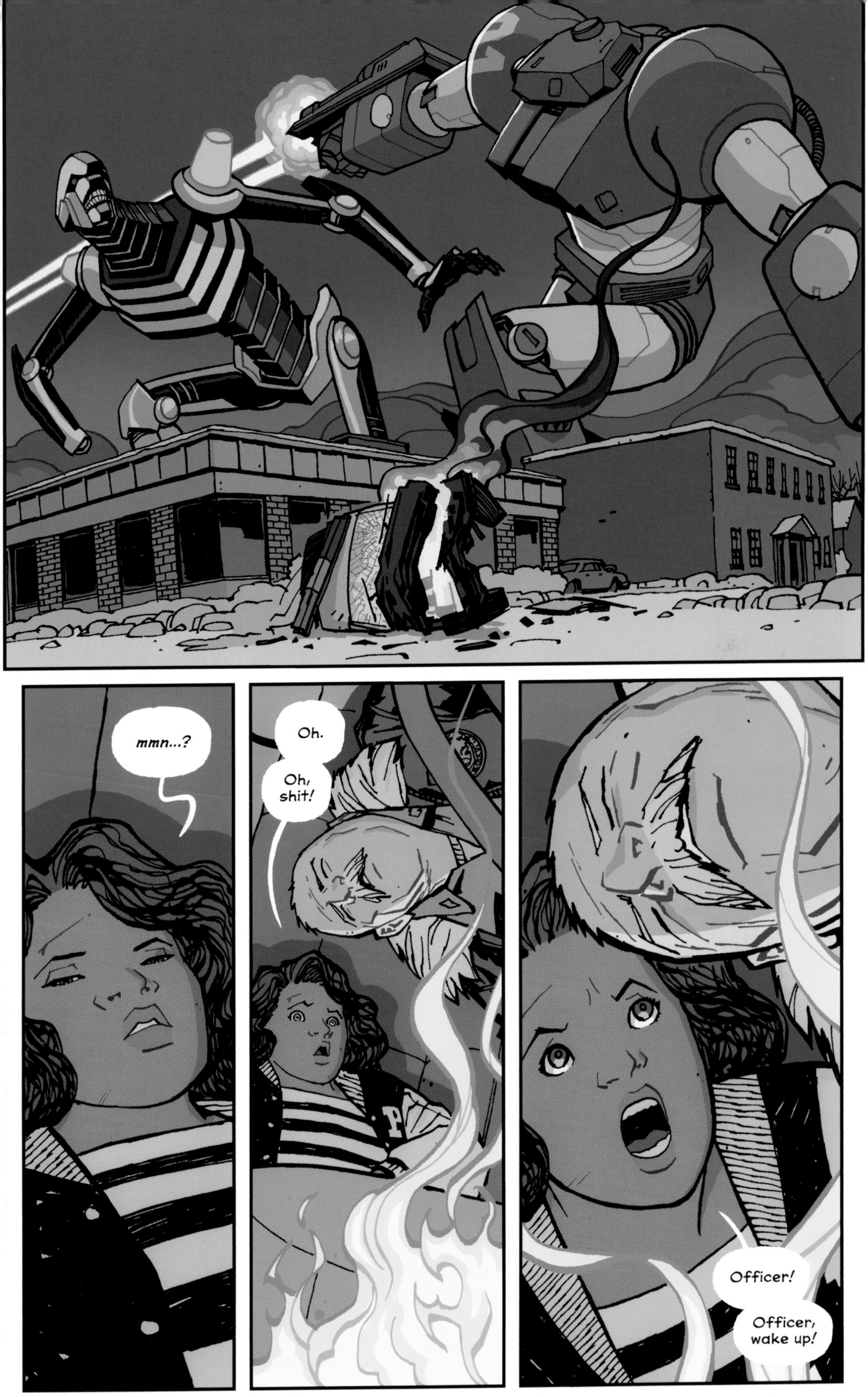
mmn...?
Oh.
Oh, shit!
Officer!
Officer, wake up!

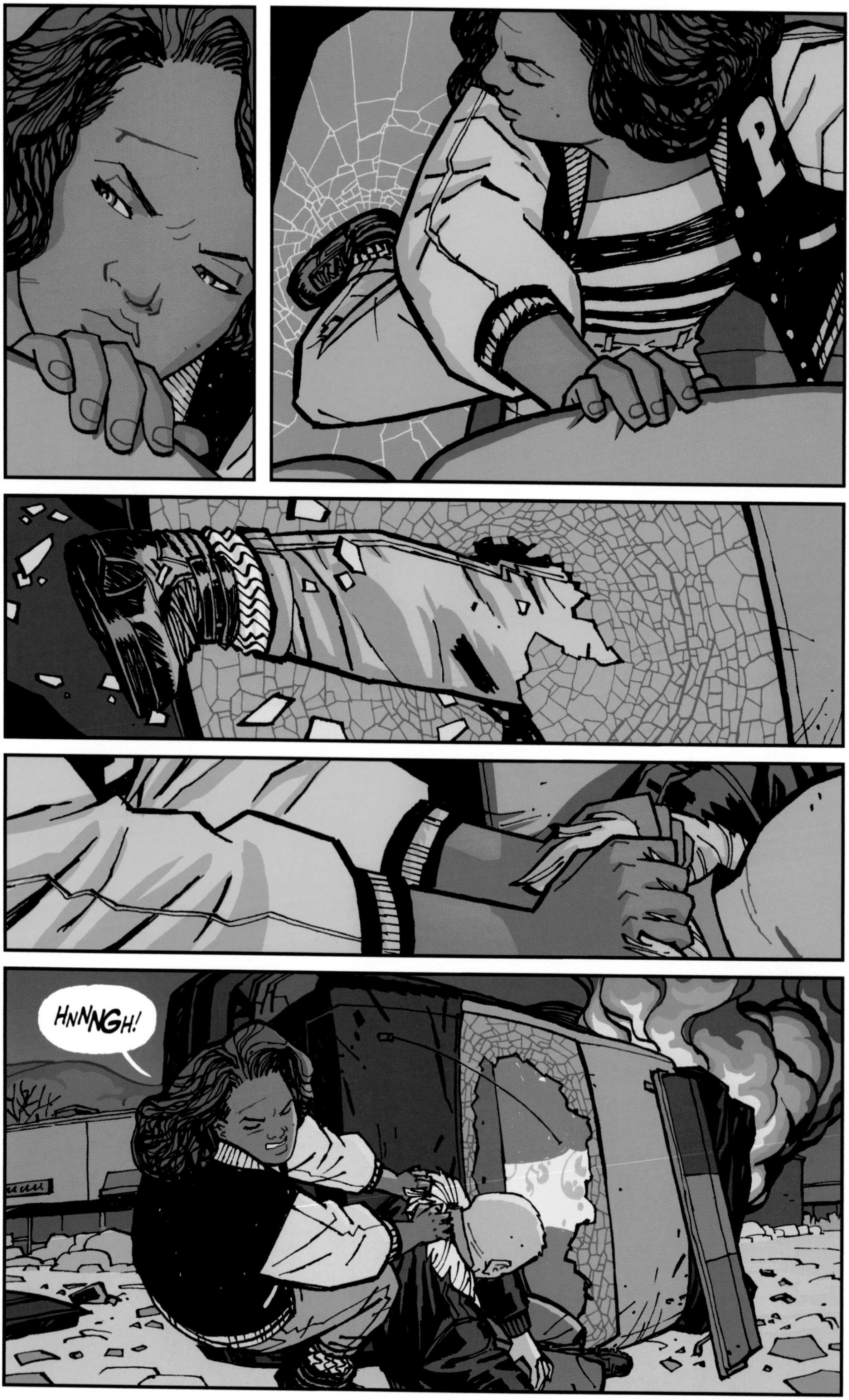
HNNNGH!

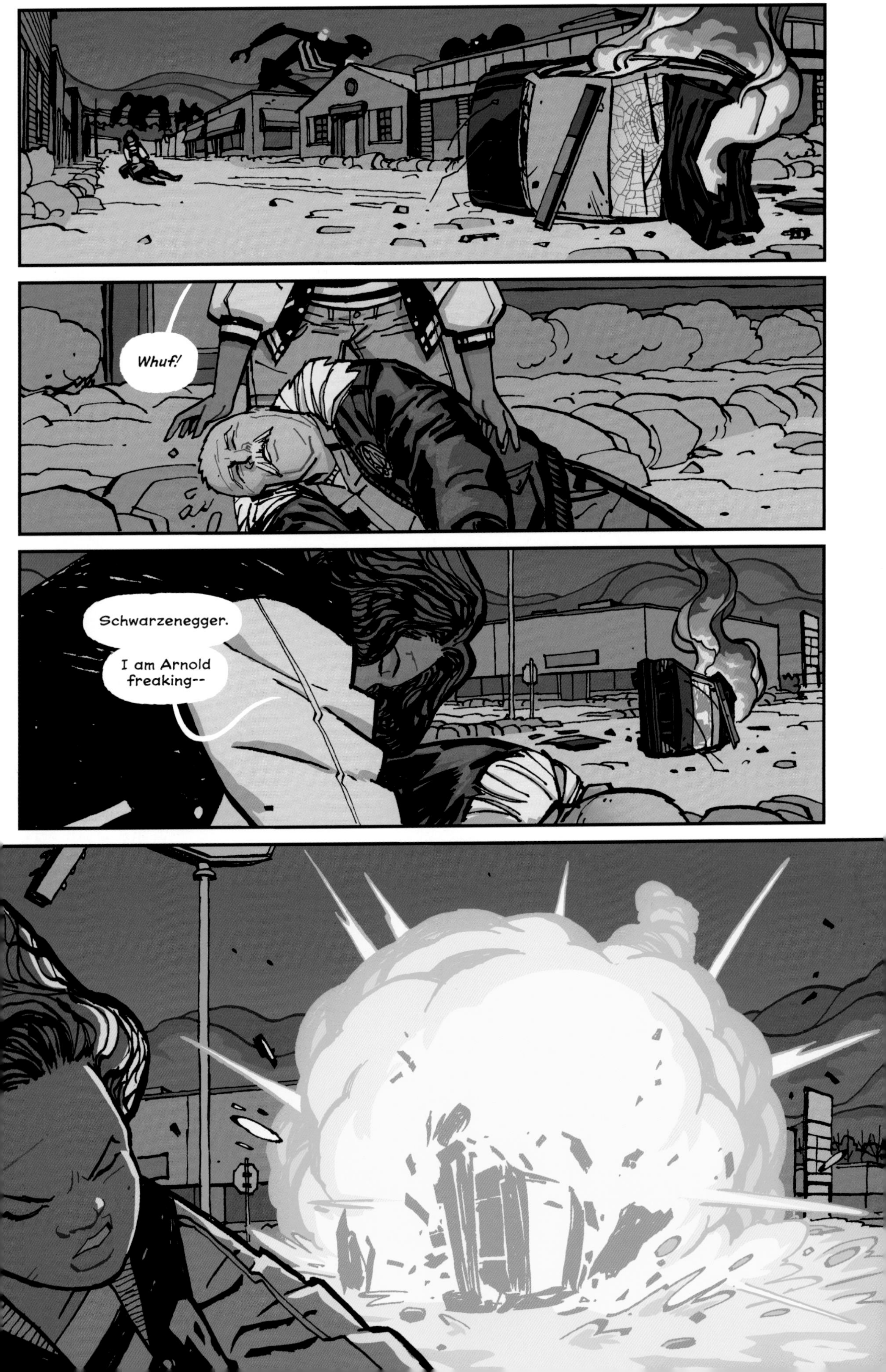
Whuf!
Schwarzenegger.
I am Arnold freaking--

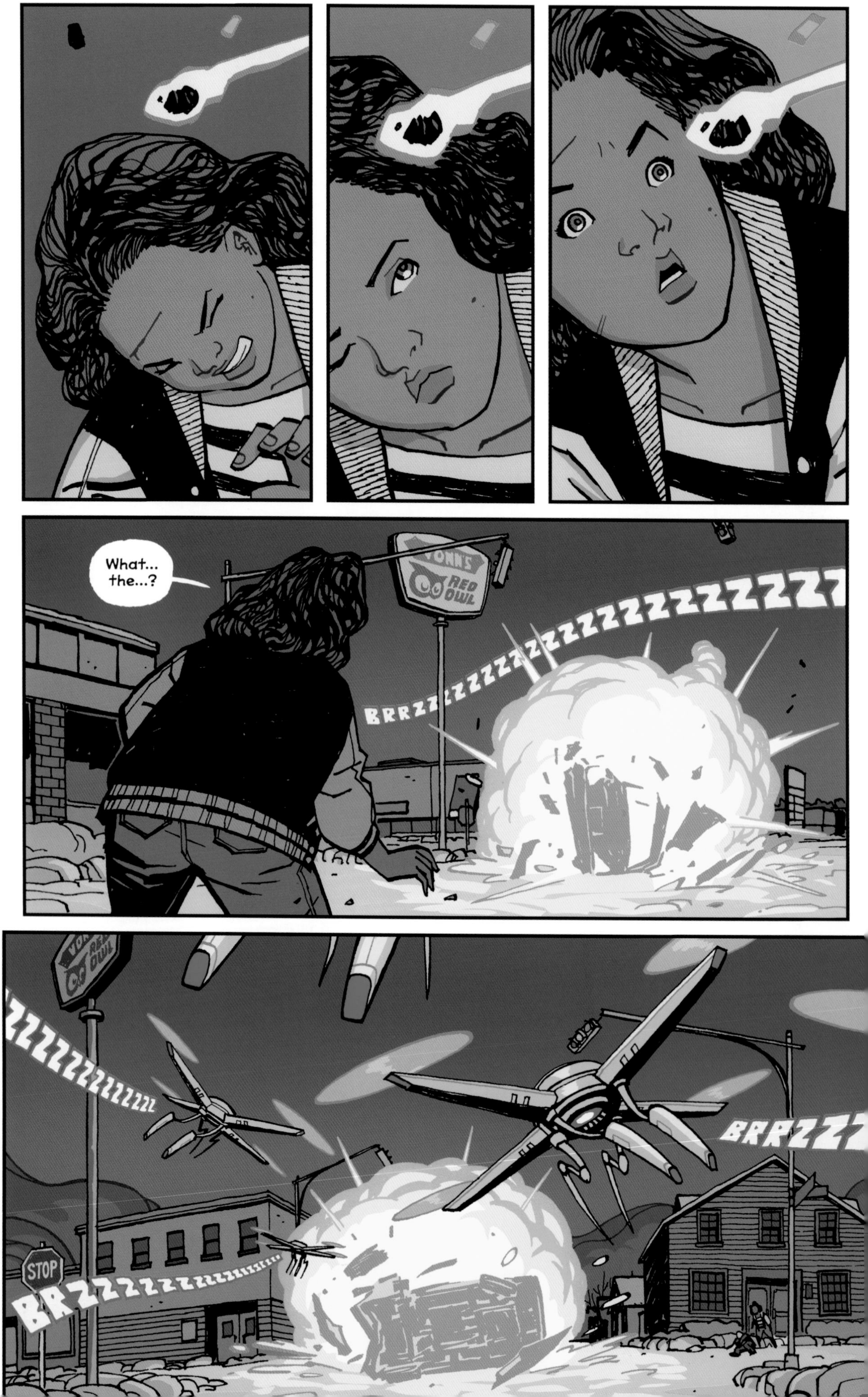
What... the...?
VONN'S RED OWL
BRRZZZZZZZZZZZZZZZZZZZZZZZZZZZ
ZZZZZZZZZZZZZZZ
BRRZZZ
STOP
BRZZZZZZZZZZZZZZZZZ

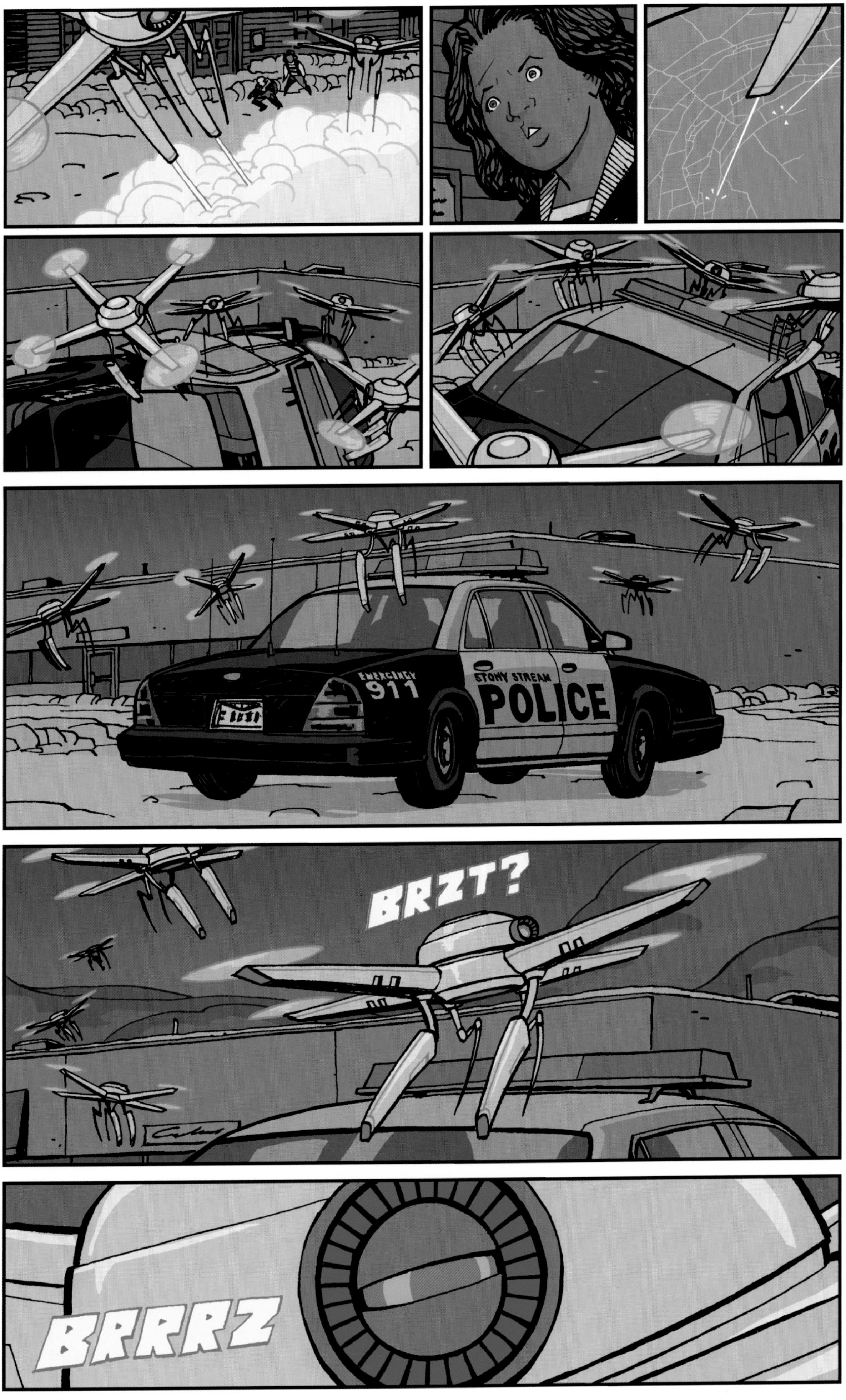
EMERGENCY
911
STONY STREAM
POLICE
BRZT?
BRRRZ

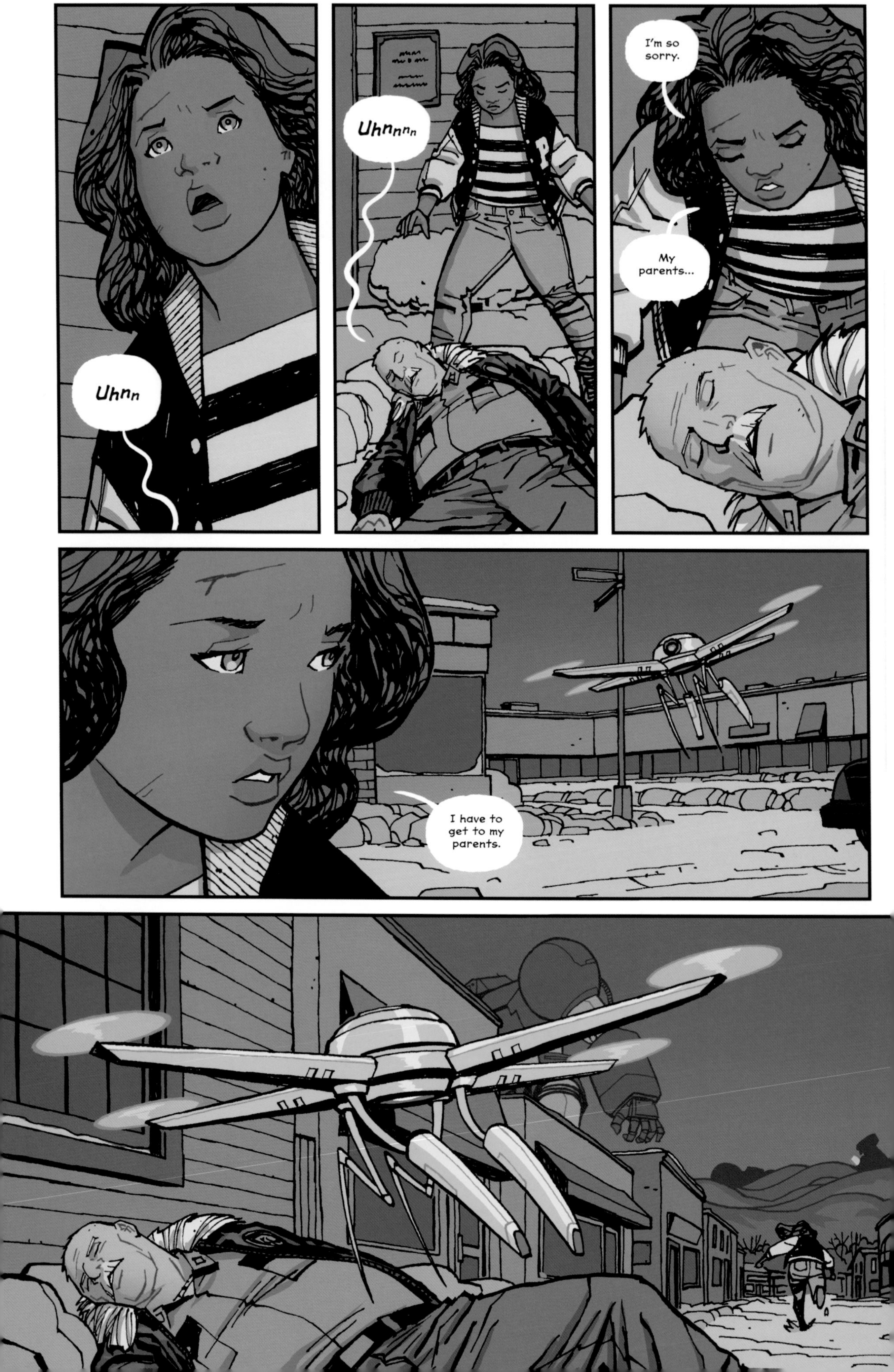
Uhnn
Uhnnnn
I'm so sorry.
My parents...
I have to get to my parents.

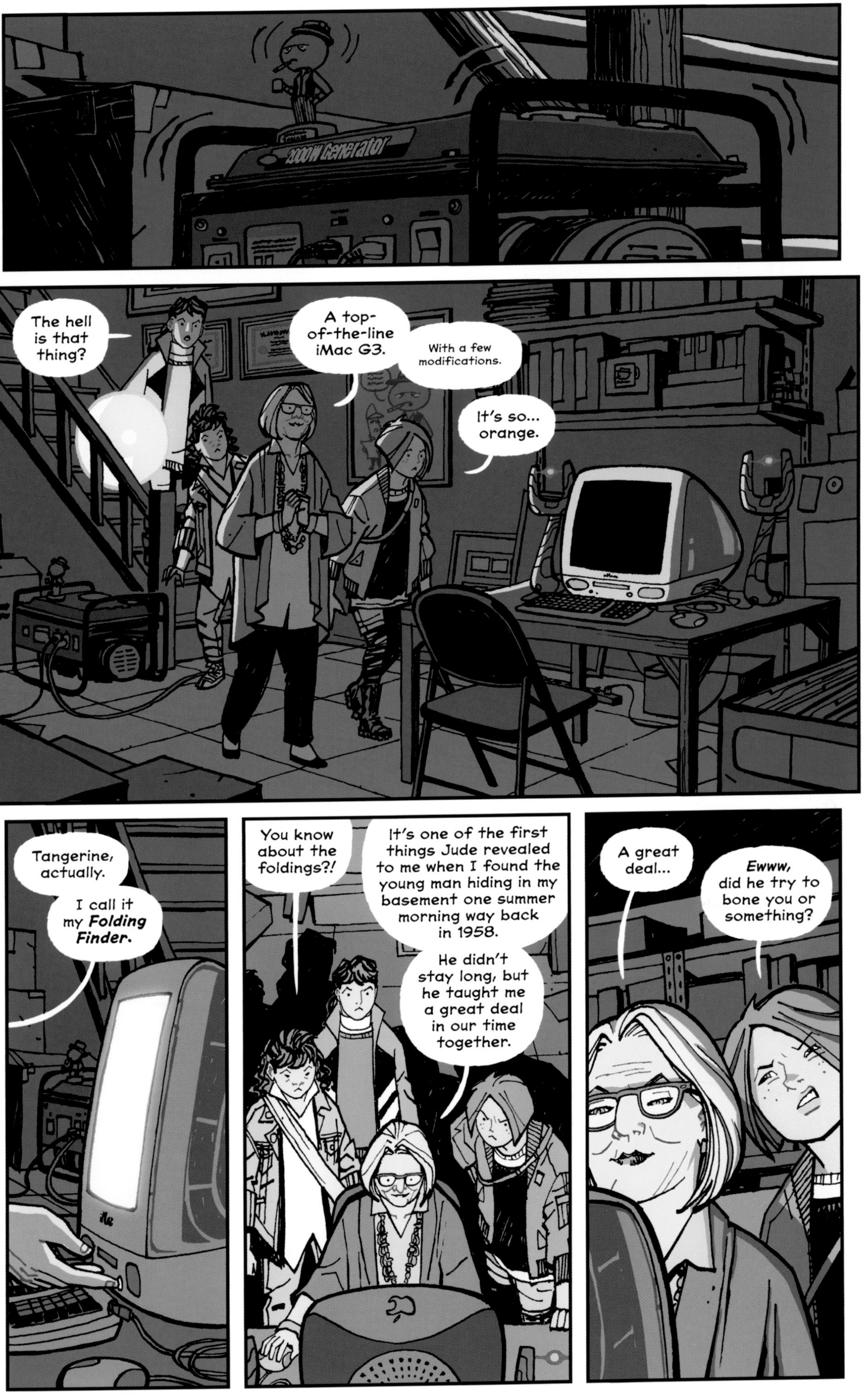
2000W Generator
The hell is that thing?
A top-of-the-line iMac G3.
With a few modifications.
It's so... orange.
Tangerine, actually.
I call it my ***Folding Finder.***
You know about the foldings?!
It's one of the first things Jude revealed to me when I found the young man hiding in my basement one summer morning way back in 1958.
He didn't stay long, but he taught me a great deal in our time together.
A great deal...
Ewww, did he try to bone you or something?

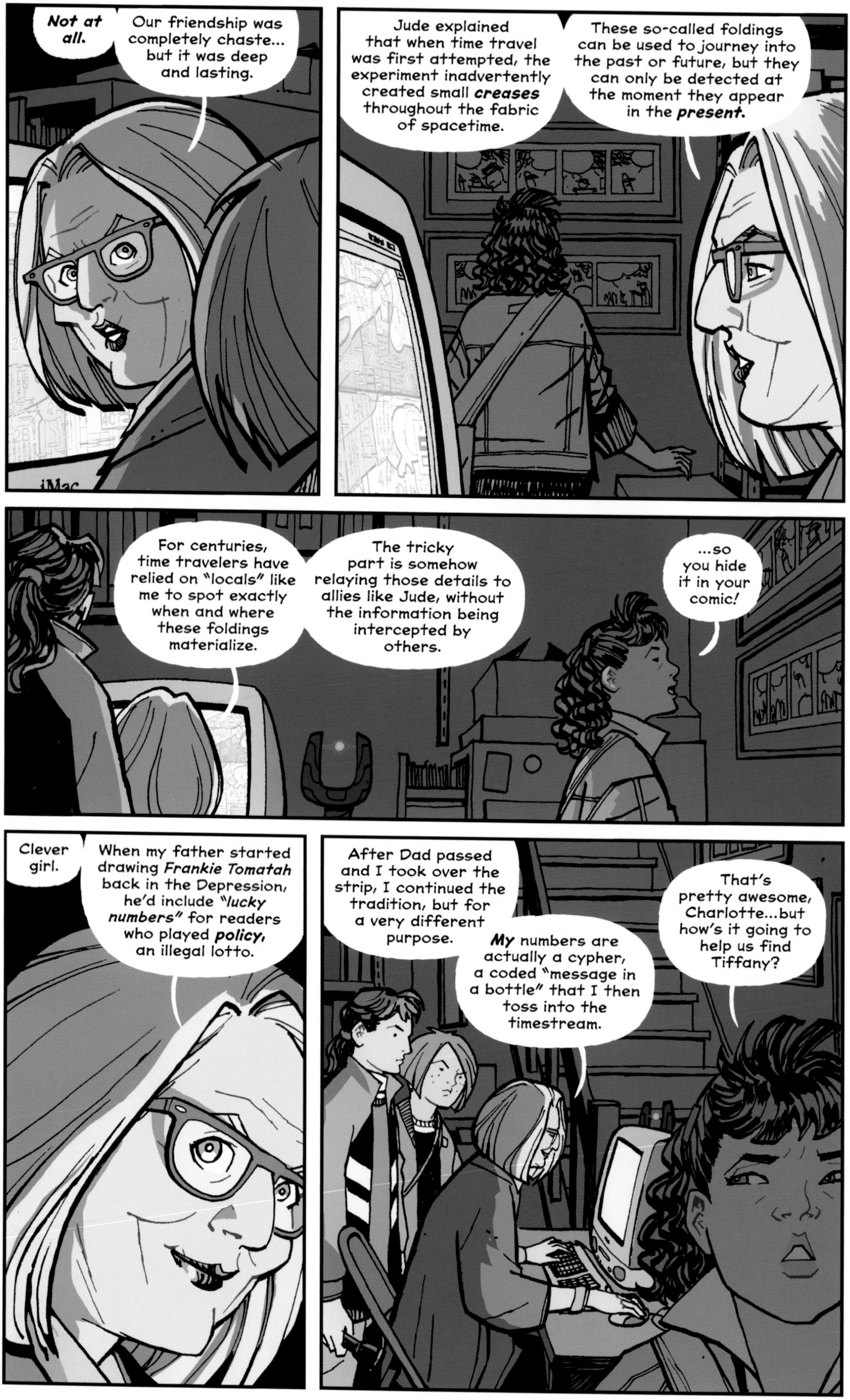
Not at all.
Our friendship was completely chaste... but it was deep and lasting.
iMac
Jude explained that when time travel was first attempted, the experiment inadvertently created small creases throughout the fabric of spacetime.
These so-called foldings can be used to journey into the past or future, but they can only be detected at the moment they appear in the present.
For centuries, time travelers have relied on "locals" like me to spot exactly when and where these foldings materialize.
The tricky part is somehow relaying those details to allies like Jude, without the information being intercepted by others.
...so you hide it in your comic!
Clever girl.
When my father started drawing Frankie Tomatah back in the Depression, he'd include "lucky numbers" for readers who played policy, an illegal lotto.
After Dad passed and I took over the strip, I continued the tradition, but for a very different purpose.
My numbers are actually a cypher, a coded "message in a bottle" that I then toss into the timestream.
That's pretty awesome, Charlotte...but how's it going to help us find Tiffany?

I don't like this, Kaje.
You see the way this crazy old lesbo is looking at Erin?
Mac, when I grow up, I think I'm going to be a lesbian.
I think maybe I'm a lesbian ***already.***
I know, right?
It's like this lady is...
The fuck did you just say?
Oh, no.

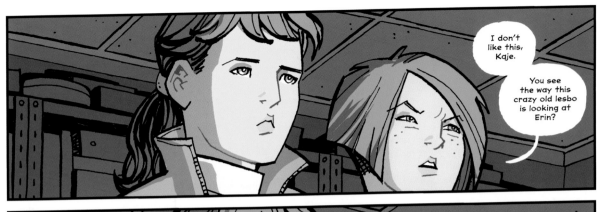

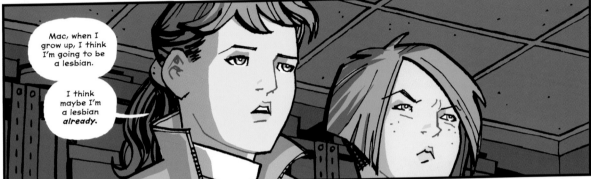

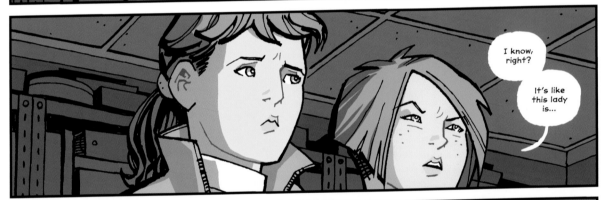

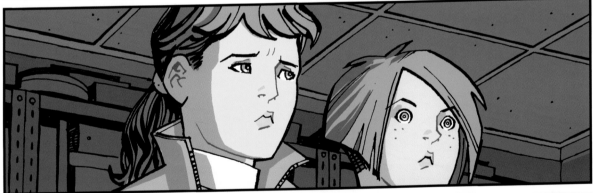

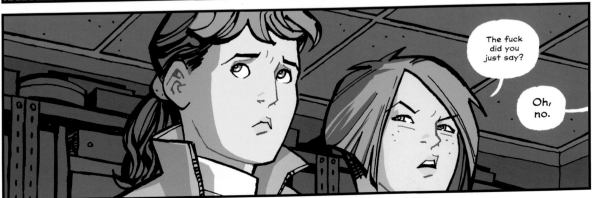

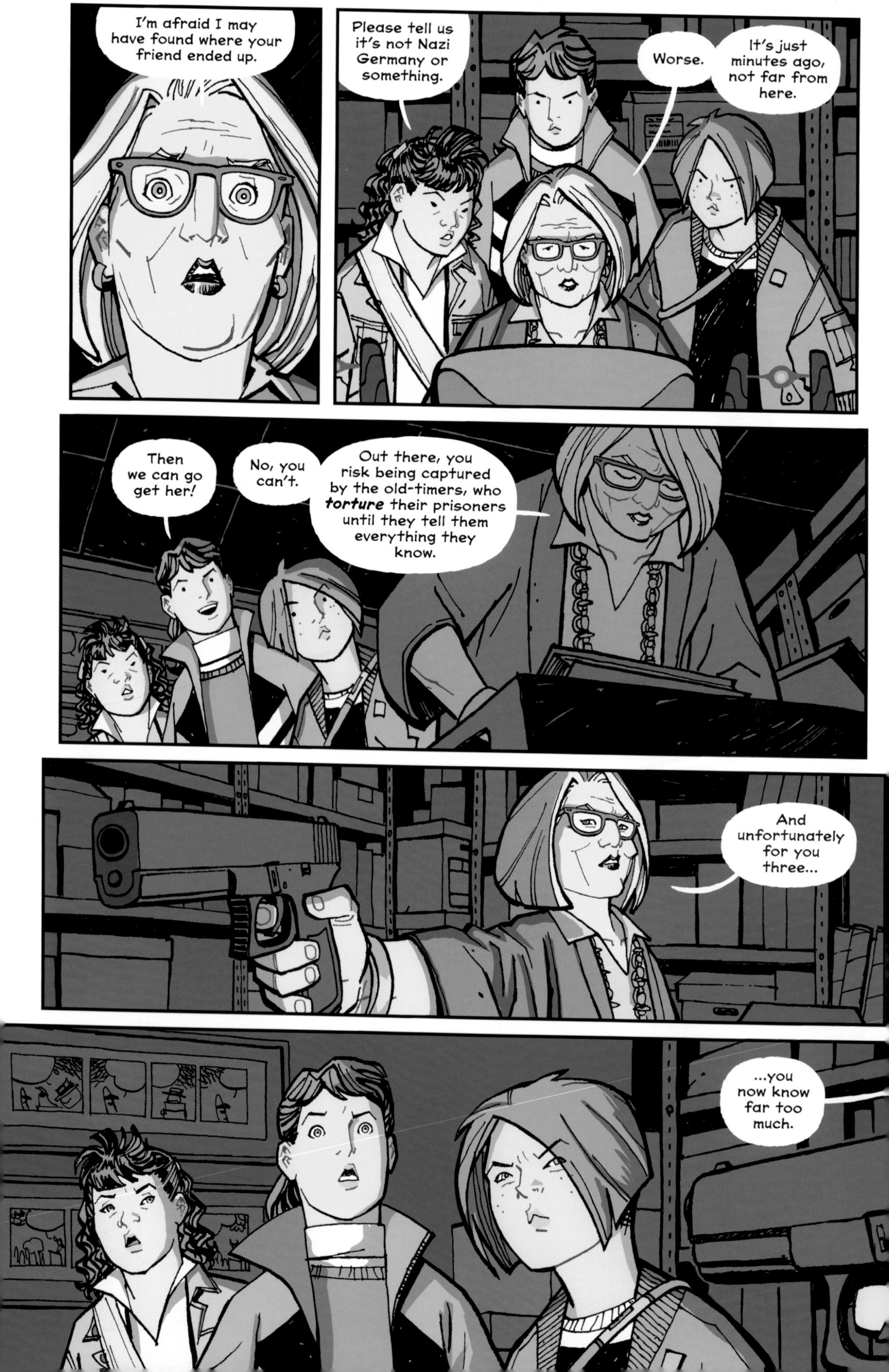
I'm afraid I may have found where your friend ended up.
Please tell us it's not Nazi Germany or something.
Worse.
It's just minutes ago, not far from here.
Then we can go get her!
No, you can't.
Out there, you risk being captured by the old-timers, who ***torture*** their prisoners until they tell them everything they know.
And unfortunately for you three...
...you now know far too much.

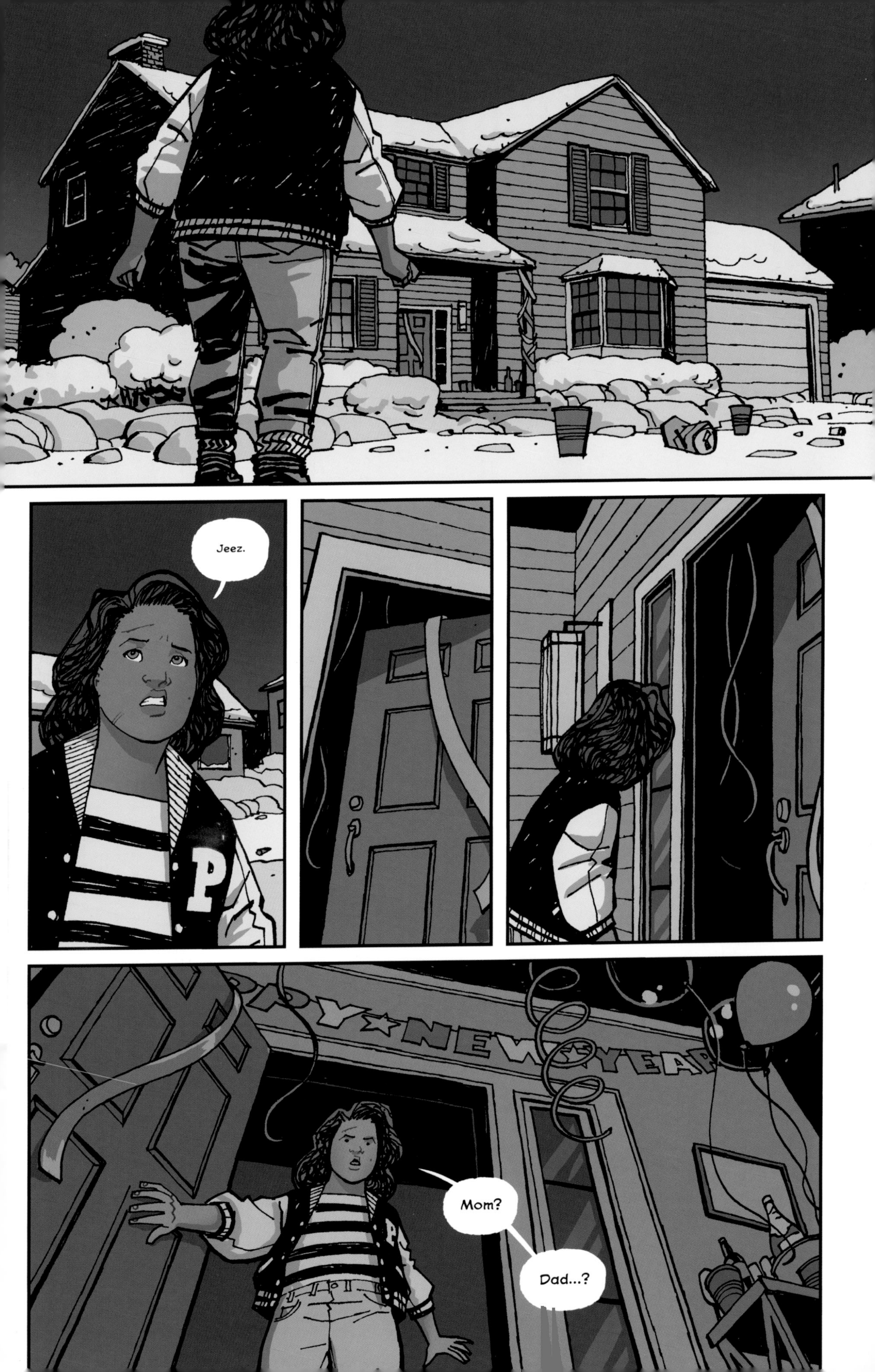
Jeez.
Mom?
Dad...?

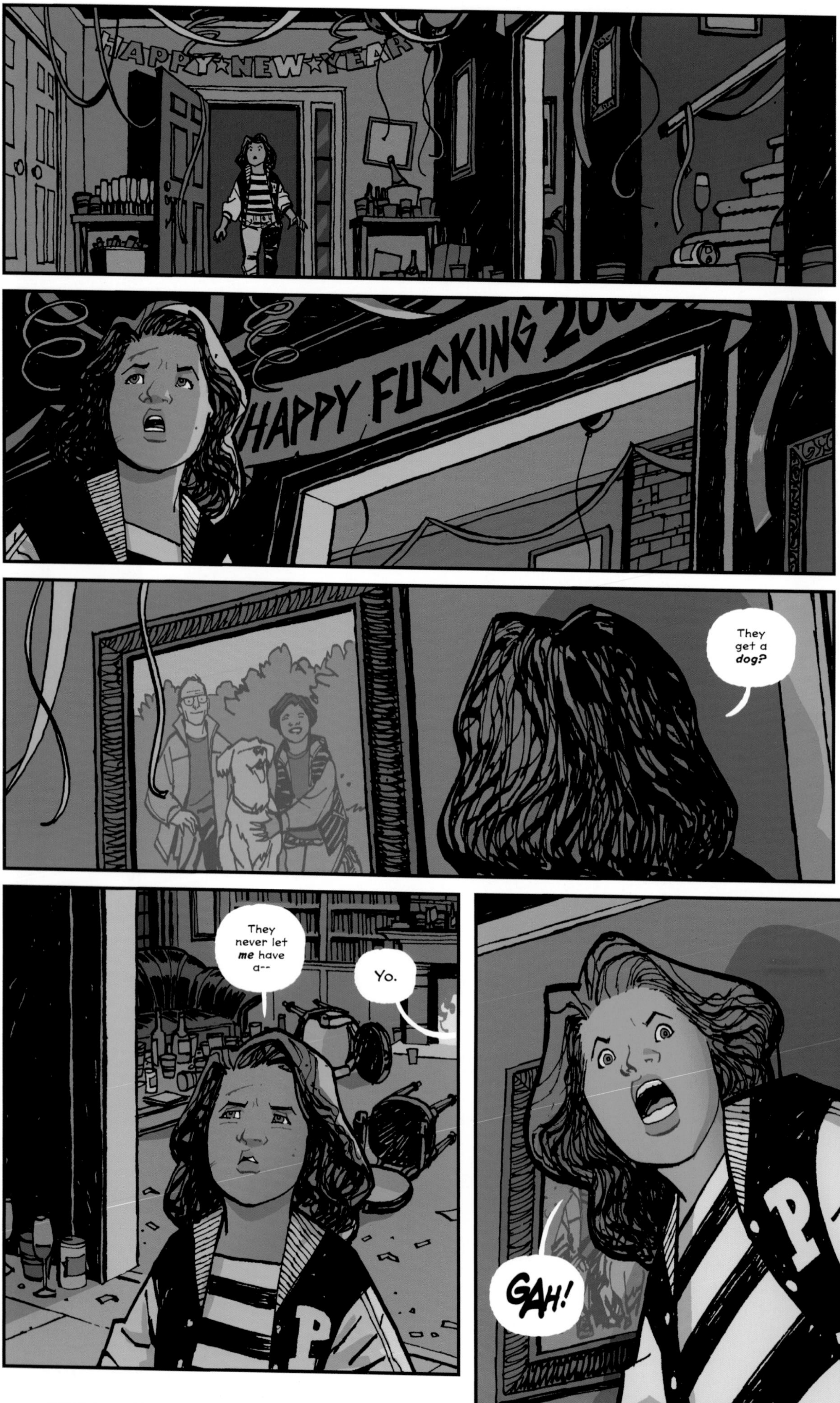
HAPPY★NEW★YEAR
HAPPY FUCKING 200
They get a dog?
They never let me have a--
Yo.
GAH!

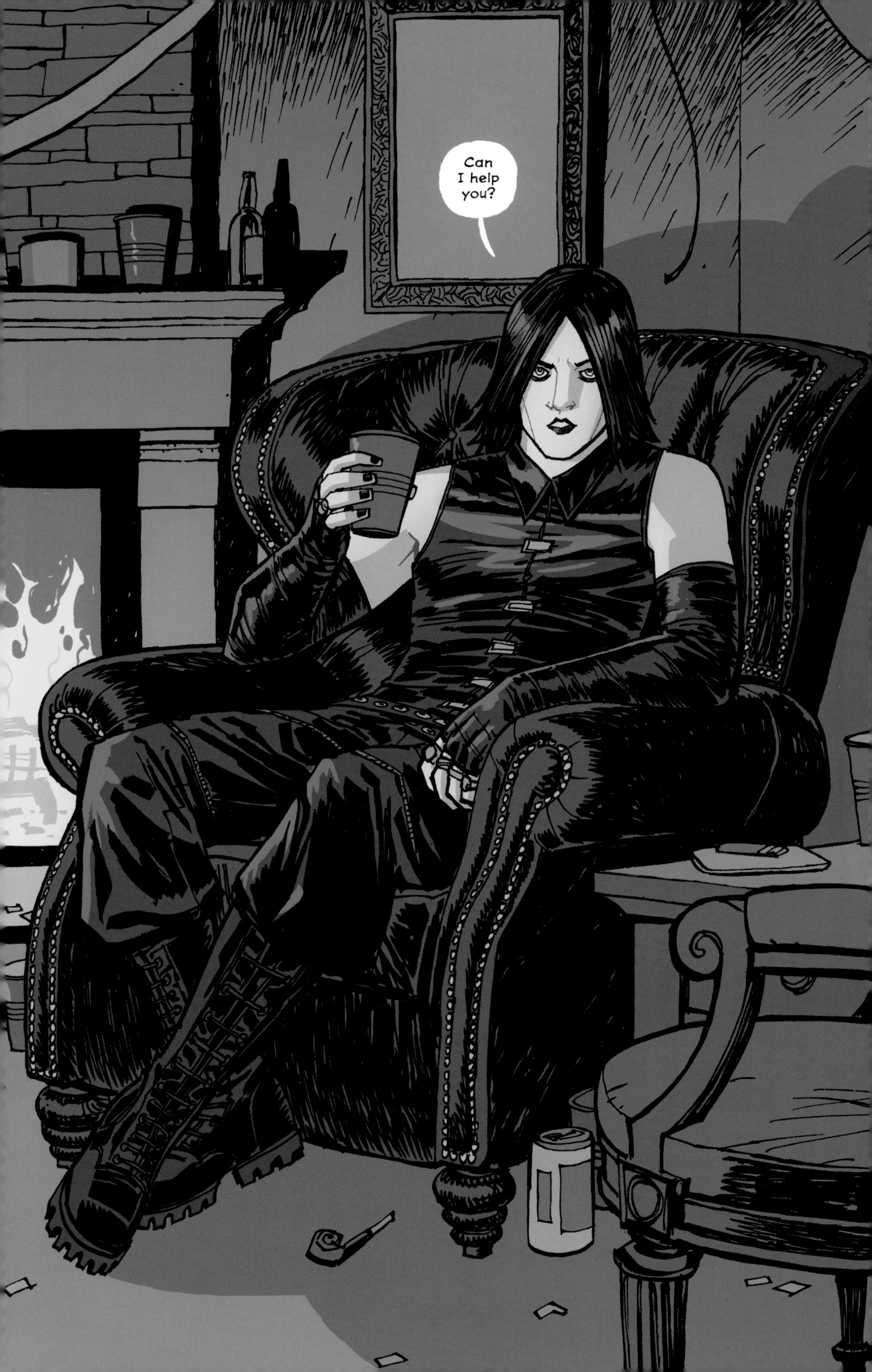
Can I help you?

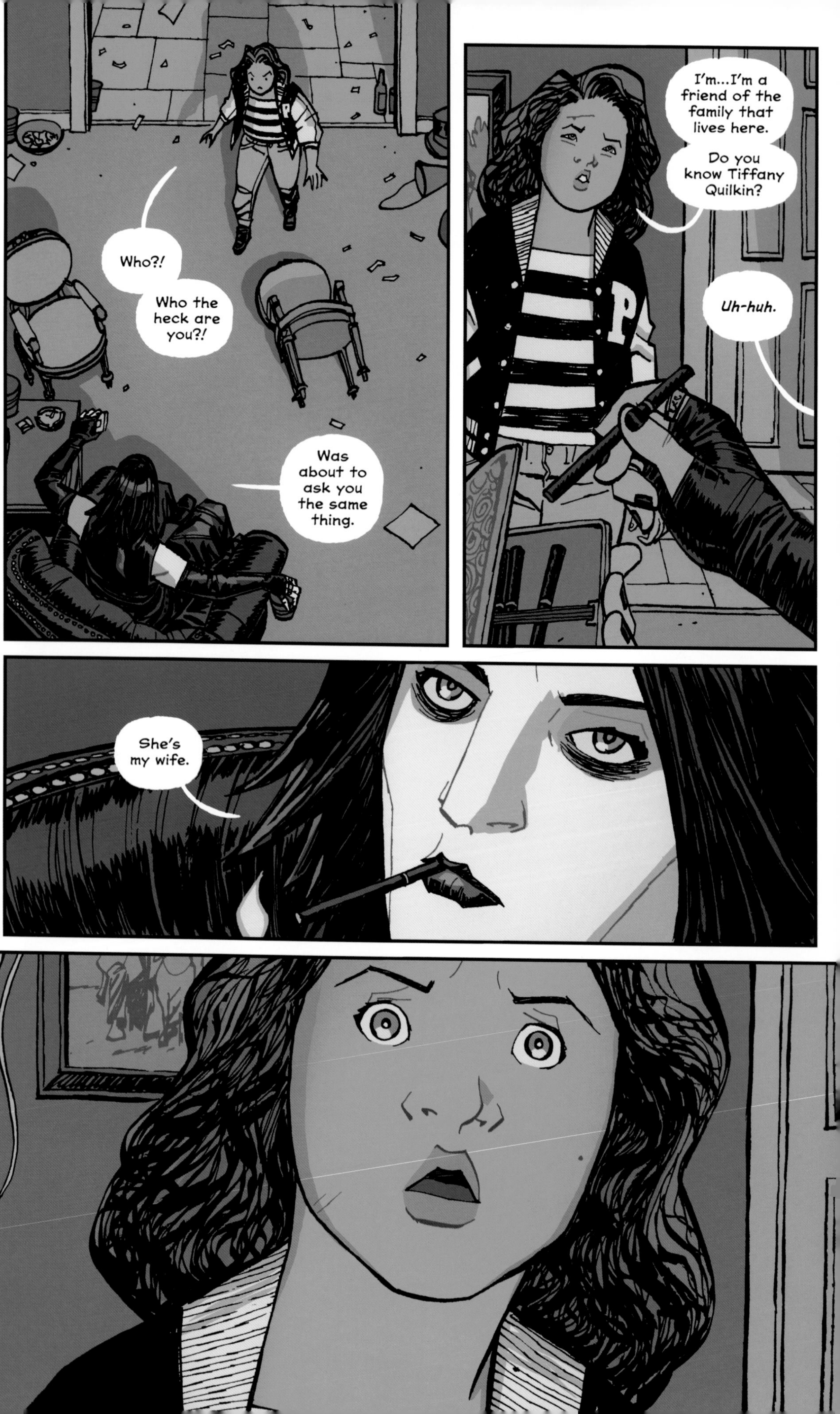
Who?!
Who the heck are you?!
Was about to ask you the same thing.
I'm...I'm a friend of the family that lives here.
Do you know Tiffany Quilkin?
Uh-huh.
She's my wife.

CHAPTER

18

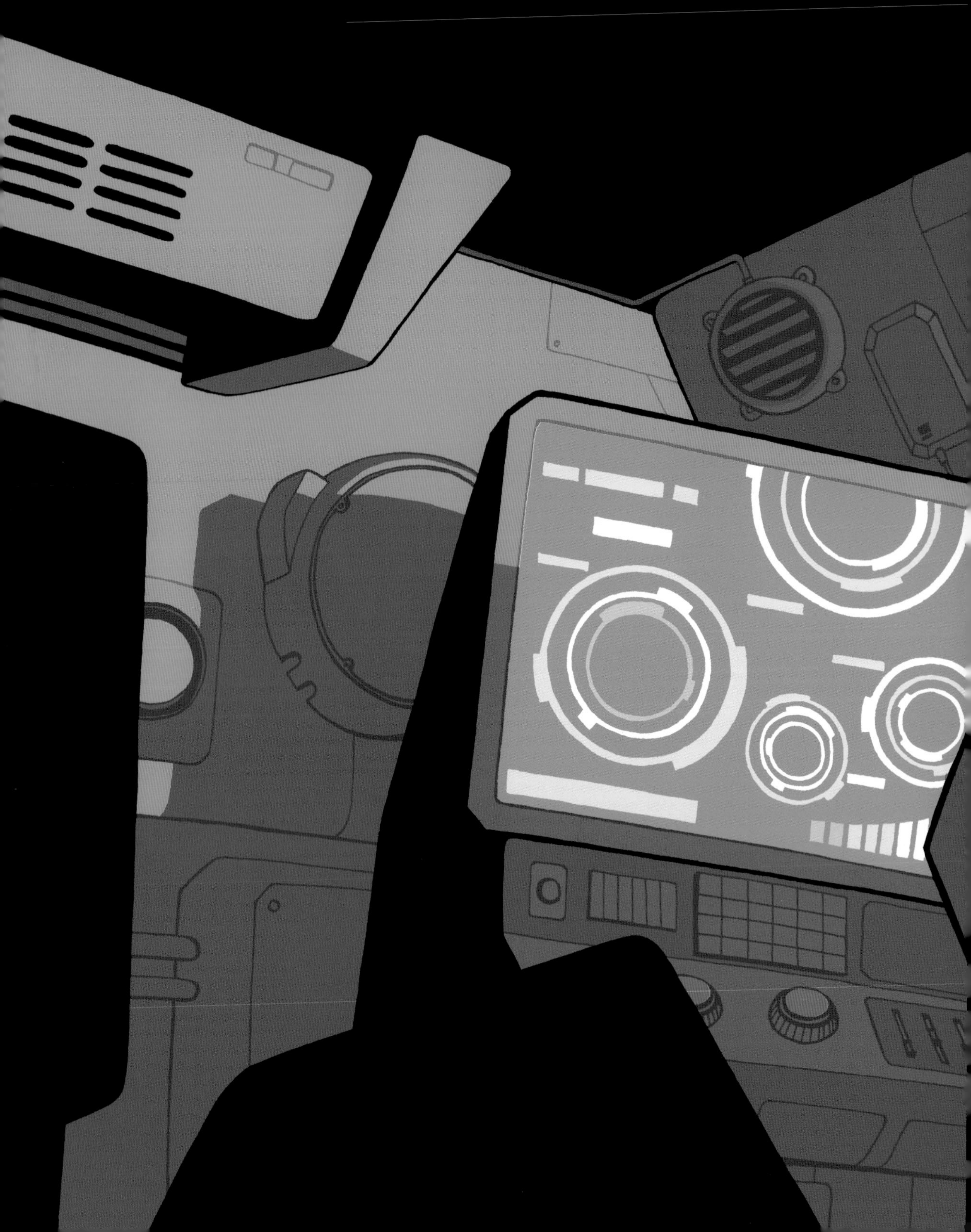

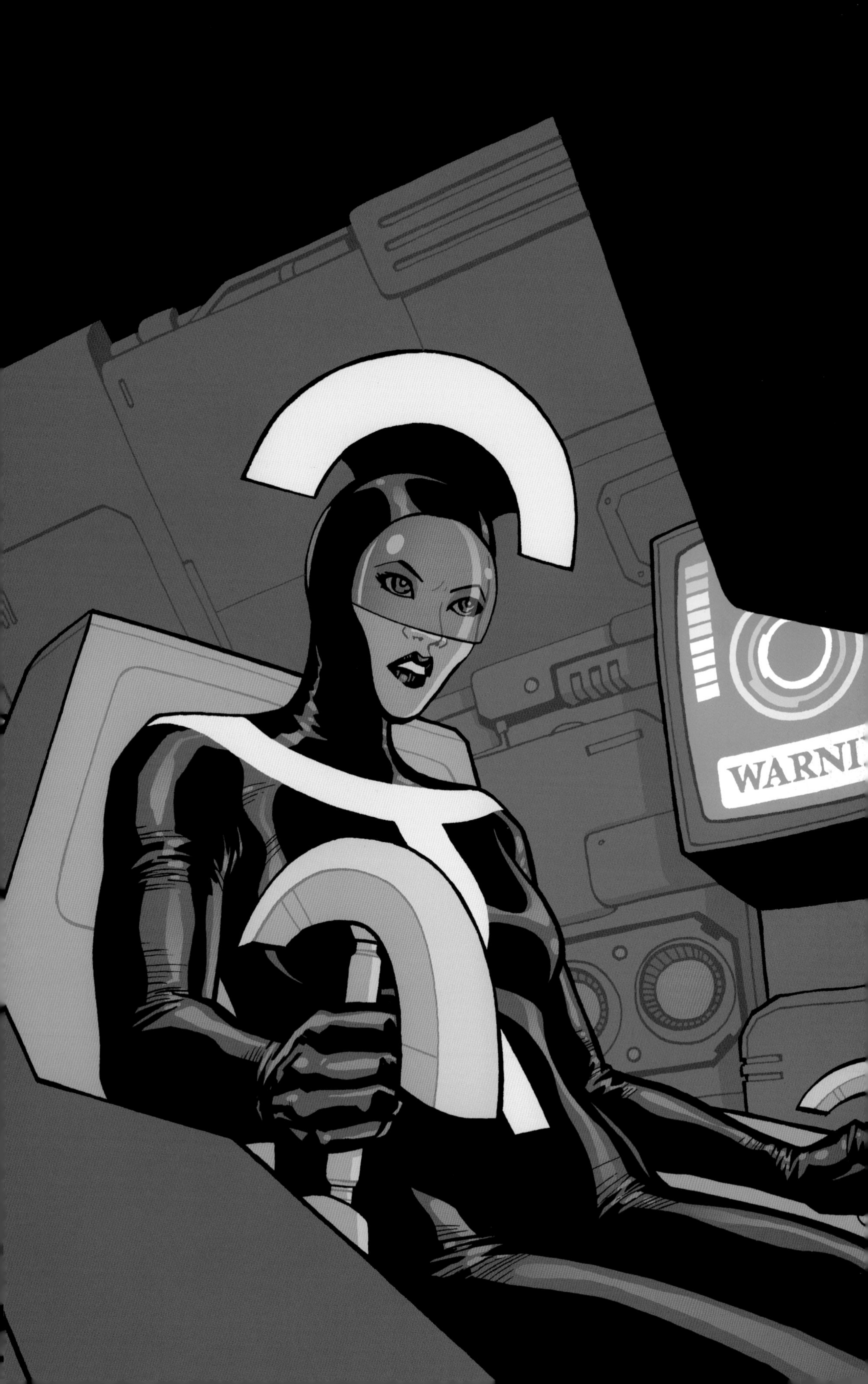

REMEMBER
Turn your computer off
before midnight on
12/31/99

-Warning Sticker from **Best Buy** circa 1999

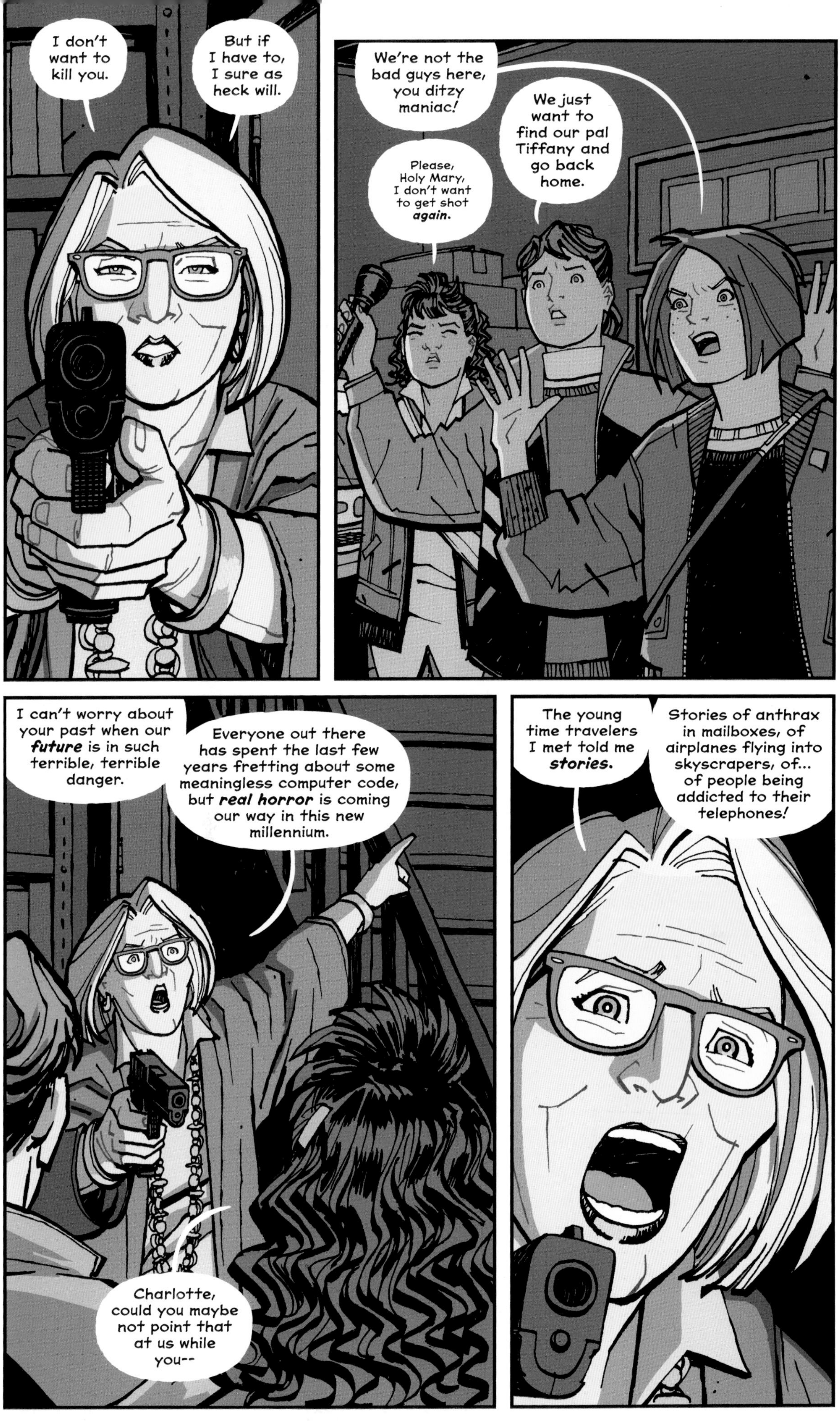
I don't want to kill you.
But if I have to, I sure as heck will.
We're not the bad guys here, you ditzy maniac!
We just want to find our pal Tiffany and go back home.
Please, Holy Mary, I don't want to get shot *again*.
I can't worry about your past when our *future* is in such terrible, terrible danger.
Everyone out there has spent the last few years fretting about some meaningless computer code, but *real horror* is coming our way in this new millennium.
Charlotte, could you maybe not point that at us while you--
The young time travelers I met told me *stories*.
Stories of anthrax in mailboxes, of airplanes flying into skyscrapers, of... of people being addicted to their telephones!

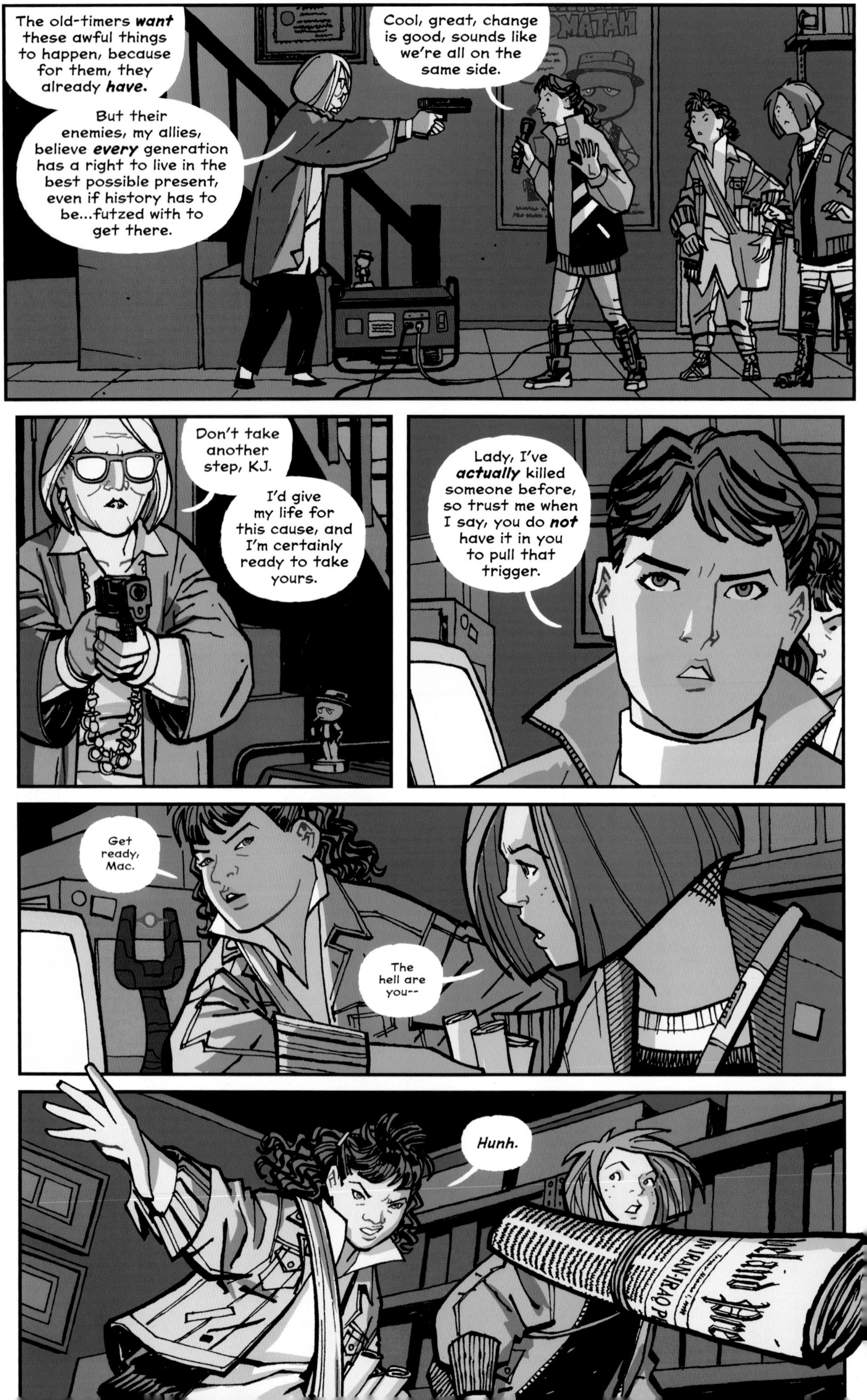
The old-timers ***want*** these awful things to happen, because for them, they already ***have.***
But their enemies, my allies, believe ***every*** generation has a right to live in the best possible present, even if history has to be...futzed with to get there.
Cool, great, change is good, sounds like we're all on the same side.
Don't take another step, KJ.
I'd give my life for this cause, and I'm certainly ready to take yours.
Lady, I've ***actually*** killed someone before, so trust me when I say, you do ***not*** have it in you to pull that trigger.
Get ready, Mac.
The hell are you--
Hunh.

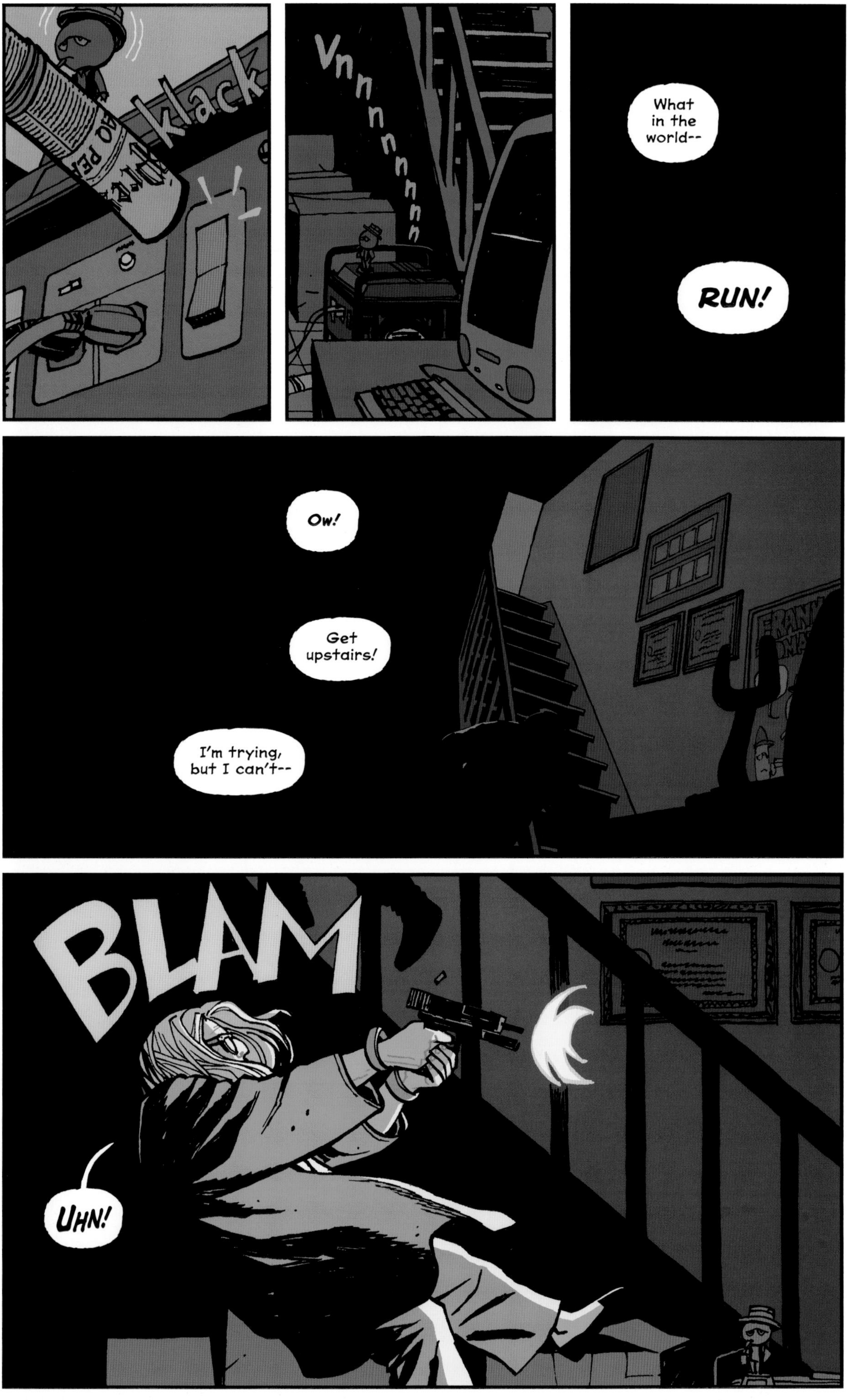
klack
Vnnnnnnnn
What in the world--
RUN!
Ow!
Get upstairs!
I'm trying, but I can't--
BLAM
UHN!

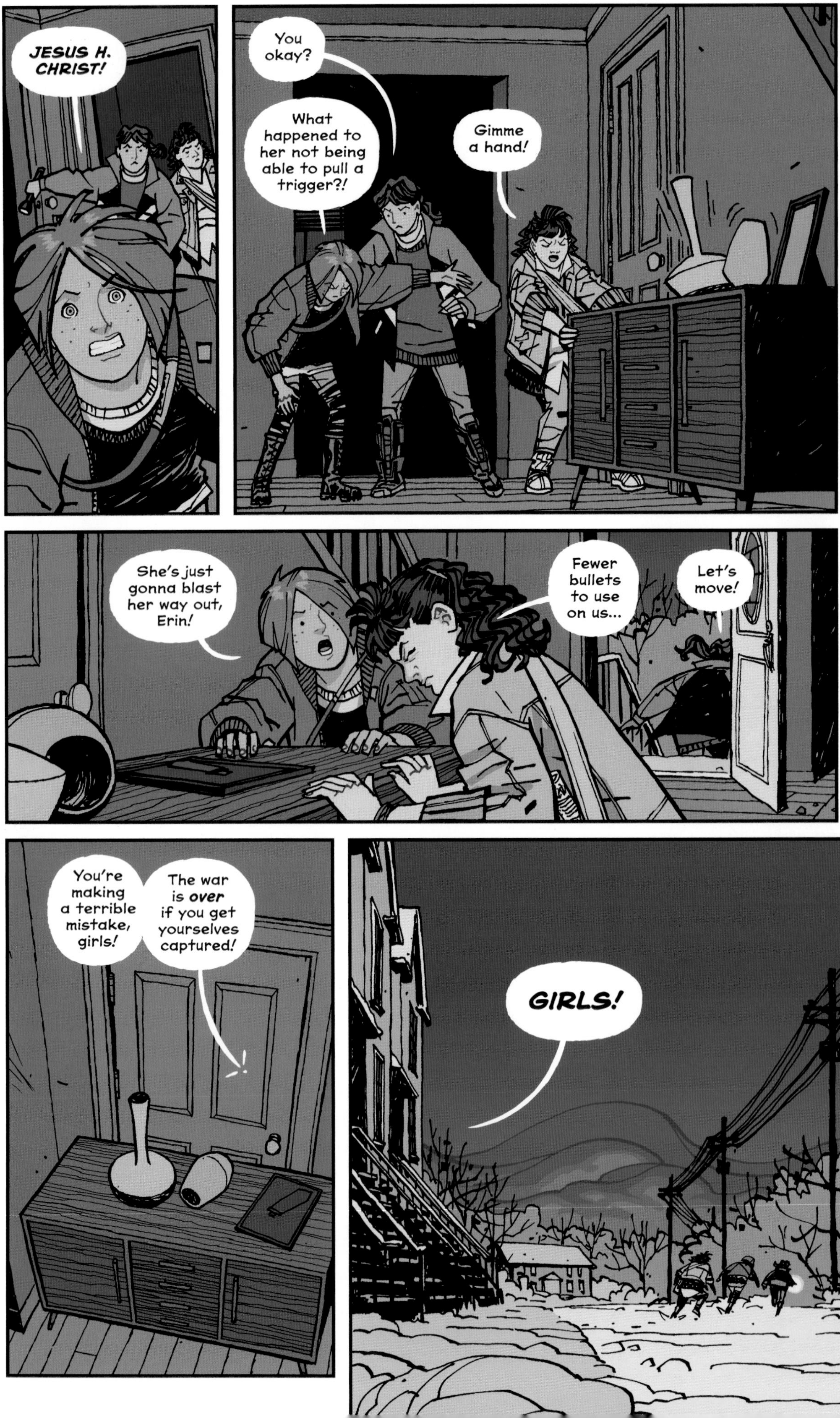
JESUS H. CHRIST!
You okay?
What happened to her not being able to pull a trigger?!
Gimme a hand!
She's just gonna blast her way out, Erin!
Fewer bullets to use on us...
Let's move!
You're making a terrible mistake, girls!
The war is *over* if you get yourselves captured!
GIRLS!

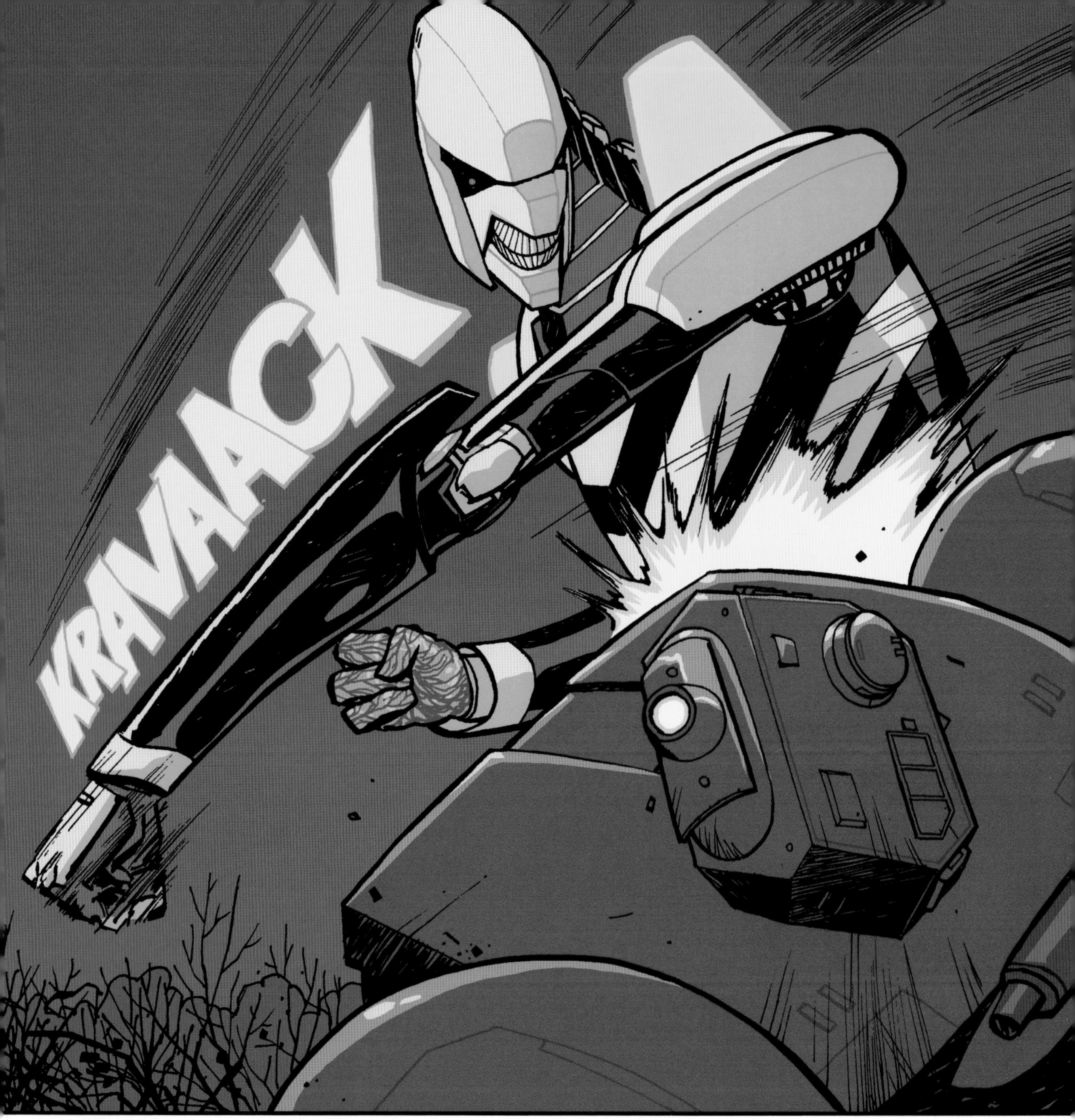
KRAVACK

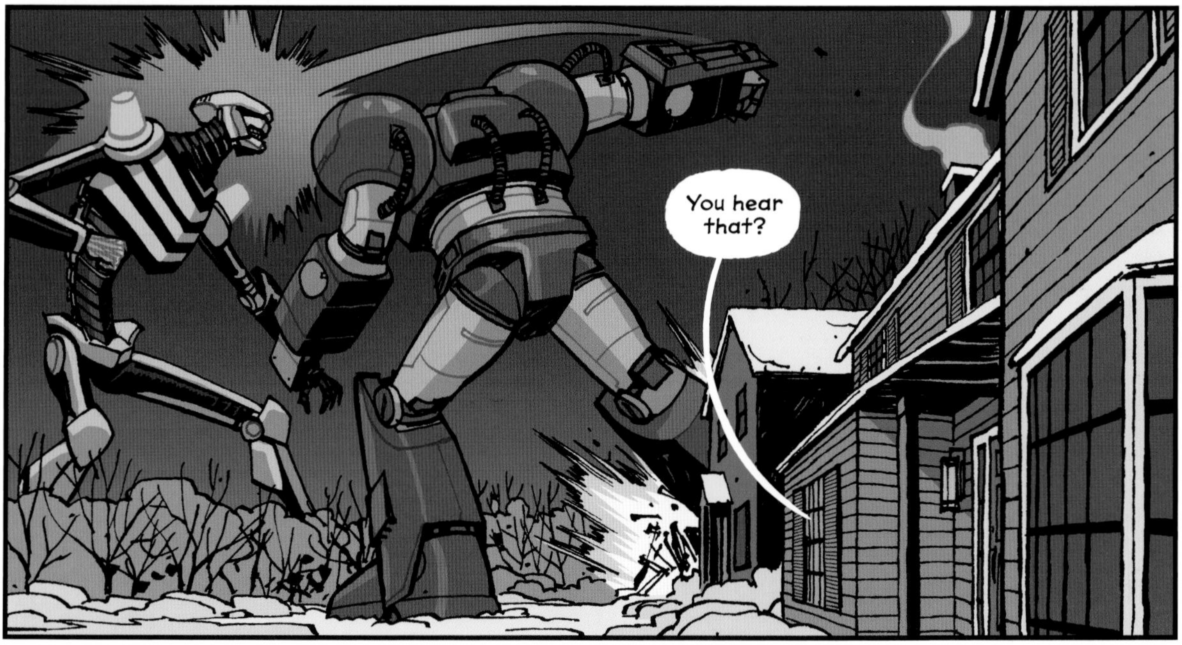
You hear that?

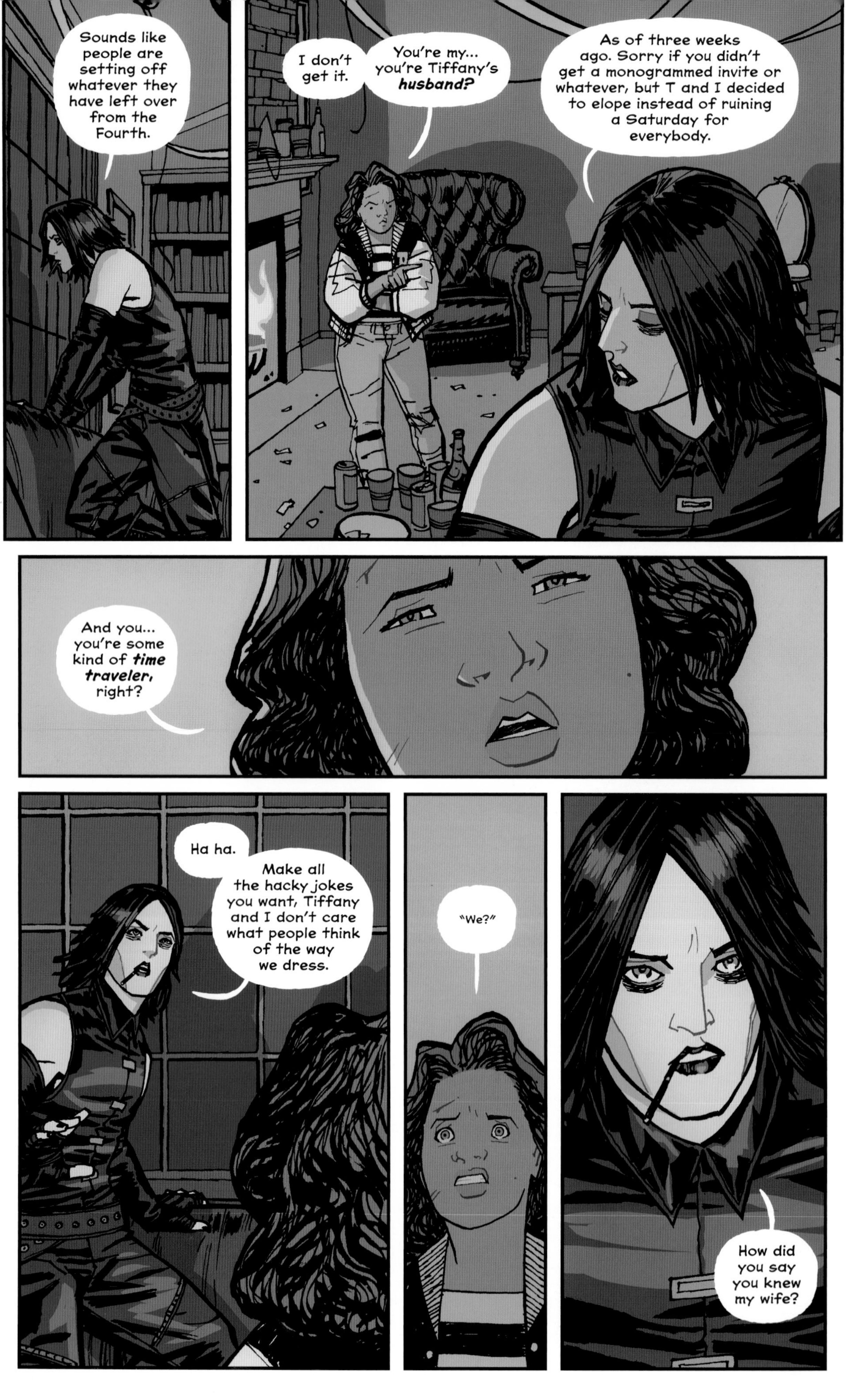
Sounds like people are setting off whatever they have left over from the Fourth.
I don't get it.
You're my... you're Tiffany's **husband?**
As of three weeks ago. Sorry if you didn't get a monogrammed invite or whatever, but T and I decided to elope instead of ruining a Saturday for everybody.
And you... you're some kind of **time traveler,** right?
Ha ha.
Make all the hacky jokes you want, Tiffany and I don't care what people think of the way we dress.
"We?"
How did you say you knew my wife?

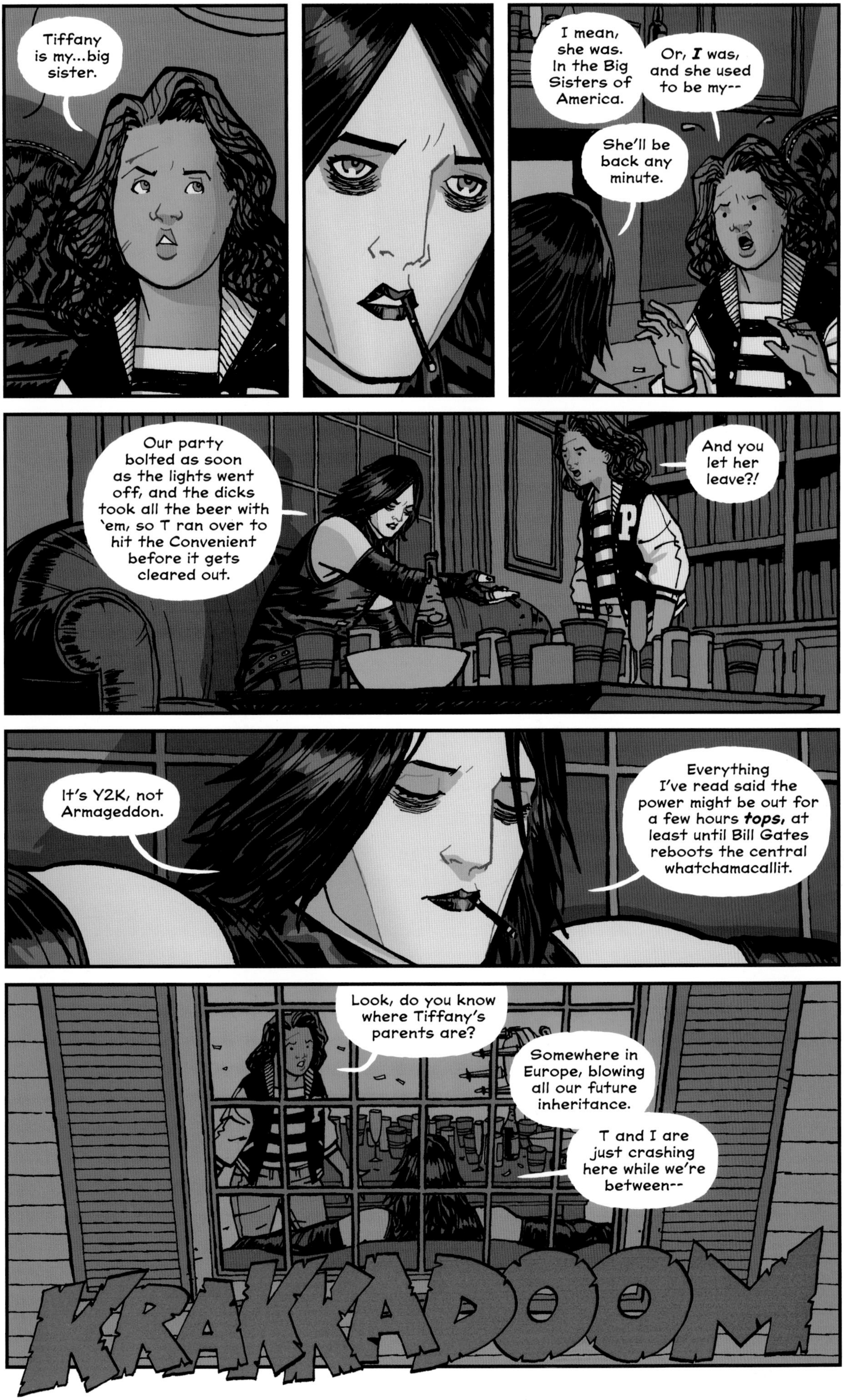
Tiffany is my...big sister.
I mean, she was. In the Big Sisters of America.
Or, *I* was, and she used to be my--
She'll be back any minute.
Our party bolted as soon as the lights went off, and the dicks took all the beer with 'em, so T ran over to hit the Convenient before it gets cleared out.
And you let her leave?!
It's Y2K, not Armageddon.
Everything I've read said the power might be out for a few hours ***tops,*** at least until Bill Gates reboots the central whatchamacallit.
Look, do you know where Tiffany's parents are?
Somewhere in Europe, blowing all our future inheritance.
T and I are just crashing here while we're between--
KRAKKADOOM

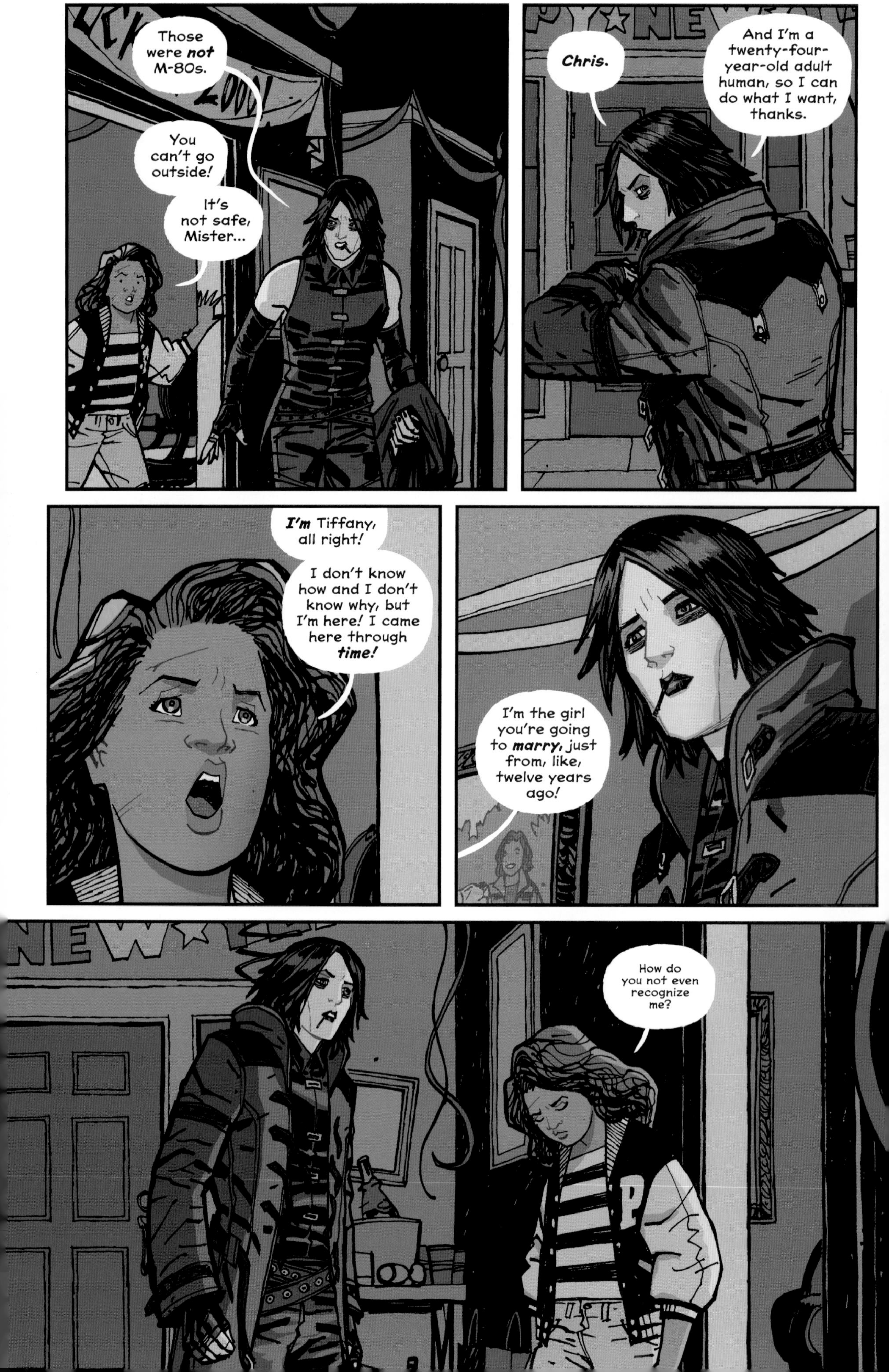
Those were *not* M-80s.
You can't go outside!
It's not safe, Mister...
Chris.
And I'm a twenty-four-year-old adult human, so I can do what I want, thanks.
I'm Tiffany, all right!
I don't know how and I don't know why, but I'm here! I came here through *time!*
I'm the girl you're going to *marry*, just from, like, twelve years ago!
How do you not even recognize me?

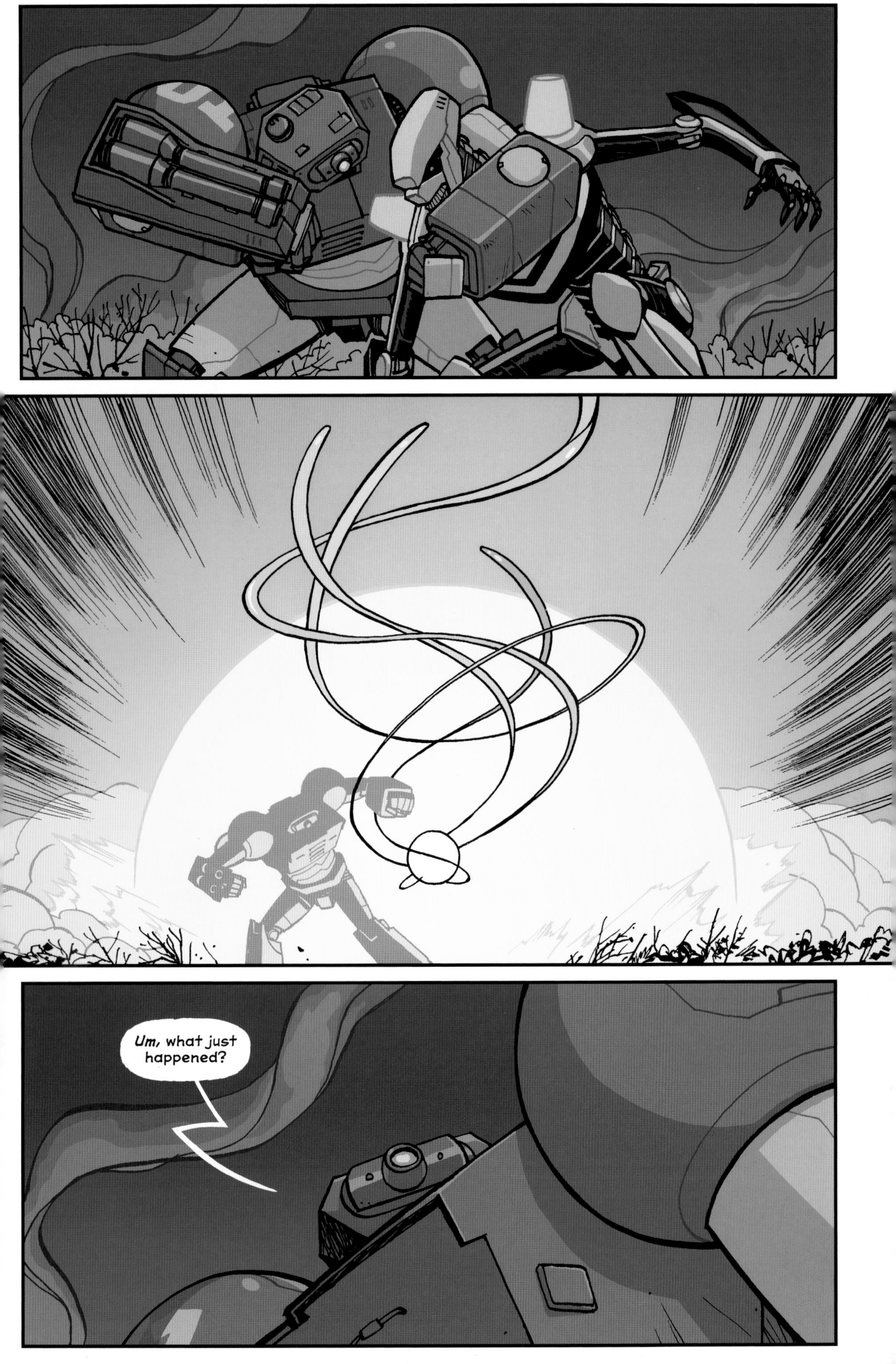
Um, what just happened?

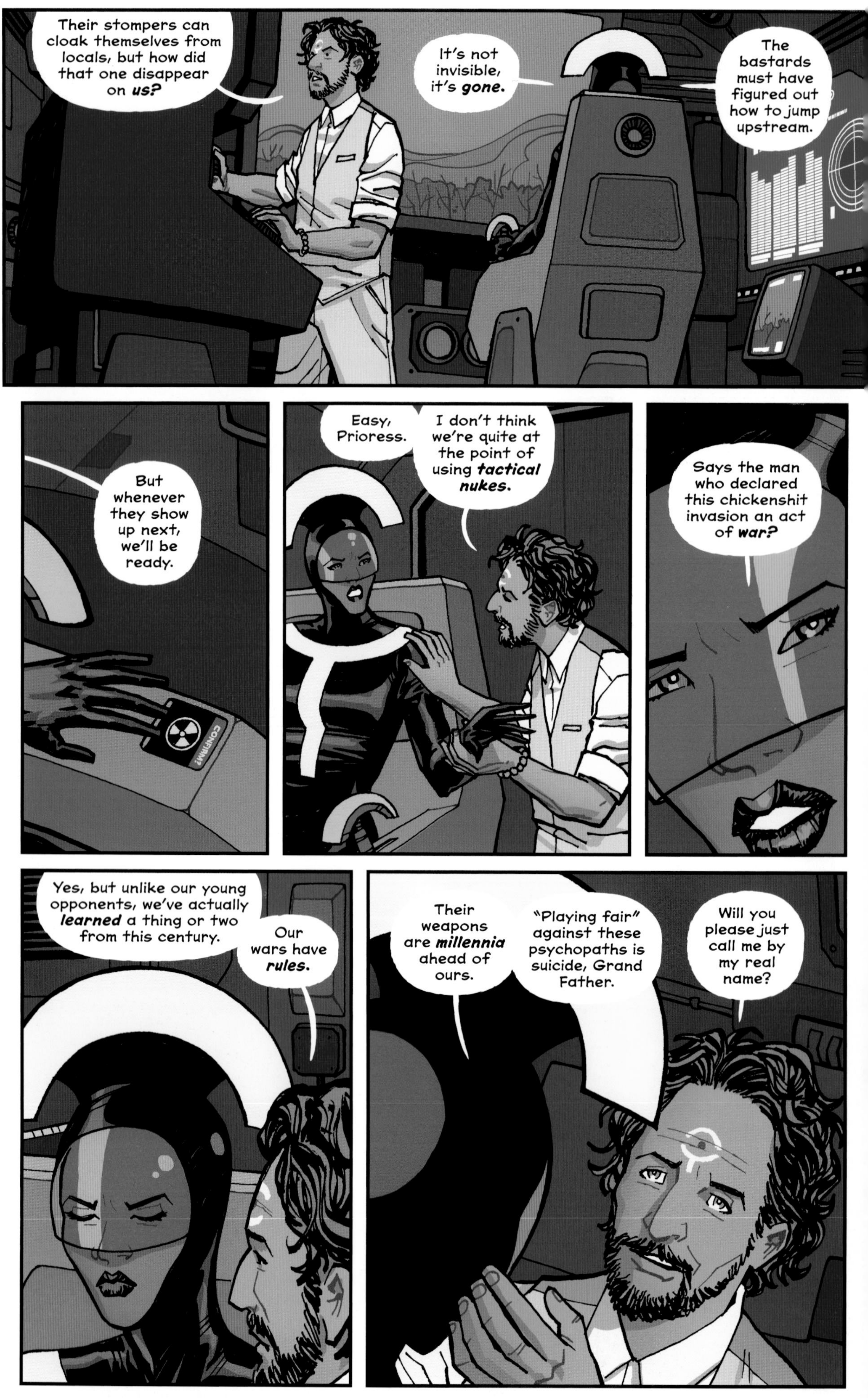
Their stompers can cloak themselves from locals, but how did that one disappear on *us?*
It's not invisible, it's ***gone.***
The bastards must have figured out how to jump upstream.
But whenever they show up next, we'll be ready.
CONFIRM?
Easy, Prioress.
I don't think we're quite at the point of using ***tactical nukes.***
Says the man who declared this chickenshit invasion an act of ***war?***
Yes, but unlike our young opponents, we've actually ***learned*** a thing or two from this century.
Our wars have ***rules.***
Their weapons are ***millennia*** ahead of ours.
"Playing fair" against these psychopaths is suicide, Grand Father.
Will you please just call me by my real name?

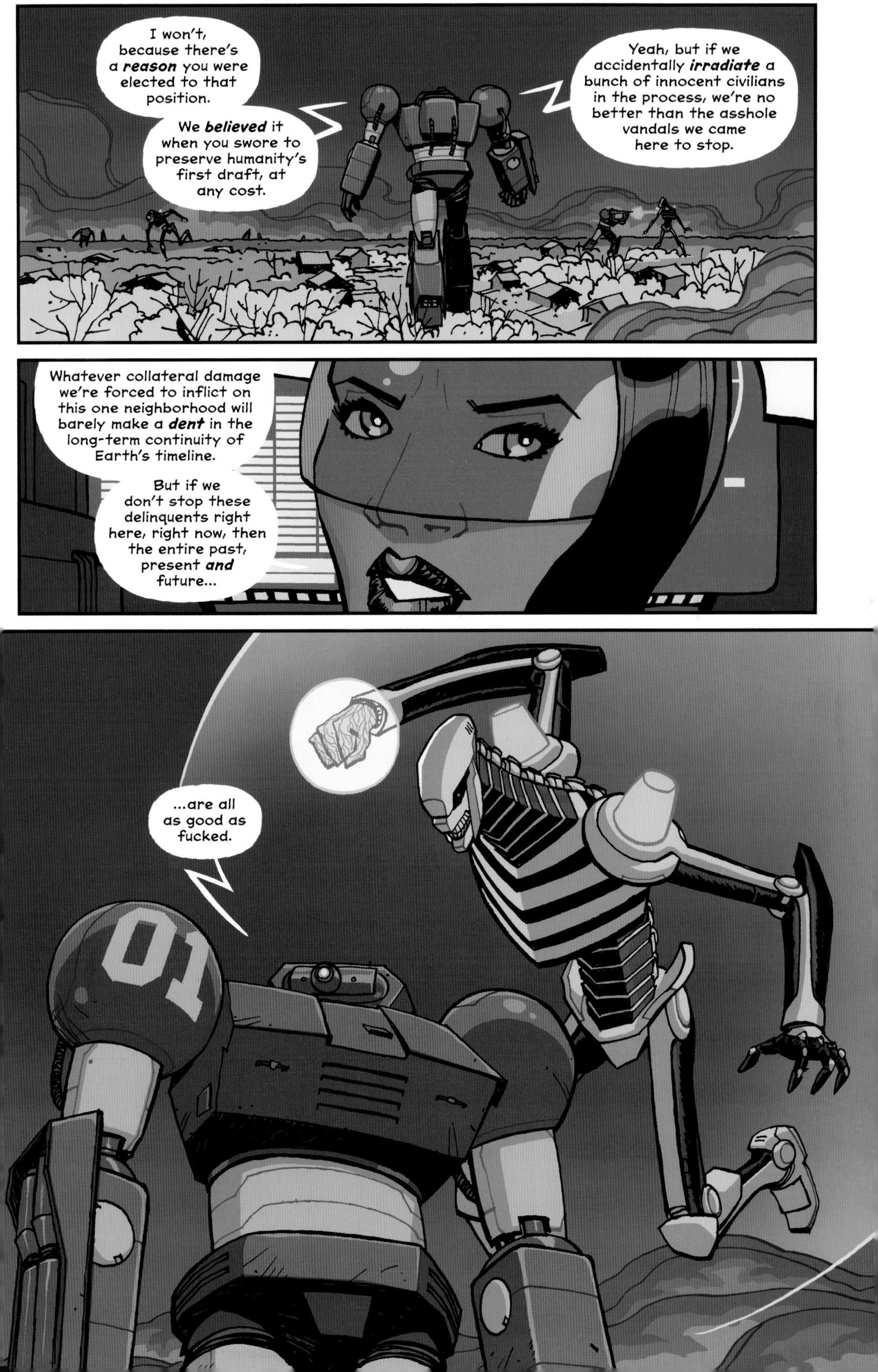
I won't, because there's a *reason* you were elected to that position.
We *believed* it when you swore to preserve humanity's first draft, at any cost.
Yeah, but if we accidentally *irradiate* a bunch of innocent civilians in the process, we're no better than the asshole vandals we came here to stop.
Whatever collateral damage we're forced to inflict on this one neighborhood will barely make a *dent* in the long-term continuity of Earth's timeline.
But if we don't stop these delinquents right here, right now, then the entire past, present *and* future...
...are all as good as fucked.
01

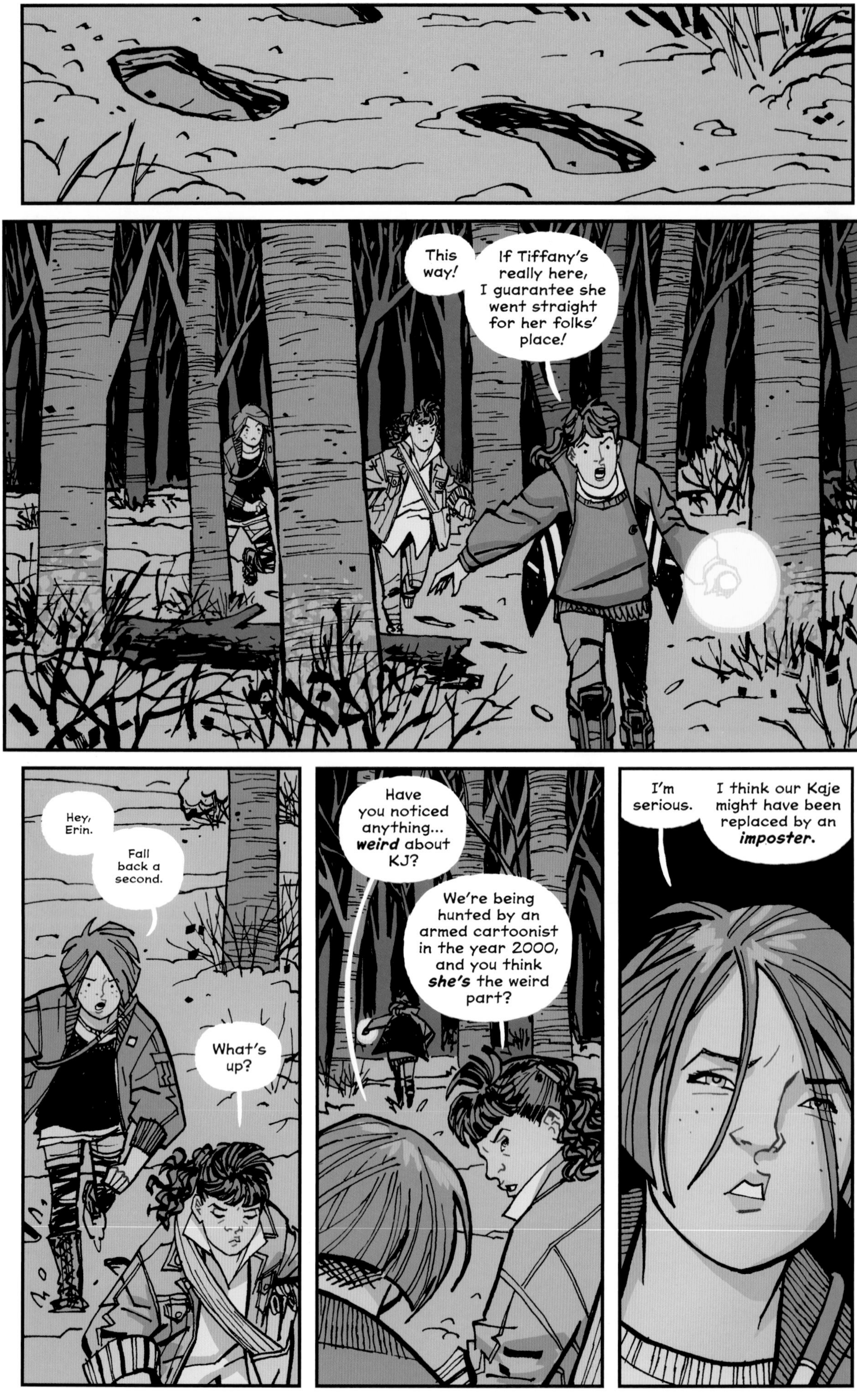
This way!
If Tiffany's really here, I guarantee she went straight for her folks' place!
Hey, Erin.
Fall back a second.
What's up?
Have you noticed anything... **weird** about KJ?
We're being hunted by an armed cartoonist in the year 2000, and you think **she's** the weird part?
I'm serious.
I think our Kaje might have been replaced by an **imposter.**

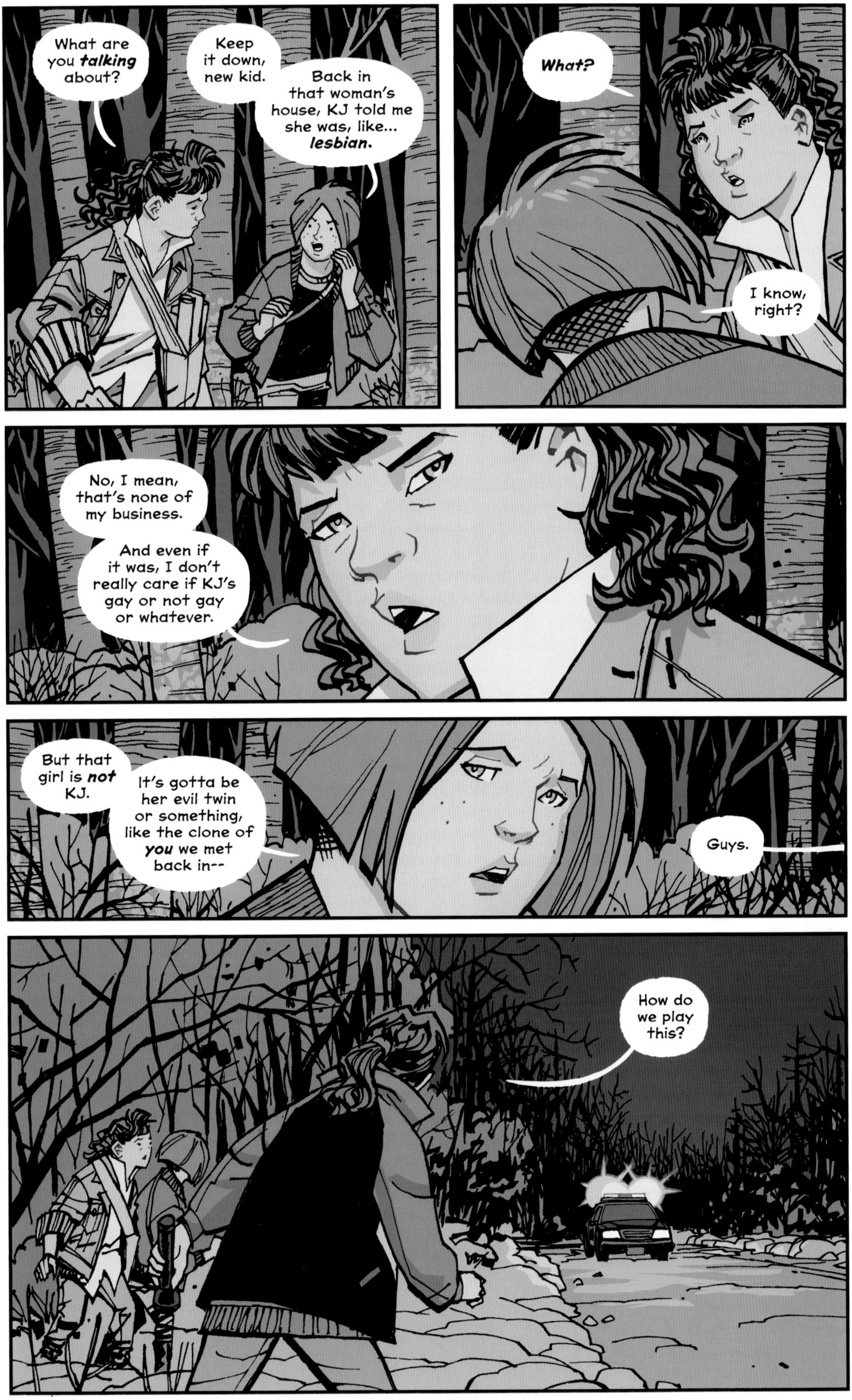
What are you *talking* about?
Keep it down, new kid.
Back in that woman's house, KJ told me she was, like... *lesbian.*
What?
I know, right?
No, I mean, that's none of my business.
And even if it was, I don't really care if KJ's gay or not gay or whatever.
But that girl is *not* KJ.
It's gotta be her evil twin or something, like the clone of *you* we met back in--
Guys.
How do we play this?

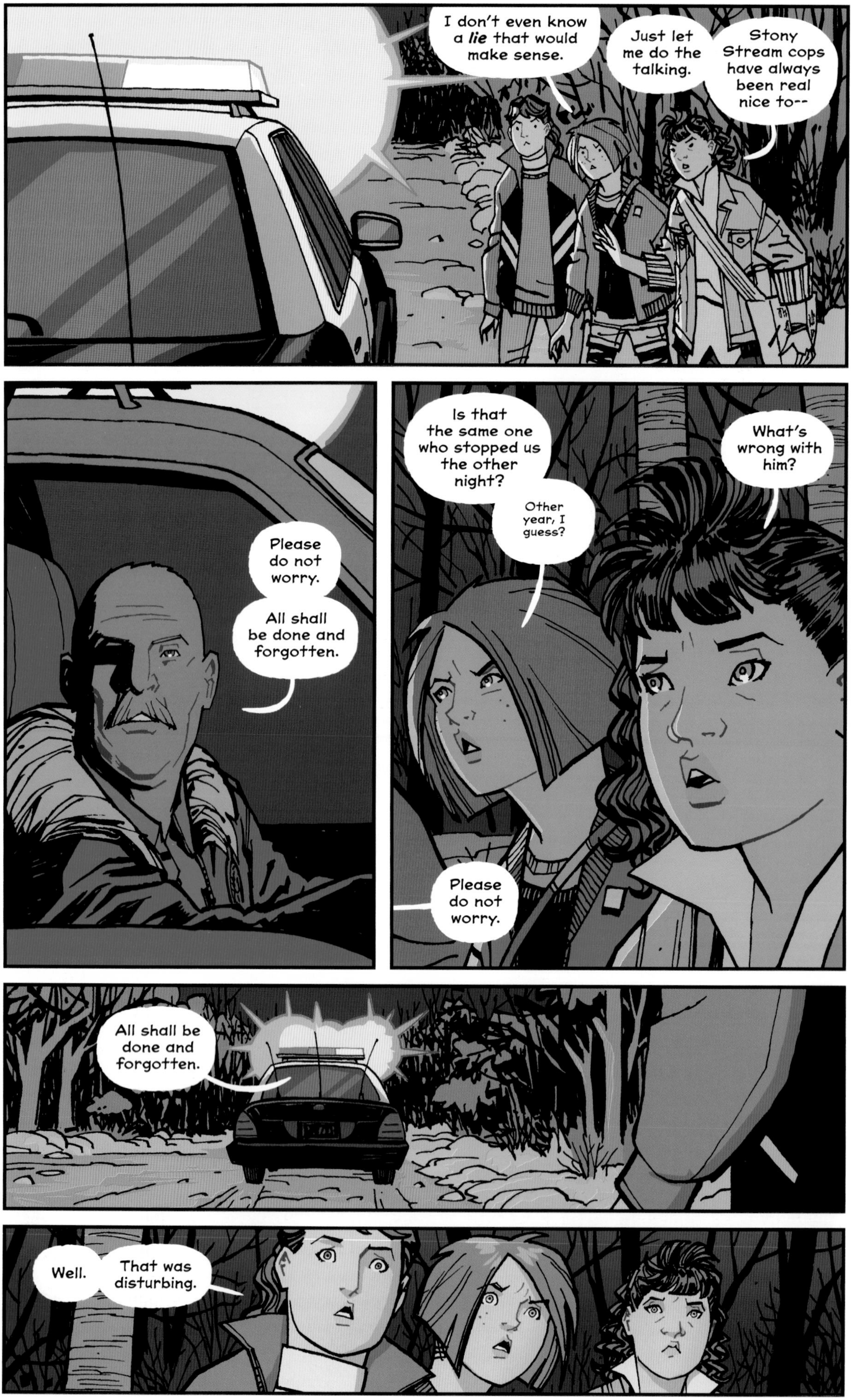
I don't even know a *lie* that would make sense.
Just let me do the talking.
Stony Stream cops have always been real nice to--
Please do not worry.
All shall be done and forgotten.
Is that the same one who stopped us the other night?
Other year, I guess?
What's wrong with him?
Please do not worry.
All shall be done and forgotten.
Well.
That was disturbing.

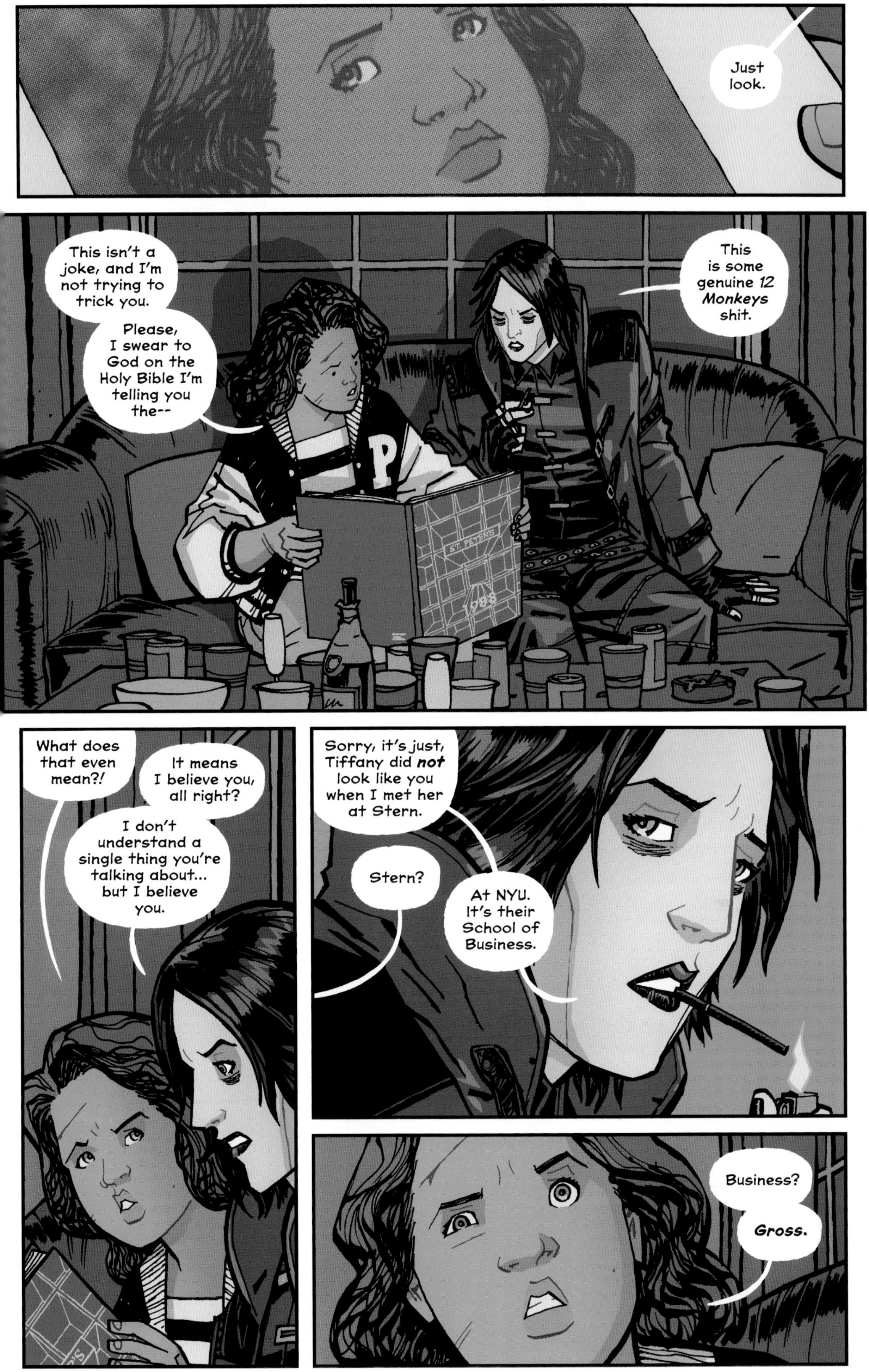
Just look.
This isn't a joke, and I'm not trying to trick you.
Please, I swear to God on the Holy Bible I'm telling you the--
This is some genuine 12 *Monkeys* shit.
ST. PETER'S
1988
What does that even mean?!
It means I believe you, all right?
I don't understand a single thing you're talking about... but I believe you.
Sorry, it's just, Tiffany did ***not*** look like you when I met her at Stern.
Stern?
At NYU. It's their School of Business.
Business?
Gross.

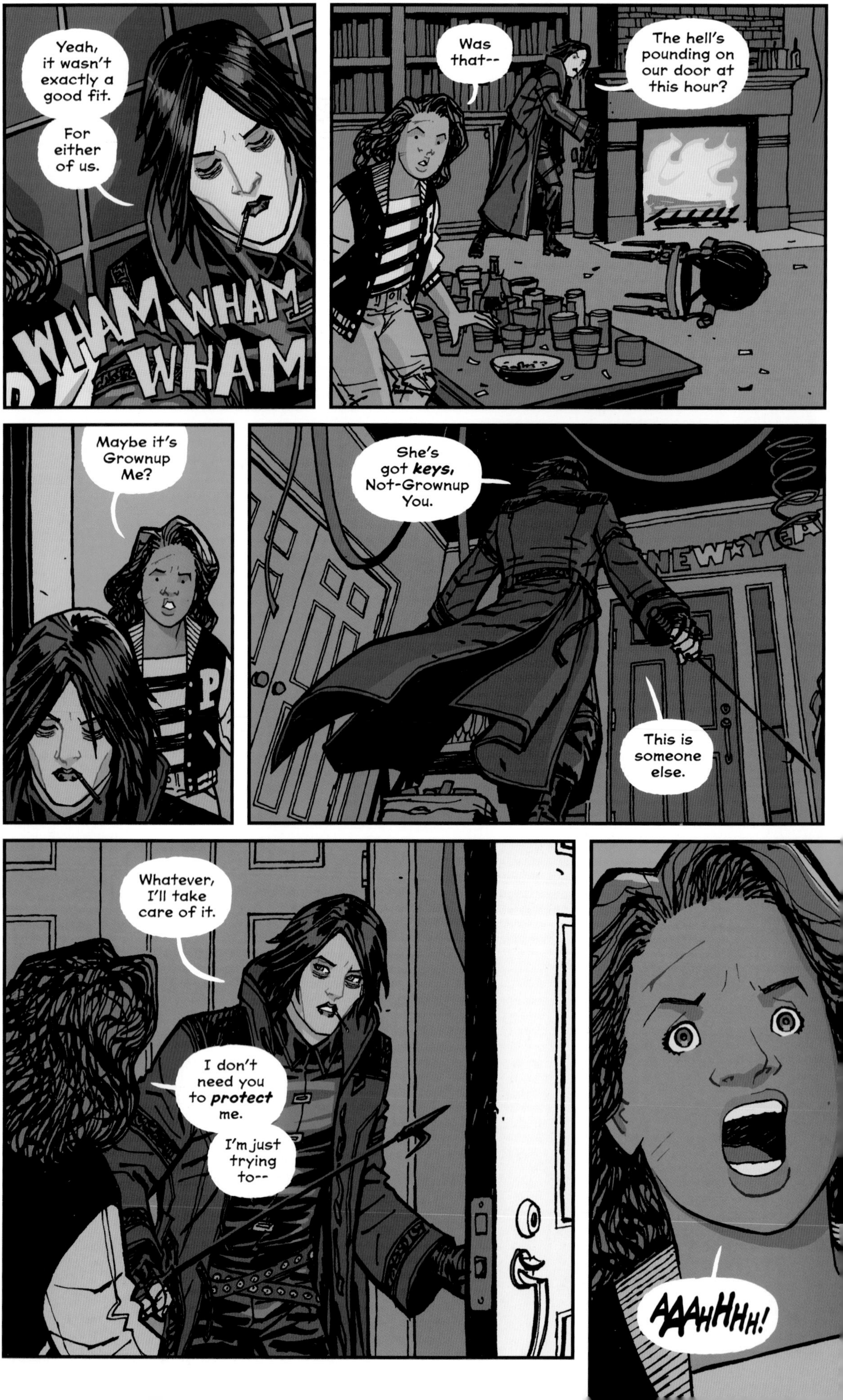
Yeah, it wasn't exactly a good fit.
For either of us.
WHAM WHAM WHAM
Was that--
The hell's pounding on our door at this hour?
Maybe it's Grownup Me?
She's got **keys,** Not-Grownup You.
This is someone else.
Whatever, I'll take care of it.
I don't need you to **protect** me.
I'm just trying to--
AAAHHHH!

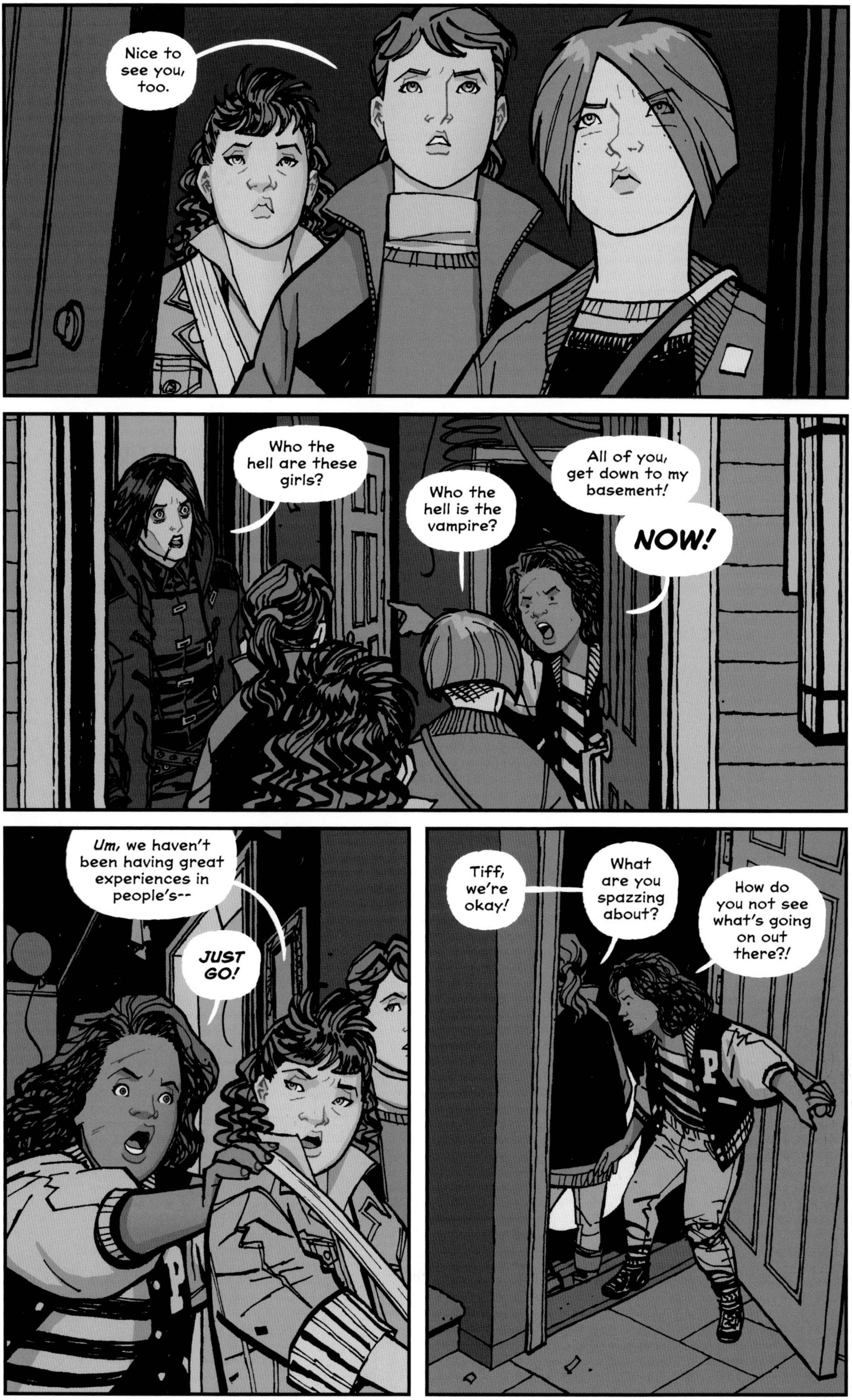
Nice to see you, too.
Who the hell are these girls?
Who the hell is the vampire?
All of you, get down to my basement!
NOW!
Um, we haven't been having great experiences in people's--
JUST GO!
Tiff, we're okay!
What are you spazzing about?
How do you not see what's going on out there?!

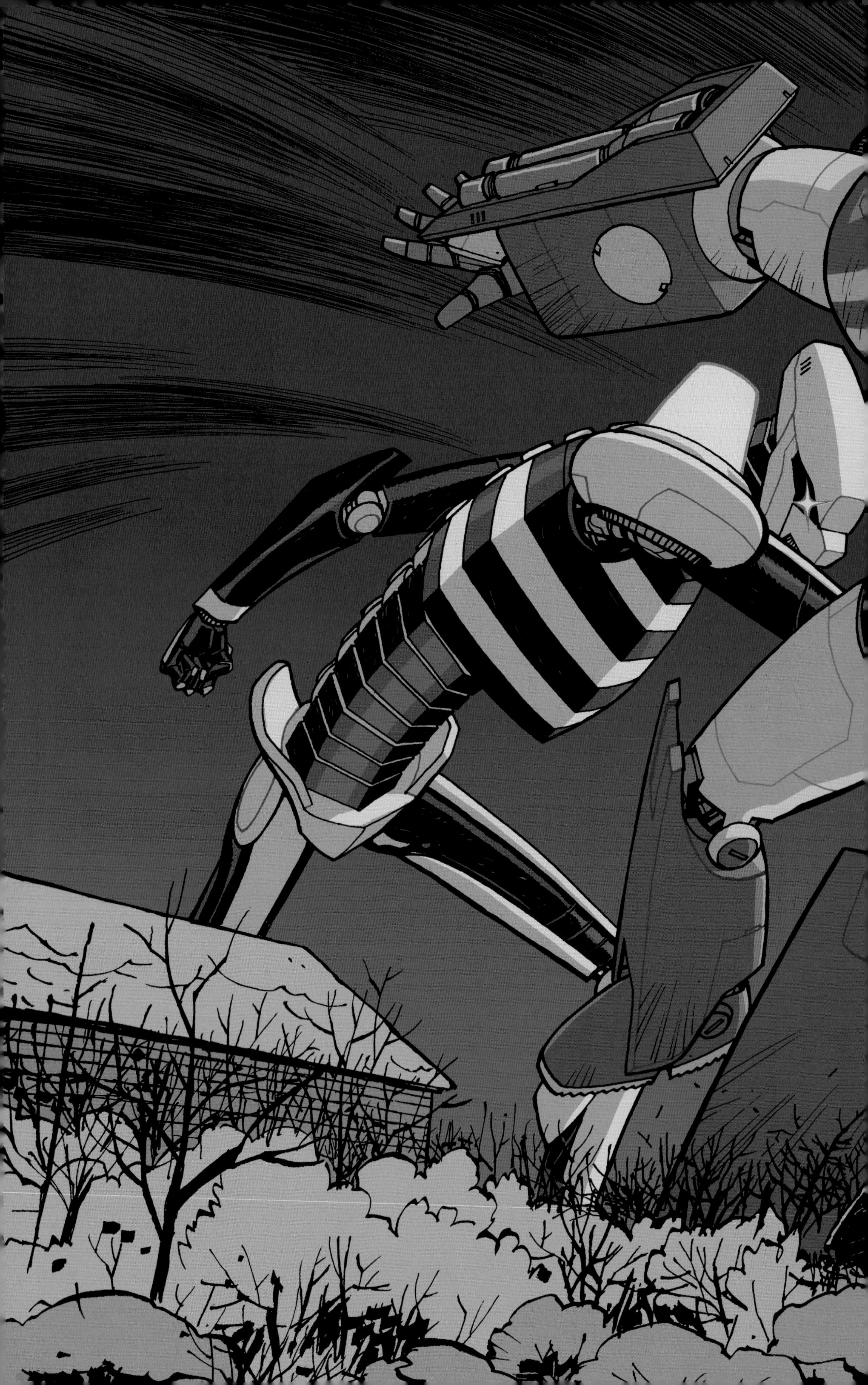

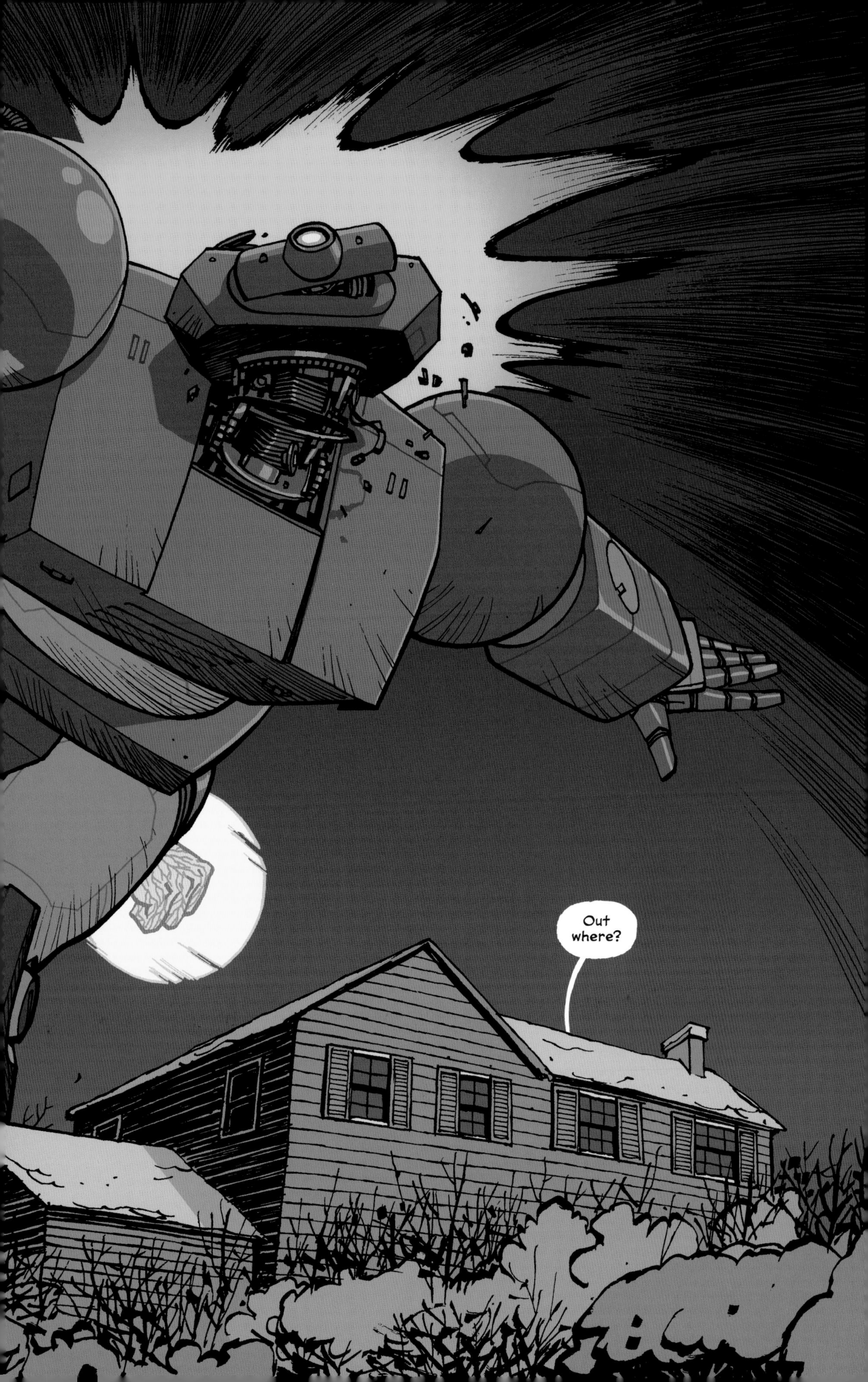
Out where?

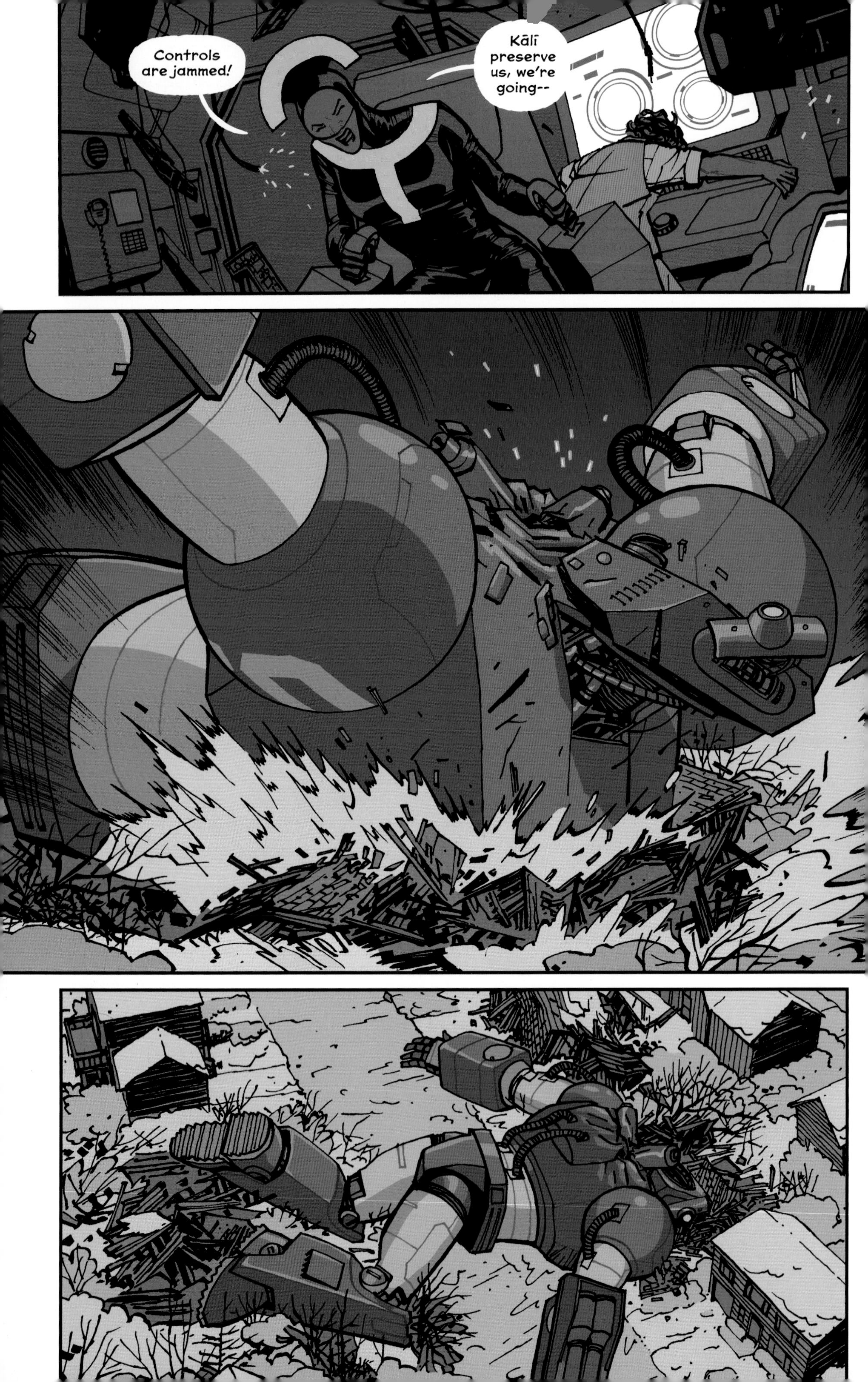
Controls are jammed!
Kālī preserve us, we're going--

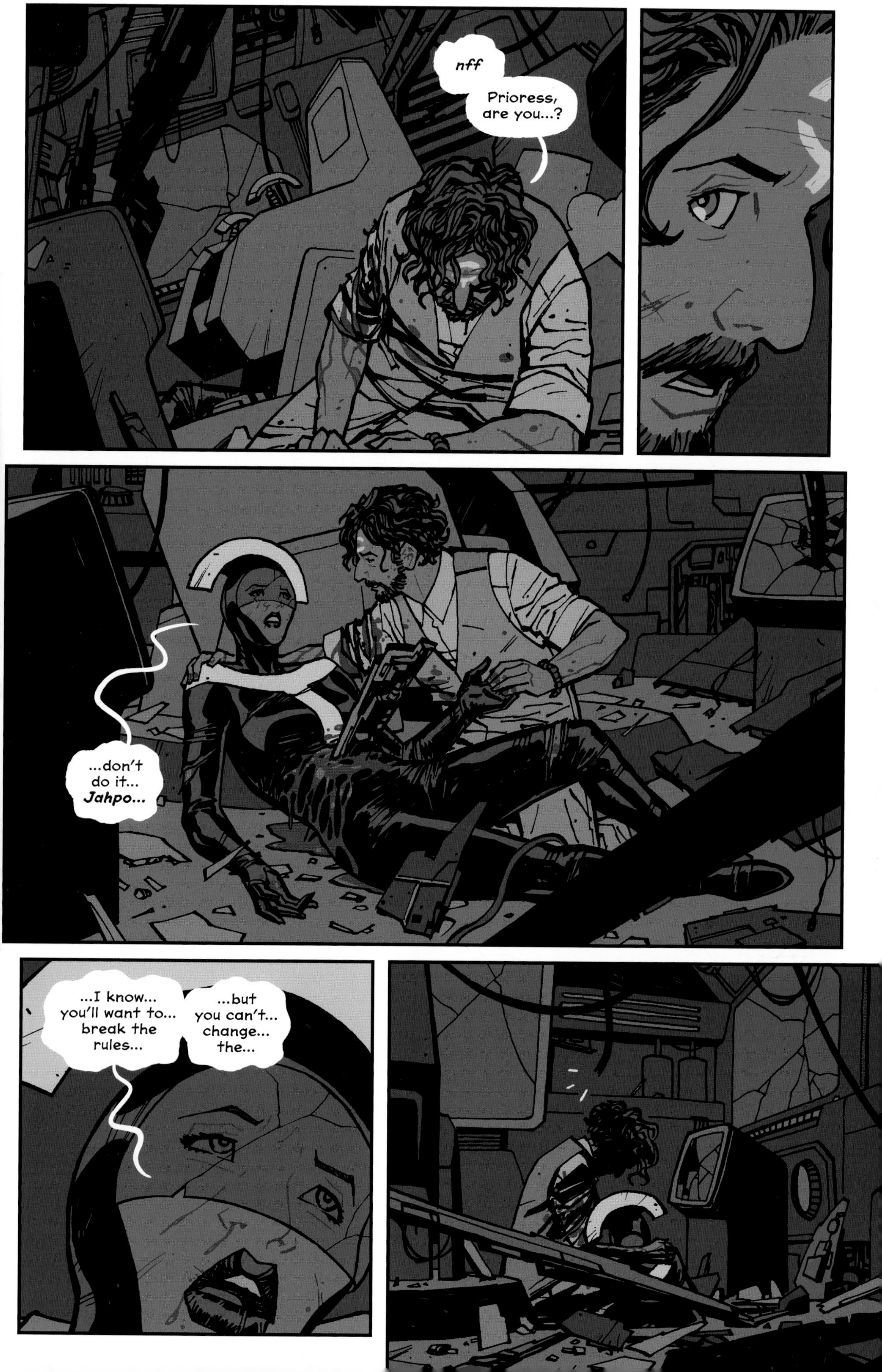
nff
Prioress, are you...?
...don't do it... Jahpo...
...I know... you'll want to... break the rules...
...but you can't... change... the...

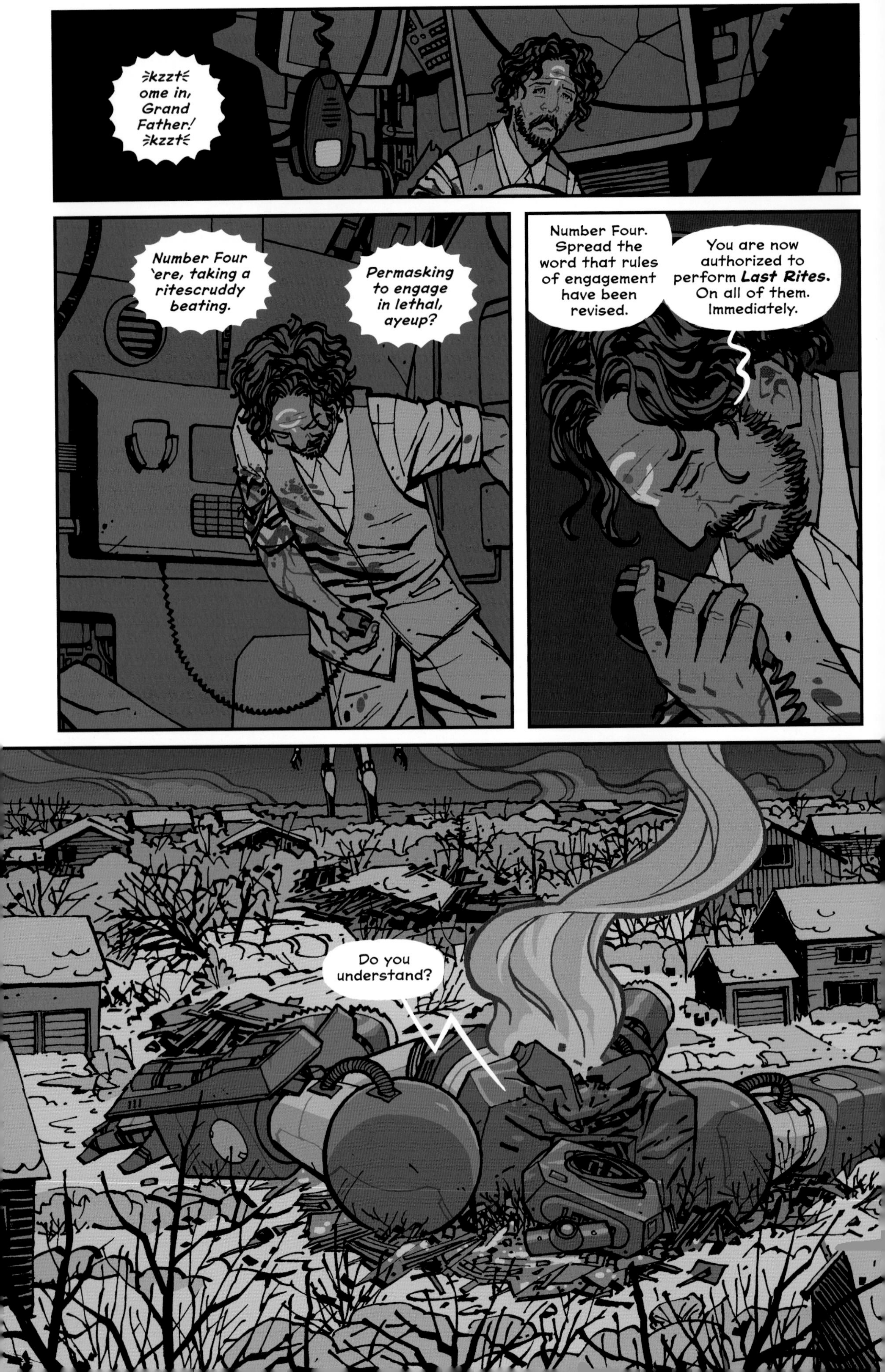

⚡kzzt⚡ ome in, Grand Father! ⚡kzzt⚡
Number Four 'ere, taking a ritescruddy beating.
Permasking to engage in lethal, ayeup?
Number Four. Spread the word that rules of engagement have been revised.
You are now authorized to perform Last Rites. On all of them. Immediately.
Do you understand?

CHAPTER

19

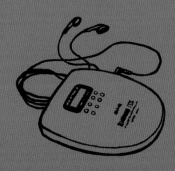

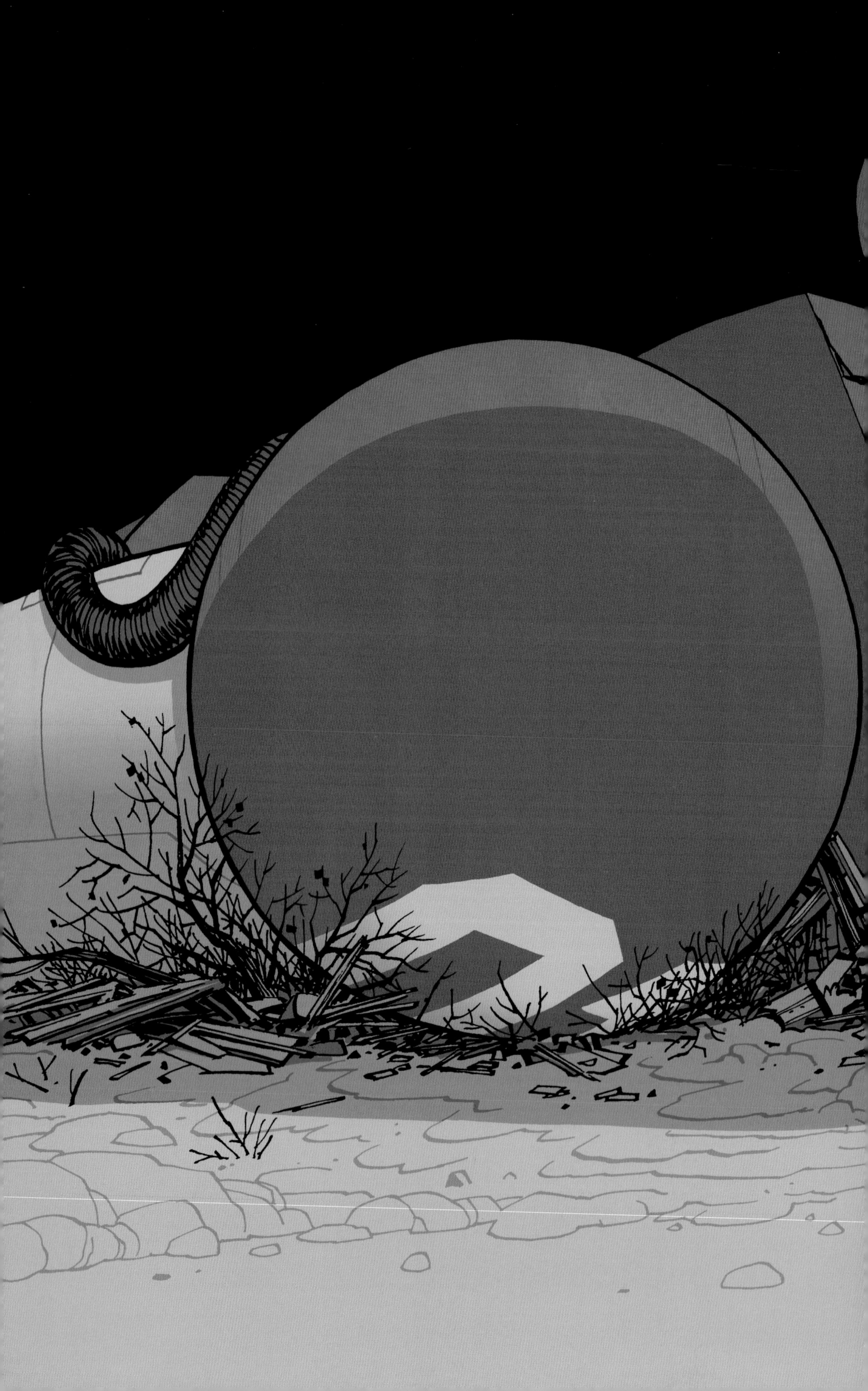

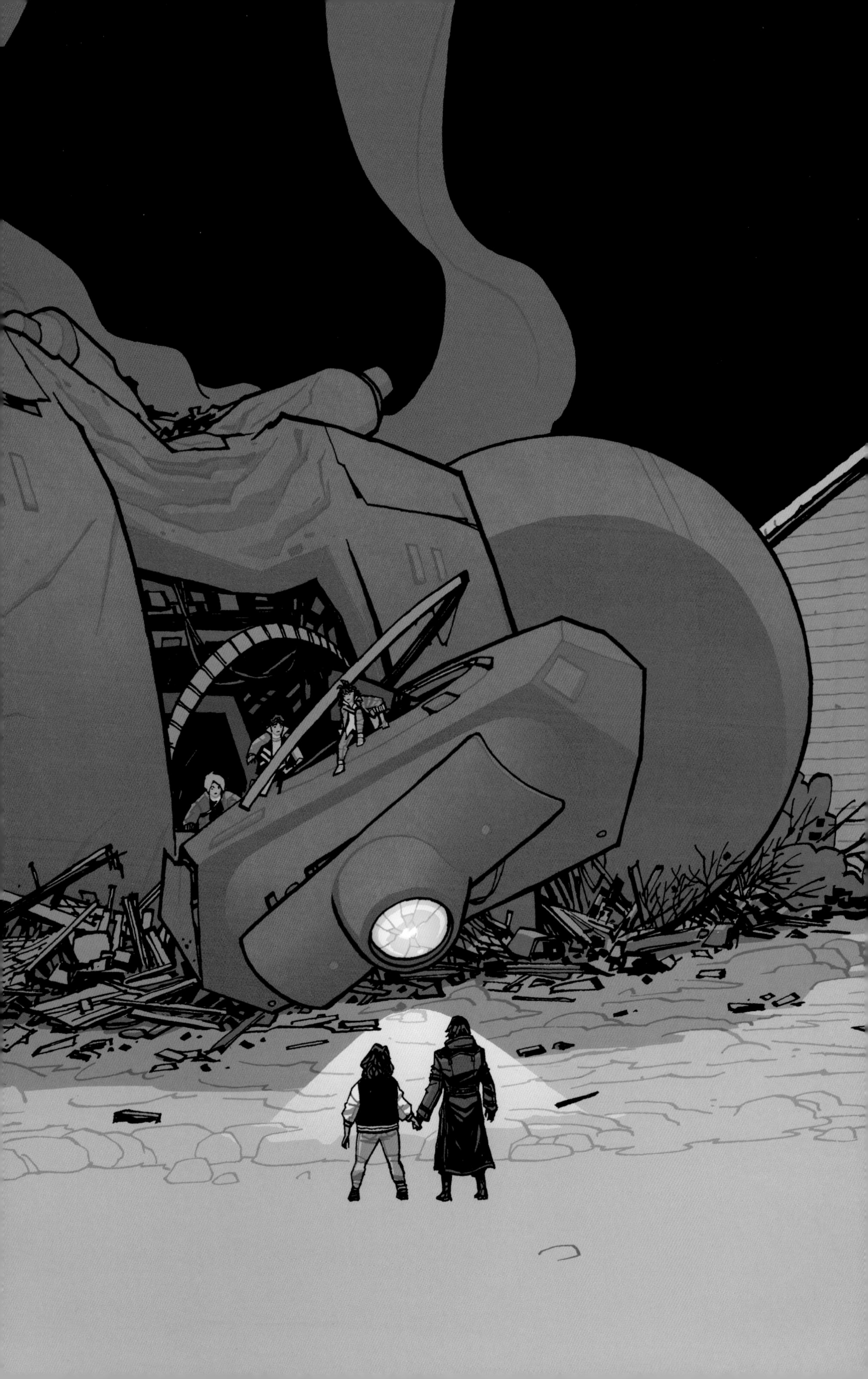

"Trump Orders Government to Stop
Work on Y2K Bug, 17 Years Later"

-**Bloomberg Politics** headline
June 15, 2017

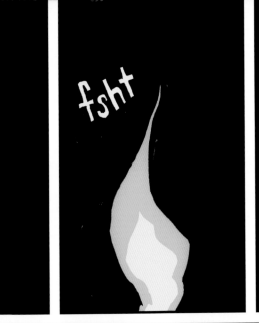

fsht

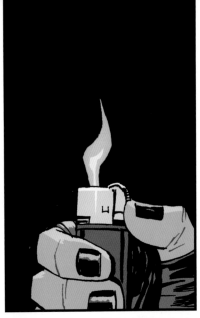

Everybody still in one piece?

What the hell just happened?

Sounded like a jumbo jet landed on Tiffany's house.

It wasn't an airplane, Erin, it was a giant killer robot!

How do you know?

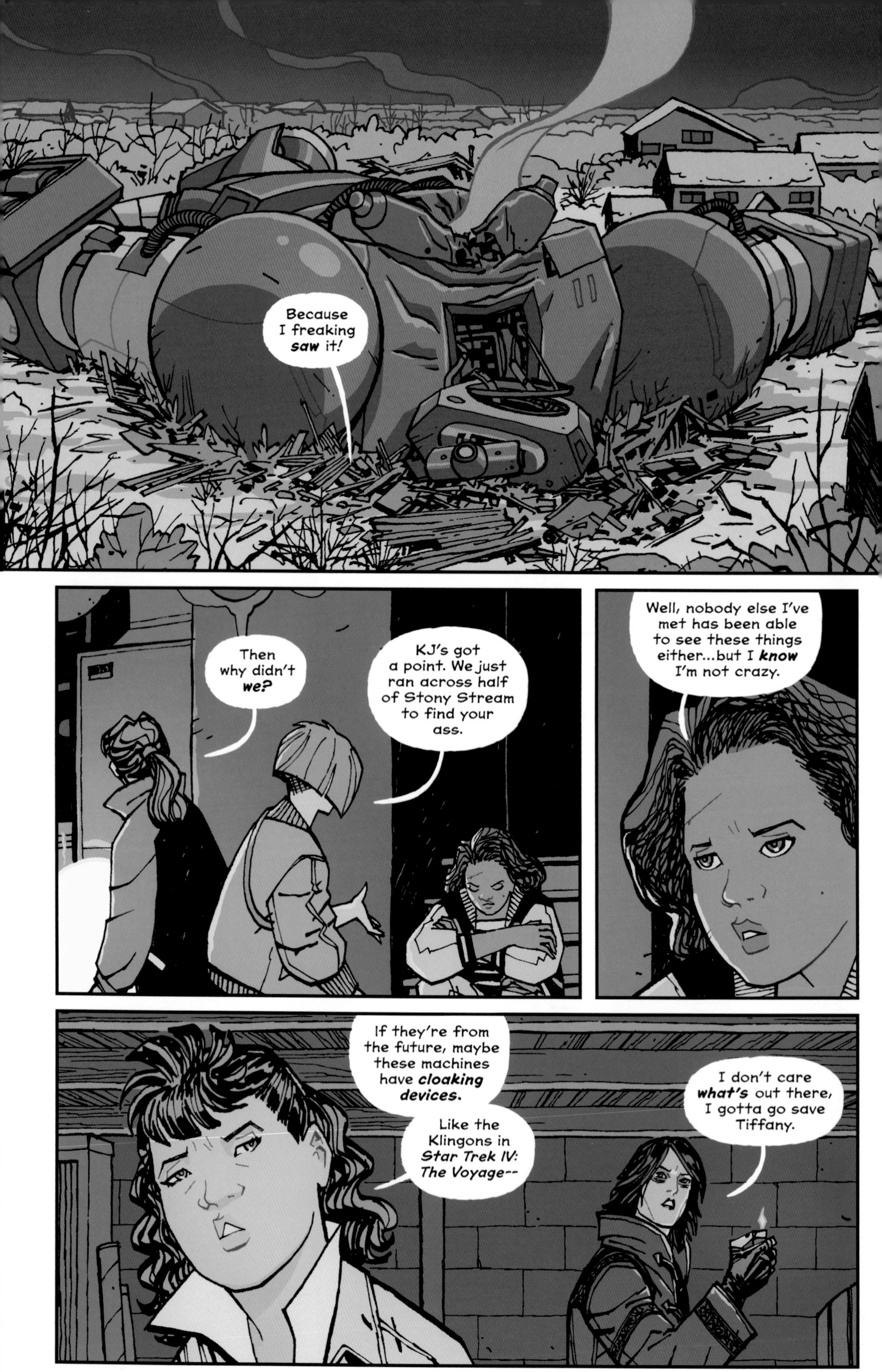

Because I freaking **saw** it!
Then why didn't **we?**
KJ's got a point. We just ran across half of Stony Stream to find your ass.
Well, nobody else I've met has been able to see these things either...but I **know** I'm not crazy.
If they're from the future, maybe these machines have **cloaking devices.**
Like the Klingons in *Star Trek IV: The Voyage--*
I don't care **what's** out there, I gotta go save Tiffany.

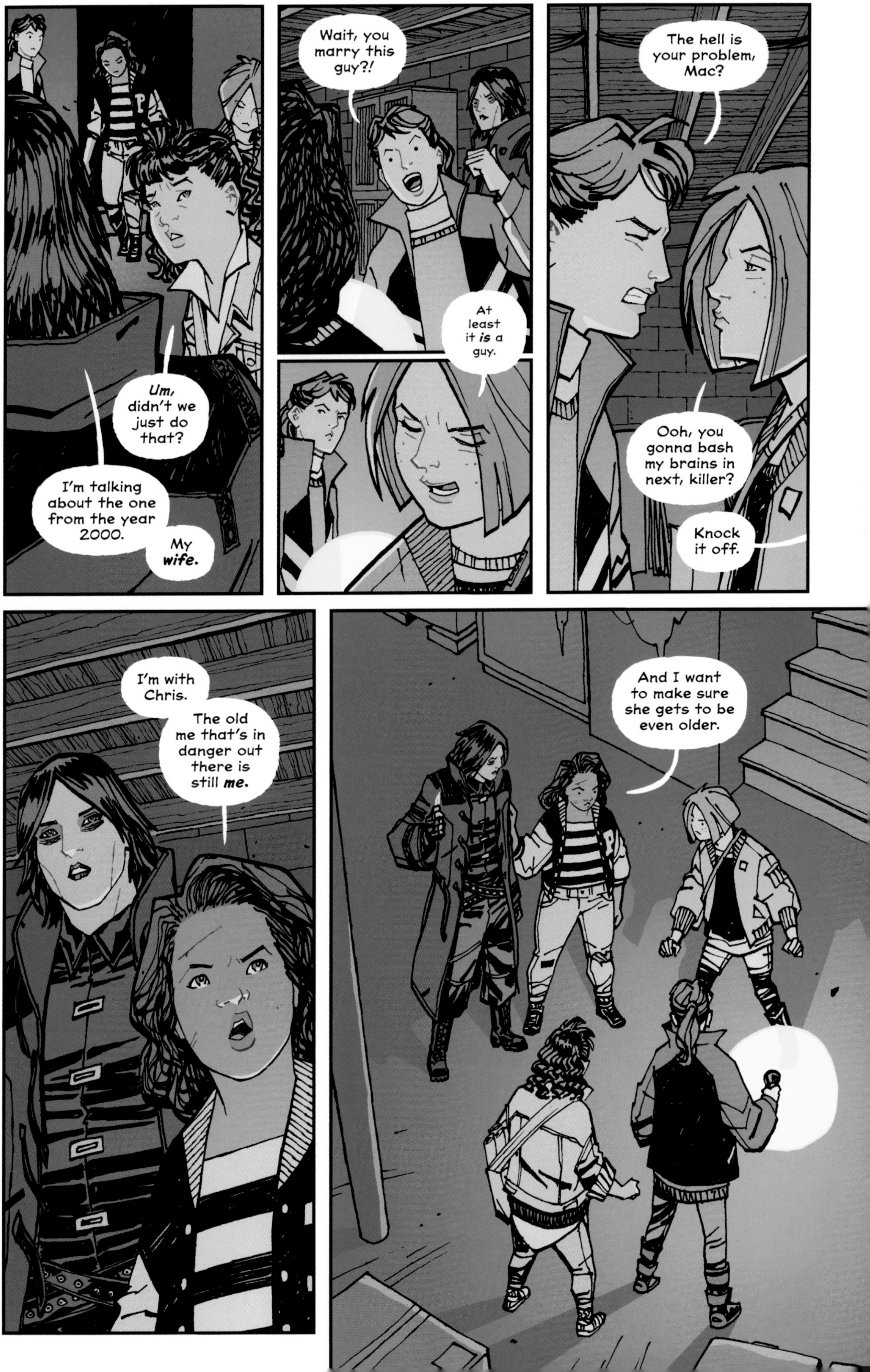
Um, didn't we just do that?
I'm talking about the one from the year 2000.
My wife.
Wait, you marry this guy?!
At least it is a guy.
The hell is your problem, Mac?
Ooh, you gonna bash my brains in next, killer?
Knock it off.
I'm with Chris.
The old me that's in danger out there is still me.
And I want to make sure she gets to be even older.

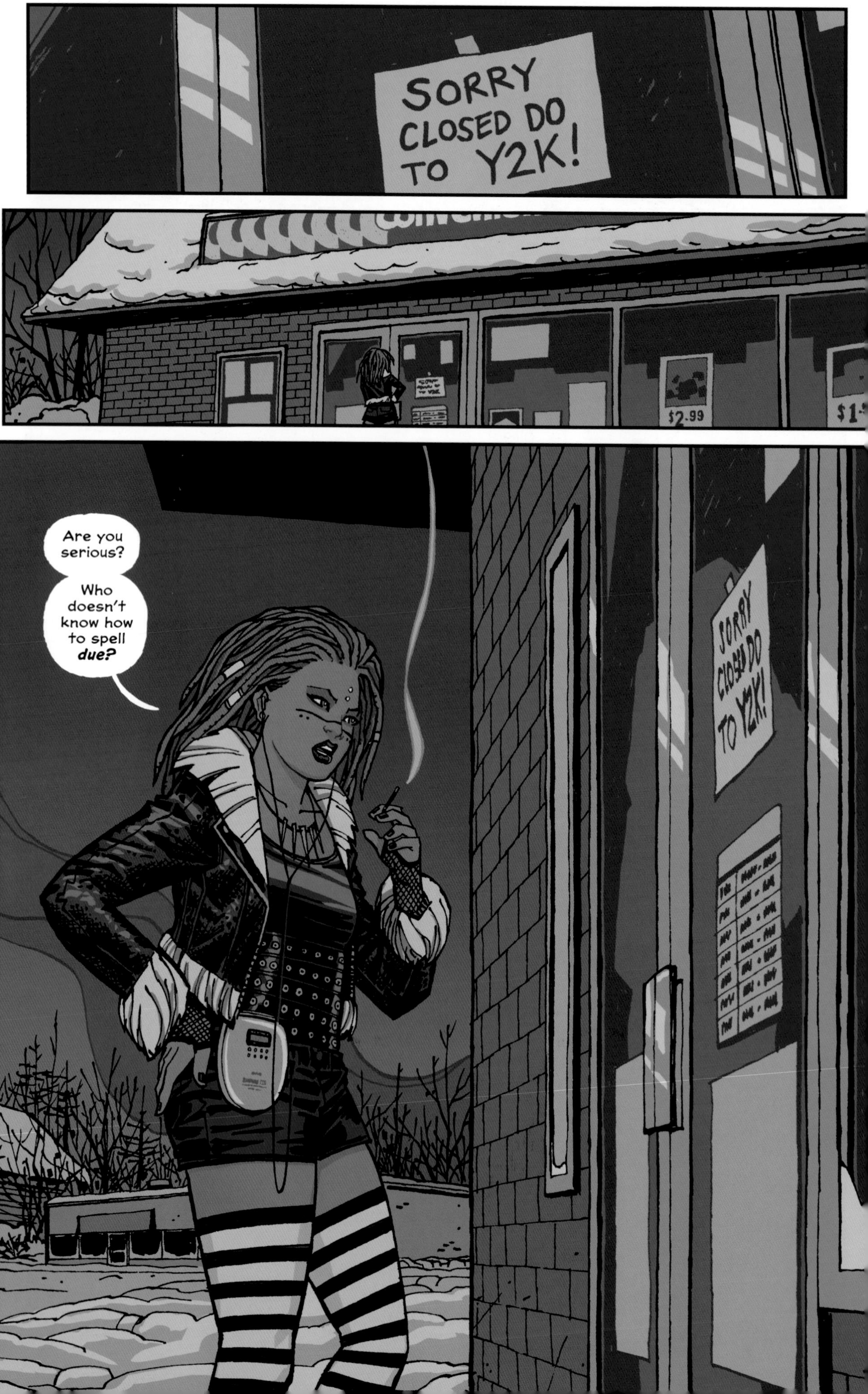
SORRY CLOSED DO TO Y2K!
$2.99
Are you serious?
Who doesn't know how to spell *due?*
SORRY CLOSED DO TO Y2K!

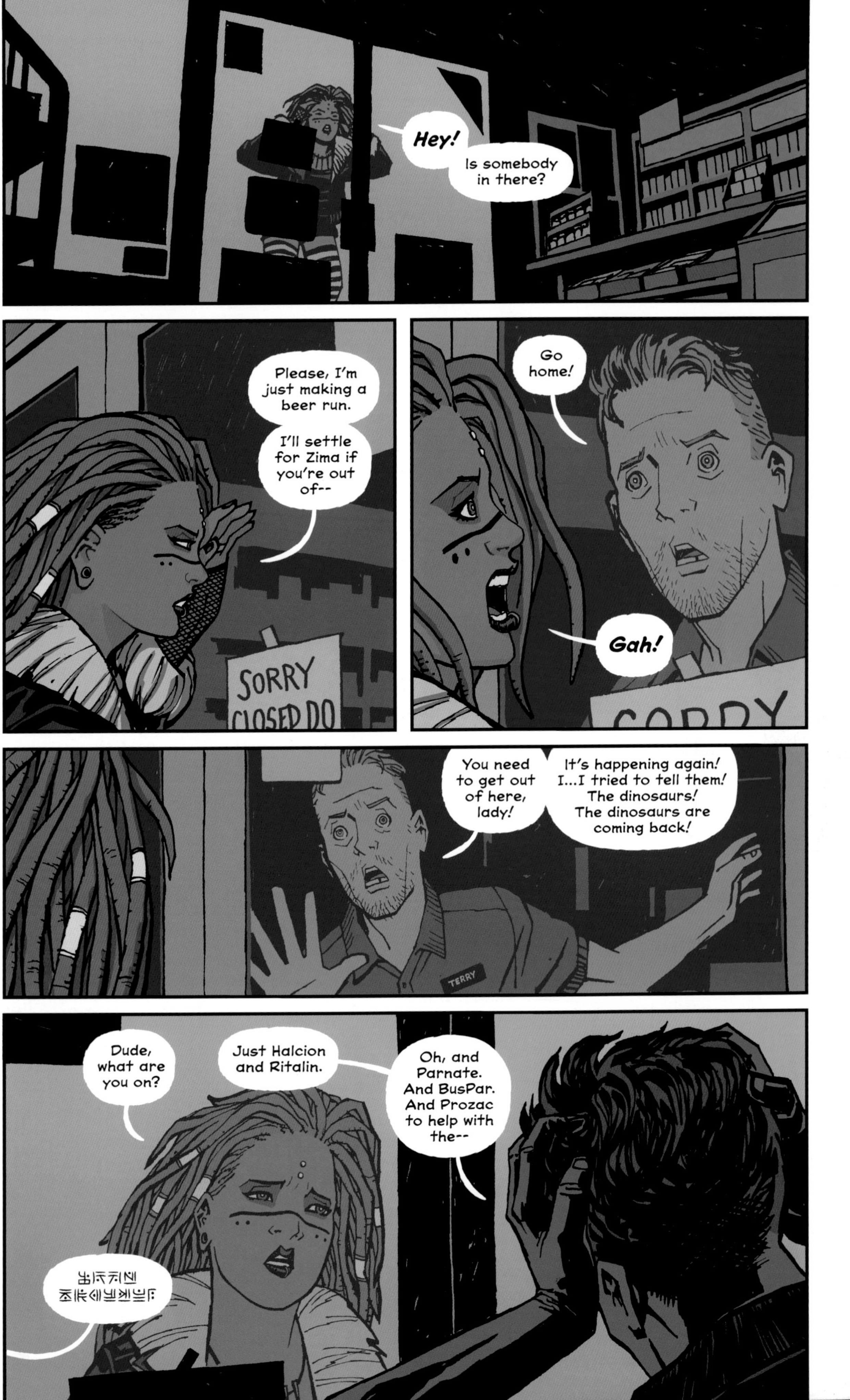
Hey!
Is somebody in there?
Please, I'm just making a beer run.
I'll settle for Zima if you're out of--
SORRY
Go home!
Gah!
You need to get out of here, lady!
It's happening again! I...I tried to tell them! The dinosaurs! The dinosaurs are coming back!
TERRY
Dude, what are you on?
Just Halcion and Ritalin.
Oh, and Parnate. And BusPar. And Prozac to help with the--

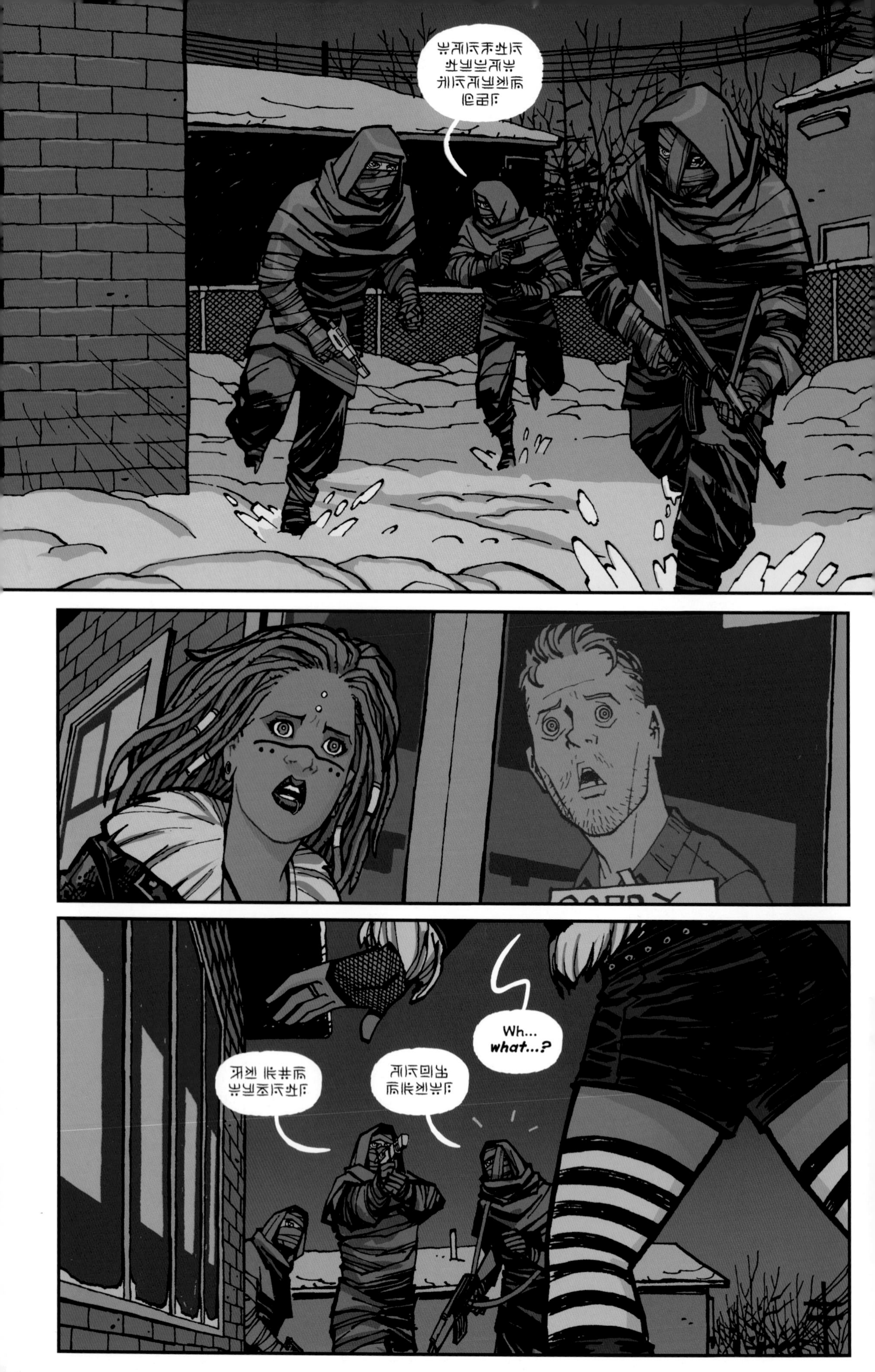
Wh... what...?

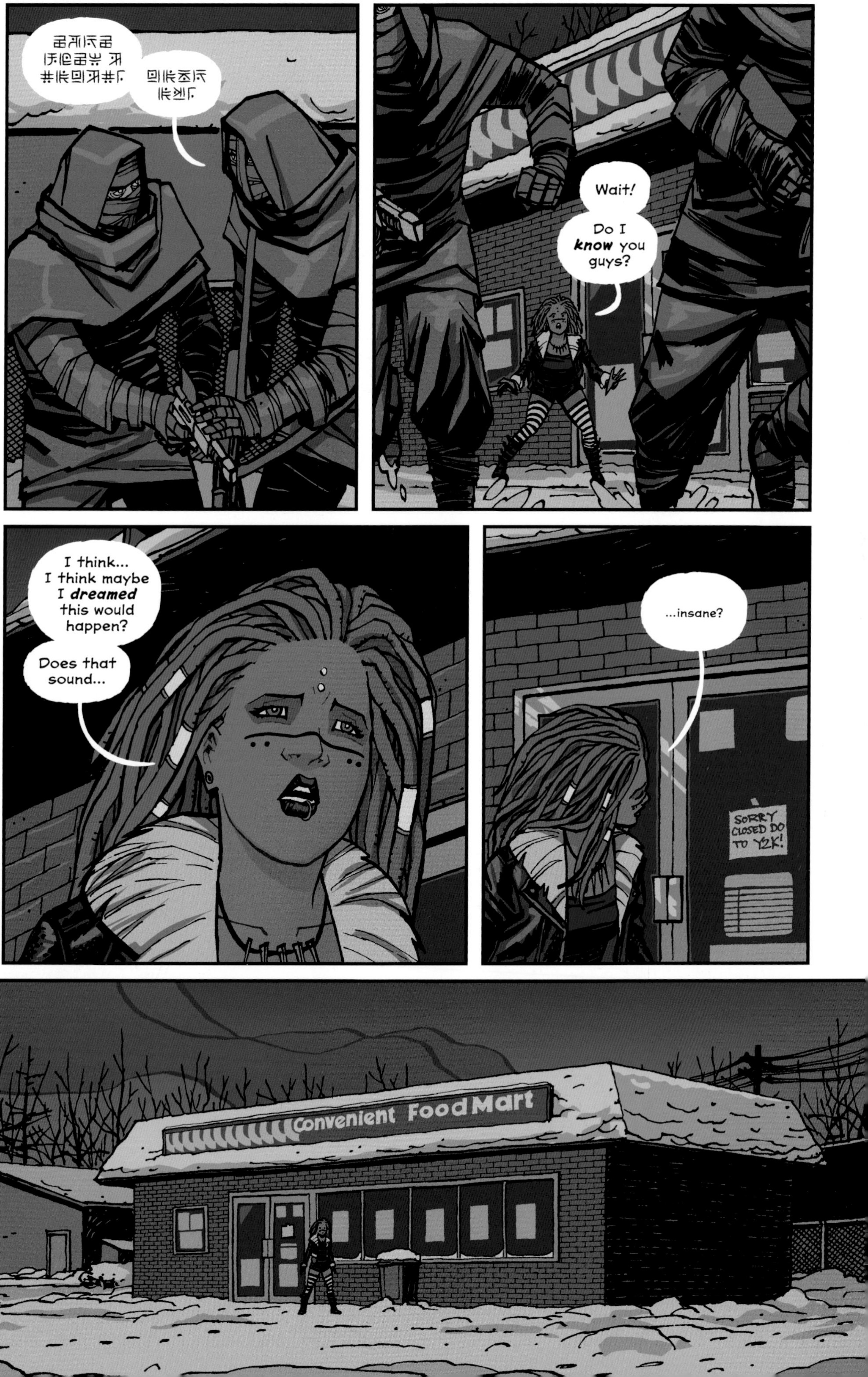
Wait!
Do I *know* you guys?
I think... I think maybe I *dreamed* this would happen?
Does that sound...
...insane?
SORRY CLOSED DO TO Y2K!
Convenient Food Mart

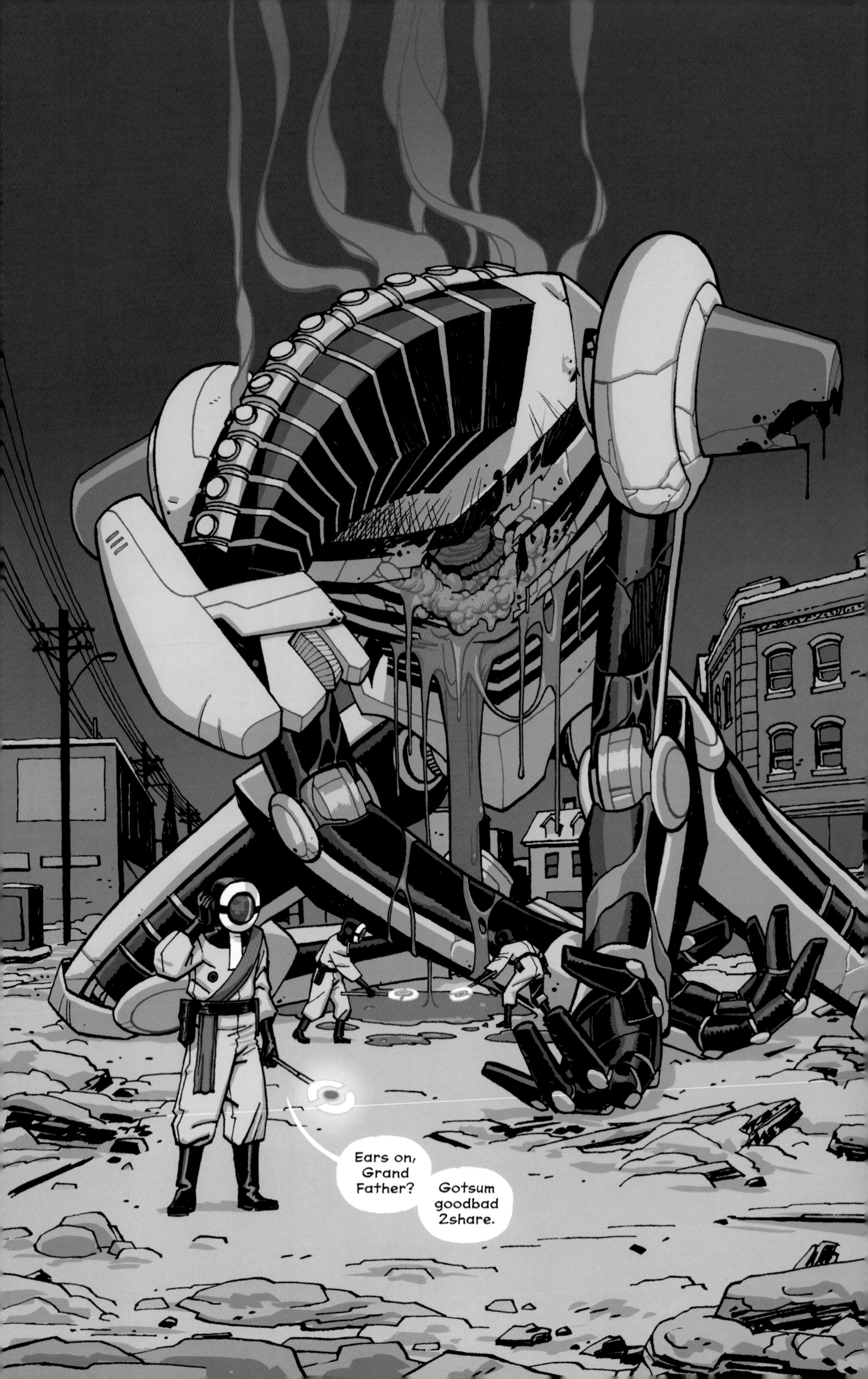
Ears on, Grand Father?
Gotsum goodbad 2share.

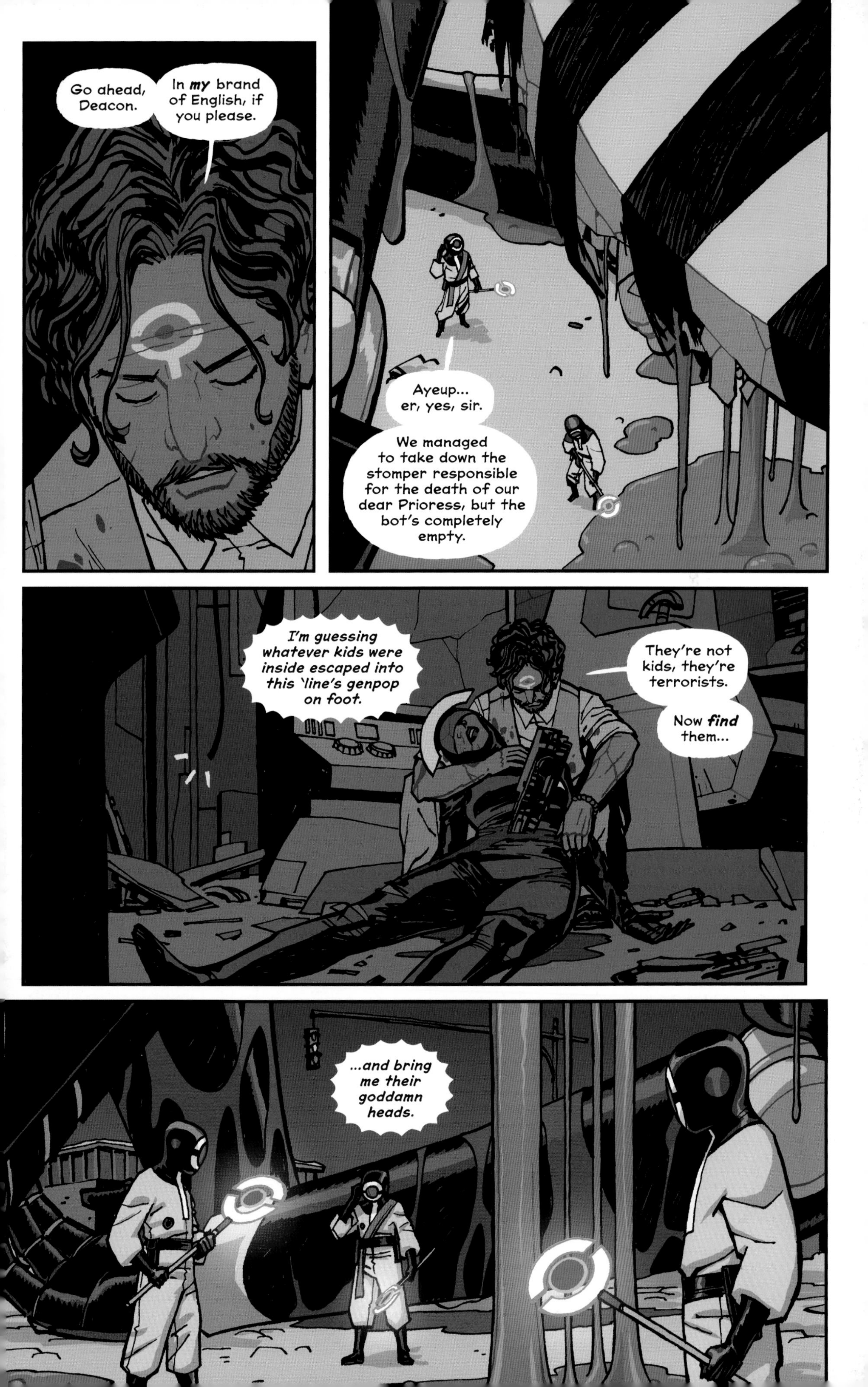
Go ahead, Deacon.
In *my* brand of English, if you please.
Ayeup... er, yes, sir.
We managed to take down the stomper responsible for the death of our dear Prioress, but the bot's completely empty.
I'm guessing whatever kids were inside escaped into this 'line's genpop on foot.
They're not kids, they're terrorists.
Now ***find*** them...
...and bring me their goddamn heads.

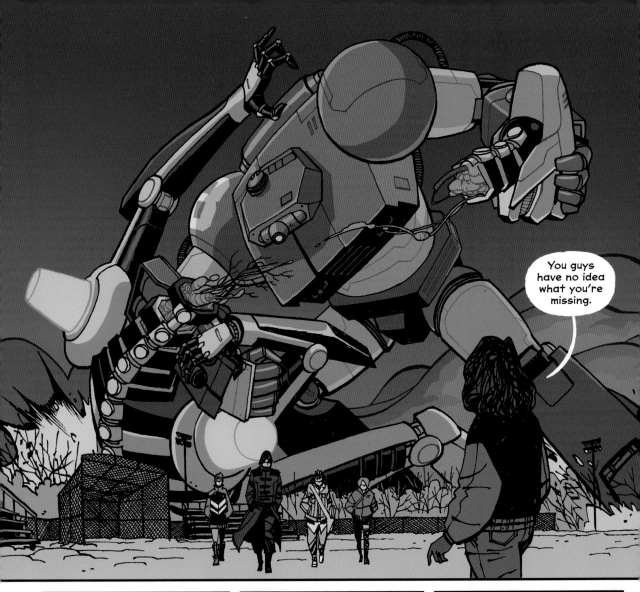

You guys have no idea what you're missing.

Why would these things want to destroy *Stony Stream?*

I don't think they do.

There are red bots and black bots, and they mostly seem to be fighting *each other.*

That makes sense, actually.

Charlotte-- the crazy cartoonist lady we met--said that we're caught in the crossfire of some kind of war between time travelers.

Yeah, dicks from the future are duking it out with dicks from the *further* future.

Holy...

What now, Tiff?

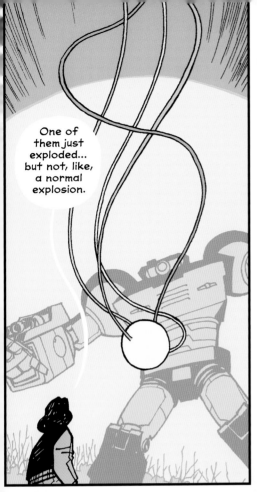

One of them just exploded... but not, like, a normal explosion.

It was more like one of the trippy blasts that launched us here.

So maybe these robots didn't use a time machine to get here.

Maybe they *are* the time machines.

If that's true, we might be able to hitch a ride on one and get back home!

Sure, all we have to do is carjack an invisible fucking Voltron.

What could be simpler?

This was the *worst* night to do mushrooms.

Chris!

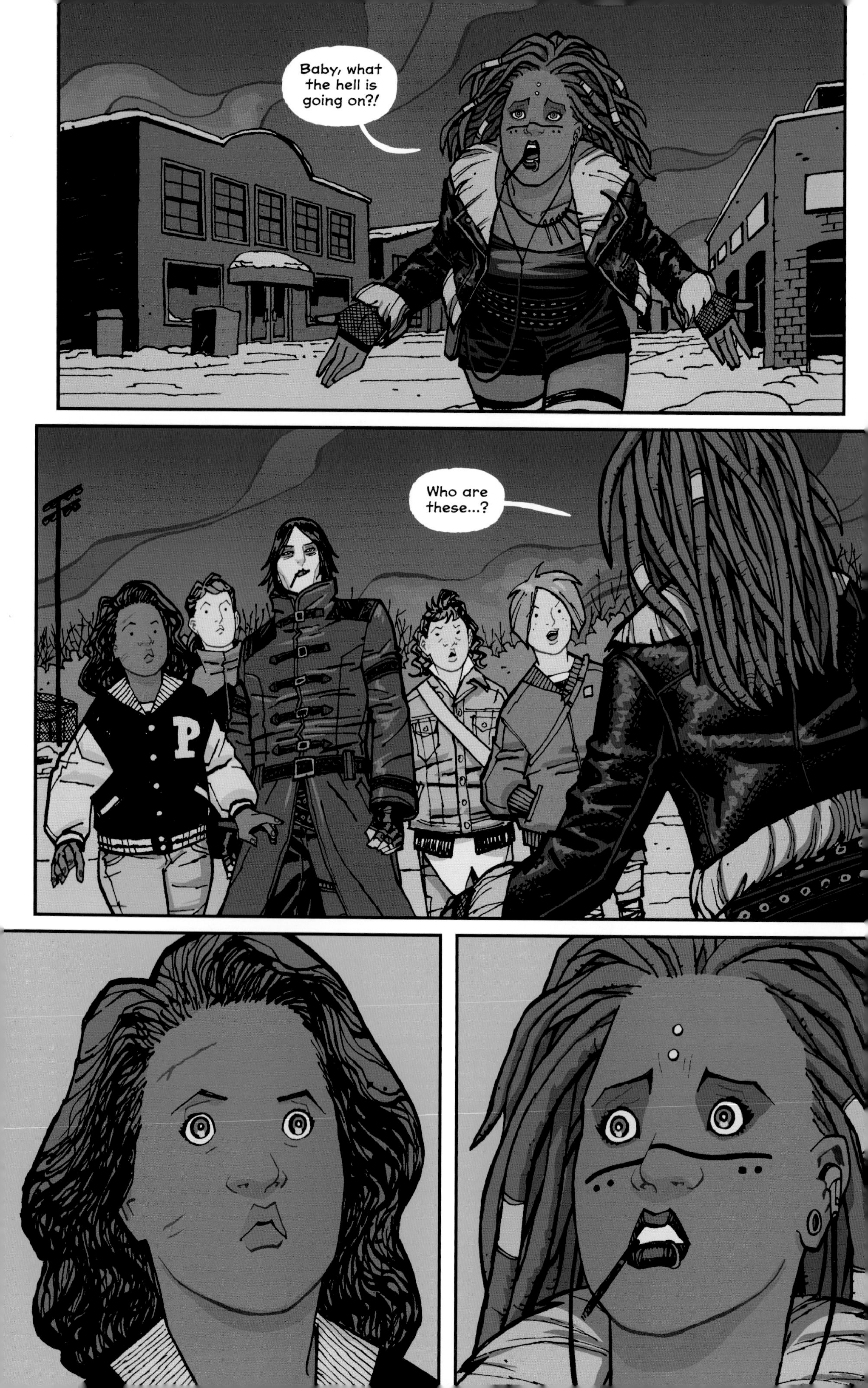

Baby, what the hell is going on?!
Who are these...?

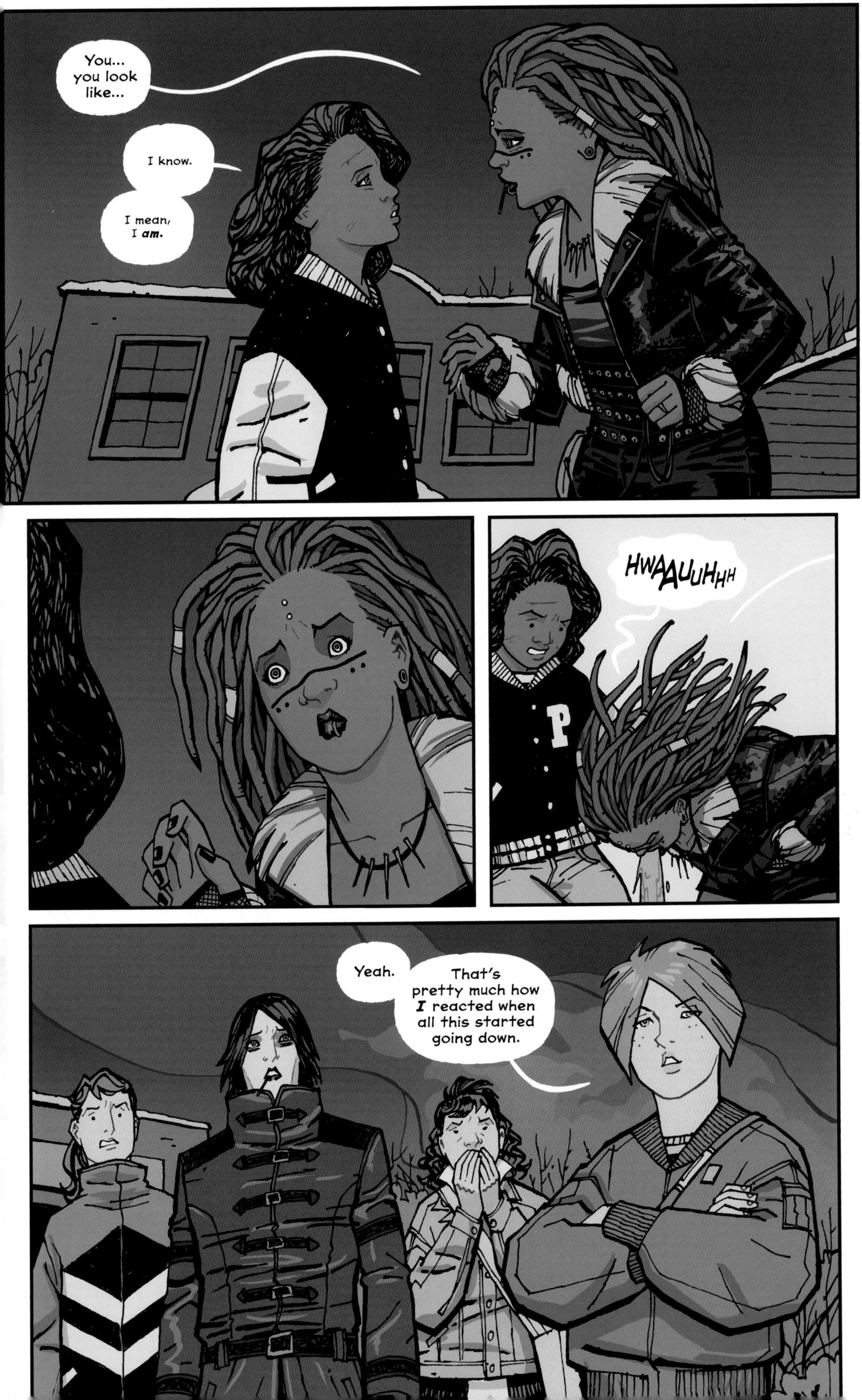
You... you look like...
I know.
I mean, I *am*.
HWAAUUHHH
Yeah.
That's pretty much how *I* reacted when all this started going down.

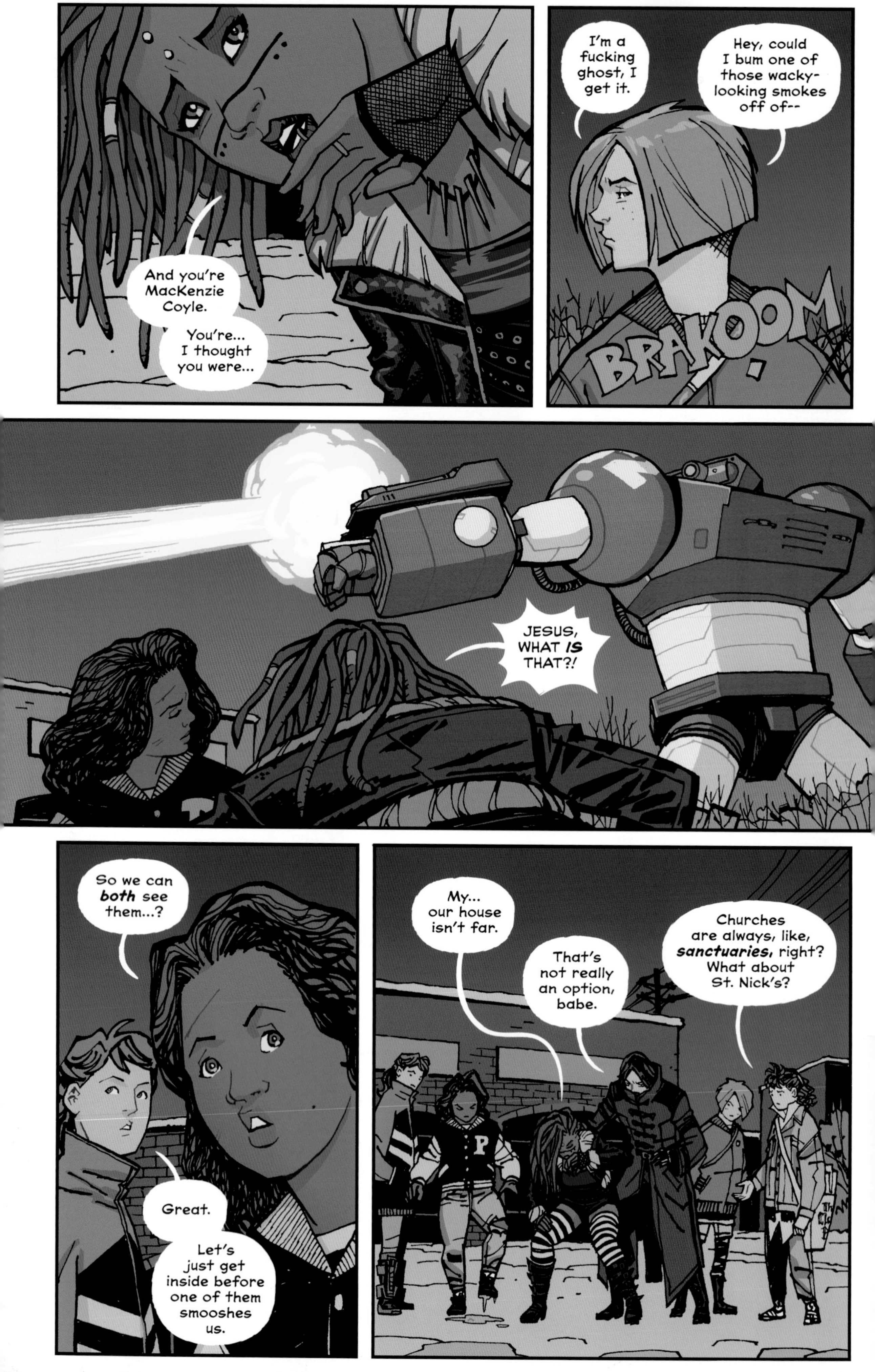
And you're MacKenzie Coyle.
You're... I thought you were...
I'm a fucking ghost, I get it.
Hey, could I bum one of those wacky-looking smokes off of--
BRAKOOM
JESUS, WHAT *IS* THAT?!
So we can ***both*** see them...?
Great.
Let's just get inside before one of them smooshes us.
My... our house isn't far.
That's not really an option, babe.
Churches are always, like, ***sanctuaries,*** right? What about St. Nick's?

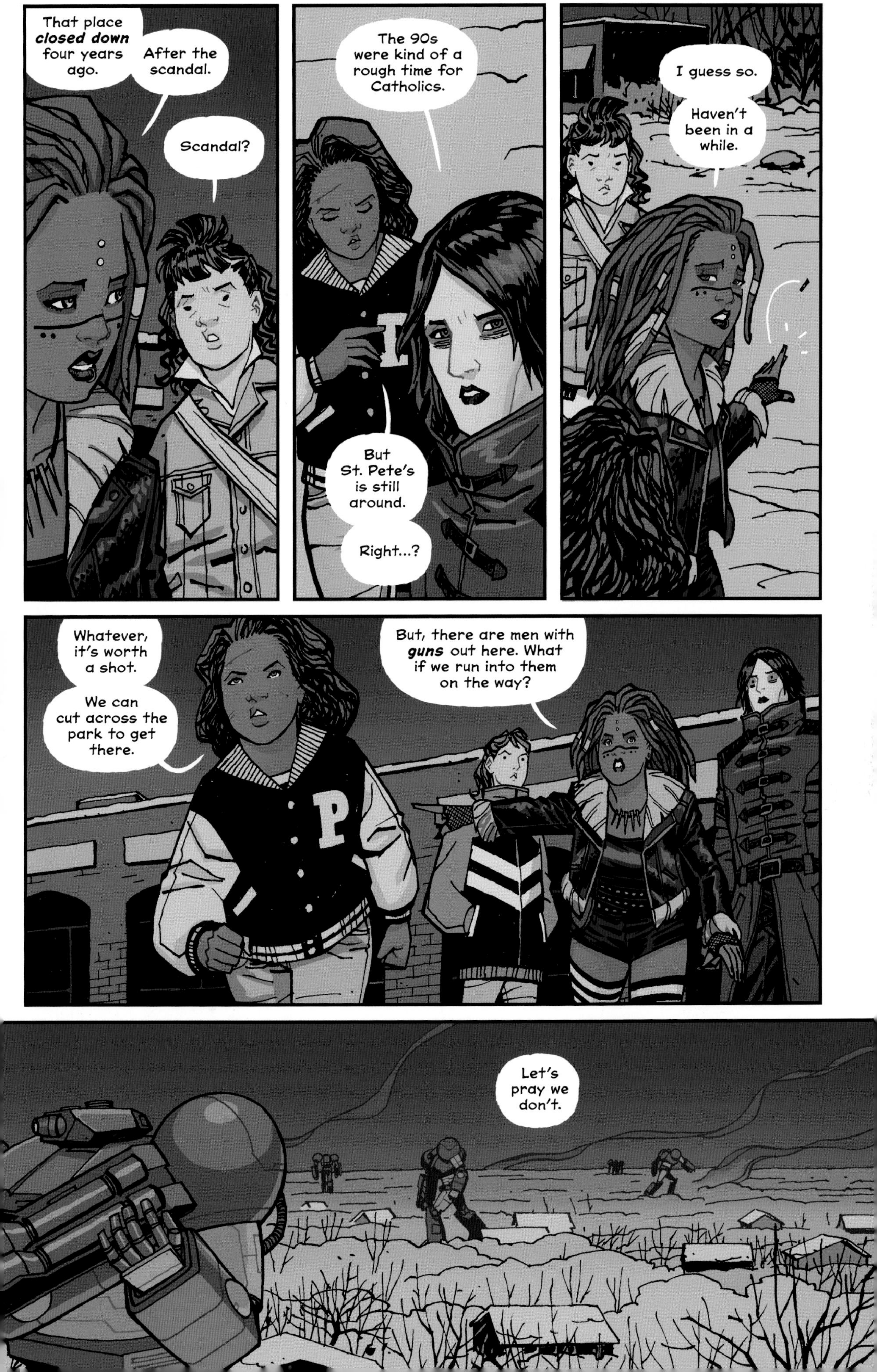
That place **closed down** four years ago.
After the scandal.
Scandal?
The 90s were kind of a rough time for Catholics.
But St. Pete's is still around.
Right...?
I guess so.
Haven't been in a while.
Whatever, it's worth a shot.
We can cut across the park to get there.
But, there are men with **guns** out here. What if we run into them on the way?
Let's pray we don't.

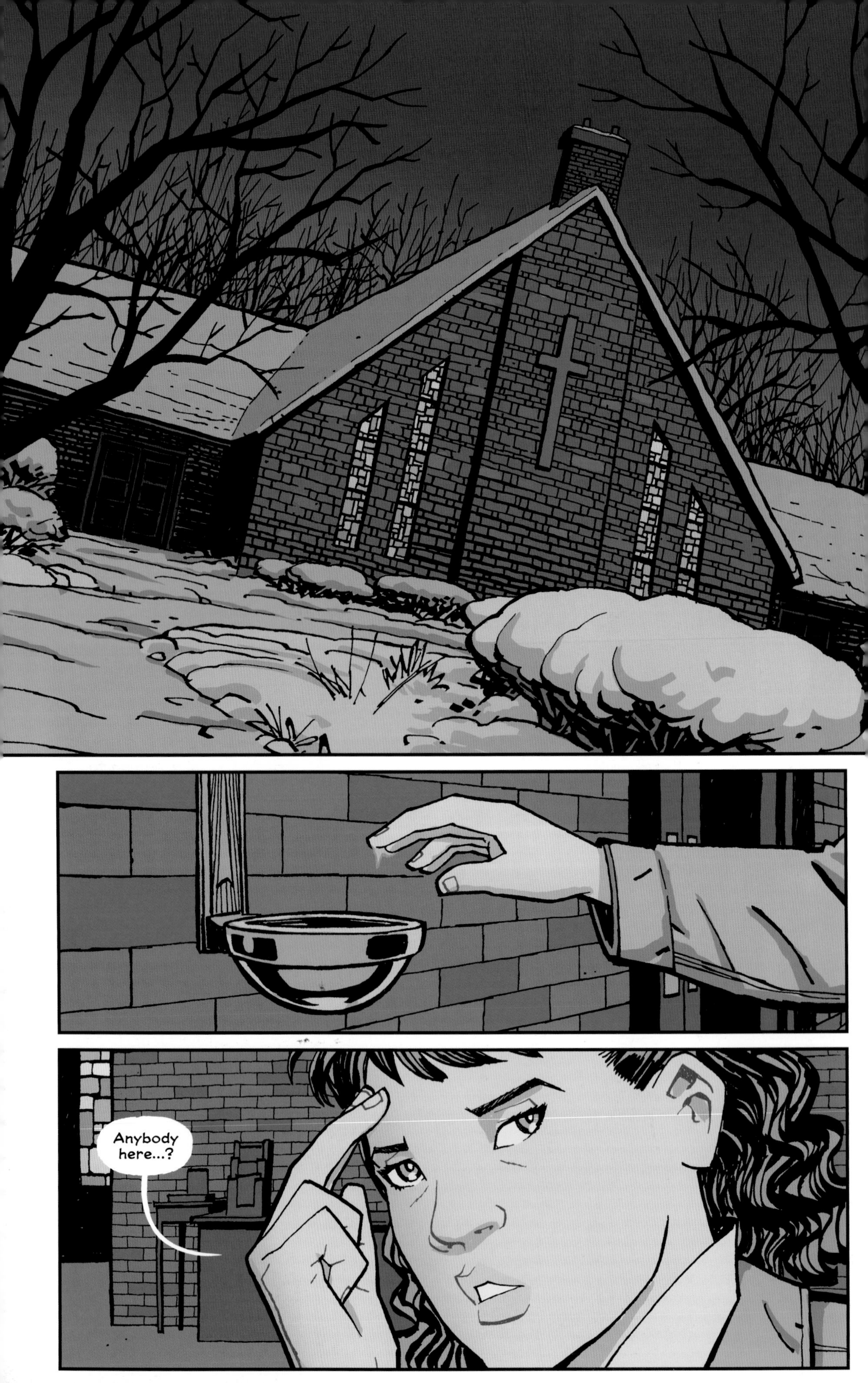
Anybody here...?

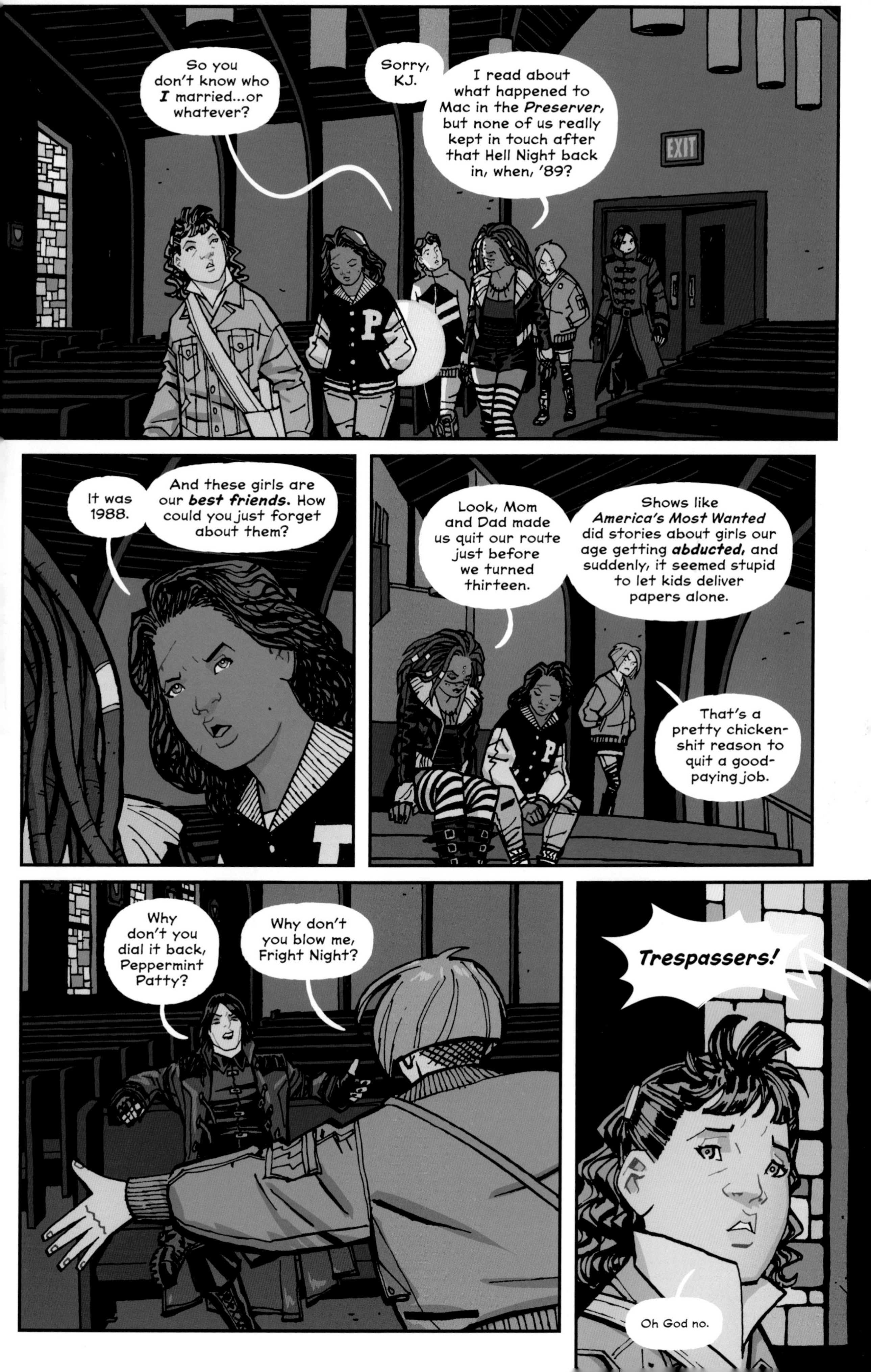
So you don't know who *I* married...or whatever?
Sorry, KJ.
I read about what happened to Mac in the *Preserver*, but none of us really kept in touch after that Hell Night back in, when, '89?
It was 1988.
And these girls are our ***best friends.*** How could you just forget about them?
Look, Mom and Dad made us quit our route just before we turned thirteen.
Shows like *America's Most Wanted* did stories about girls our age getting ***abducted,*** and suddenly, it seemed stupid to let kids deliver papers alone.
That's a pretty chicken-shit reason to quit a good-paying job.
Why don't you dial it back, Peppermint Patty?
Why don't you blow me, Fright Night?
Trespassers!
Oh God no.

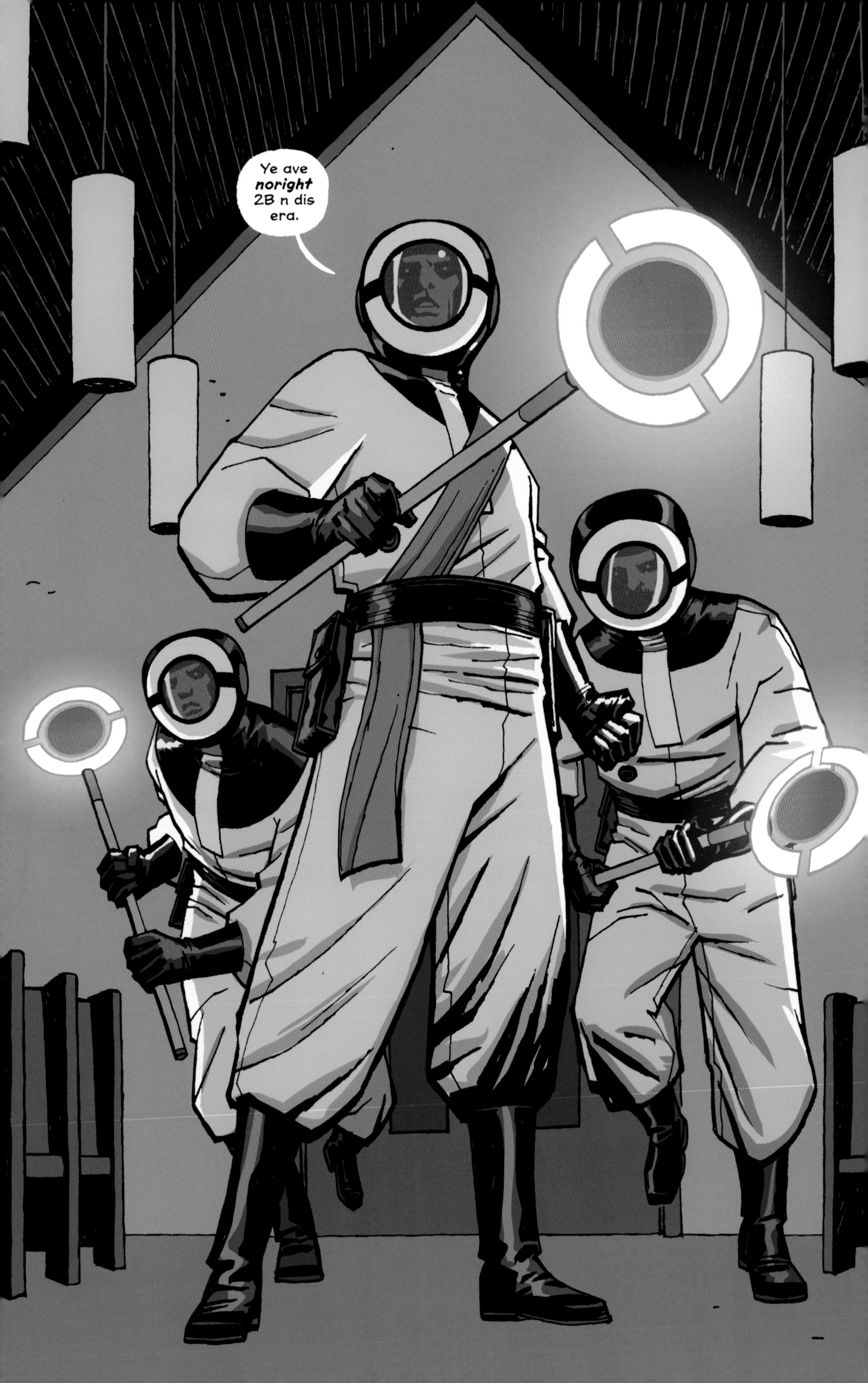
Ye ave **noright** 2B n dis era.

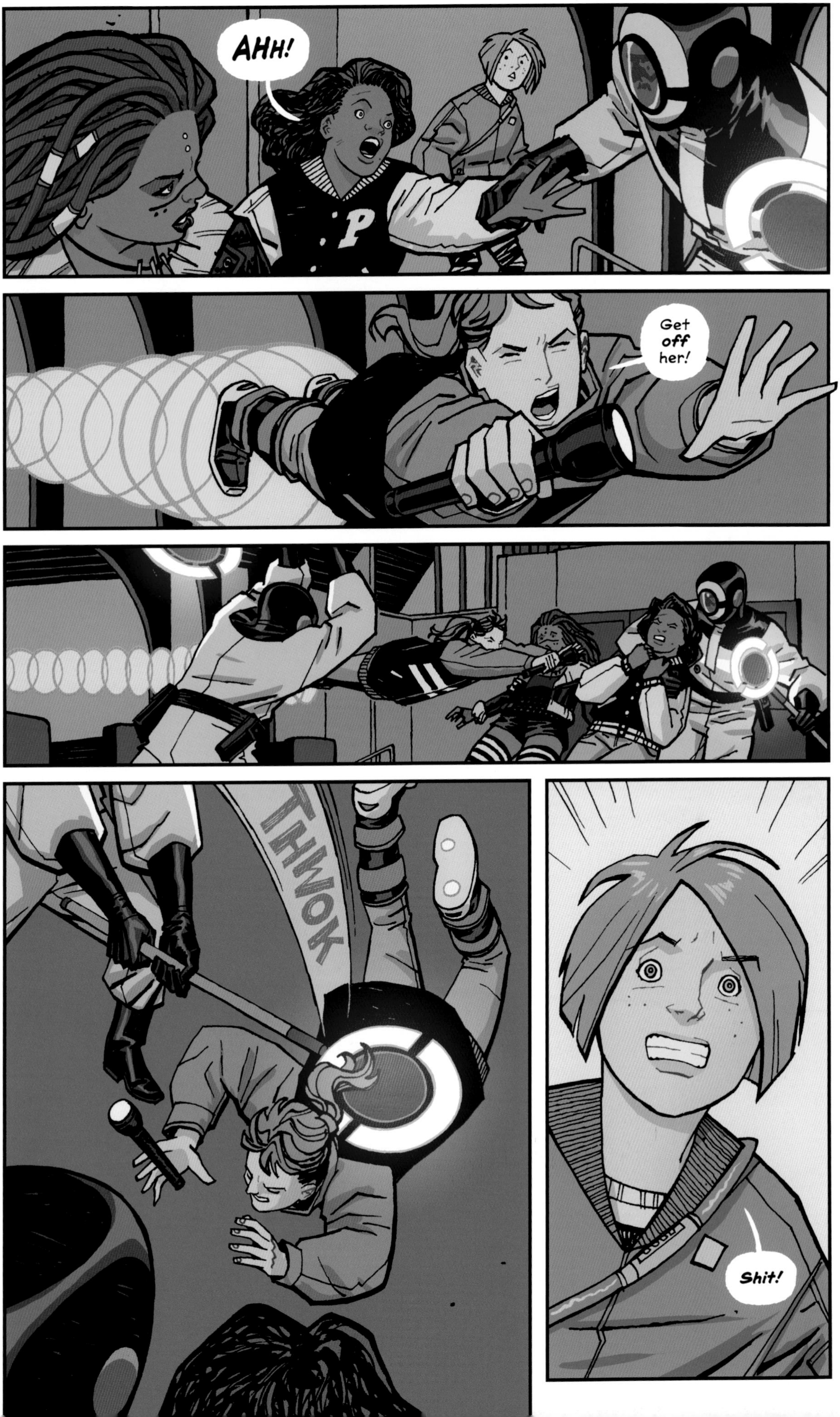
AHH!
Get off her!
THWOK
Shit!

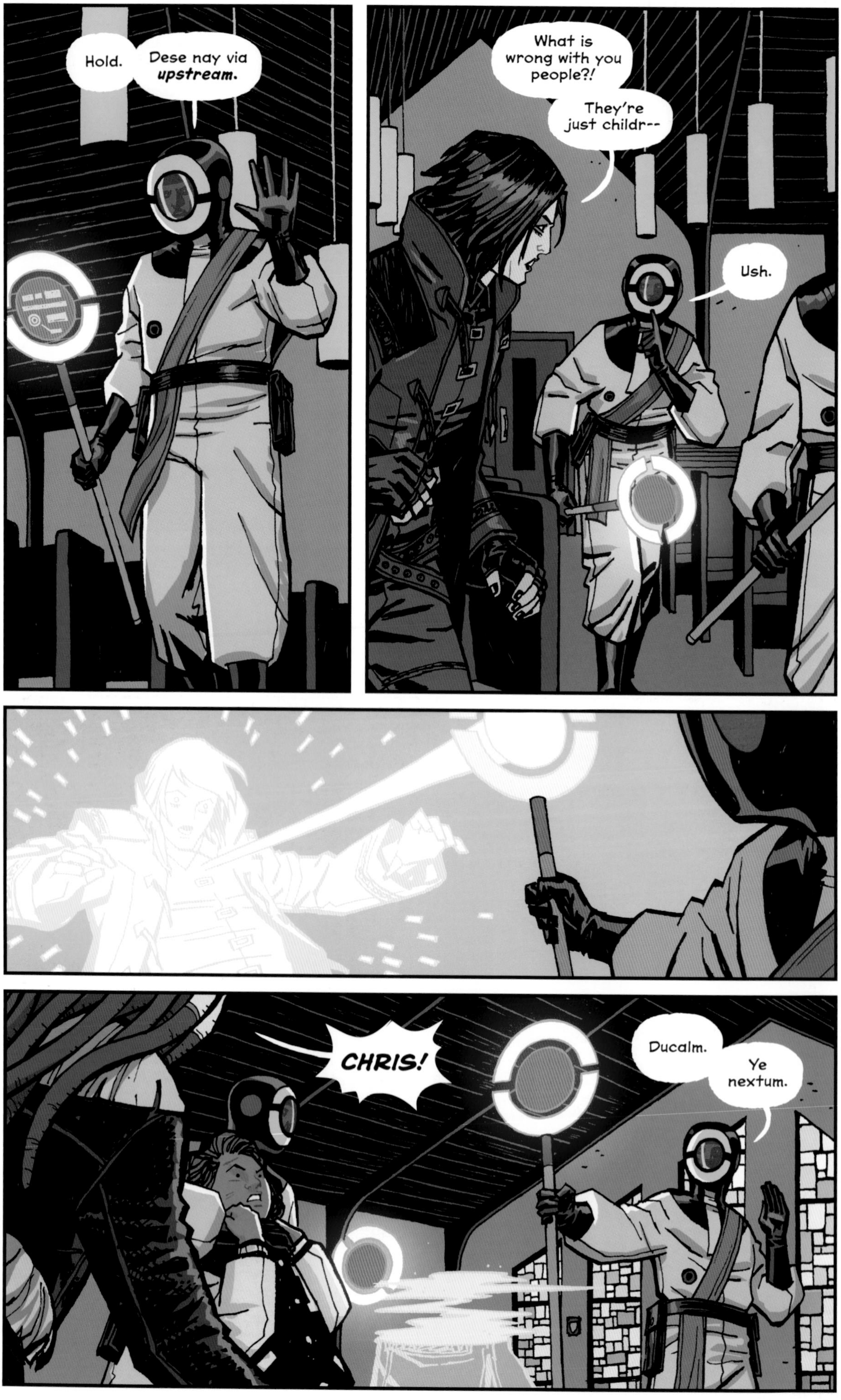
Hold.
Dese nay via *upstream.*
What is wrong with you people?!
They're just childr--
Ush.
CHRIS!
Ducalm.
Ye nextum.

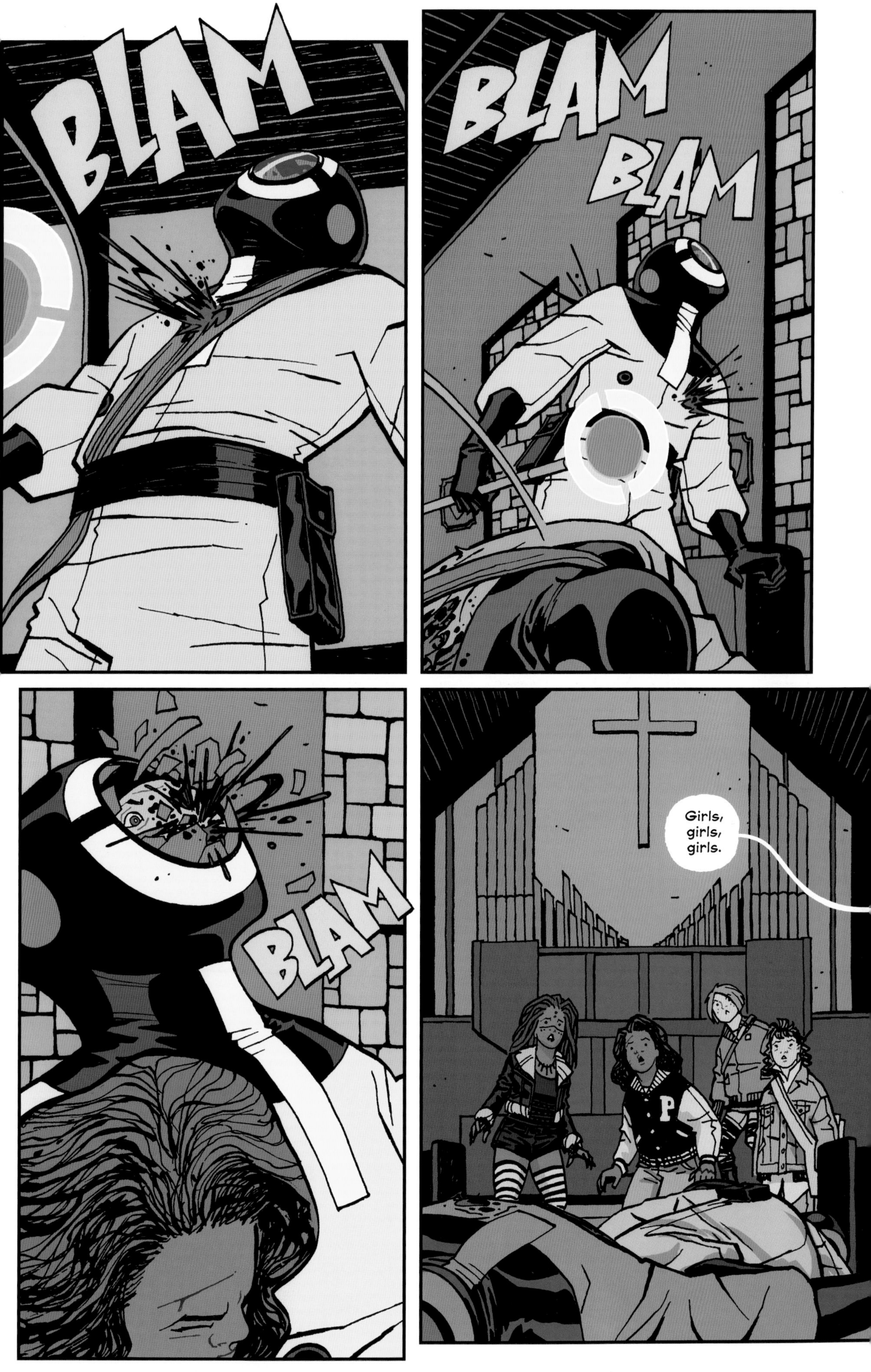
BLAM
BLAM
BLAM
BLAM
Girls, girls, girls.

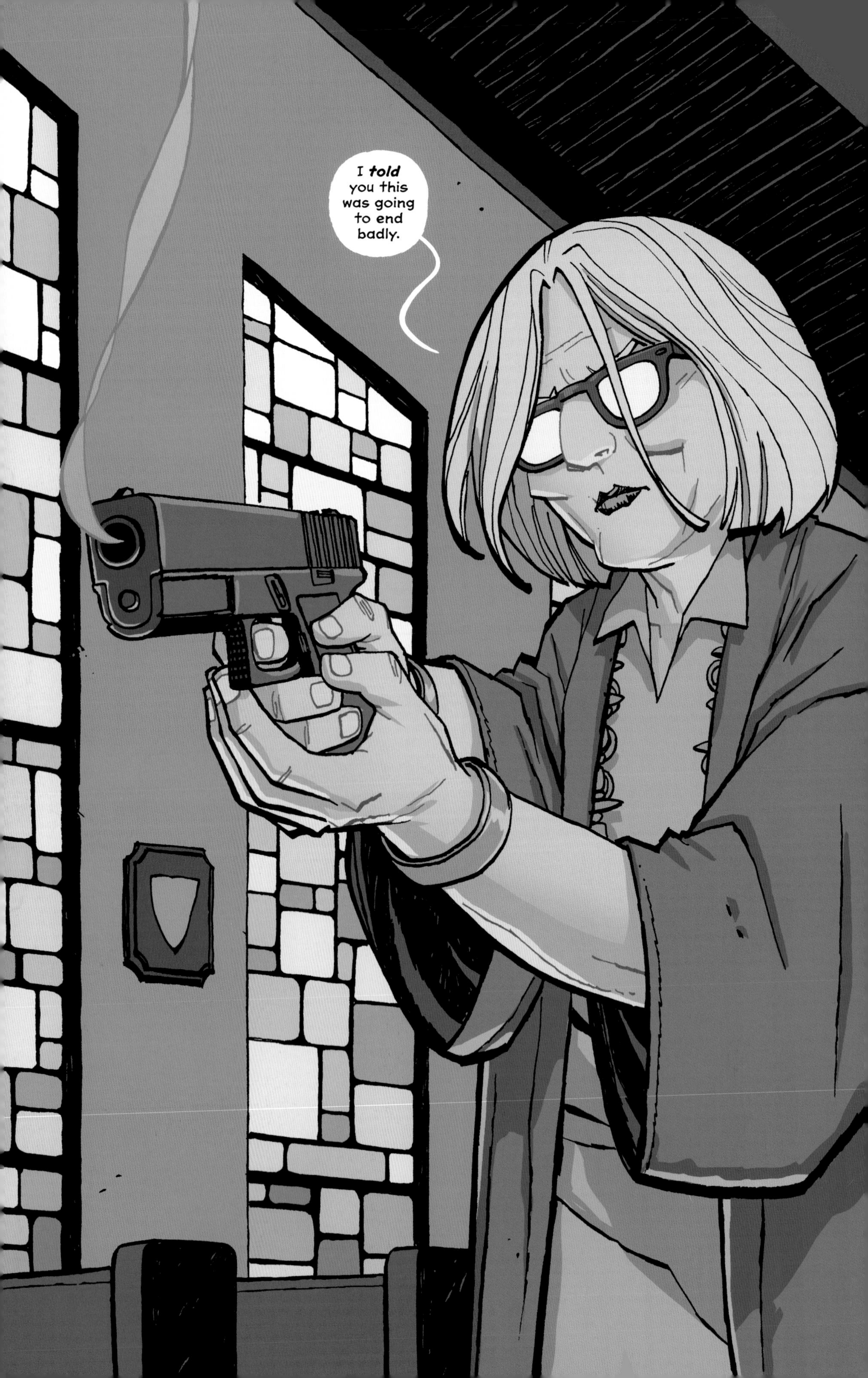
I *told* you this was going to end badly.

CHAPTER
20

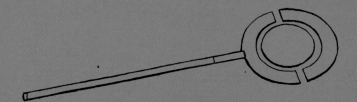

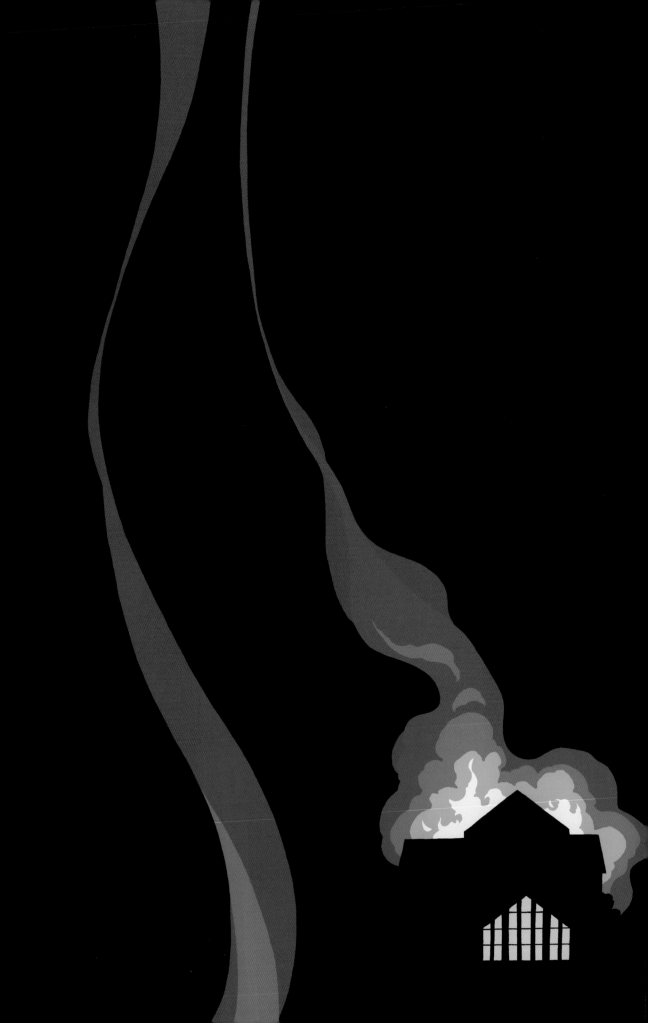

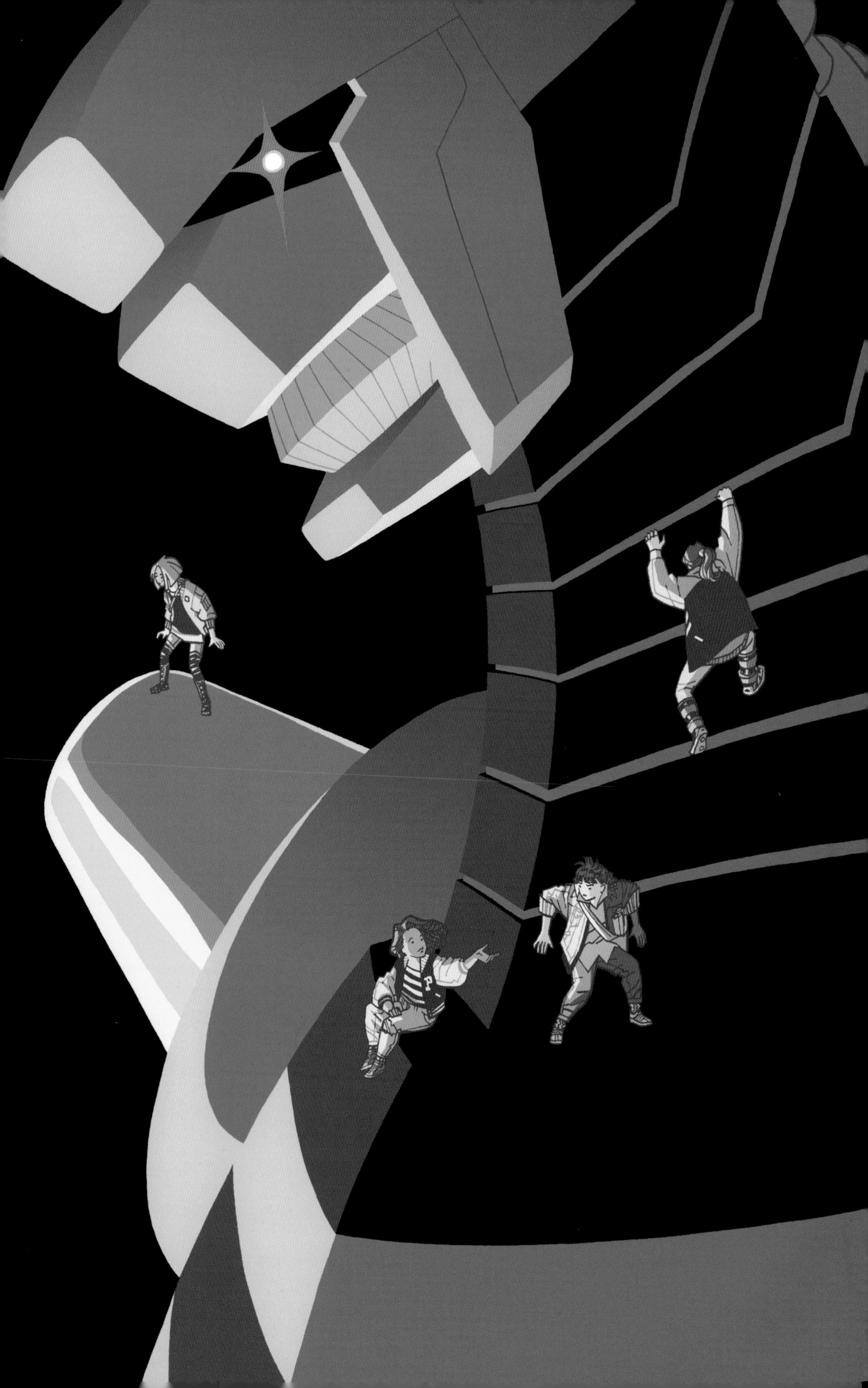

"ARMAGEDDON
Year 2000 Computer Bug
Will Turn Machine Against Man!"

—**Weekly World News** headline, 1999

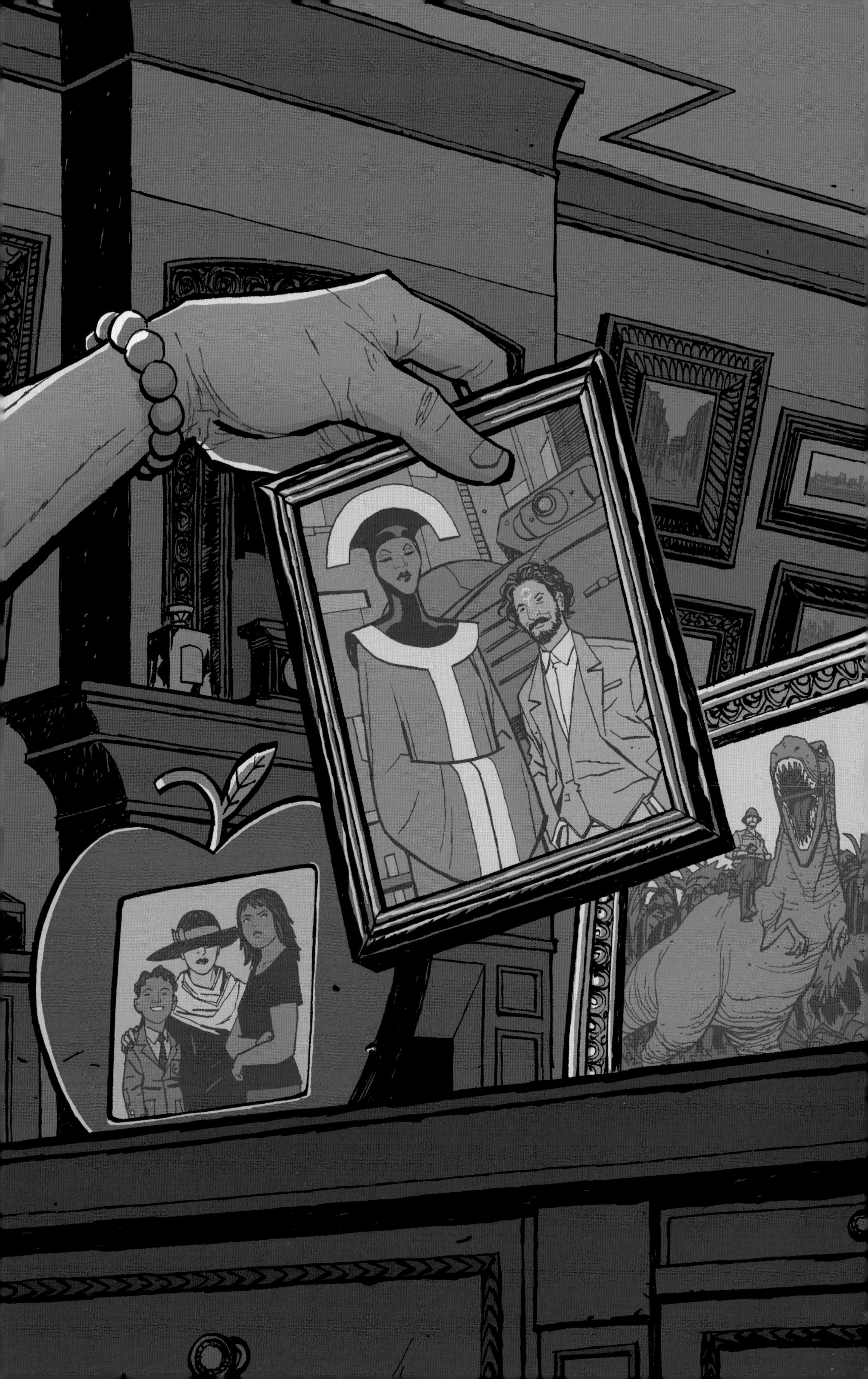

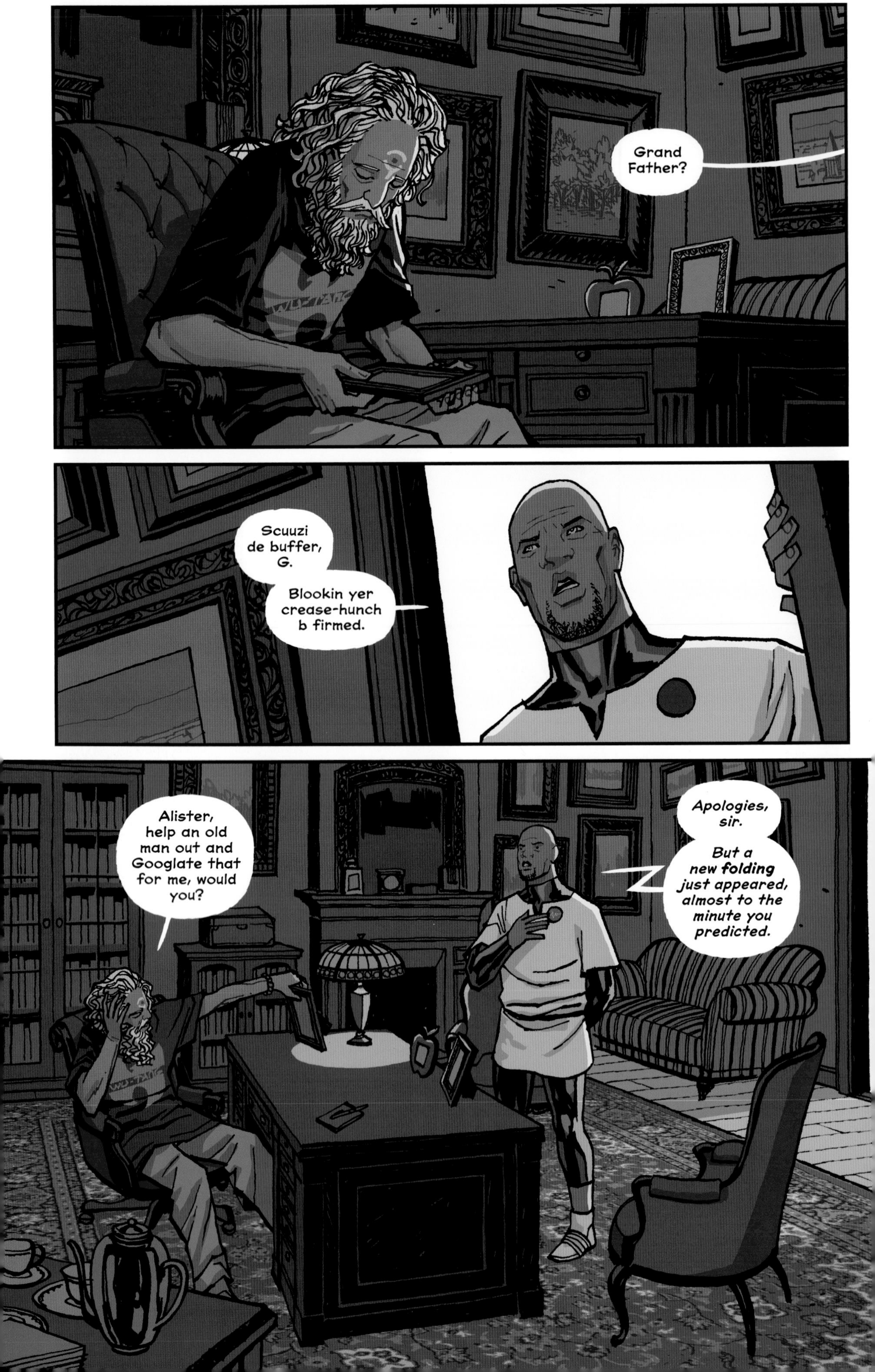
Grand Father?
Scuuzi de buffer, G.
Blookin yer crease-hunch b firmed.
Alister, help an old man out and Googlate that for me, would you?
Apologies, sir.
But a new **folding** just appeared, almost to the minute you predicted.

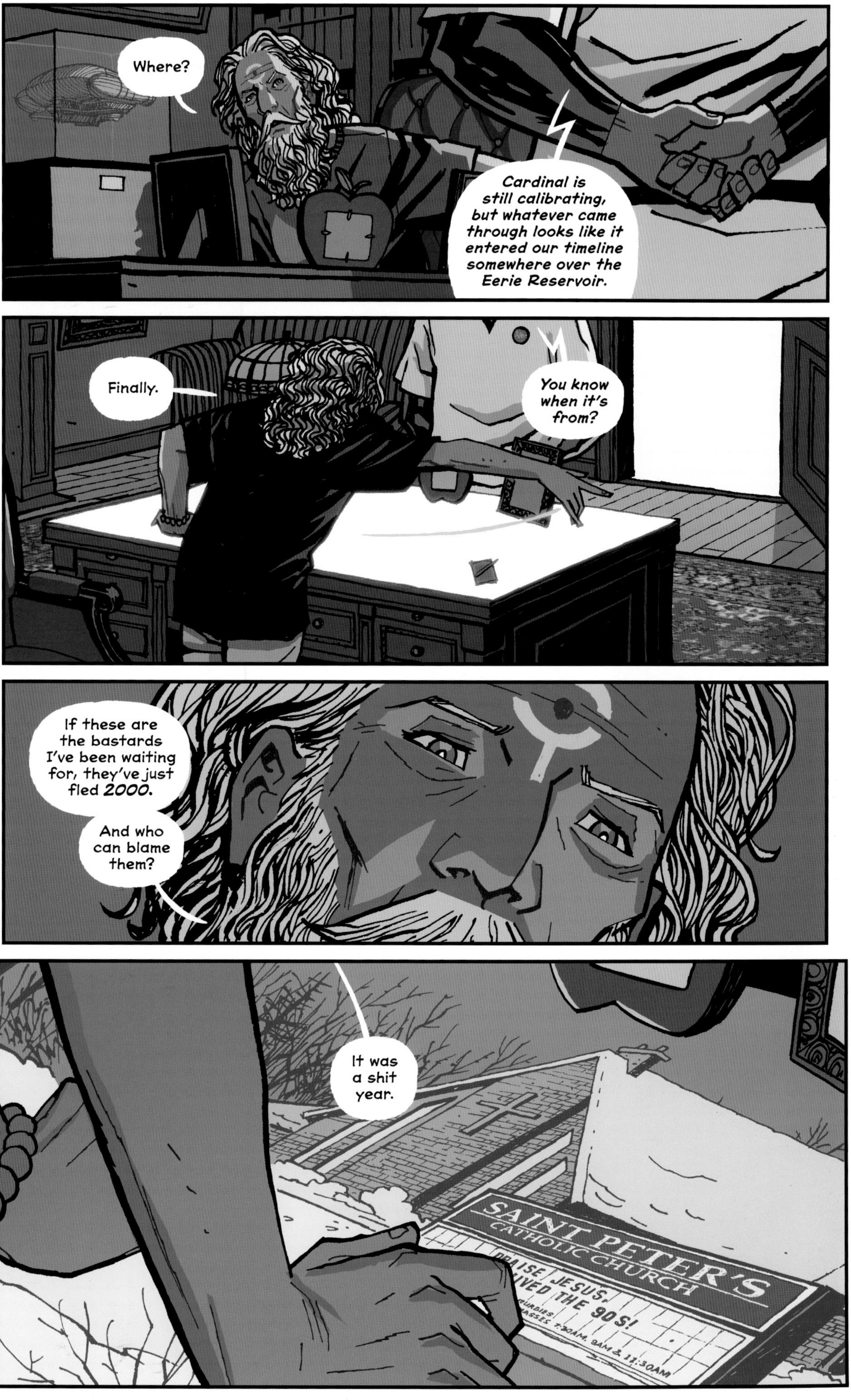
Where?
Cardinal is still calibrating, but whatever came through looks like it entered our timeline somewhere over the Eerie Reservoir.
Finally.
You know when it's from?
If these are the bastards I've been waiting for, they've just fled 2000.
And who can blame them?
It was a shit year.
SAINT PETER'S
CATHOLIC CHURCH
PRAISE JESUS,
VED THE 90S!

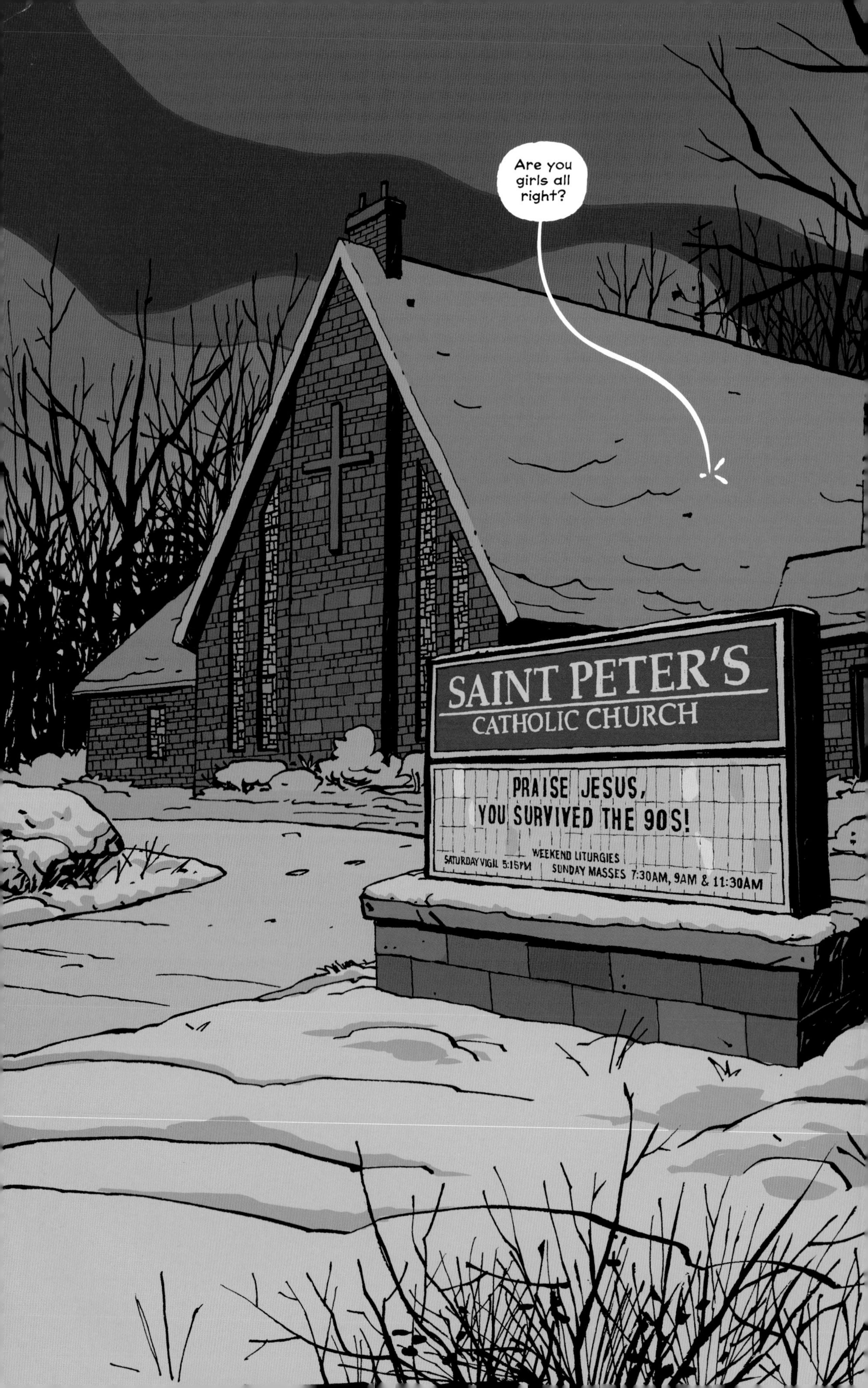
Are you girls all right?
SAINT PETER'S
CATHOLIC CHURCH
PRAISE JESUS,
YOU SURVIVED THE 90S!
WEEKEND LITURGIES
SATURDAY VIGIL 5:15PM
SUNDAY MASSES 7:30AM, 9AM & 11:30AM

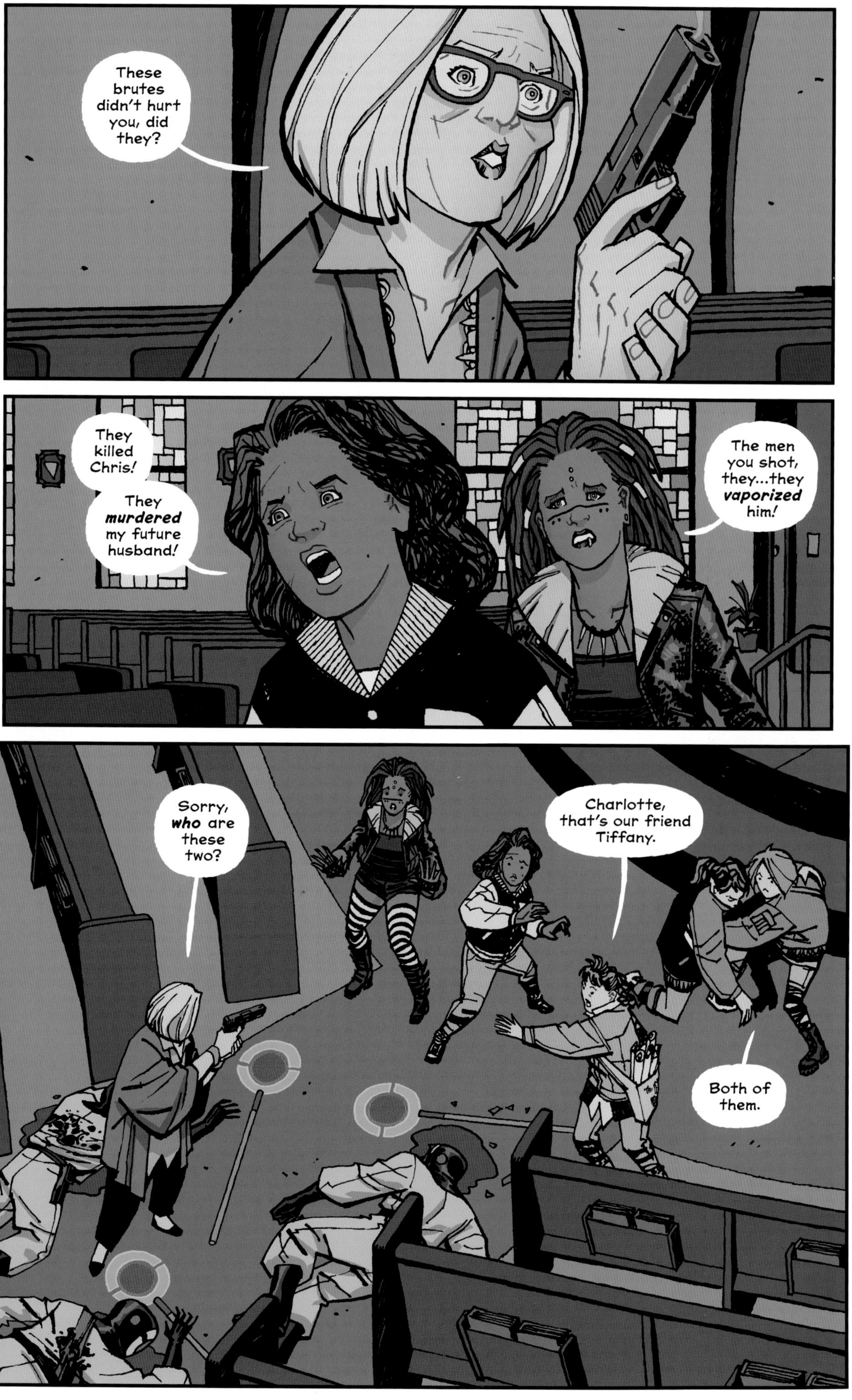
These brutes didn't hurt you, did they?
They killed Chris!
They *murdered* my future husband!
The men you shot, they...they *vaporized* him!
Sorry, *who* are these two?
Charlotte, that's our friend Tiffany.
Both of them.

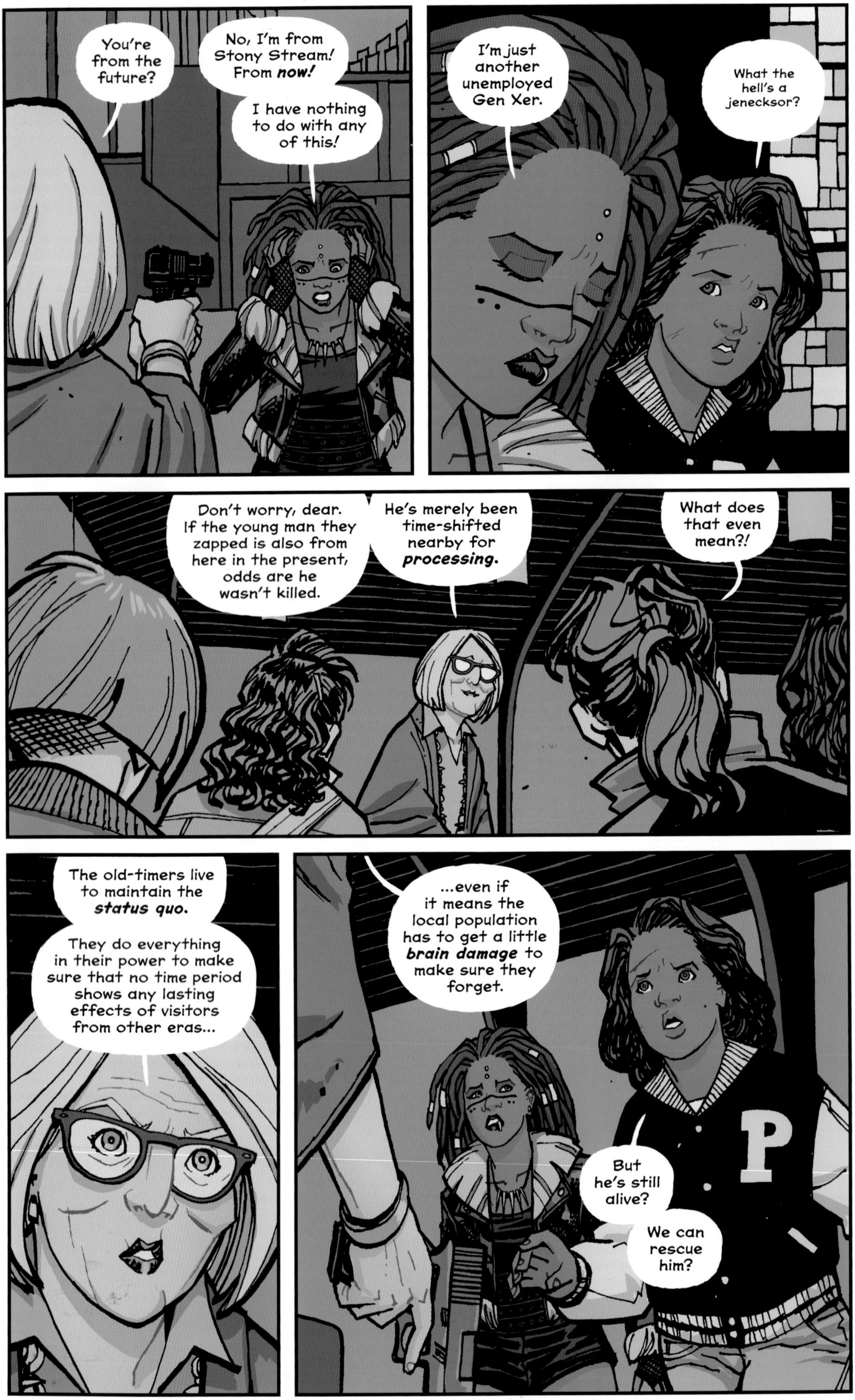

You're from the future?
No, I'm from Stony Stream! From *now!*
I have nothing to do with any of this!
I'm just another unemployed Gen Xer.
What the hell's a jenecksor?
Don't worry, dear. If the young man they zapped is also from here in the present, odds are he wasn't killed.
He's merely been time-shifted nearby for ***processing.***
What does that even mean?!
The old-timers live to maintain the ***status quo.***
They do everything in their power to make sure that no time period shows any lasting effects of visitors from other eras...
...even if it means the local population has to get a little ***brain damage*** to make sure they forget.
But he's still alive?
We can rescue him?

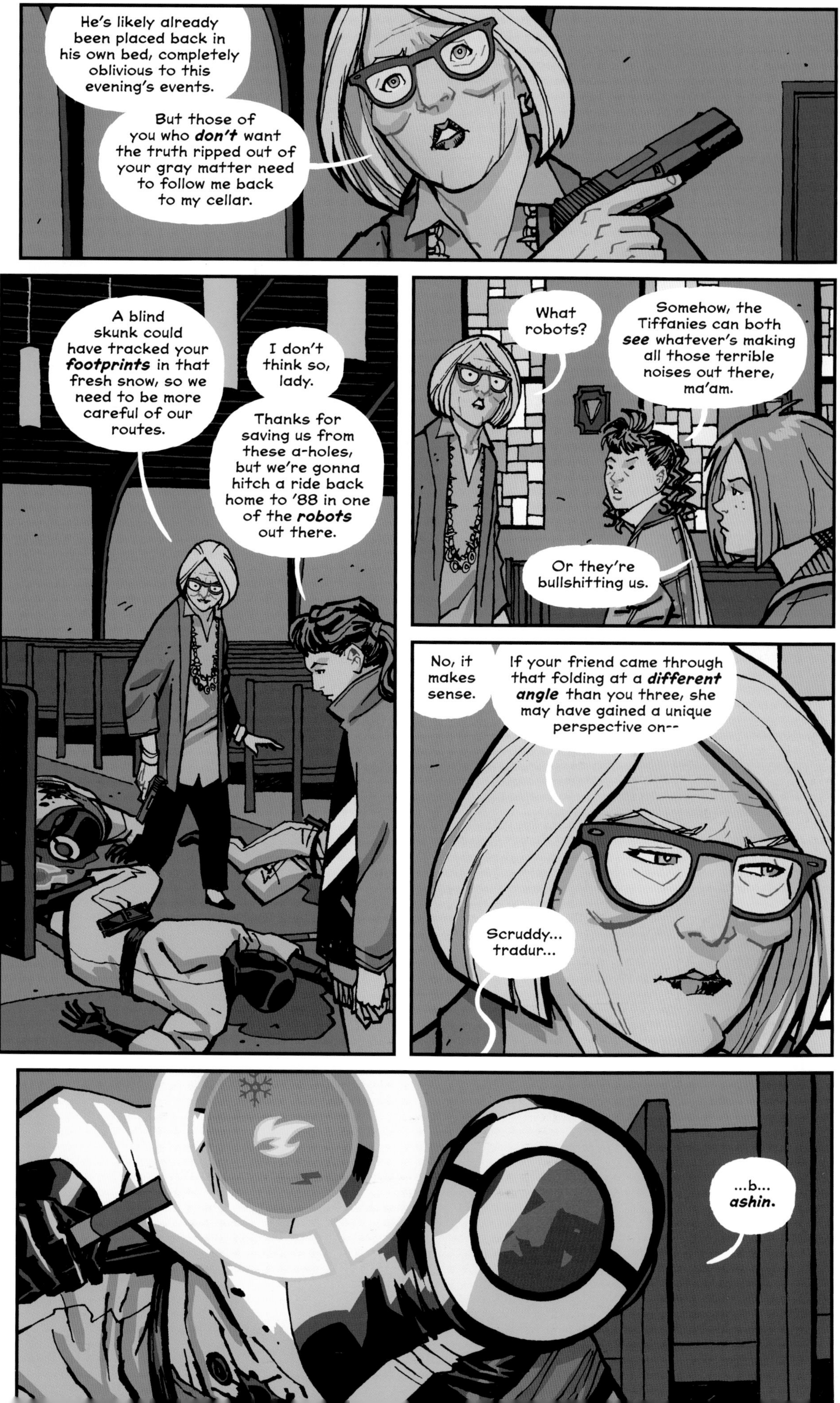
He's likely already been placed back in his own bed, completely oblivious to this evening's events.
But those of you who ***don't*** want the truth ripped out of your gray matter need to follow me back to my cellar.
A blind skunk could have tracked your ***footprints*** in that fresh snow, so we need to be more careful of our routes.
I don't think so, lady.
Thanks for saving us from these a-holes, but we're gonna hitch a ride back home to '88 in one of the ***robots*** out there.
What robots?
Somehow, the Tiffanies can both ***see*** whatever's making all those terrible noises out there, ma'am.
Or they're bullshitting us.
No, it makes sense.
If your friend came through that folding at a ***different angle*** than you three, she may have gained a unique perspective on--
Scruddy... tradur...
...b... ***ashin.***

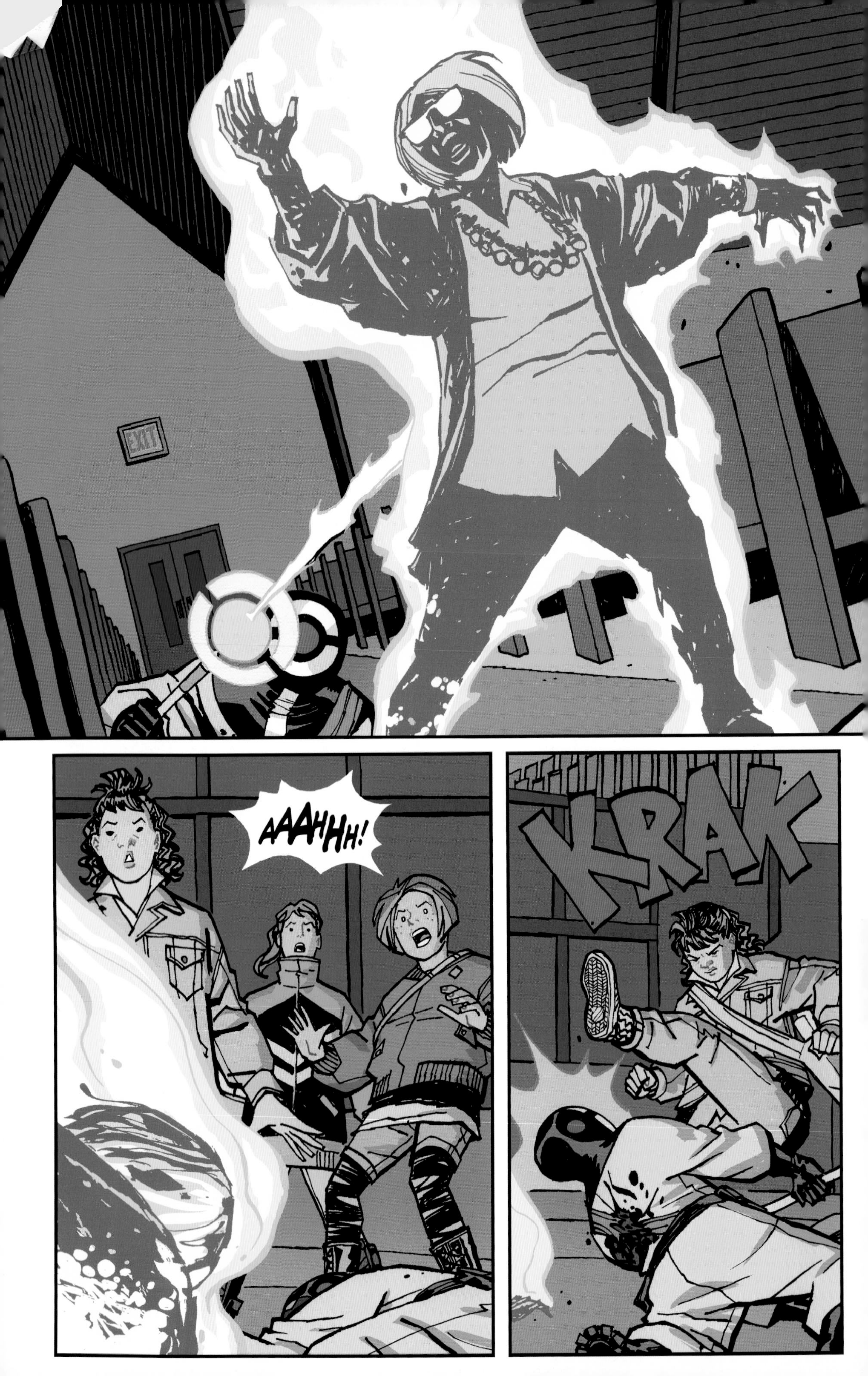
EXIT
AAAHHH!
KRAK

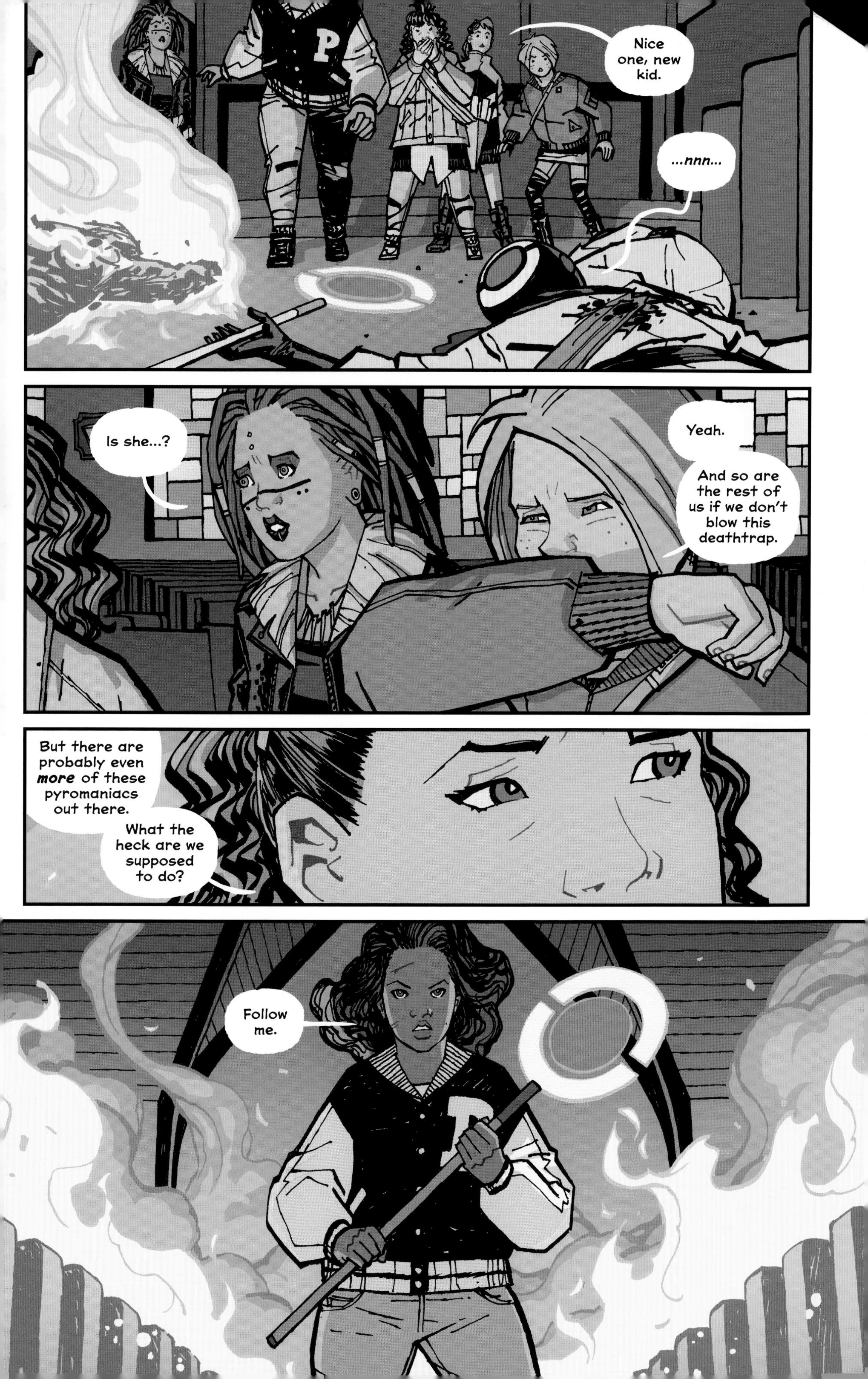

Nice one, new kid.
...nnn...
Is she...?
Yeah.
And so are the rest of us if we don't blow this deathtrap.
But there are probably even ***more*** of these pyromaniacs out there.
What the heck are we supposed to do?
Follow me.

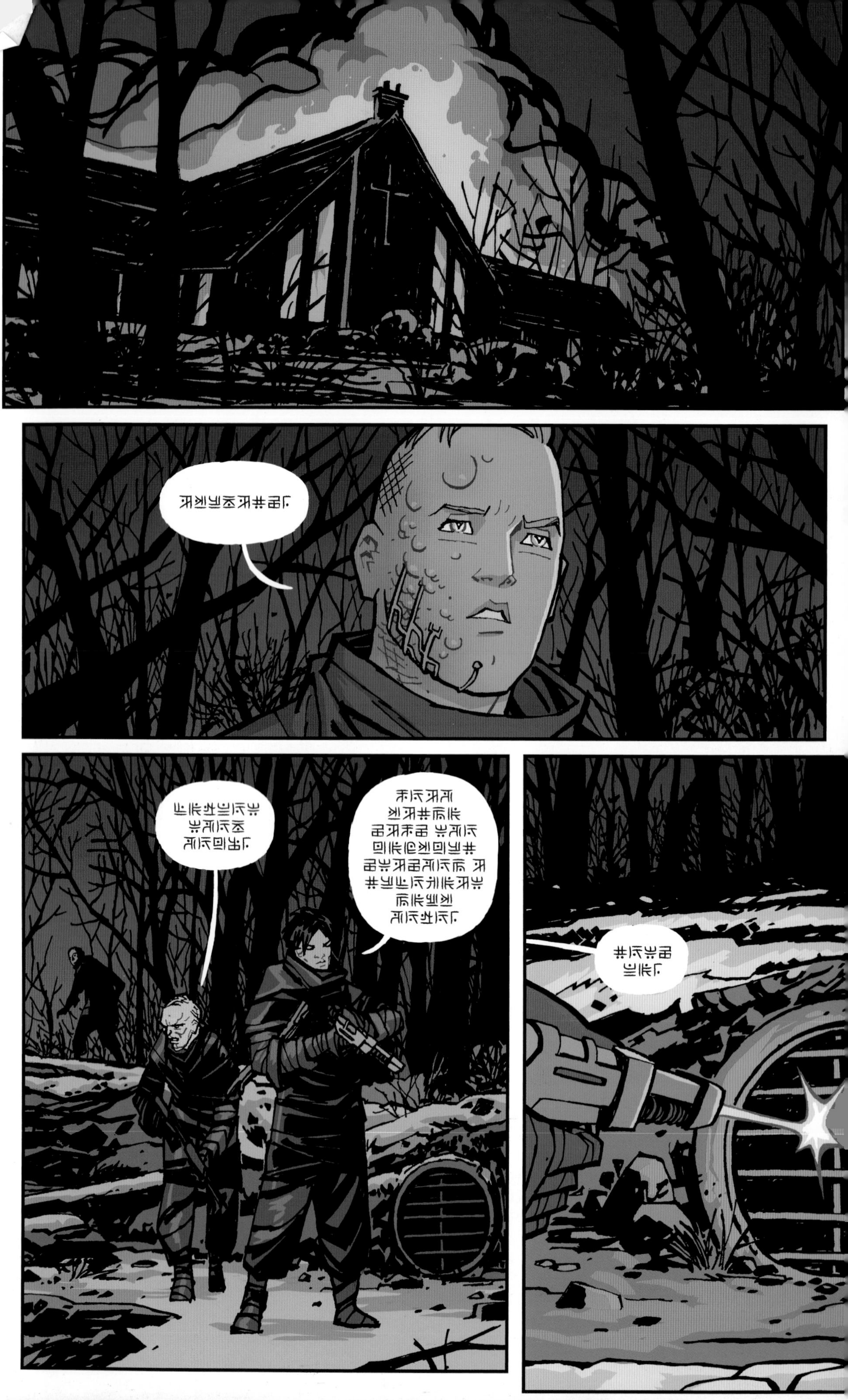

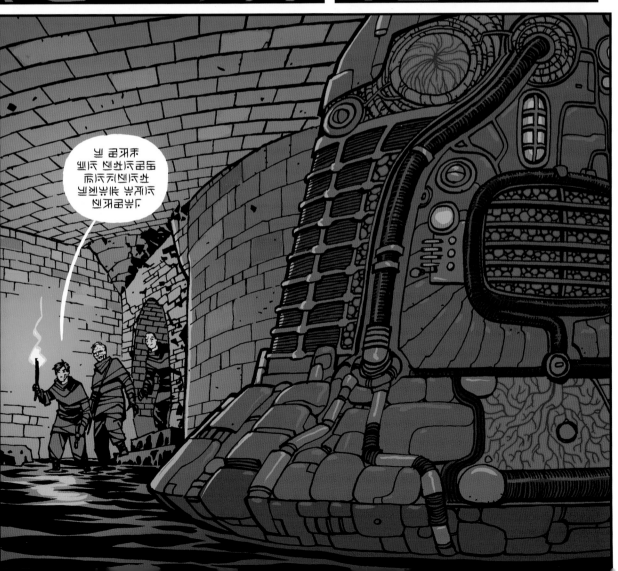

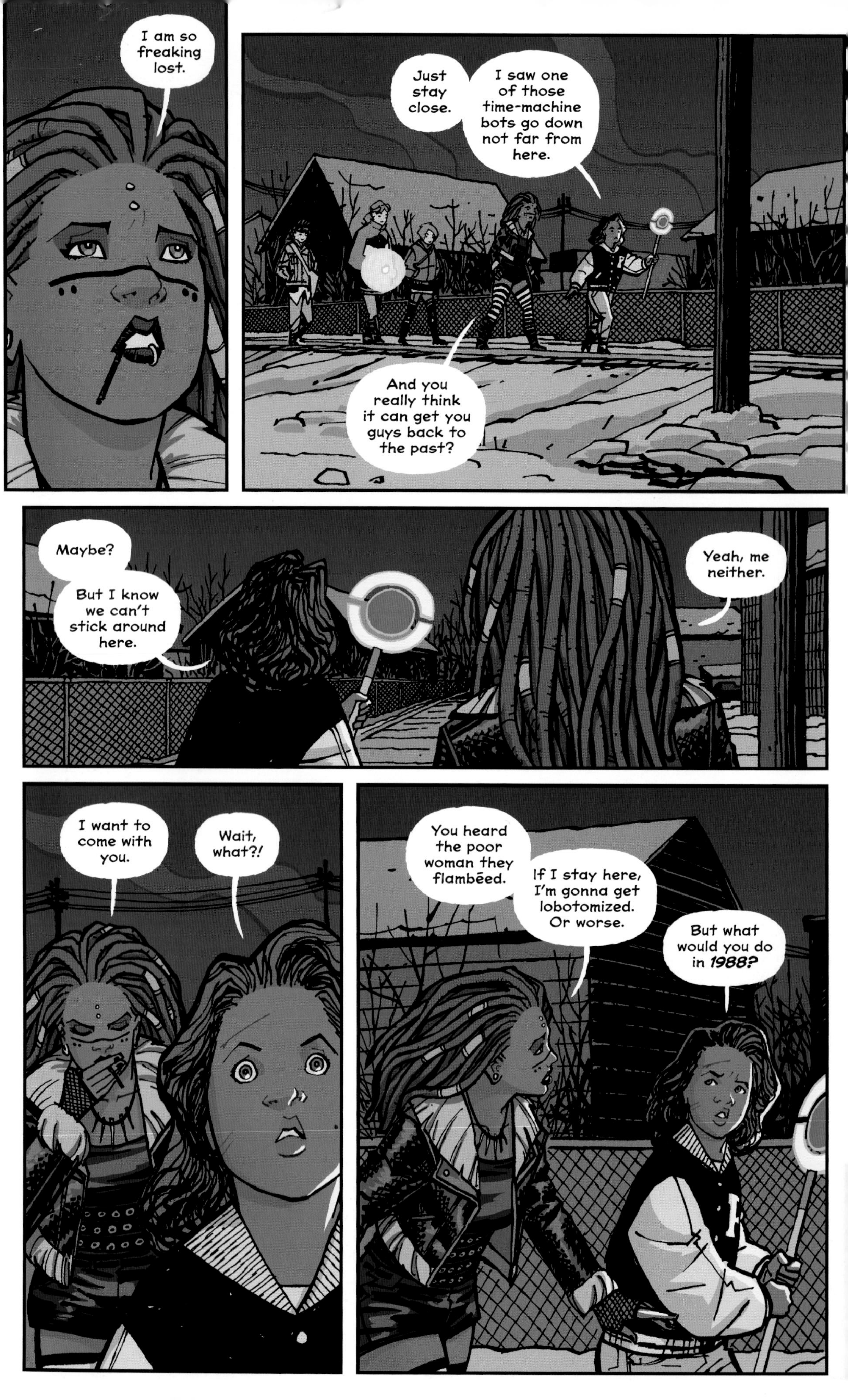
I am so freaking lost.
Just stay close.
I saw one of those time-machine bots go down not far from here.
And you really think it can get you guys back to the past?
Maybe?
But I know we can't stick around here.
Yeah, me neither.
I want to come with you.
Wait, what?!
You heard the poor woman they flambéed.
If I stay here, I'm gonna get lobotomized. Or worse.
But what would you do in *1988?*

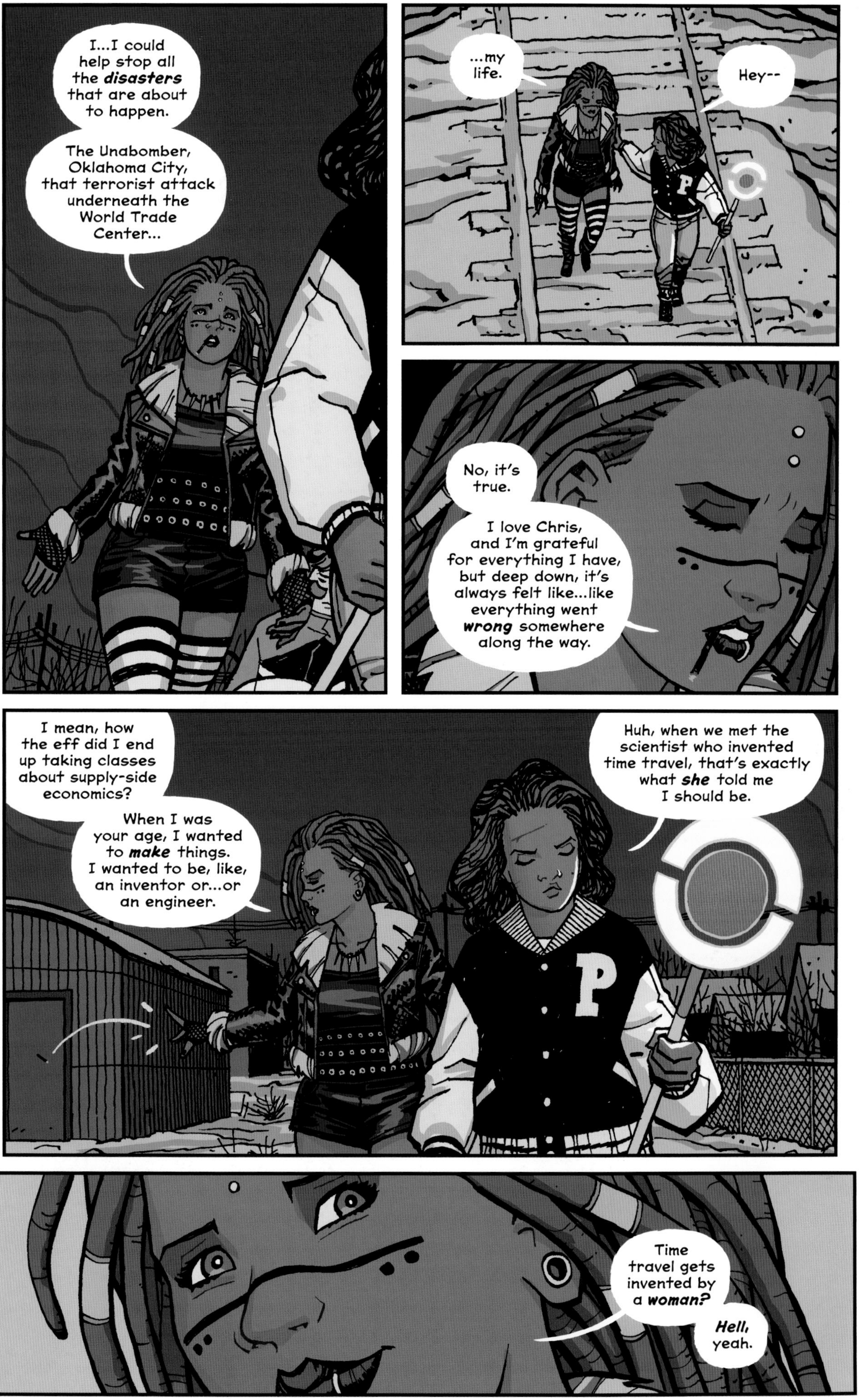
I...I could help stop all the ***disasters*** that are about to happen.
The Unabomber, Oklahoma City, that terrorist attack underneath the World Trade Center...
...my life.
Hey--
No, it's true.
I love Chris, and I'm grateful for everything I have, but deep down, it's always felt like...like everything went ***wrong*** somewhere along the way.
I mean, how the eff did I end up taking classes about supply-side economics?
When I was your age, I wanted to ***make*** things. I wanted to be, like, an inventor or...or an engineer.
Huh, when we met the scientist who invented time travel, that's exactly what ***she*** told me I should be.
Time travel gets invented by a ***woman?***
Hell, yeah.

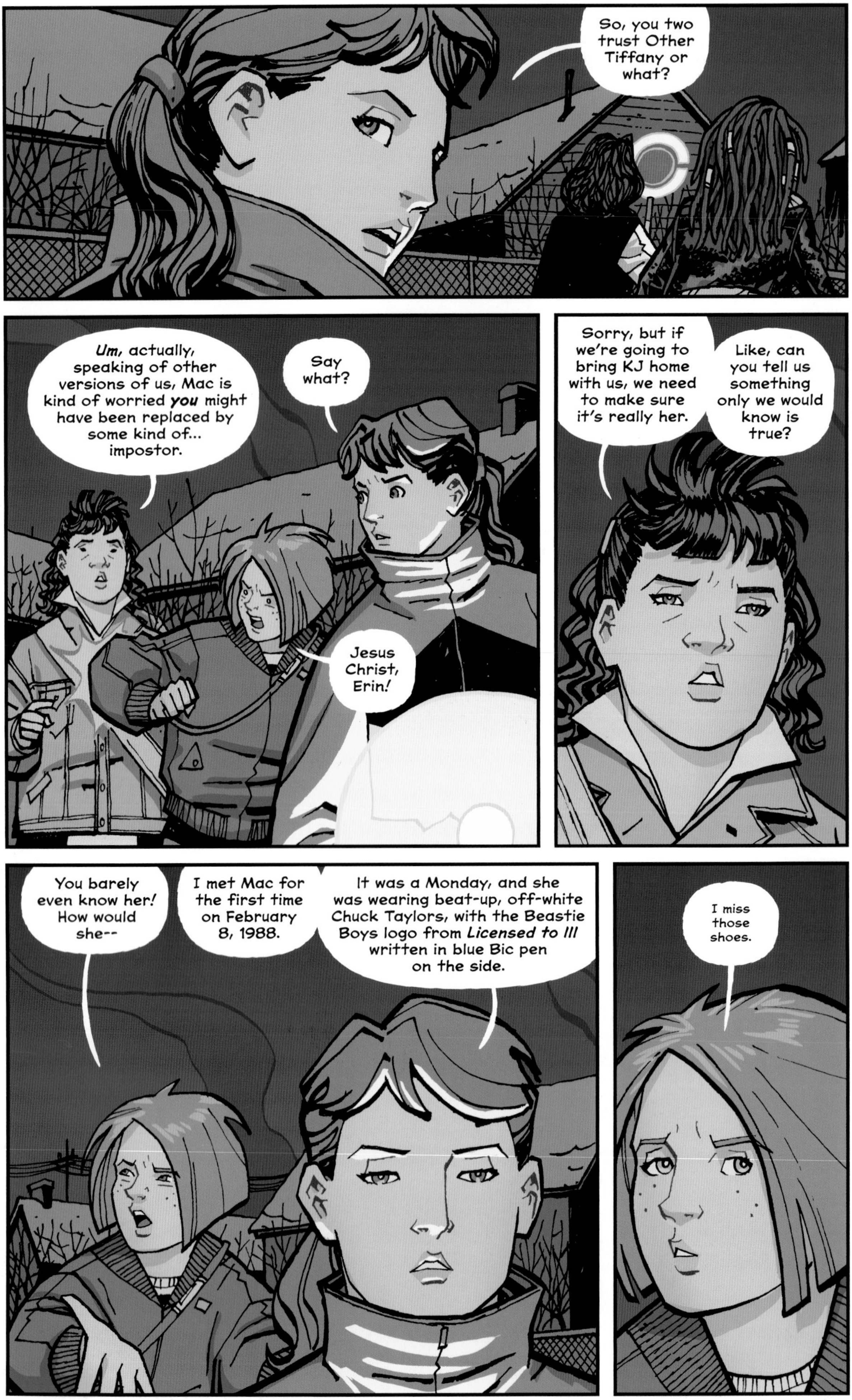

So, you two trust Other Tiffany or what?
Um, actually, speaking of other versions of us, Mac is kind of worried *you* might have been replaced by some kind of... impostor.
Say what?
Jesus Christ, Erin!
Sorry, but if we're going to bring KJ home with us, we need to make sure it's really her.
Like, can you tell us something only we would know is true?
You barely even know her! How would she--
I met Mac for the first time on February 8, 1988.
It was a Monday, and she was wearing beat-up, off-white Chuck Taylors, with the Beastie Boys logo from *Licensed to Ill* written in blue Bic pen on the side.
I miss those shoes.

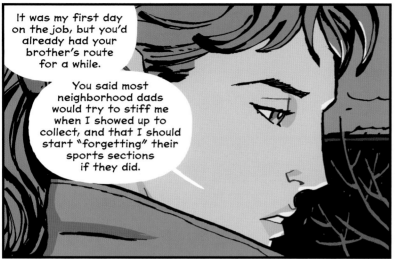

It was my first day on the job, but you'd already had your brother's route for a while.

You said most neighborhood dads would try to stiff me when I showed up to collect, and that I should start "forgetting" their sports sections if they did.

You were eating string cheese, but instead of pulling it off in strips like a normal person, you just ate it like a god-damn banana, which I thought was--

All right, all right!

It's really you, I get it.

≷Whew≷

Mac was seriously convinced you were some sort of gay pod person.

One out of two, anyway.

Cool.

Can you guys see this?

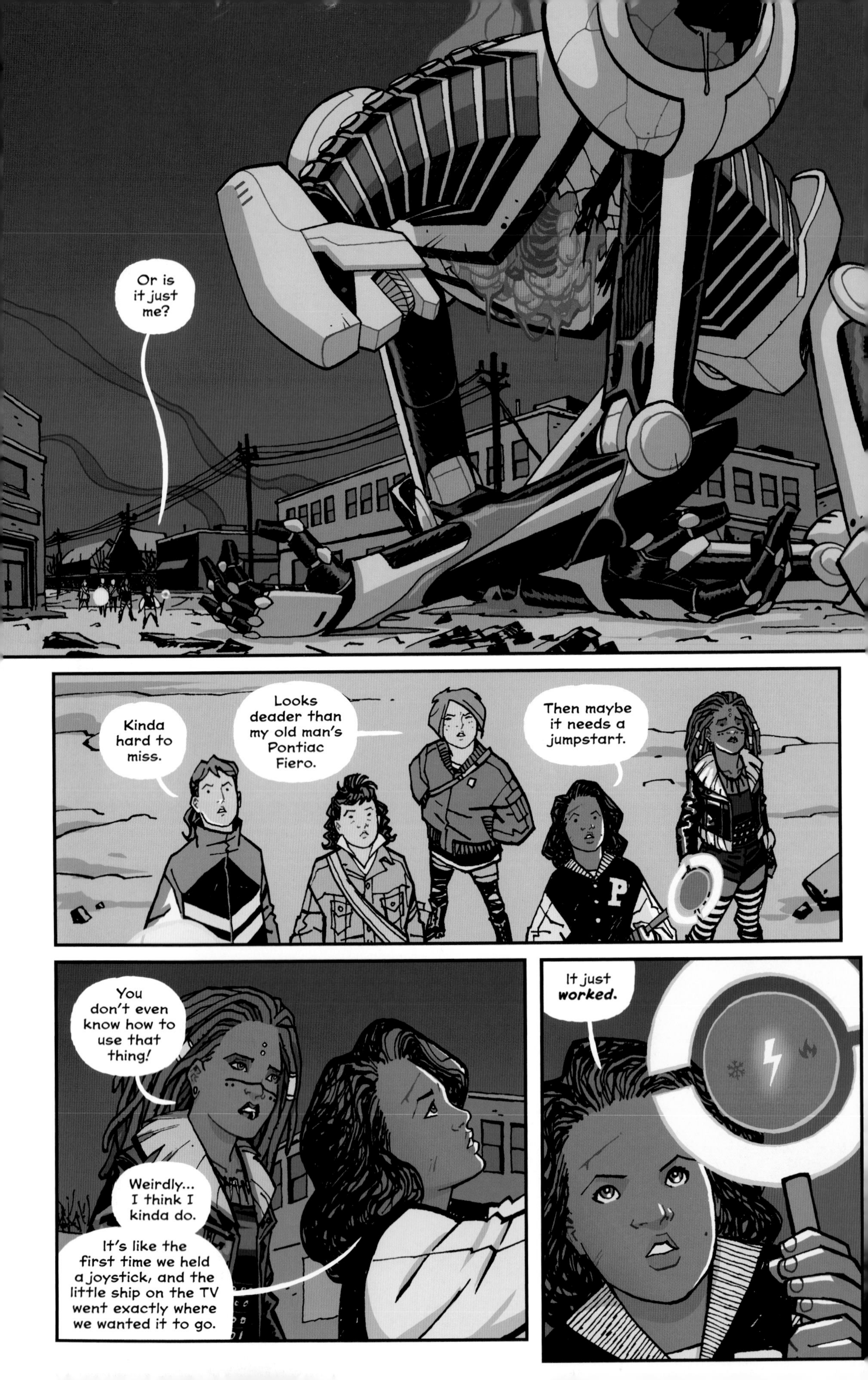
Or is it just me?
Kinda hard to miss.
Looks deader than my old man's Pontiac Fiero.
Then maybe it needs a jumpstart.
You don't even know how to use that thing!
Weirdly... I think I kinda do.
It's like the first time we held a joystick, and the little ship on the TV went exactly where we wanted it to go.
It just *worked.*

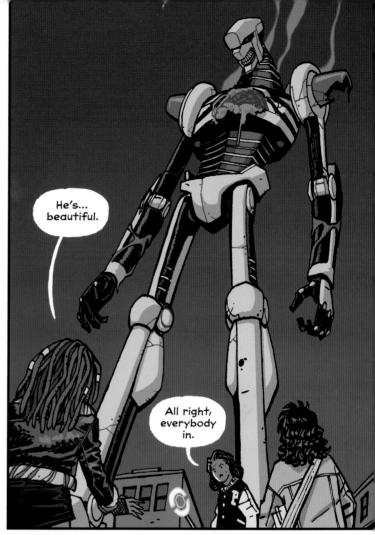

He's... beautiful.

All right, everybody in.

Everybody?

We're taking Ms. Facepaint **with** us?

What is she supposed to do when we get back to--

Oh, God.

What's up, Tiffany?

You see something?

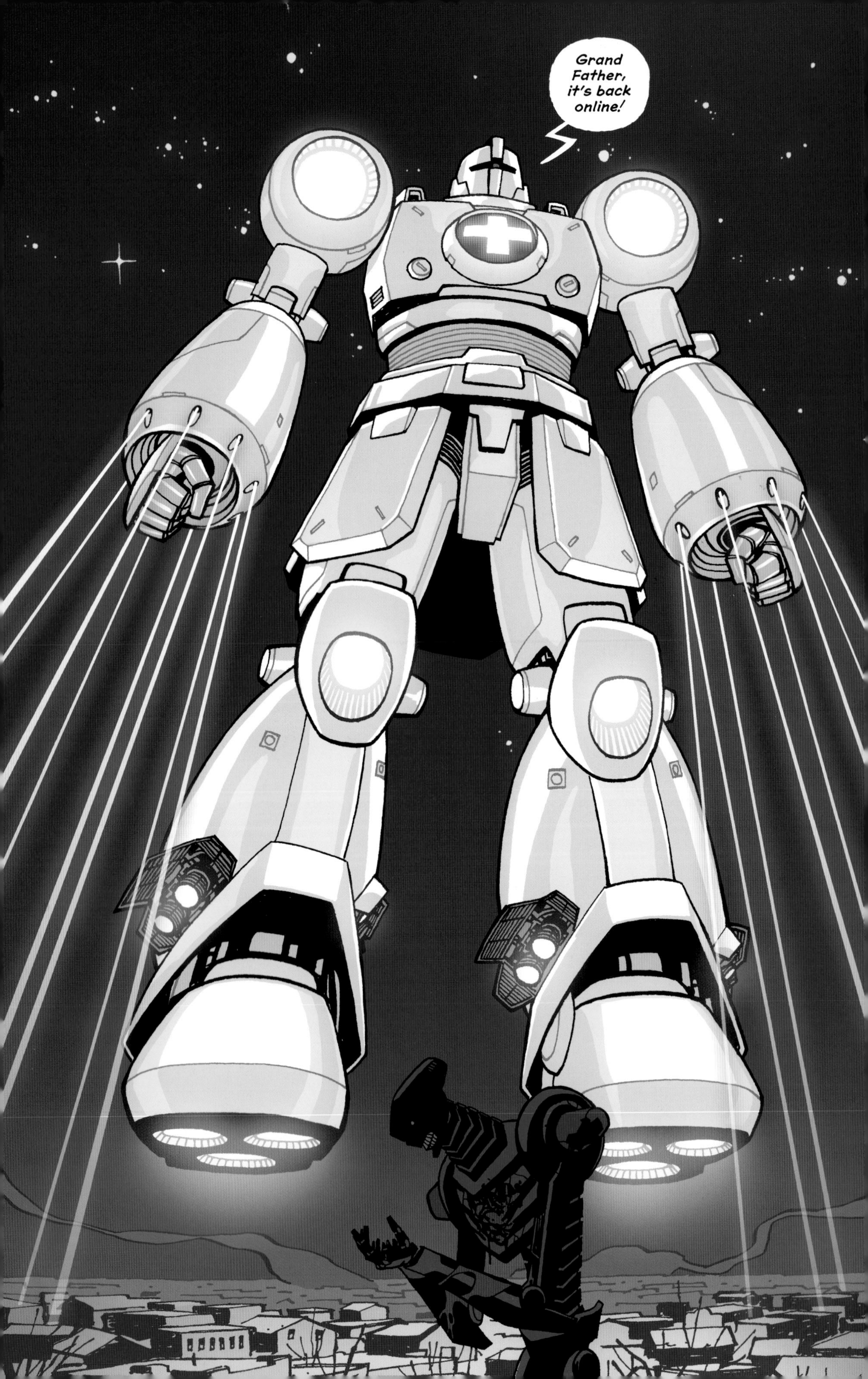
Grand Father, it's back online!

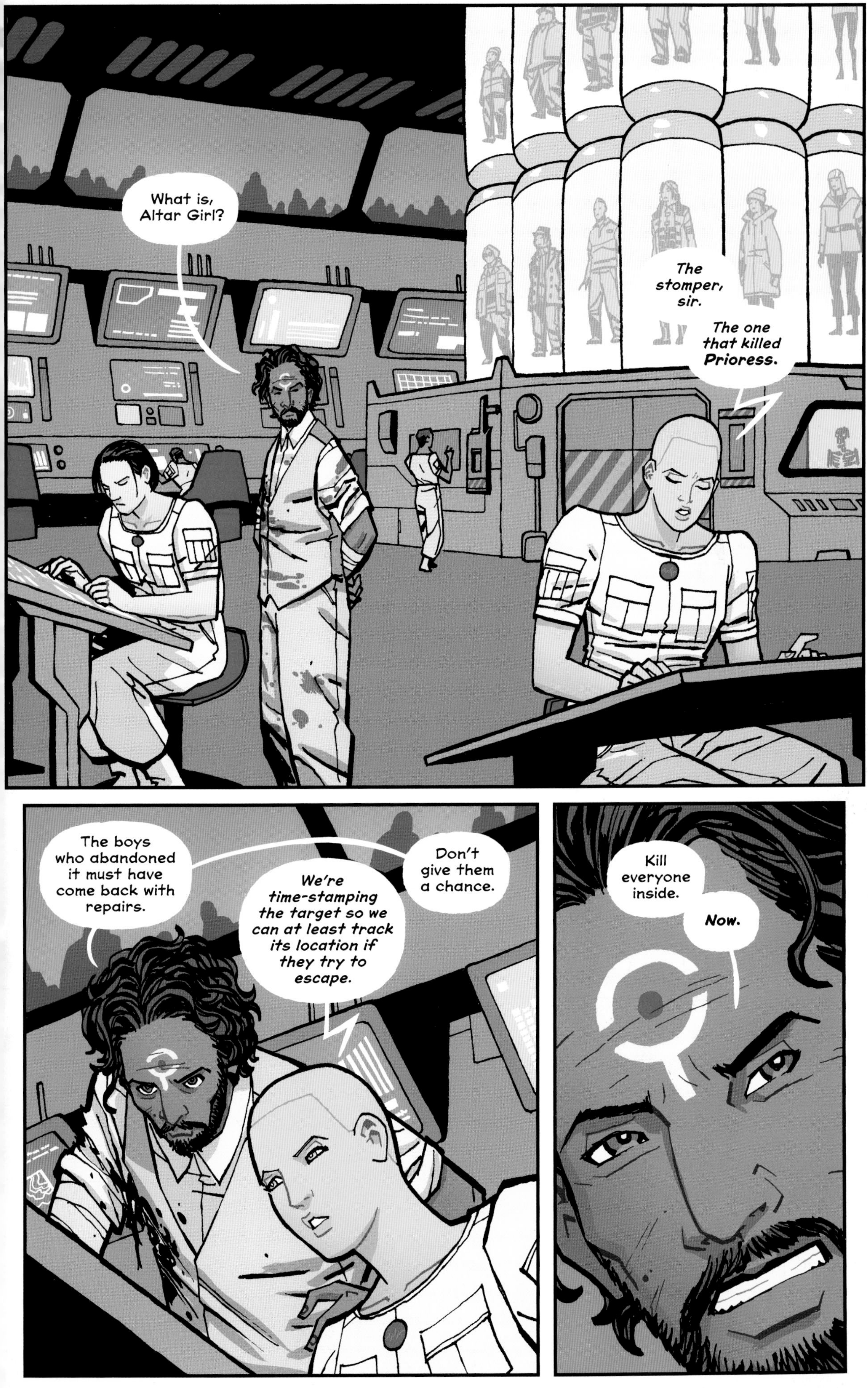
What is, Altar Girl?
The stomper, sir.
The one that killed Prioress.
The boys who abandoned it must have come back with repairs.
We're time-stamping the target so we can at least track its location if they try to escape.
Don't give them a chance.
Kill everyone inside.
Now.

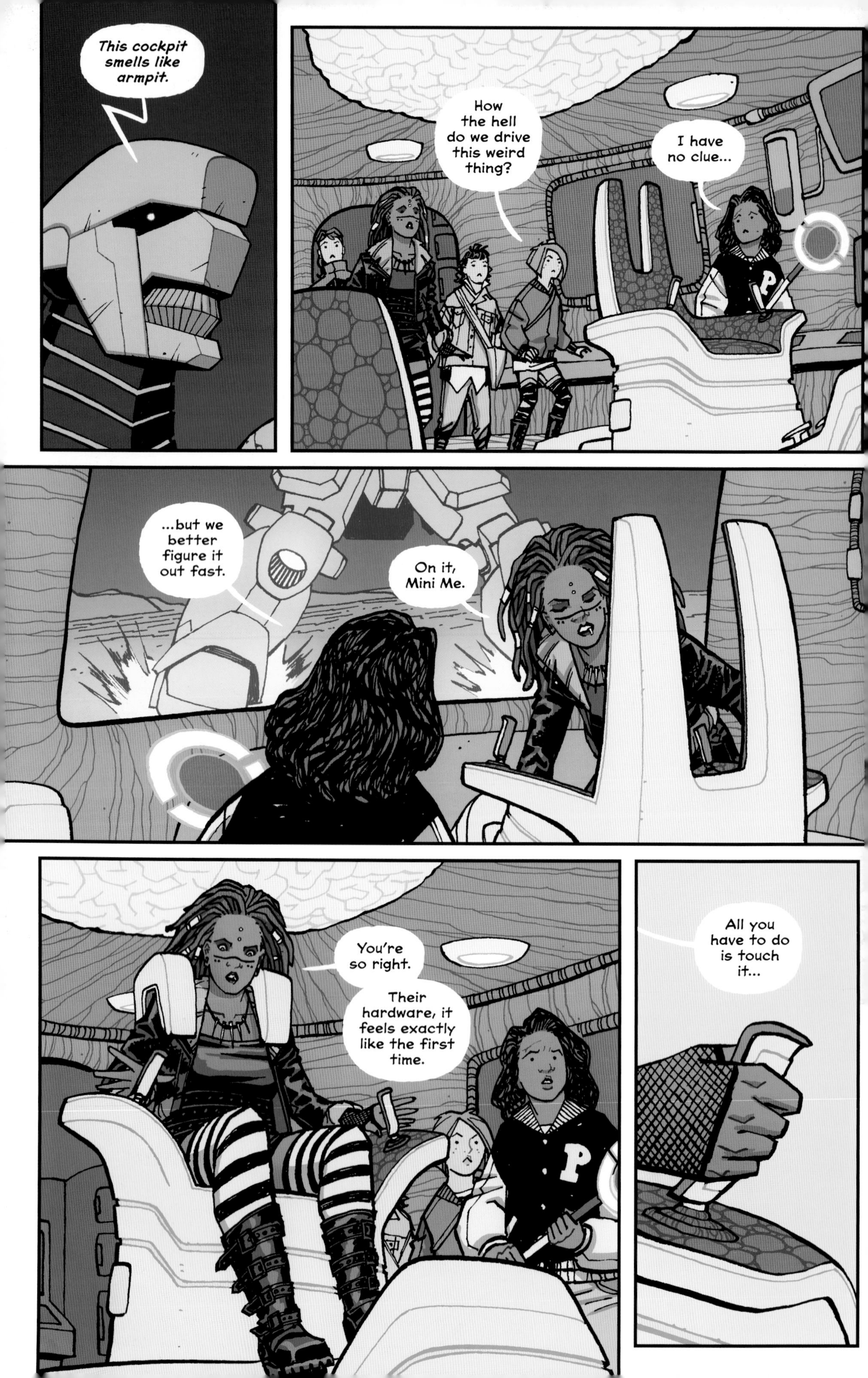
This cockpit smells like armpit.
How the hell do we drive this weird thing?
I have no clue...
...but we better figure it out fast.
On it, Mini Me.
You're so right.
Their hardware, it feels exactly like the first time.
All you have to do is touch it...

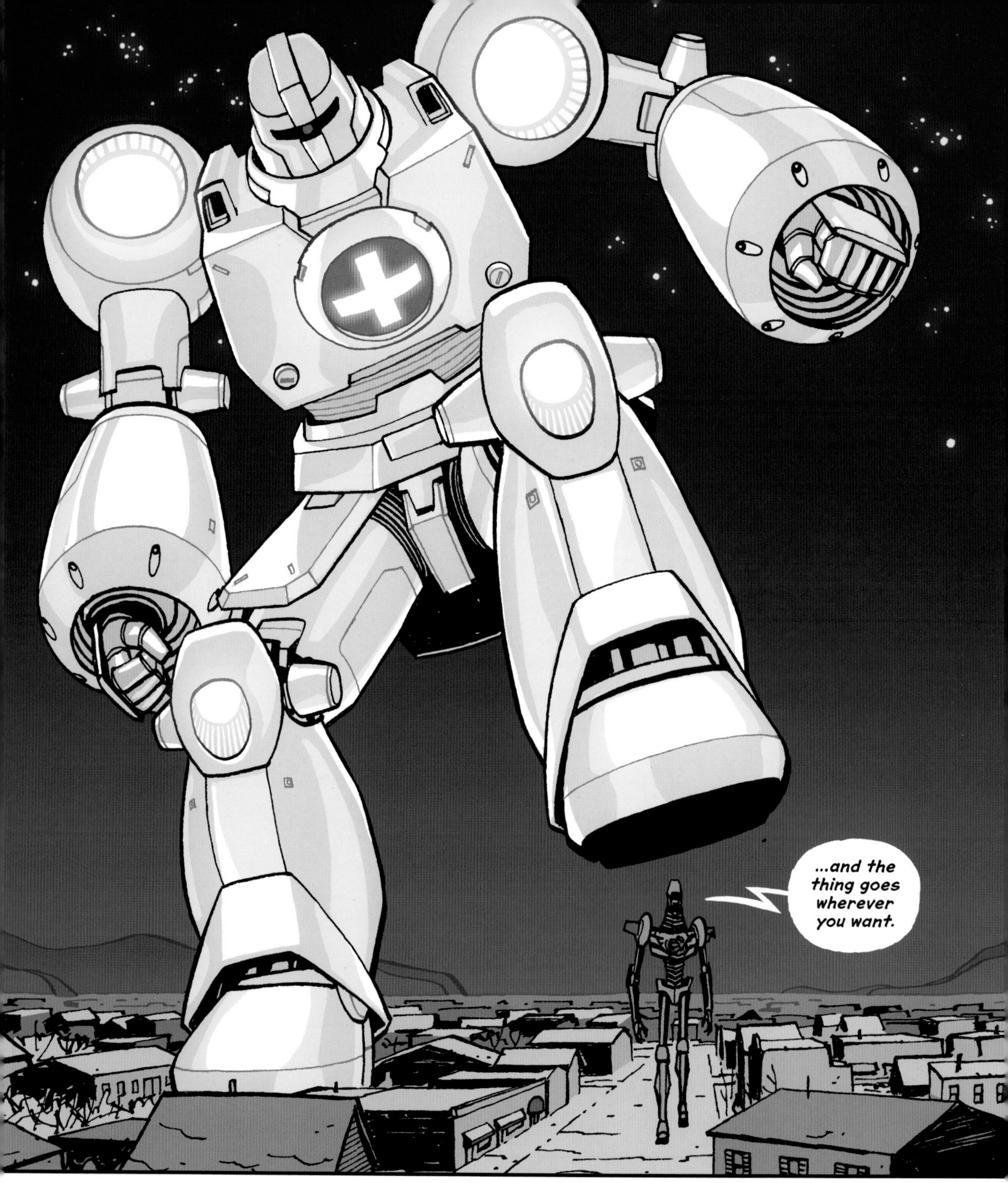
...and the thing goes wherever you want.

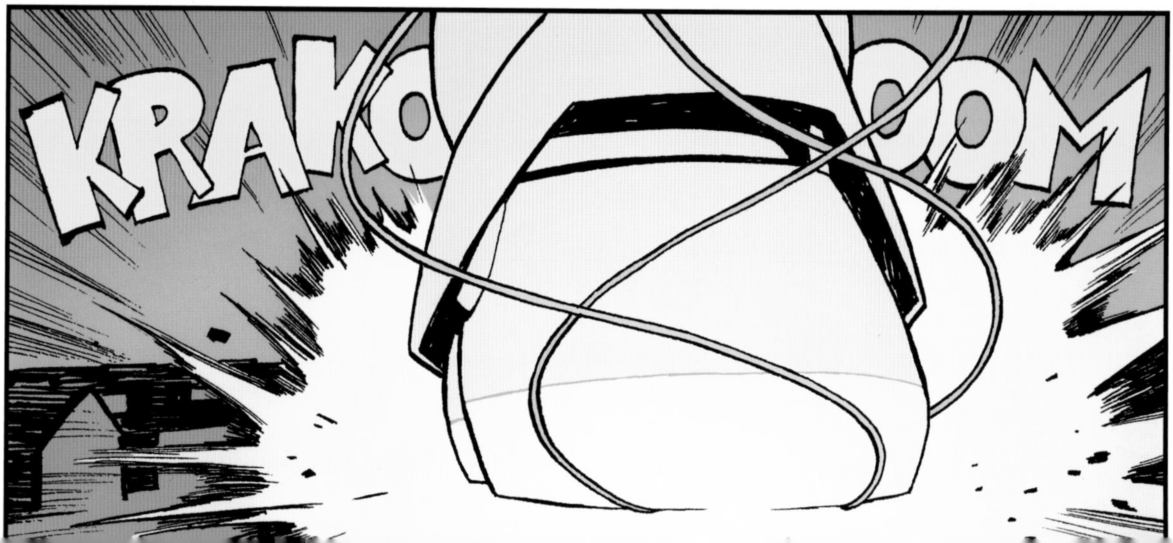
KRAKOOOM

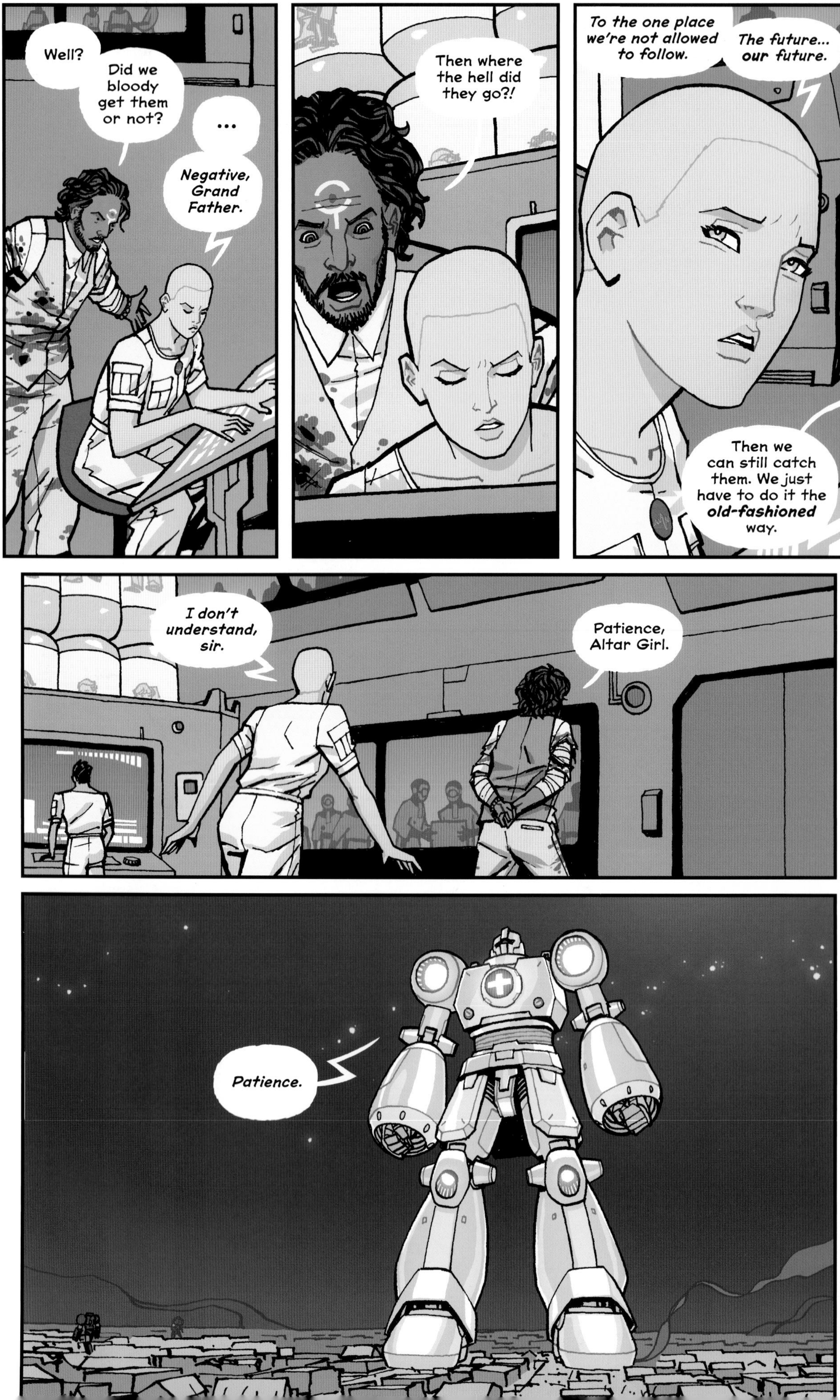
Well?
Did we bloody get them or not?
...
Negative, Grand Father.
Then where the hell did they go?!
To the one place we're not allowed to follow.
The future... our future.
Then we can still catch them. We just have to do it the old-fashioned way.
I don't understand, sir.
Patience, Altar Girl.
Patience.

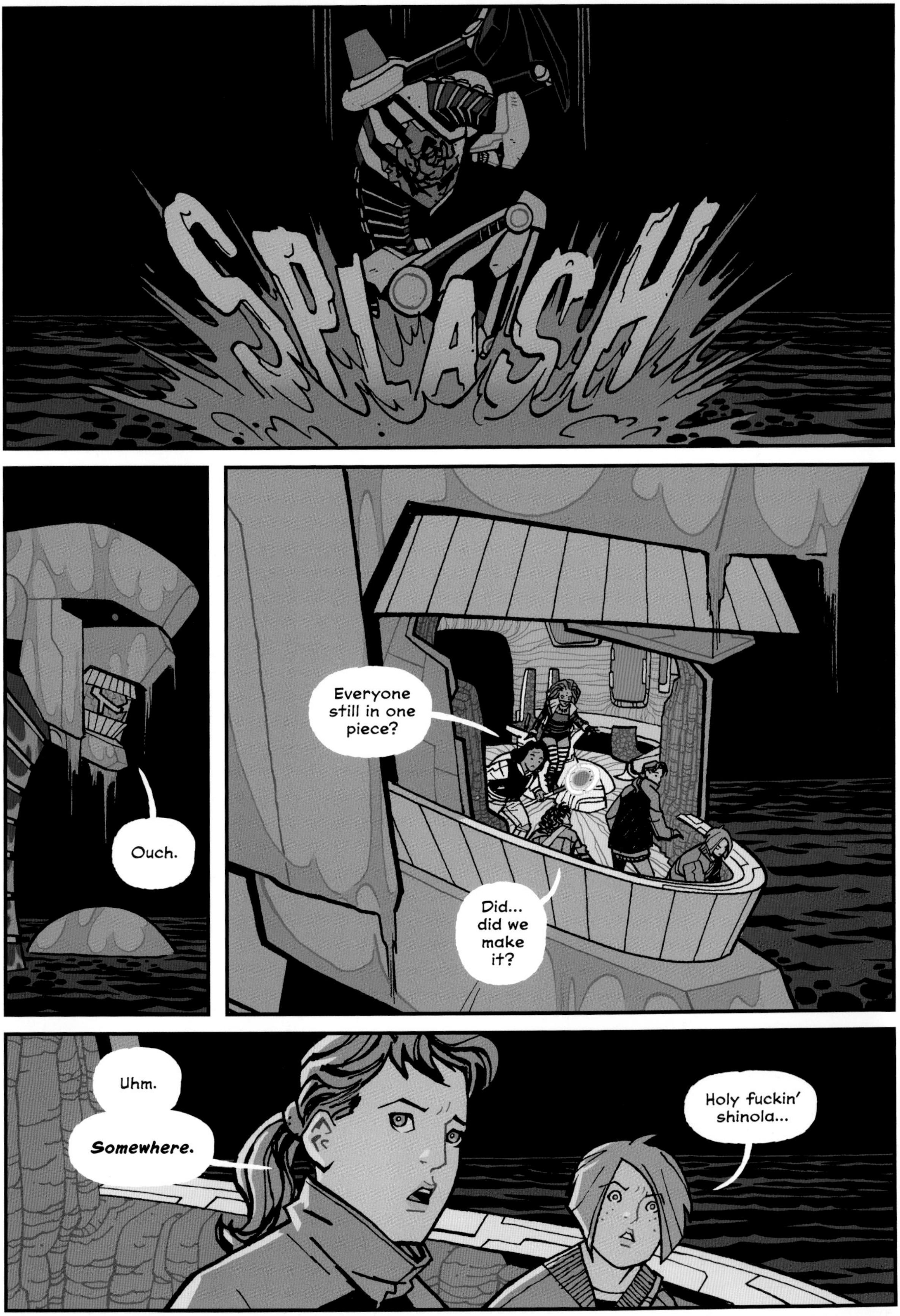
SPLASH
Ouch.
Everyone still in one piece?
Did... did we make it?
Uhm.
Somewhere.
Holy fuckin' shinola...

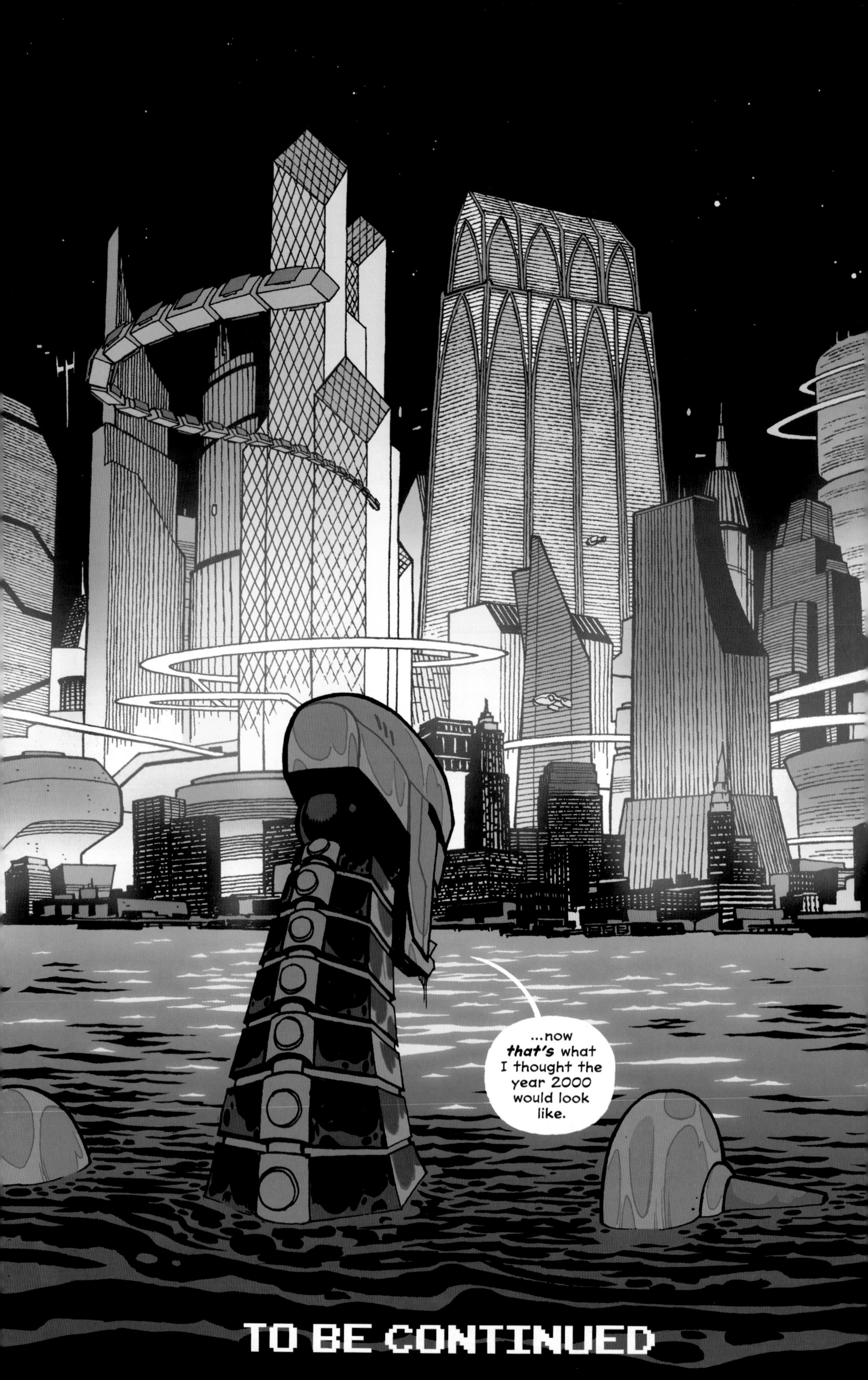
...now *that's* what I thought the year 2000 would look like.
TO BE CONTINUED

ART

Gallery

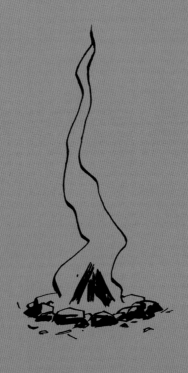

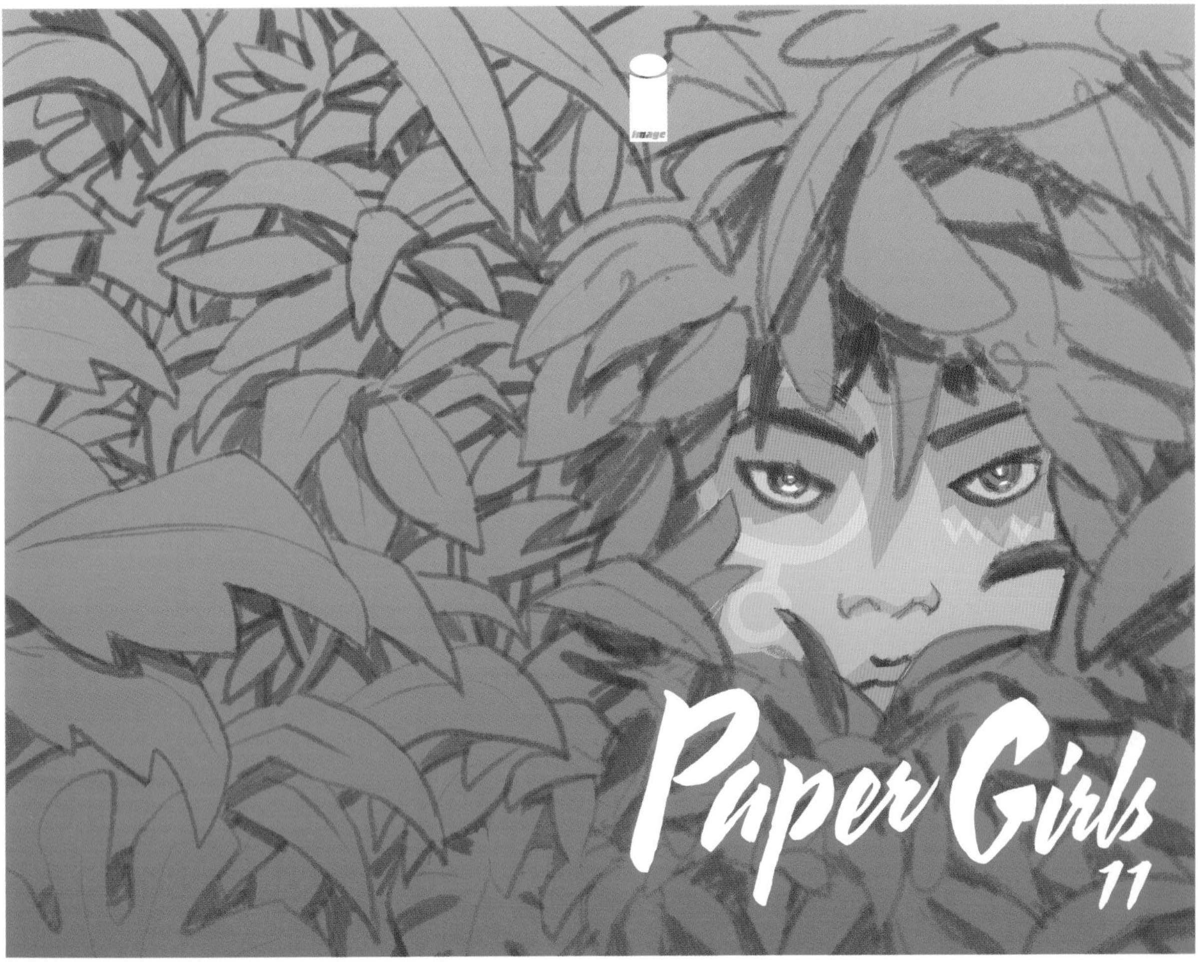
image
Paper Girls
11

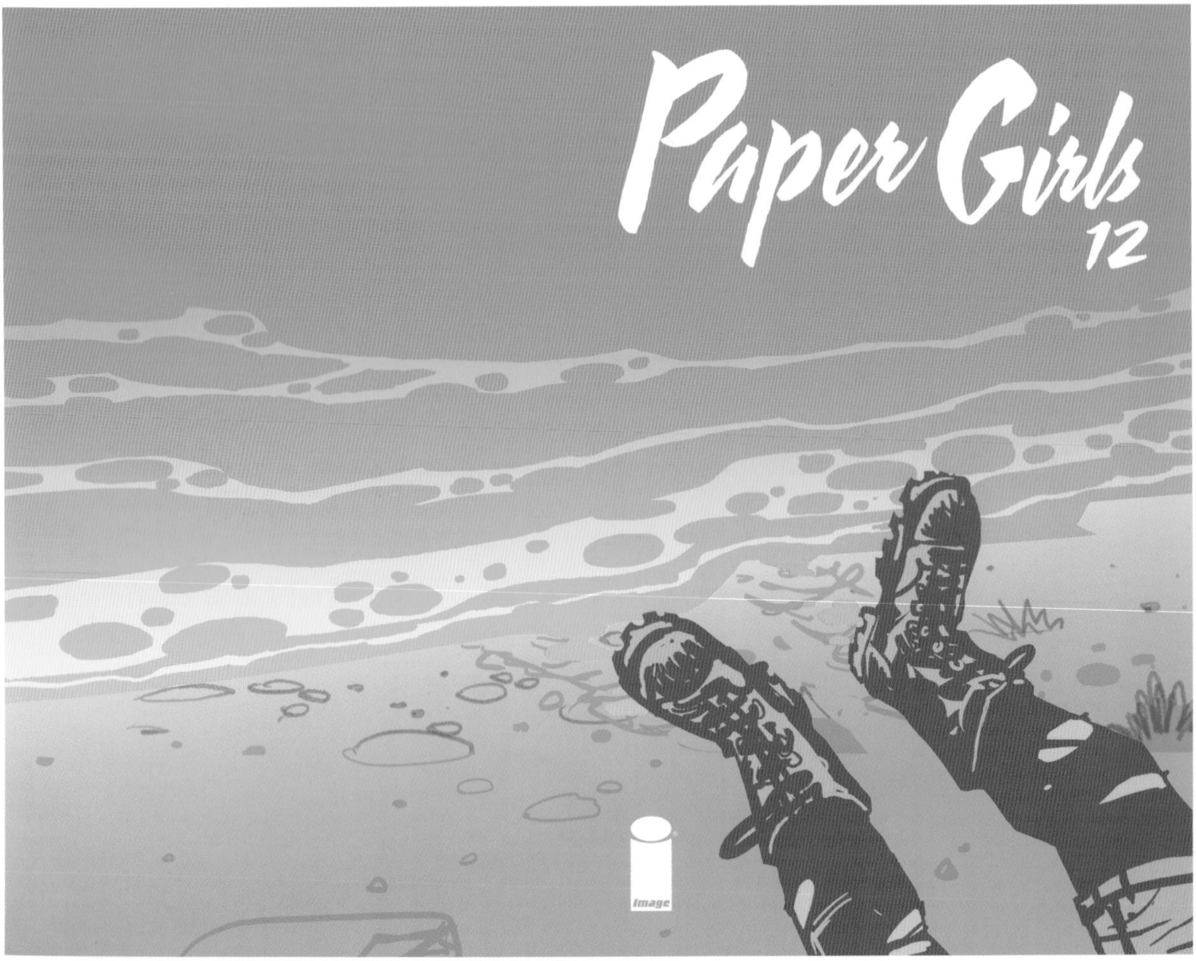
Paper Girls
12
image

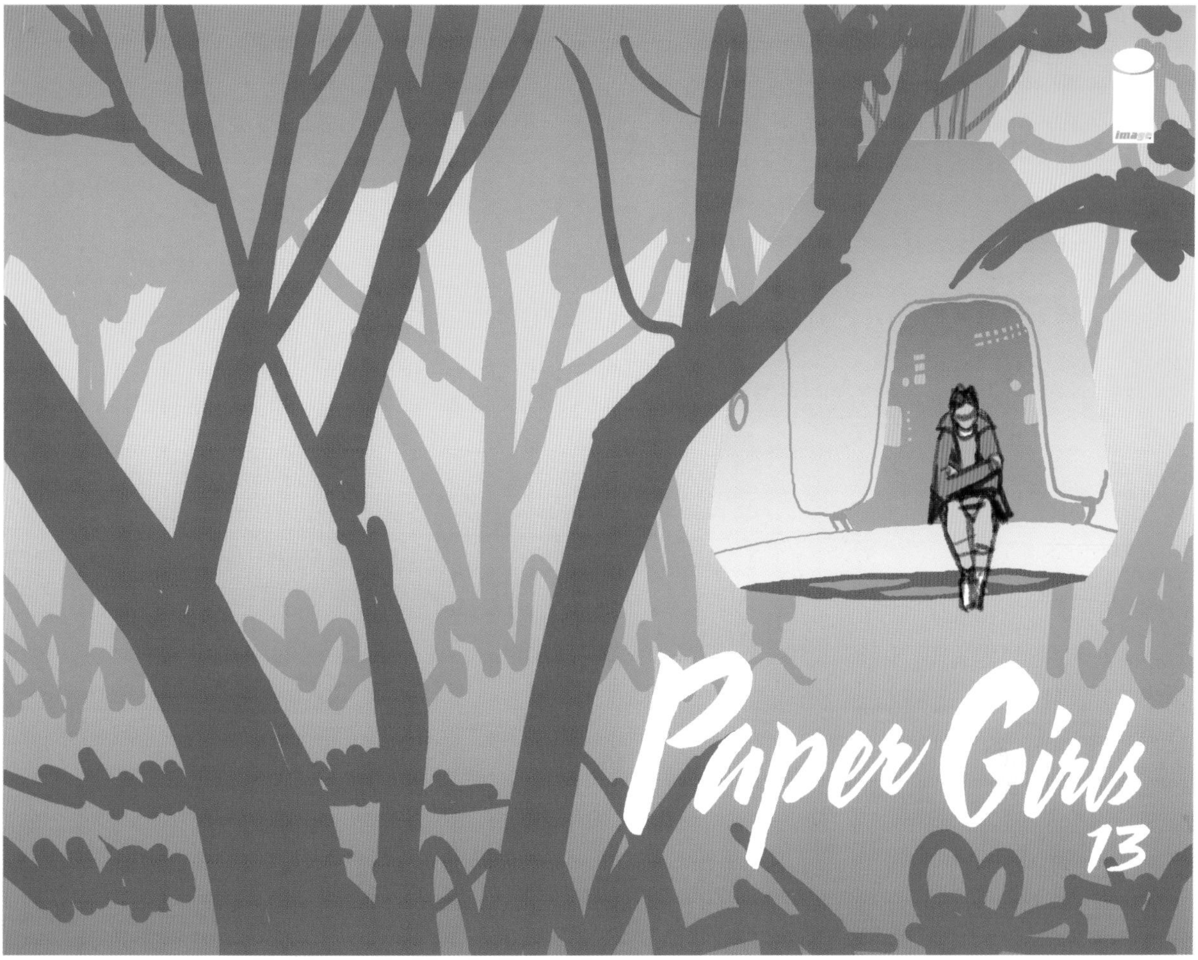
image
Paper Girls
13

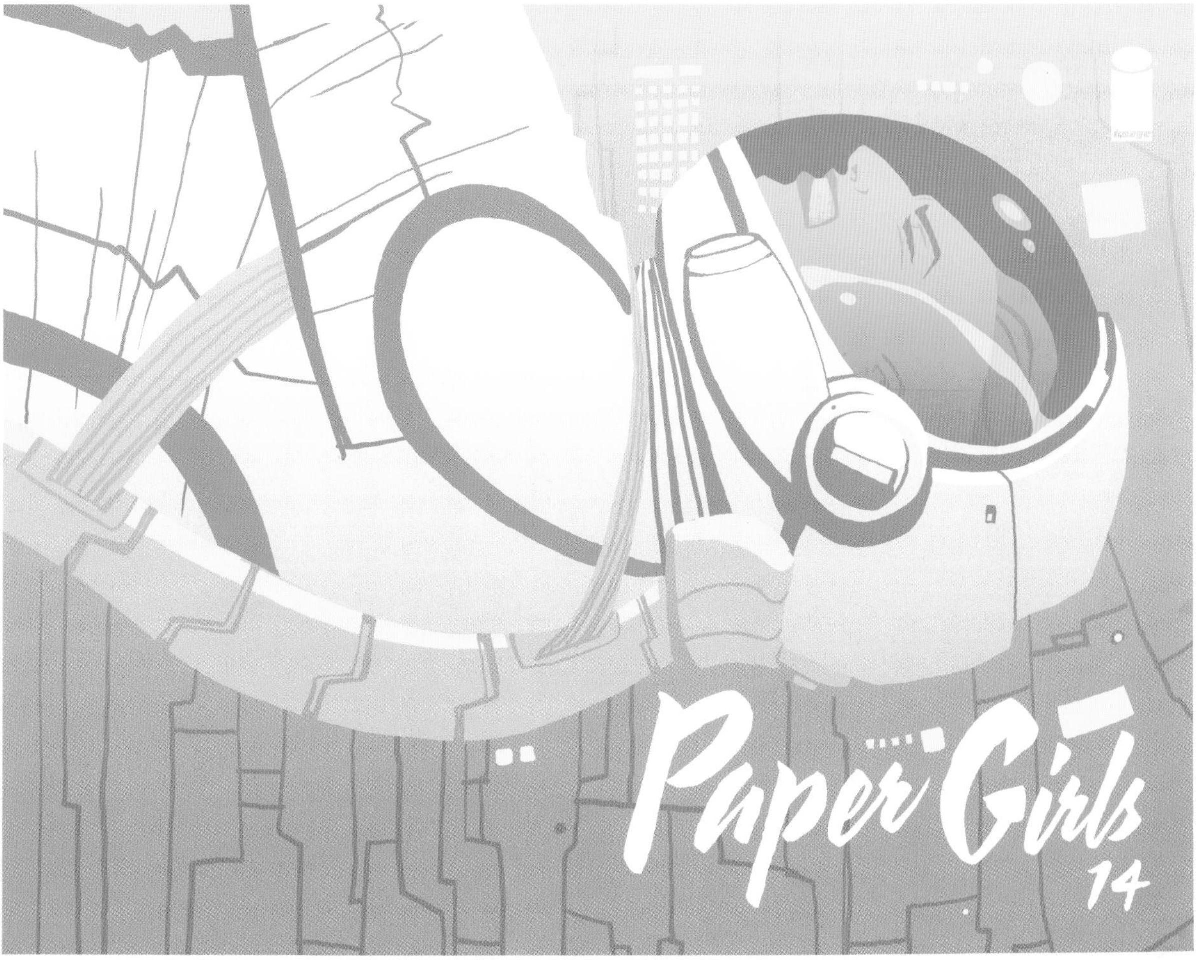
image
Paper Girls
14

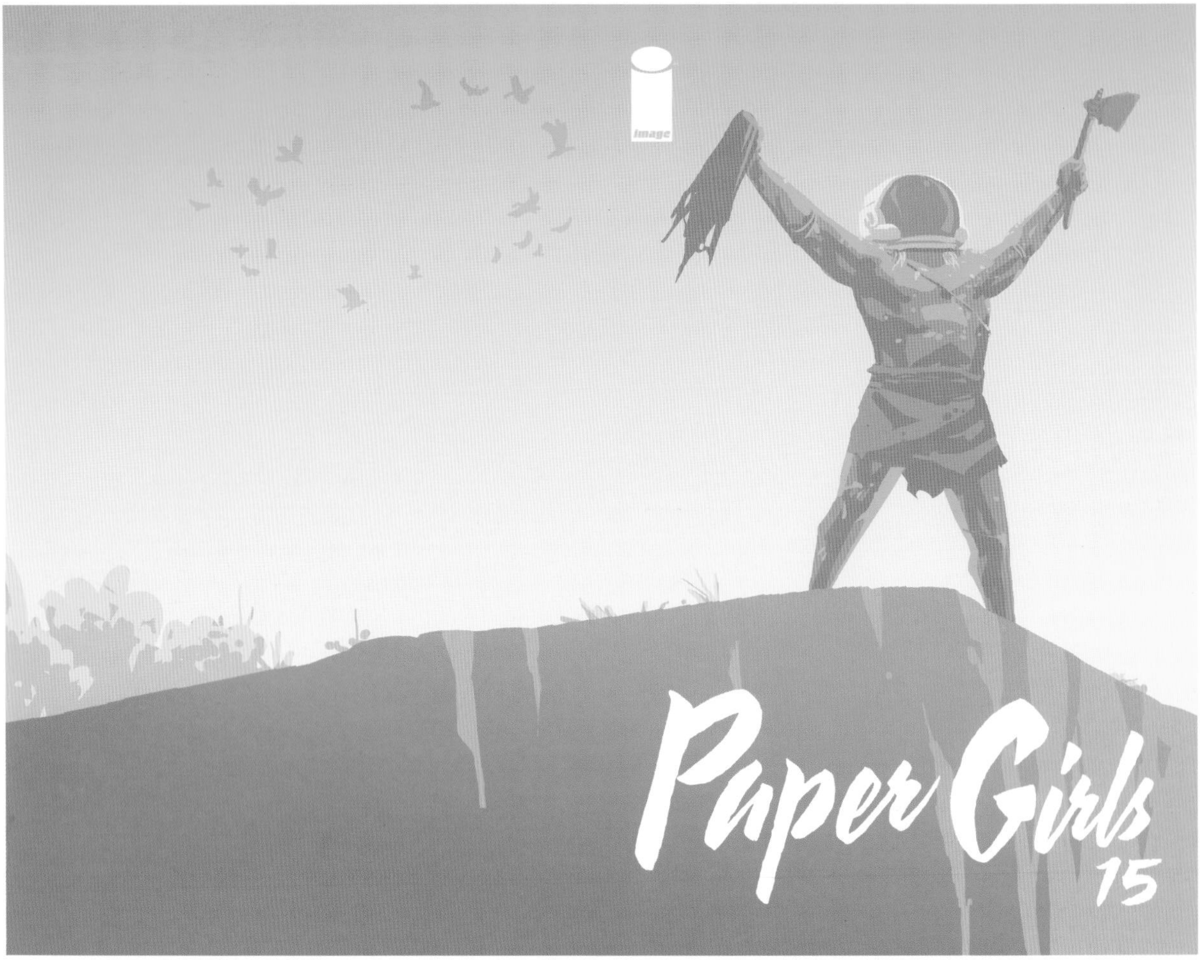
image
Paper Girls
15

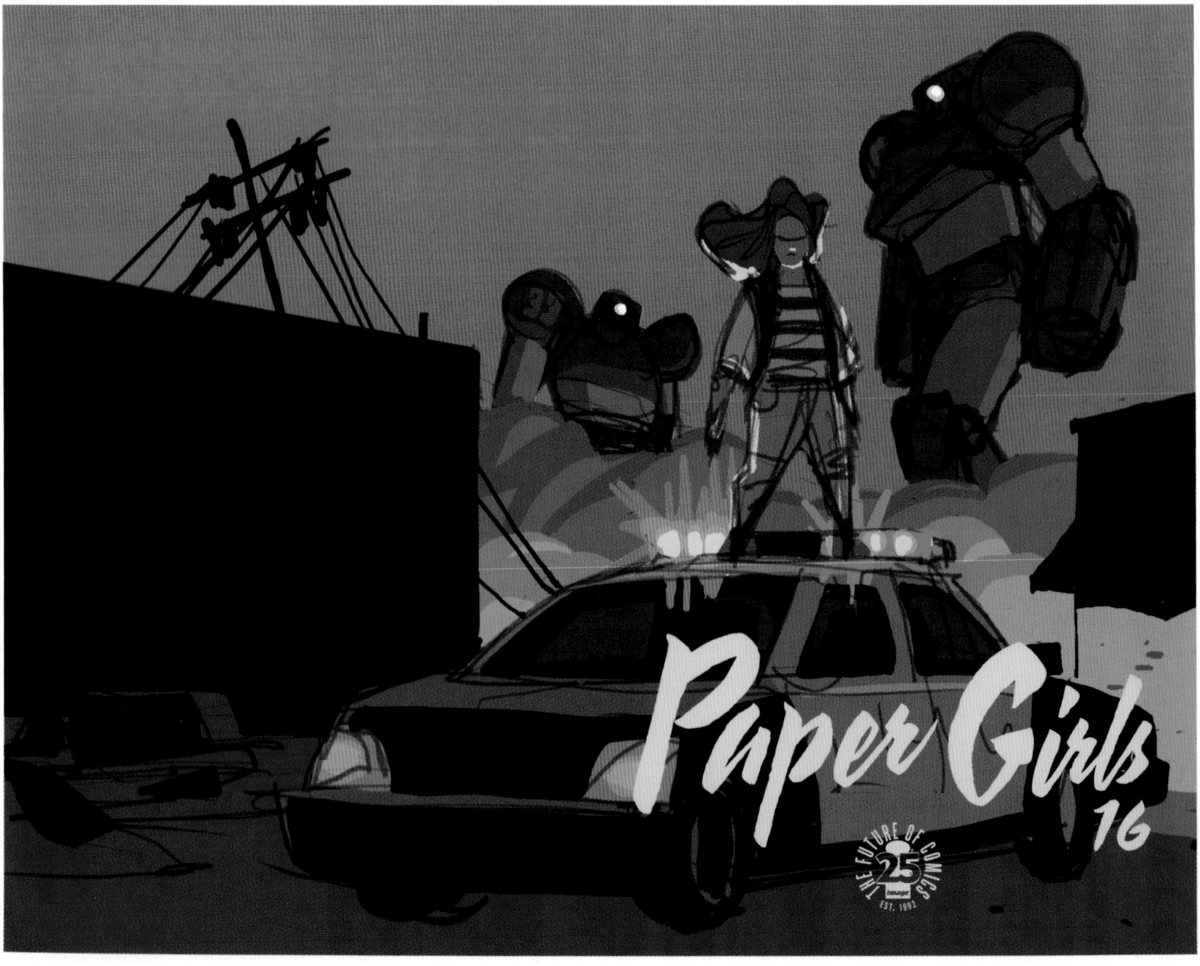
Paper Girls
16
THE FUTURE OF COMICS
25
image
EST. 1992

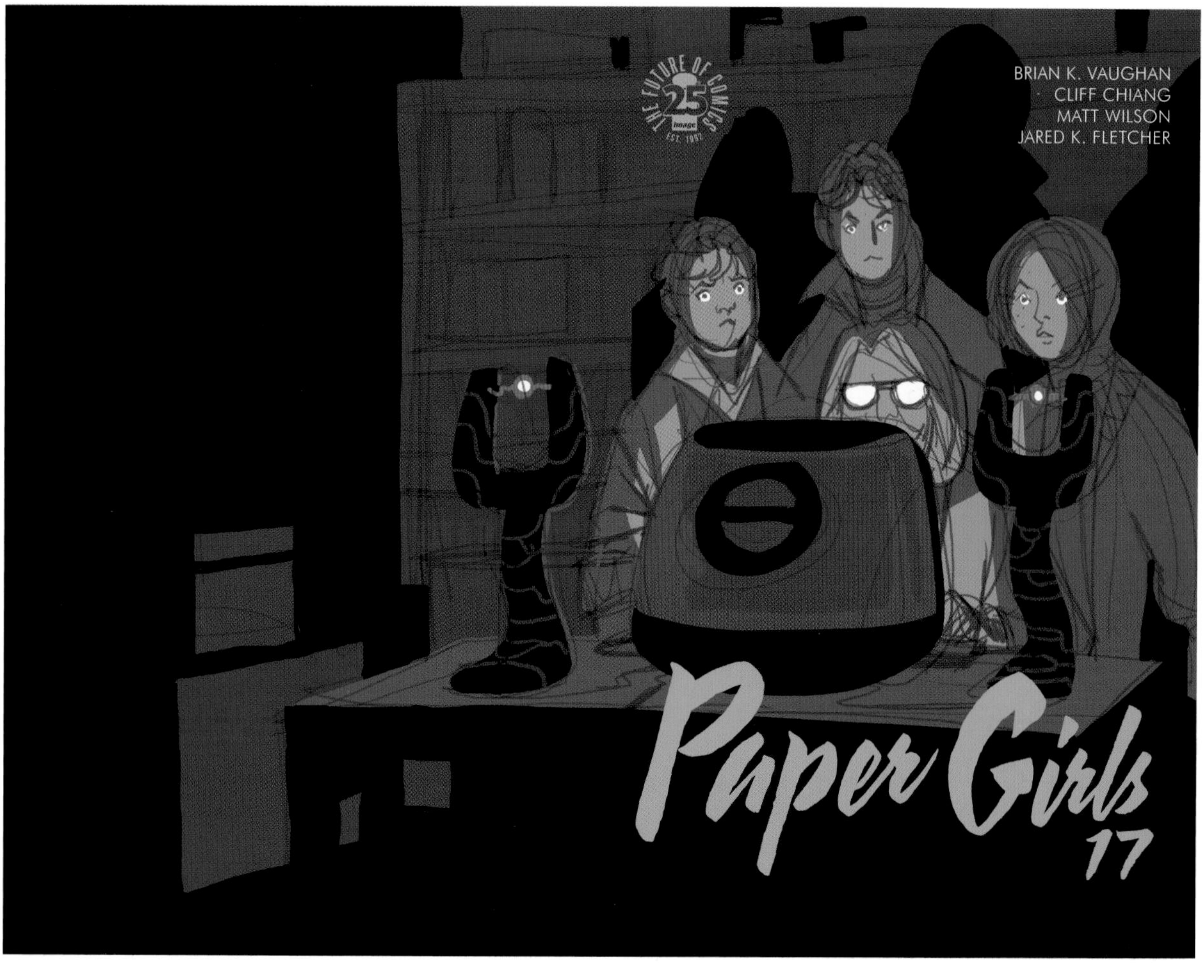
THE FUTURE OF COMICS
25
image
EST. 1992
BRIAN K. VAUGHAN
CLIFF CHIANG
MATT WILSON
JARED K. FLETCHER
Paper Girls
17

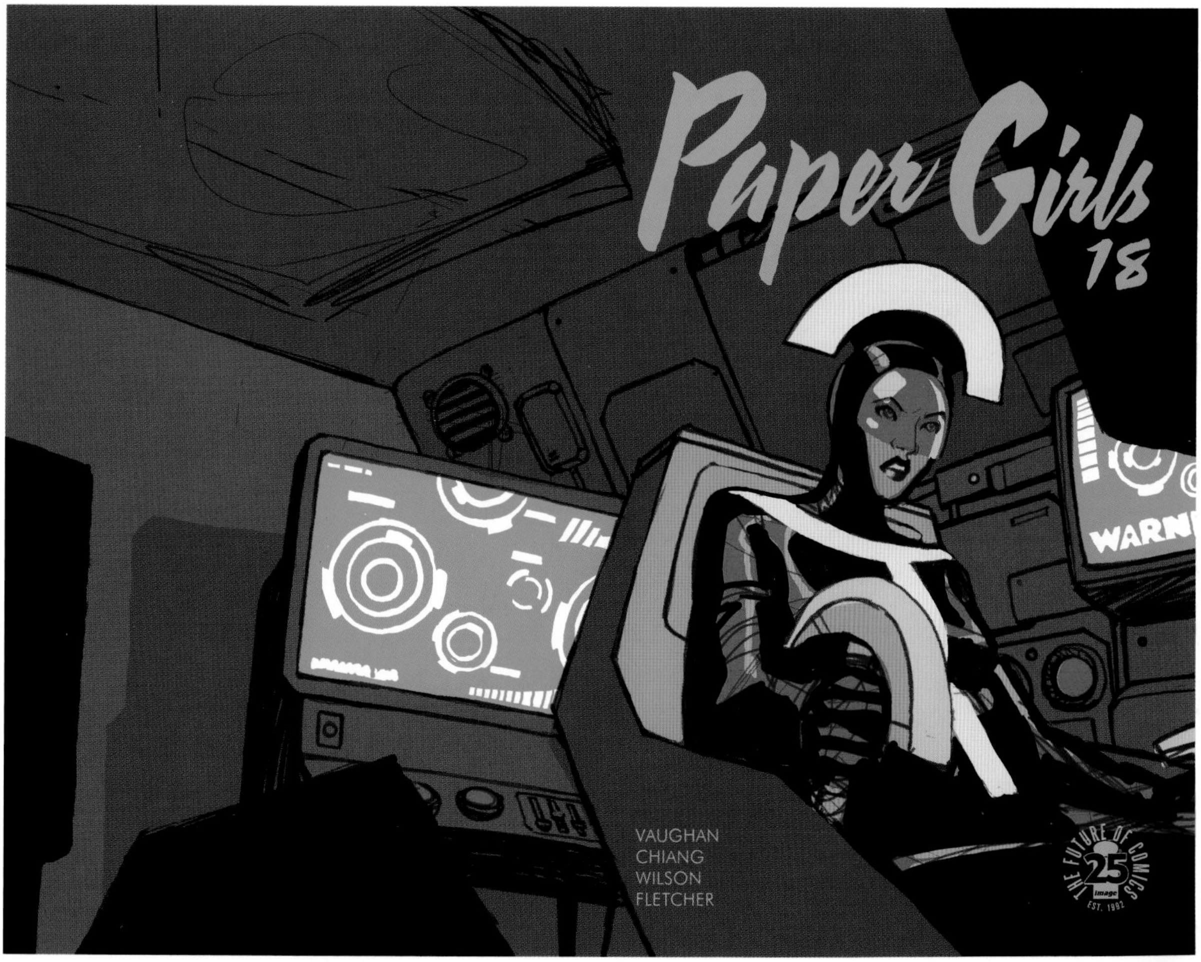
Paper Girls
18
WARN
VAUGHAN
CHIANG
WILSON
FLETCHER
THE FUTURE OF COMICS
25
image
EST. 1992

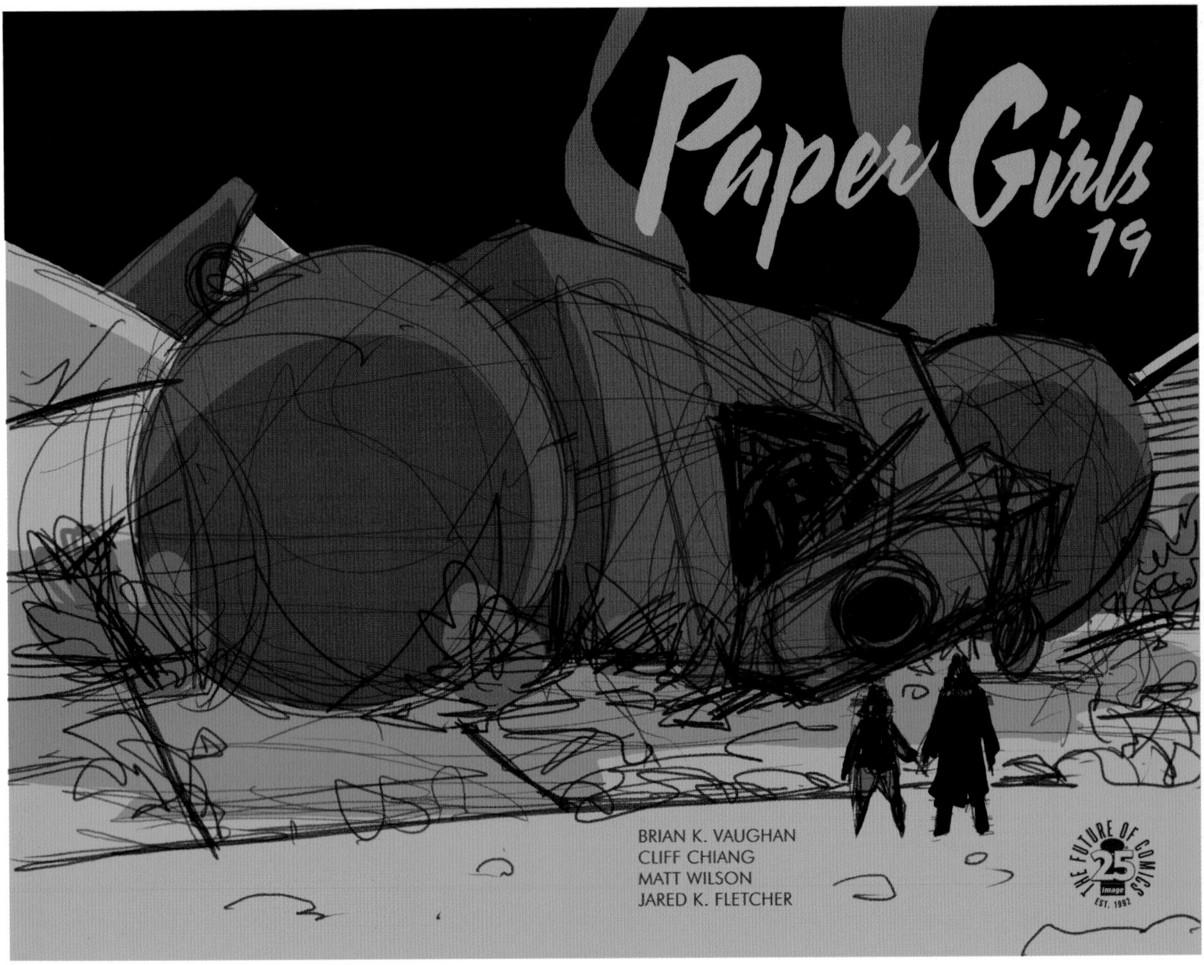
Paper Girls
19
BRIAN K. VAUGHAN
CLIFF CHIANG
MATT WILSON
JARED K. FLETCHER
THE FUTURE OF COMICS
25
EST. 1992

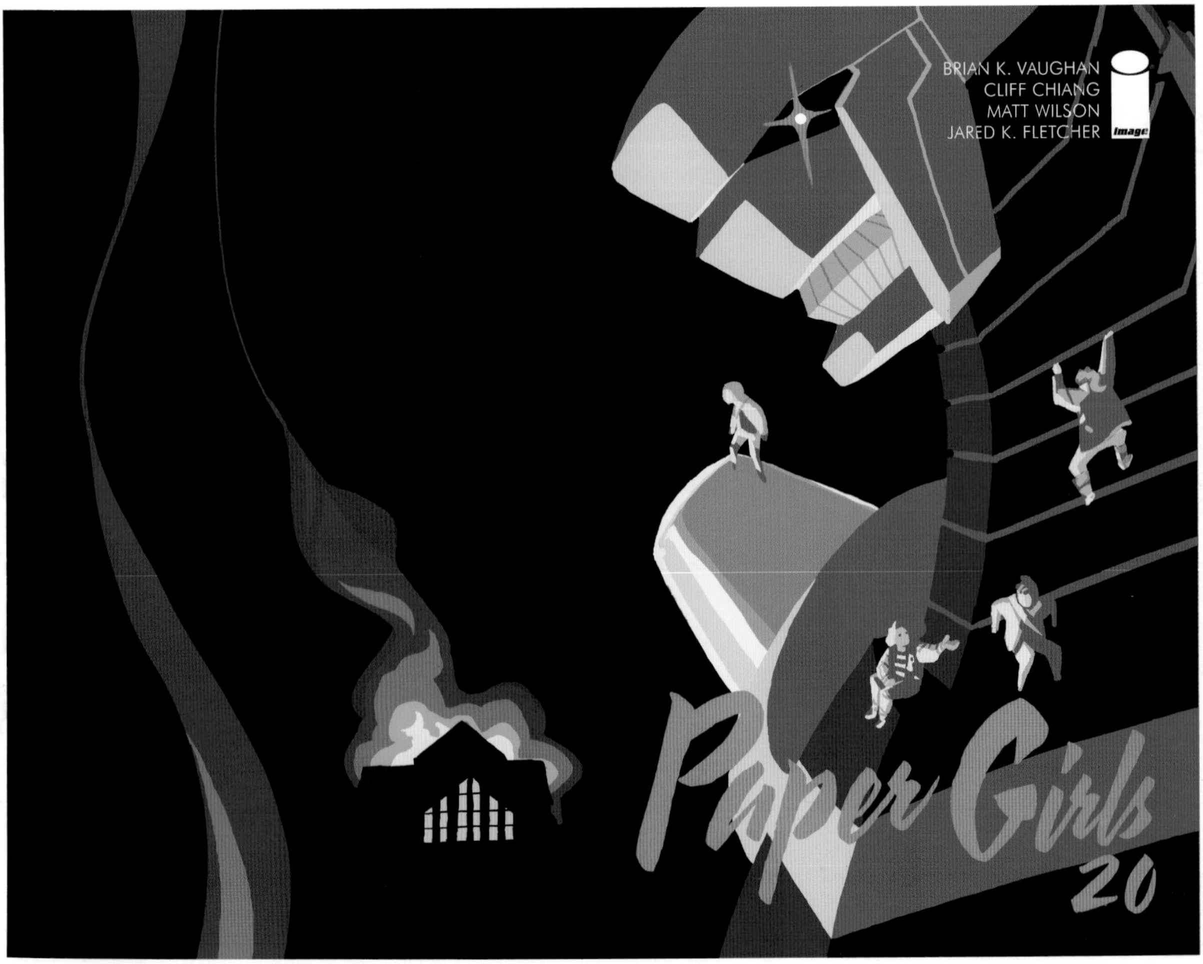
BRIAN K. VAUGHAN
CLIFF CHIANG
MATT WILSON
JARED K. FLETCHER
image
Paper Girls
20

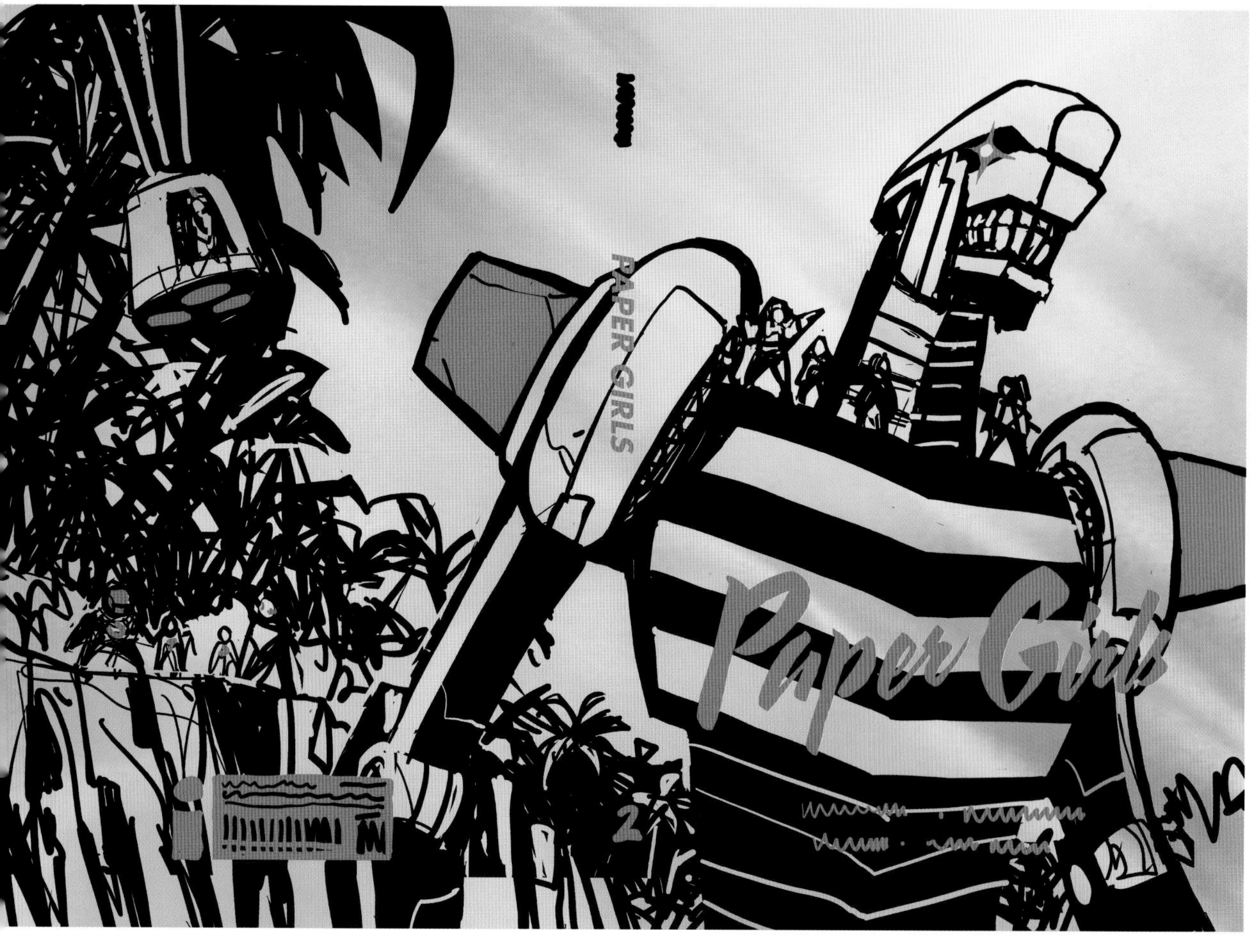
PAPER GIRLS
Paper Girls
2

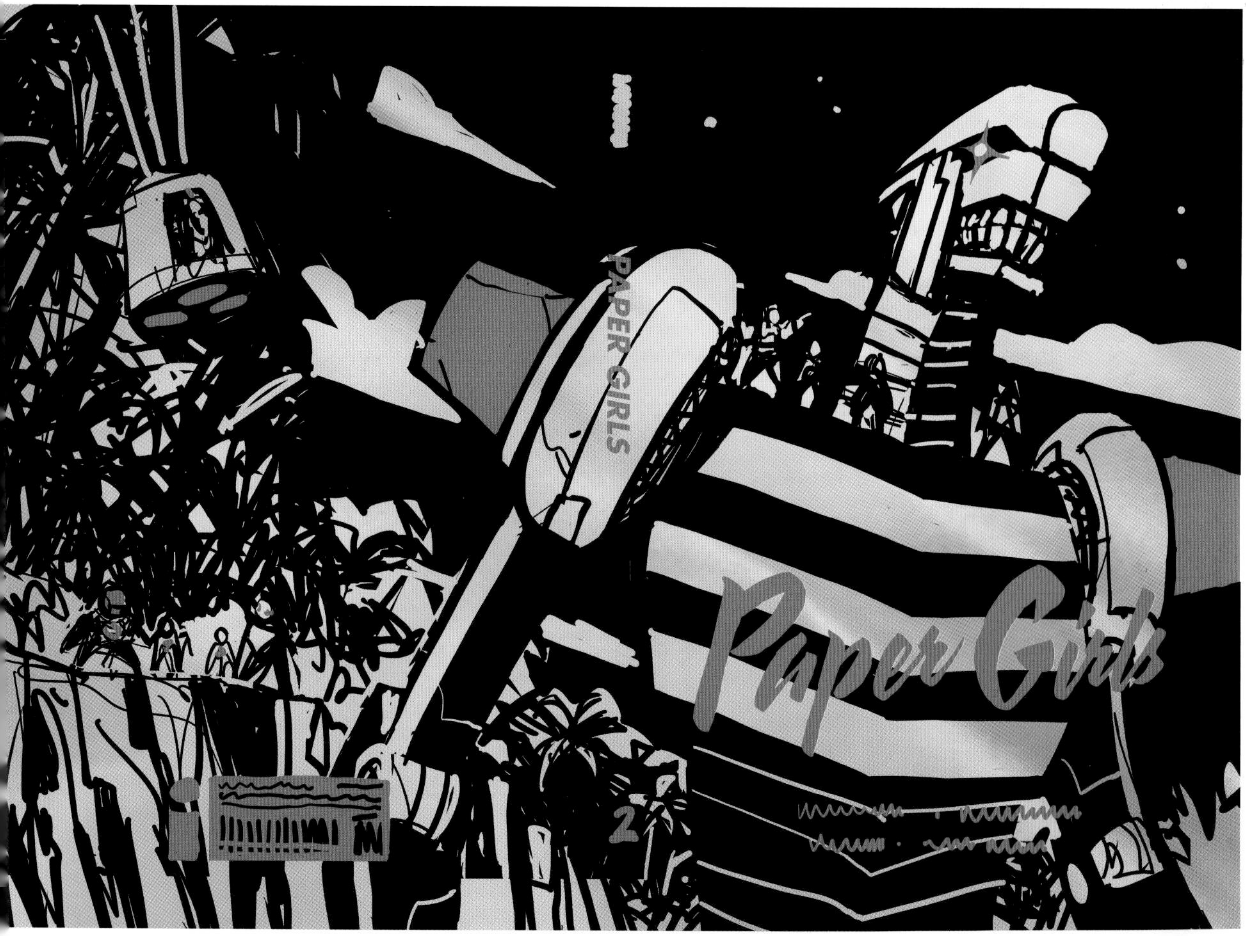
PAPER GIRLS
Paper Girls
2

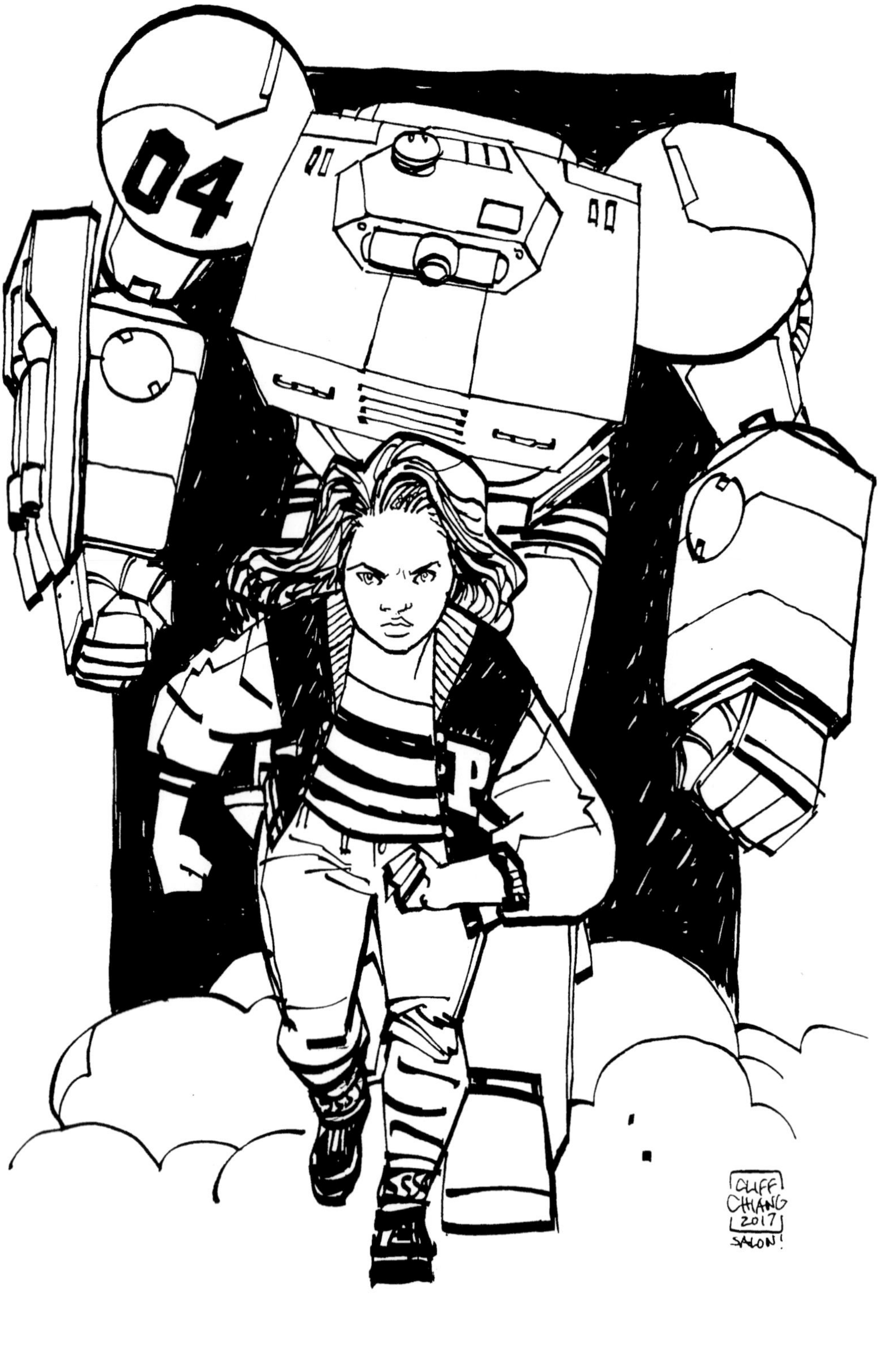
04
P
CLIFF CHIANG 2017
SALON!

Live sketch for Salon.com *streaming event*

COLOR PROCESS

Gallery

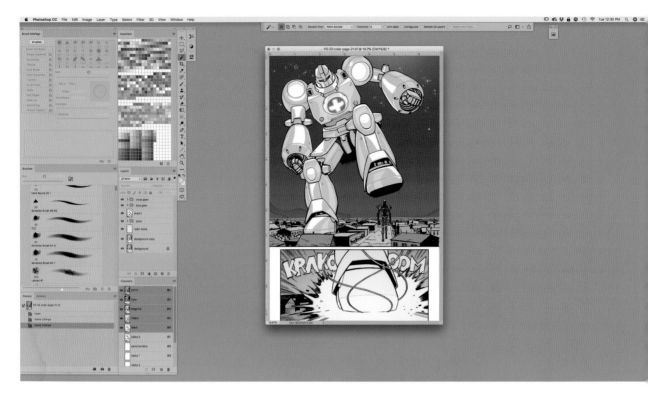

One of the most distinctive features of Paper Girls *is the striking use of color by Matt Wilson. Assisted by flatter Dee Cunniffe, Matt brings the black and white artwork to life with a restrained but romantic palette that is integral to the storytelling. In 2017, Matt was awarded the prestigious Eisner Award for Best Colorist, in part for his work in this volume. Here, Matt gives us a behind-the-scenes look at his process and some of the artistic choices that go into coloring* Paper Girls.

Matt's Workspace

This is what I'm looking at on screen when I color, pretty standard Photoshop stuff. I'm left-handed so I keep everything on the left and work in the center.

I use a 27" Wacom Cintiq tablet monitor connected to an iMac and color all my work in Adobe Photoshop.

Brushes
Size:
20
Hard Round 20 1
20
Sampled Brush #8 #2
40
[[[[[
87
Sampled Brush #4 3
70
Sampled Brush #4 1
250
Leaves #1

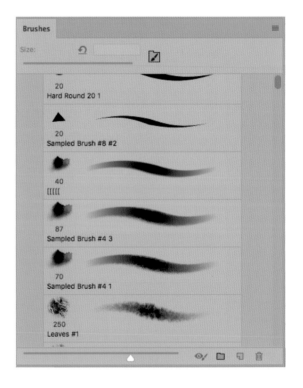

I have tons of brushes, but for *Paper Girls* I pretty much only use that triangle shaped brush to do all my mark making. If an environment calls for some dirt or grunge, I may use that Leaves #1 brush here and there. I've collected many brushes from various online sources over the years, including from a designer named Kyle Webster. Kyle makes pretty much the best custom brushes available. And while I don't use too many custom brushes on *Paper Girls,* I do use them a lot in other projects, and would highly recommend them. Luckily, Adobe now offers all his brushes in Photoshop if you're using the latest version.

Swatches

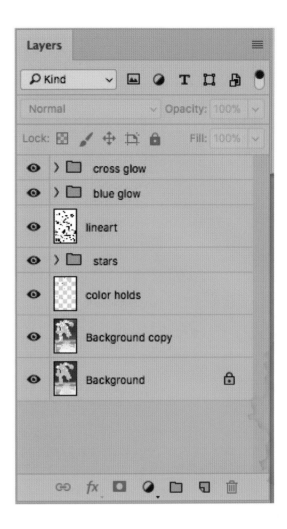

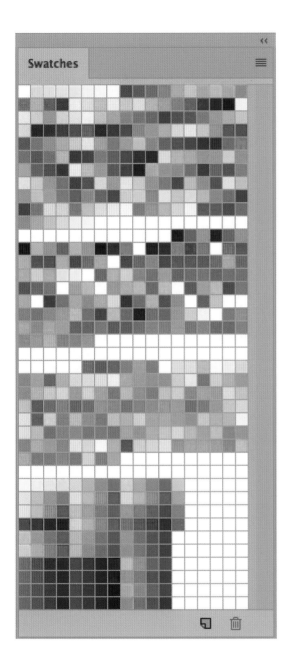

These are the base colors I use to build every palette or color choice in all my work. If I want to use any of these swatches purely at 100%, they're colors I can rely on to print nicely. I often use them at varying percentages, like filling with a color but only at 40%, to mix with the color underneath. I'll also do the same when using a brush, setting it to a percentage below 100%, or set the brush or fill to a different blending mode as well as a lower percentage, which gives me even more color mixing options.

Layers
Kind
Normal
Opacity: 100%
Lock:
Fill: 100%
cross glow
blue glow
lineart
stars
color holds
Background copy
Background

Paper Girls is one of my simpler books in terms of number of layers and special effects, and this is probably the most complicated layer setup I've had on the book. In comparison, my work on *The Mighty Thor* with artist Russell Dauterman could possibly have another dozen layers. First, I keep my flat colors on the bottom layer so I can easily select large sections without gradients or the mark making getting in the way. On the layer above that are the same colors as the layer beneath it, but this is where I do all of my main coloring work. All the gradients or rendering happens there. When I turn a black line into a colored line, that's called a color hold. In this book, they're often used for some of the lines in the girl's faces, or clouds, or some of the odd future tech. I keep the color holds on their own layer so I can easily change them. Finally, the lineart layer is all the black lines you see in the image. Those four layers are pretty common across all of my files on any book I color, but depending on the subject matter I'll have other more specialized layers. For this page that means all the various glowing elements, like the stars, cross and other glowing parts of the giant mech.

Flats to Finished

Here you see the progress of a colored page. The first step is called "flats." Most colorists send the black and white pages to an assistant to flat the page, adding flat colors so that the colorist can easily select the different elements on a page with a click rather than having to outline every element themselves. The flats don't have to be the same colors as the final colors, they just speed up the coloring process for the colorist. The next image shows how I adjusted the flats to fit the desired palette and lighting of the scene. The final image shows the finished colors, where I've added rendering using gradients in the background of panel 4 and mark making on the characters to show the shadows cast from the fire, and I've also applied color holds to things like the fire, the girls' facial features, and the tech.

Recycle! (Your Palettes)

The inside of the Stony Gate Mall has appeared in two different points in time so far. In an earlier volume, we saw the mall in the year 2016, when it was closed and run down. But in this volume, in the year 2000, it's still open for business and regularly used, so we decided to use the same palette but not include all the dirty textures. In most cases I would've been inclined to use a slightly different palette in the mall's second appearance, but here it made sense to repeat the palette, and it was a fun way to tie the locations' two different appearances together.

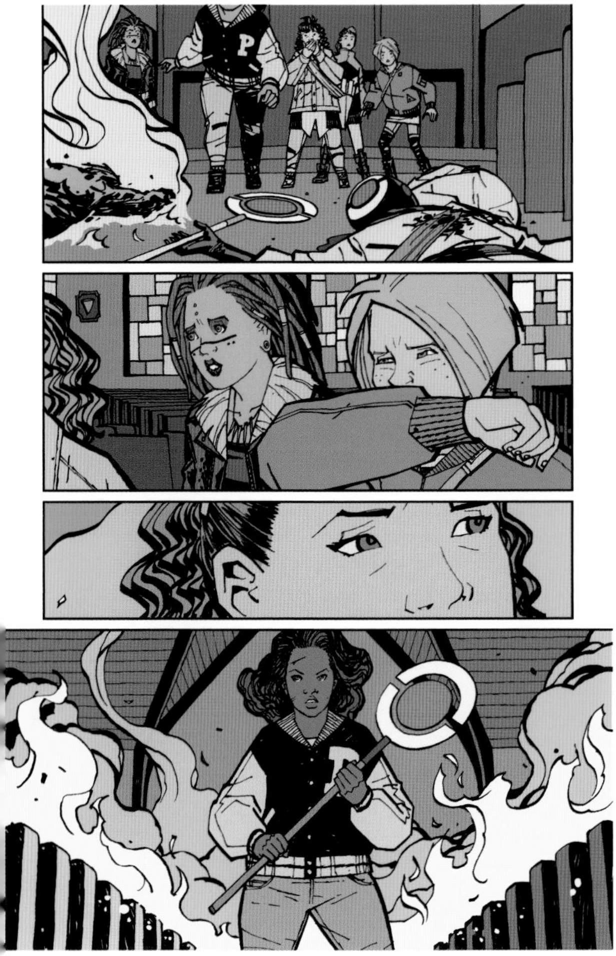

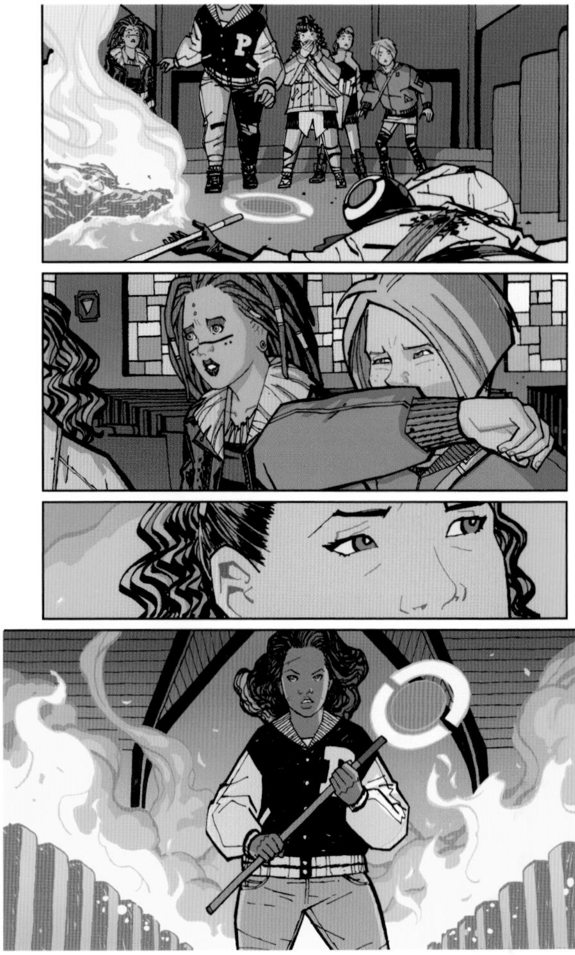

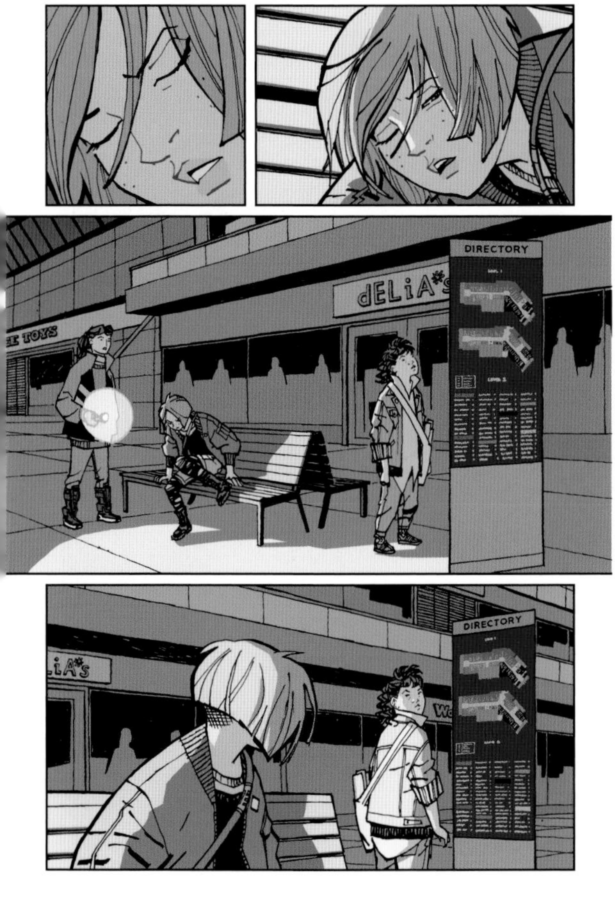
DIRECTORY
dELiA*s
DIRECTORY

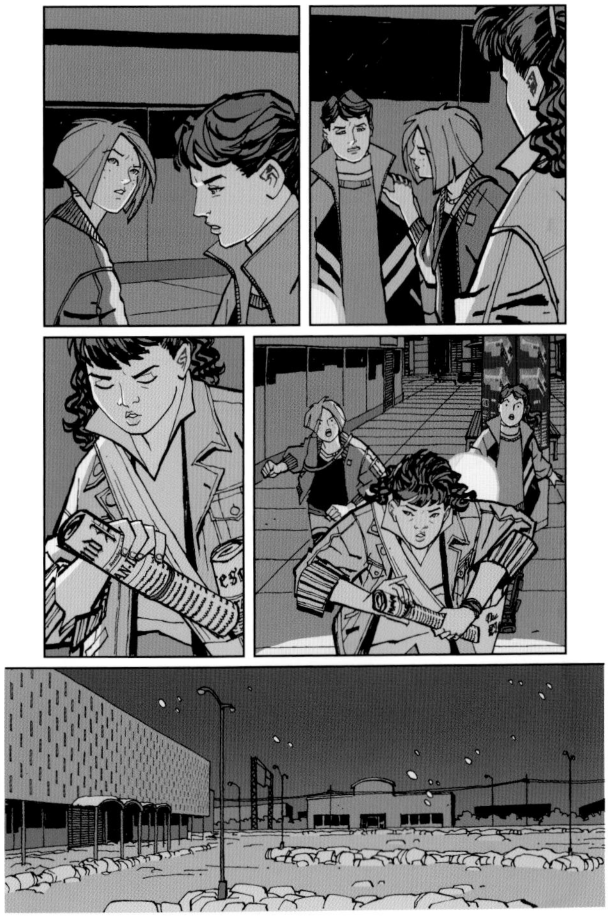

Setting the Mood

We didn't set out with the mandate to impose an overall palette on each 5-issue arc, but that idea developed slowly as the series progressed. Because the first arc took place mostly on the same night and in the same general locations, there is a dominant palette by default. So it made sense to move away from that palette in the second arc when the story progressed further in time.

By the third arc, we have a dramatic shift in the environment. Going from the urban/suburban modern world to undeveloped prehistoric forests naturally pushed the palette in a completely different direction. As you can see, a pattern has emerged where each arc's overall palettes are a reaction to the previous arc.

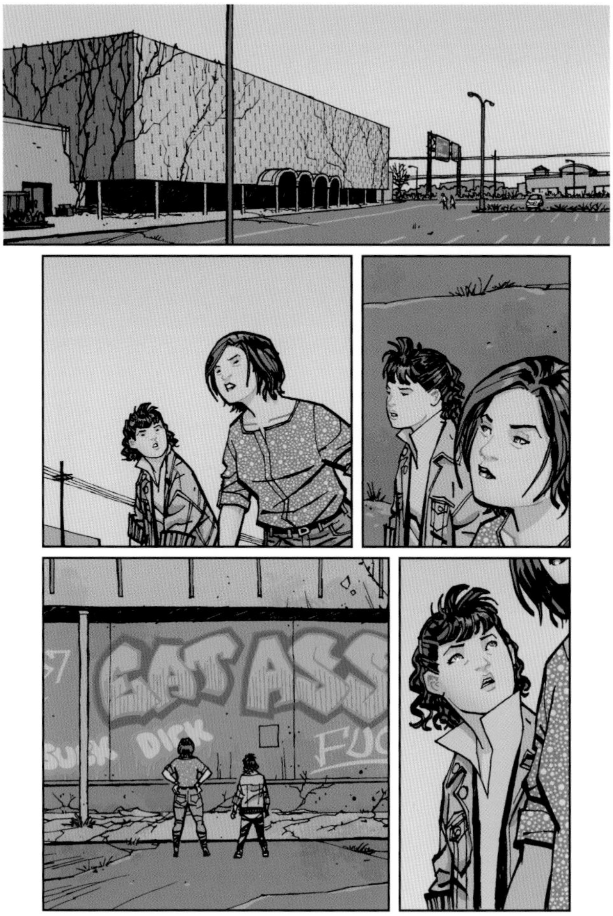

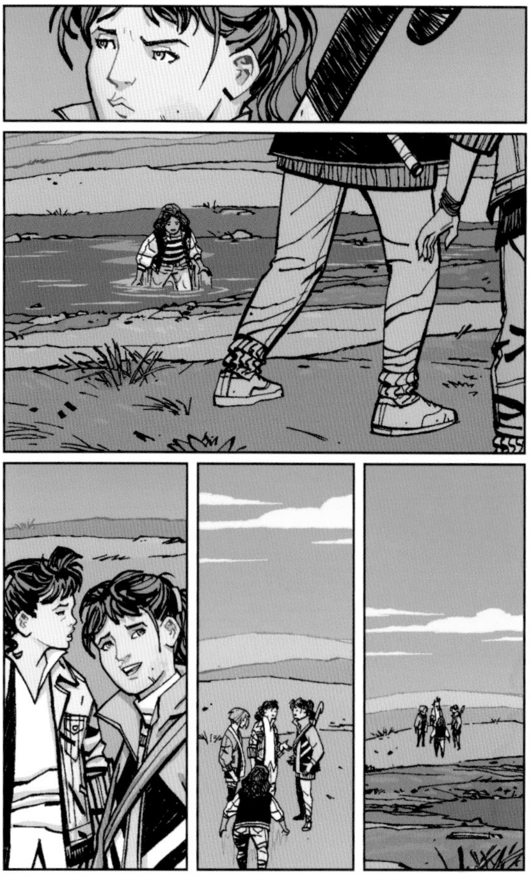

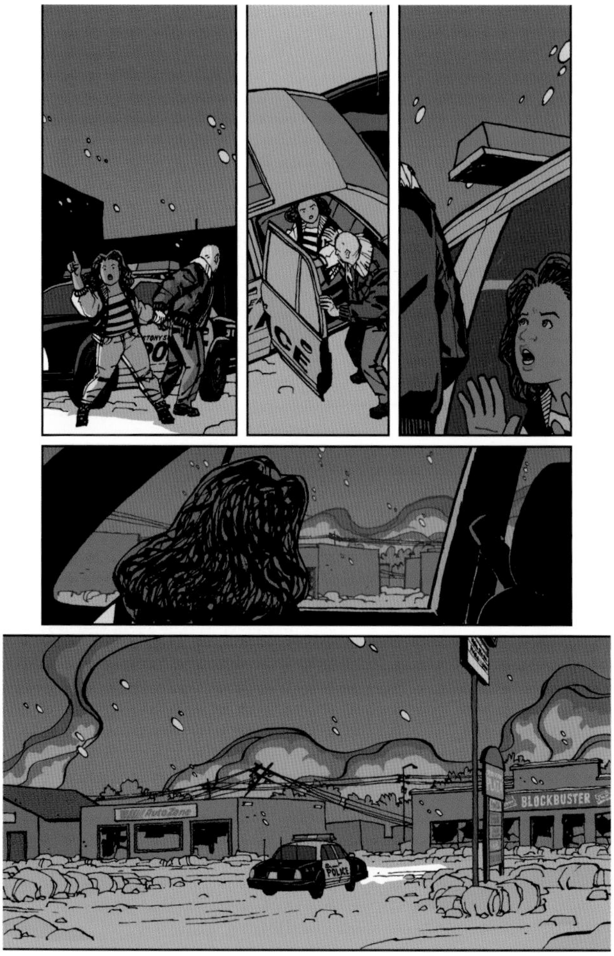
AutoZone
BLOCKBUSTER

For the fourth arc, we were back in a more modern setting. Now in the year 2000, and with the story playing with the concept of the Y2K bug, I thought it'd be fun to change directions. We transition from the lush, cleanly colored forests in arc three, to more drab and dreary grays with orange as accents to play up the apocalyptic feeling of the fourth arc.

Color Blocking

In a lot of scenes in *Paper Girls,* I try to block out sections of a panel or a scene as either being in light or shadow. In other words, I'll categorize the scenes into different areas and then assign them a dominant color. Then, as the characters move through the scene I can move those blocks of color and light to give context to where the characters are, where they were, and where they may be going next. Here you can see how the characters start by crossing the stream in panels 1-3, lit by sunlight coming through an opening in the tree canopy. Then, in panel 4, they've entered the shadows on the other side of the stream. And by panel 5, they're exiting the shadows and entering yet another light-filled clearing.

On the opposite page there's another example of how color can be used to show movement by blocking out the environment with different dominant colors. By following the red and blue accent colors from the police cruiser's lights against a very desaturated main palette, you get a sense of the police car moving through the scene.

Another way I've used color blocking is to better define what might seem like one space into multiple zones. In both of these cases it helps the reader feel the closeness and intimacy of the space the characters are inhabiting. In the fireside forest scene, I clearly blocked out what's inside the ring of fire light, and what falls outside the light. The idea is to convey how isolated and surrounded by wilderness the girls are.

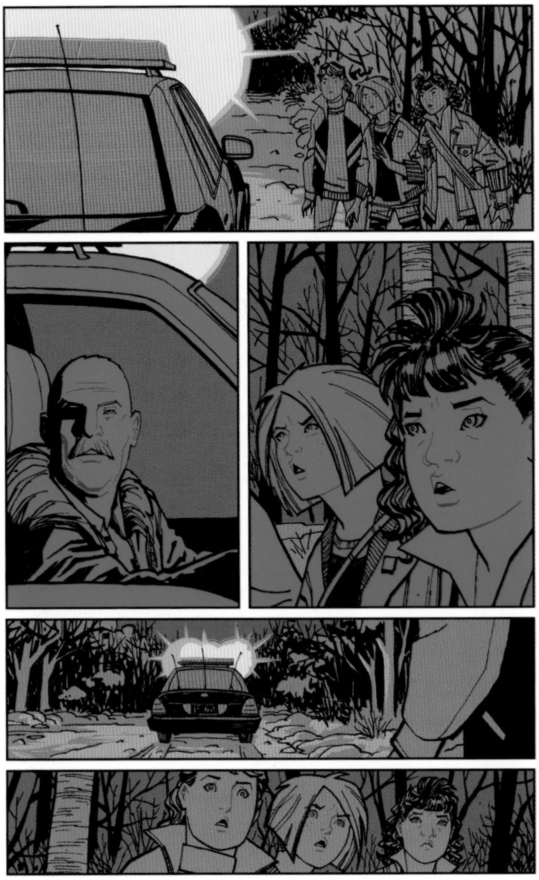

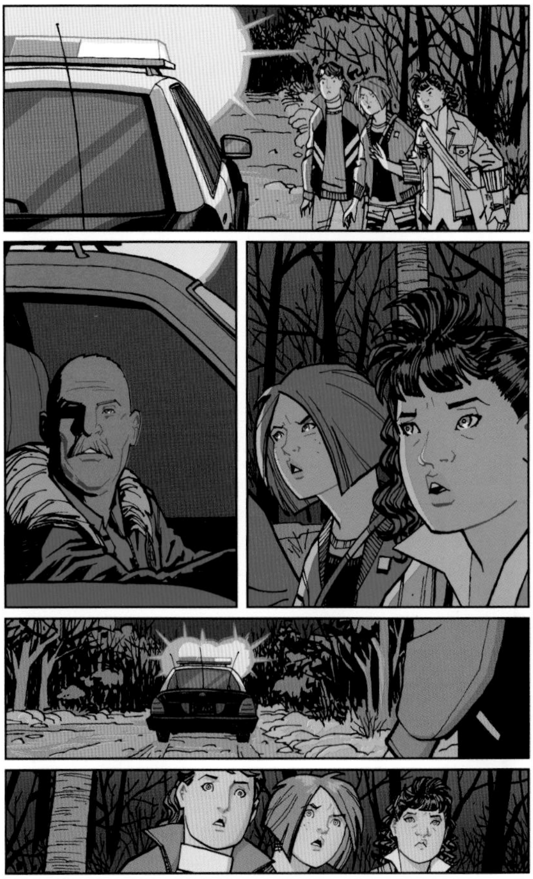

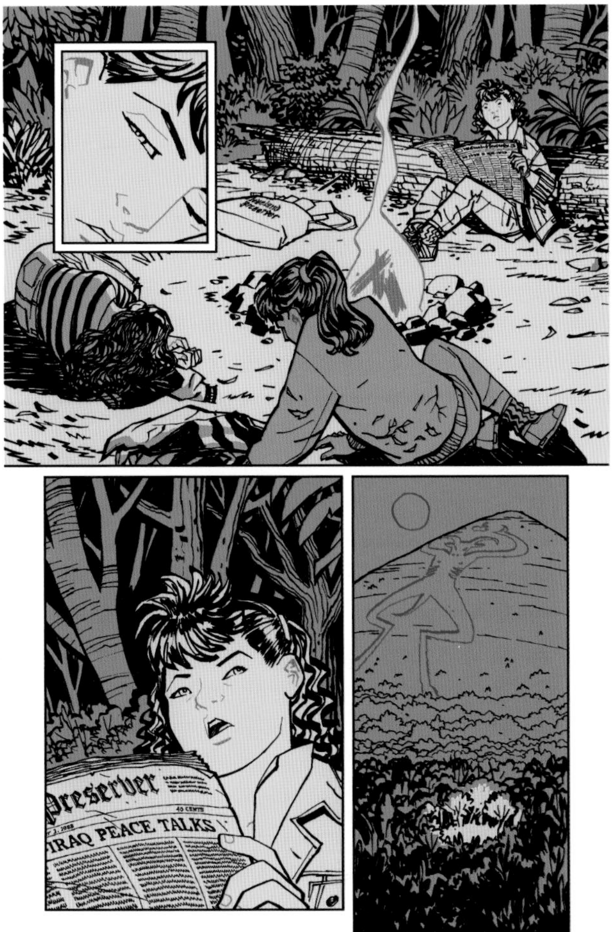

Preserver
IRAQ PEACE TALKS

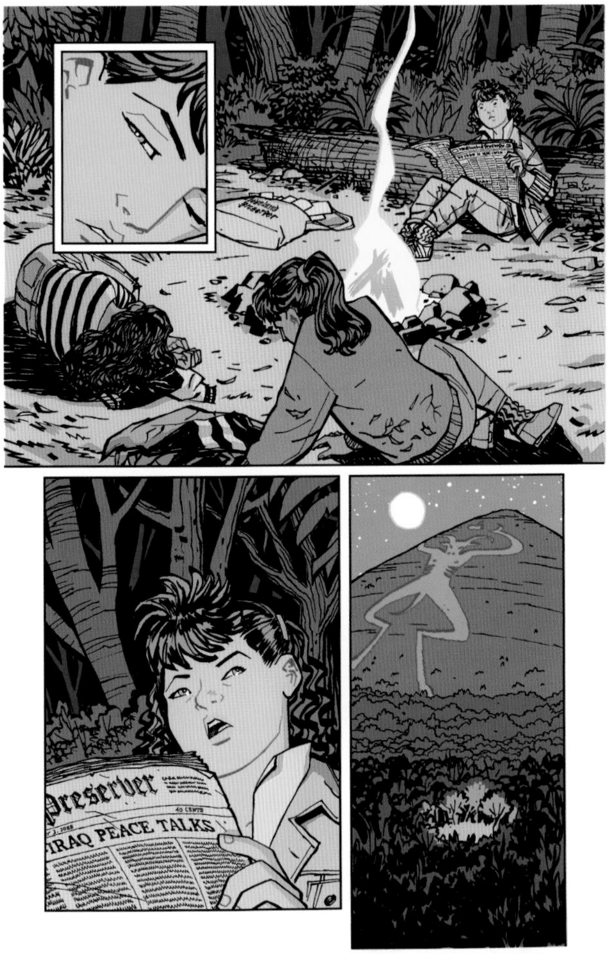

Preserver
IRAQ PEACE TALKS

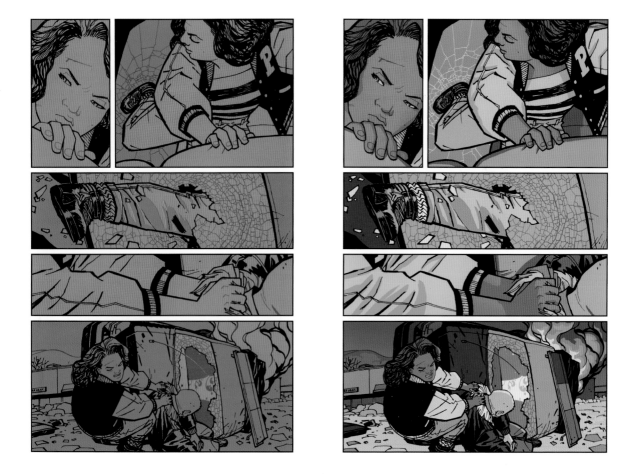

In the crashed car scene, it was important to emphasize the danger inside that burning car. Making the interior of the car a completely separate and hotter palette from the snowy exterior helped clarify when Tiff was in danger and when she had successfully escaped.

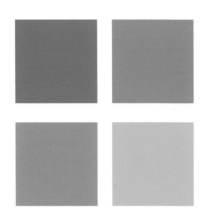

Perceptual Color vs. Local Color

Local color is the natural color of an object in ordinary daylight, without the influence of atmosphere or reflected light from adjacent colors. Perceptual color, however, is the color as perceived by the eye, changed by the effects of light and atmosphere. In the same way, for instance, that distant mountains can appear to be blue, Mac's red hair can be vastly different colors depending on the scene's palette.

CREATORS

BRIAN K. VAUGHAN
Activities: Theater, Sci-Fi Book Club,
Power of the Pen
Worst Subject: Math, P.E. (tie)
Halloween Costume: Homemade
Spider-Man Symbiote Suit

CLIFF CHIANG
Homeroom: Miss Benson
Activities: Chorus, Ski Club, French
Cultural Society, Art Club
Favorite NES games: *Contra,
Double Dribble, Metal Gear*

MATT WILSON
Homeroom: Miss Pearce
Activities: Basketball, Art Club,
Taekwondo, skateboarding
Favorite toys: Battle Beasts, M.A.S.K.,
The Centurions, G.I. Joe, TMNT

JARED K. FLETCHER
Homeroom: Mr. Chandler
Activities: Sailing, Art Club,
Wrestling, talking too much
Favorite Lego set: Space Monorail
Transport System 6990